A Shattered Glass Empire

James H. Wiggins III

Edited by Linda Wiggins

ISBN:0692328661
ISBN-13:978-0692328668

DEDICATION

To Dina: for reminding me who I am when I needed it most, teaching me what truly matters in this world, sharing knowledge, wisdom, gifts, and experiences that have defined some of the most important aspects of my life. Whenever you feel like you are drowning in an ocean of space-time, look to God's sky and remember that you are an extraor<u>dina</u>rily strong spirit, amazingly talented individual, and loved more than you will ever know. Life steals so much and gives so little in return. The one thing that can never be taken unless we allow it to be is our humanity because, "We are all the same species." - D.C.

CONTENTS

ACKNOWLEDGMENTS

This message is for all the people who have been so very dear to me my whole life; and also the new spirits which I've met along the way. You may not always be able to avoid reality, stop evil from running rampant, fix the problem, change anything, run away, or win the battle; but you can always hope to survive and have faith that the future will be brighter than the past.

ACKNOWLEDGMENTS

[illegible]

1 A Short History Of The Future

The most disturbing aspect about the flying drones is their silence. Twenty-four hours per day, they patrol the skies. Every second they take pictures and record audio of their surroundings. They upload their data into monolithic, government controlled data bases. They hover at both high and low altitudes. There is no standard size for a drone. Some are smaller than a tennis ball. Others are larger than commercial airliners.

In the year 2216, the former United States of America is a totalitarian corporate oligarchy. Socialists have completely enslaved the working class. Tax rates for some people can rise to over ninety percent of their income. Nationwide unemployment has not fallen below seventy-three percent in over fifty years. A permanently dependent welfare class comprised of apathetic, lazy citizens, and illegal immigrants; annually votes to implement draconian laws. Communist educational systems and militarized law enforcement brigades, keep the general population in perpetual ignorance and total fear. There are no lawmakers or politicians at the top of the social ladder. All policies are created and implemented by an elite group of Fascist global corporations, who are exempt from the laws which they vehemently enforce. This diabolical form of government, which is a combination of the most abominable and oppressive forms of civic rule, is colloquially called Sociofasciunism.

From birth to death, a person's every movement is monitored by some form of government surveillance. Nobody remembers the "old times", when this practice was not mandatory. The majority of humans live in a world ruined by technology. They have no idea what it means to be "free". Most people have heard the rumors. Older people talk about the long lost "Constitutional Republic". They speak of a time when people could talk to their neighbors, drive their car, or go to a public park without being monitored. They reminisce about the days when people could publicly criticize their government, without fear of being jailed. For the majority of people, these assertions are fairy tales.

Cameras are everywhere. They are in street lamps, billboard signs, personal automobiles, home appliances and public restrooms. The cameras are equipped with microphones that record every sound. They scan people and create numerous digital images of their bodies. These images are stored in multiple databases. This surveillance network is used to unfairly influence the economy. Corporations use this vast pool of data to selectively advertise products, and manipulate purchasing trends. Managing natural resources is the driving force behind this complete control grid.

The Carbon Tax Law of 2184 criminalized almost every basic form of human activity. Any action that was not heavily taxed was outlawed. Being associated with any Christian organization, questioning or denying humans' effect on planetary climate change, owning pets that did not have traceable microchips, and calling people hurtful words like "pedophile" or "foreigner", were severely punishable offenses. Heavy fines and jail time were imposed on people that violated the Carbon Tax Law. The law was created under the false pretense of reducing pollution. The politicians who sponsored the bill claimed it would help stabilize public consumption. This statement was an absolute prevarication. The law was specifically designed to reduce the average person's standard of living.

Hordes of people died within one year of the law's passage. They could not afford the rising cost of gasoline, and therefore had no means of transporting themselves to work at what few jobs remained. Burning gas fuel was considered a threat to the environment. The ban of its usage was one of the law's harshest provisions. All vehicles were required to run on electricity. This unreasonable mandate forced numerous truck driving organizations to close their businesses. Store shelves across the nation were left barren and desolate. It took over twenty years for all auto companies to complete the conversion of their vehicles.

Under the Carbon Tax Law organically grown meat, cheese, bread, milk, and produce, were strictly outlawed by authoritarian organizations like the Food and Drug Administration. They claimed that private farmers could not be trusted to properly manufacture safe food products, in a way that would not violate Carbon Laws. Therefore, black market organic food prices rivaled the price of illicit street drugs. Drug dealers started peddling items like raw milk, and cheese, at inflated prices. This led to an explosion of crime. Numerous gangs competed for dominance in the new market of "edible gold".

The food regulations led to massive crackdowns on private food businesses. Many rural farmers were jailed because they refused to stop growing and selling their own food. Numerous families, including women and children, were killed when Federal agents raided their farms. The private farming industry was destroyed. This led to a sharp decrease in the availability of organically grown food at supermarkets. Before the Carbon Tax Law was passed, healthy food was copious. Farmers around the country had once grown produce, raised livestock, refined grains, and caught fish in abundance. Supermarkets were once replete with healthy food that was reasonably priced. The only organic food currently available is sold at high class specialty stores. The food is encased behind bulletproof glass. The stores are patrolled by armed security guards.

The death of the organic food industry produced a wave of disease. Processed food is high in additives, like artificial bovine hormones. The consumption of genetically modified foods like corn, sugar, and soy, permanently damages human DNA. The lack of healthy eating choices produced an epidemic of cancer, obesity, heart disease, and many other ghastly medical afflictions. In modern times, it is not uncommon for people in their twenties and thirties, to die from poor nutrition. The rising health crisis has crippled the health care industry.

America's health laws had been reformed under the fascist Inexpensive Care Act of 2163. Because the law was written by large health insurance companies, the cost of purchasing health insurance plans skyrocketed. Even though the law required all people to buy health insurance; the rate of uninsured individuals drastically rose, because people could not afford to pay the high premiums. This forced many private doctors to close their practices. All doctors and medical care professionals were eventually granted government employee status.

The government did not have the monetary borrowing capacity to increase welfare subsidies. The nation's poorest individuals were left without any health insurance. This led to the widespread use of Death Panels. The Death Panels were always part of the ICA, but their existence was denied for decades. The Death Panels' job was to ration health care. There were a variety of reasons that patients were routinely denied medical assistance. People that were deemed too elderly, or sickly to warrant treatment, were withheld access to wellness services. Mentally handicapped, physically disabled, and comatose patients were outright euthanized.

Other sections of the law drastically changed the way businesses operated. Small businesses were not given an exemption to the law's Environmental Mandate. This provision stated that all businesses must implement certain measures to operate in a more eco-friendly manner. Costs of revamping water filtering, electrical wiring, waste disposal systems, and other building components, was the business owners' burden. Their only other option was to pay a steep Pollution Penalty. Small franchises and stores could not afford to pay any of these costs. Large corporations did not have the same dilemma. They quickly replaced the majority of their work forces with robots. Numerous professions deemed "unnecessary" like Customer Service, Health Inspection, and Accounting jobs, were immediately automated. At first, large businesses took a sharp profit decrease because of the increased production costs. However this trend was soon reversed when smaller operations went out of business, and left people with no choice but to buy their goods from global franchises.

The Carbon Tax's effect on food quality was enormous. For many food producers it was simply an extension of existing business practices. Corporations had been cutting corners in their food production methods for over one hundred years. Over the decades, they laced their food products with deadly filler ingredients. One of the earliest additives was mechanically separated meat byproduct, also known as Pink Sludge. This incredibly toxic protein slime was sold to grocery stores, restaurants, and fast food chains. Manufacturers laced the food's cardboard, aluminum, and plastic containers, with Bisphenol A. It is an estrogen mimicker and toxic artificial hormone that preserves the shelf life of packaged products.

The Environmental Defense Agency spiked the water supply with cancer inducing Hexoforicilicate and Sodium Fluoride. This practice allowed water companies to conserve more of their reservoirs. They greatly increased their supply's volume by diluting it with chemicals. These chemicals caused widespread brain damage, and reduced human intelligence. This resulted in a population with massively lowered IQ's. A mentally retarded, and physically stunted population, was easily controlled by a ruthless corporate oligarchy. This is why many Americans were unable to resist the elite's power grab. The total deindustrialization of America took only a few decades.

Big Agriculture's greatest evil was the release of Genetically Modified Food Organisms. GMOs were created in laboratories by mad scientists, who were Hell bent on unleashing chaos, disease, and destruction on the human species. Genetically Modified Foods were created from seeds that had different genetic traits woven into their plant genes. This caused the seeds to mutate, and become biological hazards. After the Carbon Tax, over ninety-eight percent of all food sold in the United States was genetically modified. GMO plants could be manipulated to carry a variety of different toxins. Some of these toxins included biological viruses such as HIV and HPV. Food companies defended these bio-atrocities by claiming the mutations acted as vaccines, which controlled deadly pandemics. Other plants grew their own pesticides. They eventually killed any bug, rodent, or human which ingested the plants. GMOs were eventually exported from America, to every civilized nation on Earth.

The human death toll from the consumption of GMOs was horrific. Cancers, diseases, infertility, birth defects, obesity, and early death became rampant in society. At one time, the average life expectancy of a normal human had exceeded age eighty-five. In 2216, the average life expectancy of a human is forty-two. Masses of people lost their ability to reproduce, due to the damage caused to their internal reproductive organs. The Carbon Tax's One Child Mandate, a clause that stated no American was allowed to birth more than one child per household, was inadvertently enforced by the GMO infertility rate.

People were so overwhelmed by feelings of joy when they were actually lucky enough to conceive a child; that they gradually forgot about the tyrannical, government enforced, One Child

Mandate. The OCM led to a drastic increase in abortions, because people did not want to risk being sentenced to life imprisonment for violating the policy. Over twenty million abortions were performed within the first year of the law's passage.

Organic farmers had higher production costs, even before the law was passed. With its implementation, farmers simply could not continue legally growing their own food. This sent a shock-wave through the economy. Unemployment and poverty became America's new social norm. Even as society crumbled, the big agricultural companies' lust for profit did not wane. Soon, they began to re-release Organic food at hyper-inflated costs. Organic food prices skyrocketed to levels that the average working class American could not afford. One pound of ground beef cost 450 Carbon Credits; the equivalent value of 700 old American dollars.

The lack of adequate health care, an abundance of poor food, and a stagnant economy, led to nationwide starvation. Desperately famished citizens resorted to eating anything they could find; including rats, domesticated pets, bark, and shrubbery. There were widespread reports that people even resorted to cannibalism. Rural areas became ghost towns. Industrial cities became overpopulated. Living conditions deteriorated across the country. Some zones were kept in good conditions, but the majority of places became slums. Cracked streets, decrepit buildings, and rotted grass were rampant in every municipality.

This societal decay further propelled the black market. Ordinary citizens committed more crimes in the hope of raising money to buy any type of food. Some groups outright stole perishables. They robbed stores, manufacturing plants, transportation trucks, and even their fellow citizens, for edible products. Rival street gangs could not supply the demand. They waged war against each other over food hustling turf. Food scarcity eventually made the gangs decide that high profits were not worth their own starvation. They maintained their empires by resuming their illegal drug, weapon, and human organ sales.

As a response to rampant lawlessness, the government ordered food production to be increased. But due to the lack of independent farms left, it was impossible for big Agriculture to produce a supply that met the demand. Food producers gave wealthy cities delivery priority. This meant that many areas of the country did not maintain a regular food supply. This inevitably led to massive food riots. With their swollen stomachs barren, people turned on each other and began destroying what remained of civilization.

The riots were tolerated for a while; but eventually the violence was quelled via swift and relentless actions by government enforcers. Rioters were beaten and sometimes killed during hostile confrontations with the police. Eventually, protesters became scared to revolt. People wanted to preserve what little remained of a peaceful society. There came a breaking point where the benefits of destruction outweighed its collective costs. As a result, the mass rioting stopped. Scores of people committed suicide to escape their desolation. Others resigned themselves to die from malnourishment.

Every State and Federal agency was allowed to become completely tyrannical. It was an inevitable conclusion, because for decades the system of law and justice had given way to corruption. Over the years big corporations slowly bought their way out of the political system. Politicians were bribed to create laws, which only benefited the Super Class. This corruption allowed a select group of oligarchs to seize total control of the markets. Oil, Food, Transportation, Technology, and many other industries, were monopolized by a small group of wealthy individuals. The only companies that were allowed to operate were the ones that were wealthy enough to buy their government issued business licenses. These unfair practices completely destroyed middle class families by bankrupting small businesses.

The economy imploded and poverty was rampant. The Third Great Depression, as it was called, was worse than the combined previous two. For most people turning to crime wasn't a choice, but a necessity. 'Food related crimes' were the most common. For many men the decision between stealing to feed their families, and watching them starve to death, was an easy one to make. Across the country, ordinary people were forced to commit petty crimes like theft and prostitution. The majority of their ill-gotten gains went to purchasing food.

Jails could not accommodate the influx of newly born convicts. The court system could not handle the revolving door of criminal prosecutions. Eventually many people, even those convicted of violent offenses, were allowed to go free. This was done to accommodate the vastly growing prison population. The only reason certain cases were ever tried, was to scare the remaining domesticated humans into obedience. Political dissidents and Carbon Tax violators were the most heavily prosecuted. Only those individuals still plugged into the mind control grid, perpetuated by Television and Video Games, fooled themselves into believing that a moral social justice system still existed. Groups of total conformists praised their rouge, kleptocratic, murderous government, for punishing these allegedly repugnant and immoral individuals.

Living conditions became so dangerous, that the government's only option became one of zero tolerance. Enforcers equipped with full riot gear routinely patrolled the streets. The line between traditional Police and Military personnel was all but erased. All law enforcement agencies were authorized to use lethal force to stop any crime they witnessed. After a few months of undeclared Martial Law, the crime rate began dropping. However the peace that came with the militarization soon faded, when cities could no longer pay the Federal Government to protect their streets. Certain areas of the country became virtual wastelands. Cities burned to the ground. It was accepted that some parts of the country, would be forever lost to poverty induced anarchy.

Carbon Credits were the next authoritarian step of the American coup d'état. To save an economy that was in ruins, the Federal Reserve Bank revalued America's money, and restructured America's debt. The Federal Reserve Bank was a private financial institution that had controlled the issuance of American currency, since 1913. At one time it issued paper Federal Reserve notes, which could be used to buy goods and services. The Federal Reserve notes were not backed by any sort of real commodity, like gold, that had intrinsic value.

For hundreds of years, America's monetary system was based upon the creation of debt. All businesses, private citizens, and government institutions, borrowed large amounts of money from different banks. The banks charged high interest rates to their debtors. This debt was repaid individually by businesses and citizens. Governments repaid this debt through tax collection revenue. All banks ultimately borrowed their money from the Federal Reserve. Every American bank was a subsidiary of the Federal Reserve.

High tax rates forced businesses to raise the price of their goods. Individuals were forced to take out more loans to pay for the products. This created a vicious pool of private debt that could not be repaid. There came a point when the Fed had created so much debt, through the printing of fiat currency, that America went into hyper-inflation.

Debtors had many pieces of paper, but the price of goods was so high, that it took large amounts of paper to purchase items. People, who already used debit and credit cards, were charged a service fee to cover the rising electronic filing costs. Large amounts of paper in circulation were considered an environmental hazard under the Carbon Tax Law. Therefore the Federal Reserve had to revalue the money supply.

The Fed responded by issuing Carbon Credits. The disposable plastic cards could be refilled at any bank. When people turned in their devalued paper dollars at a bank, they were given Carbon Credits in exchange. Carbon Credits could also be applied to a bank account, and used electronically. To cover the cost of this debt revaluation, the Federal Reserve abolished the Federal Income Tax. They replaced it with a United Nations Special Drawing Option.

Every year, in addition to paying a wide variety of other taxes, citizens paid a direct portion of their Carbon Taxes to the International Monetary Foundation. The IMF is a private global bank that is given charter by the United Nations. The IMF convinced America's creditors to revalue their paper dollars in Carbon Credits. This allowed a bankrupt American government, to avoid entering physical wars with its angry lenders.

This devaluation had a devastating side effect. The American dollar lost its status as the world's reserve currency. The IMF issued Platinum-backed global money, called the Supreme Planetary Currency. Countries kept their regional currencies, but the price of all commodities were revalued in SPC denominations. In America, the only reason people kept some of their paper dollars, was because certain items could still be purchased with cash. The dollars were considered an internal currency.

Legal items were cheaper if a person purchased them in Carbon Credits. An item that might cost $100 of paper money could be purchased with Carbon Credits, for half that price. Cash was predominately used to purchase black market items like illegal food. The Carbon Credit system was digital and their usage was tracked. All records of Carbon Credit transactions were stored in a national database. Cash was untraceable and redeemable for Carbon Credits, which made it the perfect tender for illegal goods.

But the most disturbing part about this future, are the silent flying drones. They patrol occupied American territories on both the homeland, and abroad. They have all the surveillance capabilities of the street cameras. They are fully mobile and are not controlled by humans. The drones can shoot powerful laser beams that will incinerate a human in seconds. These fully autonomous machines use sophisticated algorithms to select which targets they will annihilate. They are one of the most deadly aerial devices ever created.

The drones are the only thing that Cameron Moss feared. He knew that they could vaporize his team at any time. He had seen many people die after being hit by their directional, microwave energy beams. To Cameron, there was no worse way to perish. People misfortune enough to be blasted by a high powered drone pulse, were obliterated into a pulpy residue within a millisecond. Those that were hit with a less powerful shot had their skin seared away. They dropped to the ground and violently convulsed until their organs cooked inside of their body.

Cameron hoped that if he was ever shot by a drone, his pain would be minimal. He had reoccurring nightmares about being shackled to a bed, while getting repeatedly incinerated by a drone. He dreamt that he would get evaporated, only to be reassembled a moment later, and repeat the process. To Cameron, no vision of Hell was more frightening than this dream. When he saw the truck driving down the road, he put his fear aside.

"You ready?" Cameron asked.

"Yes. I'm jamming the drone's signal. We'll only have a few minutes before their A.I. overrides the scramblers. We have to hurry," replied Lucia Valente.

She typed commands into the holographic interface projecting above the glass screen of her hand held computer.

Cameron cracked a smile and said, "Well, we wouldn't want to make it too easy. Would we?"

He tried to steady his shaking hands, while looking at the midday sun. He vividly envisioned the truck's contents. It was filled with naturally grown organic meat, made from real animals. It was much more filling and healthy, than the synthetic cloned meat found in stores. The truck was on its way to one of the wealthy districts' markets. Cameron took one last deep breath, and tied his bandana around his face.

2 Date Night

Cameron adjusted the heavy body armor, which he wore for intimidation and protection. The pieces of his protective suit were crafted from discarded steel. The metal had been salvaged from defunct gas cars that were strewn around junkyards. Underneath the steel was a one inch thick sheet of Kevlar. It had been cut to resemble the scales of an alligator. Separating the connecting parts at the joints, allowed him maximum mobility and flexibility. Beneath the scales was a full body rubber suit, which prevented the materials from chaffing his skin. Atop his head was a black skullcap. His team was dressed in similar attire.

His team wore black bandanas to conceal their identities. They wore the suits to protect themselves from the violent gangs, and hungry hordes of fellow looters, that roamed the streets. Delivering food had become so dangerous after the collapse, that the government declared truck driving too hazardous an occupation for a citizen to hold. In 2186, it mandated that all trucks be self-driven by a dashboard mounted, computer navigation system. The trucks followed pre-programmed routes, and were guided by Global Positioning Systems. For a while, the only time humans would come in contact with the truck is when they handled the cargo.

However in 2205, food production companies bribed Congress to amend the law, and allow private security guards to accompany the trucks. Newer trucks were equipped with a limited use manual drive. The guards engaged it during emergencies by using their biometric hand print. It allowed the truck to be driven for thirteen miles, before it was automatically disengaged. The security guards were some of the only people, still allowed to own and carry guns.

Gun ownership was heavily restricted for regular citizens. Legally obtaining one was a long and arduous process. Treaties passed by the United Nations, had led to a de facto gun ban across the United States and the rest of the world. While enforcers had stopped short of gun confiscation, gun stores across America shut down, to avoid the hassle of conforming with international gun selling laws. Only a handful of specialized dealers remained. Anyone who purchased from them was subject to abide by strict government rules. This drove crime rates upward, because the black market was flooded with a wave of illegal guns. Real criminals did not care what the law stated. They obtained any gun that they desired. These illegal guns killed more people, than during any time when legal civilian gun ownership was a proud American pastime.

While there were a large percentage of food truck guards who carried guns, many found it easier to use more common items for their defense. They were usually armed with bats, metal pipes, knives, and various other easily obtained items. The team never had a violent confrontation with a fellow Food Liberationist, or truck guard, in all the years they had been stealing food. But they had been involved in a few significant battles with violent outlaws, who only wanted food for profit. The Food Liberationists were people who battled against the tyrannical Carbon Tax Law; by stealing or growing food and selling it to the poor. They were different from bandits and gangs, who selfishly hoarded it for themselves. Cameron and his team lived with the constant knowledge that any situation could become volatile.

The truck barreled down the road and started approaching the overpass. When it was within close enough range, Lucia pressed a button on her computer. The truck's engine turned off, right before it reached the overpass. The truck pulled over to the right side shoulder, near a concrete divider, and rolled to a stop. Lucia feverishly typed into her computer. A few seconds later, the guard looked down at his dashboard's screen. It repeatedly flashed the words, 'FLAT TIRE'. A corresponding graphic showed the right passenger's side tire blinking red. The guard muttered a few words to himself before exiting the truck. He had a large machete strapped to his side. He looked around cautiously, before slowly walking around to the passenger's side.

While the guard was walking, Cameron used a modified pistol to shoot a small dart into the back of the security guard's neck. The dart was filled with a non-lethal serum, which would cause a person to lose consciousness for a brief period of time. The guards felt very little pain, and generally awoke without any negative side effects. The guard grabbed his neck, and began stumbling. Vincent Oldman reached over the cement divider, behind which he had been hiding, and swiftly pulled the guard behind the concrete.

Vincent quickly jumped over the divider. He entered the truck through its passenger's side door, and moved into the driver's seat. He attempted to turn the wheel, but it was locked. Vincent looked at the overpass, through the truck's windshield. He raised his hands in a confused manner to indicate that he did not know why he could not drive.

"What's wrong?" Cameron asked Lucia.

"Calm down. I'm overriding the auto-drive right now," Lucia replied.

She typed a few more keystrokes. The truck's dashboard flashed the words, "Manual drive activated." Vincent gave Lucia and Cameron a two thumbs up signal.

"He can drive. Change the license plate number," Cameron said to Lucia.

Hardly breaking a sweat, Lucia continued typing on her computer. The truck's digital license plate sequence began rearranging itself into a new number. A few seconds later, its engine restarted.

"We've got to hurry up and get to the drop point. The GPS is dead and the plates are scrambled, but it won't be long before they know something is wrong," Lucia said.

Cameron motioned for Vincent to follow an adjacent road, which led to an abandoned rest area. Vincent started driving. Cameron and Lucia ran along the top of the overpass. When they reached the intersection, they jumped from its lowest point. They landed near the pit stop's entrance. Vincent stopped the truck. Lucia and Cameron entered through the passenger's side door. When they were all settled, Vincent followed the road back to the main highway, and sped away.

Eleven minutes later, Vincent pulled off the highway. He followed local roads until the crew reached an abandoned parking lot, located behind a decrepit building. Nakano Eiji was waiting with a large cargo van, which they would use to transport the food. Vincent pulled the truck around, so that the back ends of both vehicles were facing each other. Eiji opened the transport van's back door. Cameron, Vincent, and Lucia, exited the stolen truck.

"There you guys are. I was starting to get worried!" Eiji kindly said.

Cameron quickly walked past Eiji. He picked up an object that looked like a pen, which Eiji had left on the ground. Cameron drew a circle around the truck's back door hand scanning panel. Cameron clicked the pen's tip, and the truck's metal was burned away.

"Something I said?" Eiji asked in a bewildered voice.

"We're carrying almost two hundred pounds of stolen meat. Now's not the time to be joking around," Lucia said.

They feverishly unloaded the truck's contents into the cargo van. When they finished, Lucia and Vincent covered the meat with a large tarp. They climbed inside through the van's rear door. Eiji and Cameron entered the main cabin.

"I can't wait to get home," Cameron said.

Eiji started the engine, and the group began driving back to their compound. After a few minutes, Cameron finally took off his bandana and broke the silence.

"I can't take this shit anymore," Cameron heatedly said.

"What makes you say that?" Eiji asked.

"Don't you ever feel bad about stealing from people? I'm starting to have serious doubts about what we do with our lives. We hardly relax. We never do anything productive, or even remotely fun. It's just one robbery after another. What makes us any better than the criminals who put us in this situation?" Cameron said.

Eiji sensed that Cameron was upset, and tried to calm him down.

"I'm not excusing our behavior, but I understand why you're angry. It's pretty hard for a man to retain his sanity these days. I mean, who would have thought there would come a time when people would have to steal animal meat, because they don't want to eat its cloned version? That stuff will kill you. They grow it in laboratory test tubes. It's the awful product of deranged science experiments. Nobody should ever have to eat that garbage. I'm not saying that what we do is right. But there comes a point when a man must stand up and say, 'I am a human, and I refuse to be treated this way. Enough is enough,'" Eiji said.

"How long do you think it'll be, before we get caught? We can't do this forever. More and more, I find myself thinking that after one last good haul, I'm out. I'm done with this life. But I never make that plan a reality," Cameron said.

"Don't feel bad, Cameron. You won't be the only one going down, when our operation falls apart," Eiji responded.

"That doesn't make me feel much better, but thanks...I guess," Cameron said.

Eiji is a Japanese immigrant, who moved to America twenty-one years ago. Most of Japan was rendered uninhabitable by a nuclear accident. A strong typhoon hit several nuclear reactors, which caused them to explode. Large areas of land and water supplies were contaminated. Some Japanese believed that it was a man-made weather weapon attack. Japan helped Tibet achieve its independence from Communist China, after a four year war that ended in 2155. Two years later, the typhoon occurred. It took several decades for the radiation poisoning to become noticeable, and by then it was too late to solve the problem.

Horrific birth defects created by high radioactive levels, led the Japanese government to declare large parts of Japan nuclear wastelands. In many sections of Japan, no life will ever again be able to flourish. This led to a mass Japanese exodus. Many Japanese moved to other parts of the world, to avoid being killed by the radiation. Eiji came to America with his parents when he was thirteen. Like many other Americans, they found themselves fighting to survive in a Carbon Credit society. When he was twenty-five, Eiji joined a local Food Rebel Faction, and moved away from his parents.

The team had almost reached their destination. They lived in a very poor, and quite dangerous, part of the state. The city of Newark, New Jersey; was largely destroyed by the Welfare Riots of 2190. When inflation began rising due to the Carbon Tax Law, people on Public Assistance found that their dollar valued checks could not cover the cost of living. Eventually, people revolted. Some cities were literally burned to the ground. Others were simply left in terrible conditions. Welfare checks were eventually converted into Carbon Credits. This quelled the dependent class, because they could once again buy the items which they needed.

Newark was hit hard by social unrest and economic collapse over the past few decades.

However after a partial recovery, the city was finally able to maintain minimal electricity, running water, and sewer services, for the people that could afford them. Cameron and his friends made money by selling high quality illegal food. They accepted cash, and individual Carbon Credit cards. When they needed to convert cash into credits, they used a money launderer. The account was registered to a street artist named Sky Solomon.

Every time a person bought illegal food with cash, Sky would give Cameron's team one of her paintings. This allowed her to prove that she legally obtained the cash, when she took it to the bank. It was a very risky business. They had a close circle of buyers that did not report them to the authorities. Their customers could not afford to legally purchase organic food, so they quietly paid cash for the illegal goods which Cameron and his team provided.

Twenty-five minutes later, Eiji pulled the van into an abandoned warehouse that the team used for their operations.

"Looks like we're safe for now," Eiji stated.

Cameron and Eiji exited the van, and unlocked its back door.

"What an amazing haul! Hey, check it out. I scored a little something extra," Vincent said.

He pulled a small plastic card out of his pocket, while stepping out the back of the van.

"I lifted it from the guy, before I took the truck," Vincent arrogantly said.

Cameron flew into a rage and yelled, "Dammit Vincent, we don't steal directly from guards! They have families!"

"So what? He'll make it back double, in insurance," Vincent replied.

Cameron could no longer contain himself, and shoved Vincent.

"I don't care what he makes in insurance! It's wrong to steal directly from the guards!" Cameron shouted.

"Fuck off, Cam! You're trash!" Vincent snarled back.

He pushed Cameron back. The men stared each other down for a brief but intense moment.

"Whatever," Vincent finally said.

Vincent walked towards the spiral staircase which led out of the room.

Before he left Vincent nastily said, "Hey man, don't forget. You're a crook too."

Cameron was about to chase after him, when Lucia put her hand on his chest.

"That's not going to make you feel better," Lucia said.

Cameron lowered his head, turned the opposite direction, and walked out of the warehouse. Outside, Cameron was unable to control his rage.

"Shit!" he exclaimed.

He put his hands on his hips. After a brief moment of silence, Cameron dropped to his knees.

"Shit! *Shit!* SHIT!" he shouted while punching the ground.

Suddenly a voice behind him said, "Easy champ. Those gloves aren't easy to build."

Cameron looked around and saw a physically fit, well-aged man, walking towards him. The man had a scruffy beard. He had let his wavy gray hair grow down to his shoulders. His name is Walter Kingsley; and he is the team's leader. He is a gifted craftsman, and is the inventor of their body armor.

In Walter's younger days, he lived through the painful economic collapse, brought about by the Carbon Tax Law. Walter feels the law is unjust. He spent his life fighting tyranny by joining the Food Liberation. The group vowed to continue selling organic food on the black market. He is fifty-nine and trains younger companions to continue his work. Even though he is a criminal, Walter is an extremely moral man. He does not believe in wantonly hurting people. He is Cameron's mentor, and very close friend.

Cameron stood up, and heatedly said, "Vincent stole credits from a guard! Can you believe that? He probably only got forty or fifty credits! It's one thing to steal from a corrupt corporation that rips off its customers; but stealing from the average worker is wrong!"

"That's not good. He knows that's not our style. I will have a serious talk with him. You know I don't condone petty thuggery," Walter said.

There was a brief silence.

"I have something for you. It might take your mind off what happened today," Walter continued.

In his hand were two electronic passports.

"I had to bribe a few people a pretty zettabyte to get these made. They weren't cheap," Walter said.

He handed Cameron the passports. After closely examining them, Cameron was stricken with shock.

"These are for interstate travel. How did you get them?" Cameron asked.

"You'll want to use them soon. They'll be deactivated in a few days," Walter said with a mischievous grin.

Walter strolled away, leaving Cameron to admire the passports. Walter had created phony identification for Sky Solomon, and himself. He needed the passports, because interstate travel was only allowed with proper identification. However street counterfeiting was possible, if a person had the right connections. Walter would buy real passport cards from people he met in the streets. He would take the passports to computer hackers, who would change the digital data in them, and replace the real information with fabricated identification. After a person finished using a stolen passport he would break it, which destroyed its tracking chip.

Cameron went back into the warehouse, and walked up the spiral staircase. The stairs led to a larger section of the compound, which was used as a private dwelling. Years ago, Walter purchased it from a defunct gasoline car manufacturer, which no longer had a use for the building. Walter later hired construction workers to add segments to the warehouse, so that it could also be used as a domicile. Cameron saw Lucia and Eiji in the living room. They were separating the meat and wrapping it in cellophane.

They needed to quickly sell the meat before it spoiled. This was not difficult because finding buyers was never a problem. There was a high demand for organic meat on the illegal market. Street prices were cheaper than what was found in stores. People were quite willing to risk buying the meat illegally, so that they wouldn't have to eat the cocktail of poison chemicals found in cloned meat. Cameron walked through the living room, and went to the bedroom living area. He stood in front of his bedroom door. He placed his left index and middle finger, on the small biometric panel beside the doorknob.

"Bio-signature recognized. Welcome home, Cameron," a computerized voice said through the door's tiny speaker.

Cameron entered the room, and the door slid shut behind him. He placed his fingers on another wall panel. He slowly raised his fingers from the panel's bottom, to its middle. The brightness of the room's lights was adjusted. He walked over to a nearby table. Upon it, a glass sphere was resting atop a tripod. He placed his hand above the sphere, and snapped his fingers twice. A large holographic image began floating above the tripod.

He sat down on his bed, across from the holographic television, and listened to the endless barrage of nonsense which spewed from the TV. He picked up a small bracelet from his nightstand, and wrapped it around his left wrist. He opened his palm, and waved the back of his right hand in front of its sensor. A holographic interface appeared in his left palm. He used the interface to browse through several channels. He realized that nothing interested him so he used the bracelet's interface to turn off the TV.

He pressed another button, and a digital personal contact book appeared. He selected Sky Solomon's number and proceeded to call her. She answered his call, and an image of her face projected inside Cameron's palm.

"Hey Cam," Sky said.

"Get dressed. We're going out," Cameron said.

"Out? Where?" Sky asked.

"It's a surprise. Trust me, you'll be pleased. Be ready in one hour," Cameron said.

He closed his palm, and ended the call before she could respond. After Cameron had finished changing into his hooded sweatshirt and jeans, he left the compound and walked to a nearby bus station. Buses and other forms of public transportation were many people's preferred travel method. Very few people could afford a car. Ten minutes later, Cameron exited the bus and went to Sky's apartment building. He walked up the stairs, and knocked on her door.

When Sky opened it, Cameron said with a smile, "Hello, Rose Mathews."

"What?" Sky asked with a confused look on her face.

Cameron reached into his pocket, and handed her a passport. Sky quickly tapped the passport's touch screen panel.

"How did you get these?" Sky asked with shock.

"What can I say? Walter is a genius. We should take the train to Manhattan. It'll be cheaper than riding the bus the entire way," Cameron replied.

Sky wasted no time. She immediately grabbed her jacket, and left the apartment.

"I hear the train checkpoints are less intrusive than the road ones. I'm excited! I haven't been to the city in a long time," Sky said.

"Let's hope they don't use DNA recognition to authenticate us. The passports can only trick the card scanners. We're screwed if they ask to draw our blood," Cameron said.

"I think they only do that at airports and schools, but I could be wrong," Sky said.

They left the building and walked to the bus stop. The bus arrived a few minutes later, and the duo rode it to the nearest train station. They approached the station entrance.

"Here goes nothing," Sky nervously said.

They walked up to the heavily armed policeman guarding the door. He kept a firm grip upon his laser rifle, and pointed its barrel at the ground.

"Walk through this door to complete the scanning process," he said.

Cameron walked through the door first. He stood inside a chamber, which used lasers to take a three dimensional holographic image of his body. The door on the chamber's other side opened, and Cameron was allowed to exit. Sky entered the chamber next. Another guard was waiting on the chamber's other side. Sky and Cameron waited for the guard's computer to finish analyzing their body scans.

"Biological inspection complete. No weapons detected. No further threat assessment needed," said the scanner.

"You're free to leave," said the other guard.

Without saying a word, Cameron and Sky immediately left the security checkpoint. They walked to the elevator, and rode it up to the main platform. They walked over to the ticket dispensing kiosk, and used its holographic interface to select two train tickets.

"Interstate travel requested. Please insert passport card to verify travel privileges," the machine said.

Cameron and Sky looked at each other for a brief moment. The machines were equipped with recording devices, so they dared not speak about their plans. Cameron's hands were shaking. He inserted the passport card into the machine's reader, and anxiously awaited the results.

"Interstate travel authorized. Please insert the next passport," the voice said.

Cameron quickly removed his card, and Sky inserted hers.

"Passport verified. Please pay the amount shown on screen," said the robotic voice.

"$3,000: CASH. $1,500: CARBON," flashed on the screen.

"Damn," Sky said with disgust.

Sky inserted a disposable Carbon Credit Card, and paid for the tickets.

"Watch out," Cameron said.

He gently pushed Sky aside. He tapped his cell phone wrist band against a black glass window on the machine's front. The machine sent a textual message containing their ticket information to Cameron's cell phone.

"I've got to get Lucy to hack your phone. You shouldn't be using unencrypted cell numbers," said Cameron.

The pair made their way to the platform.

"It's getting dark," Sky said.

The train pulled into the station a few minutes later. Its body was painted a sleek color of gray. It had black, tinted windows. Its physical appearance resembled the shape of a high caliber bullet. Live-action advertisements flashed on its side. Sky and Cameron entered, and quickly found a pair of open seats. There weren't many people riding. Most people could not afford interstate travel. Shortly after they sat down, a train conductor came to their seats and asked for their tickets. Cameron fully expected the conductor to ask them questions about why they were traveling between states. To his surprise, the conductor simply extended his wrist. Cameron tapped their bands together. The conductor checked the holographic image displaying in his palm.

"Enjoy your trip," the conductor said before walking away.

"That was unexpected. I thought security would be more stringent," Sky noted.

"Yeah. They must need the money," Cameron said.

Cameron had barely finished his sentence when another policeman, armed with a laser rifle, casually patrolled the aisle. He strolled past them. Cameron saw that Sky was worried, and nervous.

"Relax, that's normal. Calm down or you'll set off the behavioral detectors," Cameron said.

Sky looked up, and noticed a small black camera above a nearby doorway.

"I feel like I'm in a Petri dish, being examined under a microscope," Sky said.

Cameron lowered his head and tried to take a nap. He had been awake for nearly fourteen hours. About twenty minutes later, Cameron was awoken by the sound of an argument at the back of the train. Sky and Cameron turned in their seats to view the source of the dispute. A young woman was clutching her purse, and sobbing. She tried pleading her case to the conductor, and the rifle-wielding police officer.

"You don't understand. I can't afford a passport. My mother is very ill. I'm only going to Brooklyn. It's not that far. I have enough money to pay the fare, and I'm already on the train. Please, let me buy a ticket," she said in a shaky voice.

The conductor genuinely looked remorseful. He looked over at the heavily armed police officer, who returned his glance with a menacing stare.

"I'm sorry ma'am. I don't make the rules," the conductor said.

He fought back tears of his own, and helplessly watched the officer remove her from the train at gunpoint. The woman cried loudly. Sky turned to Cameron, and gave him a sorrowful look.

"That poor woman. How could they be so callous?" Sky asked.

Cameron put his head back down. The dispute he had just witnessed left a burning rage in his gut. Cameron hated the way the government controlled people, but he felt powerless to take action.

"Sky, the detectors..." Cameron said, while trying to control his breathing.

Sky looked away from Cameron, so that he would not see her shed a tear. Sky did not like feeling helpless. She shared Cameron's anger, but knew he was right. If the behavior detector sensed they were acting suspiciously, it would alert the authorities. If they were discovered, Sky and Cameron would be arrested for using fake interstate travel passports.

Once they arrived in Manhattan, they started walking towards the New York City streets. They exited out a pair of Pennsylvania Station's large doors. Sky abruptly stopped walking. She looked at her surroundings, and was immediately overwhelmed by the bustling city activity. She stared in awe at the self-driving cabs, which were taking passengers to their destinations. She watched families use a holographic information center, to text message their cell phones information about tourist sites.

Large drones flew around the terrain. They hovered only a few yards above the street. She was most dumbfounded, by the graphics imbedded in the sidewalk. Numerous video clips of product advertisements, entertainment shows, and news alerts were displayed. Cameron could tell that Sky was entranced by the moving digital images.

"First time I saw those, I thought there were real people trapped beneath me. I saw some guy in the ground and thought to myself, how the fuck did he fall through the concrete?" said Cameron.

Sky hesitated a moment before asking, "How do they work?"

"They use nano-computers, and a special type of paint. They coat the street with a clear paint that contains billions of miniature projectors. You know, like the ones you have in your cell phone? Well anyway, once the paint dries they send signals to the monitors, and then the video gets displayed in the ground," Cameron said.

"That's fascinating. We don't have anything like this back home. I think it looks really cool!" Sky happily said.

Cameron smiled. He was happy that she had forgotten about the incident on the train. They walked to a local bar, where they talked and had a few drinks. After the bar, they shopped at various tourist boutiques, and Cameron bought her several trinkets. Later, they stopped at a comedy club to watch a performance. After the performance, they took an automated cab back to Penn Station. They entered the station, and located an information kiosk. They looked at the departure times that were being holographically displayed.

"Damn, we just missed one. Looks like we'll have to wait fifteen minutes for a ride," Sky said.

Cameron and Sky patiently waited in a seating area. Their chatter and laughter was disrupted by a disheveled middle aged man, who walked into a large open portion of the commuter area.

He began shouting, “Your government is killing you! My family and I are homeless, and starving to death! We can't afford to pay our Carbon Taxes to the Federal Reserve! The Federal Reserve is a private, offshore foreign bank that controls our currency! It's deliberately making us poor! They're pure evil!”

Four policemen immediately walked up to the man and intimidated him.

“Sir, you are outside of a designated Free Speech Zone! If you do not stop, you *will* be arrested!” an officer said.

He ignored the threat and continued yelling, “The Fed is *murdering* us! They've stolen our wealth, crippled our economy, bribed our politicians, and have forced us into bondage! I refuse to let my family eat three-headed cloned cows!”

Another officer pulled out a black baton, and flicked a switch. The baton's tip charged with blue electricity. Before the man could continue, he was hit with the baton. A jolt of violent current shot through his body, and he fell to the ground. While he was still twitching on the floor, the police kicked his body and beat him with batons. They eventually handcuffed him. He was picked up, and dragged away from the area. Sky stood in silence for several moments. She looked at Cameron with fear in her eyes.

“I want to go home,” Sky said.

Cameron did not speak a word. He grabbed her hand, and walked towards the New Jersey bound train platform.

3 Obsolete

By the next morning, news of the man arrested at Penn Station was one of the top stories in New York. Critics of public activism condemned the man for disturbing the peace. Proponents of free speech used his treatment as proof that America was no longer a free society. However, there was a more important story that was capturing the attention of New York's citizens. America's last printed newspaper, entitled New York Now, was drastically changing its business model. The paper stated that on Friday, November 13th, 2216, the news organization would print their last issue on physical paper. From this day forward, NYN would only be available via an online publication.

Printed newspapers rapidly began going out of business, in the decades since the Carbon Tax Law was passed. Most papers did not have the funds to pay the increased Paper Waste Tax. Papers had to raise their prices to finance their higher operating costs. The higher prices drove people to get their information from the papers' websites. With the closing of New York Now, all daily printed newspapers and magazine publications in the country would now be extinct.

Gregory Times, and two of his fellow coworkers, were all watching a holographic television in the NYN lobby. They remained silent, while watching the company's CEO deliver a press conference.

"...And so it is with great sadness that I, Robert Jones the sixth, bid farewell to the printed form of our newspaper. For over three hundred and fifty years, our publication has informed this wonderful city of current events. Today, our service to its magnificent citizens comes to a valiant end," said Robert.

Times looked at the hologram with a blank stare upon his face. He had worked for the paper for the past twelve years, in the pressing department. His job was to order the paper, ink, office supplies, and make sure the machines were in working condition. He had just been promoted to a managerial position, and received a new office last year.

His entire department was losing their jobs. Times knew that his situation was dire. He was not college educated, and there were not many unskilled professions left in America. Grunt labor jobs like Times' were extremely rare. Without a college degree, most people found they could not find adequately paying work. Times dreaded the thought of having to find a new job, but he knew it was a task which he could no longer avoid. Eventually, a shaky voice broke the silence.

"I don't know what I'm going to do. My husband and I, barely have enough money to pay our bills. I don't want to go on welfare. They control your entire life," said Cynthia, an elderly coworker of Times'.

"I heard they force you to get vaccinated every six months. If you miss a shot, they only give you two weeks to get it, or else they stop your payments. They tell you what kind of food you can buy, too," said Eric, another coworker.

"That's awful. Who can afford to live like that?" Cynthia asked.

"Apparently us," Times said.

Times had not attempted to hide the anger in his voice. Cynthia and Eric looked at Times, with deep sympathy in their eyes. They all shared a crushing feeling of hopelessness.

"Maybe it won't be so bad, Greg. You never know, we all might find new jobs quickly," Cynthia soothingly said.

Times knew she did not believe her own words. He politely pretended that what she said made him feel better.

"Yeah. Well, my wife is throwing me a birthday party tomorrow. Needless to say, you're all invited. We splurged and bought a real ham. It took us seven months to pay off the credit card bill. We finally made the last deposit yesterday. I'm picking it up, first thing tomorrow morning," Times said.

"Wow, a *real* ham? It has been more than two years since I've eaten real meat. I can't afford any. I'll definitely come over," Eric replied.

"Yes, I'm going to stop by too," said Cynthia.

"Okay, I'm leaving. No point delaying the inevitable," Times said.

"Aren't you going to the farewell party? The company bought us cake, and two percent real cheese pizza," Cynthia said.

Times looked at the holographic TV, one last time.

"No. To tell you the truth, I've always hated this place. I'm tired of the long hours, terrible pay, and power tripping bosses bitching about their stupid reports. They can keep their pity party," Times said.

He zipped up his jacket, and walked out of the building. Cynthia and Eric looked at each other for a moment, and then resumed watching the TV. Times walked down the street at an angry, fast pace. He turned the corner, and was startled by the sight of a loud, angry mob.

"Traitor!" a demonstrator screamed.

"Go back to China!" another protestor shouted.

"Tell us the truth about the domestic labor camps!" yelled an activist.

Nearly one hundred people were gathered, and attempting to block traffic. Police dressed in black uniforms and riot gear, clashed with the crowd. They shouted at protesters and threatened to arrest them if they did not move out of the street.

Times walked up to a woman and asked, "What the hell are they protesting?"

"President Cho is giving a speech at the United Nations today. His motorcade will drive down the block, later this hour," the woman replied.

"Why are they angry?" Times asked.

"The people here believe that the President was born in China. If that's true, he's not eligible to be the President under the United States Constitution," the woman stated.

"Hah! We still have a Constitution?" Times asked sarcastically.

"It's not funny. We're living under tyranny. Didn't you hear about the man that was arrested yesterday, for speaking outside of a supposed 'Free Speech Zone'?" the woman asked.

"Yeah well, what can you do? Corruption is as old, as the day is long," Times said.

He turned around, and walked in the other direction.

"Idiots," Times thought to himself.

He entered a nearby subway station. He rode the next available train to his destination. After exiting the subway, he walked a few more blocks to his apartment building. He entered the building, and took the elevator to his floor. He opened the door to his apartment by using its finger scanning panel. He heard laughter coming from his living room. He walked into the room and saw his wife, Mallory. She and her friend Brian Johnson were sitting on the couch. They were talking and drinking wine.

"...And I'll be damned if you think I'm going to pay that much, for a last generation implantable phon...Oh, hey Greg," Brian said when he saw Times.

Times gave Brian a cold stare. He suspected his wife was cheating with Brian, but he did not have any proof.

"Hello, Brian," Times said bitterly.

"Hi honey!" Mallory said while rising from the couch.

"Brian suggested that we all go out to dinner. Is that okay with you?" Mallory asked Times.

Brian stood up and said, "I'm real sorry for you, Greg. Hell of a thing, to see happen. I was hoping we could all go out and try to enjoy ourselves. Larissa and I know a great Mexican place in Midtown. Their taco meat is so good; you'd almost think it was real!"

Times stared at Brian for a second, and then looked at his wife.

"Umm, yeah. I guess that could be fun," Times said in an indifferent manner.

"Great! I'll text you the address. Meet us there at seven," Brian said.

"Yeah...yeah, okay," Times said with no emotion.

"I should go home and get ready," Brain said, after a moment of awkward silence.

Brian put his hand on Mallory's shoulder.

"Nice talking with you," Brian said.

Brian and Mallory smiled at each other. Brian shook Times' hand before leaving the apartment.

"How did it go?" Mallory meekly asked Times.

"I've had more fun at funerals," Times said.

He walked away from her, went to the bedroom, and laid his weary body upon the soft mattress.

Later that evening, Times, Mallory, Brian, and Larissa, sat around a restaurant table and ate dinner. Times remained subdued. He was wholly uninterested in their pointless conversation.

"We discovered this place last year, on our wedding anniversary. The food is *so* good!" Larissa exclaimed.

"They have some of the best genetically enhanced food in the city. It doesn't have that terrible aftertaste, like some other places," Brian said.

"I think it's good they're making people eat Smart Food. We have to do what is best for the planet," Mallory said.

"Very true. I don't know why more people can't see it that way," Larissa said.

"Everybody knows modified food is safe. I can't believe those Republican lunatics say otherwise!" Brian said.

Times listened to the three of them carry on their mindless conversation. The gibbering twits talked about absolute nonsense, like the latest fashion trends, sports teams, and television shows.

"...My favorite is 'The Yard'. Did you guys watch the season finale last week?" Brian asked.

"Ugh, I can't watch. It's too violent," Mallory replied.

"Yeah, I know! It's great!" Brian said.

"I feel bad watching it, but I can't help myself. I love that show! It's so...real," Larissa said.

"Exactly! Where else can you see real prison inmates, beat the *shit* out of each other?! I'm surprised it's still legal!" Brian said.

"You know those people actually die, right?" asked Times.

"Yes. It's really sad. Don't you ever feel bad for them, Brian?" Mallory asked.

"Naw, not at all. Those guys had their chance. They're the scum of society. Food smugglers, political activists, climate change deniers; the worst forms of trash you can imagine. I say good riddance!" Brian said with glee.

"Those food smugglers scare me. They're out of control. Did you hear that just the other day another truck was stolen in broad daylight, over in New Jersey?" Larissa asked.

"I wish our government would crack down on them. Those kids are punks. I see them every day, when I'm on my way to work. They sell bags of potatoes, right on the street corner. Nobody does anything! Who would even want to eat that food? They grow it in the dirty ground, with bugs," said Mallory.

"Disgusting. That's why I don't feel bad about watching them get their asses kicked. They're nothing but filthy animals," Brian said.

After the group finished their meal, the waitress brought their checks. She opened her palm, and pointed it at Brian.

"Eyes please," said the waitress.

Brian giggled. The waitress took a retina scan of his left eye, with her cell phone's camera. She immediately did the same thing to Times.

The waitress smiled and said, "Thank you," before she left.

The group finished their drinks, grabbed their jackets, and exited the restaurant.

"It was great seeing both of you. I can't wait for your party this weekend, Greg," Larissa said.

"Real ham. Wow, I can't remember the last time I've had one," Brian said.

The group parted ways after a few more pleasantries. It was 10:21 PM when Mallory and Times arrived back at their apartment. They changed their clothes, and got ready for bed.

"You could have at least pretended to have a good time," Mallory coldly said.

Times looked at Mallory, with pain in his heart. He fought back tears of aggression.

"Why would you say that to me? You know what happened today," Times said.

"What kind of an excuse is that?" Mallory snapped back.

She paused for a moment, and controlled her temper.

"I understand that you're upset; but you have to pretend that it doesn't bother you. You wouldn't want people to think we're in trouble, would you?" she asked.

Times sat down on the bed and told her, "Baby, we *are* in trouble. You know that jobs are scarce. Unemployment credits will help us in the short term, but they may not hold us over until I can find more work. I know you don't want too, but please consider letting me go on welf–"

"No! Don't you dare say that! I will not have you embarrassing me in front of my friends! Do you know what they will say about us?! It's bad enough that you're applying for unemployment assistance! I will *not* have people calling me white welfare trash! You had better find a job, real fast!" she interrupted.

Mallory's face burned red. Times' heart sank, and his pride shattered.

"Yes dear," he sheepishly said.

They laid down in bed. Times, felt utterly defeated.

"Room lights, off," Mallory said.

The room went dark. Mallory rolled onto her right side. Times lay on his back, and stared at the ceiling. After a couple minutes he rolled over, put his left hand on her waist, and began rubbing her backside. She coldly squirmed away.

"Not tonight, Greg. I'm tired," she said.

Times slowly removed his hand. He was hurt, upset, and ashamed that she rejected him. His sexual life with Mallory was not very active. On the rare occasions they did make love, she seemed distant, uninterested, and devoid of all desire. This was another reason why Times thought she was cheating with Brian. Times lay on his back for a while, until he heard her snoring. Slowly he arose out of bed, walked out of the room, and closed the bedroom door.

He walked to the living room, and over to the computer station. He sat on the chair, and pressed a button on a small black box. The box illuminated and began projecting a holographic user interface. He flicked another switch on the box's side, and a holographic keyboard started projecting on the table's flat surface. He began interacting with the holographic screen, by using his finger to navigate to a web browser. He browsed several news sites, and stumbled across an article about that morning's protest of President Cho Kee Ban. He opened a video of a male reporter who was giving more information about the event.

"Multiple arrests were made in upper Manhattan today. Protesters demanded that President Cho Kee Ban, release his birth certificate to prove that he was born in America. Accusations about President Cho being born in China continue to haunt his administration," said the reporter.

Times watched the video for a few more minutes, and then navigated to Glagoole, a popular internet search engine. He typed "President Cho conspiracies" into the holographic keyboard. The search yielded a few dozen articles. After browsing a few sites, he stumbled upon a site called "ChoSecretsRevealed.com." The website contained many digital documents that supposedly proved that President Cho was born in China.

He noticed that the website's owners were hosting a rally in Greenwich Village. Their meeting date was Wednesday, November 18th, 2216 at 7:00 PM. Times did not take the conspiracies seriously. But his curiosity was peaked, so he decided to attend the rally.

"I must be going crazy. Nobody in their right mind would believe this conspiracy bullshit," Times said to himself.

After using the computer for another forty-five minutes, Times shut down the machine and went to lay back down on his bed. The next morning, Mallory awoke Times.

"Hey. Happy thirty-fourth, my love," she softly said.

She pulled out a gift wrapped box from underneath the bed, and handed it to him. He unwrapped the box, opened it, and removed a dark purple trench coat. Times stood up, and admired the fine apparel. He ran his fingers along the outside of its sleeve. He looked at Mallory and smiled.

"Thank you so much, hon. It's really awesome," Times said.

Mallory smiled back and hugged him. They shared a peaceful moment of silence.

Times said, "Look, about last night. I'm really sorry. I hate fighting with you..." before letting his thoughts trail off.

"Let's not talk about it anymore. Today is your big day. You should get dressed and go get the ham. I told our guests they could come by any time after four-thirty," Mallory said.

"You're right. I should get moving," Times said.

Times spent the next half hour preparing to leave. He finished getting dressed, put on his trench coat, and went to the living room.

"You think I should bring something for protection?" Times asked.

"We don't really have anything that you'd be able to legally carry. I had to turn in our pepper spray last month, after the new state law banned it from civilian use," Mallory replied with concern.

Without saying a word, Times walked over and opened the kitchen cupboard. He removed a portable multi-tool. It contained a small knife amongst its various instruments.

Mallory began saying, "Greg. You shouldn't take that–"

"I just lost my job. I'm not about to lose my ham," Times interrupted.

He put the pocket tool inside of his trench coat's left breast pocket.

"I'll see you later," Times said.

Mallory almost asked him to leave the tool behind. She silently acknowledged that he needed the protection, and let him leave without chastising him. Violent crime was a serious problem in New York. She knew someone might try to rob him, if they found out that he was carrying real meat. Times left the apartment, and went to the subway. He rode to uptown Manhattan, on the east side of New York City. He reached the street level, and was surprised that it contained so many oriental businesses.

"Heh, Chinatown gets bigger every year," he snickered to himself.

The Chinese had taken over large parts of America, shortly after the Carbon Tax Laws were passed. China was America's biggest creditor, and held the largest number of their old Federal Reserve Notes. When the Carbon Credits were issued, America had no choice but to give the Chinese government control over large sections of the country's infrastructure. The Chinese had threatened to invade America in response to the devaluation of the U.S. dollar. As part of a treaty signed in 2189, China agreed to accept American physical assets for debt repayment. The only benefit of this massive wealth transfer was that it prevented a war between the nations.

Many cities in America looked like extensions of Hong Kong. Chinese people and businesses were prominent throughout the country. Big cities had the highest degree of Chinese influence. Most Americans hated the fact that China exerted so much control over America. Many Americans felt that their nation had become a puppet of the Communist Chinese Government. Others felt this partnership was a better alternative than fighting a grisly war, which would result in many Chinese and American casualties.

Times finally arrived at the butcher shop. An armed guard stood in front of the door and prevented Times from entering. The man was tall, and physically fit. He carried a fully automatic AR-75 assault laser rifle. He was dressed in generic military camouflage fatigues. He firmly kept his right hand, on the pistol grip of his gun.

"Sir, I need to see your identification before I let you inside," said the guard.

Times looked at a small machine that was beside the guard. It was a five foot high metal cylinder, with a black dome on its top. The dome had a sensor that could read biometric and electronic identifications. Times tapped his electronic cell phone wrist band against the dome's top.

"ERROR: Could not process Celi-band information," said the machine.

"Damn this useless piece of shit. It has been acting up all day. You'll have to use your hand print," said the guard.

Times placed his left palm on the dome's top. Seconds later, Times' personal information and photo ID was holographically displayed. Above the dome the words, "Threat Level: Low" were shown.

"Looks good. I just need to scan you for weapons," the guard said.

Times began sweating and nervously said, "Listen, I'm picking up a ham today. I brought along an, insurance policy..."

He slowly reached into his coat pocket, and handed the guard the multi-tool. The guard inspected the tool, and saw that it contained a small knife.

"You're not allowed to carry these. You can get in a lot of trouble for having this on your person," the guard said.

The guard placed the tool in his vest's front pocket. The guard then pulled a portable body scanner out of his back pocket. He held the square device upright, pressed a button, and scanned Times' image into the machine. The device was a highly powerful x-ray instrument, that allowed the guard to see the entire outline of Times' body, including his genitals. After the scan, the guard was satisfied that Times was not an immediate threat.

"You may enter. I'll give this back, on your way out," the guard said.

He removed the tool from his pocket and showed it to Times. The guard stepped aside so that Times could enter.

"Thank you, sir," Times said in a genuinely appreciative manner.

Times stepped underneath the door's sensor. It opened, and he walked inside. He was immediately overwhelmed by the store's magnificent sights, and smells. Along the walls, fresh organic animal meat sat behind bulletproof glass. The store had a restaurant area where rich customers ordered fine meats and alcohol. The smell of seared steak, pork, duck, chicken, and various other animal delicacies; made Times' mouth water and his body ache. Real animal meat was a delicacy that the average working man had rarely savored. Times walked up to the counter.

"Hi, I'm Gregory. I'm here to pick up an order," Times said to the female cashier.

She pointed to a large black section on the clear glass counter. Times pressed it with his left hand. His order information, picture, and a message indicating that he had paid for the meat, holographically displayed above the counter.

"Congratulations on making your last payment, Mister Times. The final sum is six thousand one hundred forty-two Carbon Credits. I've sent a copy of your receipt, to the cell phone number you provided with your initial down payment. I'll send someone to get your ham right away," she said.

"I need one ham for a Mister G. Times, please," she said into her wristband.

A second later a male voice replied through her device.

"I'll be there in a minute," he said.

"Please, have a seat. I'll come get you when they bring it out," the woman said to Times.

Times nodded, walked over to the bench by the counter, and sat down. After what seemed like an eternity, the woman motioned for him to return. The ham was sitting on the counter, and was wrapped in a brown package. Times assumed the bland packaging was to make it seem less valuable.

"Would you like to hire a security detail? They'll accompany you for only five hundred fifty Carbon Credits an hour," she said.

Times very seriously considered the offer. He ultimately did not accept, because he could not afford the service.

"No. No, I think I'll be okay," Times replied in a shaky voice.

"Whatever you say," said the cashier.

She placed the wrapped ham in a white plastic bag, and handed it to Times. Times left the store, and asked the guard to return his multi-tool. To Times' surprise, the guard did not hesitate to return his multi-tool.

"Good luck," the guard said.

Times briskly walked back to the subway. During the entire ride home, he was incredibly nervous. He knew that some people would be desperate enough to kill him for the ham. He tried to put that thought out of his mind. Eventually he arrived at his stop, and exited the subway.

Times immediately went to his apartment building. He raced to the elevator, rode to his floor, and ran down the hall. He sprang inside, and immediately slammed the door behind him. He took several deep breaths. Mallory arose from the couch, and approached him.

"Did everything go okay?" Mallory asked.

He stormed past her, went the kitchen, placed the ham on the counter, and unwrapped it feverishly.

"You tell me!" Times said with excitement.

Mallory and Times stared at the ham for ten minutes, without saying a word to each other.

"It's beautiful," Mallory finally said.

Times grabbed her waist, and kissed Mallory hard upon her lips.

"Let's start cooking. We're throwing a party!" he said.

Mallory smiled, and turned on the oven. Times went to the bedroom, and jumped onto his bed. He lay upon his back, closed his eyes, and fought back tears of joy. He was incredibly happy about the fact that within a few hours, he would be eating organic animal ham.

4 Let's Go For A Ride

Cameron was in the compound's gym area, practicing his boxing skills. He landed heavy blows upon the large punching bag. He controlled his breathing so that each hit would impact with maximum force. He wore a pair of training gauntlets that Walter had custom built for him. The gauntlets were heavier than the ones he wore when he was out in the field. He was training his muscles to compensate for the gauntlet's increased mass. This allowed him to have tighter reflexes during real combat situations; because his body would react more hastily when he was less encumbered.

Cameron settled into a rhythm, and proceeded to unleash a flurry of fast jabs. He sank deeper into his meditation and started throwing a series of powerful roundhouse punches. He quickly spun his whole body around, and finished his combination with a devastating backhanded blow. He panted heavily, and tried to regain his wind. He was so focused that he did not notice Lucia had entered the room. She was standing by the door, and watching him train. She eventually made eye contact with him.

"Walt wants to speak with us," Lucia said.

Cameron was still out of breath. He nodded his head in acknowledgement, and began unbuckling his gauntlets. Lucia exited the gym, with Cameron following not far behind her. They walked to a conference area in an adjacent garage. When Cameron and Lucia entered the room, they saw Vincent and Eiji. Walter stood at the end of a large rectangular table. While walking past Walter, Cameron handed him the gauntlets by pressing them against Walter's chest.

"I need a couple more ounces. They're starting to feel light," Cameron said.

Walter nodded, took the gauntlets, and placed them on the table. The team assembled at the table's opposite end.

"Great. Everyone's here. Let's get started," Walter said.

He pressed a button on a thin, transparent, computer tablet. The machine spread a holographic image across the table. It showed a New Jersey driving map. Along the map, red dots flashed in certain sections.

"Those hot spots are folks who need us to make a drop," Walter said.

Walter pressed his middle, index finger, and thumb together. He placed them on the computer screen, and expanded them outward in a triangular shape. The map was re-sized, and a more detailed outline of the terrain was rendered.

"Your first stop is Manville. The Branson farm needs a delivery," Walter said.

He slowly dragged his finger across the screen. A red line was drawn along the map's roadway. It outlined the path that Walter wanted them to travel.

"I heard that the Transportation Security Force is operating increased roadway checkpoints. You can't go the normal route," Walter said.

"I don't even know why they bother. There's barely anyone out on the roads these days," Eiji said.

"That is exactly why you have to be extra careful, and avoid them. Paul and his family are good people. They're risking their lives by growing all that produce. You can't bring them *any* unwanted attention," Walter replied to Eiji.

Walter continued, "Lucy, program the route into the dashboard, and let the car drive itself there. It'll make y'all seem less suspicious. He's going to give you four bags of potatoes. Each weighs eight pounds. You'll also get five-dozen apples, and two pounds of bananas. Give them thirty-nine pounds of ground beef, eight whole chickens, and eleven pounds of pork sausages."

"Whoa Walt, why are we giving them so much? That wasn't an easy job! By the time we take our cut of the meat and sell the fruit, we'll barely make any profit," Vincent said.

"Calm down, we have plenty of meat. There were sixty-two whole chickens in that truck. We can get at least two hundred and fifty dollars per chicken," said Eiji.

"Possibly more. I hear the Federal Reserve is currently running another one of their cash buy-back programs. They're trying to get all this old paper money off of the street. They're offering a one-to-two, dollar-to-credit exchange rate, until the end of this month. We don't know how much we'll make, once we convert the cash," Lucia said.

"Oh come on, nobody goes for those programs. Everybody knows they're a scam. They want to confiscate what little bit of untraceable currency we have left," Vincent said.

"Y'all might as well stop arguing. You know that Walt has soft spot for the Branson's. Besides, who says we're going to sell all of the goods? We have to eat too, Vince," Cameron said.

Vincent quieted down when he realized that he would not convince the group to reconsider.

"Whatever. You Orientals don't need to eat much anyway!" Vincent said in a cheerful tone.

He playfully put Eiji in a fake headlock, and rubbed the top of Eiji's head with his knuckles.

"You the one that needs to quit snackin', meat-head!" Eiji quipped back.

Eiji smiled, and pulled away from Vincent. The whole team chuckled, and Walter shut down the computers.

The team loaded the meat into the trunk of Walter's amply sized sedan car. A few years ago, Walter purchased the vehicle from a legitimate dealership. He immediately hacked its computer interfaces and Carbon Monitoring Meter. This ensured that all data sent back to the Transportation Security Federation was inaccurate. All vehicles' mileage and usage was monitored by the TSF. By manipulating the car's odometer, Walter was able to make it appear that the car did not drive very often. In addition to all motor vehicle's electric engine conversions, driving activity was taxed on a per-mile basis. This was done under the premise that driving was an environmental hazard.

After loading the last portion of meat, they entered the vehicle. Lucia sat in the driver's seat, and Cameron took the passenger's one. Eiji sat behind Cameron, and Vincent sat behind Lucia. She pulled a small rectangular card from her pocket, and placed it into the car's ignition slot. Lucia opened the glove box compartment. She removed a small black bag. It contained a handkerchief, one blue canister of aerosol spray paint, and one clear canister of aerosol spray paint. She sprayed a few shots of the blue aerosol into her right hand. She waited a moment for the mist to dry. Lucia then pressed her palm against the car's touch panel dash board. The car's engine started, and a computerized voice began speaking.

It said, "Welcome Wal–"

Lucia snapped, "Oh, shut up," before the voice finished.

She typed a series of numbers into the holographic keyboard that was projecting from the dashboard. The car's engine once again went dead, but the keypad continued projecting. She typed another keystroke sequence into the keypad. After a moment the car's internal dashboard, and external lights, flashed a few times. The car's engine restarted.

The electronic voice said, "Welcome Walter. There are zero passengers in the car. You have approximately 135 Carbon Miles, left on this card. Please use the electronic keypad in the dashboard, to input your destination."

Lucia entered the team's destination address and driving route, into the interface.

After Lucia finished the car's electronic voice said, "Bio-signature recognized. Destination set. Please fasten your safety belt, and enjoy the ride."

The car began driving. Lucia sprayed the clear aerosol spray into her hand, and wiped it with the handkerchief.

"Ow! I hate using that stuff!" Lucia exclaimed.

"Aww, pipe down you pussy," Vincent said in a joking voice.

Lucia turned around and snapped, "First of all, watch the language. And secondly, fuck you! You don't understand. That shit burns, man!"

Lucia was a tough girl that didn't like when the guys teased her, or made overtly sexist comments in her presence. All of the guys respected her, but it was not easy being the only girl in a tough, male-dominated group of outlaws.

Eiji relaxed in his seat and said, "It's amazing how you and Walt get all this high tech shit to work. I've never seen people hack machines, like you two. Spoofing bio-prints is serious business."

"Aww, don't be mad da rite man ha've better technorogy den Eiji-San!" Vincent said.

Vincent put his fingers against his eyes, to mock the slant of Eiji's face. Eiji playfully punched Vincent in his left arm. Lucia began lightly clawing at his other arm, with her fingernails.

Vincent laughed and said, "Oh! Ow! No, no! Stop! Cut it out!"

Cameron cracked a smile and said to his friends, "How about we stop fucking around, and play a *real* game!"

He activated his cell phone, and tapped its holographic screen several times. The glowing image of a square appeared. With his right fingertips, he removed the projecting square and threw it down in front of his opened left palm. The square expanded, and formed a playing field. A holographic sphere appeared in the middle of the playing surface.

"Yes! Air Ball! I love this game!" Vincent said with glee.

"Alright, alright. Calm down. Give Lucy and I, a second to adjust our chairs," said Cameron.

Lucia pressed a button on the holographic keypad. The backs of Cameron and Lucia's chairs retracted into their seats. The chairs repositioned themselves, so that they were facing Eiji and Vincent. The chairs' backsides extended in the opposite direction.

"Much better. Okay, everyone. Define your goal," said Cameron.

The four of them each grabbed a corner of the field. They extended their hands in front of their bodies, and left a small space between their fingers. They pointed their thumbs upward. Their palms were faced toward their chests. The surface calibrated itself, so that it was evenly distributed between the players.

"Lucy, start us off," Cameron said.

Lucia took both of her hands, and cupped the holographic ball. She returned her hands to the playing position. She lightly tapped the sphere, and it rolled towards Eiji. He gently tapped the sphere in a manner that reflected it off the playing surface's wall. It traveled back in Lucia's direction. When the sphere got close to her hands, she flicked her wrist, and shot the sphere in Cameron's direction.

Cameron's reflexes were quick, and he was able to swat the sphere towards Vincent. The team took turns bouncing the ball between each other. The sphere started moving faster and faster. Each player was deep in concentration. They never knew which direction the sphere would be swatted.

The sphere bounced in Vincent's direction, and he swatted it hard with the back of his hand. The sphere bounced off a wall at an angle, changed its direction, and quickly sped towards Lucia. She missed her opportunity to strike, and it touched the goal marking inside her corner of the playing field.

"Bullshit!" Lucia exclaimed with a smile.

"Owned, noob! You got to pay attention!" Vincent said in a smug, yet playful voice.

"Okay come on, give it up," Cameron said.

Cameron took the sphere from Lucia and said, "He's right you know. This game is all about..."

Cameron forcefully slapped the sphere at Vincent. It shot past Vincent's hands, which scored Cameron a goal.

"Oh, come on!" Vincent said with embarrassment.

Eiji and Lucia let out loud laughter and said, "Oooohhhhhh!"

Cameron chuckled and said, "You got to pay attention, right?!"

Vincent made a mocking face at Cameron, and the whole team laughed before resuming their game. The team spent the rest of the drive playing games, talking, and watching various music video clips on Cameron's holographic cell phone. The phone allowed images to be projected over a wide area. Cameron had set the phone to project into the middle of car, which allowed everyone to clearly see the videos. Enjoying each other's company felt good. Even though their various personality traits sometimes caused considerable tension between the group, they had developed a high level of camaraderie and trust between themselves. While browsing music videos, Cameron stumbled across a video that he despised.

"Hey look at this video. This is that crappy song, I was telling y'all about," said Cameron.

He played the video for his friends. The video showed a group of three young black males, dancing in unison. The song's lyrics were more asinine, than the oversized clothes and jewelry the males were wearing.

"UNNGGGHH MAN, I'M TALKING BOUT UNGH! WHEN I WALK IT'S LIKE, UNGH NIGGER! UNGH UNGHUNGH! See what I'm talking about! UNNGGH, it's the grunt song! Nigger, it's the grunt song! UNNGGH, it's the grunt song! Nigger, it's the grunt song....!" the lead singer screamed.

Cameron squinted his face in disgust and said, "Aren't these the most ignorant, fluoride drinking niggers you've ever seen in your entire life?"

Lucia rolled her eyes and said, "I'm sure their parents must be so proud."

Vincent and Eiji shook their heads in agreement. Cameron watched the video for a few more seconds.

"Retarded," Cameron finally said.

Cameron turned off his phone, and the group sat in silence for the next several minutes. The car's computerized voice alerted them of their whereabouts.

"Arriving at destination in two minutes," it said.

Exactly two minutes later, the car rolled to a stop.

"Destination reached. Please insert more Carbon Credits to continue driving," the automated voice said.

Cameron looked carefully at the group's surroundings. The car had pulled over, and stopped alongside the highway. Though it would be unnoticeable to passing motorists, there was a small dirt road visible a few yards away from their car.

"I hate this part of the trip," Eiji said with genuine concern in his voice.

Vincent reached into a compartment underneath his seat, and removed a nine millimeter handgun.

"Cameron, are you ready?" Vincent asked.

Cameron reached into the car's glove box, and pulled out a .38 caliber silver revolver. Without saying a word, he got out of the vehicle. Vincent exited the car, and walked toward the dirt road. Cameron accompanied him. When they reached the road's edge, Cameron pressed his hand against Vincent's chest. The duo stopped moving.

Cameron spoke loudly and clearly, "Your light calibration is too high. You can see the waves in the bushes. Turn your contrast down."

A few seconds later, a blurry image moved from behind the bushes. The blurry blob quickly dissipated. A very young girl briskly jogged towards Cameron and Vincent. Her long blonde hair was tied in a ponytail. She wore blue jeans, a long-sleeved pink sweater, and a black bullet proof vest. She carried a single barrel, semi-automatic shotgun.

"You always see me! You *suck!*" said the girl.

She playfully slapped Cameron on the side of his stomach. Cameron pretended to be hurt.

"Oh, ow! You're getting strong! Not bad, for an eight year old," he said.

"I'm eight and three quarters, *stupid!*" the girl said.

She scrunched her face, and stuck out her tongue.

Vincent was visibly flustered and said, "You scared the shit out of us, Lily. For piss sakes, we come out here all the time. You know we're not–"

Before Vincent could finish his sentence, he was interrupted.

"Watch the language. I don't like my daughter hearing such vulgarity," a southern accented voice said, over the radio attached to the vest's shoulder.

An embarrassed Vincent looked down at the ground.

"Hey Paul! What…you too good to say 'hi' to a brotha, face-to-face?" Cameron asked.

Immediately after Cameron finished his sentence, the image of a man's face began displaying across the vest. The man was smooth shaven. His short cut hair was fading to gray, but it still retained some of its light brown color. The handsome face was that of Paul Branson. Paul is Walter's longtime friend. Paul lives in one of New Jersey's last rural areas. Living in the secluded countryside allows Paul to grow organic fruits and vegetables. Even though growing food is illegal for private citizens, Paul disobeys the law in order to feed his family. Much like Walter, Paul does not enjoy being an outlaw. However, Paul feels he has no choice. He refuses to let his family eat Genetically Modified Food.

Genetically Modified Food is known to cause infertility in humans. The American population steadily declined in the decades following the Carbon Tax Law, due to the abundance of GMO food. There are only a few million Americans living across the remaining states. Most Americans live in densely crowded cities, which leave large areas of the country unpopulated. The only reason people like Paul and Walter get away with their crimes, is because there is simply no one left alive to care. Only giant prison territories, like New York City, have a heavy law enforcement presence. The human inhabitants that live in those highly populated urban areas are completely domesticated. Their lifestyle is tightly controlled.

Paul lives on a small farm in Manville, New Jersey. He is part of an illegal Constitutional Community. Certain areas of the country have unofficial Constitutional Zones. In these places, free humans try to live like their ancestors once did, “in the old days”. The residents secretly grow their own food and have small stockpiles of bartering items, which they trade between each other. Paul's house is surrounded by woods. Most of the buildings and houses near Paul's farm have long since been abandoned. The surrounding roads rarely see any pedestrian, or vehicle traffic.

Paul's family consists of himself, his wife Doreen, their three daughters, Lily (8), Abigail (14), and Samantha (20), and his son Paul junior (15). The family lives off the grid and is self-sufficient. They use rain and well water for bathing and drinking. They have numerous computers and advanced technologies, including military-grade invisibility devices. Paul stole these gadgets during the food riots, when the armories were overrun. They use solar, wind, and other alternative fuel sources, to power the house and their gear.

Twenty-five years ago, when he was a young man at the age of twenty-seven, Paul witnessed the food riots. He saw many of his friends and family starve to death. He illegally drifted up North, from his hometown of Chantilly, Virginia. His cousins stayed in Virginia, hoping that life would improve. Paul lost contact with them in 2192. In 2194, he met twenty-six year old Doreen. She was a fellow illegal drifter, who ignored the interstate travel restrictions required by the Carbon Tax Law.

Doreen had lived in Maine for the majority of her life. In 2190, her family went completely broke. The bank seized her family's house, because they could not pay their Carbon or Property Taxes. They lived in numerous homeless shelters. They stole food, and Doreen's mother worked as a prostitute to feed their family. Doreen's father was sentenced to life in prison, in 2191. He was caught smuggling raw vegetable produce across the border, from Canada into the United States. Doreen and her mother eventually found themselves living in New Jersey. Doreen met Paul by chance, one evening. Paul intervened in a public dispute between Doreen and her ex-boyfriend. They had lived next door to Paul, in a government subsidized housing project. Doreen's boyfriend was beating her in the parking lot. Paul broke the man's jaw, and stabbed him in the leg with a pocket knife.

Paul wanted to save Doreen and her mother from poverty. He went lurking around the criminal underground to find work. Eventually he met Walter, and they began committing numerous crimes of necessity. Paul and Walter made a decent living doing legitimate work, for corporations that needed temporary workers. He made additional money by doing illegitimate work, for various street gangsters, until late 2195. That was the year that Doreen's mother was diagnosed with breast cancer. She sold her body for $250,000 in Carbon Credits, to a private pharmaceutical research corporation. The company specialized in creating cancer vaccines. Their testing department paid humans large sums of money, for the permission to experiment on their bodies. People were injected with experimental drugs, which sometimes caused fatal illnesses. Doreen received $150,000, after her mother's death in early 2196. Paul, Doreen, and Walter, eventually found an abandoned farm. They originally intended to only stay there temporarily.

However, Doreen soon discovered she was pregnant. Samantha was born in late 2196, and Paul decided to permanently stay on the abandoned farm. Walter persuaded Paul and Doreen, to use a portion of the $150,000. They purchased vegetable seeds from a reputable black market dealer. They used the non-genetically modified seeds to plant an organic garden. Months later, they were growing organic fruits and vegetables. They sold the produce on the black market and made a small fortune.

Walter left the farm a couple years later, after he had saved enough money to buy the used factory in Newark. Decades ago, Paul's lifestyle would have been considered modest, and normal. However, Paul was considered a criminal in the eyes of the government. He grew his own food, paid no Federal Income Taxes, and violated the One Child Mandate. Paul was the antithesis of a domesticated human. He was among the last breed of men, who exercised what they believed to be their constitutionally protected rights.

The One Child Mandate stated that no family could conceive more than one child per person. The government justified this absurd practice, under the ridiculous guise that it curtailed carbon emissions and prevented human overpopulation. Paul lived in constant fear that one day; the State would take away his children, and send Doreen and him to prison. This policy followed guidelines implemented decades before, by the Communist Chinese government. In 2188, the Council on Foreign Relations adamantly praised this deplorable policy. The Council called the outrageous eugenics measures, extremely progressive. The Council congratulated America, for leading the world in the battle against man-made climate change.

Paul's image remained displayed across Lily's vest.

"Nice to see you again, Cameron. It's safe to drive up to the house. I don't see any drones pinging on my radar. See you soon," Paul said before his image disappeared.

"I'll meet you there," said Cameron while handing Vincent his gun.

Vincent walked back to the car, and entered. Lucia proceeded to manually drive it along the road which led to Paul's farm. Lily and Cameron walked down the path, and chatted amongst themselves.

Lily happily said with pride, "I shot a wild deer last week! Daddy took me hunting, and we shot it in the woods!"

"Wow! That's awesome. You're lucky he let you use the gun. Bullets are hard to find nowadays. We usually use our bows if we have to hunt," Cameron said.

"Daddy wants me to practice my aim. He said bows are good, but guns are the best tool to use in a sticky situation. You never know when your life may depend on you being a good shot!" Lily said.

Cameron smiled and said, "Heh, no argument from me."

The pair arrived at the family farm a few minutes later. Paul, Samantha, Vincent, Lucia, and Eiji, were standing outside and talking.

"Hello everyone," Cameron said while approaching the group.

"Hey, Cam. Lily, you and Sam head to the house, and put the gun away," Paul said.

Lily and Samantha promptly followed their father's instructions.

Paul looked at the rest of the group and said, "When's that old fox Walter, going to come visit me? I haven't seen him in months!"

Lucia chuckled and said, "I'm sure he hasn't forgotten about you. We've just been busy."

She looked down at the ground, and felt remorse in her heart. None of the team liked being outlaws. But in a post-industrial America, there weren't many alternative options.

"Eiji, why don't you give Vincent some help unloading the meat," Cameron said.

The group separated. Paul took Lucia and Cameron to the garden. The garden was surrounded by special jamming devices. The jammers scrambled the drones' cameras, and blurred the garden from aerial view. Paul had placed the group's produce in three moderately sized wooden crates. Paul had also placed a mobile hand truck with the crates, so that they could be easily moved.

Paul looked at Cameron and said, “This is our last good harvest for the year. Winter's coming soon. It'll be too cold to grow very much, until spring.”

Cameron nodded and replied, “I understand. We have enough money to support ourselves. Walter never has a problem finding us jobs.”

Lucia helped Cameron place a crate on the dolly. She proceeded to walk it back to the car. Cameron waited until she was out of earshot before candidly speaking with Paul.

He turned to Paul and said, “It's getting bad out here, Paul. I don't know if I can do this much longer. We're starting to do things of which I'm not proud. Every day, it gets harder and harder to look myself in the mirror.”

Paul fell silent for a moment and said, “So, quit. What's stopping you?”

Cameron looked at Paul, with confusion.

“I honestly don't know. I guess...I simply wouldn't know what to do with myself. I've lived this way for so long...” Cameron said, before letting his thoughts trail off.

After a moment Paul said, “Cameron, just because the country went to Hell, doesn't mean you have to be a demon. There comes a point in every man's life, where he has to look inside himself; and decide if the life he has chosen is one worth living.”

Paul put his arm on Cameron's shoulder.

He continued speaking, “We're all in this together, Cameron. Believe me; I've wrestled with my share of moral dilemmas over the years. I'm not even sure if you should be taking advice from someone like me. I assure you, I'm no Saint. Don't lose your self-respect, or humanity; and don't let the machine consume your soul.”

Cameron did not say a word. He simply looked at Paul in a thankful manner, and waited for Lucia to return with the dolly.

5 An Unlikely Encounter

Gregory Times arrived at the unemployment office in the Bronx, at 9:00 AM. It was Monday, November 18th, 2216. Times had only been unemployed for a few days, and he was already worried about his ability to pay the bills. Poverty was no laughing matter, in the new America. Times knew that if he did not receive unemployment he might not be able to afford his apartment.

Times stood in a long line and waited to walk into the processing kiosk. The kiosk was behind a small curtain, which was in front of a large rectangular machine that stood seven feet high. It was equipped with cameras, microphones, a touch screen computer interface, and various slots to process different types of plastic cards. After waiting for almost two hours, Times finally reached the kiosk. He stepped inside, closed the curtain, and stared at the screen.

"Please state your name, and the last five digits of your Social Security Identifier," the computer said to him.

Times cleared his throat and said, "Gregory Times. 9-2-9-3-1."

The machine processed his data. Fifteen seconds later, Times' photo identification and personal information was displayed on the screen.

"Is this information correct?" it said in a cold robotic voice.

"Yes," Times replied.

"All recipients of unemployment services are required by law to receive vaccinations every six months. Please place your arm in the provided slot," said the machine.

Times slowly placed his right forearm in the round receptacle. Almost immediately, he felt the slot's fabric tighten around his arm. He was painfully pricked by a series of needles.

"Ow! Is it supposed to hurt this bad?" Times cried out in pain.

With no hesitation the machine said, "Please hold still, while the vaccination process completes."

After a few more pricks, the machine released Gregory's arm.

"Vaccination complete. Issuing Unemployment ID card," said the machine.

A few minutes later, the machine produced a tiny plastic card with Times' information, from one of its slots.

"You have not yet chosen to conceive your allotted one child with Mallory Times. Should you choose to reproduce, you must report her pregnancy to the unemployment office. Please sign the Unemployment Agreement," it said.

Times barely skimmed the agreement that was displaying on the screen. He felt there was no point in reading a document which he could not avoid signing, if he wanted the unemployment money. He hesitated for a moment, and then placed his open palm on the computer screen. The screen scanned Times' hand print.

"Signature accepted. Unemployment filing process, complete. Your Carbon Credits will be automatically uploaded to your bank account, once per month. Payment will begin on the first of next month. Thank you, and goodbye," the computerized voice said.

Times stood in silence for a moment, and then walked out of the booth. He exited the unemployment office, and walked towards the nearest subway. He exited at his stop, and walked back to his apartment. By the time he entered his flat, he was feeling sick.

"Damn. I hope I'm not having an allergic reaction to the vaccine," Times said to himself.

Times went to his bedroom. He laid down, and started tossing and turning. When he could no longer suppress his urge to vomit, he went to the bathroom to release himself. After heaving a few times, he returned to the bed and slept for the rest of the day. He later was awakened by Mallory.

"You feel okay?" Mallory asked.

Times sat up in the bed and replied, "The shots are terrible. They made me sick."

Mallory gave Times a disproving look.

"Stop being a conspiracy theorist. Everyone knows vaccines are safe," she dismissively said.

Times decided the issue was not worth starting a fight.

"Yeah. I guess it must have just been something I ate. What time is it, Mallory?" Times asked.

"Five thirty," she replied.

Times was planning on attending that evening's protest of President Cho. He did not want to tell Mallory, because she disapproved of political activities. He knew she would be angry with him for going to the protest.

He got off the bed and said, "I think I'm going out tonight. Maybe I'll catch a movie. I need to clear my head."

"Okay. I was hoping we could stay home and watch TV. But I won't hold you, if you really want to leave," Mallory hesitantly said.

"I'm sorry. I'm not trying to abandon you. I just, need to figure out how I'm going to find a job. The unemployment checks won't help us out too much. It'll be enough to keep the power on, and pay the rent, but not much else," Times said.

"Well don't think too long. You need to get out there, and find a new job," Mallory said.

"I know, I know," Times said.

Times spent some time getting ready, and left for the protest at 6:00 PM. He took the subway several stops, and followed the map on his phone to find the protest site. The protest was being held in Greenwich Park, in the heart of Greenwich Village. Times saw a large crowd gathering in the middle of the park. The crowd was surrounded by policemen and military personnel. They wore full riot gear, and were armed with laser rifles. A medium sized drone hovered over the park. It routinely scanned the protesters for signs of trouble. A podium was standing on a makeshift platform. A political activist named Michelle Jacobs, whom Times recognized from internet videos, was in the middle of making a speech.

"...is why we must ask President Cho to immediately leave office! He is a foreign born Chinese citizen, and therefore ineligible to be President! Friends, ask yourselves. Why are details about President Cho's past, classified state secrets? Why did the White House seal his college transcripts, from when he attended the Ritgers-Rawnan Law College? Why can he not, after almost five years in office, produce a valid Birth Certificate? I'll tell you why. Because he was born in China, and is trying to conceal his identity!" Michelle said.

The crowd cheered loudly after Michelle stopped speaking. Times nervously moved through the crowd. He noticed an elderly man wearing glasses, a long black coat, and fedora hat. The man appeared to be in his late fifties, or early sixties. He was analytically watching the crowd. Times looked at the man, who returned Times' glance with a smile.

Michelle continued, "I am asking for all of you, to help expose the truth about President Cho! He's a foreign born citizen! Please write to Congress and demand that a *real* investigation of Cho Kee Ban's background be conducted. Let's settle the place of his birth, once and for all!"

The crowd erupted with a mighty cheer, and applause.

Michelle concluded her speech by saying, "My friends, we live in dark days. Our government has destroyed our country, and enslaved our people. The time for revolution has long passed. Crime has exploded. People are starving to death. Foreign operatives like President Cho lecture us daily about how we're not paying enough Carbon Taxes. Well, guess what? The tax doesn't go to our government. It goes to private mega banks; called the Federal Reserve and IMF. They have taken over our country through fraud, and crippled us via debt! If we don't act now, these elite Globalists will bankrupt the few of us left, which they haven't been able to kill through deindustrialization. We *have* to restore our Bill of Rights and Constitution, or we're all dead! Resist tyranny!"

The thunderous applause was long and loud. After Michelle left the podium, people began breaking into separate groups. They discussed political matters amongst themselves. Times noticed that the elderly man had not said a word the entire speech. Unexpectedly, the man walked up to Times.

"Passionate, isn't she?" the elderly man asked.

"Stupid, seems like a more accurate word. How can she even get away with such harsh criticism of President Cho? I thought the Hate Speech laws banned this type of verbal abuse," Times responded.

The elderly man smiled and said, "I'm sure the government is watching her. Most of these protesters are on FBI terrorist watch lists, even if they are not violent."

Times bit his lip, and was having second thoughts about attending the protest. He did not want to be on a terrorist watch list.

"Forgive me. I haven't properly introduced myself. My name is Webster Morgan," the man said.

Webster reached out to shake Times' hand, and he accepted the gesture.

"I'm Gregory Times. Nice to meet you," he said.

"What brings you out today? You don't look like the typical protester," asked Webster.

"I saw a few videos on the internet, which peaked my interest. Heh, to tell you the truth, I don't even know why I'm here. Morbid curiosity, I guess," Times replied.

"I see. Nothing like the intrigue of a good conspiracy, to peak a man's interest," Webster said.

Times agreed and said, "Can't argue with you. What do you think about this whole issue? You think there's any truth to what she said?"

Webster leaned closer to Times and said, "Between you and me...she makes a good point. But don't tell anyone I said that; I don't want to be taken to a forced labor camp!"

The two men laughed together.

After a moment of silence, Webster said, "You seem a little ill. Are you feeling all right?"

"I had to get vaccinated this morning so I can collect unemployment. Call me crazy, but I think the shot made me sick. My wife thinks it's just my imagination. I probably just ate something that upset my stomach," Times said.

Webster smiled and said, "I hope you feel better. Where did you used to work?"

"With the New York Now newspaper," Times replied.

"Yes, I heard they closed down. It's a shame that nobody respects the written word anymore," Webster said.

"What about you? You look too well dressed, and fed, to be unemployed," Times said.

Webster lightly tapped his belly and said, "I admit, I indulge myself."

After a brief pause Webster said, "My work is complicated. It's not a profession that is very popular, among conspiracy theorists."

"Where do you work?" Times asked.

"I own Rigor Pharmaceuticals. Over the years I've taken a modest start-up company, and turned it into a global empire," Webster firmly replied.

"Sounds nice. I wish I was a made man, like you. What's so controversial about your work?" asked Times.

"Prescription drugs have acquired a stigma throughout the conspiracy community. Obviously, I think their concerns are unfounded. It is my job to create safe and effective drugs. I feel companies like mine, are misunderstood. We have no intentions of harming anyone. After all, what company would want to hurt their customers?" Webster replied.

"You make a very valid point," replied Times.

Times and Webster hadn't noticed that the crowd was becoming restless. Heated debates, raged amongst the participants. There was a group of Cho supporters, arguing loudly with a group of anti-Cho protestors. Times and Webster, listened to emotional protesters from both sides, voice their opinions.

"You're all nuts! It's violent conspiracy theorists like you, that have destroyed our country!"

"What is it going to take for you to get out of your coma?!"

"All these laws, and taxes, help keep our liberties safe."

"*We* didn't destroy America! America was destroyed by *foreign banks!*"

"Why can't you people admit, he *is* an American citizen..."

"My kid was paralyzed after they forcibly gave her the flu shot!"

"I will *not* listen to your propaganda, about vaccines being deadly..."

"The food gangs are the real threat."

"Arrest these terrorist sympathizers–!"

"It's illegal for the military to patrol our streets!"

"How dare you. My son gave his life in Syria, to protect our freedoms..."

"You probably want a drone over every household–"

"Our government is run by corrupt foreigners–!"

The crowd's noise had reached a deafening level. Without warning, a drone that had been patrolling high above the protesters, glided down. It flew above the gathering. It was jet black, and had a triangular shaped body. It had two thrusters on the bottom of its body, and two thrusters on the tips of its wings. It had a large camera on the top of its body, which scanned the entire crowd. Some protesters left, when they noticed the drone scanning the crowd. Others were not intimidated by its presence. The drone rotated its wing thrusters in a vertical manner, so that all four of them were facing downward. It hovered for only a moment, before its computerized voice spoke and struck the crowd silent.

"Warning. This demonstration has exceeded the maximum time, allotted by the Free Speech Permit. All citizens are required to disperse. Non-compliance will result in the use of lethal force," said the drone.

Most of the crowd froze, while the drone menacingly hovered above them. In a bold act of defiance, a teenage boy picked a small rock off of the ground.

"Fuck you, robot!" the teenager yelled.

He hurled the rock at the drone. The rock had only left the boy's hand for two seconds, before a high powered laser shot the rock, and exploded it into pieces. The crowd gasped in horror. The drone turned around, and faced the boy. He was a young Mexican, around the age of sixteen. The drone shone a spotlight on him.

"Attacking a drone is a violation of the law. Violence will not be tolerated," it said.

The boy attempted to turn around and flee, but he did not move more than a few inches. Without further warning, the drone shot the young boy with a low intensity laser pulse beam. The boy fell to the ground, and writhed in pain. The laser left a small burn mark on his shoulder. Protesters, that had been angrily addressing each other only moments before, ran to the boy and tried to give him medical aid. A woman poured out the remaining contents of her water bottle, on the boy. Others tried to help him back onto his feet. Michelle Jacobs had watched the entire event unfold.

"Do you see?! This is what we're fighting! Ask yourselves. Is this the type of society, in which you wish to live?! We're not citizens, we're cattle!" Michelle angrily yelled.

Suddenly, the drone opened up two panels on the top of its body. From the panels, two laser guns extended. They began rotating in a three hundred and sixty degree angle. What the drone said next, shook the crowd to its core.

"Warning. A Free Speech Curfew is now in effect. Thermal weapons, calibrated to lethal frequencies. All persons that do not evacuate this fifty foot radius, will be met with deadly force in the next eight minutes," the drone said.

The drone's camera projected the holographic image of a clock timer, counting down the eight minutes. Several individuals began screaming. Panicked protesters started running for their lives. Fifty feet was a relatively small area, but the drone's words were deadly serious. People wasted no time evacuating the area. Military and policemen were standing outside of the perimeter. Certain ones beat and arrested protesters at random, once the protesters had cleared the drone's radius. Some protesters tried fighting back, but were quickly clobbered by the heavily armed personnel.

Webster looked at Times and said, "I'd say, it's best we leave. Follow me."

Times was overwhelmed by the chaos, which was unfolding before his eyes. Without hesitation, he ran away and followed Webster's every step. The two men bolted away from the park. Horrifyingly anguished cries, echoed in the distance. Once they were far enough away from the scene, they slowed their movement to a brisk walk. Both men took deep breaths, and slowed down their pace even more, until they came to a complete stop.

"Whew! That got my blood flowing!" Webster declared.

Times took a deep breath and exclaimed, "Are you crazy? We almost got killed!"

The two men stood in silence for a few moments, until they had both regained their composure.

"God dammit, this is going to be all over the news. The Feds have me on camera. I'm probably going to lose my unemployment. What the hell was I thinking?" Times heatedly asked.

"Calm down. You didn't do anything wrong," Webster sternly said.

Times tried to calm his anxiety.

"I guess you're right. Still, my wife is going to kill me if she finds out I was here," Times said.

Without warning, Times felt a sharp pain in his gut. The intense pain made him keel over, and clutch his stomach.

"Ow! What the hell is wrong with me?!" Times yelled.

He knelt on the ground and groaned. Webster stood behind him, and placed his hand upon Times' shoulder.

"You said you were vaccinated today?" Webster asked.

Times winced and said, "Yes, around eleven thirty this morning."

Webster reached under Times' arm, and helped him to his feet.

"Your body is having an adverse reaction to the nano-machines," Webster explained.

"What are you talking about?" Times asked with confusion.

"Nano-machines are tiny robots implanted into the vaccines' liquid. They will release additional doses of medicine into your system, over the next few months," said Webster.

"Watch it, you sound like one of those conspiracy theorists," Times said in a sarcastic manner.

Webster smiled and continued explaining, "Don't worry, they're relatively harmless. You'll excrete the remains, a couple weeks before you need to get your next shot."

"How do you know so much about them?" Times asked.

"Nanotechnology was researched by my company. We thought it was an easier way to deliver time-released doses of medication. In the end, we scrapped the idea. Focus groups showed that our customers preferred to manually take their doses," Webster replied.

The ominous answer both intrigued, and agitated Times. There was something slightly disturbing about Webster. His pleasing demeanor made Times uneasy. Webster did not appear outwardly threatening. But his cryptic manner of speaking, and mysterious way of carrying himself, made Times nervous.

"I should go home," said Times.

"Here, let me give you my cell phone number. I may have a vitamin supplement, that will help suppress your reaction to the vaccine," said Webster.

"Full of surprises, aren't you?" Times replied.

He extended his wrist, and exposed his cell phone wrist band. Webster extended his wrist, and tapped his cell phone band against Times'. The two phones beeped, which indicated that their numbers had been exchanged.

"Surprises? No, I hate surprises. That's the problem with our society. The general population thinks that everything happens by chance. I am a man who believes that there is no such thing as coincidence," Webster said.

Webster's mood became notably serious. Times was bewildered that he would make such a bizarre statement.

"What's your deal anyway? Why do you want to help me?" Times asked.

"Because you seem…troubled," replied Webster.

"You're not a fag, are you? Because I'll tell you right now, I'm not into any queer shit," Times pugnaciously said.

Webster was offended.

"Even if I were the type to seek a male suitor, don't you think it's wrong to accuse me without any proof?" Webster said.

Times hung his head in shame.

"I'm sorry. The past few days have been really lousy," Times said.

"You need to learn how to control your anger, son. Or at least, use it for a greater cause. Our society is on the brink of revolution. A man needs all the friends he can get, in these uncertain days. You seem like you could use a friend," Webster said.

Times was shocked by Webster's generous offer.

"I don't have many friends. I guess we could hang out sometime. It might get my mind off of my problems," Times said with embarrassment.

Webster grinned.

He shook Times' hand and said, "I look forward to speaking with you again, Gregory."

Webster walked past Times, and into the New York City night. Times stood on the sidewalk for a few minutes. He gazed at the sky. High above his head, he saw the silhouette of a drone, flying past the skyscraper rooftops. He wondered if it was the same drone, which he had just seen at the park. He tried to tell himself that the nervous feeling in his gut was not fear, but an adverse reaction to the vaccine. But deep down inside himself, Times knew the truth. He was terrified by the events he had just witnessed. Times was not a person who liked to dwell upon the government's overt corruption. But witnessing the protest's violent conclusion left him with fear, and rage towards his overlords.

Times knew that he was a slave to the system. He knew that he lived in a false reality. His life was nothing more than a set of artificially manufactured reactions, to a pre-programmed set of instructions. The artificial habit in which he was living kept him docile, fat, and weak. It took an immense amount of willpower, to repress the hatred he felt brewing in his soul. He thought back to all the meaningless conversations, in which he had engaged with his coworkers, over the years. He remembered how fully grown men would stand around the water cooler, drinking cups filled with poisonous fluoride; which was a chemical added to 98% of all available drinking water. They would grandstand, trying to impress one another with their knowledge of sports, video games, and comic book movies. These men were nothing but children in adult bodies.

He remembered watching all the women constantly judge one another. They repeatedly talked about celebrities, reality television shows, and the latest fashion. They injected themselves with dangerous beauty products, in an attempt to fit the mold of what society told them was attractive. They mercilessly hen pecked their husbands, and destroyed their masculinity by belittling their every action. The few people he knew who actually got married, lived loveless lives. They were either involved in swinging sex parties, or had little intimate contact with one another. Families were all but destroyed by the One Child Mandate, which had led to a massive increase in abortions. Most families wanted a male child, and eventually society had a disproportionate ratio of males to females.

Times thought back to all the years he had lost, working for the system. He felt nothing but remorse over the fact that he had wasted his life. From his childhood, he had always tried to obey orders. He studied well, got decent grades in high school, and was able to find a moderately well-paying job. His friends and family praised him for living the American dream, but Times knew this dream was a sham. He was hundreds of thousands of dollars in debt, and had no logical way to pay it back. Even if he were to find a new job, the interest accumulated from his numerous petty loans, would keep him impoverished. That was the banker's secret. They created unlimited amounts of debt, and kept inflation and interest on the debt at a high rate, so that it was impossible to repay. Times could work his whole life, and never break free from his financial prison.

His stomach felt like a boiling kettle. His knees quivered, and knocked together at the kneecaps. The comment Webster had made about the nano-machines inside of the vaccines, frightened him. Deep down inside, he knew the machines were real. He had heard stories about people having horrible reactions to the vaccines. Some people got terribly sick, and started slowly dying after being vaccinated. Doctors would not even treat a sick patient, who complained about being poisoned by a vaccine; even if that patient was bleeding out of his every orifice, when he arrived at the hospital.

Doctors believed that anyone complaining about vaccines was a conspiracy theorist. Doctors even went so far as to call the authorities on people, who claimed that the vaccines were purposely killing humans. Times remembered hearing stories about people, who went into violent convulsions after receiving the shots. People claimed that their children were brain damaged, after receiving the vaccines. He had even heard about extreme cases where people chopped off their arms after receiving the vaccine, to stop the viral infection.

It took every ounce of willpower Times had in his body, to prevent himself from vomiting. He realized that he wasn't even sick from the vaccine anymore. That nausea had subsided, for the moment. He was nauseous about the fact that he had been a human jellyfish for his entire life. After a few more moments of shaking, he pulled himself together. He walked to the subway, and went home.

6 Pay Day

"It's Sky. Leave me one," the prerecorded message said.

The phone beeped, and the voice mail started recording.

"Damn girl, pick up your phone," Cameron said.

He closed his palm, which ended the call. Cameron had been trying to call Sky for the past forty minutes. It was midday on Wednesday, November 21st, 2216. Cameron had been awake for the past few hours and he was about to leave the compound. The last time he had seen Sky was the night they both went to New York City. They had spoken by phone a couple times since that night, but they had not again met in person.

Cameron felt that Sky had become distant ever since their trip. She had rarely ever been out of New Jersey. Cameron knew that interstate travel could sometimes have negative effects on a person. In the old days, traveling by train to another state would have been a normal activity. In today's society, traveling to another state was a privilege for most people. For wealthy individuals, interstate travel was a mundane task. For people who lived in the poor districts, like Cameron and Sky, interstate travel was unnerving. For some, it was a thrill which brought unimaginable joy. They were momentarily fooled into thinking that they had escaped their poverty. For others, it was a constant reminder of how imbalanced was the American power structure.

There had been numerous cases of people being arrested, and even killed by authorities, when they tried to cross state borders. Some individuals lucky enough to have made an interstate trip became depressed after their journey. They realized that their whole world was a prison. They understood that their government had enslaved them to the point, that they were no longer allowed to travel freely. Given the depressing sights they witnessed during their voyage, Cameron wanted to make sure that Sky had not been adversely affected by the adventure.

However, Cameron's mind was not solely focused on Sky. He had to go pick up his payment, from a money launderer that helped sell the remaining meat and produce. Cameron and his team had a sophisticated operation. It involved giving local acquaintances a certain amount of food, which they sold to customers. At times, Cameron felt like nothing more than a petty drug dealer. He would acquire the food through robberies, or illegal food deals. He loaned it to distributors and then collected the majority of the profits. He let the small time hustlers keep a portion of the proceeds.

The only reason it worked so well, was because the illegal food market was a dangerous business. Cameron and his friends kept the violent food gangs out of the neighborhood, while providing fresh food to generally nonthreatening people. This allowed otherwise law abiding citizens to eat healthy, while still paying their bills. Because Walter always stressed community over profit, Cameron and his team did not make a tremendous amount of money. While it was hard to find a person in what remained of their small Newark city, who genuinely enjoyed the societal norms, the entire community had an unspoken agreement that this was the best way to support their economy. Everyone knew that the only other option was to live under violent street gang rule, or submit to government tyranny.

Cameron tried calling Sky one more time to no avail. He grabbed his black leather jacket, and exited his room. He walked down the hall, and into the living room. Eiji and Walter were sitting on opposite ends of the L-shaped living room couch. They were both using their personal holographic tablet computers. Cameron walked past them without saying a word. He went to the spiral staircase. Walter looked up from his holographic display.

"Cam? You leaving?" Walter asked.

"Yeah. It's pay day, remember?" Cameron replied.

Walter nodded his head, and returned his attention to the computer.

Before Cameron left Walter said, "Don't stay out too long. We have business to talk about tonight."

Cameron glanced over his shoulder.

"I'll try," he said.

Cameron walked through the warehouse, and exited out one of its doors. He shivered briefly, as his body tried to adjust to the cold weather. He boarded a bus at a nearby stop, and rode it for several minutes. He exited the bus, and walked a few blocks to the main street strip. The strip contained the majority of the city's shops. Its decrepit apartments and surrounding buildings gave away its true nature. It was a demoralized and decaying metropolis, which was lucky to have not descended into chaos.

Prostitutes walked the streets, liquor stores sold synthetic alcohol, and there were virtually no cars driving on the road. In the daytime, most shop owners felt safe. The strip had laundry mats, hotels, clothing and electronic stores, beauty salons, and various eateries. Most shops did decent business, due to the high volume of train station commuters that patronized their stores. However, the strip was little more than a fancy slum.

Cameron walked up to a Chinese restaurant. It was a small restaurant that mostly served takeout meals. A group of three young men in their late teenage years were outside the building. One man was sitting down, with his back leaning against the restaurant's brick wall. His friend sat upright beside him. The other man sat on the steps, which led to the restaurant's front door. Even though Cameron had dealt with them numerous times, their demeanor always unnerved him. He was not afraid of the men, but he was very disturbed by their actions.

The men all had the same look upon their faces. Their eyes were white, except for a bluish gray tint around their iris. They all drooled from their mouths, and ignored their surroundings. They were underfed, disheveled, and did not have a very pleasant style of dress. They wore hooded sweatshirts, and ragged jeans. They did not move from their spots, nor did they bother patrons, which is why the restaurant owners rarely asked them to move. Unfortunately, their behavior was all too common for people their age.

They were hardcore video gamers. They operated the games, by using special contact lenses. The lenses were miniature computers that functioned via brainwaves. Brainwave technology utilized the electronic signals that naturally occurred in the human body. The lenses would scan the player's iris, and send commands which operated the game. This type of interface deeply immersed the player in the game's fictional setting. The contacts created a portal to a virtual world, which was entirely controlled by the player's thoughts.

The gamers spent hours each day, playing the latest popular game. Gamers were even able to make a modest living by competing in tournaments. They lived in what was commonly called, augmented reality. To them, their fictional virtual identities were more important and realistic, than their own flesh bodies. They had entire alternate lives, which satisfied them more than real human interaction. They were more interested in gaining virtual currency, friends, and notoriety, than they were in trying to be successful in their real lives. Cameron walked up to the man sitting on the steps, and started speaking to him.

"Ken. Kenneth, it's Cameron," he said.

Kenneth swayed from side to side, while his mouth hanged open. He drooled from his mouth, and did not respond.

"Come on, goddammit," Cameron said.

Cameron lightly slapped Kenneth's face, in an effort to wake him from his trance.

"Ken, Ken. Wake the fuck up, it's Cameron," he said.

He continued tapping Kenneth, on the side of his face. Kenneth stirred, and slowly reacted to Cameron's touch. Kenneth closed his mouth, and licked his lips to hydrate himself. He momentarily recovered from his daze.

"Ca...Camer...on? You want to play?" Kenneth groggily asked.

"No, I don't. Stop screwing around, and talk to me," Cameron said in a visibly annoyed tone.

The bluish gray tint in Kenneth's eyes slowly faded, and returned to their normal brown color. Kenneth wiped the drool from his face. Sweat dripped from his brow. He breathed heavily, like he had just awakened from a very intense sleep.

"Hey...Ca...wha', sup?" Kenneth asked.

Cameron tried to hide his annoyance. He knew that Kenneth was not a bad person. But it was frustrating dealing with someone, who was so out of touch with reality. Cameron knew that he had to make Kenneth pay attention.

"You told me that you wanted to move those goodies. You got some money, or what?" Cameron said.

Kenneth smiled but still looked like he was half asleep.

"Yeaah. Yeeah I got you, man! I...sold it up good...to that girl, man," Kenneth said.

Cameron tried to hide his mild amusement. Though he was serious about collecting his funds, Cameron could not help but be entertained by the sight of a fully grown man, who had the mental capacity of a retarded child.

"And this girl, did she give you any money?" Cameron asked.

Still dazed Kenneth said, "Yeah man I traded it…to friend. Said she'd give me real...good deal on game gear."

"Ken *please* focus, my nigger. Did you make a sale, or what?" Cameron asked in a stern voice.

"Hold on," Kenneth said.

Kenneth put his finger to his temple. His eyes rolled back into his head, and he started blinking quickly. Cameron became uneasy, but hid his feelings.

After a moment Kenneth said, "Here...Here give me your hand."

Cameron extended his right hand and opened it, palm side facing up. Kenneth rolled up his sleeve, and touched his cell phone wrist band against Cameron's.

"It's...there," Kenneth said.

Kenneth's eyes stopped rolling around, and Cameron looked at his palm. The phone's holographic text read, "13,000 CARBON CREDITS transferred." Cameron closed the display, and covered his wristband.

Cameron eased his demeanor and said, "Sorry to bust your balls man, but that shit ain't easy for niggers to get."

Kenneth was still too dazed to give a decent response.

"No...Problem, Cam. You...the man, man. Helping...people eat," Kenneth sincerely muttered.

Cameron could tell that Kenneth was already suffering withdrawal from his game. Gamers had a tough time coming back to reality, after playing for so many consecutive hours.

"I'll have some more, real soon," Cameron said.

"Thanks...Cam," Kenneth said.

His eyes started fading into the bluish gray tint. Soon Kenneth would fully slip back into his game world.

"And stop playing that shit all the damn time. It rots your brain," Cameron said firmly.

Cameron saw Kenneth attempt to nod. His eyes fully glazed over, and he was once again immersed in his game. Cameron shrugged, and began walking back to the bus stop. He was only a few blocks away when he felt his wrist vibrate. He opened the holographic interface, and spoke to the image displayed in his palm.

"Hey. What's up, stranger?" Cameron playfully asked.

"I have to tell you something," Sky replied.

"What's wrong Sky?" Cameron asked with deep concern in his voice.

"I'm in trouble, Cameron. I think the Feds are watching me. My phone keeps randomly rebooting. My computer's web browser is moving really slowly, and my apartment lights keep flickering," she said.

Cameron felt his heart skip a beat. He tried to maintain his composure so that he would not alarm Sky.

"How long has this been happening?" Cameron asked in the calmest voice he could muster.

"Ever since that night," Sky worriedly replied.

"Sky, I'm–"

"You're nothing but trouble, Cameron. I'm not sure if we should talk anymore," Sky interrupted.

Her words deeply hurt him.

He sheepishly responded, "Walter is a professional. I wouldn't worry–"

"No! Just...just leave me alone!" Sky yelled.

She disconnected the hologram. Cameron futilely tried tapping his wristband, to maintain the connection.

"Fuck!" Cameron yelled out in distress.

Cameron took a few deep breaths and tried clearing his mind. This was not the first time Sky got angry with him. She did not like being involved with illegal activities. She would frequently fight with Cameron, but the two would always resolve their differences. However Cameron could never be sure if she was serious, when she said she didn't want to speak anymore. He never knew when their next fight would be their last.

Cameron rode the bus back to the stop closest to the compound. The entire time, he felt disturbingly violent. Cameron was scared of his violent side. He rarely committed violent acts, but the few he had committed, were very serious. He could remember three specific times when he lost control. When he was a teenager, he beat a fellow street hustler with a tire iron. The other thug had tried to rob Cameron, for a bag of oranges he was selling. Another time, he broke a man's ribs during a street fight. The two had a petty dispute over some chickens, which had been mistakenly thrown away.

His first violent outburst remained his most vivid memory. It happened when he was only eight years old. Growing up poor, Cameron was malnourished and out of shape. While he was still in a government controlled, prison preparation facility, he engaged in his first serious fight. Public schools had been fundamentally transformed into brain washing centers. The government wrote virtually all the textbooks, so they had the power to rewrite history as they saw fit. No information was taught in public school, which was not approved by the government.

Curriculums taught students the values of Communism and Socialism. Mathematics was redefined so that students did not have to give correct numerical solutions. They only had to explain why the numbers they chose made them feel good about their sexuality. Children, who picked numbers that were allegedly anti-heterosexual, were given higher grades. Shorthand words like, "hgrm" (hologram), "sftydrn" (safety drone), and "hmncbnpltn" (human carbon pollution), were considered proper English. Playing sports was banned, unless the child stated his career choice was that of a professional athlete. Scores were not kept. Children played for a set period of time, and then both teams were declared winners.

With the exception of Christianity, all religions including Satanism were embraced. Illegal immigrants were granted free tuition. When they reached kindergarten, children were taught about graphic sexual activity. These studies included lessons about masturbation, homosexuality, incest, bestiality, and necrophilia. Sexual relationships between children and school staff were allowed. The only stipulations were that the child must openly consent to the relationship, and had to be at least five years old. Pedophile teachers and faculty members, were given miniature, flying drone bodyguards. The two foot long robotic airplanes hovered above the pedophiles' heads. The drones would shoot hot particle beams, at angry citizens who tried to kill the child molesters.

Children were routinely required to use hand, eye, and vein scanners. These biometric devices were utilized to sign documents, use the restroom, and purchase cafeteria food. There were annual anti-terror drills, where attacks on the school were simulated by role-players. Commonly represented groups of alleged terrorists, were returning war veterans, gun owners, climate change deniers, food liberationists, pro-life supporters, and homeschoolers. The Bills Of Rights, and Constitution, were heavily demonized. Supporting the Second Amendment was an arrestable offense.

One day while sitting at the lunch table, a large boy named DeMarcus Barton, began teasing Cameron. DeMarcus was a twelfth generation welfare recipient. His family were staunch Socialists, who reveled in their dependence. They adamantly praised the government, for taking care of their family throughout the decades. DeMarcus was too big for his age, due to the high volume of hormone laced food that the welfare class was forced to eat. That day, DeMarcus sat down beside Cameron and ripped a juice box from his hand.

"What you eating, nigger?" DeMarcus said.

"Stop playing, Dee," young Cameron said in a squeamish voice.

"Shut up, you African booty scratcher!" DeMarcus said.

DeMarcus further examined the box. He laughed and alerted the other children at the table of the box's organic contents. Cameron's parents could not always afford real organic food, which was only available in certain stores that were licensed by the federal government. But sometimes they would save up enough money, to occasionally buy it for him.

"Eww, *this* nigger drinks *faggoty* apple juice! He's an apple faggot!" DeMarcus said.

DeMarcus made a mocking face, and continued taunting young Cameron.

"Apple faggot, apple faggot!" DeMarcus jibbed.

Cameron tried reasoning with DeMarcus to no avail.

"Stop playing, nigger. Give me back my juice," Cameron said.

DeMarcus suddenly got very serious with Cameron. He stood up, and started shouting in little Cameron's face.

DeMarcus said, "Sissy ass nigger, I *know* you ain't talking to *me* like that! Don't make me beat your ass! Yeah, I took your faggot apple juice! The fuck you going to do about it, bitch nigger? Nothing! You gonna cry, and run home to your hairy ass mothe–"

Cameron did not wait for DeMarcus to finish his sentence. He punched DeMarcus right in his mouth. A few of his baby teeth were knocked loose. DeMarcus fell down, and Cameron pounced on top of him. He continued punching DeMarcus in his face. A crude humanoid robot pulled Cameron off of DeMarcus, before any serious damage could be done. Cameron was immediately expelled from the school, and sent to another public de-education facility. His parents were fined $850 in Carbon Credits. The school nurse recommended that he be placed on anti-psychotic drugs. Cameron's parents wisely refused.

That day was the first time Cameron ever fought for his right to eat. He was forever changed by that fateful experience. He learned at a young age, that there was no place in this world for intelligent, rational people. A person had to be brutal, and follow his primal instincts if he hoped to survive.

He put the thoughts of violence out of his mind, and returned to the compound. When he arrived he overheard Lucia, Eiji, Walter, and Vincent arguing in the living room. Cameron walked up the stairs, entered the room, and witnessed the heated transaction. Their words echoed over one another.

"No way we're going...!" Lucia yelled.

"...it's a great haul..." Walter said.

"This doesn't feel right..." Eiji stated.

"...are you *trying* to get us caught?" Vincent asked.

Cameron watched them argue for a few more seconds.

"Enough! Why the hell are you all fighting?" he loudly asked.

The room went silent.

Eiji motioned to Walter and said, "Go on, tell him."

Walter pointed to a glowing red truck, on a holographic map that was projecting upon the wall.

"It's a couple days before Thanksgiving. We've got to take this truck that's coming out of Trenton. It'll be our biggest hit this year," Walter said.

"Hah! Sorry...I think I had a spot of crazy stuck in my ear. Did you say, Trenton?" Cameron asked.

Walter gave Cameron a deadly serious stare.

"Yes. What's the problem?" Walter asked.

Cameron's smile quickly faded.

"Walt, buddy, that's a *suicide* mission. Trenton is under military occupation," Cameron said in a serious voice.

"Which is why we have to take extra precautions," Walter said.

Walter pointed to the map and said, "This Federal Emergency Monitoring Association truck is leaving at 11:30 PM tomorrow. It's filled with three hundred pounds of hormone free, real organic turkeys, hams, beef, and other delicious treats. Approximately two hours and thirteen minutes later, it is scheduled to arrive in Edison. It will be delivered to the Governor's banquet. Our plan is to intercept it before it reaches the destination."

"Have you lost your damn mind? FEMA? You want to fucking rob FEMA?!" Cameron yelled.

"See! Even Cameron sees this is crazy!" Vincent forcefully interjected.

"If we get caught, they'll throw us in a damn FEMA forced labor camp!" Lucia added.

"I never said *we*, are robbing FEMA," Walter said.

Walter expanded the map, to show a more detailed view of the street.

"There will be a large crowd in the area. They have a plan to stop the truck, after it passes the toll booth in New Brunswick. We'll storm the truck as a group, and take its contents," Walter said.

Cameron broke out in jeering laughter, and chuckled until his belly hurt.

"You really think they give a shit about our strength in numbers?" Cameron asked defiantly.

"That truck will have a drone escort. We'll be lucky if they don't shoot us on sight," Lucia said.

"I agree with them Walter. This is unbelievably risky. This will only create anarchy," Eiji said in a somber tone.

Walter turned off the holographic console, and fell silent.

"What do you think you know, about anarchy? When I was a young man I saw people so hungry, that they ate the burnt corpses of fellow rioters," Walter said.

He began slowly walking around the room. The rest of his team bowed their heads in shame.

Walter continued, "Anarchy was watching families hack each other to bits with machetes, over the last slice of fresh bread. Anarchy was watching the military evacuate, because the armories were being overrun with hungry refugees."

After circling the entire group, Walter stopped at the base of the table, and continued explaining his plan.

"They have a plan to stop the truck in the middle of the road. There will be many people begging for the food. The authorities will have no choice but to abandon their vehicle, unless they want to be responsible for firing live ammunition on innocent civilians," said Walter.

"Conformation by ultimatum. Clever. It wouldn't be the first time that has worked," Vincent said.

Walter nodded his head, acknowledging that Vincent understood his plan. There was another awkward silence.

"I'm not convinced. It still sounds too risky," Cameron said.

"Yes. We have no way of predicting that FEMA will stand down," Lucia said.

Walter looked at Lucia and said, "No, we don't. We'll just have to trust that our servants will take the moral high ground, and feed their fellow man."

Cameron gave his team a cold stare. He was disgusted by the plan, and decided to voice his opinion.

"Whatever. You're going to have to do it without a wing man," said Cameron.

Cameron did not wait for a response. He turned around, and stormed out of the room.

"Cam, Cam! Goddammit Walter, look what you've done! Cameron, wait!" Lucia yelled.

She followed Cameron down the stairs, and out to the garage. Lucia quickly caught up to Cameron, grabbed him by his right shoulder, and swung him around so that the two were standing facing each other.

She fought back tears and screamed, "Are you insane?! How could you just walk out on us?"

Cameron gave her a stone cold glare.

"I'm not walking out on anybody, Lucy. That plan is bat shit crazy," Cameron said.

He paused for a moment, so that both of them could calm down.

"You know I'll follow Walter, on any job which I thought would benefit our group. But this idea is foolish and reckless. It's not even like him to wantonly risk lives," Cameron added.

Lucia tried to reason with Cameron and said, "I don't know what he's thinking. This is the stupidest idea he has ever concocted, but he seems really positive that it will work. We've got to trust him. Can't you at least come with us, to make sure all Hell doesn't break loose?"

"You ask me to save you from Hell, but what makes you think I'm not its harbinger?" Cameron solemnly asked.

He stared at Lucia for a few more seconds. Cameron eventually turned around, and exited the compound.

7 A Dangerous Proposition

Gregory Times dialed the buttons on his cell phone at a furious pace. He had already dialed the number several times that day to no avail.

Once again the automated voice message said, "Webster Morgan is unavailable..."

Times hung up the phone without leaving a message. He had already left Webster two messages. Mallory and Times had invited a small group of people to a Thanksgiving Day party. It was taking place tomorrow, on Thursday, November 22nd, 2216. Attendees would include Times' mother, Mallory's parents, Larissa and Brian. Mallory was frantically cleaning the apartment. She wanted every inch to be free from dirt and grime. Times was sitting in the living room and browsing news articles on the internet while she cleaned. She paused for a moment.

"Greg, when are you going to the store? I need you to pick up food," Mallory said.

Times started to reply, "I went last night, Mallory. Didn't you see the groce–?"

"WE ARE NOT SERVING POOR PEOPLE'S FOOD TO OUR FRIENDS AND FAMILY FOR THANKSGIVING!" she angrily shouted.

Times looked up from his computer. He was completely startled by her brazen hostility.

"It's bad enough that we had to buy a cloned turkey. The least you could do is spend a little money to buy organic side dishes," Mallory said before Times could respond.

Times looked away from her. He was devastated by her harsh words. Times hated Mallory's constant ridicule and incessant bossiness. Yesterday Times had purchased canned corn, mashed potatoes, gravy, and cranberry sauce, using his Unemployment Food Credits. Times knew they were facing a tough economic situation, and had to be careful how they spent their money. Mallory's belittlement did nothing except make Times feel like less of a man.

"I'm sorry. I'll go out this afternoon," Times sheepishly responded.

Mallory gave Times a furious stare before resuming her cleaning. Times turned off the holographic computer and readied himself for his trip to the market. He left the apartment without saying a word to Mallory, and took a subway train to an upscale store in West Manhattan. As Times walked around the establishment, he started to feel overwhelming depression. He saw wonderful organic foods on sale. Fresh yams, pies, milk, and other items, were being sold to rich customers. The food's smell was so tantalizing, that Times was almost able to ignore the heavily armed police presence. They were patrolling the inside, and outside, of the store.

Times browsed the isles, and calculated which items he could afford. He decided to purchase one gallon of egg nog, one apple pie, sixteen ounces of mashed potatoes, and a liter of gravy. He proceeded to the register. The man behind the counter scanned the items and told Times the price.

"Two hundred forty-one and thirty-seven. Carbon," the clerk said.

Times winced when he heard the outrageously high price. He extended his arm, and tapped his cell phone wrist band against the panel embedded in the counter. The clerk waited for a minute while the transaction processed.

"You're only authorized to spend one hundred eighty-four and seventy-two in Carbon, until December first. You'll have to use cash to cover the remaining tab," said the clerk.

Times reached into his pocket, and removed his wallet.

"How much do I owe?" Times asked.

"Let's see. At the current conversion rate, that will be one hundred thirteen and thirty," the clerk said.

Times pulled out a single hundred dollar bill, and a single twenty dollar bill from his wallet. The clerk gave Times a nasty look. He then used his thumbprint on a scanning panel to unlock the cash register. He handed Times his change before bagging Times' groceries. While Times walked out of the store, he felt the judgmental stares of other customers. He knew they were silently mocking him. Times felt his manhood shrivel up like a withered flower. He angrily walked towards the subway. He was one and a half blocks away from the entry point, when he heard a familiar voice.

"Doing some last minute shopping?" asked the voice.

He turned around, and saw a black sedan car driving itself a few feet behind him. Times saw Webster Morgan sitting in the back passenger's seat. Times greeted him with a passive aggressive response.

"Well I'm obviously not going to work," Times said.

"I see you have some provisions. I'm sure they're quite nice!" Webster said.

"Probably not nicer than yours," Times said, showing his obvious envy.

"Is that any way to address a friend?" Webster asked.

Times grew visibly upset and asked, "What the hell do you want?"

"I'm sorry I didn't pick up my phone earlier," Webster replied.

"Forget it, Webster. I don't even know why I called," Times dismissively stated.

Webster opened the passenger's door and said, "Step in; I'll give you a ride home."

Times looked at Webster for a moment, before walking over and entering the vehicle. Times and Webster sat in silence for five long minutes.

Times finally broke the silence by asking, "Are you some kind of freak stalker?"

"What do you mean?" Webster asked in a confused voice.

"Why are you out here?" Times asked with annoyance.

Webster showed Times his cell phone and said, "You told me to meet you. Did you change your mind?"

Times looked at the screen, and felt bewildered. Webster had a textual message displaying in his palm, which Times never remembered sending.

"Going to Belle's @ 3:30. Meet up for drinks?" it read.

Still confused, Times tried to shrug off the bizarre message.

"I must have forgotten sending that to you," Times said.

Webster responded, "If you're busy, I can leave–"

"No, it's fine. I just, haven't felt good the past few days. Heh, it seems like I can't even remember when I text people," Times interrupted.

Webster grinned and replied, "You must still be feeling the effects of the vaccine. Here, I have something for you."

Webster reached into his coat pocket. He pulled out a small vial of blue powder, and handed it to Times.

"It's a detoxifying sugar that will block the effects of the nano-machines. You can eat it alone, or drink it by dissolving it in water," Webster said.

Times took the vial from Webster, and stared at it for a moment.

"How do you know it will work?" Times asked.

"Because I make my living by selling it, Greg," Webster quickly responded.

Times felt shame for questioning Webster's knowledge. Times knew that Webster was highly intelligent, and felt embarrassed that he could not interact on the same intellectual level.

"Sorry Webster, I didn't mean any offense. I'm having a really shitty day. Hell, fuck having a shitty day. I'm having a whole shitty week...year...life!" Times said with visible agitation.

"You *must* learn to manage your anger, my good boy. I see that you have some food. You should be happy that you still have money to eat," Webster said.

"Hah! I could barely afford anything in that store. Can you believe this little bit of food cost me almost three hundred dollars in credit, or cash, or whatever the fuck these stores are using for currency nowadays!" Times said with rage.

"Are you eating any meat this year?" Webster asked.

"You're joking right? It took me seven months to pay for a ham that I could barely afford when I *did* have a job. Now that I'm unemployed, they've restricted my meat consumption. The only thing I'll be eating this year is one of those six legged cloned turkeys," Times bitterly said.

Times stared at the vial before saying, "You know what? I don't care if they say vaccines are mandatory. I want these nano-machines out of my body."

Times opened the vial, and swallowed its contents in one gulp. The powder tasted sour, and made him cough.

"I'm not going to make myself sick, just to get a few measly unemployment credits," Times said.

Times looked away from Webster. The two men sat in silence for a few minutes.

"I'm not sure if I should tell you this, but I might be able to help you get a real turkey," Webster finally said.

"Really? How much will it cost me?" Times asked with shock.

"Not one penny, my boy," Webster sternly replied.

Times did not have a response at first. He barely knew Webster, let alone trusted him. However, Times was in such a self-destructive mood that he no longer cared what happened to him. He was physically and emotionally drained.

He looked Webster in the eye and asked, "How is that possible?"

Webster wasted no time saying, "There are channels which a person can go through to obtain such goods, if he is willing to take the risk. Tell me, will you be free very early tomorrow morning? Around midnight?"

Times looked at the time on his cell phone.

"That's in a few hours..." he said weakly.

Webster began saying, "I understand if you can't make it–"

"No, no that's fine. Where should I meet you?" Times interrupted.

"Go to the Port Authority Building, on Forty-Second Street. There is an elevator in the main lobby, which leads to a parking garage on the fifth floor. Be there at midnight, and I'll handle the rest," Webster replied.

"Okay. Listen, I need to get home. My wife is waiting for me," Times nervously said.

"Of course. No problem," Webster responded.

Times exited the car. Before he closed the door, Times looked at Webster one last time.

"Hey Webster, thanks. I really owe you one," Times said.

Webster smiled and said, "I'll see you a bit later."

Times closed the door, and began walking to the nearest subway. It was 4:27 PM. Times did not have long before he had to again meet with Webster. The entire subway ride home Times desperately thought of a lie he could tell Mallory, to explain why he had to leave the apartment at such a late hour. He knew she would never believe him, so he decided to make one last stop on the way home to buy a bottle of wine. If he could get her drunk, then she would pass out, and then he could sneak out of the apartment. He went to a liquor store near his apartment, and spent $43.36 in cash for a large bottle of synthetic red wine. He asked the clerk for gift wrapping, and paid an extra $7.56 for the convenience.

Times went home and reached his apartment door. Times prepared himself to be scolded by Mallory. After a few moments he took a deep breath, and placed his fingertips against the door's lock panel. The door slid open, and Times entered the room. Mallory was sitting on the couch. She was in a dazed state. Wires protruded from her arm. A large hologram was projecting two feet from her body. Images quickly flashed. Times saw all of this, and knew she was playing a video game. Mallory rarely played video games. It was disturbing for Times to see her so heavily immersed in play.

"Hey...honey..." Mallory said, with drool dripping from her lips.

Times gently put the groceries on the kitchen counter, and began unloading the bag's contents into the refrigerator.

"Hi, baby. What are you playing?" Times softly asked.

"Oh...am sorry...it's fun...shooting...want to play?" Mallory said while appearing halfway conscience.

Times sat beside her, and kissed her gently on the lips. She tried to smile, but could not. Her body was too weak from the electricity pumping through her veins.

Times said, "You should have told me that you still enjoyed playing. I would have gotten you a new controller. Those ventricle inputs are old. They have contacts now that..."

Times stopped in the middle of his thought, so that he could admire his beautiful wife. For a moment, he could tell that she actually felt content with her life. Even if the feeling came from being placed in an artificial stasis, Times enjoyed seeing her smile.

"Play...?" Mallory asked.

She reached up, and touched his face with her left hand. The wires still protruded from her right forearm. Times could not help himself. He kissed her again on the lips, and let his left hand slide between her thighs. After a moment he moved her, so that she fell deeper into his arms.

"It's okay. You have fun," he whispered in her ear.

She stared into her husband's eyes and replied, "No...play...with me..."

Mallory pulled the wires from her veins, and started kissing Times extremely passionately. The couple sank deeper into each other's arms. Times choked back tears. It had been weeks since he had been intimate with Mallory. He wondered why every night between them could not be filled with such unbridled affection. Times soon let all rational thought slip from his mind, while the two of them explored each other's bodies.

8 Last Exit

"Fuck you, and your stupid monkey bullshit!"

"Monkey? Call me a fucking monkey again! See if I don't fucking paralyze you!"

"Fucking try it, you subterranean sack of shit!"

"FUCK YOU!"

Eiji frantically ran towards the compound's living room. Lucia and Walter raced to the room, following not far behind Eiji. Cameron and Vincent's screaming, was echoing throughout the compound. Sounds of loud scuffling, and objects breaking, could be heard from every room. Eiji was the first to reach the room. He saw Cameron and Vincent locked in a struggle. They had their bodies entangled, and were on the floor wrestling with each other. They only stopped arguing briefly, to try and gain the upper hand in their test of strength. Eiji immediately dove onto the floor, and tried to stop the brawl. He was afraid that they were going to hurt each other.

"Get the fuck out of the way, Eiji!" Vincent screamed.

"Why the hell are you two fighting?!" Eiji managed to say, while trying to separate them.

"Stop! What is wrong with you guys?!" Lucia screamed.

The three men continued to brawl in a chauvinistic and cartoonish fashion. Walter had enough of their outburst. He reached into his waistband and quickly drew the revolver, which he kept by his side when he slept. It was customized stun gun, which had an expandable rectangular holographic screen on its side. Walter quickly expanded the screen, and tapped it twice. It immediately shot a low intensity laser beam at Vincent, Eiji, and Cameron.

The laser beam only targeted Vincent and Cameron. Once they were hit, they immediately stopped fighting. They convulsed for a second, then fell away from each other and writhed on the ground in pain. Eiji stood up, and moved away from Cameron and Vincent. He checked his body to make sure he had not been hit by the laser. Walter holstered the gun, and walked towards Vincent and Cameron. They were both still reeling from the shock pulse. Walter angrily kicked Vincent twice in his stomach. Vincent gasped for breath. Walter then knelt on top of Cameron, and slapped him twice on both sides of his face.

"Does somebody want to tell me what's the fucking problem?" Walter angrily asked.

Vincent and Cameron took a few moments to regain their breath. Vincent pulled himself to his knees. Cameron sat with his back against the wall.

Panting for air Vincent said, "You gave *him* an interstate passport!"

"It wasn't just *me*, you idiot. He gave one to Sky, too!" Cameron quickly said.

Walter stared at the ground for a brief minute. He felt guilty that he had not mentioned the passports to the team.

"How did you find out about the passports?" Walter asked.

"Hah! You don't even deny it, Walter!" Vincent said while scowling at him.

Eiji and Lucia looked at Walter, with obvious hurt in their eyes. It was not usually in Walter's nature to play favoritism with his team members.

"Is that true?" Eiji asked.

"Sky is a good asset, and she seems to get along real well with Cameron. I thought it would be nice for them to spend some time together," Walter said.

Before anyone could respond Walter added, "Whatever happened between them is none of our business. Don't forget, we have a mission tonight. Instead of fighting, you should all be getting prepared. Tonight is not a joke. I don't want to see any more of this ridiculous horseplay in my house. If you want to play touch-tip and grab-ass, go do it somewhere else. I expect everyone to deliver tonight. Is that understood?"

Eiji, Vincent, Lucia, and Cameron, all remained silent. They all knew better than to challenge Walter's authority.

"Good. Now clean up this mess, and get ready to move. We leave in eighty-five minutes," Walter said.

He took one last look at the silent group, and left the room.

Lucy walked to Vincent and said, "Let me get you some ice for–"

"Fuck off," Vincent interrupted.

He pulled himself to his feet.

"This isn't over, Cameron. You may be Walter's favorite, but don't forget who is the muscle in this group," Vincent said while pounding his chest.

Cameron gave Vincent a cold stare, and remained silent. Vincent turned around, and walked out of the room.

"I'll go talk to him," said Eiji.

Lucia sat beside Cameron, and gently rubbed his thigh.

"Are things better, between you and Sky?" she asked.

"No, not really," said Cameron.

"You should speak with her," Lucia said.

She grabbed Cameron's hand. Cameron could tell that Lucia wanted him to call Sky on his cell phone. Cameron obliged, and dialed Sky's number. After a few rings, Sky's image began projecting in Cameron's palm.

"Seriously, why are you calling me?" Sky said in a shaky voice.

Sky abruptly stopped speaking, when she noticed Lucia was sitting beside Cameron.

"Hey Lucy. Sorry, I didn't see you," said Sky.

"It's all right, chica," Lucia replied.

Cameron finally spoke up and said, "Please come out with me tonight."

Sky tried to resist Cameron's charm.

She said, "Why? No..."

"I've been calling you all day. I know you've read my texts, too. I've already told you, something really big is going down tonight. I really need your help," said Cameron.

Sky paused for a moment and said, "Fine. I'll be over in a while."

Sky disconnected the holographic connection before Cameron could respond.

Lucia smiled and asked, "See? Was that so hard?"

Lucia stood up, and extended her arm to Cameron. Cameron took her hand, and pulled himself off the floor.

He said to Lucia, "Thanks. I–"

"It's nada," Lucia said.

She patted Cameron on his shoulder, and pinched his cheek in a motherly way.

"You can't keep fighting with Vincent. Like it or not, you guys need each other. The group needs you. All you're going to do is destroy yourselves and us, if you keep competing with each other," Lucia added.

Cameron looked away from Lucia, and felt ashamed for his actions. Lucia was satisfied by knowing that she had gotten through to Cameron. She exited the room.

Less than one hour later, the entire group of rebels had assembled. Sky, Walter, Lucia, Vincent, Eiji, and Cameron, met in front of the compound.

"What's our plan?" asked Eiji.

Walter opened his palm, and expanded the holographic image projecting from his cell phone. They all listened closely while Walter explained his plan.

"We're going to make a stand right here, under the bridge that connects Route One, to the turnpike. This is going to be extremely dangerous, but we won't be alone. I've talked to some of the most prominent food factions in Jersey. We all support each other. Tonight is not about proving which gang has the most street credit. Tonight, is about making a stand for the people. We need to show these tyrants that we are sick of their oppression," Walter said.

"Right on, Walt," Vincent said.

Walter closed his palm to remove the image.

"I'm an old man. Old enough to remember the last days of our Republic. I pray to almighty God, we don't see violence tonight. I have seen enough of it in my lifetime. However, we will take this truck at all costs. We will show these ruthless Globalists, that the *people* are in control. I need all of your help," Walter somberly said.

Walter spoke directly to Lucia, "Lucy, you're in control of our Suppression Technology. Use our computers to jam any incoming drone signals. Scramble all communication devices in the area that aren't transmitting on our bandwidth."

"Eiji, you're in charge of medics, and evacuation. We have to accept the fact, that there might be heavy causalities. We may need to rescue the wounded. I've left more than enough supplies in our transport van to handle any medical issues. You'll also have sonar, and flash grenades, to distract any hostile forces. If you find yourself in trouble, use them to disorient any humans, or machines, in the surrounding area. Render aid to anyone who needs it, and provide cover to those who are trying to escape," Walter said to Eiji.

Eiji and Lucia nodded. They both acknowledged their duty.

"Cameron, Vincent, now's not the time for your petty bullshit. You're the ones on the ground," Walter stated.

The entire group looked at Cameron and Vincent, who barely even glanced at one another.

"Whatever problems you two have with one another, can wait until another day. Tonight, you're riot control. I can't give you any strict orders. All I can ask is that you use your best judgment. Try to prevent this mission from turning into a bloodbath," said Walter.

Vincent and Cameron still did not speak to each other.

"Fine. You don't have to talk. Just don't scratch your armor. It's not easy for me to repair," Walter said.

The entire group stood in solitude for a few moments.

"Okay, enough talk. WILD OUT!" Walter said with passion.

The team immediately went their separate ways. Eiji, Vincent, and Cameron, entered the van containing the medical supplies. Lucia walked to Walter's car. Walter and Sky followed her.

"Walter, we have to talk," Sky said.

Walter stopped walking and Sky asked him, "Why the hell are you bringing me into this? You know I don't get involved on this level. Besides, I'm useless to you–"

"You're more valuable than you think, Sky. Everyone has a purpose. You'll be with Lucia and me, on top of the old Edison Tower. You're going to be filming everything that happens. For better or worse, we need to document tonight's events," Walter interrupted.

"That's stupid. Why the hell would you need *me*, to operate a lousy video camera?" Sky asked.

Walter tried to speak, but Sky abruptly said, "Don't bother answering me. I don't want to know your reasoning. Just...don't get me in any trouble."

Sky and Walter looked at each other briefly, before they continued walking towards Walter's car. The cavalry left the compound. The van and car sped along the highway. Their destination was New Brunswick, New Jersey. In only forty-five minutes time, they would arrive at their goal. They were now traveling the path to infamy.

Elsewhere, Gregory Times waited anxiously for Webster Morgan to arrive at the fifth floor of the Port Authority parking deck. Times felt quite agitated. He had just been thermally body scanned for weapons with the sensors located in the elevator. Even though he was used to living in a surveillance society, he did not like the idea of having to be x-rayed every time he stepped into a public building. He had called Webster's cell phone twice, and had still received no response. The time was 12:01 AM, Thanksgiving morning. He paced back and forth. Armed military guards near the parking deck's gate watched his every move. They held large laser rifles, and were dressed in camouflage. They covered their faces and heads, with bandanas and helmets.

Times was considering leaving, until he saw a black limousine pull up to the parking deck's entrance. The limousine stopped at the gate. A camera mounted on the gate's top, recorded a digital image of the vehicle. The license plates were electronically forwarded to a national terrorism database. This process determined if the license plates were validly registered. The database determined the plates were legitimate. The spiked steel strip, which was blocking the limousine's front wheels, rescinded. The limousine drove past the spikes, and rolled itself towards Times. It pulled up, and one of its black tinted windows rolled down.

Times saw Webster and said, "I thought you weren't going to show."

The limousine's back door opened, and Webster motioned for Times to enter the vehicle.

"Sorry for the delay. I didn't mean to keep you waiting," said Webster.

Times entered the limousine and said, "Fancy, fancy."

"Take us to exit nine. New Brunswick, New Jersey," Webster said.

There was no physical driver in the car, but the limousine's voice recognition devices responded to Webster's instruction. The car began driving out of the parking garage.

"Wait a minute, what are you talking about? I don't have an interstate passport. I can't leave New York," Times said anxiously.

"Relax," Webster said.

"Relax? I'll lose my unemployment if I get arrested for violating interstate travel laws!" Times angrily said.

"You said you wanted a real turkey. I'm going to get you one," Webster calmly said.

"No turkey is worth risking what little credits they're giving me. Let me out," Times said.

The limousine had reached the street, but had not yet reached the tunnel.

"If you want to leave, that's okay. Just so you know, I'm not taking you to get the meat. I have already arraigned for a turkey to be delivered to your apartment, later this morning. That is, if you still desire one," said Webster.

Times was confused.

Before he could respond Webster said, "I'm taking you out of town for another reason. I want you to see something very important, that is happening there tonight."

Times knew that he should get out of the car, but he wanted the turkey so badly that he remained in the vehicle.

"Fine. I'll go," Times said.

Webster smiled gleefully and said, "Wonderful. Drink this, my friend. It'll calm your nerves."

Webster reached into his coat pocket. He pulled out a twelve ounce bottle, which contained a bright blue liquid.

"This isn't going to kill me, right?" Times asked while taking the bottle.

"If I wanted to kill you, I could have done so already," said Webster in a cold tone.

This statement highly disturbed Times. He tried ignoring Webster's ominous words. Times opened the bottle, and began drinking. The liquid was chilled to perfection; but was not very pleasing to the palette.

After a few sips Times said, "Ugh, it tastes bitter."

"Yes, that's because it's real alcohol," Webster said.

Times continued drinking. The limousine entered the tunnel. There were very few automobiles on the road.

"What is it that you want to show me?" Times asked.

"When we met that night at the protest, I could tell there was something very unique about you, Gregory. You seem like a man, on the verge of waking from a very deep slumber. Tell me...how do you feel about the world, and its current state?" Webster asked.

Times felt weird answering such a personal question. He was not used to being asked for his opinion.

"I think it's awful. They make us live like servants. They feed us scraps, and spy on our every move. It's like this whole world has turned into a giant prison," Times replied.

"So you're not happy with the way you live?" Webster asked.

"No, not at all," Times said.

"You wish to change our society?" Webster asked.

"Yes, I suppose," Times replied.

"*That* is why I befriended you. I am a man, who wishes to bring about great societal change," said Webster.

"How?" Times asked.

"You're not required to know that, at this time. I simply want to see if you're ready for the truth," Webster replied.

The two sat in silence after Webster finished speaking. They arrived at the tunnel's underground checkpoint. All cars traveling through the tunnel had to pass a security inspection, before they were allowed to cross the border. Armed military guards were verifying identifications, and used hand held x-ray machines to body scan the cars' occupants. Before the barbed wire gate would open, the vehicles had to drive through an additional scanning tube, after they had been manually checked by the military guards. Webster's limousine eventually made it to the checkpoint. Webster rolled down his window and Times became extremely nervous.

"I need your interstate passport," said the guard.

Webster smiled and said, "Of course."

He reached his hand out the window, and placed it on the guard's hand held scanner. The guard looked at the screen, and then at Times.

"I need his, too," the guard said.

Webster chuckled and said, "I think you need to have a good look at that screen, son."

The guard carefully studied the screen.

He abruptly told Webster, "Oh, I'm sorry. I didn't realize. You can go."

Webster rolled up the window. Times stared at him in awe. The limousine drove itself through the scanning tube, and the gate opened.

"How the hell did you do that? I thought it was illegal to travel across state lines without a passport," Times asked.

"Soon you'll learn that rules only apply to those who do not possess the means, to bend them. Earlier, I updated my travel itinerary. I indicated that I was bringing an intern with me, during my travels tonight. The itinerary indicated that this intern had already obtained an interstate passport. The intern was cleared beforehand, during a trusted traveler screening," Webster said.

Times had no words for Webster. The realization that this man had enough money to manipulate his way around the law both terrified and excited Times.

"You might want to get some rest. You're in for a long night," Webster said.

Times had not felt sleepy, until this moment.

"Yeah, I guess I do feel kind of tired," Times said.

Times leaned his head against the window and fell unconscious.

Meanwhile, Cameron Moss and his friends were reaching their destination. Walter called Cameron's cell phone.

"Park the van underneath the overpass. We have to hit them right when they get off of the turnpike. We're going to park at the tower, so we can get a good aerial view of the surroundings," Water said.

Cameron acknowledged Walter's instructions.

"I hope he knows what he's doing," Cameron said to Vincent.

Eiji pulled the van underneath the overpass. The three exited the vehicle, with their guns holstered around their waists. They all were wearing their body armor. Bandanas covered their faces. They began walking around the street, which had virtually no cars. They heard a rustling in the bushes. Cameron reached for his gun.

He heard someone say, "Don't shoot us!"

A young girl walked from behind the shrubbery. Cameron looked around, and saw other people hiding in the area.

"You guys are with the Food Liberation, right?" asked the girl.

"Who are you?" replied Vincent.

"Relax. Your friend Wally told us to meet you here. We're part of the resistance," she replied.

"What's your name?" asked Vincent.

"Rachel," she replied.

Before Vincent could respond, he heard Walter's voice speak over his earpiece intercom.

"Relax, they're not spies. We're scanning everyone. There is no sign of hostiles," Walter said.

"Shit might get nasty out here tonight. I want to make one thing clear. We're not the good guys. If you fuck with us, or are trying to get us arrested, you'll be sorry," Cameron firmly told Rachel.

"We would *never* do that. We're with you," Rachel said.

"So what's the plan?" Vincent asked her.

"We have a car that we'll light on fire. We'll roll it down the road, before they take the New Brunswick exit. Wally told us he probably couldn't hack the transport truck, and remotely turn it off. So we'll have to use a good old fashioned road block, to get their attention," said Rachel.

"Sounds like a good plan," Eiji said.

"Let's get in position. They'll be here soon," Cameron said.

The team hid with the rebels, and waited. After forty minutes, they saw a black limousine exiting the turnpike.

"Who was that?" asked Eiji.

"I don't know. It looks like they're pulling into the tower," said Lucia over the intercom.

The limousine pulled into the bottom deck of the Edison Tower, and turned itself off.

"Are they Feds?" asked Eiji.

"Maybe. They appear to have a jammer in the car. I can't make out any thermal imprints," Lucia said.

"We'll keep an eye on them," said Walter.

They all continued waiting. Ten minutes later, they saw three large military trucks exiting the turnpike. The trucks were being escorted by two triangular shaped white drones. The trucks were solid black, and had the FEMA logo painted on their sides.

"This is them. Get ready for some action," Vincent said.

"Here we go. Pray that everyone makes it out safely," Lucia said.

She feverishly typed commands into her computer's holographic interface, and attempted to get a lock on the drones' signal. On the ground, Cameron instructed the other rebels to set the car ablaze, and roll it down the street. They immediately followed Cameron's request. The leading truck had to swerve to avoid hitting the flaming car. All three trucks stopped. The two drones escorting the trucks descended from their watchful position in the sky and hovered over the trucks. The leading truck's back doors opened, and eight military personnel jumped out. They were armed with laser rifles, and were dressed in black and silver camouflage. They wore combat helmets, glasses, and black bandana masks to cover their faces. The military men used their millimeter scanning goggles, and saw that there were many rebels scattered throughout the area. They aimed their laser rifles in the crowd's general direction.

"You are interfering with a military transport! Back off, or we will be forced to open fire!" shouted one of the men.

While hidden behind a bush, Cameron tossed a small transmitter out in the road. The transmitter landed on the ground, and Walter's life-sized holographic image started projecting in the street. He was filming himself, from inside of the abandoned Edison Tower. He wore a long, brown leather jacket, and custom built mask. Walter's mask had a simple design. It was a gas mask, with reflective eye coatings. The mask had enhanced optics, which allowed Walter to utilize telescopic focusing, and night vision. He used a scrambler to disguise his voice, when he spoke to the troops.

"Friends, fellow Americans, we mean you no violence. Right now, you are surrounded by almost one hundred of your fellow citizens. They have traveled from across the state, to be here tonight. They are from all different ages, races, and religions. They come here, to ask for your help," said Walter.

Slowly, people came out from their hiding places behind the unkempt bushes, decrepit buildings, and underpasses. They were dressed slovenly, and had obviously been stricken hard by poverty.

Walter continued, "We know in your hearts that you are not wicked people, but you serve a wicked government. For decades, they have oppressed the American people. The people who stand before you ask for your help, to end this oppression. These are but a small handful of the starving masses living in New Jersey. They want only one thing. A chance to eat real food."

The hungry civilians started inching closer to the military convoy. The men had turned their backs to each other, and had formed a protective circle. Their guns were still trained on the crowd.

"I'm warning you! We *will* use lethal force, if you do *not* stop approaching this convoy!" a soldier yelled.

Walter continued speaking, "You're carrying over three hundred pounds of food to a corrupt Governor, who will share it with her equally corrupt friends. They sit in their lavish offices, while we are out here starving to death. These people have had enough of this injustice. They want the food in that truck, and they are willing to die for that food. That's pure organic meat. It's something these people rarely, if ever, have tasted."

"What are we going to do? Look at some of these people. They're just kids," a soldier whispered to his comrade.

The people continued advancing, while pleading with the military to show them mercy.

"Please, help us," said an older man.

"We're your friends. Don't hurt us," said a young girl.

"We can share it with you. You don't have to starve either," said a middle aged woman.

"We're so hungry," said a frail teenage boy.

Walter continued speaking, "You can tell your superiors that you were outnumbered, and that we took the truck by force. They won't reprimand you for not firing upon innocent civilians. Your families will be proud of you, for supporting food freedom. Hell, tell the Governor that giving away the food will help her approval rating. Tell her to consider it, a charitable donation."

The black limousine, which had pulled into the lower level of the parking garage, was now going unnoticed. Inside, Webster and Times watched the unfolding standoff.

"See what I mean? These people are oppressed too, but they lack a plan. Look at them. They're a flock of peasants, begging the master for scraps. They have no conviction, no organization, and no plan of attack," Webster said.

"Why don't they just take the truck? They've got them outnumbered," Times said.

"Exactly! They refuse to act, because they are weak! They have no leader!" Webster replied.

Times looked at Webster, and absorbed the wisdom of what he was saying.

"I want to get a closer look," said Times.

"Sure, sure. Go see them. Go see the tongue, lick the boot," Webster said.

Times exited the limousine, and began walking toward the scene. The atmosphere was tense. The military did not want to fire on unarmed civilians, but the crowd was intent on taking the truck.

"We have to make a call now, sir. They're getting close," a soldier said to his team leader.

The crowd approached. The leader carefully weighed his options. The drones shone their lights upon the crowd.

"Aw, hell. Open the truck," said the leader.

"Excuse me?" another member asked the leader.

"I said open the goddamned truck. It's lost," the leader quickly stated.

The soldier reluctantly did as he was ordered, and opened the back of the armored meat truck.

"Thank you, thank you," several people said, before rushing towards the vehicle.

"Bless your heart," a woman holding the hand of her eight year old boy, said to the military leader.

"Yes! Yes! Do you feel that? That's the spirit of liberty, igniting your soul! You're helping these people in ways you cannot even begin imagine!" Walter ecstatically said.

Times had run down to one of the exit ramps, but remained a safe distance from the standoff. He watched the unfolding event, but did not want to get too close to the action. He took cover behind a bush in the overpass, and watched in horror at what happened next. The third truck, which had remained still during the conflict, suddenly opened its back doors. A four wheeled box rolled itself onto the terrain. The box's top opened, and two large mechanical arms protruded. One arm was equipped with a large Gatling gun. The other was equipped with a high powered thermal rifle.

"This is a warning to all citizens. You are now engaging in group terrorism. If you do not cease and desist, you will be eliminated," the box said in a terrorizing robotic voice.

"My God. What is that thing? It's huge!" Lucia said.

A frightened Sky said, "Those people need to get out of there right now! It's going to kill them!"

The robot menaced the crowd with its weapons. Walter tried remaining calm, and kept projecting his image.

"Please, turn the robot off! It's going to slaughter innocent people!" Walter pleaded.

The team's leader ran to the back of the box. He pressed his right palm against its control panel. It did not respond. The words, "Manual Override Disengaged," flashed brightly.

"Shit, it's locked! Everybody leave! This is not a joke! The bot is set to kill!" said the leader.

Lucia typed commands into her holographic keyboard, to no avail. Her eyes began swelling with tears as she unsuccessfully tried disrupting the drones.

"Dammit, I can't get any signal! Their jammers are too strong!" Lucia said.

People started screaming, and raced towards the truck. They quickly began looting the meat. They were orderly and fairly divided the spoils, but they all could sense that they were in grave danger. The two drones that were hovering above the crowd further lowered their positions. They readied their weapons.

"Warning has been given. Cease and desist orders have been ignored. Hostiles refuse to comply. Engaging enemy combatants," the box's mechanized voice said.

The large arm with the Gatling gun pointed towards the people looting the truck, and eviscerated them in a hailstorm of bullets. The bullets viciously tore through the crowd, and shredded their fragile human flesh to pieces. Chunks of human bodies fell to the ground, and numerous people dropped dead. Those who were not immediately killed lay in a pool of their own blood; until their last bit of life force drained from their mangled bodies.

"No! No!" Walter screamed.

Walter immediately cut the signal to his holographic projection. The bloodshed was only beginning. Many rebels no longer cared about their safety, and stole whatever they could take from the truck. Others tried to flee. Pockets of armed rebels, that had remained hidden until this point, jumped out from their vantage points, and began shooting at the robots. The military men who had been allies moments before, suddenly became enforcers. They began arresting the hungry rebels.

They walked around and shot people with a specially calibrated burst from their laser guns. The beam's plasma formed electronic nets which resembled spider webbing. People yelled for help as they fell to the ground, and the webbing prevented them from moving. Other military men decided they wanted no part in the massacre, and simply climbed back into the troop transport truck. They locked the doors, and waited for the violence to end.

"Shit! This is turning into a fucking war zone!" yelled Cameron.

"We have to stay low, and try to draw the bots away from the trucks! We need to give these people a fighting chance!" yelled Vincent.

"I'm going to the south overpass! I'll try shooting it from there! Keep everyone spread out!" Cameron yelled.

Vincent and Cameron separated, and began shooting at the drones. They would quickly fire shots, and then hide in the surrounding area. They didn't dare expose themselves for too long; for fear that they would be murdered. From his spot behind his van, Eiji threw flash grenades into the crowd. The grenades flashed multiple pulses of bright light, and were designed to disrupt the drones. Eiji tossed smoke grenades, which further aided the crowd's escape.

The large robotic arm stopped firing, and the rest of the box's contents emerged. The shape of a robotic body arose from the box. It resembled a human torso, and had a spherical camera for a head. The robot scanned the crowd, and honed its sights on the remaining targets. The box began rolling around the street. It indiscriminately fired at the panicked crowd. The drones began assisting in the horrendous assault, by unleashing horrible weaponry on the American citizens.

The drones began flying in circles above the street. One drone sprayed a densely populated group of fleeing pedestrians with a bright blue flame. They howled in pain, as their skin melted. They were quickly incinerated, and were reduced into a pile of burning corpses. Bushes and shrubbery around the road began catching fire. People, who were still trying to hide in the bushes, ran out from their hiding spots. Their clothes were burning. They screamed, and tried rolling around on the hard pavement, in an effort to extinguish the flame. The large robot shot several people who were on the ground, being burned alive. The aerial drone shot another burst of flame at additional crowd members. They shrieked, and were engulfed in a painful fireball.

The other drone shot pulse lasers at individuals who were attempting to run away from the mayhem. The pulse disseminated a severe electric shock wave through its victims' bodies. People exploded into piles of pulverized red mash. Bits of human remains flew in every direction, when the laser burst ripped apart their flesh. Several rebels, who were shooting at the drone, were violently blasted into pieces when it hit them with its powerful particle beam. The drone mercilessly vaporized a young woman, who was running away with an organic turkey that she had just stolen from the meat truck. The drone used its laser to decimate a man who was crawling around on the ground, and had been wounded by a bullet. The man's body burst into a disgusting array of blood and gore.

The scene was gruesome. Burned bodies, gunshot victims, and body parts littered the area. Some portions of the street were stained with blood. People were screaming, and crying. Those who were lucky enough to escape, ran away with whatever food they could salvage. Times shook in terror while the nightmare unfolded before him. He watched a drone shoot a young boy in the lower half of his body, which blew off his legs. He fell dead, with only his torso intact. Times began vomiting.

He started running back to Webster's limousine.

Times heard agonizing cries from burn victims, who were still breathing but were utterly disfigured. He saw sparks from ricocheted bullets that barely missed him. He willed himself to run at a frantic pace. Times shuddered when he heard the short screams of a woman, whose skin was being melted by the drone's blue flame. Eiji was hidden behind the team's van. He implored people to run towards his location.

"Over here! I have supplies!" Eiji shouted.

Some people ran by him, but others stopped for help. He handed out water and bandages. He only stopped to throw more smoke and flash grenades.

Suddenly a voice shouted, "Hey!"

Eiji looked up, and saw three military men jogging towards him.

"Leave us alone! Haven't enough people died tonight?!" Eiji screamed at them.

"We agree," one of the men said while slowing his pace.

They cautiously approached the group. The squad's leader, and his companions, pulled down their bandanas.

"Sergeant Dominic Perez, U.S. Army. Due to the circumstances, our mission objectives have changed," he said.

"What are you saying?" Eiji carefully asked Dominic.

"He's saying, *fuck* this shit! I didn't sign up to kill unarmed women and *kids* on American soil!" his Rifleman said.

"Cam, I think we have some friendlies," Eiji said over his intercom.

Cameron was hidden behind a crumbling brick building. He poked his head around the building's corner, and fired two shots at the ground combat drone.

"What the hell are you talking about, man?!" Cameron frantically replied.

"Some of the Army guys say they want to help," Eiji said.

"Tell them to cut off the signal to the fucking drones!" Vincent screamed over the intercom.

"We can't. They're programmed to override our authority during extreme emergencies," said Dominic.

"So what are we going to do?" asked Eiji.

"We can steal the truck for you. It's going to be risky. We'll have to make it seem like we're just trying to secure the goods. I think I can buy us enough time to stop at the tower, and dump the rest of food without the drones noticing," said Dominic.

"You catch all that, dude?" said Eiji to Cameron.

"Copy! We'll cover you!" yelled Cameron.

"Okay, unload the food on the first floor, and then get moving. You don't want to get caught assisting us," said Eiji.

"We can only promise to drop it off. You're on your own transporting the food," said Dominic.

"I understand. Thank you, and good luck," said Eiji.

He saluted the brave warrior. Dominic and his two teammates turned around, and ran back to the truck. The robots were still on a killing spree. The small group of armed rebels was managing to put up a decent fight against the autonomous killers. They were dealing the drones a lot of damage. The robots were having trouble focusing on them, due to the heavy smoke and light disruption from Eiji's flash grenades.

"Step out of the vehicle! I'm moving this truck to safety!" Dominic yelled at his subordinate troops, who were guarding the meat truck.

One replied, "But sir, we should stay–"

"I'm giving you a fucking order! Now move, so I can secure this truck! Wait here, and try to stop this bloodbath!" Dominic abruptly interrupted.

Dominic entered the vehicle, and drove away. Times was still fighting for his life. He continued running at a frantic pace. He briefly looked back and saw a man who was fleeing, get viciously gunned down by the combat robot. The man died, still clutching the ham with which he was running. Times ran into the tower's dilapidated parking lot, and finally reached the limousine

"Are you seeing this? The robots are committing murder!" Times said to Webster.

"Yes, they are. And the troops are simply standing around, letting it happen. They're no better than those fools who thought they could steal the food. Look at what these people have done to themselves," Webster callously said.

Webster looked into the distance. He saw a drone still shooting massive amounts of blue flame at what remained of the crowd. People's skin, melted away like heated butter. They screamed one last time, before their life was extinguished.

"What do you think about all of this, Gregory?" asked Webster.

"It's absolutely awful. But what can we do? We're helpless," said Times.

"That is where you are wrong, my friend. We *can* make a difference, by fighting the enemy!" exclaimed Webster.

"Who is the enemy?" asked Times.

Webster became agitated and said, "Can you not see it, with your own eyes? It's these damn Food Liberationists! They are the ones causing all this mindless suffering! They refuse to respect law and order! Their tireless crusades do nothing; except bring misery to their companions!"

"You're...you're right. I don't agree with some of the government's policies, but this isn't the way to solve anything. On the other hand, I can't believe that the military is letting this slaughter occur. I can't tell which party is more guilty of treason," said Times.

"That's understandable. These are complex issues. Sometimes, it is hard to spot the true villain," Webster said.

Webster and Times fell silent, and continued watching the carnage. Times winced, after watching a man get his head blown off of his shoulders by a pulse laser beam. The drones were flying around the area taking out the few remaining survivors. Dead bodies lay strewn all over the street. Many were badly burned. Some were missing limbs. Others were riddled with bullet wounds.

An escaping woman made the unfortunate mistake of exposing herself for too long. The ground robot shot her dead, in a hail of gunfire. Cameron and Vincent stealthy moved towards the tower. They were careful not to draw the drones' attention. Eiji had given away the last of his supplies, and had driven away from the debacle. He drove to an area of the highway where he could make a U-Turn. He speedily drove to the tower.

When Eiji arrived, he saw Dominic unloading the food. He quickly helped Dominic remove the truck's remaining contents. A few moments later, Cameron and Vincent arrived, panting heavily.

"That was fucking *sick!* I've never seen something so fucked up, in my entire life!" said Vincent.

"Hey, be glad we're still standing. A lot of those people didn't make it out alive," said Cameron.

Vincent noticed that Dominic was helping unload the food.

"How the hell could you serve a government that butchers its own people?" Vincent asked Dominic.

"Vin, relax. Now's not the time for politics. He made the right choice when it counted the most. He'll be tried for treason and most likely executed; if his commanding officers ever find out that he helped us," Cameron said.

Dominic did not say a word. He handed Eiji the last piece of food, and closed the truck's back door.

"I have to make up a good excuse, when they ask me to explain why there's no more meat. I have to leave. I'm already getting asked my whereabouts. I'll lead the squad south. That will hopefully give you guys a chance to escape. Head north. Make sure this food finds its way to deserving, hungry stomachs. Watch out for those drones. Good luck guys. I'm so sorry this happened," Dominic said while fighting back tears.

"You're a good man. Maybe we can return the favor, one day," Cameron said to Dominic.

Cameron extended his arm, offering to shake Dominic's hand. Dominic accepted the gesture, then quickly got back into the truck and drove away. Sky, Walter, and Lucia, drove into the bottom parking deck a few seconds later. Lucia was in the back seat, crying hysterically. Sky, was stone silent. The team did not say anything to each other. They simply packed up the food, and left the tower.

Elsewhere, Webster and Times were preparing to depart.

"Who were those clowns in the masks? I saw them when I was on the street. They seemed like the ring leaders," Times asked Webster.

"Food thugs. Some of the most notorious survivalists in New Jersey. They are total outlaws. I can't believe they have been allowed to operate for so long," answered Webster.

"How do you know about them?" asked Times.

"Earlier this year, they helped rob a seafood boat owned by one of Rigor's shareholders. I carefully studied the boat's surveillance footage, and identified one of their accomplices. She was an intern that I hired for a summer position. I have been spying on her for several months. After intercepting an incoming call to her cell phone, I learned of tonight's big event. I was originally hoping to collect evidence for the authorities. I have recently joined a special anti-terror unit that is partnered with our adept Federal government. It is called, InfraGuards. After this turn of events, I feel it is best to monitor them for a little while longer. That way, I can crush them myself," replied Webster.

Times was silent, and stricken with a complex variety of emotions. Times realized that Webster was even more powerful, and dangerous, than he first thought. Times quickly came to his senses, and realized that it was 3:17 AM.

"Oh fuck me, look at the time! We have to leave. I don't want Mallory to find out that I was gone," Times said.

"Of course. I'll have you back at your flat, shortly. Attention limousine. Please drive Gregory home," Webster said.

The limousine started driving itself back to Manhattan. Times sank into the limousine's large black seat, and closed his eyes. He tried to ignore the sounds of screaming, and the heartbreaking images of suffering, that were still fresh in his mind.

9 The Mourning After

Gregory Times did not awake the next morning, until the sound of his ringing doorbell jolted him from his slumber. He had no recollection of coming home the previous night. The last thing he remembered was the chaotic sounds of the early morning massacre. The memory of seeing people suffer agonizing pain had haunted his dreams. He could still smell the stench of burnt flesh. He could still hear the sounds of gunshots ringing in his ears. He momentarily lied to himself, and pretended he had simply awoken from a terrible nightmare, but there was no hiding from the truth.

The news was ablaze with stories of what was being called, the Thanksgiving Day Massacre. Cell phone videos from eye witnesses that had recorded the bloodshed were being posted across the internet. Traumatized survivors were being interviewed by the news media. Times exited his bedroom, and saw that Mallory had already answered the door.

"Yes, I understand. Thank you," Mallory said to the robot.

The robot was nothing but a large rectangular scanning panel, attached to a pipe. It had a crude pair of exoskeleton arms and legs. The scanning panel had a cartoonish human face rendered on its inside. She placed her palm on the panel. Her hand print was immediately accepted. The robot's poorly animated face gave Mallory an awkward smile.

The hideous contraption said, "Signature accepted. Have a nice day," before walking away from the apartment.

She closed the door and said, "It's a miracle! We've won!"

Times saw Mallory was holding a large gift wrapped package. She cradled the package under her left arm, and hugged Times with her right one. She placed the package on the kitchen table, and frantically tore away the gift wrapping. Inside, was a twenty-five pound organic turkey.

The note that accompanied the package read, "Congratulations on your good fortune! Signed, W. M."

"Who sent this to us?" asked Times.

"The delivery robot said you won a contest. Don't you remember? She said that last month, you entered a free turkey lottery sponsored by the United Nations," answered Mallory.

Times stared at the initials on the note. He knew W.M. stood for Webster Morgan. Times knew he never entered any contest, and that Webster must have sent the note to make it seem like Times randomly won the turkey.

"Yes, I guess I must have forgotten," said Times.

"I can't wait to show our guests! They will be thrilled!" Mallory exclaimed.

She began unwrapping the turkey, and preparing spices for the meat.

"Hey Mallory, this is going to sound weird, but what time did I get home last night?" asked Times.

Mallory looked confused and responded, "I don't think you left. You were asleep in bed this morning. I don't remember you leaving after we..."

Mallory let her thoughts trail off. Times knew they were both shocked at the fact that they were intimate last night.

"I'm sorry. I guess I must have been dreaming," said Times.

"You probably just dozed off watching television before you came to bed. I wouldn't be surprised if it gave you nightmares. There was a horrible terrorist attack last night in New Jersey. What a rat hole. I can't believe anyone still lives there," Mallory said with disgust.

Before Times could respond Mallory said, "You should wash up, my love. Our guests will be here soon. President Cho is giving a speech addressing the attacks, at noon. You can hear all the details at that time."

Times left the room without saying anything. He was infuriated that the media was calling it a terrorist attack. However, he did not dare tell Mallory his true feelings. He could not let her know that he had witnessed the mayhem.

Across the bay in New Jersey; Cameron, Vincent, Lucia, Sky, Eiji, and Walter, were trying to cope with the emotional impact of the savage events. They had all slept very little since the incident, and had barely spoken to each other after arriving home. Walter and Lucia had unpacked and wrapped what little meat they were able to salvage. They walked into the living room, where the rest of the group was waiting. Lucia sat on the couch, beside Eiji. Walter angrily stood against a nearby wall.

"Eighteen hams and eleven turkeys. I can't believe all those people died; and all we could save were eighteen lousy hams and..." Lucia said.

Lucia let her thoughts trail off. She did not want her friends to hear her voice cracking. She fought back tears.

"It wasn't about the haul. It was about trying to make a difference," said Walter.

Vincent said, "We made a difference, all right. We changed a lot of lives for the wor–"

"Would you stop? Just fucking stop," Cameron abruptly interrupted.

The two men exchanged aggressive looks, but did not take their anger out on one another. They both knew that the plan went terribly wrong. There was nothing either one of them could do about it; and they both knew that they had to leave their differences aside for the group's benefit.

"Can we eat any?" Sky asked softly.

The group looked at her with complete shock.

After an awkward silence Sky said, "Oh my God, I'm so sorry. That's a terribly inconsid–"

"It's okay. That's a great idea. Many people gave their lives to give us the privilege of tasting this meat. It would be disrespectful, to not honor their sacrifice," Walter interrupted.

"I have some spices in my room," said Eiji.

They all somberly started helping prepare the meal. In New York City, Times and Mallory's guests were arriving. Brian and Larissa were the first to show. Soon thereafter, Times' mom Patricia and Mallory's parents, Holly and Scott Baker, came over. The group took turns greeting each other, and exchanging pleasantries. The big topic on everyone's mind was the Thanksgiving Day Massacre.

"My goodness, it sounds so awful. I can't believe those bandits attacked the truck for no reason," said Larissa.

"Those people, and excuse my language, are damn hooligans," said Scott.

"I'm so glad you turned out the way you did, Gregory. You were always such a good boy," Patricia said to her son.

Times wore his best social mask. He pretended that he was another outsider, watching the stories unfold on television like everybody else. He repressed his feelings of rage, disgust, fear, pain, and sadness. He noticed Brian indulging on some snacks that Mallory had placed upon the dining room table. Brian picked up a large handful of genetically modified caramel popcorn. He stuffed it into his mouth, and chewed loudly. He was completely absent of manners. It took every ounce of willpower Times had, to refrain from strangling him.

"Great party, Greg," Brian said.

Brian continued loudly smacking his lips, and Times gave him a creepy smile.

"You know...you might want to slow down, and chew your food," Times said very dryly.

Times paused briefly before adding, "I wouldn't want you to choke."

Brian stared at Times for a moment, before erupting with laughter.

"Hah, hah! You're awesome, Greg! Give me five!" Brian said.

He extended his hand, so that Times could give him a slapping handshake. Before long, it was 12:00 PM. President Cho Kee Ban was on the verge of holding an official press conference. The entire country was watching. Few Americans were listening more intently, than the people in Times' and Cameron's separate homes.

"We are now going to our live feed from the White House. President Cho will be making a statement about the horrific violence, that occurred last night in New Jersey," said the Chinese female newscaster.

Times always hated the news anchors. He had worked with them regularly, before he lost his job at the newspapers. He disrespectfully nicknamed them, biological androids. Times felt they were all soulless gargoyles, who casually reported numerous deaths like it was not an important occurrence. He loathed their indifference.

President Cho's holographic image, displayed from the projector which had been placed in the Rose Garden. Two Secret Service agents in dark black suits, stood on opposite sides of the hologram. They diligently watched President Cho's hologram, and protected it from any spectators that may wish to harm the projection. President Cho's holographic image began speaking.

"Good afternoon, my fellow Americans. It is with a heavy heart that I speak to you on this Thanksgiving Day. As many of you have heard, New Jersey was rocked by a violent act of terrorism, at 2:15 this morning," said President Cho.

From their compound in New Jersey, Cameron and his crew watched the broadcast. They all scowled while listening to the contrived spin that the puppet politician was putting on the events.

"A large food faction attacked a militarized FEMA convoy, and attempted to take the goods that it was transporting. As a result, our military drones had no choice but to engage the enemy combatants. I condemn any act of violence against American armed forces. This radical and heavily armed rouge militia, left our brave men in uniform no choice but to forcefully contain the threat," President Cho said.

Lucia became irate. She spoke her mind, even though she knew that Cho could not hear her.

"Is that what you're telling people? That we attacked *you?!* Those fucking robots shot first, on unarmed women and children!" she shouted.

"What a bastard. He is totally distorting the truth," said Eiji.

"This is *sick*," said Sky.

Back in his apartment, Gregory Times could hardly contain his fury. He savagely bit his nails, while fighting the urge to grab his holographic television, and smash it against the wall.

President Cho continued, "Because of this heinous and despicable act, extraordinary measures must be enacted to preserve our nation's collective safety. That is why I am imposing a nationwide mandatory curfew."

The people at Cameron's compound exploded with rage, and began cursing loudly. Elsewhere, Gregory Times' blood boiled hot with choler. The groups watched President Cho deliver the final segment of his speech.

"All citizens are required to remain indoors, between the hours of 10:00 PM and 6:00 AM. There are no exceptions. Anyone violating this curfew will be subject to a citation, and potentially jail time. This curfew will be active, for at least the next three weeks. It may possibly be extended, until the end of the year," President Cho said.

"Is this guy for real? They publicly execute us, and then place everybody on house arrest like fucking children?" Vincent said, seething with anger.

"What a tyrant! I hate him!" said Lucia.

"Turn it off. I've heard enough," said Walter.

Eiji wasted no time complying. He waved his hand in a downward motion, in front of the television's motion sensor camera. The image quickly shut off.

"We'll talk about this later," Walter said.

Walter stormed out of the room. Eiji, Lucia, and Vincent, continued preparing dinner. Sky arose from the couch. She went to the spiral staircase, walked down it to the garage, and exited the compound. Cameron noticed his friends were glaring at him. They were surprised that he wasn't immediately following her.

"Bloody hell," Cameron said.

He arose, and chased after Sky. He arrived outside and saw she was standing against the wall, with her back facing outward. Her hands were pressed against her face, and she was obviously sobbing. He put his hand on her right shoulder.

He said, "Sky–"

She quickly turned around, and flung his hand away.

"Get *off* of me, you bastard!" she screamed.

Tears streamed down her cheeks. Cameron was heartbroken. He watched mascara run down her face.

"I'm sorry. Please forgive me," Cameron said.

He reached out to hug her. She angrily pounded his chest a couple of times, before she let herself fall into his arms. She cried against his chest for several minutes. She eventually calmed down, and backed away from his embrace.

"I'm sorry," said Cameron.

"Why do you keep saying that? You never mean it; because if you did you wouldn't keep hurting me," said Sky.

Cameron was distraught, and did not know how to respond. Sky was not officially Cameron's girlfriend. Nevertheless it was well known that they were extremely close. They had not yet decided to pursue a full-fledged romantic relationship due to Cameron's criminal activity. However, they both had a strong desire to be together.

"What do you want from me? If you want to leave...then leave. Nobody will blame you for running away," Cameron coldly said to her.

"You know what makes me so mad? You're better than this, Cameron. You don't need this lifestyle. You could be such a great person. Why do you waste your potential?" Sky asked.

Cameron felt immense guilt. He did not like disappointing Sky, but he felt trapped. Most of his life had been spent stealing food and living the life of a rebel. He liked his friends, and did not wish to quit fighting for liberty.

"Maybe I don't want to change," he said.

"That's *bullshit.* You're not happy with your life either," Sky said.

"You have too much faith in me, Sky. I'm just another broke nigger from Jersey. I'm nobody," Cameron said.

He grabbed her biceps, and resisted the urge to kiss her. They shared a long and emotional gaze. Cameron released her arms, and started walking to the compound.

"I wish you believed in yourself, the way I believe in you," Sky said before he left.

Cameron stopped for a moment, and glanced over his shoulder. Her words cut his heart deeply. With pain resting upon his soul, he hung his head and went inside the compound.

10 No Child Left Below

Times remained quiet. The angry activists around him shouted over one another.

"...can we expect to be respected, when they murder us for trying to eat?!"

"...long until it's *your* child–"

"...is the President and knows best–"

"...has abandoned us, because *we've* abandoned God!"

It was twenty-two days after the Thanksgiving Day Massacre. Webster and Times had become close acquaintances. They did not always agree on political, social, or economic issues, but they respected each other. Times had been attending political gatherings for weeks. Webster informed him of every event, and sometimes even brought Times organic food when he attended.

One angry activist shouted, "I don't care what you want to do with your life! I will not be bossed around like some kind of child! Fuck the curfew!"

Soon the activists chanted in unison, "Fuck the curfew! Fuck the curfew!"

After a few chants, the roar of the crowd quieted down. Times confronted Webster.

"They're really angry tonight," said Times.

"Who can blame them? They are victims of the greatest tyranny in human history," said Webster.

Times gazed at the crowd, but did not respond to Webster.

"Have you thought about what I said?" Webster asked.

"When? That...day?" Times cautiously said.

Webster grinned, yet remained silent.

Times spoke again, "Yes, I have thought about what you said, for quite some time. It's not me. I'm not a leader."

"I see. I can't blame you, I guess. There are few men brave enough to accept leadership," said Webster.

"It's not about bravery, friend," Times said.

"Why do you hide, if not out of fear?" asked Webster.

Times smiled happily and responded, "She's pregnant."

"Are you sure?" Webster asked.

"Absolutely. I couldn't be more sure, or happier," Times replied.

"Well, congratulations! I wish you well, young man. You must invite me to the baby shower," Webster said.

Webster extended his hand, and the men shared a strong handshake.

Times said, "I don't mean any disrespect–"

"Don't be absurd. I am not upset," Webster said in a genuinely caring tone.

He did not question Webster any further. Times took a final look at the disgruntled mob, and breathed a deep sigh.

"I hope to see you soon, old man," Times said with conviction.

"Indeed," said Webster with a smile.

Times did not hesitate to exit the meeting. He went to the subway, and returned home to Mallory. She was waiting anxiously for him. He was very happy to see that she was scantily clad in her nightgown.

"Welcome home!" she said.

Mallory ran over and hugged him immediately after he entered the apartment. Times kissed her passionately, and rubbed her stomach.

"We're both glad to see you!" Mallory said.

Times gave her a loving embrace. He kissed her one more time, upon her soft lips.

"You're everything I could ever want," Times said.

Mallory smiled and said, "We have our first ultrasound tomorrow. Let's go get some rest!"

The couple went to bed and was incredibly content with their life together.

They woke up the next morning, and readied themselves for the hospital visit. They made their way to United World Hospital, a Chinese owned and operated hospital in Greenwich Village. They were not worried about the bill. Pregnant women were given access to free hospital visits under Socialist health care laws. Times and his wife walked over to a large black kiosk that was placed in the lobby.

"Palm prints please," said the giant kiosk.

Mallory and Times put their palms against the screen.

"Welcome, Gregory and Mallory Times. Please have a seat," the kiosk's robotic voice said.

They sat in the emergency room and waited to speak with a doctor. They were too happy to notice the plethora of people entering the facility. They waited for almost two hours, while many injured people came into the hospital. Some had gunshot wounds. Others were missing appendages. All persons were required to give the giant machine their palm print, if they wanted treatment. If a person could not give his prints due to missing limbs, he was required to give a sample of blood; which was taken by a robot hospital nurse. The nurses rolled around on two-wheeled devices that resembled scooters. They had a humanoid torso, highly intricate robotic arms, and hands. Their heads were spherical cameras, which also rendered a cartoonish looking face inside of the sphere. Eventually, a robot nurse rolled up to Mallory and her husband.

"Times, party of two. Please follow me," the robot said.

Mallory and Times were escorted to a hospital room. Another man and his wife were having their small child examined. Times could tell the child was stricken with a form of Autism. The child's eyes rolled around like marbles in her skull. Another robotic nurse carefully examined the girl; who was drooling on herself. Her parents looked upon their daughter with deep concern.

"Your child is experiencing a convulsion. This is a perfectly normal response after taking a vaccine. That means the medication had no side effects. Do not attempt to touch your child," the robotic nurse said.

The girl's parents smiled awkwardly. They somehow convinced themselves that this was acceptable behavior. The robot that was escorting Mallory and Times, pressed a button on the control panel embedded in its chest. The glass wall separating the two sides of the room turned white, which gave its human occupants their much needed privacy.

"The doctor will be here shortly," the robot nurse said.

The robot rolled away, and the happy couple waited for another twenty minutes. A human female doctor entered the room, and was accompanied by the robot nurse.

"You're here for the ultrasound, right?" asked the doctor.

"Yes, we are! I'm so excited!" replied Mallory.

The doctor smiled, and typed a few commands into the robot's chest plate interface. The robot lifted Mallory's shirt, and exposed her stomach. The robot carefully sprayed a thin coating of blue paint, upon Mallory's bare midriff. After a moment the paint dissolved, and showed the inside of Mallory's womb. The doctor placed her hand on Mallory's stomach.

"Let us take a look at the beautiful baby," the doctor said.

The doctor moved her finger around Mallory's stomach, and examined the unborn child. Holographic images projected around Mallory's belly, and showed the baby's vital signs.

"Everything looks normal. I think that..." the doctor said, before letting her sentence trail off.

"Is anything wrong?" Times politely asked.

The doctor became pale, and ignored his question. Mallory and Times were worried by the doctor's demeanor.

"Uh, um. One second, I need to call my supervisor," the doctor said.

"Doctor, what's wrong?" Mallory asked.

"I have a code six hundred fifty-one, dot zero. Please advise," the doctor said into her cell phone band.

Times became agitated and asked, "Hey doc, she asked you a question. What's the matter?"

The doctor tried to cut the ultrasound's video feed. Times moved her hand, before she could stop the projection. Times felt his heart sink to the bottom of his stomach. He began sweating, and became nauseous.

Times looked at his wife and said, "Don't worry hon, it's a mistake."

Mallory pressed her stomach, and rotated the holographic image in her direction. Times tried stopping her, but it was too late.

"Don't look! Baby don't look, it's a mistake!" Times shouted.

Mallory burst into tears when she saw the image. Two tiny heads were seen floating in utero. The tiny frames of two separate bodies were visible. Small nubs of fingers, and partially formed eyes, were clearly distinguished. Mallory was pregnant with twins. In another time, this would have been a cause for joyous celebration. But in this world, the sight was a death sentence. Times did not waste a second before springing into action.

He shoved the doctor to the floor, grabbed Mallory by her hand and ran out of the room. He looked to his left, and saw two armed camouflage wearing guards. They aimed large machine guns at the couple, while running down the hall. Times looked to his right, and saw another three armed guards running down the corridor's opposite end. The overhead lights began flashing red.

"Mallory, RUN!" Times screamed.

Still clutching her hand, Times ran forward towards the stairwell. The guards turned off their guns' safety locks.

"Stop! Child Enforcement Agency!" yelled one of the guards.

Times and Mallory ran into the stairwell. They raced down one flight of stairs, burst through a door, and exited to another hospital floor. Hospital security cameras body scanned them. The camera's immediately alerted all CEA agents of their location. They ran frantically and knocked over any object or person that stood in their way. They turned a corner, and tried escaping into another stairwell. They stopped when they saw four armed patrolmen blocking their path. Mallory and Times' pictures were being displayed inside the walls. Next to them were the words, "Carbon Violators."

"Emergency. Code 651.0 in progress. This hospital is under lock-down. CEA and security personnel, check your phone for live GPS updates of the suspect's whereabouts," a voice said over the intercom.

"Go Mallory, go!" screamed Times.

He let go of her hand, and lunged at the armed men. He moved fluidly, and no longer cared about his own personal safety. He summoned a strength, which only a man desperately trying to protect his family, can muster. He grabbed one of the CEA enforcers and began biting him. The enforcer released a spine curdling scream. Times tore out a small chunk from his face, and spit it on the ground. Mallory tried to open the stairwell door. She was shot by a strong, non-lethal laser round, from one of the enforcer's guns.

Times fought valiantly. He furiously punched and kicked the men. He did not even wince, when they hit him with steel batons. He barely flinched when they grabbed his neck, and started strangling him. He viciously yanked away their hands, and began violently punching the guards. They desperately tried restraining him. Mallory tried crawling away, but the damage was already done. She felt blood drip from between her legs. Three doctors joined the armed men, and held Mallory down on the floor. One of the doctors held a needle, which contained red liquid.

"Don't touch her! I'll fucking kill every last one of you!" Times screamed.

Times broke free from his assailants. He knocked over a CEA enforcer and rushed to his wife's aid. The doctors and guards marveled at Times' strength.

One guard said, "Crap, what the hell is this guy taking? He's goddamned strong!"

Times was able to pull one last act of heroism. He tackled the doctor who was holding the needle. He pinned the physician on the ground, and smashed his head against the floor. The doctor flopped around and started having a seizure. One of the CEA enforcers used his hand held taser, to shoot a highly powerful jolt of electricity into Times' back.

Times rolled over, and twitched around on the floor. He helplessly watched his entire life, crumble before his eyes. Mallory was still bleeding, when she was forcibly injected with the red liquid. She began gasping, and quickly went into shock. The doctors and armed men, held her down.

"You are in violation of the One Child Mandate. Compulsory abortion has been applied," said a CEA enforcer.

Mallory's body violently convulsed. She heaved the contents of her stomach upon herself. The bleeding between her legs worsened. A robot nurse rolled up to Mallory, cut a hole in her stomach, and surgically inserted a tube into her umbilicus. The tube made a horrible squishing, and suction sound. It filled with blood and tiny body parts. Mallory and Times' twins were viciously ripped from Mallory's womb. After thirty-eight agonizing seconds, the robot finished. It sewed Mallory's stomach wound shut, using special foam that instantly clotted blood. The robot committed its final vile act by issuing Mallory a hospital bill, and legal citation.

"Your bank account will be charged, with the amount you see displayed on your cell phone. If you do not have enough money in your account, you will have ninety days to pay the remaining balance. If you do not pay the fine, a warrant will be issued for your arrest. In the event you are arrested, you may face additional criminal penalties," the robot said in a heartless metallic voice.

Nearby spectators gasped in repulsion. Some ran away in tears. Most people stared blankly at their cell phones and ignored the commotion. No one dared help the couple, or condemn the hospital staff's actions. The patients were too afraid that they would be equally brutalized by the merciless CEA enforcers.

"Fuck you, fuck you..." Times said.

He regained control of his body, and crawled over to Mallory. They held each other, for what seemed like an eternity. Before the doctors and armed enforcers left, they rolled a wheelchair over to their victims. Eventually, Times arose from the floor. Mallory and he were covered in blood. He picked her up, and gently placed her in the wheelchair. They left the hospital, entered a nearby subway, and went back to their apartment. They remained silent during their entire journey.

Times rolled Mallory into their bedroom, removed her from the chair, and placed her upon the bed. She was too traumatized to speak. She touched his face with her hand. She ran her fingers across his lips. She stared at him, with an awestruck look on her face. After several minutes, she passed out from exhaustion. Times walked out of the room, and closed the bedroom door. He exited the apartment. He was overcome with animosity, and started punching the walls. He hit them so hard, that he broke holes into the reinforced sheet rock. He activated his cell phone, and called the only person he still considered a friend.

Webster answered the phone and said, "Gregory, nice to hear from you. What can I do for you, my friend?"

Times cleared his throat, and said, "Tonight I've learned, that we are nothing but animals."

"What are you talking about? Are you all right?" replied Webster.

Times leaned his back against the hallway wall, and slowly let himself sink into a sitting position.

"Mallory was carrying twins," Times said in disbelief.

Webster did not need to ask why Times sounded so upset. Webster knew that America's One Child Mandate was strictly enforced. Times' tragic compulsory abortion experience, was one of thousands that occurred at government owned hospitals every year. Ten years ago, an independent hacking group called Onymous, published electronic documents they stole from hospital computers. The documents made the shocking claim that there were hundreds more abortions, secretly performed by mobile execution teams. The teams forcibly entered a person's house and aborted their offspring. All their victims were hiding the fact, that they conceived a second child.

The teams were alerted of the violation by ordinary citizens. These citizens willingly spy on their neighbors. The documents were widely available on the rouge internet, called the deep web. Downloading the documents was considered proliferation of terrorist propaganda. It was a crime, punishable by up to ten years in jail. The accuracy of the information contained in these documents was never confirmed; because too many people were scared to obtain copies of them. The only news media outlets that reported their existence were independent organizations.

"Gregory, I am so sorry. I cannot imagine how you must be feeling," Webster remorsefully said.

"We've tried to conceive before, but it never worked. We were worried that we might be infertile. We were considering trying genetic therapy, to help us reproduce," Times lamented.

After a brief pause he said, "Now, I wish that were the case. Anything would have been better..."

Times choked up, and began silently shedding tears before he could finish.

"Words will never be able to express my sorrow, at your terrible loss. Please do not think I am trying to be an opportunist, but I would like to offer you some help," said Webster.

"What kind of help?" asked Times.

"My company is testing a new drug. It is designed for patients with severe Post Traumatic Stress Disorder. We've performed several trials, on returning Syrian war veterans. The drug has had moderate success. I feel it has helped comfort many disturbed men and women. In exchange for your participation in the trials; I will offer you and your wife the drug, psychological counseling, and financial compensation," Webster said.

Initially Times was shocked by Webster's sudden generosity. The feeling almost immediately faded, because Times had come to expect phenomenal surprises from Webster.

"I don't know what to say, except…thank you," said Times.

"Stop by my office, tomorrow. I will get you started on the program immediately. We will bring your wife into the project, once you feel she is ready. I'll text you the details. Check your phone tomorrow morning," said Webster.

Times did not wait long before saying, "Okay, I accept. It's not like I have anything else to lose."

He closed his palm, and Webster's facial image disappeared. Times sat against the wall, and cried for twenty-three minutes. Afterwards he returned to his apartment, laid upon his bed, and fell asleep beside Mallory.

11 The Examination

The next morning, Times awoke early. He saw that Mallory was still sleeping. She breathed heavily. Her chest heaved after every labored inhale. He wanted to hold her, but did not want to disturb her slumber. He went to the kitchen and opened the refrigerator. The shelves were quite barren. Half a gallon of hormone laden milk, six slices of stale bread, and four slices of cloned roast beef were all that remained. Times remembered to check his phone, which he had neglected to remove from his wrist before falling asleep.

A holographic image appeared in his left palm. He placed his right finger upon the image. After holding his finger in place for three seconds, he quickly swiped it in a downward motion. The image expanded, and covered his forearm.

The image read, "Good Morning, GREGORY TIMES. You have received a gift worth 550 CARBON CREDITS, from WEBSTER MORGAN. Would you like to accept, or decline this transaction?"

Times tapped the area of his forearm that was illuminated with the word 'ACCEPT'.

The screen processed the transaction, and then displayed the words, "Thank you, GREGORY. You also have ONE (1) new Text Message. Would you like to read this message?"

Times pressed the portion of his arm which displayed a holographic button labeled 'OK'.

The message, "10:00 AM. Friday, December 14th, 2216. Meet me at 3025, West Seventy-Eight Street, 7th floor," appeared.

Times waved his right hand over his left forearm, and the holographic image disappeared. He grabbed a glass from his cupboard, and poured himself some milk. He sat down at his living room table, drank his milk, and ate a slice of bread. After he finished, he went into the bedroom to see Mallory. She was still asleep. He sat next to her on the bed. Times leaned closely to her face.

"Mal, are you awake?" Times whispered.

He gently shook her shoulders. She groaned, and rustled in the bed for a moment. He leaned even closer.

"Baby, I have to leave for a little while. I think I have a job offer. Please don't be angry with me," he whispered.

Times operated his cell phone one last time, and sent 400 Carbon Credits to Mallory's phone. Times gave Mallory a soft kiss on her cheek.

"I love you," he whispered.

Times arose from the bed. He walked to the closet, grabbed his clothes, entered the bathroom, and dressed himself. After he had put on his best sports jacket, dress pants, shirt, and tie, he exited the bathroom. He walked by his bedroom door. He stopped, and glanced into the room, when he heard Mallory whimpering.

"Baby? Are you okay?" Times asked.

Mallory did not respond, and pretended that she was still asleep. Times knew that she was crying. Her body was racked with pain, from the forced abortion. He pressed a small panel beside the door's frame, and it quietly closed.

Times exited the apartment. He took the subway to the address which Webster had given him. Soon he found himself standing in front of a huge skyscraper, in the uptown section of Manhattan.

There was no mistaking who owned the building. The words RIGOR PHARMACEUTICALS were projecting on the building's front, in large holographic letters. Times entered the structure, and walked up to the giant black kiosk in the middle of the reception area.

The text on the screen read, "Welcome. Please place your palm on the receptacle to continue."

Times followed the instructions, and held his hand in place for a few seconds.

Soon a robotic voice said, "Welcome Gregory Times. Webster is expecting you. Please go to floor seven."

Times removed his hand, and walked to the elevator tube. The tube was a wonderful silver color that looked big enough to hold at least thirty people. The tube was connected to a shaft, which ran all the way to the building's top floor. He entered the elevator with several other people. The doors shut, and it started moving. Even though Times felt well dressed, he soon became upset that his attire was not up to par with everyone else's. The men wore expensive suits, and the women wore dazzling skirts. They talked mindlessly on their cell phones, striking business deals with whoever was on the receiving end. Times loathed the corporate world. He wondered why these infantile adults, got such a thrill out of dressing like aureate birds, and fancy lads. He had nothing but disdain for the upper class. He felt they looked down upon second class citizens like him.

He arrived at the seventh floor, and started walking through a long corridor. He saw a vast amount of people working on the busy floor. Doctors in white robes could be seen working behind giant glass doors. A group of business women walked past him. They excitedly spoke about their ideas for new marketing campaigns. There were lots of security personnel closely monitoring the activities. They all wore dark business suits, and contact lenses. The optics completely blacked out their eyes' color. In their right eye, the lenses projected video streams from closed circuit cameras. They were able to change feeds by blinking in a specific manner. In their left eye, was a highly advanced form of backscatter technology. This allowed them to see through certain objects, including people's clothes. Their ears were inked with a special tattoo that was an operable communication device. Times was positive they had guns, and he did not dare make any suspicious movements.

He reached the corridor's end, and found himself in the reception area. There were chairs, a nice table, and an electronic magazine dispenser. People tapped their cell phones against the box, and downloaded free magazine publications. A friendly young female receptionist was sitting behind a large desk. Beside the female, stood a five foot tall robot. Its body was a cylinder attached to a set of four wheels. It had human-sized robotic arms, which were equipped with claws that were used to grip objects. Its head was a rectangular shaped camera, which could rotate 360 degrees. Times walked to the reception desk.

"My name is Gregory. I'm here to see Webster," he said.

At first, the female looked at him with suspicion.

"May I see your identification?" she asked.

She extended her hand. Times rolled up his sleeve, and tapped his wristband against hers.

After looking at her palm she replied, "Welcome Gregory. Webster has been expecting you. Please follow Alice."

"Pleased to meet you, Mister Times. My name is Alice. It is my pleasure to assist you," the robot said in a friendly, mechanized female voice.

The robot Alice extended its claw. Times grabbed its hand and gave it a shake. Its grip was surprisingly soft.

"Uhh, hello. Nice to meet you too...I think," said Times.

"People get a little nervous when they first meet Alice. But don't worry, she's harmless!" said the receptionist.

The robot Alice began rolling from behind the reception desk. It dutifully led the way for Times. They walked down an adjacent corridor, until they reached a set of large double doors. Alice placed its robotic claw in the door's custom built handle, and rotated its hand to the right. The hybrid scanning panel was equipped to accept human hand prints, and specifically designed robotic claws. The left side door retracted into the upper part of the frame. The right one retracted into the ground.

Times stepped inside and was awestricken by the office's grandeur. A large desk was in the middle of the room. Large windows showed the beautiful Manhattan skyline. There was a sprawling bookcase containing what Times estimated to be, well over 300 books. A small artificial fireplace was carved into a portion of the bookcase. The fireplace contained a holographic projection, which displayed the image of a wood burning fire.

A holographic television displayed on a wall, near the door's right hand side. A large couch was in an opposite corner of the room. Two chairs sat on either side of the desk. A moderately sized chair faced a larger one that was pointed at the opened doors. Webster arose from the grand chair, and greeted Times with a smile.

"Welcome, my friend! Glad you decided to join me," Webster said.

He walked in Times' direction. His crisp black business suit and red tie were accentuated by the light emanating from the windows. The two men met in the middle of the room, and shook hands.

"Webster, this...this is incredible," Times said with reverence.

While still clutching his hand, Webster patted Times on his right shoulder.

"Are you hungry? Would you like something to eat?" Webster asked.

Times had been trying to ignore the empty pit in his stomach.

"I suppose I'll have a bite, if it's not too much trouble," Times said with a slight tremble in his voice.

"Half a sandwich. Turkey, with lettuce," Webster sternly said.

The robot Alice made a series of blipping noises. It rattled around for several seconds. Afterwards, it opened a panel in the front of its torso. It removed a perfectly prepared sandwich. The oval shaped roll was approximately eight inches in length. The meat was plentiful. Webster returned to his desk, and sat upon his mighty chair. The robot Alice placed the sandwich on the desk.

Webster looked directly at Times and said, "Sit. Eat. You look malnourished."

Times reluctantly sat in the adjacent chair. It was noticeably smaller than the one in which Webster sat. Times could not control himself. He quickly picked up the sandwich, and began eating heartily. After a few mouthfuls, he found himself about to choke. Times had not meant to take such enormous bites. He had already devoured one quarter of the sandwich. It took great self-discipline to stop himself from attacking the leftover pieces. He finished chewing the remaining bits that were already in his mouth. He was so overwhelmed by the magnificent taste of the delicious organic food that he did not speak.

"Drink?" Webster asked.

Before Times had a chance to respond, Alice produced a bottle of root beer from its chest cupboard. Times feverishly drank the cool and refreshing beverage. After consuming half the bottle's contents, he placed it on the table.

"You're a very lucky man," Times meekly said.

"I don't believe in luck. A man makes his own fortune. Let us get down to business," said Webster.

After a brief pause Webster said two chilling words, "Devil's Blood."

"What?" asked Times.

"Scopolamine. It's an incredibly powerful plant. My company seeks to use it to treat severe depression and Post Traumatic Stress Disorder," Webster said.

"Yes, you mentioned PTSD last night. Why can't you get it released? Did it kill too many of your other guinea pigs?" Times asked.

Webster was not affected by Times' snide remark.

"The nickname Devil's Blood was coined decades ago. It is called that, because the plant excretes a sticky red liquid from its stems. Some cultures even call it Devil's Breath, because it can be ground into a powder. It is used to treat motion sickness, pain, and illicit drug addiction," Webster replied.

"Sounds like a miracle plant. What's the problem?" Times asked.

"Its use can produce some…undesirable side effects," Webster said.

"Go on, I'm listening," Times said with intrigue.

"Three years ago, we were on the verge of a nationwide release. We were only four days away from showcasing our findings to our shareholders. There was an incident. One of our patients had a son. He stole some of the medication, and consumed several pills one evening. At the end of a violent outburst he proceeded to hack off his right foot, with a woodcutting axe that his father kept in the house," Webster said.

"I can see how that might negatively affect sales," Times nervously said.

Webster continued, "He set fire to their condominium, before butchering himself. His adopted sisters died from smoke inhalation. His…two fathers, burned to death. He poured kerosene on their bedroom floor, before throwing a burning pack of matches into the room."

Times was noticeably shaken by the violent story.

"There's no proof the drug made him snap. People commit horrible crimes every day," Times said.

"Not when they're six years old," replied Webster.

Times was mortified by Webster's revelation.

"I see. Nobody would buy a product, that causes those types of side effects," said Times.

"Since the incident, we've modified the formula. We believe that it's possible to block the potential psychosis, induced by consuming an excessive dosage," said Webster.

Times arose from the chair, and walked over to Alice. He patted the top of the obvious camera it had for a head.

"I understand," said Times.

Before Webster could reply Times added, "The sick become well, and the well become sick. This is why you can't have normal clinical trials. I assume this type of research, borders on the limits of what the law allows."

"There may be some, ethical issues...but think of the potential! This could be one of the greatest pharmacological breakthroughs in human history! And *you* can be part of the discovery!" Webster exclaimed.

Times stopped patting Alice on its head.

"Maybe," Times said.

He gave Webster a cold stare.

"Or maybe I'm simply less of an insurance risk," Times said.

There was a brief silence before Webster said, "Alice, please escort Gregory to room three o'two. The chemic will explain the process in greater detail."

"Follow me, sir," Alice said to Times.

Before Times left the room, he said to Webster, "I don't know if it's appropriate to thank you, considering the unique nature of our relationship. But I am grateful, albeit in a morbid way, for our friendship."

"Good luck," Webster solemnly replied.

Alice and Times traversed the long hallways, and winding corridors. They eventually reached a small, windowless office. Alice placed its robotic claw into the door's hybrid panel. The door slid open, and Times followed Alice into the room. The room was well lit, and painted a marvelous shade of white.

There was a medical operating table in the middle of the room. A large glass window embedded in the back wall caught Times' attention. He recognized it was one way glass. It allowed others to see into the room, but prevented Times from seeing the opposite side. The room contained various cabinets, drawers, tabletops, and sinks. He saw a refrigerator, which Times assumed was not used to store food.

"Have a seat," said Alice.

Times removed his jacket, and sat upon the table. Alice removed a small syringe from one of the drawers.

"Hold out your arm," Alice said.

The robot connected the syringe to an open slot in its right claw. Times rolled up his sleeve, and remained steady. Alice poked him with the syringe, and began drawing his blood. After a moment the robot stopped.

"The chemic should be here any minute," it said.

Alice took Times' blood over to a small workstation, and placed a droplet of it underneath a microscope. The robot scanned another sample, with laser beams that shot from its camera. Times bowed his head, and let his mind wander. He tried to ignore the heavy pain in his heart. He thought of Mallory. He longed to hold her, comfort her, and tell her that everything would be all right. Choking back tears, he looked up at the door.

A loud thumping sound echoed from down the hallway. The sound got closer, and the sight that revealed itself in the doorway took Times completely by surprise.

"Greetings, Mister Times. I am Chemical Medic 3100. You may call me Chem-Mech, if you please. I am programmed to treat patients that are undergoing pharmacological therapies," said the robot standing in the doorway.

Times marveled at the five and a half foot tall machine. Its torso was a large square-shaped box. Two robotic arms, similar to that of a human, protruded from its torso. Intricately designed robotic claws were attached to the arms, and resembled human fingers. Its legs were comprised of two straight rods that bent backwards at the knees. The feet were rectangular rubber pads, which rested flat on the ground. Its head was a sphere, attached to a rod at the top of the box. The front of the sphere was a dark circular curved dome, which eerily resembled the dark shade of the room's one-way mirror.

"Chem-Mech. Clever," said Times.

The robot walked further into the room. Its motion was stunningly fluid. It lifted up one leg, moved it forward, and placed it on the ground; before gracefully performing the same motion with its other leg. Despite its torso slightly bouncing up and down when it moved, and ignoring the inverted kneecaps, the robot accurately mimicked human motion.

"I can have a human physician perform the examination, if you prefer," the Chem-Mech said.

It cautiously approached Times, who was absolutely stunned by its realistic interaction.

"No, it's all right. You seem very nice. I just wish Webster would have told me what to expect," Times said.

Alice rolled over to the Chem-Mech, and handed it the vial of Times' blood. The Chem-Mech inserted the vile into a small opening on the side of its chest panel.

"My patient log says you recently suffered a traumatic event. Would you like to disclose the details?" it asked.

"No, not particularly," replied Times.

"Okay," replied the Chem-Mech.

It used one of its robotic fingers to shine a light in Times' eye.

"It was a death...in the family," Times unexpectedly said.

"I am sorry for your loss," the Chem-Mech said.

It proceeded to body scan Times, using a series of lasers that projected out of its head dome. Chem-Mech curled up one of its robotic fingers. It tapped Times' left knee with its finger, to test Times' reflexes. Times' leg violently jerked outwards, and kicked the Chem-Mech in the upper portion of its right leg. The robot stared at Times for a moment, but was unaffected by the reaction. Times let out a deep breath and cleared his throat. He did not know what made him feel more bizarre; the fact that he was divulging his emotions to a machine, or the fact that he wanted to apologize for kicking its leg. Before Times could say anything, the Chem-Mech lightly grabbed his wrist. It began measuring Times' pulse.

"Has this experience made you feel unusually agitated, fatigued, or depressed?" the Chem-Mech asked.

"Yes," Times quickly answered.

"To which symptom?" it asked.

"All of them," Times coldly replied.

"Did this experience make you want to hurt yourself, Gregory?" the Chem-Mech asked.

Times let his eyes gaze towards the wall.

"No," Times eventually replied.

Chem-Mech put down Times' wrist, and placed its robotic claws upon Times' chest and back.

"Did this event make you want to hurt someone else?" it asked.

"Yes," Times abruptly replied.

Times looked at the machine and expected a response, but the machine simply tilted its head from side-to-side, while keeping its hands placed upon Times' body. The experience made Times feel uneasy. He had an eerie suspicion that the robot was trying to read his thoughts. After a moment, the Chem-Mech removed its hands.

"Thank you for your cooperation, Gregory. Please wait one moment," the Chem-Mech said.

The robot stepped back from Times. Its body began making clunking, and whirring sounds. Its chest rattled loudly, and it shook on its feet for precisely twenty-two seconds. When it finally stopped, the Chem-Mech walked closer to Times. It stood up high on its front legs. A small panel opened near the bottom of its chest plate. After some thick fog dissipated, a plastic vial containing thirty-two clear gel pills could be seen.

"Take one of these every night, before you go to sleep. Come back for a refill when the bottle is empty," it said.

Times gently removed the bottle. The Chem-Mech closed its panel, and walked to the opposite corner of the room. It sank its legs down, so that it compressed its size to two feet tall. Finally, the Chem-Mech switched itself into sleep mode. Times stared in bewilderment at the Chemical Medic 3100. He looked at the bottle that it had just produced for him. He tried his best to comprehend the outstanding experience which had just occurred.

Before he could react the robot Alice said, "Follow me, Mister Times. I'll show you to the exit."

12 A Mysterious Encounter

Cameron and his crew sat around their war table with solemn looks upon their faces. It was a cold afternoon on Tuesday, December 18th, 2216. At 4:10 PM, Walter entered the room and sat at the head of the table.

"Sorry I kept you all waiting. I was talking with Paul," Walter said.

The group did not speak.

"He has lined up an incredible deal. One of his clients is a manager on a celebrity cruise ship," Walter said.

Walter briefly paused because he was disturbed by the prolonged silence.

Walter continued, "They have clearance to travel to the State of Puerto Rico. The island is holding a celebration, to mark the seventy-fifth anniversary of its induction to the Union, as the fifty-second State. It will dock for two days. There is a rouge group of hunters that poach wild game on the island. They have–"

"We're not doing any more jobs," Vincent firmly interrupted.

"I suppose I don't need to ask, the reason behind your decision," Walter solemnly replied.

Walter looked at the team's sullen faces.

"You're *all* in agreement?" he directly asked Cameron.

Cameron glared back at Walter. Cameron felt the entire room staring at him. Cameron felt an unspoken pressure to speak on his team's behalf. Cameron did not like being the de facto second-in-command, of their group. Going against Walter's wishes felt repugnant. Cameron felt that he was betraying a member of his own family. But Cameron could not ignore the fact that his other teammates no longer had the desire to perform their duties.

Cameron took a deep breath and sternly said, "It's hard to justify our actions, after what happened on the turnpike."

His friends gave Cameron an approving look, silently showing their gratitude for challenging Walter's authority.

"We started doing what we do, to help people. What's the point of this entire struggle, if we just wind up getting people hurt?" Vincent asked.

"Vincent, there are always casualties in war," Walter replied.

"How can you call our fight, a war? We're criminals. We sell illegal goods, most of which are stolen, for profit. There's nothing heroic, or valiant about us," Vincent passionately said.

Walter sharply replied, "Horse shit! What happened out there was not our fault! Those people knew the risks–"

"That's your rationalization? It's okay, because they made a choice?" asked Eiji.

"What about those kids?! Are you saying they deserved to die?!" Lucia abruptly yelled.

"You know that's not what I meant! Nobody deserved it, but–" Walter snapped back.

Walter could not finish his sentence. The room erupted in a shouting match. The entire team began yelling angry words over one another. They all switched between verbally attacking each other, and defending their past actions. Amid the commotion and while fighting back tears, Lucia yelled something that silenced the entire group.

"I don't want to hear it, Walter! I won't help you kill anyone else!" she screamed.

Walter realized his words were in vain. He sighed deeply before making a heartfelt speech.

"You're all too young to remember what it was like, before the Carbon Taxes. You were just little kids, when it happened. Your parents protected you by going along with the tyranny. They gave you vaccines, registered your births, and kept you enrolled in public schools. They sheltered you from the harshness of the real collapse. I was twenty-six when they passed. My whole life, people were oppressed by an increasingly tyrannical government. It moved too slowly for people to realize what was happening. We helplessly watched our civil liberties eroded at the hands of fascist politicians; themselves funded by private globalist bankers," Walter said.

Walter continued, "Despite the hardship, we always knew that we could count on one thing; our food freedom. I remember when the stores were stockpiled full of affordable Organic food; when people could still legally buy freshly grown produce from their neighbors; when buying a Thanksgiving turkey that wasn't cloned in a laboratory, was something that even the most impoverished person could afford. That all changed with the implementation of the Carbon Taxes. We've all seen hard times, and know how tough it is to survive. But you have no idea what it was like, to watch society collapse. You have no idea how painful it was to watch neighbors who had lived in peace for decades; wake up one morning and start killing each other over the last bag of rice."

There was a long silence. Walter's deep wisdom laid a heavy burden upon his friends' souls.

He spoke more intense truth, "Genetically modified food is *killing* humanity. Studies conducted before I was even born proved mammals that ate only GMO food, made their species infertile in less than four generation's time. Corporations have been feeding GMO food to humans for decades. Humans consider a generation to be twenty years. GMOs have been in over ninety-five percent of the world's food chain since 2149. We are living in the last fertile generation of mankind. This *is* a war, even if you don't see it as one. It's a war, for the survival of our species."

Walter continued speaking, "The hunters will sneak the food onto the ship during the previous night. It will be packed in regular luggage. The manager will help distract the security guards, so that the hunters will not get caught. Paul was planning to help us load it into two vans, after the ship arrives back at the Jersey City harbor. It would have been an easy job that would have yielded plenty of cargo. But we will have to escape with whatever we can salvage, before the security guards become suspicious."

Walter left the team with one final emotional thought, "I love you all, like you're my own children. I'm not mad at any of you, for making this decision. We all must choose our own path in life. The boat will arrive in a little over four weeks. I assume you've all planned to move out by that time. Take whatever you need from the compound before you leave. I wish you the best of luck, in starting your new life."

Walter arose from his chair, and retired to his room. Lucia, Eiji, Cameron, and Vincent did not say a word.

The next day, the four young friends started packing their belongings. They exchanged casual pleasantries, and reminisced about the times they had spent together. They did not always acknowledge how strong the bond was between them; but now that they were on the verge of saying goodbye to their old lives, they realized how emotionally attached they had become to one another.

They had all agreed to meet later that evening for drinks at a local bar in downtown Newark.

Cameron arrived at the bar, at 8:45 PM. It was a dreary establishment. Holographic television screens imbedded into a circular panel above the bar, projected mindless entertainment for the patrons.

Live broadcasts of The Yard; a graphically violent show where convicted felons entered a cage and fought each other, sometimes to their deaths; played adjacent to broadcasts of other sports, like football, baseball, and basketball. Other screens showed news broadcasts, that were nothing but totalitarian government sponsored propaganda. The most disturbing entertainment was uncensored hardcore pornography. The pornography was the media, which Cameron most despised.

Men at the bar salivated over the sight of degenerate whores shamelessly performing acts of public prostitution. The men stated their desire to marry the wenches. They spoke with great reverence of their beauty. The men proclaimed that they yearned to be sexual studs, like the cretinous oxen whom they saw degrading the harlots. Cameron wondered how the ability to simultaneously insert several penises into her three predominant orifices, was a quality which a real man would desire in a woman.

People of both genders, hailed the sports athletes greatness. Cameron admired the professional nouveau-gladiators, who spent their lives refining actual skills. But he was horrified that some people actually wanted to enter prison, so that they could compete on The Yard. Those people's delusions rivaled that of the counterfeit savants; who worshiped the propaganda news. The faux intellectuals made horribly asinine statements. They mindlessly regurgitated opinions and talking points, which were spoon fed to them by the television.

Some claimed that they didn't support President Cho continuing the Syrian war. However, they still blindly supported the deployment of American troops, who were fighting overseas. These hypocrites parroted the opinions fed to them by the news' "professional analysts"; without fully understanding the true soldier's struggle. They had no idea what was the true cost of war, and they hadn't a single scintilla of critical thought.

Cameron walked around the establishment, until he saw his friends sitting in a booth near the back of the room. Cameron sat down beside Lucia, who was seated across the table from Eiji and Vincent.

"Why can't we ever go get shit faced at a nice family restaurant?" he said with a smile.

"This *is* a family restaurant. A couple of these waitresses are obviously pregnant. And the bouncers at the doors don't look a day over seventeen!" Vincent replied.

Vincent handed Cameron a beer from the case which they had ordered. Cameron opened it, and sipped its cool, refreshing contents.

"You know why they're so freakishly big for their age, right? It's from eating all those artificial hormones, and GMOs. I swear, the average age of puberty nowadays must be ten," said Eiji.

"True, but early blooming *does* have its advantages!" Vincent said.

Vincent flexed his left bicep muscle, and the team laughed joyfully.

"No, it doesn't! Let me tell you a story. I was chatting up this girl, a few weeks ago. She had a knockout body. Best tits you could imagine," Eiji said before playfully telling Lucia, "Way better than yours!"

Lucia returned his quip by sticking out her tongue and middle finger.

"I asked her if she wanted to go get some drinks. She said 'yes', but that she had to be back before her curfew. I asked her if she was on parole or something, and she said 'no'. She said that her mom didn't like her hanging out past nine. When I asked her how old she was, she looked me dead in the eye and told me 'fourteen'!"

The shocked crew let out uproarious laughter.

"Congratulations. That's the funniest, and creepiest, story I've heard all year," said Lucia.

"I'm surprised you turned her down. I thought your people are into those little oriental schoolgirls!" said Vincent.

"Boy, I'm glad I don't have to hear your racist jokes anymore!" Eiji mockingly replied to the coltish comment.

He tossed a rolled up napkin at Vincent.

"Now Vincent, that's not nice. Eiji can't help the fact he's a perverted Jap; any more than *you* can help the fact you're mentally retarded!" jibbed Cameron.

They all laughed at Cameron's witty joke, and took a large swig of their beers.

"Let me ask you something, Lucy. Why did you choose to join us? Some people, deranged people, might be inclined to say you're kind of cute. I know you're not a dyke. Why haven't you run off, and started a family?" Vincent said.

The sudden personal question caught Lucia off her guard.

"I haven't found the right guy," she shyly replied.

"I wasn't aware you were even looking. You've rarely dated, in the seven years I've known you," said Vincent.

"That's not true, I've had two boyfriends!" Lucia replied.

"That one nigger doesn't count. Real talk, that nigger was a booty pirate!" Cameron interjected.

"Stop! Aaron wasn't gay. I would know, you ass!" said Lucia.

"Fuck that! My nigger had a Mohawk, and *two* tongue rings. He put the 'got' in 'faggot'!" Cameron said.

All the men shared a laugh, after Cameron's obviously playful jest. Lucia gently punched Cameron's shoulder.

"Oh Cameron, stop! You're horrible!" Lucia said.

Lucia looked away from Vincent, and tried to ignore his question. He would not let her dodge the issue.

"Seriously though, I'm genuinely curious. Why would you ever want this kind of life?" Vincent asked.

Lucia gazed down at the table. She took a few sips of beer, before showing her friends an emotional side of herself, which she rarely exposed.

Lucia said, "When I was growing up, my family worked for a cleaning company. They used to service a lot of restaurants. One day, my father had to take me with him to work. I caught a mild cold after getting that year's flu vaccine, and he couldn't find anyone to watch me. The restaurant he was cleaning that day was a swanky upscale place. All the rich trendy types ate there. I was wandering around, and went to the kitchen. The chef was complaining to the delivery robot that the manufacturer had fucked up the order. They had been mistakenly shipped several pounds of cloned beef. I'll never forget his words. He said, 'God *dammit*, I can't feed them this *shit!* My boss will *fire* me if he finds out I served the customers meat, from some three headed, mutated freak!' When the robot asked what it should do with the meat, the chef said, 'I don't care! Take it back! Throw it out! Just get it the fuck out of my sight! Hell, why don't you give it to those spics that clean the toilets? They'll eat anything.'"

The team was shocked by her raw display of emotion. They sat in solitude for several moments.

"I've never heard you tell that story," Eiji finally said.

"It's one of my worst memories. I never wanted to admit that for many years, he was right," she coldly said.

The team once again became very somber.

"You think Walter's right? About this being a war?" Eiji asked.

"It sure felt like one," said Vincent.

The team knew that Vincent was referring to the turnpike massacre.

"I have no doubt that he speaks the truth. What remains to be seen, is if we will win," said Cameron.

"Are any of you reconsidering our decision?" asked Lucia.

"No. We've given enough to this rotted society. Let them fight their own battles," said Cameron.

While nobody challenged him directly, the group could tell Cameron was not wholeheartedly behind his statement. It was not easy to turn their backs on a struggle that they all believed was righteous. The team had an unspoken feeling that their work, no matter how costly, genuinely benefited society's forgotten citizens.

After a couple more hours of fraternization, the group left the bar. They planned to go their separate ways for the evening. No one had set an official date to leave the compound. Nonetheless they all agreed that they would not return, for at least a few days. After Eiji and Vincent had departed, Cameron began walking to the nearest bus station; which was only a few blocks away from the bar. The cold weather made Cameron shiver, while he waited for the bus.

Suddenly he heard a familiar voice say, "It's warmer, back at the house."

"Aren't you supposed to be going to that swanky, Hillside motel?" he asked Lucia.

"I am. But I wanted to talk with you first," replied Lucia.

Cameron looked at the bus' arrival time, which was being holographically displayed underneath a lamp post.

"Make it quick. The bus will be here in a few minutes," he said.

Lucia wasted no time telling him, "You don't have to do this, Cameron."

He tried to silence her by saying, "You're wasting your time. I'm–"

"I'll fight for you. We'll *all* fight for you," Lucia said.

He tried ignoring her, but she continued speaking, "You lead this team, in a way that we're all guilty of not acknowledging. Walter may manage the finer details, but you are the *real* leader. You are our strength. Even he knows how important you are to us. He would never ask us to do something, of which we were incapable."

Cameron silently watched the bus approach from down the road.

Lucia made one final plea, "There's no retirement for us, Cameron. We have to be one hundred percent committed. Walter's right. This is a fight for the survival of our species. This is about the survival of free humans. It's about mothers, and fathers, and good kids, who just want to live a peaceful life. Why should a small group of psychopathic elites be allowed to decide our fate? They have no right to erase us from existence."

The bus rolled up to the stop, and its doors opened.

"Hello. Please have your cellular phone, with Carbon Credits and Photo ID, ready before you enter. This bus will depart in forty-five seconds," an automated voice said.

There was not a human driving the bus. Mass transportation had been operated by a grid of autonomous machines for decades. Cameron entered, and waited on the bus' first step. The sensors in the bus' doorway began taking a digital scan of Cameron's body. Cameron angrily waited for the scanners to finish their assessment.

"What are you going to do, run away from reality?" Lucia passionately asked.

Cameron glanced over his shoulder and replied, "I wish. I wish I could get into this bus, and drive away until everything disappeared. I'd hide, until the world once again made sense."

"Scan complete. No immediate threat detected. Please swipe your cell phone, or state issued travel card, at the nearby receptacle before entering the main passenger car," said the bus' robotic voice.

Cameron turned around, and looked up at the night sky. His eyes fixated on a specific object. Lucia looked up, and saw he was staring directly at a drone. It hovered above the area making its routine patrols.

Cameron looked at Lucia and said, "But I know, that is a fool's dream. There's nowhere left to hide."

He walked further into the bus, and the doors closed behind him. Lucia watched it drive away. The cold winter air chilled her body. Cameron's words chilled her soul.

Cameron pressed a few buttons on his cell phone, and then tapped it against the bus' front window.

"You have paid for three stops," said the robotic voice.

A second set of doors opened, and allowed Cameron into the main seating area. The bus was moderately crowded, and was carrying a wide variety of passengers. Second class citizens, who were fortunate enough to work eighteen hour days, sat beside the drifters of society. Cameron seated himself near the back of the bus.

He pulled his sweatshirt's hood over his face, and leaned his head against the bus' side window. He closed his eyes, but the liquor inside him prevented him from completely falling asleep. He had only begun relaxing for several minutes, when he felt the bus come to a stop. He opened his eyes, and was shocked to see that the bus was empty. He arose from his seat, and walked to the front of the bus. He used the bus' emergency levers to open both sets of doors.

He stepped into the street, and blinked a few times. He saw small dust particles floating in the air. The particles swayed, and drifted in different directions. He was surprised to see the street was devoid of people. Street lights flickered. There was an eerie silence. Cameron thought he must be dreaming, and attempted to slap himself into awaking. He attempted to use his cell phone, but no clear image projected in his hand. The screen expanded, and only rendered a grainy static image into his palm.

Cameron became extremely frightened. He swiftly jogged to the bus' other side, and looked down the opposite end of the street. He gazed up at the surrounding buildings, and tried to catch a glimpse of its occupants. All he could see was people's silhouettes. Their movements were uneven, and broken. At first they appeared to move fast, like they were being accelerated by some unseen force. Suddenly they slowed down, and appeared like they were moving underwater.

He looked at the sky, and saw the same drone was still flying high above the terrain. It moved forward very slowly, and almost appeared to hover in place. It was out of synch with the movement of the people in the buildings. Cameron started panicking. Sweat dripped from his brow. His breathing became labored, and uneven. If this was a nightmare, he wished it would end immediately.

The wind started whipping around at a ferocious speed. The force of the gust knocked the hood from his head. The particles in the air began glowing brightly. He felt a low vibration rattling his body. He heard a faint humming in his ears. He was about to run, when suddenly a large ripple appeared above him, and distorted his view of the street!

The ripple made the same wave effect that occurs when a stone is dropped into a pond. All visible matter warped, and twisted its shape. The ripple's waves expanded. Bits of black ash spewed in every direction. The effect lasted, for only a few more seconds. Suddenly, a human figure teleported downward through the ripple, and kicked Cameron in his gut!

The blow knocked Cameron to the floor. Cameron gasped for breath. He crawled around on his hands and knees.

"Fight back!" he heard a distorted male voice say.

While panting and wheezing, Cameron slowly looked up at the Figure standing above him. The Figure was dressed in marvelous attire. He wore a suit, which looked like it was made from the finest fabric a person could imagine. The fabric resembled thick leather, but was far more durable. The fabric looked like it could withstand blazing heat, and frigid cold.

The majority of his boots were colored solid red. They had black tips on the toes, and white soles on the heels. The one piece suit was predominately red. A large white and black stripe was painted on its side. The Figure wore red gloves. They had a white and black checkered pattern on the fingers. His chest plate was solid gold. Embedded inside the plate, was a brightly colored orb. The orb was a crystal sphere, which emanated the most beautiful light Cameron had ever seen. Its pattern was astonishing.

The light faded from dim, to bright luminescence. The colors slowly changed, and transformed through all colors in the known worldly light spectrum. One moment, it would dim to a dark shade of black. Then it would slowly brighten, and turn orange. It cycled through marvelous shades of pink, blue, red, purple, and more. Its color pattern permeated through every possible hue combination. He wore a solid black helmet, which covered his entire face. A dark tinted crystal plate was imbedded into the helmet. Cameron could not see the Figure's face through the plate.

"I said, fight BACK!" the Figure shouted.

The Figure once again kicked Cameron in his stomach. The blow lifted Cameron off of the ground, and propelled him backwards. The world around Cameron seemed to slow down. His body flew through the air. He felt an odd sense of peace while he was weightless. That peace was quickly shattered when the Figure teleported forward, and punched Cameron in his chest! The blow was devastating, and slammed Cameron into the bus.

Somehow, Cameron was able to pull himself to his feet, using the bus to regain his balance. Cameron lunged forward. With his right hand, he punched the Figure in his head. The Figure's head tilted sideways, and to the right. The Figure immediately returned his head to its natural position. Cameron was stunned. He thought the powerful blow would have been more effective.

Cameron quickly formed a boxing stance. He used a left handed jab, to strike the Figure in his face. The Figure's head snapped back for a brief second, before returning to normal. Cameron was astounded. His punches seemingly had no effect. Cameron hit the Figure in the face with two quick left jabs. He followed up with a hard right handed hook punch.

The Figure blocked Cameron's hook with his left hand. He slightly crouched, and delivered an open fist palm strike to Cameron's mid-section. The blow pushed Cameron back, but he did not let the attack faze him. The Figure lurched forward, and tried shoving his left knee into Cameron's stomach. Cameron blocked the attack by countering with his right forearm. The Figure tried to strike Cameron with his right knee. Cameron stopped this move by stepping back, and using his left forearm to absorb the strike.

Cameron did not have much room to evade because he was still standing close to the bus. Cameron went on the offense. He delivered an upright standing kick to the Figure's chest, when the Figure foolishly tried attacking with another knee shot. The Figure staggered back, and slightly slumped forward. Cameron delivered a solid left handed punch to the side of the Figure's head. He followed through with a powerful right uppercut to the Figure's face, which sent him reeling.

The Figure lifted off the ground and began falling backwards. Before he could land, the Figure teleported himself back to a standing position. Cameron gasped for breath. He briefly held his arms out to his side. With his palms facing upward, Cameron looked at the Figure with frustration.

"Seriously?" Cameron asked.

Cameron resumed his boxing stance. The two men squared off, and began circling each other. The Figure attempted to break Cameron's guard. He used his left foot to throw a low kick at Cameron's shin. Cameron dodged the maneuver. The Figure quickly kicked at Cameron's other shin. This time the Figure immediately followed the maneuver, with a powerful right handed hook. Cameron absorbed the shot with his left arm. He swiftly grabbed the Figure's arm and locked it underneath his own.

Cameron began punching the Figure in his stomach. The Figure countered by punching Cameron in the side of his body. The two men wobbled, and slowly lost their balance. Cameron momentarily gained the upper hand by leveraging his weight, pushing his body forward, and knocking the Figure to the ground. The Figure was dazed and Cameron tried to maintain dominance. He knelt over the Figure and attempted to remove his helmet.

"Let's see what's behind that goddamned mask of yours!" Cameron yelled while yanking the head covering.

The Figure kicked Cameron hard in the gut, causing Cameron to stumble backwards. The Figure quickly stood up and delivered yet another kick to Cameron's chest. Cameron fell into the bus, and groaned in pain. Cameron desperately tried regaining his footing. The Figure ran up to Cameron, and began unleashing a flurry of alternating left and right handed jabs into Cameron's midsection. He grabbed Cameron by his shirt and threw him forward.

The Figure suddenly pulled a spectacular move. The Figure quickly ran up the side of the bus, turned 180 degrees in midair, and slammed his right forearm into Cameron's back! Cameron fell to his knees. He was exhausted, and resigned himself to the fact that he might die tonight. The Figure walked in front of Cameron.

"You quit too easily," the Figure said.

He extended his right hand and said, "Stand."

Cameron looked at the Figure, and slapped away his hand.

"Fuck off," Cameron said.

The Figure continued extending his arm. Cameron again smacked the Figure's hand.

"I said, fuck off!" Cameron yelled.

The Figure kept his arm outstretched. Cameron looked at the Figure for a few more seconds, before finally accepting his gesture. The Figure helped a battered Cameron rise to his feet. Cameron immediately let go of the Figure's hand, after regaining his balance. Cameron scowled at the Figure.

Cameron's pride was deeply hurt from losing the fight.

"Any specific reason why you're trying to kill me?" Cameron asked.

The Figure stared at Cameron, but remained silent. Cameron continued to ask questions.

"Why are you dressed like such a queer? Who are you?"

When the Figure still did not respond, Cameron grew angry.

"Answer me, dammit!" Cameron yelled.

"Your immaturity, and inability to control your emotions, is your biggest weaknesses. If you cannot conquer these flaws, you will remain destined to lose," the Figure abruptly said.

Cameron was exacerbated.

"Lose? Lose what? What are you talking about? WHAT THE FUCK IS HAPPENING!" Cameron screamed.

The Figure quickly teleported closer. He grabbed Cameron by his neck, and slammed him against the bus.

"Carefully choose your words, and do *not* disrespect me!" the Figure said.

Cameron squirmed uncomfortably. The Figure did not squeeze Cameron's neck dangerously tight, but the feeling was nonetheless unpleasant.

The Figure once again spoke, "You have no idea the horrors, which await you on this timeline. I have not yet seen a future in which you prevail. You fail every single time, because you lack confidence. You allow your soul to become corrupted. Your thoughts collapse under the weight of negative influence by others. Those who seek to abolish you, have lost their faith. You must not allow yourself to crumble, Cameron Moss. You *must* believe in yourself. I believe in you!"

The Figure slowly released his grip from Cameron's neck. Cameron was in complete disbelief. His mind was flooded with questions. What were these horrors, about which this mysterious man spoke? What was the strange glowing orb which he possessed? Was this experience actually happening in reality? Or was this a horrible hallucination, manifested by Cameron's imagination? Out of all the possible questions he could have proposed, Cameron asked only one.

"How do you know my name?"

"Train your mind harder, and your physical strength will follow in accordance. I expect you to put up a less pitiful fight, the next time we meet," the Figure replied.

The Figure pressed his glowing orb. A bright blue fluid began oozing out. The fluid formed a rectangular, bio-holographic shape, in front of the Figure's chest. The rectangle was embedded with picture symbols, which Cameron did not recognize. The Figure feverishly pressed the symbols inside of the blue fluid. When his fingers pressed a symbol, the fluid would rise slightly and then dissolve. It looked like his finger was tapping against watery tree sap. While the Figure pressed the buttons, a series of geometric patterns, numbers, and letters, flashed across his visor. The objects appeared to render backwards. Cameron knew this meant that the material was translucent; and that he was seeing the opposite of what the Figure saw inside the visor.

The Figure finished pressing the astonishing interface. The fluid retracted into the orb. The patterns in his visor continued projecting for a brief moment, and then ceased flashing. The orb quickly began changing its colors, and started glowing brightly. The Figure vertically arose from the ground at a slow pace. The air grew warm. Cameron felt intense heat emanating from the orb. Its colors flashed so fast that they eventually became a mass of pure white light.

"If you are wise, you will heed my warning. Your very life depends on this knowledge," the Figure said.

The Figure slowly extended his arms at his side. An instant later, the Figure teleported into the rippled, ashy void; and Cameron was transported back to his original place on the bus!

The bus' scenery was identical to the way it looked just before the encounter. People continued their mundane interactions. They were oblivious to the awesome event that Cameron had just experienced. In fact the oddest part was that they did not share Cameron's confusion; or seem to be aware anything was abnormal. The only proof that Cameron had to prove his experience was real, was the pain flowing through his bloody knuckles, and bruised face.

13 A Terrible Accident?

The days that followed were filled with somber change. Vincent had taken up amateur boxing at a local gym. The controlled competition was a good way for him to remain strong, hone his skills, and release his aggression. Eiji spent his time living in a nearby tent city, among fellow food freedom rebels. The people were completely impoverished, but they had a close knit community. They knew he had contributed a great deal of help over the years, through his food distribution missions. They were happy to let him stay for a while.

Lucia visited her cousin Tara, who was helping Lucia obtain an illegal interstate passport. Lucia wanted to visit her ailing father in Yonkers, New York. Lucia's mother died of breast cancer at age thirty-eight, when Lucia was six years old. Lucia's father was devastated, and did not remarry for many years. When Lucia was twenty, her father Carlos married his longtime girlfriend, Yasmine. Yasmine had cared for Carlos and Lucia, since Lucia was thirteen. Lucia was now thirty-three, and her father was sixty-four. He was very ill from years of hard work, and eating genetically modified food. He and Yasmine did not have much money, so caring for Carlos was a difficult task. She hoped her dad would live at least ten more years, so that he could see Lucia start a family of her own. But Lucia knew deep down inside, that he would be dead long before she bore children.

Cameron stayed at Sky's apartment. Cameron had slept at a cheap hotel the night he was confronted by the mysterious Figure. The following day he went to Sky's home. He concocted a fictional story to explain his injuries. He claimed he was drunk, accidentally tripped, and fell down the bus' stairs. Sky did not fully believe his story, but she refrained from pressing him for more information. There were many aspects of Cameron's life, about which Sky did not want to know the details. Instead, she enjoyed spending time with him, and was thrilled that he no longer wanted to be a food rebel. She wondered if they would finally start a real relationship. They had a strong friendship, and mutual sexual attraction, but neither of them knew if their lives would ever be sane enough to settle down together.

Walter spent his time selling his stockpile of food. He was doing deep soul searching over the life which he had lived. He had worked with many different people over the years, but his current team was the dearest to his heart. He had never seen such a bright group of individuals. They were focused, poised, and never used unnecessary violence to advance their struggle. He was genuinely happy that they were choosing to live clean lives. He knew they would have a tough time adjusting to life inside the control grid society. He prayed their past would not haunt them, but he knew their troubles were far from over.

Elsewhere, Gregory Times endured a different set of complications. The afternoon on which he returned from Webster's business, was a heart wrenching and emotional day. He returned home to find Mallory was still crying in their bed. He apologized profusely for leaving her alone. He held her in his arms and they cried together. They mourned the loss of their unborn babies whose lives were deemed expendable by a totalitarian government. Their children were considered to be economically, and environmentally unfriendly. Their existences were extinguished before they took one breath.

Times told Mallory about the job he had accepted from Webster. He explained the circumstances under which he and Webster had first met. At first, Mallory was angry that Times had been attending political functions without telling her, but she did not stay that way for too long. She knew Times had a passion for politics and current events, which was why Times worked at the New York Now Paper for so many years.

Times had always wanted to be a journalist. He was never able to follow his dream, because he lacked sufficient funds to afford a higher education. Times had sometimes been invited by his former coworkers, to attend certain political events. She did not know that he continued attending them, after he was fired.

Times was glad that Mallory was not mad at him for remaining politically active. But he dared not tell her the full truth about his relationship with Webster, until she was emotionally prepared. He was terrified of explaining to her, what he witnessed on the New Jersey Turnpike. However, he did not let that inevitable discussion preoccupy his thoughts.

Many days had passed since Times started his new job. It was 8:35 AM on Thursday, December 20th, 2216. Mallory and Times were sitting at their living room table. They ate a breakfast consisting of genetically modified cereal, and cloned cow's milk. Today would be Mallory's first day of participation in the clinical drug trial. Times was glad that she decided to join the program. He knew they both needed the therapy, and money.

Mallory and Times finished their meal, left the apartment, and rode the subway train to Rigor Pharmaceuticals' building. Times led Mallory up to the seventh floor. The female receptionist, and the robot Alice, greeted them at the reception desk. Shortly thereafter, Alice walked the couple to the same laboratory where Times had first been evaluated.

Mallory was startled when she first saw the Chem-Mech. She felt uncomfortable being interrogated by a robot. She reluctantly gave vague and evasive answers to the Chem-Mech's questions. After Times assured her that everything was okay, she was more willing to talk about her symptoms. Mallory eventually disclosed the fact that she was recently the victim of a government mandated forced abortion. Mallory received a dosage of prescription pills from the Chem-Mech.

After the exam the robot Alice said, “Follow me to the focus group.”

Alice led Mallory and Times down the long winding corridors, until they reached a large room. Alice used the hybrid security panel to open the door. It motioned for the couple to enter the room. Mallory looked at Times with a feeling of concern. He quietly assured her, that there was nothing to fear. Times held her hand and escorted her inside.

There was a circle of chairs in the room. Two women and a man were already seated. Mallory and Times, sat down in two empty chairs. Shortly thereafter, one more woman and two men arrived. The group sat around and uncomfortably made casual conversation. After a short time, a well dressed woman in her early forties entered the room. Her frizzy long hair was a stark contrast to her professional business jacket, and skirt.

“Good morning everyone, I am your therapist. My name is Shannon Johnson. It is a pleasure to meet all of you. Before we get started, I ask that everyone please sign the attendance sheet,” she said.

She tapped her finger against the clear rectangular fiberglass pad, which she held in her left hand. A dark square appeared next to a list of names on the pad's screen. She gave the pad to a nearby patient. The man located his name on the list, and pressed his thumb against the square. It was passed along, until everyone had scanned their print into the machine.

“Thank you. Now let's start by getting to know one another. You already know who I am.

Would anyone like to break the ice, and introduce themselves next?" Shannon asked.

The room was silent. A man in his late twenties eventually spoke.

"Nathan Miller. U.S. Air Force," he said.

"Welcome, Nathan. Tell us about yourself," said Shannon.

"I spent the last six years in Syria, fighting the war. When I came home, I had trouble sleeping. My psychiatric adviser thought it would be a good idea, for me to participate in this program."

The soldier did not continue. A few moments later, a middle aged man in his fifties decided to speak.

"My name's Ricardo Ortiz and I'm originally from Mexico. I hosted a popular internet talk show, in my home country. One day the drug gang, Los Hermanos Muertos, demanded I start paying them half my check. They want the money, once every pay period. They call it a protection fee. Every two weeks, half of my pay gone to drug dealers. They extort me and call it a 'tax' on the road," he said with a thick accent.

Ricardo continued, "I spoke out against this travesty, and they murder my family. They hang my wife from a tree by her own intestines. They dismember my son, and put his remains in a suitcase, outside of his school. By the grace of God, I was able to escape the city. I fled to the state of South Arizona, with my middle daughter. I have not heard from my oldest or youngest daughter, for almost two years..."

Ricardo choked back tears while finishing his story. After a few moments of silence a teenage girl, who happened to be sitting next to Mallory, spoke.

"I'm Amanda Ross. I'm struggling with depression, and self-harm. I accidentally got pregnant by my ex-boyfriend. He was angry at first, but he supported me having the baby. One day the CEA told us I had to have an abortion. They said our parents made too much money collectively, to qualify me for welfare," she said.

Times winced while listening to the girl's story. He was well aware of the eugenics provisions in the Inexpensive Care Act of 2163, and the Carbon Tax Law of 2184. The laws stated that people under the age of eighteen were required to have abortions; if they did not meet the minimum financial requirements the government decided was necessary to raise a child. If a person could not produce an income of $80,000 Carbon Credits per year, either by working or through welfare entitlements, then having an abortion was mandatory.

People of low social-economic status, routinely had their pregnancies terminated, because they were deemed too poor to raise a child. Their babies were considered burdens on society, because the Federal government could no longer afford to completely assist them. Welfare and other entitlement programs had their funding drastically reduced by a bankrupt American government. The United Nations supported these policies, because they felt that under-supported babies were a planetary environmental hazard.

Amanda continued her story, "I became depressed, and started cutting myself. I started hanging out with a bad crowd, like video gamers and food outlaws. I started doing electronic drugs, and became addicted to nanites. I overdosed on nano-nasal spray, and heavily modified pear extract liquor. My dad found me passed out, faced down in our pool. The paramedics said I would have drowned, if my epidermal skin implant hadn't alerted his cell phone that I wasn't breathing."

Mallory was deeply affected by Amanda's story. Mallory gently reached over, and held the young girl's hand.

"I'm Mallory Times. My husband Gregory and I have also been affected by the One Child

Mandate. A few weeks ago, our pregnancy was terminated. I was carrying twins," Mallory said.

Mallory gave Amanda a heartfelt look, and released her hand. Amanda seemed grateful for the gesture. The introductions continued.

A heavyset Negro man said, "I'm Byron Phillips, twenty-seven years strong. I have diabetes, high blood pressure, high cholesterol, gout, hypertension, and practically every other dietary disease you can imagine. I used to think I got sick from eating GMO food, and drinking GMO diet soda. But my physical therapist assured me, that's just a conspiracy theory. There's no proof that GMO food causes disease. I was recently diagnosed with a stomach tumor, which the doctor told me is inoperable cancer. My name is on the transplant list, and my doctors are hoping that I get selected for an operation. They thought it would be a good idea, for me to join a support group in case..."

Byron's thoughts trailed off, but his message was clear. He was going to die, before he ever had a chance to live. Lastly, a couple in their early forties told their story.

"I'm Emma," the woman said.

"I'm Todd," her husband said.

"We're survivors of the Thanksgiving Day terrorist attack that occurred in New Jersey," Emma continued.

"It was horrible. Gang members attacked a FEMA food transport truck, for no reason! The resulting carnage was unspeakable," Todd said.

Times was shocked by their false statements. Times had not yet revealed to anyone, that he had personally witnessed the Turnpike murders. He was furious that the couple was distorting the truth about the events. His first inclination was to curse at them, and decry their untruthfulness. For a moment, Times thought that these people were crisis actors. Crisis actors were sometimes used in the aftermath of a disaster, to corroborate an official government story.

Crisis actors usually helped shape public opinion after a highly controversial event; like an alleged terrorist attack. Despite his doubts, he could not directly speak about the incident. If he did, he would be arrested for concealing knowledge about terrorist activity; which was a crime punishable by up to fifteen years in jail.

Instead Times callously said, "Yes. Our media has made us well aware of the imminent danger, posed by starving teenage militants. I think it's great that they were executed, for stealing turkeys and chickens."

The room fell silent. They were all surprised by Times' harsh, and controversial words.

Shannon arose from her seat and said, "I think that's a good place to take a break. Come back in fifteen minutes. Everyone remember, this is a diverse group of people. All of our experiences are unique. Please be sure to respect each other during our conversations."

Times immediately left his chair, and exited the room. He found himself overcome with rage. He wanted to strangle Todd and Emma until they repented; and told the truth about what happened that early Thanksgiving morning. He rapidly walked down the hallway. His breathing was labored. Times held up his left wrist, and spoke into his band.

"Call Webster," he said.

Webster did not answer his phone. Times looked directly into the phone's camera.

"Webster, it's me. We have to talk. I feel, strange. Anxious..." he said.

Times realized that he was rambling. He cut the signal, and sent Webster the visual voice mail. Times entered a restroom, and rushed over to the sinks. He swiped his hand in front of the small black receiver above the faucet. Water began flowing, and he splashed it upon his face. He closed his eyes, and let the cool liquid refresh him. Suddenly, a voice broke his concentration.

"You feeling okay, mister?" asked the voice.

Times looked up, and saw Nathan's reflection in the mirror. Times again swiped his hand in front of the panel. The water slowed until it ceased to pour. Times, his face still cold and wet, turned around to face Nathan.

"I'm fine," Times calmly replied.

He walked over to the wall near the restroom's entrance. He placed his hands and face, in front of a large metal grating embedded into the wall. The hot air dried the moisture on his body. Nathan used a urinal, and then washed his hands.

"How long have you been with your wife?" Nathan asked.

Nathan walked beside Times, and began drying himself in front of the metal grate.

"Six years, married four," Times replied.

"Nice. I'm real sorry, about what happened to you two. You seem like a very sweet couple," Nathan said.

Times could not concentrate well enough to give a proper response.

"Thanks. I'll see you inside," Times indifferently said.

He left the restroom, and returned to the group session. Not long after Times returned, the session resumed. Mallory was annoyed that Times had caused an incident earlier; but she did not publicly chastise him. The group spent the rest of the day studying the psychology of trauma. Shannon skillfully steered the discussion's flow. They concluded their session two hours later. The robot Alice reentered the room, and escorted the patients back to the lobby. Not long after arriving, Times saw a familiar face.

"Gregory! How are you, my boy?" Webster asked with a smile.

He briskly walked up to greet Times.

"I'm well, my friend," Times cheerfully replied.

The two men shook hands.

"I'd like you to meet my wife, Mallory," Times said.

"She's even more beautiful in person, than you've already described," Webster said.

Webster gracefully shook Mallory's hand. She blushed, after hearing the generous compliment.

"Thank you. Greg has told me a lot about you. He says you're a good man. We're both very grateful that you're helping us," Mallory said.

"It is really my pleasure. My only goal is to make you well. Listen, I'm terribly regretful to cut our conversation short, but I've a meeting to attend. Alice, follow me," said Webster.

The robot Alice rolled itself over Webster.

"No problem. Nice seeing you," Times said.

Webster and Alice started walking, and rolling away. Webster waved at Nathan as they passed each other in the hallway. Nathan approached the elevator, in front of which Mallory and Times were standing.

"I didn't know you were friends with Webster," Nathan said.

"We haven't known each other long, but he's definitely been very kind to me," replied Times.

Mallory rubbed her husband's back in a supportive manner. The elevator arrived, and all three of them entered.

"Fuck yeah, Webster is awesome. He's the one who convinced my therapist to enroll me in the program," Nathan said a moment later.

"Oh, really? How did you meet him?" asked Times.

"A few months ago, I helped escort him and a few of his colleagues, through a really rough part of town. My unit got a call, and our commander told us we needed to extract some VIP's. A flash riot had broken out in front of the U.N. headquarters. I think they were protesting mandatory vaccines, or some other bullshit. I joked that Manhattan was the new Damascus. Anyway, after we got them out, Webster asked me for my contact information. He could tell I was still stressed about the war, so he convinced the V.A. administrators to enroll me in this program," Nathan answered.

"That's quite amazing. He sounds like he truly has a passion for helping people," Mallory said.

The elevator reached the ground floor, and they went their separate ways. Mallory and Times went back to their apartment. After they entered, Times gently grabbed Mallory by her waist and affectionately caressed her.

"Are you all right?" Times asked.

Mallory gently kissed her husband's lips.

"That was pretty intense. It was painful hearing all those sad stories. At least we know we aren't the only people with messed up lives. I'm not sure how I feel about this program, but I trust you with my life," she answered.

She kissed him again and said, "It was nice meeting your friend."

"I'm glad you met him too. He has taught me a lot about the world. Hey, have a seat on the couch. I have a surprise for you," Times said.

Mallory sat, and Times went into their bedroom. He returned a moment later, with a small white envelope.

"For you," he said while handing her the envelope.

She opened it, and removed the small plastic cards inside. They were two tickets to the Madison Square Garden Theatre for the Saturday, December 22nd, showing of: 'Scien-Circus; Featuring the Animals of Tomorrow!'

Mallory excitedly said, "Gregory, how did you pay for these? They must have cost a fortu–"

"Don't worry. I didn't spend more than we can afford," Times interrupted.

Mallory relaxed and hugged Times.

"We're going to make it, Greg. I know eventually we'll be okay," she said while hugging him.

Times remained silent, and held her tightly. Her warm embrace comforted his soul.

Saturday arrived. Times and Mallory rode the subway to Pennsylvania Station. They exited the subway station, and went to the street to watch the free parade that was occurring before the show. Thirteen years ago, Scien-Circus had become an annual New York City event. The show was a new age carnival with a twist. All the performing animals were genetically modified creatures.

There were many acts, including: a group of primates cloned from a single chimpanzee; three foot tall miniature adult elephants, giraffes, and bears; prairie dogs whose fur was infused with the bio-luminescent abdomens of fireflies, so that they glowed in the dark; chimera unicorns, which were ponies spliced with rhinoceros and ostrich DNA to give them a horn and wings! While all the animals were a breathtaking sight to behold, the main attraction was the three headed Pliger.

The Pliger was a very large beast, which contained DNA from three different feline species. Its body was predominately brown, with marvelous black and white stripes. Its left head was that of a black Panther. Its right head was one of a white Tiger. Its middle head was the golden brown head of a Lion, complete with a silky smooth mane! The Pliger was considered by the scientific community, to be the crowning achievement of modern genetic engineering.

Times and Mallory walked around the sidewalk and tried to find a good spot to view the parade. They finally found a decent viewing place at the corner of Thirty-Fifth Street, and Seventh Avenue.

"It's marvelous!" exclaimed Mallory.

Various animals and human performers marched down the street. The couple watched in awe with the rest of the crowd, at the stunning man made creations. However, not everyone shared in the crowd's bliss. A few blocks away, a very large group had gathered to protest the parade. They shouted obscenities and ridiculed the event.

"How the fuck can you support these atrocities?!"

"These freaks are abominations!"

"You're *all* sinning against the Lord!"

"May God have mercy on you, for your affront to His creations!"

"You bastards are abusing these poor animals!"

"End genetic experimentation!"

"How long before they do this shit to *humans?!*"

The protesting crowd had been contained to a Free Speech Zone, with a half mile radius. Heavily armed National Guard units kept a close watch over the citizens. Flying drones circled the area. Armored trucks blocked off sections of the street. Security was heavy, due to the fact that there had been violent incidents during past parades. Previous protests had resulted in numerous human and animal deaths. There had been no causalities in the nine years since the military began operating security, but every year there was high tension, fights, and mass arrests of protesters. Times could tell the protesters were making Mallory nervous, even though she seemed to be enjoying the parade.

"Come on, let's go get something to eat," Times said.

He cradled Mallory's hand, and started walking. The couple found a food vending truck operated by humanoid robots, not far from the Madison Square Garden Theater.

"Wow! The hot dogs here contain two percent real meat!" said Mallory.

"Not bad. And they're only fifty Carbon Credits a piece," said Times.

They purchased two hot dogs, and two six ounce sodas, for $125 Carbon Credits. After finishing their meal, they walked to the theatre. They stood in a long line, and waited to enter the facility. The show started at 8:00 PM, but they arrived two and a half hours early, so that they would have enough time to clear the security checkpoint. All patrons had to submit to thorough examinations, which included presenting identification, emptying the contents of their pockets, and being body scanned by a thermal imaging machine.

The Federal Transportation Authority conducted the searches. They were formerly called the Transportation Security Administration, and were only used at airports. In 2139, after a group of Iranian terrorists used suicide bombers to attack a subway station, the TSA was renamed and given the authority to conduct security procedures on highways, movie theaters, shopping malls, train stations, and other mass public gatherings.

Most patrons were quickly scanned, and allowed to enter. Modest amounts were subjected to a brief groping, which included all areas of their body. A small few were given cavity searches. Even small children, were not immune to any of these alleged safety inspections. A little over an hour after they had entered the line, Mallory and Times were about to pass security.

"Step up to the scanner," said a large, overweight female FTA agent to Times.

Times stepped inside a giant rectangular box. The woman tilted her head and put her left eye, in front of the machine's retina scanner. The clear shape of Times' body, including his genitals, was projected as a holographic image on the machine's right side.

"You're okay," the fat woman said.

Times walked out of the box, stood on the other side, and waited for Mallory. She entered the box, and was scanned. A light on the machine's top, flashed red.

"Warning. Scan indicates target may be armed," a robotic voice said.

"I'm going to have to pat you down," the FTA agent said.

Mallory cringed, but only muttered, "Okay," to the agent.

The agent did a brief sweep of Mallory's body, and instructed her to once again walk through the machine. The machine flashed red for a second time.

"I'm going to need to conduct a more thorough search," said the ogrish woman, while cracking a sick smile.

Mallory became scared and said, "What's wrong? I'm not a crimi–"

"It's not up to me, ma'am. I'm just following procedures," interrupted the woman.

The woman began putting on a pair of blue plastic gloves. She looked at Mallory, and licked her lips.

Times said, "Wait, there has to be something wrong. I've been with her the whole day. There's nothing–"

"SIR! Step *back*, and lower your voice! This is an official investigation!" the trollish wench interrupted.

Two male FTA thugs began menacing Times. They stood next to him in an intimidating manner. They firmly rested their right hands upon their holstered laser pistols. Times knew that he had to defuse the situation.

"Mallory, do you want to leave?" Times asked.

Before Mallory could answer, one of the male goons shouted, "Hey! She told you to be quiet! Now shut your fuckin' face!"

Times began scowling at the man, who had just yelled at him. He was fat, and disgusting, like the slug who was about to grope his wife. Times began breathing very heavily. He heard a strange buzzing noise in his ears. For a moment he thought himself crazy, because he heard unintelligible whispers in his head.

The fat she-beast began molesting Mallory. She slowly rubbed her grimy paws over Mallory's stomach. She massaged Mallory's breasts, and tweaked Mallory's nipples through her clothes. The two male FTA agents began giggling like retarded little boys. A few people in the crowd aimed their cell phones at Mallory, and recorded the incident with their cameras. Mallory started shaking, and felt nauseous. The woman ran her hands down Mallory's buttocks and thighs. The agent began cooing, and making creepy, satisfied, moaning sounds.

"Hell yeah! Give that sweet piece of ass some good lovin'!" one spectator said.

Times began coughing. He felt the whispers becoming louder. A sharp pain shot through his chest. The woman moved her hands along Mallory's hips. Times looked at the disgusting society in which he lived. A whole crowd of people chuckled while his wife was being raped in broad daylight, by tyrannical government thugs. All around him, people marveled at crimes against nature, while paying to view the monstrosities. He felt his brain burn like hot acid. The whispers got louder. The woman started cupping Mallory's vagina, and prepared to stick her hand down Mallory's pants. Times glared at the goon, and felt a fire burning in the pit of his stomach. His lips barely moved and no one around him heard a sound, but Times knew that he muttered a single word to the vile slag.

"Die..." Times whispered.

A second later, the woman abruptly shivered. This momentarily stopped her from further hurting Mallory. She brushed the feeling off, and tried resuming her sexual assault. She attempted to put her hands down Mallory's pants, but again she shivered. The woman grunted and her face contorted in pain. The woman gasped for air, and she started clutching her chest. She violently convulsed, fell to the floor, and writhed in pain. Witnesses started screaming. The two male FTA agents, rushed to their coworker's aid.

"What's wrong? Are you okay?" one of them asked.

The woman howled while convulsing in pain. She wildly twitched, while her arms and legs, flailed chaotically.

"Help! I think she's having a heart attack!" screamed one of the male FTA agents.

Mallory stepped back from the woman, while Times stood in shock. He watched the woman thrash about, and foam at the mouth. People began crying, yet they still held out their opened palms and recorded every moment on their cell phones. A few moments later, paramedics rushed to the fat woman's aid. They pushed Times out of the way, which snapped him out of his daze. They proceeded to perform CPR on the woman.

Times, still dumbfounded, knew it would be no use. He knew that the woman would die. He wanted her dead, and was happy that soon she would be no more than a flaccid pile of skin. Times looked around, and feared that someone had heard his thoughts. After he saw that no one was paying attention to him, he stealthily walked past the dying woman.

Times grabbed Mallory's hand and said, "We're leaving."

They quickly walked away from the unfolding situation, and entered the nearest subway station. The entire time he was walking, Times felt the ringing in his ear, and heard the whispers. He was frightened to his core. Times let out a brief scream, before falling to his hands and knees. His breathing was short, and labored.

Mallory knelt beside him and said, "Oh my God. Greg, what's wrong?"

He concentrated hard and calmed his nerves. Mallory helped him to his feet.

"I'm fine," Times said in a labored voice.

Times winced in discomfort, and rested his back against the wall. After a moment, the noises in his head subsided.

Mallory frantically asked, "Greg wha–"

"Did that bitch hurt you?" Times hastily interrupted.

Times grabbed Mallory tightly by her shoulders.

Mallory immediately replied, "Ow! No. Greg, stop. You're hurting me."

Times quickly loosened his grip.

"Mallory...no...I'm sorry. I didn't mean to grab you so hard," he said.

He pulled her close, and pressed her head against his chest.

Time softly whispered in her ear, "I'd never hurt you."

He hugged her tightly, while staring into the distance. He whispered again, so softly that she barely heard him.

"I'll never again, let anyone hurt you," Times said with a hardened look upon his face.

14 A Disturbing Revelation

Times spent the rest of the next morning obsessively researching telepathy. He used his personal computer to read dozens of digital articles accessible through internet databases. After two hours, he was exhausted and disgusted by the lack of credible information available about the phenomena. Most documents dismissed telepathy as nothing but science fiction conjecture. Only a few scholarly research papers lent credence to the hypothesis that one could manipulate objects, or people, using his mind.

Times discovered an article which suggested that brainwave technology had the ability to create artificial telepathy. During the mid-twenty-second century, brainwave interfaces were invented as an alternative method for humans to control computers. Specially designed headbands, utilized electrical signals naturally occurring in the human brain, for an input source. Humans did not have to type on a keyboard, or run their fingers through holographic beams of light, to operate the machine. Instead, they thought about what they wanted the computer to perform, and it carried out the request.

However by early 2182, the technology had all but disappeared from the emerging market. Conspiracy themed websites compared the brainwave anti-revolution to the decade's long conspiracy by the auto industry and big oil companies, to suppress alternative fuel technologies. Energy efficient cars that ran on various cheap alternative fuels, like corn oil and hydrogen, had been invented over one hundred years in the past. The inventors of those technologies had their patents purchased by big auto and oil companies. The companies then shelved the technology which prevented it from being released to the public.

Over the years, corporate monoliths sabotaged any effort to make fuel efficient cars until the Carbon Tax Law was implemented. The law granted billions of dollars to select automakers and covered their electric engine conversion costs. It was no coincidence that only companies, whom had donated millions to elect politicians that passed the bill, received Carbon Bailout money. It was also not surprising that the cost of owning a vehicle tripled in price after the conversion.

Power companies were also given billions to help them cover the expense of expanding their power grids. The companies eventually started limiting the amount of electricity that people could use. This was made even more offensive by the fact they charged people higher rates, for less service. The companies were also allowed to pay an extremely lower income tax rate; making the debt created by the bailout impossible to repay. People routinely died of heat stroke during hot months and hypothermia during cold months; because they were not given adequate amounts of electricity to heat or cool their homes. Blackouts that covered large sections of the country and lasted for weeks at a time, were a common occurrence across all parts of America.

The most egregious exploiters of the Carbon Tax Law were the oil and coal companies. Trillions of dollars were given to their industries in exchange for their promise to responsibly go out of business. Hundreds of coal plants, coal mines, oil rigs, and oil refineries, were closed. Their land was seized by the government, declared nature preserves, and donated to the United Nations World Heritage Centre. UNWHC allowed thousands of land acres that could have been used to grow new crops, or build new areas for human civilization, become barren wastelands. Shockingly, members of the corporate environmental movement praised the land seizure as a positive development. They falsely claimed that preventing human activity helped preserve the Earth.

A similar fate befell the brainwave industry. Inventors and small companies had their ideas purchased by billionaires, who quickly stifled the full capabilities of the technology. Currently, brainwave technology is only used by a select user group. People, who have lost mobility in certain parts of their body, use brainwave interfaces to operate medical devices like prosthetic limbs. Other brainwave interfaces are used to operate video game inputs. Current conspiracy theorists wonder how long it will be until brainwave technology is mandated in public use; the same way that occurred with environmentally friendly technology.

Times had arraigned for Webster to perform some tests on him after the group met for their final session of 2216, on Thursday, December 27th. The session concluded gracefully and Times told Mallory he would meet her back at their apartment. Times waited in the reception area for twenty minutes, until the robot Alice escorted Times to Webster's office. Once there, Times sat in the chair across from Webster's desk.

"Thanks for seeing me on such short notice," Times said.

"You're welcome. I admit, you have me worried, Gregory," replied Webster.

"Why?" asked Times.

Webster paused for a moment and then answered, "Because we're both aware of the risks involved with taking this medication. You sounded vague and frantic when we last spoke. You were rambling nonsense, and now you've asked me to perform some neurological scans. What is it you're hoping to accomplish?"

Times took a deep breath and said, "I'm not sure you'd understand, or believe me, if I told you the truth. I can barely believe how bizarre some of these experiences have been."

"Entertain me," said Webster.

Webster crossed his arms, and sat back in his mighty chair. Times took another deep breath.

"I think the meds are having unintended side effects. The weird part, is that I don't mind them," Times said.

"What are you experiencing?" asked Webster.

Times continued, "I feel, different. More focused. I have more energy and stamina. My muscles are tighter than they've been, since I was a teenager–"

"These hardly sound like side effects!" Webster interrupted.

"It's not that simple. I'm also feeling more aggressive, and violent. For example; sometimes a person will bump into me, ever so slightly. And I'll want to do nothing more, than smash their face with a brick. I also think that I may be...projecting my emotions onto others. I think...I may have unintentionally hurt someone," Times quickly replied.

Webster was taken aback by Times' confession.

"Have you told anyone else?" Webster asked.

"No," replied Times.

"Not even your wife?" asked Webster.

"No," Times once again confirmed.

Webster did not wait long to say, "Alice, take Gregory to research lab seven, dash A two. Tell the Chem-Mech to meet you there. I'll be there shortly."

"DNA confirmation required for restricted area clearance," said the robot Alice.

Webster rolled up his sleeve. Alice pricked him, and drew his blood with its right robotic claw.

"Identification confirmed. Access granted," Alice said a second later.

Times followed Alice out of the room. She took him to the elevator and they rode to the thirteenth floor. When he exited the elevator, Times saw a large research laboratory. Heavily fortified doors blocked access to rooms throughout the long winding corridor. Times followed Alice through the corridors until they reached a lab at the end of a hallway. The lab had a camera and small laser gun mounted above the doorway.

"Automaton is being accompanied by an unknown human. Identify, and state business," said the camera's robotic voice.

Alice began making a series of whirring, and buzzing sounds. A light on the top of its camera head flashed several times. Seconds later, the door unlocked.

"Authorization accepted. Access granted," the door's voice said.

The robot Alice rolled into the room. Times followed it inside, and looked at the room's layout. There were numerous holographic computer workstations and monitors. Swirling lines of test tubes, inside of which flowed colored liquid, were placed on a large tabletop counter.

The counter covered the entire width of a wall. A reclining examination chair was in the middle of the room. Times sat in the chair. Several minutes later, Webster arrived with the Chem-Mech. Webster handed Times a plastic headband with electronic sensors.

"Wear this, so we can monitor your brainwave activity. Chem-Mech has a pill you need to ingest, so that we can monitor your internal vital signs," Webster said.

The Chem-Mech opened its chest compartment and presented a single white pill to Times. Times grabbed the pill and swallowed it whole.

"Ugh, god *damn.* Why does it taste so bad?" asked Times.

"It's coated with seaweed extract. It'll help your body more easily digest the pill's embedded nano-monitor," Webster said.

Times reclined in the chair and asked, "How will this work?"

"You should start by relaxing. After you're ready, try to recreate the emotion you were feeling at the time the event occurred, which you say worried you," replied Webster.

Times closed his eyes and began concentrating.

"Patient's vital signs are normal. Projecting statistics," said Chem-Mech.

The Chem-Mech used its mounted head camera to project a holographic image of Times' blood pressure, heart rate, and brainwave activity, above Times' body. Times envisioned the fat woman who had sexually assaulted Mallory. He felt anger that his wife was abused. He was also filled with a sense of relief. Times felt that she got what she deserved.

"Physical vital signs remain stable. Neuro-signals are slightly elevated, but not abnormal," Chem-Mech said.

Times twitched, and tried remaining focused. He struggled for a few minutes, and desperately tried to make something extraordinary happen.

"This isn't fucking working!" Times finally exclaimed.

"Heart rate, elevated. Blood pressure, rising. Neurological activity, significantly increased," Chem-Mech said.

Times felt the blood vessels in his brain pulse with adrenaline. Times screamed and abruptly sat up in the chair.

"What happened?" Times asked Webster.

Webster placed his hand inside the holographic image and made several gestures. A more detailed breakdown of Times' body readings was displayed. Webster rotated his hand and removed a three dimensional holographic image of Times' brain. The image illuminated in different sections with purple, red, and yellow colors.

"See for yourself, Greg," said Webster.

Times arose from the chair, and moved closer to him. Webster held the three dimensional rendering in his palm.

"These areas of the brain control speech and emotion," said the Chem-Mech.

It used a small laser beam from its camera head to highlight specific portions of the 3D model.

"They showed stronger than average signals during the test," said Chem-Mech.

"That makes no sense. What would that, have to do with tele–"

Times stopped speaking immediately. He did not yet intend to tell Webster his true reason for requesting the test.

"Tele? Tele, what?" asked Webster.

"Telepathy," Times said in an embarrassed voice.

"So, that is what you're researching," said Webster.

He collapsed his palm to close the image. Webster began slowly pacing around the room. He eventually stopped near the door where Alice was standing.

Times became uneasy and said, "If you need me to reimburse you for the service, I could–"

"This event you mentioned. Did you speak aloud, before it occurred?" Webster interrupted.

"Yes, I did," Times replied.

After a brief silence Webster said, "You actually may have a valid theory."

Times was stunned.

"What do you mean?" Times asked.

Webster replied, "Words are a powerful tool. Some would say that they are mankind's greatest achievement. Communication, has allowed humans to share the magnificent secrets of science, and express our emotions through literature. Language has helped us clarify our God given rights, and enshrine those rights with law. Speech has the power to evoke joy, through the use of eloquently crafted sentences; or to evoke hostility through the utterance of sole obscenities, like the word 'nigger'."

Times was speechless. He had never heard such deep philosophy.

"How does that relate to my situation?" Times asked with intrigue.

"I have a theory, but it requires a stretch of the imagination," Webster replied.

"Tell me," said Times.

"If the drugs are somehow enhancing the strength of your brainwaves, it may be possible that you're able to project sounds into the minds of others. This could be considered a mild form of telepathy," Webster said.

"I'm not sure I understand," Times said.

"Brainwave technology has been around for quite some time. It is well documented, that sending signals via electrical impulses made by the normal functioning of our brain, is possible. There is also a sonar aspect. Devices that literally make a person feel he is hearing sounds inside of his own head, have been around for decades. The technology was mostly used in military mind control experiments. Eventually it was released to private corporations for advertising purposes. This manipulation is commonly known as the microwave auditory effect. It's fundamentally based off the physics principle of directed acoustic energy. I believe that if your brainwaves were enhanced enough by the drug, then it's possible that you could perform a similar feat. Research papers have already proposed that this type of synthetic telepathy is possible. But there are no studies, that have officially observed the effect on humans," Webster said.

The fantastic idea seemed very plausible to Times.

"What could I do, to enhance these effects?" Times asked.

Webster skeptically replied, "We're not even sure if my theory is correct. Even if it were–"

"I thought you said that all this technology already exists," Times interrupted.

Webster said, "Yes it does but–"

"So what's the problem?" Times snapped.

"You could be jeopardizing your health," replied Webster.

"The benefits outweigh the risks," said Times.

Webster said, "You're being unreasonable. There's no way I–"

"I thought you were a man of science!" Times forcefully interjected.

Webster did not again speak. He looked down at the robot Alice, and patted its camera head. He gazed around the rest of the room, and marveled at the wonderful technology surrounding him.

"Indeed…I am," Webster solemnly said.

Webster walked closer to Times and the Chem-Mech.

"What would you do with this technology, if you could get it to work the way you want?" Webster asked.

Times thought critically about his intent before replying, "I'd use it, to protect what is rightfully mine. I would not let innocent people be abused. I'd make sure that atrocities, like the massacre we witnessed in New Jersey, never again happen in my presence."

"That sounds very noble. May I be honest with you, about why this technology intrigues me?" Webster asked.

Times nodded his head and said, "Of course."

"If my hypothesis is correct, this experiment will allow you to become an extraordinarily powerful, and dangerous man," said Webster.

"That was not my intention," Times honestly replied to Webster's observance.

"I understand, but your intentions are irrelevant. The only thing that matters is the final result. There are entities, both public and private, that will pay lots of money for this type of powerful technology," said Webster.

Times uneasily asked, "What are you trying to say?"

"Individually, we both have an item which the other needs. I need to be able to utilize your gift for financial benefits, if I am going to fund its research. You need my resources, to enhance your ability," said Webster.

"What are you suggesting?" asked Times.

"A mutually beneficial business endeavor. I'll provide the assets you need. In exchange, I may ask you to use your abilities for my benefit. Influence some prestigious investors, persuade a few important lobbyists, show my detractors the error of their negative smear campaigns; these are the ways in which you could repay me," Webster said deviously.

"You want me to help you gain an unfair advantage in the marketplace," Times observed.

"If you want to put it in blunt terms, yes. That is correct," Webster acknowledged while walking closer to Times.

"Why would I agree to be your servant?" Times asked in a confrontational manner.

"This has nothing to do with serving me. In fact, I am offering you the opposite of servitude. I am offering you…freedom," Webster said defensively.

"Sounds a lot like blackmail," quipped Times.

"It very well may be, my friend. But what great life achievements are obtained, without mischief's guiding hand? All truly great inventions are suppressed at the time of their creation. The benefits of ingenuity are always enjoyed by a select few, before they are released for mass consumption," said Webster.

Times did not speak.

"I do not need to lecture you, about the hierarchy of society. But I think understanding my mindset; will make my intentions more clear. There are only four classes. The Prey, the Workers, the Elite, and the Super Elite. The decadent and privileged like me are quite different from you. We view the Workers, like you, as necessary tools to complete our life missions. We sympathize with you, because many of our parents or grandparents shared your burden. You are forced to build items, and serve your job's bosses; knowing that they will never let you be part of the solution in the final equation. You are the human resources, to be used until you are retired," Webster said.

"However, you are nothing like the Prey; whose only purpose is to be used as a tool to menace the working class. The Prey has their growth purposely stunted from birth. They bring about social control; by using their inability to provide for themselves, as a means to extract wealth from the working class, through taxation. We view them as mindless dumb animals. They are hyper domesticated, and amount to little more than criminals, welfare recipients, or both. We use them to gain political support. They are the reason for, and cause of, our obsession with exploiting alleged law and social equality," Webster said.

Times was so shocked by what he was hearing, that he could not reply.

Webster continued, "The Elite are a special breed. We may start our lives from humble means, but we *work* to achieve our success. Whether we make our fortunes through artistic or scientific means, it makes no difference. We are the few who have escaped the Worker class, themselves children of the Prey class, to build great fortunes using nothing except our raw *willpower*, and *ideas*. Even *we* are termites, when compared to the powerful Super Elite. These are people, not born into *money*, but *status*. They quite literally control the supply of money. They are three hundredth generation royalty. The word 'no' does not exist in their vocabulary; lest it be used to deny another man his birthright. They are *dangerous* people. Most are criminally insane. They are responsible for all the atrocities, which are released on the unwashed masses of society. GMO, fluoride, radioactive disasters, economic ruin, television; all these were created by the Super Elite with the intention of controlling the population, and softly killing the public. They do not function in the same reality as you, or I. Which is why I believe it may be in everyone's benefit, if you obtained greater abilities."

"A wild card, to put a check on their power. This is what you intend to make me?" Times asked.

"*Exactly!* You have no idea how valuable an asset you would be to me, if you helped me keep them in line. My reasons are not purely selfish. Unlike the Super Elite, who only seek to destroy those they feel inferior to themselves; I wish to uplift my fellow man. I do not agree with my colleagues' methods of enforcing order upon the lower classes. I understand their philosophy; that to truly have a free society, there must be a system where one man wins, when another loses. But I feel that not everyone must lose. And not every loser must lose all the time. You are a man who has lost enough in his life, to know that opportunity is an elusive mistress. I am offering you an end to your loss. I am offering you a place, among the Super Elite," said Webster.

Times reflected intensely upon Webster's philosophy. Part of him resented Webster for having such a flippant attitude towards people less fortunate than him. However, the possibility of obtaining such power was far too alluring for Times to casually dismiss. He felt that having control over others, would finally give him control over his own life.

"I'm not going to be your puppet. I won't be manipulated, and I won't help you make deals with this pathetic rouge corporation, that masquerades as our government. But if you need to persuade a few people in your inner circle of friends and detractors, that they need to see the light of reason, then you shall have my help," Times finally told Webster.

Webster smiled very widely and said, "Wonderful. I knew you could be trusted, Gregory."

"What happens next?" asked Times.

"I'll need at least a week or more, to research, gather supplies, and prepare the device. My robots will be able to assemble it within a few days. We'll resume testing in two weeks," said Webster.

Times reluctantly extended his hand, which Webster promptly shook with his own.

"Why do you continue to help me?" Times asked.

"Because I believe that with the right tools, any man can rise to power. Whether he chooses to wield that power for destructive or creative purposes, is his own decision. I'm anxious to see the path a man like you chooses," Webster said.

"Chem-Mech, double our friend's dosage. Add any chemical component that may help increase brainwave activity," Webster sternly said.

"Yes, master," it replied.

The Chem-Mech went to work. Eight minutes later, it produced a new bottle of pills for Times. The men exited the room, followed by their automaton companions. They all eventually returned to the main office reception area. They wished each other well for the upcoming holiday season and parted ways.

15 Close Call

Cameron was still asleep when he started coughing. The coughs were light at first, and barely disturbed his slumber. Sky began coughing, soon thereafter. Hers were more labored and heavy. Within minutes, the two of them were violently hacking and wheezing. Cameron awoke and tapped the back of his hand against the window on the wall above his bed. The window changed to clear transparent, from the solid cream color which it used to blend with the wall. Cameron panicked when he saw the wet yellow mist outside.

"Chem-trails!" he screamed while choking down a cough.

Cameron immediately dove to the floor. He pressed his thumb against a small square panel on the side of the wooden drawers propping up his bed. He moved back while the drawers opened. Among the assorted guns, technological devices, money, and clothes, was a gas mask. He quickly handed it to Sky.

"Put it on, quick!" Cameron said.

Sky coughed deeply and said, "Cameron, my lungs hurt!"

"I know. Put the mask on, and you'll be okay!" Cameron said.

Cameron grabbed a cloth neck warmer from the clothes pile. He quickly wrapped it around his face. He took deep gasps of air, and tried to steady his breathing.

"Get up! We have to go help the others!" Cameron yelled.

The two quickly threw outside wear over their nighttime attire. Cameron burst from his room, with Sky following closely behind. They raced down the hall.

"Walter, Walter!" Cameron screamed.

Cameron saw Vincent running into the living room. Vincent was wearing his own gas mask.

"Why the fuck isn't the alarm going off?" Vincent asked.

"I don't know, the whole comp–" Cameron attempted to reply, before he was stopped by his own coughing.

"Shit, Cam! You need to put on a fucking mask! You're going to get sick!" yelled Vincent.

Sky draped Cameron's right arm over her shoulders, and put her left arm around his back. She used her body to help him keep his balance.

"Vince, where are the masks?" Sky frantically asked.

"We should have more in the warehouse. Follow me!" said Vincent.

The trio ran into the warehouse. Vincent located a locker on the wall, and attempted to use his palm print on its scanning panel to unlock the door. The panel did not respond. Vincent tried again, without success.

"Shit! Stay here. I'm going outside," Vincent exclaimed.

Vincent quickly pulled off his mask, and let Cameron catch his breath. After a few seconds, Cameron returned the mask. Cameron sat on the floor near the locker, and took turns sharing the other mask with Sky. Vincent ran outside. The air was thick with yellow mist. Vincent's skin itched, from the toxic chemicals in the air. He saw Lucia on the roof. She was wearing her own gas mask, and using a Geiger counter to measure the amount of radioactivity in the air.

He looked at her and asked, "What the hell is the problem? None of the electronics in the compound are working!

"The chemstorm is frying all the systems. The drones must be using a heavier dose of radioactive isotopes in the mixture," said Lucia.

"Cameron needs a mask, and the locker won't open!" Vincent said.

Lucia reached into her tool belt, and threw Vincent a rectangular key. On its top was an open circular dome with tiny pins on the inside. It had a small push button on its side.

"Open the panel on the side of the locker. Jam that in the keyhole, twist left, and then push the button," Lucia said.

Vincent quickly ran back into the compound. He saw Cameron was still sitting on the floor and coughing. His coughs were not as severe due to the fact he had been sharing a mask with Sky, but it was obvious that he was in great discomfort. Vincent followed Lucia's instructions, and was able to give Cameron a gas mask from the opened locker. Cameron put it on, and a couple minutes later, was able to breathe well.

"That fucking sucked!" exclaimed Cameron.

Vincent and Sky helped him to his feet.

"Lucy's outside taking radiation readings. Have either of you seen Eiji, or Walter?" Vincent asked.

"No. We were going to ask you the same thing," replied Cameron.

"Let's go talk to her," said Vincent.

They all went outside, and saw Lucia was climbing down off the roof. The yellow particles stuck to their clothes.

"Where are the boys?" Vincent asked Lucia.

"They'll be back soon. They took the car out to see if the drones are purposefully attacking the power grid. Or if the signals are being distorted because of the Chem-trails," Lucia replied.

"I haven't seen Chems sprayed this heavily in months," said Sky.

Sky looked up and asked, "Can any of you tell which way the drone is flying?"

"No. The motion sensors are having trouble tracking them. They must be using scramblers to disrupt the radar," replied Lucia.

"What's the radiation level? Should we go inside and get the suits? I have one at my apartment, if you don't have a spare," Sky said.

"We should, if this goes on for much longer. The levels I was picking up were pretty high," Lucia grimly replied.

The group was under attack by chemical aerosol spraying called Chem-trailing. Chem-trails had been sprayed over American territories since the early 2100's. They were originally used as crop pesticides. Over time companies began putting high dosages of lethal toxins into the mixture. Modern day solutions contained ingredients like aluminum, mercury, fluoride, depleted uranium, and other horrific elements. Drones dispersed the poison above all cities, and rural areas.

The federal government sanctioned the spraying, and even mandated it under the Carbon Tax Law. They falsely claimed that Chem-trails reduced diseases spread by bugs. This erased decades of political activism, which had managed to get Chem-trail spraying banned in certain parts of the country. By the mid 2190's, every American who could afford a gas mask and radiation suit had purchased one. The masks were necessary to protect oneself from the cancer inducing Chem-trail cocktail.

Vincent saw Walter and Eiji, pulling up in Walter's car.

"Hey look. It's them," said Vincent.

They exited the vehicle and Eiji said, "This is a bonafide shit storm, if I've ever seen one! The roads are horrible, and there are blackouts all over town. I don't think this is an accident. The drones are probably releasing short EMP bursts; to disrupt any tracer weapons that could help shoot them down."

"Motherfuckers," Vincent angrily said.

"Doesn't look like there's anything to do, except wait out the storm," said Walter.

Walter began walking back to the compound and the group followed.

"There are some spare clothes in the lockers. Throw them on real quick, and then go change for real, upstairs. We should avoid dragging this toxic shit around the house," Walter said.

Sky and Lucia entered the compound first, and took their time cleaning themselves. Forty-two minutes later, they opened the doors and ushered the males inside. The guys wasted no time stripping to their boxer short underwear. They were loud and raucous; made crude jokes, and engaged in horseplay.

"Stop acting like grunts! We are *not* living in a cave!" Sky said to them while the men were running upstairs.

She snapped a wet towel in their direction when they ran past her. The entire group eventually reconvened in the compound's living room.

"What a shitty way to end the year," said Eiji.

"Are we going out partying tonight?" asked Sky.

"Yes. That's a great idea," said Lucia.

"Be careful. There are more drones out on New Year's Eve, than any other night of the year. They're going to be cracking down on anyone violating curfew," Walter said with concern.

"I thought curfew ended this week, so that people could celebrate. What happened?" asked Cameron.

"President Cho extended it until January fourth. He said it was in response to the threat of terrorist rioters," said Eiji.

"Bullshit. That yellow fuck is just trying to lock down America, indefinitely!" Vincent proclaimed.

Vincent awkwardly looked at Eiji and said, "No offense."

"Don't worry; the Japanese have been at war with the Chinese for generations. We know they were behind the weather attack of 2157. I'll let that one slide," Eiji said.

The two men bumped fists as a sign of peace.

"It wouldn't be the first time an American President used a temporary Executive Order, to permanently take away the citizens' rights," Walter added.

The group silently acknowledged the wisdom of Walter's words.

Walter did not wait long before saying, "I hope you enjoy yourselves. I won't be joining you. I have to take care of some business, here at the house."

Everyone immediately protested Walter's absence. They all spoke at once.

"No way!" said Cameron.

"That's not happening..." said Lucia.

"...hang out with us," said Eiji

"Don't be a hermit!" said Vincent.

"...we want you there!" said Sky.

Walter was overwhelmed by the unanimous response. He laughed, and raised his hand.

"Hah hah, all right...*all right!* I'll have a few drinks!" Walter said.

His friends happily cheered Walter's decision.

After the brief celebration Walter said, "Okay, y'all are talking too much. Save your oxygen. We've still got to wait a few more hours, before it'll be safe to remove our gas masks."

The group agreed to leave at 7:00 PM that evening. After some more casual conversation, they all temporarily parted ways. Sky and Cameron returned to his room. He playfully tackled her onto the bed.

"Roar! I'm a radioactive dinosaur! Watch out. I bite you, while I glow in the dark!" he said.

He began tickling her with his hands. She went along with it, at first.

"No! Cameron, that's not funny!" Sky playfully said.

"Yes it is! I have sharp teeth, and can cook potatoes on my forehead!" Cameron said.

He continued touching her, and she kept giggling. She started resisting and pushed him away, when he tried to pull her close in an affectionate manner.

"What's wrong?" he asked.

"This is weird," she replied.

She squirmed underneath him. He moved to allow her space, and they both sat upright.

"Is it the masks?" Cameron asked.

Sky suddenly became very serious and said, "Stop it, Cameron. You know what I mean."

"No I don't, Sky. I'm not a fucking mind reader," Cameron snapped back.

"You don't have to be mean to me," Sky strongly said.

"I'm not being...look, what do you expect? We screw around with each other, on and off, for years. When I finally try getting serious with you, you pretend that you're not into me," replied Cameron.

"Oh Cameron, you're so romantic! I can't believe it took you this long to woo me!" Sky sarcastically said.

Cameron cleared his mind, and focused his thoughts calmly.

"I don't want to fight with you. We hang out all the time. You crash at my place, and we don't even fuck. It's not that I even care about fucking you. I mean I want to fuck you...shit, that came out wrong," Cameron said.

Sky was getting visibly upset with Cameron's horrible attempt at being a wordsmith. Cameron decided to stop speaking, so he would not further annoy her.

"All I want to know, is why you're so hesitant about being with me," Cameron said.

"I don't know if we should have this conversation right now," Sky weakly said.

"Look, I'm a bastard. Forget all that shit I just said. Sky, seriously, why can't we talk about this?" Cameron said.

"Because we're hanging out with everyone tonight. I don't want there to be any problems between us," Sky replied.

"They won't care. What's the big deal?" snapped Cameron.

"I don't think you're going to like what I have to say," Sky answered.

"Sky, you know that you can tell me anything. Why are you being so evasive?" Cameron asked with frustration.

Sky knew what she was about to say, would break Cameron's heart. But she had to be honest with him.

"I don't know if you're the right guy for me," Sky said solemnly.

Sky's words devastated Cameron.

After a long silence he said, "I understand, believe me. I know it hasn't been easy, putting up with our lifestyle for so many years. Sky, you have to understand, that part of my life is over. I'm not that guy any more. I told you, I'm out. I'm done. No more bullshit."

Sky fought back tears and said, "You think it's that easy? Cameron, do you have any idea how many laws you've broken? You will do serious time when the Feds finally decide to bust you. You can't just wake up one morning, and decide your past doesn't exist!"

Cameron was at a loss for words. He could not argue the truth behind what Sky said. He took time to formulate a coherent response.

"You of all people should know that our situation is very complex. It's not about law. It's about survival, and helping people. Isn't that why you got involved with us, five years ago?" Cameron asked.

"That's not fair. I was a twenty-three year old, naive girl, who was sick of starving. I had no idea that helping people meant being an abject criminal. People have *died* because of what you do, Cameron," Sky coldly replied.

Cameron's feelings were crushed. He felt no more significant than an ant in the middle of the desert. He had been chastised by many people during his life. But when the woman closest to him shared her unbiased criticism, the truth of her observations cut a hole in his manhood.

After a long pause Cameron said, "I'd like to think, that I've caused people more happiness, than harm."

"You sound just like Walter," Sky callously replied.

Cameron knew that comparison was not a compliment. He ignored the comment, and appealed to her empathy.

He took a deep breath and said, "I find it amazing that a person like you would ignore how fucked up the world is around you, when you wear the proof of its injustice upon your face."

The two stared at each other for several tense moments.

"You're right, Cameron. The world is a fucked up, awful place. That doesn't mean that we have to be fucked up, awful people," Sky finally said.

She lowered her head, arose from the bed, and began walking to the door. Cameron swiftly pounced to his feet, and grabbed her arm.

"Sky, wait..." Cameron said.

She jerked away from him and said, "Stop. Don't make this harder on either of us. Just let me go."

He slowly released her arm. She left his room, taking her coat and a piece of his soul with her.

Sky left the compound, and walked to a nearby bus station. She rode the bus back to her apartment, and went inside. She felt the weight of the gas mask straining her neck. She had been wearing it for over two hours. She decided to remove it, and put on a smaller surgical mask. It did not offer the same protection as the gas mask, but it prevented her from coughing profusely. Exhausted, she laid down on her couch to rest, and soon fell asleep.

She awoke four hours later, at 6:48 PM, and decided to check her cell phone. She knew Cameron would have called to find out if she was still meeting with him. She put the back of her right hand near the receiver on the bottom of the phone, which was strapped to her left wrist. She waved her right hand upward, and the hologram illuminated in her palm. She briefly browsed the text messages Cameron had sent, and then closed her left palm to make the hologram disappear.

While contemplating her response, she heard commotion outside. She looked out of her window, and saw that there was a large group of people gathered outside of her building. She could not get a good look at the crowd from her room's window, so she went downstairs to further investigate the situation. It was very cold outside. The Chem-trails had dispersed, and the air was marginally safer to breathe. She moved her mask so that it hanged around her neck. She was startled when she reached the ground floor, and saw that a crowd of around seventy people were gathered in front of the building.

They were furiously yelling at the caretaker. Sky's building was officially classified as government subsidized housing. The state owned the property, and assigned different caretakers to manage the everyday affairs. The caretaker was desperately trying to reason with the furious crowd.

"It's not my fault! I don't control the thermostats!" the caretaker said to the angry mob.

A middle aged man named Charles was the group's key spokesperson.

"We don't care! Get the power company on the phone, and tell them this bullshit has got to stop!" Charles said.

Sky moved through the crowd. Sky walked over to an older woman, whom she knew lived on her floor.

"Missus Betty, what's happening?" Sky asked.

"The power company is rationing our electricity again. There's no heat in the entire building, and they say they're going to be shutting off the lights at midnight," Mrs. Betty responded.

"Why? It's one of the coldest nights of the year," Sky angrily asked.

"They said that's exactly why they're turning it off. They don't want too many people using the system at once. They say it puts too much stress on the grid," replied Mrs. Betty.

"That's rubbish. We're going to get frostbite!" Sky heatedly said.

"I know child, I know," Mrs. Betty somberly replied.

Sky saw the group was becoming more irate. The unruly crowd was yelling at the caretaker.

"I have a small child. Do you want her to catch pneumonia?" an enraged woman asked.

"You've tried to kill us enough for one day!" a young man shouted.

He held up the surgical mask, which most people were wearing.

"There's nothing I can do! The Green Meters are programmed to stop producing power during peak hours!" the caretaker yelled.

Sky was heartbroken at the suffering which she was witnessing. The people were begging for heat, but their tyrannical government was not going to give it to them. Eco-fascism had driven these people into poverty, and now their wish to have warmth would go unfulfilled.

"Please, just go back inside and try to stay warm!" pleaded the caretaker.

"Go to Hell! You're a spineless government twat! Fuck the Green Meters, and fuck *you!*" screamed Charles.

Charles began walking towards the side of the building. Some of the group followed, while others stayed behind and tried to talk some sense into the caretaker.

While Charles was walking he angrily shouted, "Goddamn motherfuckin' *tired* of this shit! Motherfuckers want to chemically attack us, and then expect us to freeze! Well, I'm not on that bullshit! They can suck my *dick!*"

He located the large rectangular Green Meter attached to the side of the building. It was the size of small car. He picked up a nearby rock, and used it to smash the meter.

"Fuck it; if they want us to freeze, then we'll freeze on our own terms!" Charles screamed.

The crowd cheered, and more people began rushing towards the commotion. Sky and Mrs. Betty walked closer, but kept their distance from the core of the group. The caretaker ran over to the crowd, and tried to prevent them from destroying the meter.

"Stop! Are you fucking crazy?" asked the caretaker.

People in the crowd shoved the caretaker away, and helped Charles vandalize the oppressive technology. The meter was encased in thick steel, and had a computer monitor inside. The monitor had various bar graphs and text messages projecting across its screen. A bulletproof glass sheet covered the monitor. It allowed people to see the readings, without causing it damage. It was very common for people to vandalize Green Meters, even though doing so was a crime.

Some of the tenants went back inside. Others rushed to the scene with crude, makeshift weapons. They carried baseball bats, metal pipes, and shovels. They mercilessly pummeled the Green Meter. The crowd cheered, while the freezing citizens continued their assault. They started denting the metal, and chipping the thick bulletproof glass.

"This might get ugly. We should go inside," said Mrs. Betty.

Sky knew the wise old woman was right, but she could not stop watching the drama unfold.

"They have no right, to treat these people with such disrespect," Sky said in a weak voice.

"I know. But I'm a lot older than you are, child. You can't crusade forever. Eventually, you have to learn how to be happy with what you have; and be glad that God lets you make it through another day," Mrs. Betty said.

What happened next shocked the entire crowd. The meter started projecting a holographic image above the monitor. It displayed the face of a computer generated Chinese woman.

"Destroying Green Meters is against the law. Please cease and desist, or corrective measures will be taken to ensure your safety," the projection said.

"Shut up bitch!" Charles said.

Charles threw a rock at the image, and it briefly distorted after being stricken.

"Group terrorism is a crime. You are required by law to stop," the animation said.

"You're the goddamned terrorist!" a young woman shouted.

She ran up, and clubbed the meter with a hammer. The group followed her lead, and continued their assault.

After a moment the artificial woman said, "Threat level assessed. Pain compliance is required."

The meter quickly flashed, and released a low resonant hum. Everyone who was wearing a cell phone on their wrist was immediately hit with a low level shock. The pulse wave jolted their body, and caused three seconds of moderate physical discomfort. The group screamed, and some people were frightened into running away.

Charles growled and said, "Ohh, you son of a bitch! You think that stings?"

He pulled his phone from his wrist, and threw it to the ground. The meter once again began shocking the crowd.

"Ow!" said Sky.

She ripped her band from her wrist, and let it fall to the floor. To Sky's surprise, Mrs. Betty chuckled.

"Lord, I'm glad I never got me one of these things," Mrs. Betty said.

Mrs. Betty took off her gloves, and used them to pick up the wristband.

"I know they're useful for communication, but I don't want that nonsense zapping me!" she said.

Mrs. Betty wrapped the band in her gloves, and handed them to Sky. Sky could feel the band vibrating through the gloves, but the shock did not affect her because the phone was not touching her skin. The frequent blasts distressed the remaining members of the crowd. Many people left the scene, and soon only a small group remained. Those who were still around had removed, or were in the process of removing, their wrist bands. Suddenly, the mass tasering stopped.

"Pain compliance applied. Threat of group terrorism, reduced," said the animated woman.

Charles rubbed his wrist and asked, "So that's how you make us obey? By torturing us, like animals?"

The animated woman did not reply.

"Okay, that's fine," said Charles.

He looked at the group and screamed, "I am *not* a fucking *animal!*"

The crowd once again cheered, and the remaining people resumed their violent assault.

"Hostiles refuse to follow instructions. Drone assistance requested," said the animated woman.

The crowd suddenly grew very silent.

"What did that piece of shit just say?" asked a young boy in the crowd.

"It just requested a drone strike. We need to leave, right now," said another man in the crowd.

"Go on then, leave! You fucking pussies scared of a little bitch ass drone? I'm going to beat this goddamn thing down, until it gives us some motherfucking heat!" shouted Charles.

The group ceased their uprising. A friend of his came over to Charles and comforted him.

"Stop it man, you're going to get yourself killed," he told Charles.

"He's right. Don't do this. You don't want to die," another man whispered to Charles.

"I don't fucking care anymore! Death is better than this shit! You're going to have to *kill* a nigger out in this motherfucker, to make me stop! You understand? You're going to have to kill me, motherfucker! Kill ME!" Charles said.

Charles began sobbing uncontrollably, and his friends escorted him back into the building.

"That was amazing. You're a hero," one of them whispered.

The faint sounds of a few hands clapping were heard as Charles was led back into the building. Sky was heartbroken at what she had just witnessed.

Before Sky had time to reflect on the event, Mrs. Betty said, "Lord, I'm tired of watching them suffer, child."

"Do you think this will ever end? Do you think they will ever let us be free?" Sky asked.

"I pray that one day, it will. For years, my people asked the same question. They cried and pleaded for someone to save them from their bondage. Eventually they realized that help was never going to come. So they took matters into their own hands," Mrs. Betty replied.

Sky was not convinced and said, "I don't see how that's possible. We can't fight the entire system. It's too big."

Mrs. Betty said, "I think you're wrong, child. No system is too big to fight. Tyranny can be defeated, but the people must decide when the revolution happens. Nobody *lets* you be free. Freedom is God given. It is up to the individual, to exert that gift. The people have to ask God for strength. Once they make the choice to no longer live like slaves, then things will change child. I believe, God willing, one day people will choose to be free."

Mrs. Betty's words had a deep emotional effect on Sky. She believed Mrs. Betty spoke a passionate truth, and it gave Sky hope for the future. Sky cracked a thankful smile.

"Have a good night, Missus Betty," Sky said.

"Thank you, child. You too. Don't stay out too late!" Mrs. Betty said.

Mrs. Betty walked back inside the building, and Sky walked away from the apartment. She wanted to call Cameron, but she was reluctant to wear her phone after experiencing its taser effects. After calming her nerves, she mustered the will to use the device.

Cameron answered her call, "Hey, I didn't think you were going to–"

"Are you still at home?" Sky quickly interrupted.

Cameron could tell Sky was upset by the quivering tone in her voice, and the worried look upon her face.

"Yes. Sky, what's wrong?" Cameron replied.

"Is it okay if I come over?" Sky asked.

Cameron responded, "Of course, but why do you sound–"

"Thank you. I'll be there soon," Sky again interrupted.

She cut the signal, so that Cameron could not further respond. Sky caught a ride from a bus at the local station. She became nervous when she arrived at the stop near Cameron's home. She saw through the windows, that the streets were filled with people. Some were only rowdy party-goers. Others seemed mischievous, malevolent, and quite violent. She exited the bus, and saw Cameron pushing through the crowd. He wore a surgical mask around his face. He pulled the mask down to his chin, and waved at her.

"Hey! Sky! Over here!" Cameron said.

Sky quickly walked to him, and asked, "Why is everyone acting crazy?"

Cameron grabbed her hand, and began walking briskly away from the angry mob.

"The whole town is going fucking nuts. The power companies are rationing everything. Heat, lights, and plumbing, are all being restricted. We need to get inside. There are going to be riots soon," Cameron said.

They walked past a group of people, who were burning a small effigy of President Cho.

"Why are they doing that? Are they protesting the curfew?" Sky asked Cameron.

"Does it really matter? Who doesn't have a reason to hate that idiot?" Cameron replied.

They reached the compound a few minutes later. They entered, and went to the living room. Eiji, Vincent, Lucia, and Walter, were socializing and drinking.

She overheard Vincent say, "I'll call it right now, for your ass. The Hulks are winning the Mega Bowl this year. No more excuses. They will be world champs, I guarantee!"

Sky heard Eiji say, "That's total bullshit! New York has no quarterback! I bet they won't even make the playoffs...oh, shit. What's up, Sky? Cameron said you weren't coming. It's great to see you!"

"Hello Eiji," said Sky indifferently.

She walked past him, and picked up a large bottom of rum that was sitting on the living room table. She twisted the cap, and began chugging the raw fluid straight from the bottle. After a few large gulps, the group became concerned about her.

"Yikes, that's a huge sip!" said Eiji.

"Slow down, hermana!" said Lucia.

Vincent sprang from his chair and playfully said, "Whoa, whoa! Easy there, girl. You're going to make yourself sick!"

Vincent gently pulled the bottle from Sky's hand. Sky walked over to the couch and sat beside Lucia.

"Do you have any weed? I want to get fucked up tonight," Sky said.

Vincent chuckled and said, "All right, that's what I want to hear! Hey, do you like Vodka? Let me make you a screwdriver. I'll use organic orange juice!"

Vincent went to fix the beverage. Walter was less oblivious, and knew that Sky was upset.

"Everything all right?" Walter asked Cameron.

Cameron made a baffled look, and waved his hands in a back-and-forth manner, which expressed his lack of knowledge as to why Sky was upset.

Vincent returned from the kitchen with Sky's drink, a box of filtered marijuana cigarettes, and a special lighter.

"Here you go, girl. North Dakota's finest!" Vincent said.

He handed her the items. Sky took a few sips of the drink. She lit the stogie, by placing the thin sheet of lighter paper between her thumb and index finger. She snapped her fingers together, and her palm briefly illuminated. She cupped the flame in between both hands, to light the cigarette. The Smart Light, as it was called, quickly extinguished after three seconds. It did not burn her skin in the slightest way. After taking a long drag, she exhaled.

"I find it hilarious, that the only domestically produced crop still left in the country, was illegal for almost one hundred fifty years," Sky sarcastically said.

Sky continued smoking while Lucia said, "It still is, in some states."

Eiji smirked and said, "Yeah, the shitty ones."

"They all fucking suck. Fifty-two shades of the same bullshit!" said Vincent while sipping his beer.

Sky took another long drag and said, "They almost called in a drone strike, on my apartment tonight."

The group was stunned into silence for several moments. Sky continued smoking, and drinking away her anxiety.

"Why?" asked a concerned Walter.

"Some of the residents attacked the Green Meter," Sky replied.

Lucia commented, "Gosh, that's fucking bold. In public? Why are you...?"

She let her thought trail off, but Sky knew what Lucia wanted to ask.

"Not dead? Dumb luck, I guess. They taser shocked us, through our cell phones. It didn't even faze the crowd. Even though people were hurting, I didn't think they were going to stop. That is, until they heard the machine call for an air strike," Sky replied.

Sky remembered she was still wearing her phone bracelet. She quickly removed it, and threw it on top of the table.

"God damned dog collar," Sky said with disgust.

"Shit chica, that's pretty heavy," said Lucia.

She patted Sky on the back. The group's mood became extremely somber.

After a period of silence Sky said, "I'm sorry. I didn't mean to spoil the mood."

Walter replied, "It's cool," then took a long sip of his drink.

Cameron was visibly disturbed by the events which Sky described. His emotions were a mix of rage, sadness, and helplessness. He felt trapped in an invisible prison, with no realistic way to escape its grasp.

"No, it's not. The way we are forced to live, is not right. We are living in an artificial habitat; created and managed by a group of authoritarian control freaks," Cameron said.

Cameron looked at Walter and continued speaking, "I know why see yourself as a soldier, and say that we are in a war. It's true. We are under attack in every way imaginable. You know the reason it has gotten so bad? People can't recognize an enemy, unless it's dressed up in a uniform and attacking them directly. They've poisoned our food, water, and air. They've devalued our currency, stolen our money through taxes, and forced us to disarm ourselves with draconian gun control laws. This didn't happen overnight. The people let it happen, over many decades. You know why? They couldn't see the tyranny. They refused to acknowledge the evil which lurked inside their government, until it was too late. Now it has gotten so bad, that we let them execute us at will...and no one even complains."

The group was stunned by Cameron's words. While he was always a vocal opponent of the oppressive American regime, he rarely codified his thoughts into such concise statements. The group was once again silent. It was now Cameron's turn to feel embarrassed, for creating a depressing atmosphere.

Cameron said, "Shit. I'm sorr–"

"Everyone needs to stop fucking apologizing. Stop saying 'sorry', or feeling guilty for pointing out the truth. Living in reality is difficult. You all need to stop feeling bad, for stating the facts. I wish you all had made better decisions, and not chosen such rebellious paths, but those were your calls to make. You all can't change your past, but you can fight for your future," Walter said.

Eiji played coy and asked, "What are you saying?"

"Stop acting retarded. You know what he's saying. He wants us to keep fighting with him," Vincent sternly said.

Vincent looked Walter in the eye and continued, "But for whatever reason, he won't come out and ask us directly."

There was little hesitation before Walter said, "I'm not going to put you in that position. Whatever decision you make, you need to make it with a clear conscience, and without my influence."

"The past few weeks have changed me. I've realized that we're not the bad people, no matter what anyone tries to say. These government pigs may kill us, or put us in jail for the rest of our lives. I won't let the possibility of that, stop me from doing what I know is right. Psychopathic technocrats wrecked society, not us," Vincent said.

Vincent took a long swig of his drink, before he said, "I'm going with you on the run this weekend."

"So am I. I've been spending a lot of time in the slums. You should see how bad it has gotten in some sectors. People don't eat for days at a time. A lot of folks have trap doors and hidden crawl spaces in their homes. Kids sometimes have to hide there, when the Child Enforcement Agency does random inspections," Eiji immediately added.

Lucia was horrified at what Eiji had just stated.

"My God, does the CEA ever take them from their parents?" Lucia asked.

Eiji remained stone silent, and refused to look Lucia in her eyes. When she realized he wasn't going to answer her, Lucia put her head down.

"Those poor kids..." Lucia said with sadness.

She knew that Eiji's silence was a grim confirmation of her question.

"I don't think this is an appropriate time for this conversation," Cameron said.

Sky knew that he was indirectly referring to her presence in the room. They rarely spoke about their operations in front of her, because they did not want to involve her in their affairs, any more than was absolutely necessary.

"I'm sorry. I should leave," Sky said.

"Nonsense. Cameron is right; it's the last day of the year. We should at least *try* to enjoy ourselves," said Walter.

"Amen, brother. That statement deserves a toast," said Vincent.

He raised his glass, and so did the rest of the group.

Vincent smiled and said, "To saying 'fuck you' to tyranny!"

"Fuck *you*, tyranny!" said the friends.

They tipped their glasses, and solidified their resolution with a drink.

16 Keep Your Friends Close...

Four days had passed since the dawn of the New Year. It was Friday, January 4th, 2217. Times was in the same research room, where Webster had first brought him almost two weeks earlier. A small white mouse was frantically running around inside a large glass observation cage. Webster closely watched its movement.

"Another direction. Good, move it left! Once more, yes!" he excitedly said to Times.

Times deeply concentrated, while he repeated a string of commands.

"Here, that way, over..." Times said to the mouse.

After a couple more commands, Times grunted loudly, and ceased speaking. Times put his hands to his face, and took very deep breaths.

"Astonishing. Even though the mouse doesn't understand your words, it reacts to the sound of your voice. This is one of the most amazing experiments I've ever performed," said Webster.

Webster walked across the room, and over to where Times was standing.

"Can we move it closer? I'm having trouble seeing him," Times asked.

"That's part of the experiment. We have to figure out, at what distance you can still be effective," replied Webster.

Times removed the headband that he was wearing. Times handed it to the Chem-Mech, which was standing next to him. Times walked over to a nearby chair, and sat down.

"I need a break. Tell me what you've discovered," Times said.

"Chem-Mech, display your results," said Webster.

The Chem-Mech projected a holographic image of various neurological readings, block graphs, and numbers.

"Patient is exhibiting highly abnormal levels of neurological activity. Spatial auditory manipulation effects observed on test subject," said the Chem-Mech.

"Is there a button to make it translate that stuff into English?" asked Times.

Webster laughed and said, "Here, let me explain."

Webster touched the image of Times' neuro-scans. He enlarged the image, and projected it in front of Times.

"These are the old readings," Webster said.

He projected a second image, next to the one which Times was viewing.

"You were already showing higher levels of brain activity, before we started these tests. The device, combined with your increased dosage of medication, has sent your brainwaves to unprecedented levels! Look at these scans," Webster said with excitement.

He closed the brain images, and showed a digital scan of the room. The scan showed the room as a silhouette, similar to a print of a photo negative. Red and blue sine waves protruded from Times' position, to the mouse's cage.

"The faint blue wave is your voice print, being picked up by the Chem-Mech's hyper sensitive microphones. That large red one is your actual brainwaves!" exclaimed Webster.

Times was visibly impressed, but still remained skeptical.

"That's amazing. But how can you be sure that the mouse was reacting to me?" Times asked.

"While a rodent has no comprehension of human language, I believe it was instinctively reacting to the electromagnetic disturbance, created by a combination of these waves," Webster replied.

Times arose from his chair and said, "Explain."

"Do you know the feeling you get, when you're walking down the street on a cold windy day, and a sudden gust of wind blows? Your body shivers, and you react. Maybe you cover up; maybe you tilt your head. Maybe you move to another side of the street, or turn the corner to avoid its blast. That's what I believe is happening with the mouse," Webster said.

"That makes sense. The mouse feels the energy of my brainwaves, and the vibration of the sounds," Times said.

"Exactly!" Webster exclaimed.

"How do we know it will work on people?" Times asked.

Webster seemed shocked that Times would suggest human experimentation so early in the project.

"That's a tough question. Proceeding with human trials presents an entirely different set of complications. I'm sure you're aware of the legal and ethical concerns, involved with that type of human experimentation," Webster replied.

"Of course. I'm not stupid," said Times.

Times walked over to the Chem-Mech, and retrieved the headband. He examined it closely, and was highly impressed by its intricate design.

"How long did it take you to make?" Times asked Webster.

"Not long. I used a modified video game controller. I uploaded numerous schematics, and a whole library of science and math books, into Alice and Chem-Mech's memory banks. They constructed it very quickly," replied Webster.

"The machines built this? I thought you were a programmer," said Times.

"I am an old man, with limited skill. My machines...my, children...can accomplish more in one hour, than I can in one year. They can analyze enormous amounts of data, and make changes to their internal applications with very little reprogramming," Webster said.

"Self-programming machines. Damn, these robots are getting real. I hope they don't decide to wipe us out one day," said Times.

"Hah! Not a chance. They may be advanced, but I assure you, they are by no means sentient. Besides, they can always be stopped by disrupting their electrical power sources," said Webster.

"Good point," said Times, while marveling at the headband.

The band was a thin, U-shaped, silver colored, plastic ring. It had transmitters on its tips. A black LED strip was embedded into the device. The strip flashed a combination of blue and red lights, in small square blocks, around the band.

"How do I change the batteries?" asked Times.

Webster chuckled and said, "There's no need. It generates power from the eminence of your body heat."

"No shit! That's really awesome," Times said, while admiring the beautifully crafted device.

"We should continue," said Webster.

Times returned to the corner of the room, where he was originally standing. Webster's cell phone received a call.

"Excuse me a minute, Greg," said Webster.

Webster left the room. Times continued inspecting the headband for a few more moments, before placing it upon his head. Times stared at the mouse in its cage. He went to the cage, and picked up the tiny creature.

"Hey there little guy, don't be scared," Times said softly.

Times cupped the mouse in his hands, and gently petted the rodent. Times stroked the mouse upon its head.

He said, "I hope they feed you well. You're a cute little bugger, aren–"

Before Times could finish his sentence, a sudden bolt of electricity from the headband, sent a shock-wave through his body. He fell unconscious to the floor, before he even realized what had happened. The mouse fell from his hands, and scurried away in fear.

When Times finally started awakening, his vision was blurred and he was in a serious daze. He could only see the outlines of objects, and small flashes of light. His ears were ringing, and the voices which he could hear around him, were faint and muffled. He was strapped to a mobile stretcher, and was being rolled down a dimly lit hallway. He was disoriented and could not move his body. The feeling was absolutely horrific. He tried crying out for help, but he could only muster faint groans.

Times heard blips, and a heavy thudding sound. He sensed that the Chem-Mech was following not far behind. Times was rolled into a small and poorly lit room. His vision had still not yet fully returned. He saw that the stretcher was being placed next to a large experimentation device. The device looked like a large chemistry set. It had several tubes filled with different colored liquid. Smaller tubes were intricately woven with larger ones.

Times heard the thudding stop, and rolled his head to the left side of his body. Through hazy vision, he saw the Chem-Mech menacingly standing beside him. The blur of a human shape walked in front of his stretcher, and over to the experimentation device.

"Synching vital signs with the Chem-Mech," said the human.

He could tell the voice was female, but he did not recognize her. The woman sounded like she spoke with an Eastern European accent. Times rolled his head to his right. He was horrified to see the woman was starting to insert small tubes into his veins. She placed several intravenous drips into his arms. The needles pricked his skin, and caused him intense pain. The liquid from the tubes burned when it flowed into his veins. Times tried yelling at her to stop, but he could only groan. The feeling of helplessness was unbearable. He was paralyzed, and could not communicate his unwillingness to consent with whatever this person was doing to him. He felt a single tear run down his cheek.

"Start the mental recalibration," said another distinct female voice, with a British accent.

"Stop...please," Times mumbled.

His pleas for mercy went unacknowledged. The burning sensation from the liquid abruptly stopped. The sensation turned into an equally painful cold. Times felt like was in a freezer. Soon, Times was completely numb.

"No...you...killing me," Times pitifully murmured.

"He's all set. We'll keep a close watch on his vital signs," said the Eastern European woman.

"Make sure that you do, simpleton. This experiment is extremely important, and dangerous," said the British woman.

Times heard their footsteps begin fading. The door slammed shut when they left the room. Suddenly, the room went completely dark. Only the dim lights emanating from the Chem-Mech, and the experimentation device to which Times was strapped, were illuminating. Times was terrified.

"Mallory...Mallory," Times groaned in agony.

Unfortunately for Times, his love would not be coming to his rescue. His nightmarish journey was only just beginning. Times wondered if this had been Webster's plan all along; or if Webster was even aware of what was happening. Times did not have long to ponder these questions. A focused light beam began shining upon his face.

"Who's...there?" Times tried saying.

The light began flickering at a controlled rate. Times felt his heart beating rapidly. The flickering lasted for what seemed like an eternity. The flicker pattern consistently changed its speed. At first, it would be very slow. It would then gradually move faster. The rates modulated between fast and slow; until eventually the pattern remained at a steadily fast pace. The flickering made Times' brain feel like it would explode.

"Ahh!" Times screamed.

Holographic images began flashing inside of the light beam. They lasted several seconds before changing. Times could not completely gauge how fast they were switching. The images were static at first and did not seem to make any sense. He was shown pictures of an aircraft flying ablaze through the sky; a cheeseburger with a rat stuffed between the meat and bread; a baby wearing a gas mask while sitting in a puddle of dirty water. Times' breathing became panicked, and uneven. He once again cried out in agony.

The images continued flashing, and soon were playing at an accelerated speed. Images of a six-eyed fish; a burning building; a violent car crash; a school room with crying children and teachers huddled in the corner; all played to Times. The distressing images were sending Times into a frenzy. He was overcome with grief, sadness, and despair. The images turned into graphic video clips. A group of young women in bathing suits jogging on a beach; packs of wolves mauling a deer; a sports car being driven down a country road by skeleton occupants; a farmer with a burning tire around his neck; all played in front of Times' face.

Throughout this ordeal, Times' emotions varied depending upon the images and videos which he was shown. When the videos were not disturbing, Times' emotions would range from entertained, to pleased, to indifferent. He was unimpressed by the sight of a muscular bodybuilder doing a promotional advertisement for a sports drink. When disturbing videos were shown, Times felt anger, fear, and rage. He squirmed when he saw a video of a man being executed by a laser firing squad. His heart rate fluctuated when he saw a suicide bomber detonate himself inside an Israeli bank. The Chem-Mech kept a silent watch over Times, and never let Times' vital signs go into dangerously erratic levels.

The picture and videos began mixing together. A still image of a football player lifting a trophy above his head; a video of a large snake eating a child; a still image of a group of burned human corpses; were all implanted into Times' mind. Soon, he could not tell the difference between the moving, and still images. The entire horrific slide show became a blur. A video of a dazzling actress in a stunning blue dress, being photographed on a red carpet, started playing.

The normalcy of the video soon shattered when she turned sideways. Seeing that her left arm was completely amputated, and the left half of her face was removed so that only the muscles could be seen, sent a shiver down Times' spine. For a while, Times was overcome by blind fury. He eventually resigned himself to the fact that he was completely helplessness. Soon, Times felt no emotion, except emptiness.

"Why?" Times asked.

His body started violently shaking, and he had a seizure. Times passed out, and remained unconscious. During his slumber, Times' dreams were tainted by the memory of what he had just witnessed. Horrific images, like that of a child with her lower mandible blown off, haunted his thoughts.

Times eventually awoke, and found himself in a small white room. The room had two chairs, padding along the walls, and no windows. He remained strapped to the stretcher. The restraints seemed unnecessary to Times, because he still felt paralyzed and his whole body was weak. Times heard the door open. The sound of light footsteps became louder as they moved closer to Times' stretcher.

"Put him in the chair," said the voice of a British woman.

Times heard the unmistakably clunky sounds of the robot Alice, and the Chem-Mech, moving around the room. The robots removed Times' restraints, and placed him in a chair that was near the stretcher. The robots bound his wrists and ankles to the chair. Times had an exasperated look upon his face. He was too weak to move, and his breathing was labored. The British woman walked in front of Times, sat down in the chair across from him, and crossed her legs.

Times thought she would be a great beauty, if she was not doing the work of Satan. Her shoulder length blonde hair was well kept; though her dark roots were partially showing. She wore a slick, one piece, woman's business skirt. Her lip gloss was silky, and shiny. It gave her mouth a slightly pink glow, which matched the color of her cheeks. The woman looked at Times, and gave him a creepy smile.

"How are you feeling?" asked the British woman.

Times thought she was playing some kind of queer joke. He was obviously in agony, and her sardonic comment made him want to violently rape her.

"Fuck you, bitch!" Times screamed with a sudden burst of strength.

The woman giggled like a schoolgirl.

Times yelled, "Why! Oh God, why..." before he began crying.

The restraints on his body prevented him from moving too much. Times also realized for the first time that the chair in which he was sitting, was bolted to the floor. The British woman made a satisfied smile, and then feigned concern.

"Oh no, that's not nice! You shouldn't say such naughty things," she said.

She arose from her chair and walked over to Times. She turned around and sat on his lap. Times squirmed uncomfortably. He did not want this vile wench anywhere near him.

"You're too stressed, Mister Times. You must learn to relax," the woman said.

She caressed Times' face and began kissing his cheek. Times turned away in discomfort, which excited her.

"If you're going to be naughty Mister Times, at least make it amusing!" the British woman said.

She slid from his lap, to the floor. She came to a rest on her knees. She knelt with her back arched, and began massaging Times' thighs. Her actions made Times extremely uneasy.

"See? Isn't this a much better way to respond, when someone asks you a question?" the British woman said.

She moved her right hand upward, and stroked Times' groin. Times momentarily allowed himself to feel the warmth of her hand through his clothes, before regaining his sanity.

"FUCK! WHAT THE FUCK IS WRONG WITH YOU?!" he yelled.

Times violently rocked back and forth in the chair. The woman licked her lips, and was obviously incredibly aroused by Times' suffering. Times began screaming in short bursts. He was unable to formulate any words that described his pain. The British woman quickly arose from the floor.

"Mister Times, you are out of control! You need to learn how to behave!" she said.

While saying her last word, she leaned forward and lightly punched Times in his crotch. Times let out a quick yell, then wheezed, lurched forward, and coughed. The British woman became more aggressive. She formed her left hand into a claw, and squeezed Times' face between her thumb and fingers.

"Listen to me, Mister Times. I am your therapist, and it is my duty to make sure that you are well!" she sternly said.

Times whimpered, and tried pulling away from the woman. She responded by slapping him hard across the face with her right hand.

"What do you want?" asked Times in exasperation.

The British woman responded, by draping her legs across Times' lap and straddling him. She leaned forward and put her arms around his back, so that she was hugging him.

"I want you to realize your purpose," she whispered in his ear.

She sat there upon his lap, and began gently kissing his lips. Times kept his mouth closed, and frowned.

"What's the matter, Mister Times? Do you not find me attractive?" she smugly asked.

Her eyes became wild with bliss. She began grinding her hips into Times, in an effort to sexually arouse him.

"Please, let me leave. I won't tell anyone! I swear!" Times said.

"Why would you want to leave, Mister Times? Is there something wrong with me?" the British woman asked.

She started grinding him faster. She caressed him, and licked her tongue across his face. Times began crying again.

"Aww, you're so sweet!" the British woman said.

She licked his tears, and then dismounted him. She cupped his face in her left hand, and smiled in a sadistic manner. Times gave her an exasperated look.

He said, "Please–"

Without warning, the British woman punched him hard in his nose.

"Mommy and I are one!" she screamed after delivering the blow.

Times sobbed loudly, and heavily.

"Find the reptiles, down the economic hole!" the British woman said.

She punched him across the jaw with her left hand.

"Deliver us from the snow maker!" she shouted.

She forcibly took Times' hand, and made him cup her vagina. She rubbed herself with his hand for a moment, and then spit in his face. She leaned forward, and bit his right ear. Times screamed in agony. She did not show him mercy.

"The Clockwork Knights, guide us through the light," she whispered in his right ear.

She smothered his face in her breasts, and then leaned closer to his left ear.

"The Midnight Elves will do your bidding," she whispered.

"Help me!" screamed Times.

She responded, by driving her elbow into his stomach. She proceeded to punch Times three times in his face.

"The freedom of *some*, is not for all! The freedom of *some*, is not for *all!* THE FREEDOM OF SOME, IS NOT FOR ALL!" she wildly screamed.

Blood oozed from Times' nose. He felt his face begin swelling. The woman looked at the Chem-Mech, who quickly injected Times with a needle full of clear fluid. After a moment, the British woman unbuckled Times' straps. She grabbed him by the shirt, pulled him forward, and threw him to the floor. Times tried to crawl away from her.

She kicked him and said, "Don't move, my love."

The British woman used her right foot, to roll Times over on his back. She performed a disgusting act, by standing over him and urinating in his face. Times felt his blood boil, but was once again paralyzed by the powerful drugs. Suddenly, Times no longer felt the urge to cry. Instead, he was filled with uncontrollable rage.

"I'll fucking *kill* you! I fucking kill you *all!* You fuck! You cunt! I'll chop off your tits, and shove a fucking knife up your cunt!" Times screamed at the top of his lungs.

Times writhed in pain while laying helplessly upon the ground.

"I think we've had a breakthrough today, Mister Times. Overall, it was a good session. You have a lot of anger issues. I am looking forward to helping you. I'll be back later, to check on your progress," the British woman said.

Times continued screaming obscenities, "You're a dead little bitch! I fuck you in your ass, make you suck my cock! Fuck your diseased twat with a chainsaw, you dirty slut!"

The Chem-Mech and the robot Alice lifted Times off the floor and restrained him in the stretcher.

"Fuck you, robo-fuck! You're dead too, you metal fuck!" Times screamed.

The Chem-Mech gave Times an unemotional look, and was not affected by his vulgar outburst. Once Times was fully restrained, the Chem-Mech illuminated its robotic hand, and delivered Times a severe taser shock. Times stopped screaming, and passed out. The robots, and the perverted British woman, left the room.

Times awoke from his slumber, hours later. He was still in the white room, but was surprised to find that it had been cleaned, and his clothes had been changed. He felt incredibly weak, and he could barely talk. The sound of the door opening caught his attention. He could hear heavy footsteps getting closer to his stretcher. The footsteps eventually stopped near the right side of his stretcher. He used what little energy he could muster, to tilt his head to his right. The sight of Webster standing next to him sent a wave of panic through his body.

"Help...help..." Times meekly said.

"Hello, Gregory," said Webster in a somber tone.

"You...monster..." Times painfully said through labored breaths.

Webster put the headband on Times' chest and said, "This device, is brilliant. I wish I had thought of it myself."

"Help...help, me..." pleaded Times.

"I *am* helping you," Webster coldly replied.

Webster slowly walked to the bottom edge of Times' bed.

"Until now, mind control was such a convoluted process," Webster said.

Webster stood by Times' feet, and stared straight at him.

"Mass brainwashing, is so ineffective. Sure, it's easy to poison the food and water, with chemical additives. It's not a problem, to teach Communist and Socialist propaganda in schools. Creating mindless television programs, fake news reports, and addicting video games, are no harder than lifting a finger. All these methods separately; are effective tools that control and retard the population. Even with all these distractions, people still hold on to those last stubborn remnants, of free will," Webster said.

Times did not respond. Webster began walking around the stretcher, and approached Times' left side.

"The problem is that people, who decide to awaken, can break free from those systems of domination. They only work on people that choose to be consciously deceived. Once a person decides to look past the lies of these artificial constructs, and fully discovers reality, those methods of control are rendered ineffective," Webster said.

Webster slowly leaned forward and said, "But I believe you've solved that quandary."

Webster smiled sadistically. Times noticed that he no longer felt paralyzed; but he was still too weak to fight back.

"What the hell is wrong with you?" Times asked.

Webster picked up the headband from Times' chest, and placed it upon his head.

"This device has the ability to override free will. Here, let me show you," Webster said.

Webster unbuckled the strap that was restraining Times' left arm. Times immediately tried to grab him. Webster jumped back, and laughed. Times squirmed around, and continued reaching out towards his captor.

"Hah, hah! I figured that you'd be a little fractious. Perhaps, you should take it out on *yourself?*" Webster said.

While speaking his last word, Webster used the device to make Times raise his free hand. Times was forced to slap himself in the testicles! Times howled in pain.

"Very good. You see, your brainwaves have become hypersensitive. The nano-machines inside the medication's experimental chemical formula have created an unintended side effect. They have given you an increased ability to manipulate others, but you can also be easily manipulated yourself. It is quite possible that you are capable of doing things, which most people would consider extraordinary. In fact, I believe your experience at the show, was the first manifestation of these abilities. I need to study you further, so I can perfect the formula. I want to transfer your abilities to myself," Webster sadistically said.

Times tried pleading with Webster and said, "Listen, let me go, and I swear I'll never again bother you! I won't tell *anyone* about what you've done to me! I *promise!*"

"That is not possible, I'm afraid. Besides, I need you to work tomorrow. We have to handle, a bothersome problem," Webster quickly replied.

Webster grabbed Times' hand, and strapped it back to the stretcher.

"I wish you could understand the bigger picture. I wish you knew why it is so important, to keep the world in order," Webster dutifully said.

Times began sobbing and said, "Please, you don't have to do this..."
Times let his words trail off.
"Goodbye Gregory," Webster callously replied.
Webster left the room. Times' distressing cries for help, went unfulfilled.

17 Harbor Hostility

The afternoon of Saturday, January 5th, 2217, was bitterly cold. There was a light flurry of snow in the air. Cameron Moss barely noticed it while sitting on the bench at a local Newark public park. He had been there for over an hour, collecting his thoughts, and waiting for Sky to meet him. Sky arrived eight minutes later.

"God *damn*, Cameron. Why did you ask me to come all the way out here, to talk? It's freezing!" Sky asked.

She sat beside him, and playfully punched him in his shoulder. Cameron briefly smiled, and then quickly returned to his somber mood.

"Sorry, girl. I needed an appropriate visual back drop, to help me illustrate my point," Cameron said.

"Next time, pick a warmer back drop!" Sky said.

"What do you see?" Cameron asked.

"Don't play mind games, Cameron," Sky replied.

"No, I'm serious. What do you see?" Cameron replied.

"I don't know. Park stuff? Trees, benches, people. You know, normal things," Sky said.

"Look closer. Those kids over there are so fat they can't even run. Those of them, who haven't been rendered brain damaged and retarded by vaccines, just kind of waddle around grunting in shorthand text message slang. Their parents aren't paying attention to them, or each other. They're too busy fucking around with their cell phones. All the playground equipment, sculptures, artwork, and structures, including this bench, are made in China," Cameron said.

Cameron looked up at the flying drone that was patrolling the area.

"All while those death machines fly above us, and spy on everyone," Cameron finished.

Sky sensed that Cameron was very upset.

"That's life, Cameron. It sucks. What's your point?" Sky asked.

"You know what you don't see? Animals...pets. That's one of the first things they say disappeared, after the food riots. People ate their pets, before culling what few wild animals they could find. I was fifteen, before I saw a domesticated dog in person. One summer, some friends and I bought train tickets to New Brunswick. We got the money by selling raw tomatoes, which we were secretly growing in the woods. We were walking around the bourgeoisie college campus. We all almost had heart attacks, when we saw this young lady walking her six legged poodle. It was weird. We all knew it was a genetically modified freak and not a real dog, but it was so strange to see someone whom actually owned a pet," he said.

Cameron's story made Sky want to cry. She continued listening to his heartfelt speech.

"I know there will come a day, when I'll regret having to live with every poor decision I've ever made. But I can't stop fighting this war, Sky. Not yet. Not while they make us live in this high tech prison," Cameron said.

Cameron gently cupped Sky's face with his hand, and stroked her cheek with his thumb.

"You're so beautiful," Cameron said softly.

Sky turned away slightly, and Cameron removed his hand. Sky put her head down and felt deep sadness.

"You're going on a run tonight, aren't you?" Sky said.

"Yes," Cameron regretfully replied.

"I don't know how much longer I can do this, Cameron," Sky said.

Cameron replied, "I'm not asking you to–"

"I understand why you feel that you can't stop. And I don't blame you, for wanting to help people. I just wish you cared about *me*, enough to stop," Sky interrupted.

"I am doing this, *because* I care about you, Sky. I care, that you and I will never have a normal life together, if we don't defeat this evil," Cameron said.

Sky looked up, and locked her eyes with Cameron's. They gazed into each other's souls. Cameron put his left hand in Sky's lap, leaned close to her, and gently kissed her lips. He slowly pulled his head away.

"I have to leave," Cameron said with compunction.

"I know," Sky said.

"I'm sorry," Cameron told her.

"I know," Sky replied.

Cameron gave her two more soft kisses on the mouth, then arose from the bench, and left the park.

It was 4:53 PM by the time Cameron made it back to the compound. He entered the garage. Lucia, Vincent, Eiji, Paul, and Walter, were waiting for him.

"Almost five, on the dot. You're a very punctual man, Cameron," said Paul.

"Nice to see you again, Paul. It's been too long," said Cameron.

He walked over to the large rectangular holographic display around which they were all standing. A large map of the New York, and New Jersey bay area, was projecting.

Cameron wasted no time asking Walter, "So, what's the plan?"

Walter tapped the edge of the hologram, and then used two fingers from both hands to expand the image. The map zoomed out, and showed a detailed view of the Atlantic Ocean. Walter placed his finger on the island of Puerto Rico, and moved it up to the tip of the Atlantic Highlands Island. A blue line was drawn, tracing the path of his finger.

"Right now, the ship is leaving the Atlantic Highlands port. It's the last stop that will be made before it travels north, and heads our way," Walter said.

Walter continued tracing a line on the map.

"By eight thirty tonight, it'll be traveling along the New York bay. It will dock at the Statue of Freedom, where a big celebration will be occurring. While that's happening, ferries will be routinely traveling from Jersey City to exchange passengers and luggage. Paul and myself, will board one of those ferries. We'll load the cargo from the cruise ship at the statue, to boats that will be returning to Jersey City," Walter said.

Walter stopped drawing and said, "Cameron and Vincent will unload the goods in Jersey City. Eiji will arrive at the dock, with two large cargo vans. Give him the luggage, but pretend that you don't know him. Once the vans are full, go get Lucy. She'll be in the Liberty National Park. She'll text the exact coordinates to your cell phones. The text is going to seem like an advertisement, so pay close attention to the numbers. Those will be her latitude and longitude. Use the Global Positioning

Systems on your cell phone maps, to find her. Once you're all together, drive the vans to the Bayonne drop point. Paul and I will take the train and meet you there, once we can safely return to New Jersey."

The group was intimidated by Walter's enormously complex plan. None of them spoke for several moments.

"This plan, it's..." Eiji finally said.

Eiji did not have the heart to finish his sentence, so Vincent did it for him.

"Crazy."

"It has been a long time since I rode with Walter, on a job of this size. You have no idea the amount of people we can help, with that much food. There will be items on that ship, that most people will never have another chance to eat in their entire lives," Paul said.

Vincent said, "Hell yeah. Two cargo vans full of fresh, real animals! We'll probably make a quarter mill–"

"You know it's not about the money, Vincent. Don't take this mission lightly. It will be extremely dangerous, and we have to remain incognito. Meaning, we won't use any masks," Walter interrupted in a scolding tone.

Vincent turned his head away in embarrassment. He was sorry that he had let his excitement, cloud his judgment.

"We should get ready to leave," Cameron said.

Before they disbanded Paul said, "I'd like to say a word, if it's all right."

Walter nodded, and Paul held out his hands. The group quickly formed a prayer circle, and interlocked hands.

"Lord, forgive us for the sins that we are about to commit tonight. Bless us, while we do your work. Please let no one in this room, come to any physical harm. Watch over our families, and those who we love. Pray for our enemies, so that they may yet renounce their wickedness; and one day join you in the eternal kingdom of Heaven. Amen," Paul said.

The group affirmed Paul's prayer, and then began making the final preparations for their mission. Shortly thereafter, they drove away from the compound, and traveled to meet their destiny.

Elsewhere, Gregory Times was being prepared against his will; for a task that he did not yet know would change him forever. Times lay in his bed trying in vain to squeeze out of his restraints. He had no clue for how much time he had been imprisoned. Whatever the duration, it was far too long. He thought about Mallory, and how worried she must be about him. Times' mind was an unfocused blur of emotions. He hypothesized that his total confusion was the intended result of the brutal torment that he was receiving.

The sound of the door opening momentarily distracted him from his thoughts. Webster, the Chem-Mech, and the robot Alice, entered the room. Webster walked up to the left side of Times' bed.

"It's time to leave, Gregory," said Webster.

Times spoke no words and instead showed his defiance by spitting in Webster's face. Webster responded by using the brainwave headband to make Times hear a loud ringing sound in his ears. Times screamed in pain, and Webster stopped the ringing after three seconds.

"That was a very mild taste, of how terrible I can make your suffering. I'm going to remove your restraints. Get up, and take your clothes from Chem-Mech. I trust you have no objections," Webster said.

Times glared at Webster, but did not verbally respond. After a moment, Webster removed the restraints and Times followed Webster's instructions. Times finished putting on his gray pants and the purple trench coat which he had been given by Mallory.

"Blindfold him," Webster said.

Before Times could react, the Chem-Mech used its robotic claw to spray Times' eyes, with a yellow foam. Times winced in discomfort. The foam quickly caked over his eyes, and blocked Times' vision.

"Don't worry. I'll guide you," said Webster.

Times then heard Webster's voice whispering inside of his head.

"Turn around. Walk out the door. Follow the sound of my voice," Webster telepathically said to Times.

Times tried ignoring Webster's voice, but had no choice except to comply. Times was forced to walk down a seemingly endless corridor of hallways until he reached an elevator. Times felt the ominous presence of Webster and his robots, following his every step. After taking the elevator up several flights, Times was instructed to walk a little further. Eventually he reached a car, and was forced into its backseat. Webster entered the vehicle, and closed the door behind him.

"I assume we're in your limo," Times said bitterly.

"Correct, my servile animal," said Webster.

"I always thought it was an ugly color. Black is so, bland," Times said, openly showing his defiance.

Webster chuckled, and ignored Times' comments. The car began driving.

"I suppose it's okay for you to remove the blindfold. I'll just tint the windows. Go on, try to relax," Webster said.

Times reached his hand to his eyes, and peeled away the foam. When he opened his eyes, the sight of Webster sitting across from him, drove him mad with rage.

"It has been a while since we've ridden together," said Webster sarcastically.

"Fuck you!" Times yelled.

Webster let out a full bellied laugh and said, "You *must* learn to relax, Gregory; or you'll make yourself ill! It's a shame you never took my advice. I always told you that you needed to control your anger."

"Why are you doing this to me?" Times asked with sincerity.

Webster leaned back in his seat, tilted his head to the left, and attempted to ignore Times' question.

"Answer me," said Times with obvious animosity in his voice.

Webster slowly turned his gaze toward Times.

"I'm sixty-three years old. I'll be sixty-four in August. I was twenty-eight years old in 2181, when I graduated from Deimos University, with a Ph. D. in bio-mechanical engineering. For my dissertation, I wrote a paper about the future of nanotechnology in the medical field. I hypothesized that in the future, virtually all pharmaceuticals would contain nano-machines. Every pill, powder, and fluid, would contain tiny computers. They would perform an almost unlimited number of tasks. Every form of consumable drug, from generic store purchased cough syrup, to powerful hospital sedatives, would be laced with these machines. The medicines containing these nano-robots, would find their way into consumers' bodies. My desire was for the entire world to consume nanites. I spoke, of their limitless potential," Webster said.

For the first time since they became acquaintances, Webster showed Times sincere emotion.

"Nasal sprays that monitor air pollen counts, and increase or decrease their dosage depending on the levels detected. Vaccines, that only need to be injected once after birth; and can provide a patient with lifetime immunity to that disease. Orally indigestible pills that traverse the entire human body; and use tiny cameras that allow a doctor to find infections. These, were some of my ideas for inventions. I funded my research by using government grants. I maintained a perfect 4.0 Grade Point Average. I felt there was nothing, that I could not accomplish," Webster said.

Times shifted uneasily in his seat while listening to Webster.

"One day I had the privilege of attending a lecture, being given by guest speaker John Thurswell. Even though he was in his early eighties, he was in outstanding physical shape. He was the most eloquent speaker, I've ever heard. I'll never forget the knowledge he bestowed upon us that day. After regaling us with his conquests of the scientific world, he was the first private citizen to walk on the surface of Mars mind you, he posed a very unique question," Webster said.

"Many people believe that he faked the Mars landing," Times rebutted.

Webster ignored the comment.

"He looked at the alumni of '81, and asked them, 'Why do you waste technology?' There was a small fit of nervous laughter. People tried to grasp the true meaning of his question. After a while, the laughter descended into an awkward silence. He then said, 'I'm serious. Why do you frivolously waste the marvelous technologies around you?' No one in the room could answer his question. A young male, a rather uppity Negro, asked him if it was a trick question," Webster said.

Times, intent on trying to understand every insane word which Webster spoke, continued listening to his rant.

"Mister Thurswell continued with his brilliant speech. 'You think I am mad? Prove me wrong. Cell phones, computers, the vast knowledge of the internet; all these gifts have been bestowed upon you, yet you do nothing with this technology, except use it to play children's games,' he said. It was a startling revelation. Many a grown man hung his head, ashamed of his pride in the fictional virtual multi-player statistics, to which Mister Thurswell referred. The young Negro once again spoke and said, 'You're crazy man, video games are the shit!'" Webster said.

"The majority of the crowd let out an uproarious laughter. After the laughs once again settled into silence, Mister Thurswell shocked the audience to its core. He said, 'None of you can answer my question. *That* is why the future does not need you.' He proceeded to lecture us about grand technologies, which awaited the elites of the future. He spoke of massive hovering cities, flying far above the oceans. These floating fortresses would make New York seem like a modest single bedroom domicile, in comparison," Webster said.

"He explained that all of our DNA would be uploaded to a giant database, so that it could be analyzed for genetic defects. This database would lead to mandatory abortions, for any person deemed genetically derelict. He told us that entire industries would be owned and operated by robots, rendering human labor obsolete. Yes, robots *will* achieve a social status equal our own, and he was emphatically supportive of this fact. Robots will one day have all the rights which humans currently enjoy, and more. He claimed that due to all these scientific advancements, the collective human species would simply cease to remain relevant," said Webster.

The magnitude of what Webster said was difficult for Times to accept. Was this truly the elite's philosophy? Did they really believe humans, were nothing but a burden on planet Earth? Times did not have a chance to pose any questions.

"This is when it all became clear to me. Here was a man, who had stood upon the surface of Mars, and was openly expressing his disdain for humanity. He was truly a god amongst men, and was not afraid to openly admit humanity's overall uselessness. He ended his speech by saying, 'By the year 2300, there will be two distinct species of homo sapiens left in our world. One will have risen to the stars; and will be charged with the daunting task of populating space. The other will be nothing more than malformed pavement apes, using our technological scraps to grunt at each other; while they live in a micro-managed artificial stasis, controlled by robots with sentient artificial intelligence. So again I ask you, why do you waste technology? Is it because you are too preoccupied, with your education? Is it because you are too busy, spending time with your families? No. You waste technology, because you are unable to grasp the complexity of reality's true nature. You waste technology, because evolution has left you behind,'" Webster said.

Times was frightened to his core, by the elite's anti-human philosophy. Times was horrified by the fact that they wanted to create a separate society strictly for themselves.

"After the lecture, I sought out an apprenticeship with Mister Thurswell. I wanted him to bequeath every ounce of his knowledge. It took me two full years to gain Mister Thurswell's trust. He finally agreed to mentor me, in the winter of 2183. He was impressed by my experiment, which proved that nano-viruses replicated themselves, using biological signatures from their host. I injected a small snake with a cancer virus. I designed the virus to implant the snake with nano-machines, which caused the cancer to subside. But only if the snake relentlessly continued eating," Webster said.

"I released the snake into the few marshes that remained in California, after the Great Quake of 2178. The snake thrived, eating whatever it could find. The snake grew from a mere seven inches, to an astonishing thirty-five feet. In total, it weighed over two hundred pounds. Eventually the tumors in its body caused it to become too fat to hunt. Its solution was to eat itself. This obviously destroyed both the tumor, and the snake. I thought my work was a failure; until Mister Thurswell told me that I finally understood the true meaning of life," said Webster.

Times was confused and asked, "That doesn't make sense. How did you prove that the virus was a success?"

"Because it eventually overpowered the snake's natural survival instinct. The need to quench its hunger became so intense, due to the machine's constant replication; that the snake eventually did not care whether it lived, or died. It only cared about its next meal. My nano-machines infected the host, and regenerated at such an accelerated rate, that the patient had no choice but to choose self-termination, over survival. That is why Mister Thurswell said I finally understood. He told me that humanity was no different from the snake. He said that humanity would eventually eat itself, metaphorically and physically. We will not evolve quickly enough, to match technology's rapid growth rate," Webster quickly replied.

Webster grew even more solemn while continuing his lament.

"The food riots started a few months later, in the late summer of 2184. Once again, Mister Thurswell was proven right. Gregory, there is no way for me to articulate, how quickly society deteriorated. One night while we were driving through Philadelphia, I saw Mister Thurswell's prediction come true. We were passing a group of young children, huddled around a makeshift fire.

They had set ablaze the remains of a defunct car. The smell of the meat they were roasting was so volatile, that I shudder at its thought. The sight chills me to this day. They had chopped up one of their companions, he couldn't have been more than twelve years old, and they were eating him. Do you understand me, Gregory? They killed him, and then they ate him," Webster said with disgust.

Times felt sick, but could not stop listening to Webster's story.

"I knew then that the only solution was to do my part, in helping cull the general population. Mister Thurswell died three years later in 2187; at the age of 89. He left me in charge of his burgeoning pharmaceutical company. From that day forward, I dedicated my life to the eugenics movement. I helped lobby for the implementation of the Modified Water Act of 2195. It required that all public drinking water contain drugs, which inhibit a person's ability to feel emotion. I created the Chem-Mech in 2205 and his sister Alice in 2207. Their stupendous prowess will render what remains of traditional physicians, obsolete," Webster said.

"I took Mister Thurswell's vision, and formed a pharmaceutical empire that now controls over eighty-seven percent of the prescription drug market. But there was a problem with my success. I could not willfully make those who disagreed with my vision, submit to my desires. I always had to deceive my enemies, before I crushed them. However, that is all about to change. If my experiment with you is a success, then I will have achieved something greater than any man before me. Not only will I be able to *subdue* the population through chemical warfare, but I will also be able to *control* them. I will be able to *control*, those who seek to stifle my vision. I will be able to *control*, the unwashed masses. I will be able to *control*, everyone," Webster said.

"So what the fuck are you going to do with me?" Times finally asked Webster.

Webster took his time answering the question.

"Beyond proving that telepathic communication is a reality, I am going to solve a very serious problem. You will recall that eating is a central theme of our discussion. Those are the people, whom have caused me the most trouble all these years; the useless eaters. It amazed me that no matter how many laws were passed, or how many drugs were forced upon the population; unlike the snake many people retained their will to eat, and survive. Sure, some were forced to dine upon their fellow human cattle. But those who refused to heed that macabre call, were then guided by a higher purpose," Webster eventually said.

Times was confused, but listened closely to Webster.

"There were a surprising number of people, who would rather starve to death instead of cannibalize. These people formed a movement, which continues to bring scores of self-righteous vagabonds hope; that they will once again live in a free society. You've seen them before, that night in New Jersey. They have gone by many names, and their numbers continue growing each decade. They are the rebels, outlaws, and survivalists; who cling to the last remnants of the old Republic. They are, the Food Liberationists. It is unclear how they were first founded. But it is absolutely certain, who is now their unofficial leader," Webster said.

Webster tapped the side of the limousine's window with his left hand. A holographic image of a man began projecting in the space between Webster and Times' seats.

"Walter Kingsley; fifty-nine years old. He has led numerous resistance groups over the past three decades. His latest group of disciples, are his most effective to date," Webster said.

Webster again pressed the window. Lucia, Vincent, Eiji, and Cameron's images, also began projecting.

"This group is different. They should have been imprisoned years ago, like Walter's other lackeys. The authorities refuse to prosecute them. Do you know why? It's because of their stupid, mask wearing gimmick! They've become folk legends, all because of those goddamned disguises! They all come from different backgrounds, and most likely would never have chosen such a reprehensible lifestyle, if they were given a real choice. Their bodies have not rotted and withered, like those of their peers. They have withstood the assault from the lethal chemicals found in the food, water, and air. They represent the greatest danger to people like me. They represent the fighting spirit, which makes the common man believe he can change the system!" Webster said.

Times began saying, "I think you're just mad they stole your food–"

Webster reached out, and angrily punched Times. The old man's feeble hands barely affected Times' strong jaw.

"You think this is some kind of game? These are *violent* terrorists, who will destroy the utopia which countless amounts of individuals have worked to build!" Webster said.

Times was puzzled by Webster's peculiar choice of words.

"Utopia? You call this rotten, slovenly, hellish world, a fucking utopia? Utopia, for whom?!" Times angrily asked.

"A utopia, for the next generation. Those who survive this time of great tribulation will inherit a new and improved world. They will inherit a world free from pollution, disease, illness, and overpopulation. Those unfit to live, will no longer burden the rest of society with their undesirable gene pools," Webster replied.

Times was enraged.

"Let me guess. People like me, my wife, and our murdered children, are from these 'undesirable gene pools'," Times said in a cold voice.

"It's nothing personal," Webster callously replied.

Times' breathing was unsteady, due to the fury which he was containing. He looked Webster directly in the eye.

"I want you to listen to me very closely, old man. Technocrats like you, are the reason why the world is such a discordant, bereaved cesspit. You're the lowest form of filth; whose only achievement was having the extraordinarily good fortune of falling backwards, kicking and screaming, out of your mother's asshole. I saw my wife, molested. I saw my children, murdered. People like you, feel nothing but contempt for the innocent lives you destroy. I want you to know, that when I kill you...it will be in the most painful way that I can imagine," Times sternly said.

Webster leaned back in his seat, and absorbed the magnitude of Times' brutal threat.

"You and I, have more in common than you think. You could have been a great man, with the proper guidance. It is a shame that we did not meet under different circumstances; and that you are unworthy of joining the illuminated ones," Webster finally said.

The two men remained silent. The self-driving vehicle continued toward its destination.

It was 8:30 PM by the time Lucia, Vincent, Paul, Walter, Eiji, and Cameron, had arrived at their separate destinations. At 8:31 PM, Lucia sent an encrypted text message to everyone's cell phones, from her portable computer. She informed them that her GPS monitor, which was tracking the location of their phones, indicated they had all made it safely to their designated posts.

Eiji silently acknowledged the message from his position several blocks away from the dock.

"It's go time, brother," said Vincent to Cameron.

The two of them began walking up to the luggage drop zone. They were wearing stylish red suits, ties, and white shirts. The apparel had been given to them by Walter, who had obtained them from his informant on the ship.

"I feel like a damn fool, wearing this stuff," said Vincent, while awkwardly adjusting his tie.

"So in other words, you feel like your normal self?" Cameron jokingly said.

Cameron and Vincent walked up to the loading bay's entrance.

"Be cool. I'll talk to him," Cameron said.

They walked up to the security guard, who promptly said, "ID's, gentlemen."

Cameron looked at Vincent, and the two men quickly rolled up their sleeves. Vincent was the first to tap his cell phone wrist band against the side of the computer tablet, which the guard was holding. The tablet was a large, thin, rectangular band, which was completely hollow in the middle. A flat holographic image projected in the hollow area.

"ID accepted. Ted Freeman is allowed in Cargo Bay three. Interstate travel, not approved," said a robotic voice from the computer tablet.

It displayed the corresponding words on its holographic screen. Cameron tapped the screen with his wristband. The computer confirmed his fake identity, was Brent Thomas.

"You're all set. Give me a second," said the guard.

He pressed several holographic buttons. Moments later a clunky, primitive robot rolled itself to their position. It was equipped with an oval shaped camera-head. The head was connected to a small square body. It had a pair of three-pronged claws, attached to skinny human-like arms. It rolled up on a flat box, which had four wheels on its bottom.

"Follow the Pathfinder. He will take you to the loading bay," said the guard.

Cameron could not help but speak out against the guard's misuse of terminology. One of Cameron's biggest pet peeves was the fact that people tried to humanize the robots.

"It; not he. You called it, 'he'. It's not a '*he*'. It's a machine, not a human," said Cameron.

The guard gave Cameron a dirty look. Cameron could tell that they were on the verge of a verbal altercation.

"Chill, Brent. He can call *him* whatever he wants," Vincent swiftly said.

Vincent put his arm around Cameron, and looked up at the night sky. Cameron followed his gaze, and saw several aerial drones patrolling the area. Cameron knew that he had to maintain his composure, so that he would not blow their cover.

"Whatever. We have work to finish," Cameron begrudgingly said.

The men followed the Pathfinder to the loading bay. They anxiously awaited Eiji's arrival. Walter and Paul had no trouble getting to the Statue of Freedom. Their fake identifications masterfully fooled the scanners, and they were swiftly ferried to Freedom Island. They saw that the cruise ship had almost reached the island. It would be arriving within a few minutes. After they had successfully made it off the ferry, Walter and Paul stopped for a moment, to gaze at the statue.

In the year 2195, the statue had been remodeled by a Chinese construction company. The Chinese workers repainted the entire statue, but it came with a heavy price. As part of the deal, the statue and the grounds upon which it rested were ceded to the Chinese government. The Chinese paid an astronomical fee of over three trillion Carbon Credits for the statue and land.

Knowing the Statue's history made staring at its beauty that much more difficult for Paul and Walter. The silver robe the woman wore was decorated with an array of blue and red stars. The stars were embedded in the white ribbon around her shoulders. She clutched her brown book between her soft, peaches-and-cream colored arms. Her crown was painted a magnificent gold color; and had silver tips on its spiked edges. She held Liberty's torch, high above her head. The torch's handle was a dark shade of black. A bright holographic flame was burning at its end.

"You remember how she used to look? All green and rotted from the elements?" Paul asked.

"Yeah. I used to love seeing her on television, when I was a kid," Walter sadly replied.

"She looked terrible back then; like a battered, drug addicted, rape victim, who had been wandering the streets for generations. But she looks even worse, now that she's a Dragon prostitute," said Paul.

"Yeah," was all that Walter could say to Paul's somber observation.

"Don't worry. We'll take you back one day, girl," Paul said softly.

The two men took one last look at the statue. Paul looked around, and saw that the ship was docking on the island.

"That's our cue," said Paul to Walter.

They began walking to the vessel. The sounds of people partying, and music playing, were heard from the ship's deck. Paul and Walter made their way to the cargo loading dock that was located near the ship's rear. They crossed the docking bridge. When they reached the ship, they saw an armed guard. He was holding a semi-automatic bullet rifle.

"Where's your identification?" asked the guard.

"Our passports were already checked, before we came to the island," said Walter.

"This is an intercontinental boat, with a lot of celebrity passengers. Everyone has to give a DNA sample before boarding," the guard sternly replied.

Paul and Walter grew extremely nervous. DNA tests were one of the few technologies that could not be spoofed. Certain forms of identification, like legitimate interstate passports, required a user to give a blood sample. The sample was an additional security feature that could be used to verify the identification, in the event that its authenticity was questioned. Since the technology became available in the 2180's, there were numerous lawsuits challenging its legitimacy. By many, it was considered an unacceptable invasion of privacy. That is why other biometric identification methods like eye scanning, thumb, and hand printing, were more widely used.

"Hey Darrin! What are you doing?" said a middle aged black woman, while running up to the guard.

"These guys are with me, they're fine. Besides, they've already cleared security," she said.

The guard scowled at Paul and Walter.

"Rules are rules, Jen," the guard said.

"Seriously Darrin, stop being an asshole. I need their help. We've got a lot of luggage to unload," said Jennifer.

Darrin gave Paul and Walter one last dirty look.

"Fine. They are your responsibility," Darrin said.

He stepped aside, and allowed the men to walk past him. Paul and Walter quickly followed Jennifer away from the security checkpoint.

When they were out of Darrin's earshot, Jennifer asked Paul, "What's your cover?"

"I'm Sam. He's Rick," whispered Paul.

"That was too close. I think he's going to be suspicious. I hope he doesn't start harassing us," whispered Jennifer.

"We won't be long. Don't worry," said Paul.

"Too late for that, I'm afraid," Jennifer said.

Jennifer led them through the magnificent ship. The ship was decorated with moving holographic paintings. Gorgeous running waterfalls, burning fireplaces, and shifting clouds, were rendered beautifully by special projectors. Sections of the boat's infrastructure had been carved out, to give the paintings maximum depth. The ship's cream colored walls were a wonderful compliment to the velvet red carpets lining the hallways. Well-dressed butlers served the high class patrons exquisite food. It was free from genetic manipulation, and ingredients.

"This is amazing. How much does a ticket cost?" asked Walter.

"Per person, it's twenty-two million credits for a seven day trip," replied Jennifer.

"Satan be damned! It must be nice to be that rich!" Walter said.

"Vanity is a prison. These people may be some of the wealthiest bankers, business tycoons, and socialites in the world...but their money will never buy them God's love," said Paul.

The group arrived at the luggage room a few moments later.

"The VIP suitcases have red bands around the handle. There are approximately eighty-six of them," Jennifer said.

Jennifer spoke in code so that she did not reveal their plan, to the microphones inside of the wall that were listening to them. Walter used his phone to send Cameron a text message with the information Jennifer had just relayed.

"Sounds great. Thank you so much for hiring us," Walter said slyly.

"Don't thank me. Just get it out safely, and make sure it gets to the right people," said Jennifer.

"We will," Paul coyly said.

"I have to leave. I'll be back later to check on you. Call my cell, if you need anything," said Jennifer.

She hugged Paul and Walter, and then quickly left the room. It took the men almost twenty minutes to load the first shipment of cargo on the ferry returning to New Jersey.

When the ferry arrived, Vincent said to Cameron, "Look alive, man. The boat is docking."

Cameron and Vincent spent a few minutes locating the bags with red ribbons. Once they found the luggage, they returned it to Eiji, who was waiting near the dock. After Eiji had loaded a few bags, he went to the back of the van. He discretely opened a bag, peeked inside, and saw several coolers. He inspected a cooler and saw fresh meat, tightly wrapped in cellophane. The meat was packed in ice, to keep it cold. The next time Vincent and Cameron returned with more cargo, Eiji subtly nodded his head to them. The team all smiled proudly, and knew they were taking the right bags.

The team was blissfully unaware that Times and Webster had driven to a nearby location at the Jersey City port. Times was amazed how Webster once again easily used his passport to get both of them past border patrol. At the port, Webster removed a small square box from his inner coat pocket. He opened the box, and inside was a small drone which was shaped like a mosquito. Webster pressed a button on the mosquito drone's tiny head. It made a bleeping sound, and its eyes illuminated. Webster cracked the car's window, and tossed the mosquito into the air. The drone flew off towards the horizon. Webster closed the window, and then tapped his finger against its glass.

The window projected a view from the drone's camera. Webster tapped the screen again, and a holographic image expanded into the car. Times and Webster saw that the drone was quickly flying over the bay. The drone zoomed in its camera to get a closer look at people's faces. The drone outlined the shape of people's bodies, in a blue vertical rectangle. It redrew the rectangle as a square, when it zoomed in on their faces. Times was impressed by the advanced spy technology.

"What is that contraption?" Times asked.

"Nothing special. Just some old spy technology that I acquired from a friend in government," Webster replied.

"What agency?" asked Times.

"Stop talking," Webster coldly said.

The drone flew over the docking area. After a few moments, it focused on three specific targets. Webster and Times saw the images of Eiji, Vincent, and Cameron, loading their cargo.

"We must hurry," said Webster when he saw the group.

Webster zoomed the camera out. He used his finger, to highlight a section of the dock, on the window. The car quickly started driving toward the coordinates which Webster had just defined. Ten minutes later, it reached the destination.

"Go find them, Gregory. Expose these terrorists to the world," Webster said.

Webster used his mind control headband to force Times out of the vehicle. Times heard the sound of Webster's voice, ringing inside his head. This experience was extremely painful, and distressing to Times. He tried resisting Webster's commands, which were guiding him towards the dock. Times felt the mosquito drone land on his shoulder. Times tried swatting it with his hand, but the drone quickly avoided his strike.

"Don't do that again," Times heard Webster's voice say to him.

A harsh ringing sound stung the inside of Times' ear. Times winced in pain, and continued walking. He nervously approached the loading dock. Times walked up to the armed guard, who had earlier inspected Vincent and Cameron.

"This is a restricted area. Show me your ID," the guard sternly said to Times.

Times said to the guard in a soft, weak voice, "Please, help me..."

"What the hell is wro–?"

The guard slapped the side of his neck, before finishing his sentence. Times saw the drone flying away from the guard. The guard's face distorted, and he twitched for several seconds.

"God, help you," whispered Times.

Eiji, Vincent, and Cameron, noticed the weird transaction taking place between Times and the guard.

"Any idea what that's about?" Cameron asked his friends.

Both Eiji and Vincent shrugged their shoulders to indicate that they did not know what was happening.

"Something is wrong. I think we should leave," said Cameron.

"Stop being paranoid. Stay focused," Vincent said.

Cameron watched Times and the armed guard begin walking down the boardwalk, towards a ferry. They were stopped by another armed guard at the boat. Times said something to the guards, which Cameron could not hear. A few seconds later, the two armed guards boarded the ferry. Times walked away from the boat, and went back across the boardwalk. While he was walking, Times turned his head and glared directly at Eiji, Vincent, and Cameron. Times gave them a stone cold stare. He cracked a slight smile, then looked away, and continued walking.

"What the fuck?" Eiji whispered.

"We have to call this off. Something is not right," said Cameron.

Vincent used his cell phone to call Lucia.

Lucia picked up and said, "The fuck are you doing?! No contact until–"

"I need to show you something. I think we have a problem," Vincent said.

Lucia paused for a moment before saying, "Use your phone's camera, but be discrete."

Vincent put his thumb and index finger, on the side of his face. He held out his wrist, so that the camera could project images back to Lucia.

"That guy in the purple trench coat gave us a really disturbing look. Any idea who he is?" Vincent whispered.

"Shit. Your camera's optics aren't strong enough. There's no way for me to run a facial scan," said Lucia.

Cameron tapped Vincent on his shoulder, and pointed in the ferry's direction. He saw that the boat carrying the two guards was departing to Freedom Island.

"I'll have to call you back," said Vincent.

Cameron thought for a moment, before telling Eiji, "We're leaving. Pack up what's left, and drive us to the park."

"Cameron, what the hell? You can't start barking out orders, just because you got spooked! Walter said he would text us, after they finished loading everything," said Vincent.

"Why do you have to be such a goddamned hard ass, all the time? Trust me, we're not safe!" Cameron snapped.

Vincent looked at Eiji, who said; "Sorry man, you know I want to..." before letting his thoughts trail off.

"Suit yourselves," Cameron defiantly said before leaving his friends.

"Shit! Why the fuck is he always so irresponsible?" Vincent asked Eiji.

Cameron slowly followed Times away from the pier. Cameron sped up his walking pace.

"Hey!" he shouted at Times.

Times turned his head slightly and looked over his shoulder, but ultimately kept walking.

"Hey! I'm talking to you. What's your name?" Cameron yelled at Times.

Times suddenly stopped walking, turned around, and faced Cameron. He jogged up to Times.

"What was that look about back there, man?" Cameron asked him.

Times stared at Cameron with fire in his eyes.

"Why? Why does he care so much about you?" Times abruptly asked.

Cameron was puzzled and asked, "What are you talking about? Who cares about me?"

Times suddenly grabbed Cameron by his collar.

"You have no idea, what I've been through. Tell me. TELL ME WHY YOU'RE SO GODDAMNED IMPORTANT!" Times exasperatedly said.

Cameron pushed Times back and said, "Get the fuck off me, you freak!"

Times put his head in his hands and whispered, "No. No, I can't."

Cameron started backing away and said, "Listen, never mind. Sorry to bother you."

Times looked up at Cameron and said, "Please, help me. Make him stop. He can *hear* my fucking *thoughts!*"

"What's wrong with you? Are you high?" asked Cameron.

"I'm sorry," Times softly said.

Times then punched Cameron very hard in his stomach! Cameron wheezed from the intense blow, before dropping to his knees. Times punched Cameron twice across both sides of his face!

"You bitch!" screamed Times.

Vincent saw what was happening and said, "Holy shit! Eiji, that crazy asshole just attacked Cam!"

Vincent started running to help Cameron. The scuffle had attracted the attention of two armed guards, and three unarmed guards. They jogged over, to investigate the commotion. Vincent and the guards simultaneously arrived at the scene. The unarmed guards restrained Times, while Vincent helped Cameron to his feet.

"You don't understand! They're terrorists! Food Liberationists! Look at their cargo, you'll see!" Times screamed.

Cameron and Vincent grew very nervous. They gave each other worried looks, and knew that the situation needed to be diffused.

"This guy is obviously mentally ill. He flat out attacked my friend, for no reason," Vincent calmly said.

Times was still struggling with the guards.

"Look at their cargo, if you don't believe me!" Times yelled.

One of the unarmed guards, who was a woman, asked Vincent, "What's he talking about?"

"I don't know. I told you, he's bonkers," Vincent quickly said.

"That man just made a pretty serious allegation against you. I think I should have a look at what you're unloading into those vans," the female guard said.

Vincent and Cameron's pulses began racing. Times calmed down, and started laughing.

The two guards, whom Webster had placed under his control using the drone and headband system, were arriving at the statue. They had glazed looks upon their faces. Drool dripped from their open mouths. One guard exited the boat, and began walking around the island. The other guard entered the cruise ship, and went to a dining area. He aimlessly wandered around for a few moments. He stopped to admire an attractive waitress, who was sitting in a chair at the bar.

"You're really pretty," the guard said to her in a daze.

"Thanks," the waitress politely said.

She gave the bartender an exasperated look. The bartender knew that the waitress wanted him to get rid of the guard.

"Hey Tasha, can you go to the freezer, and get me some more ice? We're running low," the bartender said.

The waitress gave the bartender a thankful look, before getting up and walking away. The guard looked at the bartender in a totally lobotomized manner.

"Do you have the time?" the guard asked.

The puzzled bartender checked his cell phone and said, "Yes, it's nine–"

He did not have a chance to finish his sentence. Without warning, the guard pointed his rifle at the bartender, and shot him in the forehead. Blood and brain matter sprayed the back of the bar. The bartender immediately fell dead. People began screaming, and started running around the diner. They desperately searched for an exit.

With accurate precision, the guard began calmly walking around the room and shooting random people. His semi-automatic rifle made loud popping sounds when he pulled its trigger. The guard targeted a frightened woman who was sitting at a table. The guard had just shot her dining companion in the back of his head. A bloody body, with half of the cranium missing, was slumped forward on the table. The woman looked up and screamed briefly, before the guard put three rounds into her chest.

The guard casually removed the twenty round magazine from the rifle. He removed another clip from his front jacket pocket. He quickly reloaded and the carnage continued. The guard fired five shots at a fleeing elderly couple. The couple was struck in their legs, and shoulders. They fell to the floor, sobbed, and were in obvious pain. The guard callously walked past them. He knew that they would soon bleed to death from their wounds. He went out to the hallway and began shooting fleeing passengers. Blood lined the floors, and the walls. A ten year old boy was holding his hands to the back of his head, to give himself the illusion of cover. He was crying, and cowering in the corner. The guard did not fall for the ploy. He shot the young boy several times in his body. On the island, screaming could be heard from the boat.

"Oh my God, are those gunshots?!" a frightened man loudly asked.

The other armed guard under Webster's control, held up his rifle. He began indiscriminately firing into a crowd of people that were taking pictures near the statue's base. Several of the shots hit separate victims. One woman managed to escape with only a wounded leg, but another female was fatally shot through her neck. The guard slowly walked around the statue. He manically laughed, and shot his targets without aiming. A few of his bullets wounded several unfortunate people. A young mother was shot through her stomach. Her intestines spattered over the crying baby that she was holding. Three shots mangled a twelve year old girl's leg. She crawled along the ground, and tried to escape from the mayhem. The guard showed no mercy to a man who was on his knees, and hiding behind a garbage can.

"No! Please, don't!" the man yelled.

He shot him in the stomach, while the man cowered in fear. Paul and Walter were horrified. They faintly heard the shots from their position inside the luggage room.

"Paul, please tell me that's not..."

Walter could not finish his sentence. His eyes began swelling with tears. The screaming and gunshots were very distinct. Even though the sound was muffled by the room's walls, they had a horrible feeling that they knew exactly what was happening.

Back at the dock, Eiji, Vincent, Cameron, Times, and the rest of the guards, watched the mayhem unfold.

"What the fuck are you doing? Go over there, and help those people!" Cameron shouted at the guards.

"You see?! It's the Food Liberationists! They're attacking innocent civilians!" Times gleefully yelled.

"Weapons hot! Don't move!" the female guard said.

She motioned for the guards who were not restraining Times, to aim their weapons at Vincent, and Cameron. The men held their hands high above their heads. They slowly knelt upon the hard ground.

"Fuck," Vincent whispered.

Eiji saw that the situation was out of control. Eiji quickly got into the van, started the vehicle, revved its engine, and immediately called Lucia.

"Something terrible happened! People are getting shot! Our friends are being arrested!" Eiji said.

"You have to get out of there," Lucia frantically replied.

"Fuck that, I'm not leaving them!" Eiji replied.

"Please, don't argue with me," Lucia said in a shaky voice.

Eiji thought for a split second before saying, "It's bad enough, that we have to leave the other guys. I'm not about to lose the whole fucking team! Activate the other van's auto-drive, and send it to the drop zone. I'm going to come get you, after I save our friends!"

Before Lucia could protest, Eiji hung up the phone. He switched the van into manual drive mode, and left the loading bay. He drove the van several yards, and parked a few meters away from Cameron and Vincent. In his rear view mirror, he saw bloodied people diving off the boat, and island. They leaped into the water, in a desperate attempt to save themselves from being slaughtered. Eiji skidded his tires, and quickly drove the vehicle in reverse. He pressed the automatic door release, and the back door swung open.

Eiji skidded to a halt, right in front of the armed guards. The sudden change in momentum caused some of the bags to fall out of the van. The distraction gave Cameron and Vincent, just enough time to escape. They jumped up, and quickly climbed into the van. Eiji stepped on the pedal and sped away. Vincent and Cameron barely closed the doors, in enough time to avoid the guards' gunshots.

"Incompetence! Fucking *incompetence!*" Times yelled.

The mosquito drone pricked the two armed guards in their necks. Times pointed to the three unarmed guards.

"Finish them, then yourselves," Times said before he started walking away.

The lead woman yelled, "Stop! You're under arr–"

She did not finish her sentence. The two armed guards blasted the woman, and her two companions, into bloody masses. After they finished they put their guns to their own heads, and pulled the triggers.

Paul and Walter were still in the luggage room when Jennifer burst through the door.

"You guys have to get out of here! The guards have gone crazy! They're on a killing spree! Follow me!" she said.

The group wasted no time leaving the room. They followed Jennifer through a series of corridors. She ran down a flight of stairs and reached the bottom portion of the ship. Their path was blocked by a door. She quickly put her palm on the door's scanning panel, and was granted access.

"Almost there," she said.

They entered the room. She rushed over to a section that contained small lifeboats.

"These are only accessible by crew members. If you ride one back, you may have a chance to avoid the authorities. They will be distracted by the shooting," said Jennifer.

"Jen, please come with us," said Walter.

"No. I can't. It's too risky. I've already jeopardized my entire future by helping you get this far. I don't want to spend the rest of my life in prison," Jennifer solemnly said.

Walter nodded his head, indicating that he respected Jennifer's wishes. Jennifer gave Paul and

Walter one final hug.

"Good luck, you two," she said to them.

The two men opened the escape hatch, turned the lifeboat upside down, jumped in the water, and swam underneath the boat. They heard the frightening sounds of gunfire, while they swam. They used the boat to shield themselves from any stray bullets that might fly their way.

The scene on the ferry and the island was gruesome. The guard on the ferry aimed his gun over the side of the boat, and began shooting people who were swimming to safety. Some survivors were fortunate enough to avoid the deadly barrage. Others, like a young teenage girl, had their heads split open like broken melons by the high caliber bullets.

The guard on the island had run out of ammo and was resorting to beating people with his gun. He ran up to an elderly woman. He viciously bludgeoned her in her head and torso with the folding stock of his gun. The woman fell to the ground and started convulsing. The guard stomped her head into the pavement numerous times. He used such force, that the bones in her face broke. Her lower mandible jaw detached itself from the rest of her head. The guard was covered in blood. He cackled like a wild hyena at the gory and repulsive sight.

The whole ordeal had been taking place for several terrifying minutes. The waters in the ocean began rumbling. A massive hybrid drone surfaced from the bay's waters. The drone used its thrusters to lift itself out of the water. The middle of the massive triangular shaped drone's body was slightly curved upward. It had a hypotenuse length of over sixty feet. It was painted a dark black color. It was equipped with heat seeking missiles, thermal cameras, holographic projectors, audio recording, and playback devices. It had a Gatling gun mounted to its belly, and two laser guns on each of its wings. The combat drone's main purpose was to patrol the waters. It routinely killed people who did not voluntarily surrender, when they were caught trying to cross the New York/New Jersey border. It started flying towards Freedom Island. When it arrived, the drone hovered above the guard who was turning the island into a bloodbath.

"Terrorist identified. Eliminating threat," it said in a loud robotic voice.

The drone fired a hot laser beam at the guard's chest. The beam blasted a hole, eight inches in diameter, through his entire body. The guard fell dead instantly, while his wound bled profusely. The drone flew over to the ferry. The other guard was still firing at people, while they swam in the water. He shot a woman in her neck. Her bullet wound gushed blood, and she drowned.

"Additional enemy combatant spotted," the drone said.

It released another hot laser beam, which ripped a hole in the guard's chest. The guard dropped dead upon the ferry's deck. The drone started slowly flying around the area, and surveyed the damage.

"No further threats detected. Cross border contamination suspected. Area is now under lock-down," it said.

It continued flying, and photographed its surroundings. The aftermath was an absolute nightmare. Bodies riddled with bullet holes lay sprawled out in the water. The ghastly amount of blood had turned some sections of the ocean red. People were crying, and survivors were comforting each other. People lay mortally wounded, fighting for each one of their last breaths. The attack had only lasted a few minutes, but its impact was devastating.

Paul and Walter had almost arrived at the New Jersey dock. They had successfully shielded themselves by keeping the boat tilted at an angle. They used a narrow field of vision to guide themselves while they were in the water. They knew they didn't have much time before the rescue mission officially turned into a crime scene investigation. They pushed the boat to a part of the dock which did not have any human activity. They swam from underneath the boat, climbed up the dock's wooden ledges, and on to land. They breathed heavily.

Paul said, “Come on, old boy. We've got to keep moving,” while helping Walter to his feet.

They saw every moment of the horrific event. People were fleeing in every direction. Firefighters, EMTs, and police, were rushing to aid survivors. Two smaller drone aircraft were flying around, performing additional surveillance. Paul and Walter began jogging away from the bay. Once they felt they were far away from the site, the two men ceased jogging. They quickly took off their suit tops and discarded them. They walked to a nearby train station. The television screens embedded into the station's walls, were already reporting news of the deadly attack. Walter and Paul purchased two train tickets to Newark. They waited inside the station, and watched news coverage of the slaughter.

Paul put his head down and whispered, “God, save our souls.”

18 My Friend In The Snow

The sounds of loud sirens blared in all directions. Eiji swerved down residential roads, near the New Jersey bay area. He desperately tried to avoid detection by the authorities.

"How much further?" Vincent asked in a heated tone.

"She'll be close to the park entrance," said Eiji.

"Slow the fuck down. You're going to get us busted," said Cameron.

The group saw a caravan of heavily armored urban police tanks, followed by a flying combat drone, race down an adjacent street.

"Holy shit. Holy *shit!* We have to ditch this fucking van!" Vincent said in a very concerned tone.

"Calm down. They're busy–"

"*Fuck* you, Cameron! Don't you fucking tell me to calm the fuck down!" Vincent angrily interrupted.

"Nigger, who the fuck you think you talking to like that?" Cameron snapped back.

"I'm fucking talkin–" Vincent began saying.

"Fucking shut up! *Both* of you! Now's not the time for your retarded fighting!" Eiji interrupted.

Vincent and Cameron heeded Eiji's words, and did not escalate their argument. Even though they were giving each other menacing looks, they did not continue their verbal altercation. Four and a half minutes later, Eiji drove to the front of Liberty National Park. They saw Lucia was running out of the park. Cameron opened the van's side door, and Lucia jumped into the passenger's seat. Eiji barely waited for her to close the door before he sped away. He immediately drove through some more isolated residential streets.

"What the hell happened?! Where are Paul and Walter?!" Lucia screamed.

"We don't know. We left in a hurry. Some niggers went crazy and started shooting everyone!" Cameron said.

"I know. I saw the whole thing over the satellite feed. What set them off?" Lucia said.

"Not a clue. One minute, some faggoty ass white boy rolled up, and started beating the shit out of me. Next thing we know, shots are getting fired," Cameron stated.

"Who the hell was that guy? He knew exactly who we were, and what we were doing there," Vincent said.

"Maybe he was a cop," Lucia said.

"Nah, this guy wasn't a law man. He looked absolutely crazy," Vincent said.

"The guy was tweaked out of his mind. His eyes were bloodshot, and he was mumbling something about not being in control of himself," Cameron said.

"Did he know your names?" Lucia asked.

"I don't know; but he called us terrorists and Food Liberationists," Cameron replied.

The group grew very concerned, and did not speak for several moments.

"We've got to find Paul and Walter," Lucia finally said.

"We need to ditch this van first. We're going away for life, if they catch us packing this much food," Vincent said.

"You're right. Eiji, pull over," Lucia replied.

Eiji stopped the van on a deserted residential street. Lucia removed a medium sized hand held computer from her backpack. The computer was a one quarter inch thin, single transparent piece of fiber glass. Lucia removed her cell phone from her wrist. Lucia tapped it against the computer's glass. Both devices' holographic displays illuminated. A holographic screen vertically projected from the tablet computer.

The transparent area illuminated with keyboard letters. Lucia typed several commands into the computer. She then took her cell phone and changed some of its settings. She swiped her finger in a downward motion along the transparent keyboard's side. The holographic image retracted into the machine. Lucia placed the phone on top of the tablet computer.

The screen flashed the words, "Synching devices."

After twenty seconds Lucia said, "Almost finished. Give me one more second."

Lucia took the cell phone, and placed it on the van's holographic dashboard panel.

The dashboard flashed the words, "Synching Global Positioning System route."

After fifteen seconds, the van's robotic voice said from the speakers, "Route synched."

"Okay, we can leave. I programmed a new route for it to follow. It's going to drive itself to an isolated part of Newark. We'll have to pick it up later," said Lucia.

"We need to ditch these uniforms, and find out what happened to Paul and Walter," Cameron said.

The team exited the vehicle. The males discarded their jackets in some nearby trash receptacles. They put on some dirty hooded sweatshirts, which they had left in the van. They made several attempts to contact Paul and Walter via their cell phones. Neither man answered their calls.

"Shit. Do you think they got caught?" Cameron asked.

"Lord, I hope not," Eiji said.

"We have to go to the Branson's house. They have a right to know what happened," Vincent said.

"Lucy, what did you do with the other van?" Eiji asked.

"I sent it to Bayonne. It was still with you, when you left the dock. I didn't get to reprogram its route," Lucia replied.

"That's a good thing. Having the vans in separate locations will make it tougher to track us," Cameron said.

"How are we getting to Manville? No trains or buses stop near their house," asked Vincent.

"We can't take Walter's car. He gave Paul a ride to the compound. He'll need it to drive him back," said Lucia.

"Assuming they even made it off the island," said Eiji ominously.

"We can't think about that right now. We need to get the meat back to the compound, and let Paul's family know what happened. I think we should catch a train to Bayonne, pick up the van, and take it back to Newark with the other one. We'll unload the goods, and then stash the vans somewhere safe. Once we're done, we'll figure out how we'll get to the Branson's," Cameron said.

The group agreed. The team started walking to the nearest train station to proceed with Cameron's plan. By the time they reached the station, it was on a high security lock-down. The team saw numerous police and military personnel patrolling the area. The officers searched every passenger attempting to enter the station. Large mobile body scanners had been rolled up to the entrances. All people entering the station were required to pass through them.

"This is not good. Word has gotten out about the attack. Traveling by train is too risky," Lucia said.

"We'll never make it past security. Even if we use our real ID's, they might confiscate our computers," Eiji said.

"We need to find another route," Vincent replied.

"Pull up a bus station schedule on your computer," Cameron said to Lucia.

Lucia retrieved the materials and said, "There's a station about one mile from here. If we take the bus to Hoboken, we can transfer and take another one to the Harrison station. After that, we'll catch another bus to Newark. We'll have to hurry. The last bus out of Harrison leaves at one-thirty."

"That's plenty of time. Let's move," Cameron replied.

The team began walking to the bus station. It was almost 10:30 PM by the time the crew reached the first bus stop. They were tired and out of breath, due to the fact that they had jogged half of the way there. The bus arrived at 10:32 PM. They entered without incident after briefly being body scanned in the bus' front stairwell. The bus was not very crowded. Everyone communicating on their cell phones, or to each other, was all talking about the shooting spree at the Statue of Freedom. News reports said that the unprovoked terrorist attack was the work of Food Liberationists. President Cho was going to give a speech at midnight addressing the events.

"This is not good. They found some of the food at the bay," Lucia whispered to Cameron.

"It's not the first time the Food Freedom Movement, has been wrongfully blamed for inciting violence; and it won't be the last," said Cameron in a reassuring tone.

The team traveled to the next station, and waited for their second bus. The time was 11:22 PM. They boarded the next bus at 11:45 PM, and rode to the Harrison station. They exited the bus at Harrison, and boarded the final bus en route to Newark. It was 12:31 AM by the time they boarded their final bus. They all found seats in the back, and slumped into their chairs. They were exhausted by the day's traumatic events.

"My eyes are burning. I haven't wanted to sleep this badly, in ages," said Vincent while rubbing his left eye.

"Hang tight. We should be home in about an hour," said Lucia.

The bus arrived at its last stop, which was one half mile from the group's compound. The time was 1:19 AM. The group walked to the compound, and arrived shortly before 2:00 AM. They entered, and went to the main living quarters. There was no sign of Paul or Walter.

"Do you think they made it back?" asked Vincent.

"Walter's car is gone. That's a good sign," said Eiji.

"Lucy, how far is the van?" asked Cameron.

"Not far. About a mile," Lucia replied.

"Will I need anything to drive the vehicle?" said Cameron.

"Type AE34MQ22 into the dashboard, when it prompts you. That will engage manual drive," Lucia said.

"Okay. I'm going to pick up the van," said Cameron.

"Alone? No way. We're going with you," said Vincent.

"No. It's too risky. We're not sure if it has been cased by the authorities. You all need to sleep. I'll do this by myself," said Cameron.

The team fell into an uncomfortable silence for several moments.

"I'll be back soon, I promise. Besides, you all need to get in touch with Paul and Walter. We'll figure out what to do about the other van in the morning, after we've had time to rest," Cameron said.

"Call me, if the code doesn't work. I'll remotely hack into the dashboard, and override the locks," Lucia said.

"Sure. Text the coordinates to my phone. I'll use my GPS to find the van," Cameron replied.

"Good luck," said Eiji.

"Ditto," Vincent said.

Cameron grabbed a jacket, left the building, and began walking to the van. Cameron was so tired, that he had trouble keeping a brisk walking pace. He wanted nothing more than to curl up in his warm bed next to Sky, and sleep for a very long time. Cameron activated his cell phone. He searched for footage of President Cho's midnight speech. He located a video and expanded the image, so that it covered his whole palm. He watched President Cho address the attacks.

"Today, we are reminded of the dangerous threat that domestic American terrorist organizations present to our society. This evening, shortly after 9:00 PM; the Statue of Freedom and a commuter ferry, were attacked in what is believed to be a coordinated assault. This heinous act was committed by a group of ruthless Food Liberationists. Packaged meat was found in several suitcases, on a nearby New Jersey dock. The death toll has reached sixty-one, and is expected to climb higher. All terrorists were killed, and we are in the process of starting a manhunt for their collaborators. These violent radicalized extremists, will be brought to justice," President Cho's hologram said.

"Holy shit," Cameron whispered to himself.

Cameron was furious that President Cho was not telling a remote version of the truth. He did not know Gregory Times' identity, but Cameron was sure that Times was involved with framing the group. Cameron had no way of knowing that Times was simply a pawn, being played himself. Cameron was angry that the media was trying to demonize Food Liberationists. Even though there were a few individuals, who sometimes engaged in crimes that gave food freedom activists a bad reputation; the overall resistance was comprised of decent people. Cameron did not make excuses for his own actions, but he was completely confident that the overall food movement's intentions were positive.

Cameron was incredibly nervous when he approached the van. Cameron was shaking from the cold weather. He looked around the street to make sure that he had not been followed. He was pleased to see that there were no drones in the sky. However, he was also aware that the drones might be using stealth technology, to conceal their presence. Cameron took a deep breath, and opened the van's door. He got behind the wheel, and used his thumb to trigger the ignition. Cameron typed the code which Lucia had given him. He was immediately granted manual driving access.

Cameron was so weary that he was barely able to keep his eyes open. It started snowing while he was driving back to the compound. He blinked his eyes repeatedly, and yawned with fatigue. He noticed that the snow was falling in an unusual pattern. The flakes would fall slowly for a short time, and then suddenly drop very fast. Bits of flakes seemed to hover in the air. Cameron noticed the van's computer panels were flashing, and seemed to be malfunctioning. His vision was becoming obscured. He was immediately stricken with terror when he saw the strange, black, ashy ripple suddenly appear! The mysterious Figure fell forward. He landed on one knee, only a few yards in front of Cameron's van!

Cameron immediately hit the brakes, skidded slightly, and came to a stop. He used the wind shield wipers, to flick away some falling snow. He looked down the street, but did not see the Figure. Cameron hoped that his imagination was running rampant. He had still not reconciled if the event, in which he was first attacked by the Figure, had actually occurred in real life. Cameron did not have long to ponder the thought. The ripple quickly appeared next to Cameron's driver's side door. The Figure ripped open the door, grabbed Cameron, and threw him onto the street! Cameron hit the ground with a hard thud.

Cameron coughed before saying, "No! Not you agai–"

The Figure kicked Cameron in his stomach before he could finish speaking. The Figure pulled Cameron to his feet, and threw him against the van. The Figure began unleashing a powerful flurry of punches into Cameron's midsection. Cameron did his best to block and absorb the strikes. His body was too weak from exhaustion to prevent many of the punches from reaching their target. Cameron gasped for air. The Figure momentarily stopped his assault.

"Why are you still so weak?" the Figure asked.

Cameron felt his fighting spirit return.

"I'll show you *weak!*" Cameron yelled.

Cameron drove his knee into the Figure's gut. The Figure groaned in pain. Cameron grabbed the Figure, and smashed his helmet covered head into the van. Cameron delivered two quick jabs to the Figure's side. The Figure regained control by swinging his body around, and used his right arm to club Cameron in the side of his face. Cameron stumbled backwards. He quickly regained his footing, and stood in a boxing stance. The two men began circling each other.

"Why do you want to fight me? What did I do to you?!" Cameron yelled.

"Because someone has to knock some sense into you!" the Figure replied.

The Figure quickly teleported behind Cameron. He performed a sweeping ground kick which knocked Cameron down on his backside. The Figure tried leaping onto Cameron and delivering a dropping punch to his chest, but Cameron quickly rolled out of the way. The Figure grunted from the pain caused by slamming his hand against the hard ground. Cameron tackled the Figure to the floor. He smashed the Figure's helmet visor, twice with his forearm. Cameron struggled to remove the Figure's helmet.

"Take off that fucking *mask!*" Cameron angrily said.

The Figure suddenly teleported out of Cameron's grasp. Cameron stood up and looked around, but did not see the Figure anywhere. Cameron began laughing.

"Is that your only trick? You're a joke!" Cameron said.

"You're the only one laughing," the Figure said.

Cameron spun around and saw the Figure had reappeared behind him. The Figure teleported forward, and delivered a strong knee shot to Cameron's stomach. Cameron winced in pain, and fell backwards to the ground. The Figure tried stomping on Cameron's chest, but Cameron rolled away and avoided the blow. Cameron arose to his feet. The Figure attempted to deliver a standing sideways kick with his right leg. Cameron grabbed the Figure's leg, and spun him around. The Figure dropped to the floor.

The Figure quickly arose and went back into his fighting stance. The Figure threw two, quick left handed jabs, at Cameron's head. Cameron immediately countered. After the second jab, Cameron saw an opportunity to strike. The Figure tried lunging at Cameron, but by doing so, he left himself vulnerable to attack. Cameron delivered a powerful, standing roundhouse kick with his left leg. The Figure was hit hard in his side, and lost his balance. Cameron ran forward, and started raining punches upon the Figure's chest and face mask. After Cameron had landed a series of punches, he went for a hard right handed uppercut. Cameron could not believe what happened next.

"Time stop!" the Figure yelled.

Cameron felt an enormous encumbrance upon his body. Gravity's weight felt so heavy, that Cameron thought it would pull him through the concrete. He breathlessly watched his punching arm, move extremely slowly through the air. Everything fell deathly silent around him. Cameron could not fathom why he was not moving at his normal speed. The Figure started moving at an extraordinarily fast pace. He began running circles around Cameron. The Figure ran so fast, that he became a blur.

The Figure positioned himself next to Cameron. The Figure briefly glanced at Cameron, who was still in the middle of his slow motion punch. The Figure took his right index finger, and lightly tapped Cameron's clenched fist. Suddenly, the two men began moving at the same speed. Cameron felt intense pain. His arm rapidly swung its motion in the reverse direction!

Cameron screamed, while his body violently swung around. Cameron stumbled, and fell upon the hard cement. The Figure quickly placed his mighty boot atop Cameron's neck. Cameron gasped for air. He was certain that the Figure would execute him. However, death did not find Cameron Moss on this night. The Figure slowly removed his boot, and extended his hand to Cameron.

"Better; but you still lack true strength. Get up, Cameron," said the Figure.

Cameron reluctantly accepted the Figure's gesture. Cameron arose, and breathed heavily.

"What are you? A robot? An alien? A deity?" Cameron asked.

"I am only a man," the Figure casually replied.

"Bullshit! What the hell kind of man, has that much power?" Cameron asked.

"What you perceive as humans, are some of the most powerful beings in this dimension, and galaxy," he replied.

Cameron was visibly flustered.

"I don't know of any *human*, capable of something that spectacular. My entire body was burdened. I couldn't move. Yet I watched you run around so fast, that I could barely see you. You randomly appear, literally out of nowhere, and teleport around like it's normal," Cameron said.

"I suppose my travel methods may seem odd, to those who haven't experienced it themselves," the Figure replied.

"Odd? You call that incredible power, *odd?* Hah! Whatever, man. Why don't you take your little device, use it to find a place called Fuck-off, and go live there," Cameron heatedly said.

Cameron's words did not seem to have the mordacious effect which he had intended.

"Your anger is a burden. It poisons your thoughts, corrupts your emotions, and makes you squander your talents. You are completely nescient to your importance in this world. Will you stand up, and claim the life which is rightfully yours? Or will you wither away and have your name forgotten; long before your bones have turned to dust? You must make this decision quickly, Cameron Moss," the Figure said with commiseration.

"I don't know who you think I am. I'm not some kind of great leader. I'm just a guy, trying to find food that doesn't kill him. It sucks that I have to be a criminal to do that, but that's life," Cameron snapped.

"You contradict yourself. You claim that you're no leader. But you help lead many good people, in the fight for your food freedom," the Figure said.

Cameron paused for a few moments before saying, "That may have once been true, but not anymore. That part of my life is over. It *has* to be over. Are you aware of what happened tonight?"

"Of course," the Figure decisively said.

"Then you know that this is not a battle worth fighting. People are dying. It's no longer worth sacrificing innocent lives, to prove a point about food rights," Cameron replied.

"The lives of those who are lost, will not be in vain. The true test will be your ability to endure through these tough times. The best men are those who conquer asperity. Those who have never faced hardship have never truly lived. Because to truly live, is to experience the joy that comes with defeating adversity," the Figure said.

"Why don't *you* do something? You certainly have the capability to help," Cameron asked.

"It's not that simple. Traveling like I do has severe consequences. Basic physics dictates that no action is without a counter reaction. You have no idea how much my presence here, and contact with you, jeopardizes numerous other time lines," the Figure replied.

"So why would you bother me, if you refuse to help?" Cameron asked.

"Because I know that the next ten years, will decide the next one thousand. Humanity is at a critical junction. There will be *dire* consequences, if people simply sit on the sidelines at this point in their evolution. I believe you are a true warrior, and have the strength to endure any tribulations that await you. The clock is already accelerating. Today's events are a mere foreshadow of the coming nightmares, if my predictions on this time line are correct," the Figure said.

"So, tell me what I can do to help. Tell me how to solve the problems," Cameron said.

"You are not listening. I cannot simply give you solutions, or tell you what to do in a given situation. I can only guide you, and hope that you make the right decisions, when it is time. Time is something, of which *I* have plenty. *You* on the other hand, are not so fortunate. Your time grows short. All I can say, is that you are not a person who is easily persuaded," the Figure replied.

Cameron was baffled by the Figure's ominous words. He felt the Figure spoke in riddles, and it annoyed Cameron. The only thing more disturbing than the Figure's words was its presence. Even though Cameron saw with his own eyes that this Figure was able to bend forms of matter, time, and space; Cameron could not bring himself to believe that such a magnificent achievement was possible.

"Assuming you're not a total figment of my imagination; how is it that you're performing these fantastic feats? Is it possible? Can you really travel through time?" Cameron asked.

"Time is nothing more than a unit of measurement. Strictly speaking, it does not exist in a linear fashion. True time is one's spatial displacement, and velocity, at any given point in space. A brilliant poet could write a world changing sonnet, within a few minutes. A ne'er-do-well could waste hours sitting in one spot, and never attain significance. This is why the underachievers, and naysayers, believe time only moves in one direction. They measure time, solely by a clock's lapsing numbers," the Figure replied.

"That can't be all to the story," Cameron said.

"Yes, there is more. But like I said, your time is running out. If we are lucky, you will still be alive at a later distance, for me to explain it in further detail," the Figure replied.

Cameron said, "You know my name, and claim to know my future–"

"I know certain *aspects*, of your future," the Figure interrupted.

Cameron rephrased his question and said, "What I am saying is that you know a significant portion about my life, and the inner workings of the multiverse. I know nothing about you. Will you at least tell me your name?"

The Figure bowed his head, and tapped the glowing orb upon his chest. Blue fluid began oozing from the orb. He typed a series of commands into his bio-holographic plate. The fluid retracted into the orb.

"You will come to know me very well, over the next few cycles," the Figure said.

The Figure's helmet visor began flashing a series of words, number patterns, geometric shapes, and geographical locations. The Figure began vertically rising, very slowly. Cameron put his hands in front of his face, to shield himself from the orb's spectacular glow and emanating heat.

The Figure said, "Until then, all you need understand; is that there is only a limited amount of time to change the future. I am watching all events within my visible light spectrum. I pray there is a future, to which I can return. I pray there is a past, from which I can decipher knowledge. There is no human too small, to shape the fate of the world. I know this, because I have seen many time lines. I have seen occurrences so mighty, they have devastated entire planets. I have seen insignificant transactions, lasting for but a nanosecond. I *know* a great evil, will rise in this dimension. I *know* this darkness is combated with a force, greater than all the love in every galaxy. I *know* these statements are true. For I, am Rasheed Wallace; THE TIME SHIFTER!"

In an epic display of might, the man who called himself the Time Shifter; teleported into the black, ashy ripple! Cameron felt gravity pulling him towards the blinding hot light. He resisted its suction, by falling backwards onto his right knee and elbow. The gravitational force lasted for only a fraction of one second, before the ripple disappeared. After a moment, Cameron stood up on both feet, and looked at his surroundings. The van was not scratched one bit. The only visible remnants from the encounter were skid marks from the van's tires; and footprints, freshly made in the falling snow.

19 A Grave Miscalculation

Gregory Times awoke with a painful headache. He had not slept well in several days. In his waking daze, he held a sliver of hope that the horrific events which he was enduring were nothing but a terrible nightmare. The shackles around his wrists and feet, which kept him chained to his bed, shattered any delusion that these experiences were imaginary. He did not know what time it was, or how long he had been imprisoned. He tugged at his restraints, in a vain attempt at freeing himself from his confinement. He heard the door to his room open, followed by the light sound of swift footsteps.

"Hi, my love!" said the sadistic British woman, who had previously tortured him.

She jumped on the bed, and cuddled next to Times.

"Oh, *fuck!* Not *you!* Somebody, help!" Times screamed.

The British woman giggled, then rubbed Times' chest with her hand. She straddled Times' leg, with hers.

"Aww, why must you be so mean? I thought you would miss me, sweetie!" she said.

"*Fuck* you, you crazy cunt! Get the *fuck* off me!" Times passionately said.

The British woman laughed loudly before saying, "You sound stressed! How about I help you relax?"

She lifted off the bed for a moment, and then positioned herself on top of Times, in a way that placed their genitals in each other's faces. Times turned away. She grinded her vagina into his face.

"Yes, I think this is a wonderful cure for depression!" she said.

She started rubbing his thighs, and crotch. Times growled in anger. He momentarily had revenge by biting the woman's left buttock. The woman screamed, and pulled away. She rolled off the bed before Times could sink his teeth further into her flesh. For the first occasion he could recall in days, Times smiled widely with sincere pleasure.

"What's the matter bitch? I thought you liked it rough," Times snarled.

The British woman had a stern and disapproving look upon her face.

"That was seriously naughty!" she said.

She grabbed Times' testicles through his clothes, and squeezed them very aggressively in her hand.

"Ow! Shit!" Times yelled.

He gasped with intense pain. The woman slightly loosened her grip, and began gently rubbing his crotch.

"You owe me an apology. What do we say, when we've been a bad boy?" she coyly asked.

Times responded by spitting at her. She wiped the saliva from her face, and became aggressive. She used both hands to strangle Times. Afterwards, she slapped him three times in his face.

"Mister Times, your attitude is *unacceptable!*" said the British woman with visible anger.

Times defiantly spit at her again, this time hitting her chest. This second display of disobedience enraged her.

"BEHAVE, YOU LITTLE SHIT!" yelled the British woman.

She lifted up Times' shirt, and started biting his right nipple very hard. Times screamed loudly.

He shouted, "Fuck you, demented whore! You'll never break me!"

The British woman, angered by Times' resistance, proceeded to bite his left nipple.

"You're all dead, you fuckers! You have no idea how badly I'm going to fuck up your world!" Times shouted.

The British woman stood up, and backed away from him. Times began spitting wildly at her, so she moved further away. She activated her cell phone wrist band.

"He's really wound up today. You should get down here, immediately," she said into the phone.

"I am very disappointed in you, Mister Times. I felt at the conclusion of our last session, you were on the verge of making real progress. But today you've been extremely uncooperative, and unresponsive to my attempt at helping you. I want you to reevaluate your attitude. I expect you to be on your *best* behavior, the next time we meet," she said.

She started walking away from Times.

"Hey, you sadistic tramp. You have really nice eyes," Times abruptly said.

The British woman gave Times a confused look.

Before she could reply Times added, "I can't wait to get a better look at them."

He gave her a maniacal smile. She turned around and left the room. A short time later, Webster entered the torture chamber.

"You should kill me now, old man. You won't have too many more chances," Times immediately said to him.

Webster smiled sadistically, and walked to Times' bed.

"Don't be so impatient. There is still work to finish," Webster said.

"Why do you even need me? You've already proven your device works," asked Times.

"Because you are still very important, Gregory. I told you, your brainwave activity is quite remarkable. You are an amplifier of my power source. The device only has a limited wavelength. I have discovered that I need to be within auditory range of my target, to induce mind control. With you, that is not the case. Your brainwaves are extremely sensitive. You have already seen that I can control you from a great distance. Using your neural receptors, in conjunction with my drone's nano-machine viruses; increases the device's effect radius. Therefore I can use you as a surrogate, to deliver my orders; while never having to get near my victims. You are the ultimate marionette. And I, am your puppeteer," he said.

Times was shocked by Webster's diabolical scheme.

"Do you have any idea, how obdurate you are?" Times asked.

"I have a surprise for you. Consider it a reward, for cooperating," Webster said with a devilish grin.

Times was so enraged that Webster would derisively call Times' torture and coercion a form of cooperation, that he did not dignify the statement with a response. Webster activated his mind control headband.

"Let me make sure that you're still compliant," Webster said.

Times groaned in agony when the loud, painful ringing pierced his ears.

"Perfect," Webster said.

He removed all of Times' restraints and said, "After you,"

Webster extended his arm towards the room's door. Times' body felt extremely weak. Times forced himself to rise from the bed. Times stumbled out of the room, while moving at a slow pace.

"Where am I–" Times began asking.

He heard Webster's voice rattling the inside of his head.

"You need to stop being so inquisitive," Webster telepathically said.

After briefly creating a painful sensation in Times' body, Webster started directing his movement. Times walked down a dimly lit corridor. Times was horrified by the revelation, that on the surface, Rigor Pharmaceuticals appeared to be a normal office building; but that was only a facade. This edifice was a satanic dungeon. Times wondered how many illegal and immoral experiments had taken place in this nightmarish laboratory.

"How much does the government pay you, to run this torture chamber?" Times asked.

"Why do you think I am involved with the government?" Webster replied.

"It's bad enough you're abusing me like a dog. Don't insult my intelligence, by pretending I'm stupid. There is no way you could run a facility like this, without receiving serious cash and protection from powerful authorities," Times said.

Webster and Times stopped walking.

"You are a smart man. I've told you before, that I chose you because you are unique. However, your understanding of the world is incomplete. You think the government, and corporations, are separate entities? Corporations *are* the government. There is no Court, Congress, or President. There are only Shareholders, Boards of Directors, and CEO's," Webster said.

Webster and Times continued walking down the long corridor.

"Everything you see here was funded by the only true government. The government, called money. Ordinary people do not rise to power and become prominent public figures; unless they are funded by big banks, monolithic mega-corporations, or wealthy private individuals. There is no vote which cannot be bought; no trial which cannot be rigged; no law too unjust and oppressive to the people, that it cannot be passed! With enough wealth and power, a man can buy the world! In fact the entire form of fractional reserve banking, so eloquently invented by Eric Nathaniel Raithchild in 1815, proved that a man can purchase an entire *country* for pennies on the dollar, if he is cunning!" Webster said.

"You can't take your money with you to the grave, old man," Times said.

"Perhaps. But who is to say that there *is* a grave, Gregory? The technology finally exists, which can render even death itself, *obsolete*. Entire memory banks of the human brain can be downloaded into a computer hard drive. This can theoretically allow a person, to live forever. Life extension technologies, such as cloning, can replicate and replace entire failing organs," Webster said.

"You believe that money can buy you out of anything? Even death?" Times asked.

"Yes. If a man has access to all of these great technologies, I believe that it is possible...to live forever," Webster smugly said.

"You are a fool. The only thing your money and evil deeds will buy you, is a reservation in Hell's playground," Times said with stern commitment.

Webster did not continue speaking. The two men continued walking until they reached a split in the hallway. The hall divided into three portions at the split. The path on Times' left, led to a spiral staircase. It appeared to lead upwards into the building. In front of Times were two large silver doors, which appeared were capable of sliding open sideways. To Times' right, was a single wooden door.

The door's simplicity disturbed Times. It seemed out of place in such a magnificent maze of corridors. It had no markings, and only a twelve inch rectangular panel was located on its front. Webster placed his hand upon the panel for a few seconds. The panel scanned his imprint by forming a holographic shape around his hand. The panel flashed the words, "ACCESS GRANTED," before swinging open.

Webster motioned for Times to enter the room. Times walked slowly into the completely dark space. Times heard the door slam shut behind him. The room was painfully cold, and pitch black. For a brief moment, Times enjoyed the peaceful silence. It was the first serene moment he had experienced since beginning his harrowing ordeal. He was happy to feel like his thoughts were truly his own.

"Just kill me," Times whispered to himself.

"Why would I kill you, son?" said a lone voice.

He violently shivered, because he recognized the voice. The room slightly illuminated and Times saw his mother Patricia, sitting on a chair in a far right side corner.

"Mo...Mom?" said Times weakly.

Patricia extended her arms and said, "Aw, baby. You look tired. Come, give me a hug."

Times did not move. He gave Patricia a cold stare.

"You're not real," Times said.

Patricia lowered her arms and said, "Why would you say that, son? I–"

"STOP FUCKING WITH ME!" Times screamed.

Times covered his face with his hands.

"This is not real. This is not real..." he repeated to himself.

He forced himself to regain his sanity. Times eventually looked up, and saw nothing but an empty chair.

"If you have hurt my family, I swear, I'll torture you ten times harder than you did to me!" Times yelled.

Times heard maniacal laughter echoing throughout the chamber.

"Isn't technology wonderful, Gregory?! How do you like my latest trick?" Webster wickedly asked.

Suddenly, Patricia's image reappeared in front of Times!

"You've always been a disappointment, Gregory!" her counterfeit representation said.

The phony Patricia started walking closer to Times. He walked backwards, and desperately tried avoiding her.

"I can't believe your father and I, wasted our one child on such a miserable failure! We would have had you *aborted*, if we had known you were going to be such a goddamned disappointment!" Patricia's spectre said.

Times stopped walking, and once again put his hands to his face.

"GET OUT OF MY HEAD!" Times screamed.

Times swung his fist at Patricia's image. It distorted, and disappeared. Again, Times heard Webster laugh.

"Modern day holograms are amazing! They look *so* realistic!" Webster said.

"I hate you!" yelled Times.

The door opened and Webster entered the room. The mysterious British woman followed him. Times was stunned to see Webster was wearing a highly detailed mask! The mask was marvelous, and made from solid silver, which glistened beautifully. It was a full face covering with dark red, tinted fiberglass eyes, and a small nose. Four straps on each side of the mask, held it steady upon Webster's face.

The pattern created by the straps, resembled a spider's legs. The mouth and jaw area was equipped with a small circular plate. It protruded slightly out of the mask. The circular plate was covered with complex mesh netting. The mask formed neither a smile, nor a frown. It was a perfectly emotionless disguise.

"What do you think of my latest invention?" asked Webster.

"You can go straight to *Hell!*" yelled Times.

Webster chuckled and ignored the comment.

"It's only a prototype. I must mold a better model. I will use hologram technology to make it resemble a real face. When it is done, I will be able to change my facial pattern. I'll use it, in conjunction with its voice manipulator, to become any person I want! I will be able to discretely manipulate anyone, by using an endless array of identities!" he replied.

"You're crazy! That will never work!" said Times.

"I beg to differ, Gregory. All my life's experiments have been wildly successful. There is no reason to think this one will end in failure," said Webster.

"Why? What sense does this make? You can retire, and enjoy your wealth in complete privacy! Why go through all this trouble to mess with people?" Times asked.

"Because money is only one piece of the puzzle. Most people would be happy to retire, with billions of dollars. That is only because they are *weak!* They do not understand the importance of exercising raw, unparalleled, power! Do you think the elites, of which I am one, do not fight amongst ourselves? The only reason our plans sometimes go awry, is because there is a struggle for *power!* The Super Elites are the most ruthless predators, ever born into this world. Enhancing myself will give *me* the power, to enslave them. They will bend to my every desire. I will rule them, the way they rule society! To rule the Super Elite, is to rule the *gods!*" Webster replied.

Times was completely shocked by Webster's stark raving lunacy.

"You are so turtle shit insane, that I don't even know what to say to you at this point. Elites? Power? Gods? Fuck, you are *totally* mad! You have *no* connection to reality!" Times said.

"Believe me; I do not expect you to understand. The Globalists, and our intentions, are not meant to be understood by the common *swine!* Only those who have accepted the true Luciferian Doctrine can be fully illuminated," said Webster.

"You're right. I don't care about *you*, or your fucked up plans, or your psychotic Globalist friends! All I want is my life back!" Times said.

"I am afraid that will never happen. You obviously know, that we cannot let you leave alive. There is one special treat I would like to give you, before I terminate your service," Webster said.

Webster tipped his head, and gestured to the British woman. She walked over to the room's left side wall. She tapped the middle of it with the back of her hand. A small holographic keyboard began illuminating. The British woman typed a series of numbers into the panel, and the wall became transparent. Times was horrified to see Mallory was in the other room! She was blindfolded, and laying on a medical examination table. Her hands and feet were bound with shackles. Mallory was crying and quivering in terror. Times rushed over and banged his fists against the divider.

"Mallory! Mallory!" Times screamed.

"I'm afraid that won't work. That is one sided glass. She can't see, or hear you my love," the British woman said.

Times looked at Webster and said, "Let her go!"

"That's obviously not possible, either," said Webster.

Times violently punched the wall. His pulse raced with anxiety. Webster removed his mask, and spoke to the British woman.

"There is no rush. You may have fun with her, if you wish," Webster softly said.

"Thank you," the British woman said.

"Don't you touch her, you diseased slag! You'll be sorry if you harm one hair on her head!" Times yelled.

She walked over to the door. The British woman giggled, and gave Times a mocking wave. She held her left hand upright, and flicked her fingers twice into her palm.

"Bye bye, sweetie!" she said before closing the door.

"Please. Goddammit, PLEASE! If you have a soul, let her go!" Times frantically said to Webster.

Webster was indifferent to Times' torment.

"Beautiful, is it not?" Webster selfishly asked.

He held the mask, and marveled at its beauty. Its brightly glistening surface, contrasted the room's dim lighting.

"It is pure silver. I modeled it after a mask that I purchased when I returned to the California Islands. It was one of the first trips I made out of New York State, after Mister Thurswell's death. How I miss our...connection, to this day. I treated myself to a gift, to celebrate my one year anniversary as president of Rigor Pharmaceuticals," Webster said.

Times did not care what Webster was saying. Times began whimpering, while tears flowed down his face.

"What a terrible tragedy. I can't believe it has been almost forty-three years, since that horrible earthquake tore most of the state into the sea. In hindsight, it was probably for the best. Radiation from Japan's Fakutori nuclear disaster had already devastated the state. It was a decaying wasteland, long before I visited in early 2187. The cancer rates there are astronomical. I would not be surprised if one day, what is left of it, will be completely uninhabitable. I suppose nature solved the problems of man, on his behalf," Webster said.

"For the fucking love of God, don't kill her!" Times cried.

Webster ignored him and said, "A poor Mexican family was selling ceremonial masks, along the Nevada border. They crafted them by hand. They were fashioned from old beams of steel that they salvaged from the collapsed Golden Gay Bridge. Even though they are a dirty and repugnant people, I admire their resourcefulness."

Times momentarily took his gaze off of Mallory.

"Enough of your nonsense! Fuck you, and your bullshit stories! I don't fucking care! Let her go! She is my *wife!*" he shouted at Webster.

Webster grew enraged and said, "You need to learn some MANNERS!"

He used the headband to flood Times' mind with excruciating pain. Times fell to his knees, and let out a strong howl. After Webster let his pain subside, Times turned his attention back to Mallory. Times knew that she was terrified. Her whole body was twitching. She struggled to break free from her shackles, but it was a futile effort. Webster leaned close to Times' left ear.

"Do you want to know the meaning of life, Gregory?" Webster callously asked.

"Please...we've lost so much already..." Times said while sobbing heavily.

Webster stood up straight and placed his right hand on Times' left shoulder. He stood triumphantly above his demoralized and defeated prisoner.

"The meaning of life is domination, ruthlessness, vulgarity, and *control.* Our lives mean nothing, if we do not take control of our own environment. This is why I have risen to the class of the Super

Elite. I understand that human suffering is a necessity. Only those who ruthlessly support the degradation of their fellow man, are worthy enough to rule the world," Webster said.

Times watched the British woman enter the room. She mercilessly shouted obscenities at Mallory.

"No! Stay away from her you fucking sewer slut!" Times yelled.

Webster used his headband to cause Times more pain. Times shivered, and watched in horror, while the British woman tormented his precious Mallory. The British woman slapped Mallory's breasts very hard with her hands. Mallory winced from the pain. Times could not hear what the British woman was saying. But he was sure that she was filling her head with the same vile propaganda, to which he had already been exposed. Times watched the British woman pull Mallory's hair, and forcefully bite her atop her head.

"I want you to watch. Watch how my pet controls the situation. Neither you, nor your wife, have ever been in control of your lives. *That* is why you find yourselves in this position," Webster maliciously said to Times.

"Mallory! Don't listen to her! I love you, baby!" Times screamed at the top of his lungs.

"How does it feel, to be helpless? How does it feel, to watch her being abused at this very moment? How does it feel to know that you cannot save her; the same way you could not save your children?" Webster viciously asked.

Times felt his body begin going numb. In an instant, he heard Webster's voice fade away. Times' life flashed before his eyes. The memories of the horrible experiences, which he had endured the last few months, filled him with a burning rage. Unbridled animosity coursed through his veins like hot lava. His body grew hot. His breathing became slow, and steady. He looked up, and saw the wretched slag laughing. She pulled up Mallory's shirt, and began kissing her belly. She massaged Mallory's breasts, and vagina. Times eventually heard nothing except his own beating heart, and the familiar whispers. A strange peace came over him. He slowly tilted his head upwards, and stared directly at Webster's face. He smiled deucedly, when he saw the look of pure unrepentant evil in Webster's eyes.

"You've underestimated me," Times calmly said.

With a blinding speed, Times momentarily broke free from the mind control. He punched Webster in his genitals, using every ounce of force he could muster! Webster let out a loud yelp, and immediately flinched forward. Times seized the opportunity to stand, and while doing so, tackled Webster to the ground! Webster screamed, and tried using his mind control headband to will Times back into submission. The effort was in vain. Times rolled on top of Webster, and slapped him twice in the face! Webster was instantly disoriented. Times used the opportunity to pull the headband from Webster's cranium! Times quickly rolled away.

He heard Webster yell with panic, "Dear God...no...!"

Times arose slowly. His breathing was heavy, but focused. He held the beautiful headband in his hands, for only a moment. He calmly placed it upon his head, and turned around. Times saw Webster reaching for the mask, which he had dropped during the scuffle. Times confidently stepped on Webster's hand. Times felt happiness when he heard the old man's brittle bones break. Times picked up the mask, and put it on his face.

The straps automatically wrapped themselves around the back of his skull. The cold metal felt like a warm soothing medicine to his soul. Times let out a deep, bellowing scream. The sound reverberation shook the room, and cracked the fiberglass wall! Times stared into the adjacent room.

Its lights were flickering. He saw that the British woman was startled by the commotion. She walked over, and tapped on the wall.

"Everything okay?" she asked from behind the glass.

Times walked up to a mortified Webster, who was blubbering like a baby.

"Oh God...what have I done?" Webster whimpered.

Times picked Webster up by his collar, and placed his back against the glass wall. With his right hand, Times grabbed Webster hard around his neck, and stared at him. The cold unforgiving mask reminded Webster, that the pain he was about to endure was brought upon by himself.

"Mercy...please...mercy..." pleaded Webster.

Times looked downward, and to his left. He pondered Webster's request. After a moment, Times looked back at Webster and released him. Times slowly ran his hand along Webster's shoulder. Times pulled him by his collar, so that their faces where inches apart. Times uttered only one word.

"No."

Times shoved Webster into the glass! Webster broke through to the other side, with an amazingly loud sound. Webster landed at an awkward angle. The fall broke his right shin. The British woman released a shrill scream. Mallory was crying profusely. Webster rolled around in the broken glass. The jagged shards deeply cut his skin.

"He...help..." Webster started moaning.

"Please, don't hurt me anymore!" Mallory shouted.

Times knew Webster was sufficiently disabled for the moment. The British woman started running towards the door. Her efforts to escape were futile.

"Nice try," Times said.

He caused the woman to experience the horrible ringing sensation in her ears. She fell face first to the ground. The fall broke her nose, and some of her front teeth. Times slowly walked over to Mallory. She was trembling. Times gently placed his hand upon his wife's forehead.

Mallory said, "I don't want to di–"

"Shhh..." Times whispered.

Times telepathically removed her fear. Mallory slowly stopped crying, and remained calm. Her blindfold was soaking wet with tears.

"Please, let me out. They are going to kill me," Mallory said.

Times spoke in a deep, raspy, distorted voice, which was manipulated by the changer.

"No, they won't. You are safe, my dear," Times said.

Times freed her from her restraints. Mallory tried removing the blindfold from her eyes. Times stopped her, by gently grabbing her forearms.

"Stop. There's nothing for you to see," Times said.

Mallory said, "Please, I have to–"

"Shhh..." Times interrupted.

He softly placed two fingers upon her lips. He used his telepathy to help her calm down.

"You will make it home alive. Trust me," said Times in his deep, authoritative voice.

Times looked at Webster and said, "Use your phone. Tell your robots to meet her outside of this room. Tell them to thoroughly cleanse her wounds. Make sure they cater to her every need. Ensure she is well fed, and has adequate sleeping accommodations in your private quarters. They will take her home, after she is well rested. Understand?"

Webster feebly muttered, "I can't–"

"I asked you a fucking question," Times interrupted.

Times made Webster hear the ringing, accompanied by a painful burning sensation in his face.

"Yes! Yes!" Webster screamed.

Times walked over, and opened the door. The British woman frantically moved away from him, and cowered in the corner.

"Follow the sound of my voice. You may remove your blindfold, after this door closes," Times told Mallory.

Mallory trembled in shock, and slowly walked out of the room. Times shut the door. He walked over to the British woman, and triumphantly stood above her.

"That looks like it hurts," Times said.

The British woman placed her hand against her face, and felt the warm blood that was freely flowing.

"I...I'm sorry," she said.

Times looked at her with complete stolidity. The cold unforgiving mask was a perfect representation of his indifference to her suffering.

"Too late for apologies, my love," Times said.

Times used his right hand to place a strand of her tattered hair around the back of her left ear.

"It may be slightly damaged, but you still have a very pretty face," Times sternly said.

The British woman looked at Times, with tears streaming down her cheeks.

"If you weren't such a hellish bitch, I'd say you were a very attractive woman," Times said.

He caressed her cheek while she sobbed. Times used his thumb, to mix together her blood and tears.

"What's your name?" Times asked her.

The British woman sniffled and replied, "Amanda."

"Amanda. What a lovely name," Times said.

Times lightly slapped her cheeks, and pinched her nose. Amanda was well aware that she was being dominated.

"I still can't believe how remarkable, your eyes are," Times said.

Amanda breathed heavily, and felt absolute fear. Times grabbed her hair, and violently jerked her head back.

"I would like them, as a token of your remorse. I'll consider your debts paid, if you give them to me," Times said.

Amanda began sobbing even more heavily. Times shoved her head to the right, and released his grip.

"Give them to me. Give me your *eyes!*" Times said in a chilling tone.

Webster watched in sheer terror while Amanda slowly arose to her knees. She cried hysterically. Unmitigated fright coursed through Webster's body. He watched Amanda scream madly. She slowly reached her hands to her face. She started using her own fingers, to pick her eyeballs from their sockets! Blood poured down her cheeks. Amanda let out another blood curdling scream. She dug her nails deep into her flesh. Her visual orifices oozed blood. Terminal pain shot through every nerve in her body.

A horrible squishing sound was faintly heard underneath her spine curdling screams. Her nails moved deep into the pulpy pits of her face. With a nauseating popping sound, she pulled her eyes from their resting place. She vomited onto herself. She tugged the eyes, optic nerve and all, from her skull. She held the two eyes in each hand, and offered them to Times. Her body shook violently, while she hyperventilated and released short squeals.

"Hurry up and eat them, before you pass out," said Times ruthlessly.

Amanda shoved the severed organs into her mouth. She chewed for a brief second, before attempting to swallow. The bloody eyes became lodged in her throat. She grabbed her neck, and gasped for air. She tipped over, and fell on her left side. She convulsed; and choked to death on her own blood, and severed optical systems. Pus, vomit, and blood, slowly oozed from her mouth. There was a huge bulge in her neck, where the remains of her eyes were stuck. Her face was swollen. Her hands were bloodied. Blood streamed from her gaping recital muscles. Her dead body lay sprawled on the floor. It twitched slightly. Times turned and looked at Webster, who was utterly pale with fear. Times walked closer to him.

"Please! Not me!" Webster shouted.

He urinated upon himself while Times approached. Times knelt down next to the cowering, terrified man.

"Men like you, deserve the Hell which they create," Times said.

Times briefly looked over at Amanda's dead body.

"You are products of your own twisted desires. How ironic is it, that your technologies will be your demise? It is amazing to see how quickly your lives, can take a turn for the worse. Unlike ordinary people, you have no humility. You cannot see the folly of your twisted philosophy, until it comes back to rape you one thousand times over. You enjoy the thrill of searching for monsters, do you? Well, congratulations. Now you will be able see a real one," Times said.

20 The Lone Voice

"I can't believe I trusted you! I feel like an idiot!" yelled Sky.

"Sky, calm down. I already told you, I didn't know any of this would happen," said Cameron.

"Why not? Haven't you gotten it through your thick skull, that your actions *hurt* people?" asked Sky.

"It's not what you think. Somebody planned this attack to try and frame us," said Cameron.

"That's not the point. None of this would have happened, if you hadn't been there in the first place!" Sky said.

"No news reports have mentioned any of us by name. We don't even know if they suspect that we were involved," said Cameron.

"They won't announce to the world that they're going to take you out. They're going to kick in your door, and arrest you!" Sky yelled.

The early morning of Monday, January 7th, 2217, was filled with high tension. It had been two days, since the attack at the Statue of Freedom. Corrupt politicians, and their marionette media collaborators, had been relentlessly demonizing the Food Movement since the attack. Government leaders from around the nation praised the Federal Government's creation of a special task force, to deal with the Food Liberationists. The task force's goal was to infiltrate alleged terrorist food cells. They were authorized to arrest, or kill their leaders.

President Cho signed an Executive Order, which legalized the use of ten thousand new combat drones, to patrol streets all across America. The drones consisted of aerial stealth fighters, which used orbital space satellites to spy on every inch of the terrain; humanoid combat infantry armed with powerful laser guns; and mobile crowd control vehicles, like the one used during the Thanksgiving Day massacre.

Sky and Cameron had been fighting all morning. She showed up at 10:13 AM, after Cameron had called her cell phone, forty minutes earlier. He had told Sky he needed to speak with her in person about what happened at the Statue.

"All you had to do was stop going on runs, when you said you would! You could have been out, and avoided this mess!" Sky said.

"You don't understand. I think the attack would have happened, regardless of whether or not we were at the Statue. I think someone planned to kill those people, and blame it on the food movement," Cameron said.

"There you go again, being a conspiracy theorist," said Sky sarcastically.

"How is it conspiracy? The media has been trashing the movement hardcore, since the Thanksgiving incident. They are trying to cover up the fact that their relentless oppression of people, is what led to these violent outbreaks," Cameron said.

Sky said, "Cameron, it doesn't matter. People are dying, and even if it wasn't your fault, the public will turn on the food movement. Most people don't understand the reasons why you fight. Soon, they won't care. All they know is that they are tired of seeing bodies pile up in the street. If you needed any reason to stop–"

Sky was interrupted by a knock on Cameron's door.

"It's unlocked," said Cameron.

The door opened, and Eiji delicately entered the room. Eiji, Lucia, and Vincent, had heard the argument raging for the past twenty-eight minutes.

"Hey. Sorry to disturb you, but Paul just called. He wants us to come by, immediately," Eiji awkwardly said.

There was an uncomfortable silence. Sky gave Cameron a disapproving look.

"I'll be out in a minute," Cameron said solemnly.

Eiji nodded, and quickly left the room. Cameron let out a deep sigh.

"I have to leave. We've finally gotten in touch with Paul and Walter. Thank God, they are safe. I won't be back until later. You can hang out here, or go back to your place. It's your decision," he said to Sky.

Sky folded her arms, and angrily gazed out of Cameron's window.

"I can't believe you're going out there. I don't know if you've heard a word I've said," Sky said.

Cameron walked to her, and put his hands on her shoulders. He stared at her, and then gently used his hand to lift up her chin. He moved closer and tried to kiss her lips. She turned her head away. Cameron looked away from her. He was quite hurt by her rejection.

"Come here," Cameron softly said.

He pulled Sky close and hugged her. At first, Sky did not uncross her arms. But after a moment she started crying, and then embraced Cameron. While they held each other, the two shared a passionate kiss.

"All I want is for you to be safe," said Sky.

Cameron wiped away a tear from her cheek.

"There's nothing safe about this world, Sky," Cameron said.

Sky toughed her demeanor and said, "This doesn't mean that I forgive you. I'm still mad."

"That's fine. All that matters, is that you're still my girl," Cameron replied.

Cameron gently kissed her once more upon her soft lips. He slowly let her go, and left the room. He walked down the hallway and into the main living quarters. Eiji, Lucia, and Vincent, were waiting for him.

"Is everything okay?" asked Lucia in a caring manner.

"Sorry Lucy, but I don't feel like talking right now," Cameron replied.

Lucia nodded her head and respected his wishes.

"Walter said the car should be here soon. I don't know why he didn't want us driving the van," Vincent said.

"It's too risky. Besides, it's safer that we keep the meat separated. There's no telling what could happen over the next few days. No reason to lose the entire stash, if something were to go down," said Eiji.

The team took several belongings, including personal computers and firearms, before going outside. They waited for about fifteen minutes, in the back of their compound. They finally saw Walter's car drive itself up to the building. The team opened the car's doors and entered the vehicle.

"Unidentified occupants. Please produce your credentials," said the car's robotic voice.

Immediately, Lucia inserted a rectangular Carbon Credit card into its ignition. She rebooted the car. She used the blue aerosol spray kept in the glove compartment box, to replicate Walter's fingerprint signature.

"Welcome Walter. There are, zero, passengers in the car. You have approximately 78 Carbon Miles, left on this card. Destination identified. Driving to programmed location," the car said.

Lucia wiped her hand clean with the clear aerosol spray.

"You have no idea how much I hate using that shit! It feels like acid!" she said.

"Thanks for enduring it, Lucy," said Vincent, from the back seat behind her.

Lucia smiled with gratitude. The car began driving to its destination. Eiji shifted around in the passenger's seat.

After a little while Eiji asked, "Anyone feel like listening to some mainstream news?"

"Not really. I hate that government produced bullshit," said Vincent.

"We all do, but I think we should hear the latest developments," said Eiji.

"Relax; we'll be there in less than an hour. I'm sure Walter and Paul will have plenty of updates," said Lucia.

The drive was extremely tense, and unnerving. There was civil unrest in the streets. The team drove past a large protest, near New Brunswick. The protesters were burning effigies of farmers.

"Kill the food terrorists!" they shouted.

Heavily armed combat drones were flying at low altitudes, over densely populated areas. When they got closer to the rural sectors, they saw groups of poor and slovenly people, walking along the roadway. Cameron knew the large group of men, women, and children, were refugees.

"This is getting bad. They must be busting the local resistances. People don't normally travel this far outside of the tent cities without provisions, unless the Feds have raided their communities," Cameron said.

The entire team was extremely disheartened by the suffering which they witnessed. Terrible crimes like looting, robbery, fighting, and arson, were being allowed to run rampant. After another twenty-three minutes, the car approached the unmarked dirt road near the Branson's farm.

"Those guys look like trouble," Cameron said.

He noticed that there was a disheveled group of five men and two women, gathered near the Branson's dirt driveway. Cameron could tell the group did not realize that they were loitering near the private property.

"Pull over," Cameron said.

Lucia overrode the car's auto drive mode. She stopped the car on the side of the road, and parked it about thirty feet from where the group was congregating. Cameron and Vincent looked at each other with concern.

"It looks like they're just hanging out. It doesn't seem like they're casing the farm. Lily would have shot them by now, if they had tried to take the property," Vincent said.

"Call the Branson's and let them know what's happening," Cameron said to Lucia.

Cameron concealed his .45 magnum revolver, and Vincent concealed his 9mm pistol. The duo exited the car, and began walking towards the group. Two of the men saw Cameron and Vincent exit the vehicle. They started walking to meet them by the car. When Cameron and Vincent got close enough to the men, Cameron held out his hand.

"That's far enough," Cameron said.

They all stopped walking. Cameron sensed trouble. This looked like a group of Rouges. Rouges were outlaws that did not live by any sort of moral code. They stole anything they could find. Food, weapons, drugs, and prostitution, ran rampant in their circles. They were not Liberationists, and did not fight for any specific political cause. They were mindless ruffians, whose only goal was the incitement of anarchy. Cameron looked at the nearby shrubbery. The drifters did not notice it, but a small translucent blob, quickly scurried amongst the bushes.

One of the men, a young fellow, said, “Nice car. Is it for sale?”

“You look like you've been out here a while,” Cameron replied.

The second man, a wild-eyed older bloke, said, “Hey, nigger. My buddy asked you a question.”

The rest of the group gave Cameron's whole team, extremely dirty looks. The whole group was Caucasian. It was a well-known fact that various racially oriented gangs had always caused problems in American society. These gangs were very prevalent before the initial collapse in 2184, and they remained a strong counterculture to this day.

However, the collapse did not care about a person's race. People of all nationalities, were economically decimated by America's downfall. The racial gangs were extremely prevalent in the country. They banded together, around their ideals of race purity. There were many different race based gangs, but the most powerful were the Latin and Asian gangs. They believed that integration of the races was responsible for the collapse of society. They were totally ignorant to the fact that a multiracial group of totalitarian oligarchs was responsible for society's breakdown. The younger man pointed to the vehicle, where Lucia and Eiji were still sitting.

“Hey, look at that. They're traveling in a rainbow convoy,” he said.

The gang was unaware that Lucia was using the car's custom built thermal-scanner to check them for weapons.

The younger man looked at Vincent and said, “You look strong, brother. You would make a fine soldier. Why are you hanging around with this mixed bag of colored trash?”

Cameron glanced at Lucia, who gave him a concerned look. Her scanner had detected that some of the group's members, were carrying real firearms. Cameron looked to his right. He saw that the blurry blob had moved closer to the commotion, but was still concealed by the bushes.

Cameron took a deep breath and said, “Look, it's obvious that both our groups are armed. We don't know you, nor do we have any reason to fight. There's a small town, less than a mile from here. It's located past the remains of an abandoned strip mall. They have good food for sale. They'll probably let you stay the night, for a small fee. Keep walking north, until you get to the next exit. Follow the signs, and you'll find it easily.”

“That's a sweet ride. It's rare to see autos on the roads. You all look a little young, to afford a car that expensive. You must be trust fund kids, or something,” the older man said.

Cameron and Vincent noticed that the rest of the gang was approaching their position.

One of the approaching men mockingly said, “Maybe he's nigger rich. On welfare, getting free socialist hand-outs and shit. Did the gub'ment gibb you dat whip, you little house nigger?”

“We don't have time to fuck around with these knuckleheads,” Vincent said to Cameron.

“Yeah, I know,” said Cameron.

“Hey! You'd better watch your mouth, boy! You need to learn some respect, you fucking race traitor!” the older man said to Vincent.

Cameron saw the situation was getting volatile.

“Use rubber rounds, Lily. This asshole isn't worth wasting a good bullet,” Cameron said.

Before any of the men could react to what Cameron said, a loud bang cracked though the air. The younger man was hit in the side of his body, with a non-lethal rubber bullet from Lily's shotgun. The man screamed and fell to the ground in a daze. Cameron and Vincent quickly drew their weapons, and began yelling at the group.

“Next shot is going to be full of real hot lead, motherfuckers! Empty your fucking pockets!” yelled Cameron.

The gang was reluctant to comply.

"You brought this upon yourselves. We fucking tried reasoning with you, but you decided to act ignorant. Now follow his instructions, or else our snipers will light you up like Christmas trees," Vincent sternly said.

The gang begrudgingly threw the meager contents of their pockets, onto the road. The key items produced were, two handguns, two mid-sized pocket knives, assorted bags of illegal narcotics, several single use Carbon Credit cards, and various personal trinkets. Cameron picked up the money, and weapons.

"You can keep the rest of your bullshit. We don't want your junk," Cameron said to the gang.

Cameron knelt beside the man, whom Lily had shot. The young man was groaning. He clutched his side, where the rubber bullet had hit.

"What the fuck is wrong with you? The whole country has turned into a giant cesspit. You want to waste time fighting over meaningless race nonsense? You're a damn moron. That's why you're sprawled out on the side of the road, getting your shit took," Cameron said.

Cameron arose. The gang was surprised when he extended his arm, and offered to help the young man stand. The man briefly hesitated before accepting Cameron's offer, which further shocked the gang. Cameron briefly stared at him.

"Don't come back this way. You understand?" Cameron sternly asked.

The man gave Cameron a nasty look, before directing his gaze to his feet.

"Good. Now get the fuck out of here," Cameron said sternly.

The gang collected their belongings, and walked away. They went the opposite direction of which Cameron had advised. Cameron watched the gang disappear from sight.

"Nice shot. Your contrast settings are a lot better. I didn't see you, until you were almost on top of us," Cameron said.

A blurry blob emerged from the bushes. It dissipated, when Lily deactivated her bulletproof vest's cloaking device.

"Cam, that was so scary! Are you all right?" asked Lily.

She slung her shotgun over her shoulder, ran up, and hugged Cameron around his stomach.

Cameron said, "I'm fine. How–"

Cameron was interrupted by Paul, whose image flashed across Lily's vest.

"What happened, princess? I heard a gunshot," Paul asked with concern.

"Lily had to put a rubber in one of them," said Cameron.

"Were they part of a larger group?" Paul asked.

"Maybe. They looked pretty worn out, but they weren't starving. They might have stable quarters within a few miles' radius," Cameron replied.

"Come by the house when you feel it's safe," Paul said.

Cameron acknowledged Paul's request. He swiped his finger across Lily's shoulders, and the transmission ended. The team waited for another twenty minutes, before Cameron let them drive to the Branson's farm. Cameron walked through the forest with Lily, along the winding dirt path. Cameron was silent the entire time he and Lily were walking.

Lily broke the silence by saying, "You're too quiet."

"I'm sorry. I have a lot on my mind," Cameron replied.

"You seem sad. Everybody has been sad, since Daddy and Uncle Walter came home," Lily said.

Cameron stopped walking, and Lily did the same.

"You're lucky, to have such a strong family. Your parents are *awesome*. They've sacrificed more than you'll ever know. They have risked their lives to make sure you, and your siblings, are safe. I'm sorry that you had to deal with that situation, back there. Believe me you'll see much worse if anyone, especially the government, ever finds out about the farm," Cameron said.

Cameron knelt down, so that he was closer to Lily's height. He put his hands on her shoulders.

"I'm not sure what your parents have told you, about the world outside this farm. You're probably aware of a lot more social issues, than other children your age. I wish I had been home schooled, like you. I was in a government indoctrination center until I was fourteen years old. I dropped out when our teacher made us write a paper, saying why we hate the Second Amendment. She wanted us to explain why it's a good thing that guns are so heavily regulated," he said.

"No matter what happens, or what you hear anyone say, know that your parents are good people. They're *real* people. They are the types of people that made our country great, at one time. They are the types of people, that will take back our Republic," Cameron said.

Cameron stood up, and continued walking. There was another awkward silence.

"Cam, can I ask you something?" Lily abruptly asked.

"Anything," replied Cameron.

"Are we terrorists?" asked Lily.

Cameron immediately stopped walking. He was appalled by the nature of her question.

"Who said that to you, Lily?" Cameron replied.

Lily looked embarrassed, like she had done something wrong.

"I'm sorry. Don't be mad. I heard my mom and dad fighting about it, the other day. They were in the living room. They thought I was asleep, but I snuck out of my room. I was at the top of the stairs, listening to them. She was really mad at him. She said drones are going to kill us, because the United Nations says farmers are terrorists," Lily said.

Cameron was so heartbroken, that at first, he could not reply. He did not know how to explain to a small child, the complexity of the global political situation. There was no way for him to describe the scientific tyranny that had spread throughout America, and the rest of the world. Again, Cameron knelt down.

"Hey, look at me. I don't care what you hear from illegal governments, like the United Nations of Criminals; or FCC controlled propaganda machines, like the Communist News Network and Must Show Nothing But Crap. Farmers are *amazing* people. We are *not* terrorists. I never want to hear you talk like that again, okay?" Cameron reassuringly asked.

Lily nodded her head, acknowledging that she understood Cameron. Cameron arose, and the two resumed their walk. A few moments later, they arrived at the house. Doreen was outside with Paul Jr. and Samantha. Doreen had an exasperated look on her face. Lily put her shotgun on the ground. Doreen rushed up to Lily and began hugging and kissing her; the way any loving mother does, when she is elated to see her child.

"Lily, Daddy told me what happened! Thank God, you are safe!" Doreen said.

While Doreen clutched Lily, Cameron picked up the gun and handed it to Paul Jr.

"Your sis is one hell of a shot. Dude is lucky she used rubber bullets, or else he wouldn't have a torso," he said.

"She has a long way to go, before she can out-shoot me!" Paul Jr. said.

Paul Jr. playfully tapped his younger sister on her back. After a moment, Doreen led the group inside of the house.

"Your friends are downstairs," said Doreen.

Cameron walked down the hallway, and opened a door on the left hand side of the wall. He descended the stairs and saw Lucia, Paul, Walter, Vincent, and Eiji, congregating in the middle of the room.

"Never been more happy to see you two old boys, in my life!" said Cameron to Paul and Walter.

"The feeling is mutual, kid," said Walter.

He walked over and shook Cameron's hand. Paul gave Cameron a nod, and a subtle two finger salute.

After a brief moment of silence Cameron said, "Enough with the sentimental bullshit. What happened out there?"

Paul spoke first, "We were still loading food, when the shooting started. There was no time to get all the packages, onto the ferry. Jennifer got us out in a lifeboat. It is a miracle that we made it back alive."

"After we arrived in Jersey, we were able to catch a train to Bayonne, before the security got heavy," Walter said.

"Not us. We had to use the bus," said Eiji.

"We decided to wait until morning, before moving the goods. We didn't know if we were being followed. We drove back to the compound, and split the food between us. Paul and I drove separate vehicles back to his house. We hid the van in the woods, and stored the food in Paul's greenhouse refrigerator," Walter said.

"We were able to salvage some of the goods, before the shooting started. Eiji had to spill some out at the dock, but he saved our asses," Vincent said.

"Lucia told us you saw something at the dock. What happened?" Paul asked.

Cameron and Vincent looked at each other for a brief moment.

"This really creepy guy in a trench coat, told security that we were trafficking food. This was after he decided to attack me for no reason," Cameron said.

"I went to help Cam, and that's when the guy started accusing us, of smuggling meat," Vincent said.

The group's mood became very somber at this revelation. They all exchanged worried looks.

"He was crazy, and totally whacked out of his mind. He muttered something about not being in control of himself, and asked me why I was so important," Cameron said.

"Those were his exact words?" a confused Walter asked.

"Yeah. It was totally bizarre," Cameron replied.

"What information has come out about the shooting?" Lucia asked.

"Well I don't trust mainstream media, but from what I've been able to piece together from multiple sources; two psycho security guards opened fire on innocent people. They were allegedly part of the Food Movement," Paul replied.

Vincent remembered seeing Times talking to the guards, before the incident occurred.

"That's why Cam wanted to talk with that guy in the first place. He was walking around, speaking to a bunch of guards, right before all this started," Vincent said.

The whole group was deeply troubled by Vincent's revelation.

"This is not good," Eiji said.

"Any theories, Walt?" Paul asked.

Walter paced around the room for a few moments, thinking deeply about Paul's question.

"I really have no idea what to make of this situation. Everything we've discussed seems related; but our evidence is circumstantial. My theory is that it may have been a false flag attack, to demonize the Food Liberation," Walter said.

"What's a false flag attack?" Lucia asked.

"Sometimes when a group wants to demonize their opposition, they will run a coordinated attack, and blame it on the group that they want to vilify. It originates from the old days, when wars were still fought on the high seas. One side would paint up a friendly ship, fly the enemy's flag over the mast, and use it to attack another friendly ship," Walter replied.

"Wow, that's hellishly diabolical. Why would they kill their own people?" Vincent asked.

"Because some folks are absolutely vicious. In fact, the truth about the attack's origin is usually discovered by the public. False flags have been used for thousands of years. One of the biggest false flag attacks in this nation's history, involved using a controlled CIA funded terrorist cell, to hijack airliners and crash them into buildings. It was a heinous crime that also involved rouge elements of British, Saudi, and Israeli intelligence organizations. When I was a kid, we almost went to war with China; when they alleged rouge elements of the U.S. government used heat seeking missiles to shoot down airliners over Hong Kong," Walter said.

"Yes, I remember reading about that, when I was a little girl. That's one of the reasons we had to give them so much of our land. We didn't want an invasion," Lucia said.

"Those Chi-com's have been running false flags against the Japanese people, for years. Some people even think that the typhoon which caused the nuclear disaster, was proliferated by China; to punish us for helping fund the Tibetan revolution," Eiji said.

"Regardless of who attacked the ship and why, they know that organic meat was part of its cargo," Vincent said.

"Yes, and whoever was behind it, may have specifically been targeting us. They were certainly targeting the Food Movement, as a whole," Cameron said.

There was a long and uncomfortable silence.

"So, what's our plan?" Paul eventually asked.

"We have to get rid of the food. It's too dangerous to keep this haul any longer," Walter said.

The outraged team spoke simultaneously.

"We can't do that, Walter!" Vincent said.

"No way, people died for that meat!" said Eiji.

"He's right, it's not safe," Paul said.

"We can't let it go to waste!" said Lucia.

Walter said over the commotion, "I know you all feel passionately, and I hate to pull age rank here, but Paul and I have been doing this a long time. We've seen these types of dirty tricks used in the past. Sometimes, like in any war, there are unavoidable casualties. There's nothing to do but cut our losses and move forward with our mission."

Vincent kicked the floor and loudly said, "Horse shit!"

The group hated the idea of wasting the meat, for which so many had risked their freedom, and given their lives. Cameron paced around the room, rested his right forearm against a wall, and put his head down. His back was turned to his teammates, but he could still hear them arguing.

"There *has* to be an alternative," said Eiji.

"I agree. This is *not* fair," said Lucia.

"You don't understand, I don't feel there's another way," said Paul.

"Send it to a vote. We have that right. We risked our necks for this food," said Vincent.

"You do not understand the bigger picture," said Walter.

Cameron looked over his shoulder. He had heard enough of their bickering.

"Enough! Stop fighting!" Cameron shouted.

The group quieted down.

"I don't agree with him, but Walter's right," Cameron said with exasperation.

"Not surprised by that statement," Vincent muttered.

Cameron turned around and said, "We're all in grave danger. I have a bad feeling about what is happening to the Food Movement."

"I know this is hard, but we can't risk getting captured. We need to stay alive and out of jail, so we can keep helping people," Walter said.

"Exactly. That's why I can't let you all risk getting caught disposing of the meat. I'm getting rid of it, alone," Cameron said.

The group was stunned that Cameron would make such a bold offer.

Paul said, "Cameron. That's really not necessary. We're all—"

"Paul, stop. You have a family to worry about. You and Doreen will be in more than enough trouble, if they ever find your four kids and home garden. Same goes for the rest of you. You've all risked too much, to get tripped up over such a stupid task. Paul, take whatever meat you want for your family. We'll drive the van back to Newark, load some of the food we have at the compound, and I'll handle the rest," Cameron interrupted.

Walter walked closer to Cameron and asked him, "Are you sure about this, Cameron?"

Cameron put his hand on Walter's shoulder.

"It will be dark soon. We should get moving," Cameron said.

Walter placed his hand on Cameron's shoulder, and gave Cameron a look that indicated Walter was proud of him. Thirty-seven minutes later, the team had unloaded Paul's share of the meat from the cargo van, and were about to leave. Vincent, Lucia, and Walter, entered Walter's car. Eiji and Cameron planned to ride in the van. The Branson family was on their front porch, seeing the team off on their journey.

"Be easy, little lady. Remember what I said to you," Cameron said to Lily.

"Bye Cam!" said Lily, while giving him a big hug.

The team traveled back to Newark. Once they reached their compound, the team took their share of the meat, and loaded the rest into the van.

"I don't know whether to thank you, or talk you out of going," Eiji said to Cameron after they finished.

"You know the second one isn't going to happen," Cameron said.

Cameron used Lucia's holographic tablet computer interface, to program the van's GPS route.

"I just finished loading the last of the meat. Damn, I still can't believe you're going out alone, Cam," Vincent said.

"No reason for us all to get busted dumping illegal waste," Cameron replied.

Cameron's team huddled around him. They all solemnly acknowledged his brave decision.

"Be careful, brother," Eiji said.

"Thanks Eiji. I will," Cameron said.

"Okay, no use standing around wasting time. I've got to roll out," Cameron said.

Lucia hugged Cameron and said, "Good luck, hermano."

The rest of his team wished him well, and Cameron left the compound. He was incredibly nervous. The van barreled down the road. Before arriving at his destination, Cameron disengaged the automatic drive, and pulled the van over to the side of the road. He grabbed a large duffel bag which he had brought with him, and stepped out of the van. Cameron steadied his breathing, opened the duffel bag, and removed its contents.

Inside were Cameron's favorite long, black leather jacket, body armor, gloves, an unloaded shotgun, a hand grenade, a small spherical hover video camera, and a very special mask. The grenade was a six inch rectangular box. It could be detonated by flicking a switch on its side, and then holding one's finger against the black thumb scanning panel, on its top. Cameron put on his armor and leather jacket. He got back into the van and drove to his final destination; Sky's apartment complex.

Cameron parked the van in an isolated area near the back of the building. He positioned the van so that it was facing adjacent to a hill, in the back of the apartment complex. The hill led to a small forest, which was the complex's designated Green Zone. Green Zones were sections of urban areas, where limited shrubbery was allowed to grow. All Green Zones had to be approved by the United Nations, and were subject to its regulatory authority. Vandalizing a Green Zone was considered an international crime, and was punishable by life imprisonment.

"You can do this, Cameron," he told himself.

He activated his cell phone, and dialed Sky's number. It rang four times before she answered.

"I'm still mad at you. Can you just leave me alone for a while?" she said.

Cameron tried to hide his feelings of sadness, at her cruel response.

"That's no way to talk to your boyfriend," he arrogantly said.

Sky immediately said, "Cameron, no. Stop saying we're–"

"Listen, I don't have a whole lot of time. I need to tell you, that I am sorry we were never a real couple. I've treated you badly, and I apologize. I've done some really fucked up shit in my life," Cameron quickly interrupted.

Sky did not respond. He saw from the expression on her face, that she was fighting back tears.

Cameron said, "I'm not the type of nigger, that's real good with sentimental speeches. I just want you to know, you're the most special girl I've ever met. You're a phenomenon. A miracle. I...I–"

Cameron lost his confidence, and he also choked up with tears. He wanted very badly to tell Sky how he truly felt.

Instead he simply said, "I'll see you soon."

Cameron immediately hung up his cell phone, and exited the van. He ripped his cell phone off of his wrist, threw it to the ground and stomped on it; until it was shattered to bits on the cold asphalt. Cameron took long and shaky breaths. He strapped the shotgun to his back. He put the grenade inside his coat pocket. He removed his immaculate mask from the duffel bag. Cameron held the beautiful mask in both of his hands.

The color of its metal had been spray painted black. The tinted blue eyes, were made from a pair of modified polycarbonate, mirror coated goggles. The mask had a well-shaped nose and mouthpiece, which formed the shape of a diamond. The entire mask was contoured to fit the shape of Cameron's face. It had three straps fashioned to its side that held it in place when he clamped them around his head. He had never appreciated how much work Walter had put into making the mask, until this moment. On the fifth anniversary of their team's founding, Walter had given his friends, custom masks. Cameron's hands stopped shaking, and his breathing slowed. He placed the mask upon his face, and fastened its straps. Cameron opened the van's back door. He began throwing the suitcases full of meat onto the ground.

He noticed two black females talking to each other near the back of the building, but they did not see him. One lady was wearing a brown coat, and gray jeans. The other girl was dressed in a stylish, pink cotton jumpsuit. It took Cameron only eight minutes to unload all of the suitcases. After the suitcases were removed, he opened three of them, and placed some meat inside the empty duffel bag. He looked up into the night sky. He saw the faint outline of a triangular drone, flying many miles above his position. He extended his thumb so that it covered his line of sight to the drone.

"Yeah, I see you motherfucker," Cameron said to himself.

Cameron pressed the clear plate of glass on the camera's iris, and it illuminated.

"Here we go," said Cameron.

He tapped twice upon the glass. The camera projected a holographic display, in front of its iris. Cameron quickly used a fake internet ID, to access a popular deep web video sharing site. Cameron configured the camera's settings, to upload the video's stream to the website in real time. He sent electronic mail messages to other dummy accounts, which his friends used to communicate. Cameron tapped twice against the iris, and the holographic display vanished. Cameron was now broadcasting live to the entire digital world!

"I don't know if I'll be alive when this is finished recording. Hopefully I'll complete my mission, before my time on Earth is over," Cameron said.

He twirled his thumb around a small panel that was located on the camera's top. Cameron slowly released the camera from his palm. It began hovering in mid-air. It was eye level with him, and remained two feet away from his face.

"I've set this video to run a little over ten minutes. I know you all have a short attention span out there in internet land, but *please* pay attention!" said Cameron.

Cameron picked up the duffel bag with his left hand. He swung the shotgun around, so he could hold it steady with his right hand. He began jogging towards the two women that were standing outside of the building. The camera followed him across the terrain. This was one of the only times Cameron could remember, that he did not fear being followed by a flying drone. The woman in the pink jumpsuit saw that Cameron was running in her direction.

"What the fuck is that nigger doing? That nigger came out of nowhere!" she said to her friend.

"I don't know. Why is he wearing a mask?" the friend replied.

Cameron got closer, and the woman in the brown jacket saw he was carrying a shotgun.

"Oh shit, that nigger's packing heat!" she yelled.

Cameron heard the panic in her voice.

"Calm down! I'm not a jacker! Don't call the cops!" he shouted.

Cameron stopped running, and shifted the gun to his back. He threw the duffel bag on the floor, and it landed a few feet away from the women.

"Nigger, get the fuck out of here!" screamed the woman in the pink jumpsuit.

Cameron quickly put his hands in the air, and attempted to reason with them.

"Listen, listen! I'm not going to hurt you! I'm here to give you free food! It's organic, no lie! I'm not bullshitting you!" Cameron said.

The two women looked at each other with confusion. Cameron was glad that he had caught their attention.

Cameron broke the silence by saying, "I'm not going to shoot you. Check the bag, please."

He laid down his gun. The woman in the brown coat nervously approached the bag. She opened it and saw that it was filled with a whole duck, two alligator filets, a slab of wild boar, and a small quail. All the meat was neatly wrapped in plastic cellophane!

"How the fuck..." said the woman.

She motioned for her friend to come over, and look inside the bag. The woman in the pink jumpsuit cautiously approached her friend.

"I don't have time to explain. Text your friends in the building. Tell them there are suitcases full of fresh meat, outside that van," said Cameron.

He picked up his gun. He saw the camera's holographic timer, indicated that it only had six minutes and twenty seconds left of recording time.

"What are your names?" Cameron asked the women.

"Tamikea," said the woman in the brown coat.

"Mikala," said the woman in the pink jumpsuit.

"Okay. Tamikea, Mikala, say 'hi' to the world. You're on a live internet broadcast, right now. I need you two lovely ladies, to help me do something incredible!" said Cameron.

"Nigger, who are you?" asked Mikala.

"That's not important. The only thing that matters is that you *share!* Set up a grill, and have a barbeque. Make sure everyone gets a plate. You can do this, ladies. You can help me save these people!" yelled Cameron.

He secured the gun around his body, so that it was spread across his back, with its muzzle pointed at the ground.

"I have to leave. God bless you both," Cameron said.

He swiftly bolted away and ran into the building. The two women looked at each other, for only a split second.

"You heard him, girl. Let's help that crazy ass, mask wearin' nigger!" Tamikea excitedly said to Mikala.

The two women started typing feverishly into their holographic cell phones. They sent text messages to their friends, informing them about the food. After they finished, they quickly ran towards the suitcases full of meat. Cameron raced through the building's first floor, and banged on the tenants' doors.

"Free food! Organic meat! Go outside *right now*, if you want to eat!" he yelled.

"Weapon detected! Threat level, extreme! Authorities alerted!" a robotic voice said over the building's intercoms.

Alarms sounded throughout the complex. Cameron ignored the machine, and continued his uprising.

"Food Liberationists are *not* terrorists! The Food Revolution is here! Free organic meat, outside!" he loudly yelled.

Cameron ran through the door at the end of the hallway, and exited to the front of the building. The camera drone flew closely behind him. It recorded his every move, and continued uploading the video stream to the internet. Cameron saw that the police had already pulled their cars in front of the building, and were exiting their vehicles.

"Stop! Terrorist!" a policewoman yelled at Cameron.

"Oh, fuck!" Cameron said to himself.

Cameron ran back through the front door. He saw that people were exiting their apartments.

"Food! Organic! Outside! Go!" he continued yelling.

He pushed past the people, raced upstairs to the second floor, and banged on additional doors.

"Food Liberationists are your friends! Don't believe the corrupt, State-sponsored media! It's all lies!" he shouted.

Cameron reached a split in the hallway's path. He saw police with their guns drawn, entering the corridor.

"Stop! Terrorist! Police!" they yelled.

"Holy shit!" Cameron exclaimed.

He quickly turned left, and raced down the adjacent hallway. A shot rang out, and a bullet clipped the wall in back of him. Sirens from the building's alarm system blared all around him. The halls were starting to fill with people. This gave him the cover that he needed to escape from the cops. He climbed out a window at the end of the hallway. Knowing the building's layout helped him escape. He started descending down the fire escape ladder. He looked up, and saw the police screaming, while they pointed guns at him. He immediately released his grip upon the ladder, and fell towards the ground!

"Ahh!" Cameron screamed.

Cameron twisted his body, so that he would land on his right side. He fell twenty-three feet, and hit the hard cement. He wheezed, and struggled to catch his breath. He forced himself to stand, fight through the pain, and quickly run away. He ran in a jagged manner to disrupt the police's aim. Behind him, he heard shots being fired. Bullets flew by his body, and ricocheted off the ground. They chipped the body armor on his legs. Sky heard the commotion, and exited her apartment building. She hurriedly walked down the hallway, and saw Mrs. Betty Winslow.

"Missus Betty! Are you okay? I heard shooting!" Sky asked.

"Child, you haven't heard? There's a masked man with a shotgun running through the building! He was screaming that he had organic meat! The police are trying to kill him!" Mrs. Betty said.

Sky knew, the only person crazy enough to perform such a bodacious act of rebellion, was Cameron.

"We have to get downstairs," Sky quickly said.

Sky grabbed Mrs. Betty by her hand, and raced towards the stairwell.

Mrs. Betty chuckled and said, "Lord, have mercy!"

Cameron reached the back of the building. He saw that Tamikea and Mikala had kept their word. Mikala was setting up multiple homemade charcoal grills, to cook the meat. Her fellow residents helped her with the task. He saw Tamikea handing wrapped meats to the residents gathered around her.

"Don't push! Act correct, or else we won't feed you! There's enough for everyone! Don't worry, all y'all niggers gonna eat!" Tamikea said.

Cameron shoved his way through the crowd. Several people were startled by his appearance.

"Watch out! I need to get through!" Cameron said.

Cameron climbed atop the van's roof. Cameron saw the killer drone was descending from the air. It was only about ninety yards from his position. Cameron looked at the video drone, which was thankfully still following him. Its holographic clock indicated that he had exactly one minute and fifty-eight seconds, of recording time left. Cameron saw the police were having a tough time moving through the crowd. Hungry civilians blocked their path, and did not let them get close to the van.

"Get the fuck out of here!" yelled an older woman.

"Stay back, and let us eat!" shouted a Caucasian boy, while he stood in front of the police.

"You have no right to stop us!" shouted a teenage black girl.

Cameron took a moment to catch his breath. The video drone hovered in front of his body. All around him, he saw people civilly disobeying tyranny. The smell of charcoal permeated through the air. People orderly walked up to Tamikea and Mikala, and received their piece of real organic food. People shared laughs, while excitedly devouring the meat. Cameron noticed many people recording him on their cell phones. He was sure that footage of his heroic act would reach more people than he could possibly imagine. Cameron savored the beautiful sight, for only a moment.

"Everybody! Quiet down! This is a message from the *real* Food Liberation!" Cameron said.

The entire crowd grew silent, and all eyes focused on Cameron. He wasted no time delivering a heartfelt speech.

"I know the media has been calling us terrorists, ever since the Thanksgiving Day massacre. I assure you, nothing those bastards are saying is true. I ask you, what terror do you see here, tonight? None! These are normal people. They are feeding their neighbors, and helping their friends. These people want nothing more than to eat food which will not kill them!" Cameron passionately said.

The triangular shaped drone continued lowering its altitude. Cameron knew that it wouldn't be long, before it reached him. He looked directly into the camera, and continued his speech.

"They call us murderers, outlaws, and criminals. What crime have we committed? The crime of eating real meat, that won't give us cancer? The crime of sharing a laugh with our family? The crime of socializing with our neighbors? No, we have not committed any crime. The real crime is that our government has oppressed and domesticated us. They have criminalized every form of natural human behavior. They have criminalized human *life*," he said.

There was only forty-one seconds of video left. Cameron saw the killer drone was getting dangerously close.

"Everybody, clear the area! Get back!" Cameron yelled.

He reached into his jacket pocket and removed the grenade. People screamed and moved away from Cameron's van. Out of the corner of his eye, he saw that Mikala and Tamikea were helping move the crowd back to a safe distance. Twenty-eight seconds of video remained on the hovering video camera. The killer drone lowered itself, so that it was eye level with Cameron. The human and the machine stared at each other.

"Terrorist located. Threat level, imminent. Preparing to eliminate," the killer drone said in a cold robotic voice.

Cameron saw the crowd had moved far enough away, and they would not be harmed by what he planned to do next. They were still holding the police at bay. Cameron saw that the video drone only had twenty-two seconds of film remaining. Cameron started slowly walking backwards. He teetered on the van's edge. Cameron knew the drop into the shoddy forest would hurt, but it did not matter. He only cared about the completion of his mission. The killer drone in front of him armed its weapon and readied its hot laser beam. The video drone started counting down the final twelve seconds of its filming life.

"We're not the criminals, or villains. We're not the ones who force you to live in filthy rat holes, stacked on top of one another," Cameron said.

The last eight seconds of video was broadcast to thousands of internet viewers. The frightened apartment complex crowd began yelling at Cameron. They pleaded for him to run away, or give himself over to the authorities. They knew the drone was preparing to kill him. Cameron looked over at Sky, who had pushed her way to the front of the crowd. Cameron armed the grenade.

"We're not the terrorists. We're the motherfucking Icons!" Cameron said with utter conviction.

He skillfully lobbed the grenade upwards. Cameron stepped off the van, and began falling towards the cold, hard ground. The internet world beheld a spectacular sight, while witnessing the final three seconds of Cameron's video broadcast. The killer drone attempted to shoot Cameron with a pulse laser, but it had not planned on Cameron's sudden movement. While Cameron was suspended in mid-air, time standing still; he saw the pulse beam narrowly miss his outstretched body. The grenade exploded and hit the drone with a powerful blast wave! The killer drone was blown away from the van. It flew backwards, and crashed into the street in a spectacular burst of flames!

The blast propelled Cameron hard into the ground. He violently tumbled down the hill. The video drone was incinerated during the explosion. It only captured a split second of the blast, but that was more than enough to powerfully end Cameron's video. For several moments, the crowd screamed and panicked. When they were assured that no one was injured, they let out a triumphant cheer! Some spectators rushed to the decimated killer drone, and began stomping it into the ground. The police were helpless to contain the crowd. People pushed them backwards. Some were menacing them with bats, and other homemade weapons. Residents ordered them to leave the building, and the police were forced to oblige.

Cameron crashed against a tree at the hill's bottom, and fell unconscious. He laid there motionless, and was unaware that his video was being shared by thousands of people. By the time morning came, the video would have reached millions. The barbeque continued throughout the night. Sky and everyone else, ate until there was no food left.

Cameron was unaware that several hours later, Gregory Times watched a replay of the entire incident; from Webster's lavish New York City office. Times finished eating an organic chicken leg, and threw the bone at Webster's foot.

Times smacked his lips and said, "A very amusing show."

He licked his fingers, and arose from Webster's office chair. The lab rats, which Times had already allowed to gnarl off the toes on Webster's right foot, scurried to the discarded chicken leg. Times stood over Webster. He knelt down, and pressed the broken bone protruding from Webster's right shin, inward. Webster screamed in pain.

"I believe it is time for us, to share our gift with the world. Any objections?" Times manically asked.

Times pushed the bone deeper. He smiled widely, when Webster's cries grew more anguished. Times stood up, and licked his bloody fingers.

"That's what I thought," Times callously said.

The rats continued eating the discarded food, and were temporarily turning their attention away from Webster's foot. Times walked over to the desk, picked up the mask, and placed it upon his face. It fit perfectly over the headband, which he had not removed since stealing it from Webster. Times used the changer to manipulate his voice.

Times said in a cold raspy tone, "Now, the real horror begins."

21 To Punish, And Avenge

"Good Morning, I'm Mei Jia. It is Wednesday, January ninth, 2217. The nation is in shock this morning. Disturbing events depicted on a video recorded late last night, are spreading like wild fire via internet media," said the young female Chinese reporter.

"I'm Chao Bo. You're watching Chinese News America. The unsettling footage shows an armed masked terrorist, running around a New Jersey apartment complex, distributing what appears to be a massive quantity of illegal organic food," said the young male Chinese anchor.

"Even more distressing, was the reaction by some of the apartment's tenants. They can be seen on camera, assisting the masked terrorist with dispensing the meat, and clashing with local police. It is not yet clear, if those tenants are part of a larger terrorist sleeper cell," Mei Jia said.

"No one was injured during the assault. The armed offender, with the assistance of collaborating extremists, destroyed a Neighborhood Aerial Protection Unit during the attack. We are going to show you an excerpt from the video. Please be warned, it is graphically violent," Bo said.

The news channel played a brief video clip, from Cameron's late night food distribution rebellion. The clip showed the killer drone exploding. Gregory Times watched the newscast on a holographic projector. He had placed it in the room which Webster had previously used to imprison Times. Webster was strapped to the bed and writhing in agony. Times sat by his side eating an apple.

"Law enforcement officials have not yet ruled out the possibility, that the attack was connected with Saturday's massacre at the Statue of Freedom," said Mei Jia.

Webster groaned, and feebly said to Times, "Greg...my leg...it hurts."

Times looked at Webster's leg. The area where he had sustained his injury was swollen, discolored, and oozing pus.

"Doesn't look too bad to me. I suppose if it's bothering you, I could have it fixed," Times casually said.

Times waved his hand in front of the projector to turn off its power. He pulled his chair closer to Webster's bed.

"All right, old man. Let's talk," said Times.

Webster bit his lip nervously, while staring at him. Times grinned devilishly, and enjoyed his dominance.

"First, I want to commend you on your recent stroke of good will. It was very nice of you to transfer command of your robots and automobiles to me. It was also quite generous to give all your employees a paid vacation, until further notice. I'm sure they understand that Rigor needs some time, to work out its management issues. I'm proud of you, Webster. I really feel you've matured as an individual," Times said.

Times patted Webster's chest with his hand, and gave him a pompous smirk.

"Gregory, please. I'm sorry for everything I've done. What do you want? I'll give you anything you desire," he said.

"Oh, I know you will. There are a few more tasks which I need you to complete, before I allow your suffering to end. Mallory still has not left your private quarters. She is a prisoner of her own free will. That ends today. After I get your leg fixed, I'll need you to help me make some modifications to the device. After that is completed, you will be free to leave. Understand?" Times said very seriously.

"I...I understand," Webster feebly said.

"Good! I'll summon Alice and Chem-Mech," Times said.

Times pressed several buttons on his cell phone. Webster's machines had installed an application on it, which was used to control the robots. A few minutes later, the robot Alice and the Chem-Mech brought a wheelchair and blanket to the room. Alice and Chem-Mech unstrapped Webster from the bed, and placed him in the wheelchair. They covered his legs with the blanket. The Chem-Mech injected Webster with a pain killing drug.

"I did some research on your personal finances. With an estimated net worth of over 2.3 billion Carbon Credits, I believe it is safe to say that you're a very wealthy man," Times said.

Times tapped another button on his cell phone, which opened the Chem-Mech's chest compartment. Inside was a plastic Carbon Credit card, and Webster's cell phone.

"You are going to fill this card, with approximately 1.8 billion Carbon Credits. You will place the card in Mallory's name, and label it unconditionally confidential, so that the bank will not question the transfer. You will classify the transaction as a personal injury lawsuit settlement; to fully ensure there is no dispute," Times said.

Webster begrudgingly took the card and cell phone from Chem-Mech's chest compartment. A few minutes later, he had fulfilled Times' request.

"Very good. You can take him to see her," Times said to the robots.

Webster said, "Gregory, you won't get away with extort–"

Times furiously slapped Webster across his face, which stopped him from speaking. Times clutched Webster's jaw, between his thumb and fingers.

"How *dare* you claim to be a victim! How many people have you tortured? Killed? You have no one to blame for your misery, except yourself!" Times said.

After staring at Webster for a brief moment, Times released his grip, and turned away from Webster.

"Get him upstairs, before I kill him," Times angrily said.

The robots began taking Webster to see Mallory. Times closely followed them, and carried the mask in his left hand. He monitored a video feed that Alice was projecting from its head camera. He closely watched Mallory, laying upon Webster's large bed. The men and machines, used the elevator and rode it to a higher floor, where Webster's private penthouse was located. They walked through the lavish living space, until they reached the bedroom area.

"You will give her a sincere apology, for the Hell through which you've put her," Times said to Webster.

Webster nodded, and the robots wheeled him into the room. Times put on his mask, and waited around the corner. He was hidden from their sight, but was able to hear every word. Mallory was laying on the bed, and was curled up in a ball.

"Missus Times, may I speak with you?" Webster asked.

Mallory did not respond. She rustled in the bed, and pretended to be asleep. Webster cleared his throat.

Webster said, "I don't blame you for being upset; but if I could just have a moment of your–"

"What kind of sick demon are you?" Mallory interrupted.

Mallory slowly sat upright and faced Webster. She looked at him with deep distress in her eyes.

"What have you done with my husband?" asked Mallory.

Webster winced. He heard Times' voice, telepathically direct his response.

"Gregory is dead. I killed him, with my own hands," he was forced to say.

Mallory covered her mouth, and choked back tears. Webster handed Mallory the Carbon Credit card.

Webster said, "Please. Take this card–"

"HOW DARE YOU!" screamed Mallory.

She furiously slapped the card from Webster's hand. Times used his telepathy to subtly calm Mallory's emotions.

"Shh...It's all right. Everything will be okay. Take the card," Times whispered.

Even though Mallory did not hear Times' voice as audible words, she slowly started calming down.

"I...am sorry. I don't know what else to say," Webster said.

Webster actually showed real emotion. His eyes swelled with tears, and he started whimpering. After a moment, Mallory picked up the card.

"You are a very sick man. I don't know what you did to my husband. But don't think your money, is going to stop me from having you arrested for murder," Mallory said.

Webster put his head down and said, "The Chem-Mech will show you the way out. Please, forgive me."

He continued blubbering, and wiped away a few of his tears. Mallory spit on Webster, before storming out of the room. Times did not allow Mallory to see him when she left. Times remained far away from the door, and once again subtly used his powers to manipulate her.

"Keep walking. Go home," Times whispered.

Times heard her exit the penthouse. He became overwhelmed with sorrow, and began crying. His tears stained the inside of the mask. After a moment, Times composed himself and entered the room. Webster was sobbing profusely.

"Please! I did what you wanted! Let me go!" Webster said.

"Indeed. You followed your instructions quite well. We should go fix that leg. Alice, subdue him," Times said.

The robot Alice used its robotic claw to inject Webster with a powerful sedative. Webster was rendered unconscious.

Webster awoke, and saw that he was strapped to an operating table. The Chem-Mech and the robot Alice, were performing various medical tests, and monitoring Webster's vital signs. Times stood at the end of the table. His frightening mask was devoid of emotion.

"Oh God, no! What are you doing?" Webster asked.

"Fixing your leg, my friend," Times said.

Webster looked to his right, and was horrified to see a portable electric saw resting upon a tabletop counter.

"Please, no more! We're even!" Webster screamed.

"Even? How are we, *even?*" Times asked.

Times picked up the saw, turned it on, and began walking towards Webster.

"You have over one billion credits, for piss sakes! You can take the money, and leave me alone! No one will ever know what happened to you!" shouted a frantic Webster.

"Money is important; but power, is the true goal of a successful man. *You* taught me that, old friend. You sought to have this power for yourself. You made me, and my family, your guinea pigs. Your *arrogance* made you lose your power. I won't make the same mistake," Times coldly said.

Times started lowering the saw to Webster's right leg. The saw began tearing through Webster's appendage, just below his knee. Webster howled in tremendous pain. The bone crunched when it was sliced. The surrounding meat was cut clean. Blood sprayed in every direction. Webster passed out from the trauma, while Times finished severing the limb.

"Make sure he doesn't bleed out, then chain him back to the bed," Times told the robot Alice, and the Chem-Mech.

Times left the room, and went to change his bloody clothes. After he changed, he went to the garage, and entered Webster's limousine.

"Three twenty-eight, Bleecker Street," Times said.

"Route acknowledged," said the limousine's artificial interface.

The vehicle left the parking garage, and Times stared out of its darkly tinted windows. Times reflected on the events which had occurred over the past few months. He focused on the tragedy that had befallen Mallory and himself. Surprisingly, he did not feel any sadness. Times only felt a cold lust for revenge. The view from the limousine, reminded Times of the disconnect between society's classes. He saw people huddled around burning garbage cans, in areas of New York like Broadway; which had once been thriving centers for tourism, and employment.

The buildings were now mostly condemned. The few remaining businesses were guarded by a militarized New York City police force. Drones flew area patrols. Street cameras on lamp posts barked orders at passing citizens. One young woman threw an empty candy bar wrapper towards a garbage can. She missed the receptacle. While she was bending over to pick up the wrapper, a robotic voice from the trash bin's audio device spoke to her.

"Carbon violation. Improper waste disposal detected. Issuing fine," said the receptacle's robotic voice.

"No! Wait, dammit! I missed by accident!" the woman said.

Her plea for leniency went unfulfilled. The garbage can sent a text message to her cell phone. She checked her phone, and saw that she had received a citation for 189 Carbon Credits.

"Son of a bitch," the woman said.

She carefully placed the wrapper into the receptacle. During the ride, Times had over an hour to think about the decision which he was about to make. Times was preparing to embark on a journey that would forever alter the course of his life. He knew there was no way of returning to his world of blissful ignorance. His eyes had been opened to a truth so startling, that it shook him to his very core. He had seen a glimpse of the deeply sadistic elites that controlled society.

They were wealthy, powerful, and were indifferent to human suffering. The limousine pulled into the parking garage of the United World Hospital. Times prepared himself for his mission, by looking at several pictures on his cell phone. He looked at photos of Mallory and himself, during their happier days. When he was ready, he turned off the cell phone's holographic projection by closing his palm.

Times had the limousine park itself in an isolated spot, near the back of the hospital's garage. Times opened a small box that he had previously placed on the back seat. Inside was Webster's mosquito drone. Times activated the drone, by pressing a small button on the top of its small robotic head. He held the drone against the limousine's window. The words, "Synching devices," displayed.

A green progress bar spread across the window. After the devices had been synchronized, Times engaged its manual flight mode.

Times tossed the drone out of the window. He began flying it around the building, using a brainwave interface that he controlled with his headband. He flew through the reception area, and landed the drone on the directory kiosk. Times saw that the Child Enforcement Agency was located on the hospital's third floor. He flew the drone high, near the ceiling. Patrons and hospital staff were completely unaware of its presence. The drone hitched a ride on a nearby elevator. Times pricked an unsuspecting nurse, who was already inside, with the drone's needle. The mind control serum infected her.

"Three," Times telepathically whispered to the nurse.

The woman felt a sudden chill shoot through her body. She pressed the button, and then shook her head. The chill went away, and the woman was not harmed. She was confused as to why she had the compulsive urge to press a button for a floor to which she was not going. The doors opened, and the mosquito drone flew away completely undetected. Times flew the drone through the CEA's main office doors.

Times selected one of the several armed CEA enforcers in the office, as his first target. Times used the drone to prick the enforcer in his neck. Times was disgusted by the enforcer's militarized appearance. The enforcers had semiautomatic sub-machine guns strapped to their chests, and 9mm pistols were fastened to their legs. Times found it abhorrent that these professional hit-men were allowed to use deadly force, to uphold the One Child Mandate.

"Find the most senior officer," Times telepathically commanded the enforcer.

The enforcer was in obvious discomfort, and was not sure why he was hearing Times' voice. He was disturbed that he was being forced to follow Times' instructions. Times used the enforcer to locate the floor's senior officer. The official was in his office watching pornography on his holographic computer. Times quickly jabbed him in the side of his neck, with the drone's needle. The lower level enforcer stood drooling in front of the senior officer's desk.

"Sir. There are...have been...possible threats..." he said to the senior officer.

"Threats made...against correction doctors. I...know. Must...secure area," said the obviously dazed senior officer.

Times instructed the two men, to discretely lock the CEA office's front doors. Once they were locked, Times made the senior officer use his cell phone to communicate with the other CEA enforcers.

"Possible situation. All units, report to central office," the senior officer said in his voice message.

Times commanded the senior officer to send a textual message, to all active abortion doctors and their assistants, currently working inside the hospital.

"Immediate facility lock-down. Possible terrorists violating OCM," the message stated.

Times then made the senior officer walk to the elevator. The mosquito drone landed on the officer's shoulder. The senior officer entered the elevator and went to the hospital's sixth floor, where the main security headquarters resided. Three nurses and four doctors received the message which the senior officer had sent, a few moments ago. The staff went to the CEA's main office. Once the group was assembled, Times made the low level enforcer unlock the door, and lead the hospital staff into the CEA's command center. The low level officer locked the door after the group was inside.

"What is the meaning of this nonsense? I was in the middle of a video conference with United Nations diplomats! Why are we being detained?" the senior doctor asked.

"Sir...move to back room...many threats made," the low level enforcer clumsily said.

The senior level doctor said, "I don't care what threats–"

"I SAID MOVE!" the low level enforcer shouted.

He pointed his semi-automatic rifle at the senior level doctor.

"Your superiors will hear about this atrocity!" the doctor said.

The group began walking to the CEA's main abortion room. The abortion rooms were described by many whistle blowers, as chambers of horrors. The rooms contained numerous tools of inequity, like scissors, pliers, and abortion inducing vaccines. One of the most disturbing items, were buckets of water. Babies were routinely tossed in these buckets and drowned, when they were aborted late in their mother's term. Despite numerous lawsuits, and sometimes violent protests, the One Child Mandate was strictly enforced in America. For many, it was the ultimate confirmation that the formerly great Constitutional Republic was now completely governed by Communist law.

The senior enforcer reached the sixth floor with no trouble. Times made the mosquito drone wait at the top of the elevator. The doors opened and the enforcer was greeted by a giant, weaponized robot. The robot had a large, oval shaped head. Its arms were equipped with two circular laser Gatling guns. It had a medium-sized body frame, which resembled a human torso. Its legs bent forward at the knees, and its feet were big, square-shaped bricks.

"DNA required to proceed past this point. Confirm identity," the robot said.

Times made the senior enforcer hold out his right arm. The robot used the camera mounted on its head, to take a full holographic body scan of the senior level enforcer. From its chest compartment, the machine extended a robotic arm equipped with a needle. The needle pricked the senior level enforcer, and drew his blood. The arm retracted into the drone's chest. After a moment, the robot projected a holographic image with its camera head, and displayed the man's credentials.

"Thomas Mason, age forty-nine. Access level: HIGH. State your business on this floor," the robot said.

"Threat...abortion doctors. CEA facility lock-down. Authorization code, M dash twenty-four," Thomas said.

"Good. You're handling this quite well," Times said from the limousine.

The mosquito drone quickly flew past the giant robot, and hovered high near the ceiling.

"Authorized. Limited access is now granted to this floor. Access permit expires in seventeen minutes," the robot said.

Times made Thomas walk to the large desk in the middle of the floor. There were two armed security guards sitting behind the desk. There was a series of computer terminals, and security camera monitors, all around the desk.

"What brings you up here, Tom?" asked one of the guards.

Times used the mosquito drone, to prick the guard's neck that spoke to Thomas. The prick was quick, and precise.

The second guard started to say, "Everything all–"

Times pricked the second guard's neck, and he did not finish his sentence.

Times made Thomas whisper, "Disable everything. Get that robot first."

The two guards briefly looked at each other. They began manually overriding all the cameras, microphones, security systems, and robots, inside of the hospital.

The robot began saying, “Unauthorized override. Disengaging–” before it was disabled by the security guards.

Times made Thomas say, “Follow me, after you're done disconnecting the grid.”

The guards obediently followed Times' commands. When they were finished, Thomas and the armed guards took the elevator down to the parking garage. They walked to an ambulance, parked not far from the limousine. Thomas and the two guards opened the back of the ambulance, removed a rolling stretcher, and a thin white sheet. Times exited the vehicle.

“Took you long enough,” Times arrogantly said.

Times was wearing his mask, purple trench coat, gray pants, and brown leather gloves. Times laid upon the stretcher, and made the guards cover him with the white sheet. Times instructed the men to roll the stretcher inside of the elevator. The group traveled to the third floor, and entered the CEA's main office.

There was a total of four doctors, three nurses, two hospital security guards, and four CEA enforcers; in the CEA's abortion room.

“Who is that, on the stretcher?” asked a female nurse.

“Why is he covered? Is he hurt?” asked a female doctor.

“You had better have a good reason for detaining us,” said the angry senior level doctor.

“Sir, what threat has been made against the organization?” asked one of the security guards.

“You're a chatty agglomeration of murderers,” said Times in his intimidating deep raspy voice.

Times sat upright in the stretcher. The sheet was still covering his body, and face. Times slowly stood up, and pulled away the sheet. The room let out a collective gasp of horror, when they saw Times' terrifying mask!

“Freeze!” said one of the CEA enforcers.

The CEA enforcers not under Times' control drew their weapons, and pointed them at Times.

“Gentlemen, put your little toys DOWN!” Times said.

As Times finished his sentence, he used his mind control technology to create the tremendously painful ringing sensation in their ears. They dropped to their knees, and covered their ears with both hands. Their guns fell from their hands, and the two enforcers spoke simultaneously.

“Holy *fuck!*”

“Make it *stop!*”

Times walked over to them and picked up their guns. He put one gun in his inner coat pocket, and held the other one in his hand. Times looked at Thomas, the low level CEA enforcer, and the two armed security guards.

“I'll take yours too,” Times said to them.

Times waved his gun at the stretcher. The guards tossed all their weapons onto the stretcher. Times briefly marveled at the impressive array of sub-machine, and hand guns.

“Please, don't hurt us!” a frightened nurse said.

Times ignored her and said, “I've never used one of these. I had to read internet articles, to learn how they work.”

Times looked at the gun, and located its safety latch. Times pressed the latch, and the safety switched off. Times racked the gun, so that a bullet was placed in the chamber. Times held the gun up to the ceiling, and stared down its sights.

"Fascinating," said Times.

After a moment, Times quickly aimed the gun at Thomas and fired a shot into his face! The bullet tore through Thomas' right cheek, and exited out the back of his skull. Thomas dropped dead to the floor. All the nurses began screaming. One doctor vomited.

"My God, why did you kill him?!" another doctor asked.

"Everyone be *quiet!*" Times yelled.

He used the mask's audio device, to send a shock-wave through the entire room. He momentarily caused everyone except himself, to hear the horrible ringing sound in their ears. Several people dropped to their knees. After a moment all Times heard, was sobbing from crying people. The doctors and nurses huddled together, and tried to comfort one another.

"Much better," said Times.

"What do you want? Money? Drugs? Please, take whatever you want, just don't kill any more people!" a whimpering doctor said.

Times knelt close to the woman.

"How many years have you worked here?" Times asked her.

"A little over four years," the doctor nervously said.

Times began asking her, "How many..."

He briefly choked up, while remembering his own forcibly aborted children.

Times finished his question, "How many procedures, have you performed in those four years?"

"Fifty-one thousand, two hundred and seventy-eight," the doctor meekly replied.

"You *monster!* You've murdered over fifty thousand children, in four years?!" Times said with disgust.

The doctor began sobbing and said, "You don't understand, some of them needed–"

Times slapped the woman across her face.

"Save your crocodile tears!" Times said.

Times noticed that doctor was a colored woman.

"It's even more shameful for someone like you, to be a part of this genocide. How many of your own people, have you killed?" Times asked.

"I don't know!" the frantic doctor replied.

"How many?!" Times loudly yelled.

"Please, I don't know!" the doctor responded.

The doctor cried profusely. Times lightly clutched her neck. His unforgiving mask, sent chills down her spine.

"Did you know that over fifty-two percent of black babies are aborted? You contribute to the mass murder of your own people; and then have the nerve to ask that I spare your life. You're pitiful," Times said.

Times released the woman's neck, stood up, and looked around the room. He focused on a young male nurse. The man was clenching his hat in his hands. It was a dark black fedora hat, with a gray stripe around its rim.

"You're a nurse, son?" Times asked.

"Yes, sir," the male nurse feebly said.

"What's the matter? Couldn't cut it as a doctor? Nurses are traditionally female. Are you a faggot?" asked Times.

The puzzled male nurse said, "I don't see what–"

"Shut up! It doesn't matter. Your crimes against the unborn, not your perverse bedroom behaviors, are what has brought you judgment this day," Times interrupted.

Times grabbed the fedora hat, and placed it upon his head. He adjusted the hat, and then his trench coat's collar.

"Looks rather good on me. Don't you agree?" Times smugly asked.

The male nurse did not reply. Times looked at the low level enforcer, of which he had originally taken control.

"Look around the room. Find me alcohol, a large bag for the guns, oxygen, and nitrous oxide tanks," Times said.

The black doctor grew terrified and said, "Oh my God. What are you planning?"

"I am going to perform a little procedure of my own," Times replied.

One of the CEA enforcers said, "You have to sto–"

Times became enraged. He created the painful ringing in the man's ears, and prevented him from speaking.

"Haven't you learned that you're *not* in control of this situation?" Times angrily asked.

Times then asked the crowd, "Which one of you can upload streaming videos to the internet, like that fellow on the news today?"

The crowd was silent. They dreaded his dastardly intentions.

"No one? I find that hard to *believe!*" Times said.

Times made everyone, except the low level enforcer gathering the supplies, hear the painful ringing.

"I can! I can!" a middle aged blonde nurse eventually said.

Times made the ringing stop and said, "Good. Get it ready. You will start recording when I tell you."

The frightened blonde woman activated her cell phone's camera, and signed into a video sharing web site. The low level enforcer finished gathering all the supplies.

"Douse them, and yourself," Times said.

The enforcer began pouring alcohol over all the people in the room. He then doused the tanks with the alcohol.

"Open the tanks," Times said.

The enforcer twisted the nozzles. The compressed chemicals were released into the air.

"This guy is fucking *crazy!* Somebody please help us!" screamed the senior level doctor.

Times kicked the doctor in his testicles. The doctor howled in immense pain.

"You may begin," Times said to the blonde nurse.

The blonde nurse, her hands trembling with fear, pressed a holographic button on her cell phone. She pointed her open palm at Times, and began recording. Times looked directly into the camera, and began speaking.

"The One Child Mandate, is one of the most abhorrent provisions of the Carbon Tax Law. Today we are going to learn a few facts, about the reality of abortion," Times said.

Times began walking around the room. He addressed the different groups.

To the doctors, Times said, "You pervert science. You are rapists of women, and murderers of children. You play God, like mad scientists."

To the nurses, Times said, "You assist with these Hellish practices. You are not like the honorable caregivers, who help the weak, and infirm. Instead you proliferate suffering, and deliver death."

To the CEA enforcers, Times said, "You follow illegal orders, and enforce draconian laws. You help destroy the innocent lives of decent families. You are nothing but stuttering grunts. You embody the epitome of cowardice."

"You all stand upon rivers of dead children. For this, your souls have been corrupted. I have no doubt you will eternally burn, in the bowels of Hell," Times said to the group.

Times looked at the black female doctor and said, "Tell us, doctor. What was your preferred method of killing?"

The doctor wanted to remain silent, but the fear of being tortured by the horrible ringing in her ear, made her speak.

"Scissors. I had to perform a lot of the operations, with scissors," she nervously said.

"That sounds crude," Times said.

Times walked over to a medical operating tray. He picked up a pair of scissors, and threw them on the ground, near the doctor. Times grabbed one of the CEA enforcers by his collar, dragged him over to the doctor, and forced him to lay on his stomach.

"A demonstration," said Times.

The doctor covered her mouth in horror. She knew what Times was commanding her to perform.

"Oh, God. No..." the doctor muttered.

"Please, I insist," said Times cold heartedly.

The CEA guard began crying, and looked at the doctor.

"I don't want to die!" he told her.

"I'm sure those little babies felt the same way. Have you read the stories, about these abortion clinics? Babies, not able to talk or walk, will fight for their lives when they realize they are about to die. Babies have been observed on ultrasound, while still in utero, attempting to move away from the suction tube which eventually rips their tiny bodies apart. Nurses have reported that skinless infants are yanked out of their womb, at four months old. They flop around the table on which they've been placed, and make horrific screaming sounds with their small, undeveloped mouths. Right in this room, babies are dropped in buckets of water. They thrash wildly; in a heartbreaking and vain attempt at swimming to safety. You have all supported these atrocities. Now please, doctor. Show us your procedure, and explain how it works," Times said.

The CEA enforcer and doctor were both crying.

"Kiss the floor, asshole," said Times to the CEA enforcer.

The sobbing enforcer placed his face, flat against the ground. He tucked his arms underneath his chest.

"I would remove the specimen by its feet. I left the head partially inside the birth canal," the crying doctor said.

The doctor picked up the scissors. She grabbed the enforcer's head, to hold him steady.

"I would, oh sweet Lord...I would take the scissors, and insert them into the base of its neck, to sever the spinal cord!" the doctor said.

While finishing her sentence, the doctor shoved the scissors through the back of the enforcer's neck. He flopped around violently. Blood spurted from the back of his head. The entire room was wailing, and in tears at this point.

"Is that all?" Times coldly asked her.

"Oh please, NO MORE!" yelled the doctor.

"I asked you a question," said Times.

The doctor whimpered, and grabbed the officer's bloody head. The officer was still twitching. She grabbed the scissors' handles.

"To complete the...God help me...process...I would pull the scissors apart, like *this!*" she said.

While speaking her last word, she pulled the scissors handles away from each other. A huge gash was opened in the back of the man's neck. Blood splattered everywhere, and the man died in unbearable pain.

"As you can see, that's not a nice way to kill a person. The shameful part is that you've probably never felt any guilt about doing it, until today," Times said.

Times looked at the two security guards from the sixth floor. He pointed at the rolling stretcher.

"Take that, and go wait outside," Times said.

The guards packed up the guns in a large bag, and left the room. Times gazed at the remaining CEA enforcers, nurses, and doctors.

"I feel that you've all learned a valuable lesson today. I think that for the first time in your miserable existence, you've learned the value of human life," Times callously said.

He looked directly at the camera, which the blonde nurse was still holding in her trembling hand.

Times said, "Unfortunately, I don't think your sacrifice here today, is enough to make people fully grasp the magnitude of evil we face in this country. There are those who are still blind to the truly demonic forces, which we allow to ruin our lives. They have unleashed Hell upon our streets. That will all change, soon enough. Soon, we shall make the tyrants pay for their wanton criminality. Soon, the sleepwalking population will be broken from their comatose trance. Soon, a ferocious wave of righteousness will sweep across this defiled nation. Any man, who has but the slightest amount of wickedness in his heart, will tremble in fear of his impending judgment. Soon, like I, you shall all find that we live, IN TROUBLED TIMES!"

The man, who now called himself Troubled Times, slowly raised his shaking fists into the air while finishing his sentence. Troubled Times slowly lowered his arms, and was breathing heavily. Troubled Times turned around, and began walking towards the door. Before he left the room, Troubled Times gave the low level CEA enforcer a handgun.

"Four minutes, then ignite," Troubled Times said to him.

Troubled Times left the room.

He said to the security guards, "Lock them inside," while walking past them.

One of the guards placed his hand on the door's palm scanning panel, and the door locked. Some of Troubled Times' victims rushed over, and began banging on the door. Everyone desperately wanted to escape. Troubled Times laid down upon the stretcher, and covered himself with the white sheet. He instructed the guards to take him downstairs. The scene inside the room was chaotic. Everyone was panicking, and they all began shouting at the CEA enforcer.

"Snap out of your trance!"

"Give us the gun!"

"I'm too young to die!"

The CEA enforcer drooled and mumbled, "Stay...back. Must contain...threat."

He pointed the gun at the helpless group of abortionists, and their collaborators. The blonde nurse began speaking into her camera.

"Goodbye mom, dad, my husband Joey..." she said.

She made what she would knew would be her final remarks in this world, through a heavy stream of tears. The black doctor and young male nurse were hugging each other. They sobbed on the ground, near the mutilated CEA enforcer's dead body. Troubled Times had almost reached the elevator.

He was commanding the security guards to yell things like, "Out of the way! This man has been shot! We need to get him to the ICU, immediately!" so that they could run down the hallway, without arousing suspicion.

They reached the elevator, and pressed the button to open its doors. Back in the room, the yelling continued.

"You don't have to listen to him!"

"You're going to die too! Don't you understand?"

A moment later, the elevator reached the third floor. Troubled Times was wheeled inside by the guards. They ordered everyone out of the elevator. They reset the destination, so that the elevator would not stop at any other floors. They quickly set the elevator, to stop at the ground floor. Inside of the room, the senior level doctor decided he would take his chances.

"Enough of this shit! Give me the fucking gun!" the doctor screamed.

The doctor tried to rush forward, and tackle the enforcer. The enforcer pulled his gun's trigger. The spark from the muzzle, combined with the bullet piercing the nitrous oxide tank, ignited the chemicals in the air. The room exploded with a loud bang. The people inside, began burning alive. Flames and smoke consumed the entire room. The smell of seared flesh filled the small abortion chamber. The screaming would take several minutes to subside. Burned corpses, and flailing bodies, littered the room.

The explosion caught the local hospital staff's attention. Other armed patrol guards raced towards the sounds of chaos. Alarms began ringing throughout the entire hospital. The guards and other doctors were able to gain access to the CEA's main office. They peered through a small window, on the door where the explosion had occurred. They saw one burning person, crawling around on the floor, writhing in pain. The person's skin was melting off of his body. The person was surrounded by an inferno. There were burnt dead bodies, and body parts, spread throughout the room. One doctor began vomiting, after seeing the gruesome sight. A guard spoke into his cell phone.

"There has been an explosion in the CEA central office! Heavy causalities! Send all available personnel to the third floor!" he said.

Troubled Times and his manipulated accomplices reached the parking garage.

"Hurry up, you imbeciles!" he said from beneath the sheet.

The two guards quickly ran to the limousine. The sound of sirens blared in all directions. Troubled Times leapt off of the stretcher, with his bag of guns.

"Sir, what do you wan–"

The guard did not finish his sentence. Troubled Times shot him in his face, with a gun he held in his right hand. Troubled Times was exhausted. He momentarily lost the mental connection with the remaining guard. The guard began snapping out of his daze.

"Wha...holy fuck!" he said.

Troubled Times promptly shot the guard in his chest. Troubled Times threw the bag of guns into the limousine's trunk. Troubled Times entered the vehicle, and swiftly gave it driving directions. The limousine left the parking garage, and started returning to Rigor Pharmaceuticals. Troubled Times removed his mask. He saw helicopters, and combat drones, flying towards the hospital. Armed military personnel raced down the street. The green and black camouflaged Humvees flashed their overhead lights and blasted their sirens. Times looked out the back window, and saw that police were starting to block off the surrounding areas. After the limousine had driven a few blocks, Times pressed the window to his right. He used the car's user interface, to turn on its television.

Times heard a frantic reporter saying, "We have word of an explosion, at the United World Hospital! We are trying to find out how many have been injured! There are at least two people reported dead–"

Times cut the signal to the news feed. While riding in the lavish automobile, a sense of bliss came over him. He reveled in the pandemonium which he had just created. A smile began forming on his face, when he thought about Mallory. Times knew that he could never go back to his old life. The sadness he felt in his heart lasted for only an instant. It was replaced by an unrepentant lust to obtain retribution, and manifold disorder. His transformation into Troubled Times was complete.

22 Without A Home

"The borough of Manhattan is on complete lock-down tonight! I am standing in front of the United World Hospital; which has just been stricken by a terrorist bombing! There are at least seven people confirmed dead–"

Sky Solomon waved her hand in front of the holographic television projector, in the middle of her living room. The device's volume lowered. The hysterical news reporter on the screen was momentarily silenced. Sky frantically dialed the numbers on her holographic cell phone. Cameron did not answer. It had been almost eighteen hours, since she had last spoken with him. It was only three hours after Troubled Times' shocking attack on the United World Hospital. Sky sat down on her small living room couch. She raised the television's volume by once again waving her hand.

She watched the Chinese news reporter say, "At 7:00 PM this evening, the mayor enacted a city-wide curfew. The National Guard has deployed Automaton Safety Units throughout the region. Troops from several allied countries have surrounded the United Nations' headquarters. They have vowed to stop any further acts of terrorism directed at U.N. interests. President Cho has authorized the New York City police, under the National Defense Authority Amendment, to use lethal force against anyone violating curfew. Several riots have broken out in all five boroughs. Protesters are burning down portions of neighborhoods–"

Sky once again lowered the television's volume. Watching the tyrannical power grab by State and Federal governments, made her feel nauseous. Sky's cell phone rang. The caller identification displayed the words, "UNKNOWN." She answered the call. A scrambled image comprised entirely of static, rendered itself in Sky's palm.

"Hello?" Sky asked.

"How many are outside?" asked Lucia in an incredibly serious tone.

Sky went to her apartment window, and tapped on it with her fingertips. A solid, gray colored area of the wall, turned transparent. Sky peered out of the window. Sky saw heavily armed police and military units patrolling the building's perimeter. There were large groups of people outside, protesting the government's occupation. The crowd was loudly yelling profanities at the authorities. Weaponized combat drones, flying only twenty feet above ground, patrolled the area. Brush fires burned in the United Nations' forest preserve. Sporadic bursts of gunfire rang out in the distance.

Sky said, "There are too many to count. They are everywhere. I–"

"You're not safe. It's time to execute our contingency plan," Lucia interrupted.

Sky heatedly snapped, "Are you insane? They're threatening to execute everyone who is still outside. Drones are everywhere. I'd be shot before I reached the perim–"

"I'm hacking the signal to your TV. Be at those coordinates in eleven minutes, or we can't help you," Lucia said.

Sky looked at her television projector. The image distorted, and a crudely drawn map was rendered. The map was a copied blueprint of Sky's building. A green trail showed the escape route that Lucia wanted Sky to travel.

Sky began saying, "This is craz–"

"You need to hurry," Lucia once again interrupted.

Lucia hung up the phone, leaving Sky to carefully study the map. Sky saw that she needed to descend one flight of stairs, and climb down the fire escape near the east side of the building. Once she made it to the ground level, her next destination was the building's Laundromat. Sky did not know what she was supposed to do when she reached the laundry room. Sky was very concerned. She saw the route would take her dangerously close to the preserved UN Green Zone. Nevertheless, Sky continued studying the map. A few seconds later, the map distorted and the newscast resumed.

"...Cho would not say on record, if today's attack was related to the bombing in New Jersey. However, Pentagon officials warn that these heinous crimes, might lead to larger food attacks–"

Sky could no longer listen to the government's propaganda. She swung her arm downward extremely fast, and the projector turned off. Sky spent exactly two minutes and thirteen seconds, gathering a few meager belongings from her apartment. She took several pairs of undergarments, three small bottles of water, some organic food, and stuffed them into a backpack. She grabbed a form fitting brown leather jacket, and a baseball cap. Sky took one last look around the apartment. A tear began forming in her eye. She wiped it away, composed herself, and threw her cell phone against the wall. It shattered. She wiped away another tear, and exited her apartment.

She briskly walked towards her destination. Sounds of excitement, fear, and confusion, filled the hallway. It was rare that Sky saw so many residents outside of their apartments, and actually talking to one another. She saw a group of five black youths, smoking marijuana cigarettes and congregating near the stairwell. She casually approached them.

Sky heard one of the youths say, "That nigger was wearing a mask, and shit. He blew that motherfucker up like, POW! Metal head fell to the floor like, boom! No lie nigger, raw talk. I seen that shit myself. Matter fact, I–"

The youth stopped talking when he saw Sky. She tried to keep her head down, and quickly walk past the group.

"Hold up girl. You look mad fine. You over in three twenty-two, right? I seen you before," the youth said.

Sky tried to descend the stairs, but another youth blocked her path.

"What up? Where you going?" asked the youth whom had first spoken to Sky.

Sky tried to be polite.

"Hey guys, why are you smoking that out here? There are way better places to puff, than on the stairs," she said in a faux playful voice.

"We ain't worried about no pee-po's. Why don't you take a hit?" the main youth said.

Sky cleared her throat and said, "That's okay. I wouldn't be able to enjoy myself, with all these drones flying around. They can really kill a girl's buzz, you know?"

Sky and the main youth stared at each other for a moment. The situation was very uncomfortable.

"Besides, I wouldn't want to leech off of your stash," Sky quickly added.

The youth looked at Sky like she was a fresh piece of meat on a spit. She could tell the young thug was eying her voluptuous body, and having lustful thoughts. After a moment, a youth with long dreadlocks offered Sky assistance.

"Yo'...move," the dread-locked youth said to the boy blocking Sky's path.

The youth in Sky's way, gave his friend a puzzled look. The boy talking to Sky was also surprised by this request.

"God damn...I said *move* nigger," the dread-locked youth said in a forceful tone.

He gave the boy in the stairwell a defiant glare. The youth moved out of Sky's way, and she walked past him.

"Hey!" the main youth said to Sky.

Sky briefly looked back.

"I'ma see you," the main youth told her.

Sky ignored his comment, and hurried down to the next floor. Sky hastily walked to the fire escape. When she arrived, she glanced out of its window. She saw a drone fly by the window. It was being monitored by two military guards, who were holding laser assault rifles. Sky hesitated a moment, and waited until her path was clear. When she was ready, Sky ventured onto the fire escape and climbed down its ladder. When she reached the bottom, she let herself dangle above the ground. She let go, and dropped ten feet to the floor.

She stumbled slightly, but maintained her balance. Sky looked around nervously. She was worried that the noise had alerted the authorities. Her fears were quickly laid to rest, when she realized that no one had heard the commotion. Sky swiftly walked along a nearby paved walkway. She reached the laundry room, opened the door, and went inside. She shut it behind her, and pressed her back against the door. She took two deep breaths. Her heart raced from the stress. Sky removed her boot and smashed the door's control panel, which temporarily disabled its lock. Sky put her footwear back on and walked between the large, monolithic, washing and drying machines.

"What the hell does she want me to do next?" Sky whispered to herself.

Sky walked until she reached the end of the room. She put her back against the wall, and carefully peered out the room's back window. She saw a group of small children being body scanned by a drone. The children held their hands straight up, while the drone hovered above them. The drone scanned them with low intensity laser beams. Two armed police women pointed their laser handguns at a group of frantic parents. The parents loudly shouted, and asked why their children were being detained. Several of the children had wet their pants in fright. Sky looked away, slid down the wall, and sat down. She put her hands to her face, breathed deeply, and resisted the urge to cry. Suddenly Sky heard two loud banging sounds, very close to her position.

At first, Sky thought that the noises were coming from outside. However, she soon realized that the sound had originated from beneath the floor. Sky crawled over and inspected the spot from which the banging emanated. Sky noticed a portion of the floor was slightly askew. Sky tapped her hand several times against the peculiar spot. There was no response for a moment. Without warning, two more loud bangs resonated. Sky was startled and quickly moved away. She rested on her hands and backside. The ground began rumbling. One second later, part of the floor slid back into the wall. Sky was shocked and did not move. Dust arose from the newly created opening. Sky heard the sound of a female voice coughing.

"Aw, shit!" the female loudly whispered.

Sky saw a thin green light, pointing upwards from the ground. The beam disappeared after several seconds.

"Push!" the woman said.

"Keep climbing!" Sky heard a strained male voice say.

A woman dressed in a form fitting, full body leather suit, slowly arose from the cave. She wore a black bandana that covered her face and head. The mask was a simple cloth covering, which only left her eyes visible. The woman rolled forward and removed the gun from the holster strapped to her leg. She knelt in a combat ready position, and aimed her gun around the room. The gun's green laser optic focused in any direction it was pointed. The holographic backscatter scope on its side, scanned for additional threats. She pulled down the front piece of her mask.

"Hey! Come on, Sky!" said the woman.

Sky's nervousness subsided, when she saw that the woman was Lucia Valente. Sky crawled to the floor's opening. She peered down and saw a man wearing a black short-sleeved shirt, and black jeans. Fingerless black leather gloves firmly covered his hands. He was wearing a mask, similar to Lucia's. A large semi-automatic assault rifle was strapped to his back. Sky sat up, and Lucia tapped Sky's chest. Lucia then made a replication of legs, with her index and middle fingers. She curled them so it appeared that the legs were in a sitting position. She then moved her hand forward, and extended the legs. Sky understood that Lucia wanted her to dangle herself over the ledge, push forward, and fall straight down.

Sky positioned herself for the drop. She pushed off, and fell four feet. The man at the bottom braced her fall by opening his arms, and grabbing her waist. The man grunted, stumbled backwards, and helped Sky land on her feet. Lucia took a quick look around the room, to ensure that no one had seen them. Lucia holstered her gun, and performed the same maneuver. She brought a large amount of dust down with her. The man grunted loudly, and coughed. After helping Lucia make a smooth landing, the man removed his mask and wiped the dust from his face.

Vincent said to Lucia, "You've got to stop eating all our stash! You're getting fat–"

Lucia unlocked her gun's safety trigger, and held it by her side. Its particle chamber grew hot, and the holographic display expanded. Vincent cracked a wide smile, and playfully held up his hands.

"Our society places far too much scrutiny on the female body image," Vincent said.

Lucia grinned, and reset the gun's safety. The holographic display and laser beam disabled.

"Let's get moving," Lucia said.

Lucia handed Sky a pair of goggles, which Sky quickly strapped around her eyes. Lucia and Vincent put on their goggles, and activated them. Lucia showed Sky how to activate the night vision glasses. Lucia took her index fingers, and rubbed them in a clockwise circular motion against the front of the eye lenses. Sky performed this action, and her goggles activated. She saw the room illuminate in a bright green light. Vincent typed a sequence of buttons on a control panel embedded in the wall. The cavern's exit hatch closed, and the tunnel went pitch black.

"Where are we?" Sky asked.

"Shh," Lucia whispered.

Lucia put her right index finger to her lips, and pointed at the tunnel's ceiling. Sky heard the unmistakable sound of a drone flying overhead. It was steadily scanning the terrain. Lucia, Sky, and Vincent, began rapidly walking through the underground corridor. Lucia led the way, with Sky and Vincent closely following. When they passed certain sections, Vincent typed a sequence of numbers into small rusty wall panels. This caused the tunnel's sliding doors to shut behind them. They traveled a great distance through the maze. Eventually, they reached a large metal door.

"Go ahead," Lucia said to Vincent.

Vincent removed an aerosol canister from the waistband tool belt he was wearing. Vincent shook it, and sprayed. A blue mist emanated from the can. A hidden number key panel appeared on the door. Vincent knocked on the door in three quickly timed bursts. Four slow knocks came from the other side. Vincent replied with two slow knocks, before he entered a numeric code into the panel. Seconds later, the door opened. Another masked man was waiting on the other side. The man pointed a large shotgun at the crew. He quickly lowered it, after he saw that they were his friends. The man removed his bandana mask, and revealed his face.

"Great job. The exit is not far. Let's hurry. We don't want to stay here too long," Walter said.

The group continued their journey through the passageway. Sky noticed many different sections where the road parted ways. Walter used his cell phone's GPS, to navigate through the labyrinth.

"Walter, what is this place?" Sky asked.

"Welcome to the New Underground Railroad. Construction on these tunnels began in 2167, and continues to this day. There are vast amounts of these tunnels all around the country. They are used for smuggling highly sensitive goods like food, drugs, weapons, and political refugees," Walter said.

"I don't want to be a political refugee," Sky said.

Walter abruptly stopped walking. The rest of the group followed suit.

"Is that truly your desire? We'll take you back home, if you want," Walter said.

Vincent said, "Goddammit, I told you this was a bad idea. She is not–"

"What are we going to do, abandon her? She is our friend, and has helped us for years," Walter interrupted.

Vincent said, "Walter, these passageways aren't safe. It has taken us almost two hours to get her this far. We don't know what might happen, if–"

Lucia interrupted, "Vincent, that's enough! How can you be so cruel? We–"

"Stop fighting," Sky sternly interrupted.

There was a brief silence until Sky said, "I don't want to be a refugee, but I don't have a choice. My building is swarming with cops. They're about to conduct searches of every apartment in the building. If they find something that links me to all of you, we will all get caught. I can't go back there. Not yet. Not until this situation cools down."

"So, are we going to keep moving?" Walter asked Sky.

Sky nodded her head in confirmation, and the group continued walking. They eventually reached a ladder, which led to an escape hatch. Walter climbed up the ladder and pounded three times. Walter heard two distinct knocks emanate from the other side. Walter entered a pass code, into a panel embedded in the hatch. Walter jumped down off the ladder, and readied his gun. The door opened, and the group saw Eiji. He quickly lowered the semi-automatic sub-machine gun, he was pointing at them.

"Thank God! You guys are okay!" Eiji said.

Walter let the women ascend the ladder first. Vincent followed them, and Walter was the last one out of the tunnel. Vincent took out the aerosol can, and sprayed it on the hatch's side. Another secret panel was temporarily revealed. Vincent pushed its buttons, and the door closed. Sky looked around, and saw they were miles away from her apartment complex. They were at the edge of a drainage ditch, near the bottom of some decrepit woods.

"How large are the tunnels?" Sky asked.

"Miles. Some cover entire states. There are a lot that intersect with each other. Like I said before, these tunnels are a constant work in progress. Most people don't know it, but America has a long history of building underground passageways, and facilities," said Walter.

"Some underground tunnels in Wilmington, North Carolina, even date back to the Revolutionary War," Eiji said.

"Many military facilities like the infamous S-9, Area 77, lead to deep underground government bases. Mexican drug cartels have even built underground roadways, for international narcotics smuggling," Lucia said.

"That is amazing! How do you get the codes for the doorways?" Sky said.

"Through trusted associates. Not all codes work everywhere. Different factions use different passage routes, and codes. Most friendly routes, like the ones used by food smugglers, use the same ten digit number," Vincent said.

"You mean, anyone with the right connections knows them?" Sky asked with confusion.

"It's no secret. All patriots know the year when all men became free," Walter said.

Sky thought for a moment and said, "0-1-0-1-1-8-6-3; the day the Emancipation Proclamation became law."

Walter smiled and said, "You're a smart girl. The creators of these tunnels felt it was a good homage to the original Underground Railroad. It captured the spirit of rebellious slaves, which unfortunately we all have become."

"The date is also less obvious than the original Independence Day. The knocking is what makes it personal. Anyone traveling in a team agrees to a different knocking pattern. It's simply a way to let your friends know, that you are part of their convoy," Vincent said.

"It's pretty dangerous down there. One can never be too sure what's on the other side of those doors," added Lucia.

"Okay everybody, I hate to break up the history lesson, but we need to leave," Eiji said.

"Agreed. Let's get to the car," Walter said.

The group walked up the hill, and through the forest. It eventually led them to a dirt road. The group walked along the road, until they came to an abandoned parking lot, where Walter's car was located. They entered the vehicle, drove back to the compound, went inside, and entered the living room. A familiar face arose from the couch and greeted them. Cameron held his side, and slowly walked towards his friends.

"Hey..." Cameron weakly said.

"Cameron!" Sky yelled.

She rushed over, and gave him a big hug. Her loving squeeze sent a twinge through his tender, swollen muscles.

"Ow! Be gentle! I banged myself up pretty bad last night," Cameron said.

"How the hell did you make it out?" Sky asked.

"I owe it all to these guys. I fell back into the woods, and smacked my head. I passed out, for a couple of minutes. I got up and dragged myself half a mile, with a concussion and bruised ribs. I used my GPS to find my way out of the woods. I exited the preserve near the abandoned industrial facilities. I was exhausted, and trying to plan my next move. I almost had a heart attack when Walter's car rolled up to me, forty minutes later," Cameron said.

"I pinged the homing beacon Walter installed in his shotgun. The minute the GPS stopped long enough at one location, I sent the car to get him. We remote controlled the van he used, and drove it to an abandoned Newark neighborhood. We'll pick it up, when we are sure it hasn't been tracked," said Lucia.

"I was shocked. I had no idea they would come looking for me," said Cameron.

"Of course we went searching for you. We knew you'd need help the second we saw your video," Vincent said.

"Yeah, you doofus. You should have told us your plan. You know we would have helped you," Eiji said.

"It was too risky. I couldn't take the chance that something would go wrong," Cameron said.

"It doesn't matter. All that counts, is that we're all together," Sky said.

The team all crowded around Sky, who was still hugging Cameron, and engaged in a group hug. Cameron felt slightly crushed, by the pressure of all the people pressed against him.

"Oh! Ow! Bruised ribs, remember guys?" said Cameron.

Everyone laughed, and gave Cameron some space. Cameron gazed lovingly at Sky, who was still embracing him.

"Hey. We're about to have a serious talk. You want to stay?" asked Cameron.

Sky slowly released her embrace. Sky stroked the bottom of Cameron's chin, with her index finger.

"Well, it would be rude to kick me out! *You're* the reason I'm homeless!" Sky said.

Cameron uneasily said, "Uhh, about that...I'm sor–"

Sky placed her finger over Cameron's lips.

"Shh, we'll talk about it later," Sky whispered.

Sky asserted her place in the group, by standing strong at Cameron's side.

"Well everyone...I'd love to talk about the great victory we achieved for the Food Movement. But we have more serious problems on our hands," Cameron said.

Cameron waved his hand at the sensor on the wall. The holographic projector began displaying television images. The news was ablaze with stories about Troubled Times. The news media was continuously showing edited portions of Times' video. Every station condemned Times' actions. The team watched a reporter divulge the latest updates.

The news anchor said, "Whether this disturbing attack is related to the horrific massacre on Liberty Island is too soon to be determined. President Cho has authorized the spending of an additional fifty billion dollars to support the National Terrorism Defense fund–"

Cameron slowly waved his hand in front of the projector. The television's volume lowered.

"So who the fuck is this psycho, calling himself Troubled Times?" Cameron asked his friends.

"Unfortunately, there isn't a lot of information available about him. What we *do* know, is that Troubled Times killed at least nine people in this attack. The media is doing everything they can to connect him with the Liberty Island shooting, and the Food Liberation Movement," Walter solemnly said.

Lucia said, "I did some data mining on the deep web. Nobody knows his true identity. However, I did find some footage from the hospital. Most of the security cameras were disabled during the carnage. I did see one video that..."

Lucia let her thoughts trail off. She was not sure how to explain what she had observed.

"What did you find, Lucy?" Eiji asked.

Lucia hesitated before saying, "I think...I think Troubled Times may not be working alone. The video I watched showed hospital guards actually *helping* him."

"Do you think they were fanatical, Muslim jihadists? Or anti-Tibetan sympathizers?" Sky asked.

"That's doubtful. It sounds like Times was the only one who made it out alive," Vincent said.

Walter briefly covered his mouth with his hand, and experienced a feeling of great concern.

"Explain your theory, Lucy," Walter said.

Lucia walked over to the projection terminal. She placed all of her fingertips together, and formed her hands into the shape of a triangle. She quickly flung her arms away from each other. Several holographic screens began projecting across the wall. Dozens of tiny square windows, with videos that she had saved to the television's memory bank, began projecting. Lucia took her right index finger and tapped on a small holographic window protruding from the projection. The window enlarged.

"This is the one I found," said Lucia.

The video showed the masked man known to the world as Troubled Times, commanding the CEA enforcers to douse his helpless victims, with flammable solution. The video only lasted eighteen seconds, but its contents startled the team to their core.

"You are sure this video is legit?" asked Eiji.

"Yes. I'm afraid it is, Eiji. It happened before the explosion, and was stolen from a hospital server," Lucia said.

"If hackers are the ones who released this video, it explains why the media hasn't shown it to the public. There's no way a video with this type of bombshell information would ever be shown on the counterfeit media," said Walter.

"Why would the CEA openly help Times commit these atrocities?" Vincent asked.

"I don't know. My theory is that it was a false flag attack," Lucia replied.

"What's that?" Sky asked.

"It's when a group attacks itself on purpose, and blames their political opposition," Cameron said.

"I'm not sure that this is one of those events. False flag patsies are never allowed to survive. The ringleaders would kill an asset like Troubled Times after an assault of this magnitude. I disagree with you on this one, Lucia. I think Troubled Times is a real terrorist," said Walter.

The group was shocked by Walter's statement. The idea that Troubled Times was a rouge criminal scared them.

"A *real* terrorist? I don't know if I believe that, Walter. Real terrorists on this scale are like comic book characters. They don't exist," Cameron said after a brief silence.

"That's not true, Cameron. Real terrorists are everywhere. America has a distorted view of what is a real terrorist. They have been brainwashed to think that terrorists are simply radical lunatics, who belong to a specific political group. Real terrorists are sometimes wanton, rouge individuals, or groups. I could give you countless examples of less obvious forms of terrorism. For example, would you agree that real terrorists are the ones who poison our food?" Walter replied.

"Fair enough," Cameron said.

Walter operated the projector, and returned to the television's multiple video selections. He used his right index finger to select a live television news feed which began holographically projecting. Walter waved his hand, which raised the volume.

"The rash of American terror attacks has caused great concern in mainland China. Officials in the Chinese government are worried that the attacks will spread to the homeland. President Cho has stated that he will work with Chinese authorities, to ensure that no violence reaches their country," the female Chinese news reporter said.

"Unbelievable. Americans are dying in the most brutal ways imaginable, and the media is worried about what happens to some Chinamen," Vincent said.

"Even if it *wasn't* a staged event, numerous government agencies will use it to increase their power," Sky said.

"Including that Hong Kong motherfucker, Cho," Eiji said with seething bitterness in his voice.

Walter raised both his arms in front of the projector and quickly swept them in a downward motion. All the videos turned off, and the group exchanged exasperated looks. They knew that these events would result in dire consequences.

"What do you think we should do?" Lucia finally asked.

"I hoped we would have more time. You all may not yet realize it, but this is a significant turning point for the Food Movement. If Cho and other government stooges have their way; they will use these attacks as an excuse to arrest, or kill, every rouge organic farmer left in this country," Walter solemnly said.

The team was horrified by Walter's words. They all feared that their lives were in serious jeopardy.

"How should we proceed?" Cameron asked.

"I don't think we have the means to do anything about Troubled Times. Our job is to make sure that the Food Movement remains a positive symbol of resistance. The past few months have taught me a lot. People are more willing than ever to fight, and even *die*, for their food rights. It's something I haven't seen since the collapse. We *have* to capitalize on this sentiment," Walter said.

"It's too dangerous for everyone to stay here," said Vincent.

"I agree. Sky, how would you feel about temporarily living with one of our most trusted friends?" Walter asked.

"What other option do I have? I don't want to see Cameron, or any of you, get killed. I'm part of this team now, and I'll do whatever it takes to help," Sky said.

"Wonderful. Vincent, you're going with Eiji and Sky to the Branson's. It's not just about keeping Sky safe. They're going to need protection. They have a big family; but with so many young children, they won't be able to handle an assault. I will talk to Paul before you arrive. He will be mad that I am asking him for a favor of this magnitude," Walter said.

"What about us? We'll have a tough time protecting the compound with only three people," said Cameron.

"We'll manage. We have to keep the group separate until we can formulate a better plan. We can't risk getting the entire crew arrested," Walter said with a heavy heart.

"It's not like this is the end. We *are* going to beat these people," Eiji said.

"Hell yeah, we will. Fuck the New World Order!" Lucia said.

"Are we ready?" Walter asked the team a moment later.

They all agreed to the plan. Cameron was obviously apprehensive. Sky gently rubbed his back to calm his nerves.

"Good. Be ready to leave in one hour," Walter said.

Within forty-five minutes Eiji, Vincent, and Sky, had packed one of their spare vans with all the supplies that they would need. Computers, food, weapons, money, and grooming items, were among the van's cargo. Outside of the compound, Sky and Cameron shared a warm embrace.

"I didn't want to say this in front of your friends. I don't want to leave you, Cameron," said Sky.

Cameron gently stroked away a strand of hair, from her face. He softly caressed her hips.

"It's not going to be for that long. I'll be there, the first chance I get," Cameron lovingly replied.

"I hope you appreciate how much I'm sacrificing to be with you. Part of me, thinks I've gone completely insane. I never dreamed I'd become a Freedom Fighter," said Sky.

"Very few people make a conscious decision, to rebel against tyranny. This life has a morbidly humorous way of choosing *you*. Not the other way around," said Cameron.

Cameron stared deep into Sky's eyes. He felt blessed to be fighting alongside such an incredibly strong woman.

"Hey, remember the first time we met? I was making a drop to a friend that used to live in your building. You walked around the corner, and into the hallway, right when I was showing him my stash. It was an awesome haul. I had a bag of freshly picked organic oranges, grapes, and chicken breasts. I was so scared you were going to call the cops that I gave him the bag without even taking the money. He called me a couple hours later and laughed at me. Dude said it was the most hilarious thing he had ever seen," he said in a soothing voice.

Sky giggled and said, "You looked like you'd seen a drone! To tell you the truth, you scared me. I didn't know you were selling food. I thought it was nano-drugs!"

"I asked him about you. He told me where you stayed, and that you were cool with the Food Movement. I remember how scared I was to approach you. You intimidated me. I had never seen a more beautiful girl in my entire life. For the next three weeks, I knocked on your door and left you an apple. Every Friday night, at seven thirty, I'd leave it nicely gift wrapped on your doormat. One day, you were finally waiting outside. Remember what you said?" Cameron asked.

Sky breathed deep said, "I said, 'The least you could do, is tell me your name if you're going to leave..."

"...contraband on my doorstep!"

Cameron finished the last four words with her, and they shared a laugh. Cameron held her waist, and kissed her.

"I felt like such an idiot. My whole life, I had tried to be super discreet when I dealt with food. But there I was, leaving it around like an idiot. I was so happy to meet someone so magnificent; that didn't judge me before they got to know me. You're the first person that truly made me feel my work is important," Cameron said.

The couple affectionately ran their hands, along each other's bodies.

"I know it hasn't always been easy. But I *promise* something good will come from all of this, Sky," said Cameron.

Sky leaned into Cameron, and the two shared a passionate kiss. A moment later, Eiji came around the corner.

"Good grief, she won't be gone *that* long!" Eiji playfully said.

Cameron and Sky laughed heartily. Sky kept her lips pressed against Cameron's.

"Oh, shit. Looks like we're busted!" Sky said.

"We're coming out now, Eiji!" Cameron promptly said.

"Relax, relax. I was only teasin'. Take your time," Eiji said.

He walked away, and gave them their privacy. Once more, Cameron gently kissed Sky's delicate lips. Seconds later, Cameron forced himself to stop.

"It's time," Cameron finally said.

Sky looked at Cameron with a deep passion in her eyes.

"You had better not break your promise," Sky said.

"I won't," Cameron reassuringly said.

They released their grip upon each other's bodies, and walked to the front of the compound. The group met in front of the van. They all took turns shaking hands and wishing each other well. They did not want to admit it, but there was a very real possibility that they may never again see each other. Lucia gave Sky a big hug.

"Don't worry chica. I'll keep him out of trouble," Lucia said.

Vincent sat in the van's driver's seat. Eiji sat in the passenger's side, and Sky climbed into the back.

"Guess this is goodbye for now, friends. Be safe," Vincent said.

"Y'all don't bring too much attention to yourselves, understand? Stay off the main roads, and listen to what Paul tells you. We'll be in touch soon," Walter said.

Vincent tapped the van's side twice with his left hand. Walter knew Vincent would heed his advice. Vincent started the van, and began driving away from the building. Lucia, Walter, and Cameron, stood outside of the compound. The cold January night chilled their bodies. Walter gazed longingly at the heavens.

"I wish we could see more stars. When I was a kid, before the drone's dirty burning fuel polluted the skies, there were stars everywhere. Now we're lucky to see any," Walter said.

Lucia and Cameron looked up at the empty night sky. Cameron put his hand on Walter's shoulder.

"We'll see them again, one day," Cameron said.

Cameron noticed far in the distance, that a drone was slowly patrolling the area. It flashed numerous lights, while ominously flying through the air.

"Shit. That drone is almost blacker than the night itself. It must be using urban stealth technology," said Walter.

"This is bad. If that's the type of drone I think it is, it's more than just a standard surveillance drone. It's using ground penetrating radar and taking thermal pictures of our bodies. They must be using it to calculate how many people are actually living in the city," Lucia said.

"Cho has been talking about imposing Martial Law, ever since the Thanksgiving Day Massacre. This is probably the first step. They'll create a three dimensional computer map of the terrain, and then send in drones to lock this place down. They'll have choke points strategically placed around the town. They'll execute anyone trying to escape," Walter said.

"Are they trying to start a civil war? I know the general public isn't intellectually astute; but I don't think they're going to put up with Martial Law," Cameron said.

"There have been isolated stretches of Martial Law ever since the Carbon Taxes were implemented. I remember when I was around your age; the Marines patrolled the streets of Trenton for ten weeks. They said it was in response to the starving rioters that were starting to burn down Capitol buildings," Walter said.

Lucia and Cameron could not believe the magnitude of the subjects about which they were talking.

"What can we do about it, Walter? How do we win?" Lucia asked.

Walter had a deeply sad look upon his face. He waited several seconds, before replying.

"Survive."

Walter spoke no more words. He slowly walked back inside the compound. Lucia and Cameron remained silent for quite some time.

"Do you think we have any chance?" Lucia eventually asked Cameron.

"At what?" Cameron replied.

"Surviving," said Lucia.

Cameron stared at the drone, and was overwhelmed by enormous grief.

"No," Cameron solemnly replied.

Lucia was very upset by Cameron's words.

"Why, Cameron? Why are you so pessimistic? Walter would never speak so negatively!" she said with frustration.

Cameron sighed deeply and replied, "Walter is one of my best friends. He has been like a second father to me. My parents have been gone almost thirteen years. I miss them every day. I wish that I would have gotten to know them better. I wish I had told them how much they meant to me, and how much I loved them. They were always busy working, while I spent my young life locked inside a government training facility, fictitiously called a 'school'."

Cameron rarely talked about his past. Lucia was intrigued, and listened to Cameron's heartfelt revelation.

"I don't think they would be very proud of me, if they were alive today. They would never have wanted to see their only son join the Food Liberty Movement," Cameron said.

Lucia choked up and asked, "How did they–?"

She could not bring herself to finish her question. Cameron had a stone cold look of sorrow upon his face.

"It's not important," he finally said.

They both looked back up at the stars, and watched the drone fly off into the horizon.

Cameron took a deep breath and said, "Walter is a good man, but he's fighting a losing battle. Until now, I wasn't ready to admit that ours is a lost cause. In a few weeks, I'm going to Paul's house and getting Sky. We're not coming back."

Lucia turned away from Cameron, so that he would not see her wipe angry tears from her eyes.

Lucia cleared her throat and said, "The war's not over yet, Cameron. It hasn't even started. I don't give a fuck about Cho, or Martial Law, or Troubled Times. I'm going to keep fighting. I *have* to keep fighting!"

Cameron admired Lucia's warrior spirit.

"I know," Cameron said.

He patted her on the shoulder and walked back into the compound. Lucia waited for twenty-two minutes before she went to her room. She laid upon on her bed, closed her eyes, and cried herself to sleep.

Eiji, Sky, and Vincent, arrived at the Branson's house shortly before 12:30 AM. The group waited near the entrance of the small dirt road until they were able to contact Paul.

Paul answered his cell phone by saying, "How many?"

"Three," Vincent said.

"I've already talked to Walt. He didn't want to say too much over these tapped cell phone lines. Apparently there's something very serious happening," Paul said.

"That's putting it mildly," Vincent said.

"Sam will be there in a minute," Paul replied.

A few moments later, a large blurry figure uncloaked itself in front of the group's van. Samantha Branson waved at the group, and motioned for them to continue driving down the road. Samantha was equipped with a high caliber, semi-automatic assault rifle. She again activated her cloaking device, and Vincent slowly drove down the road. Samantha could not be seen, but Vincent did not worry about hitting her. He was sure that Samantha would stay out of the van's way. Vincent finished driving to the Branson's house, and the team exited the van. Samantha again deactivated her cloaking device. She used her holographic cell phone, to call Paul.

"We're outside, dad," she said.

"Give me a minute," Paul responded.

Paul soon exited the house, with a .22 caliber handgun holstered at his side.

"Tell me why you've got us all awake and out here at such a late hour, Vincent," said Paul in a stern tone.

"This is Sky Solomon. She's helped us a lot, over the years. She doesn't deal with food directly, but she helps us launder capital. She's incredibly loyal to our plight," Vincent said.

"Sounds very noble. But why is she here?" Paul asked in a confrontational manner.

"I lived at the apartment complex, where Cameron distributed food and shot a drone the other night. Did you see what happened?" Sky asked.

"Don't let the appearance of this old ramshackle homestead, fool you. We have our fair share of electronic devices. We use hacked technology very sparingly when we need to communicate. We use encrypted connections through old wireless signals, from when the internet used to be public. Heh, I tell you, I'm never surprised at our government's stupidity. The frequencies that Wi-Fi and radio signals broadcast on don't go away, simply because they switch to new ones. Yeah, I saw the video. Hell, half the world has probably seen it at this point. It was beautiful, watching that metal piece of shit getting stomped into the ground. It was over twenty-five years ago, the first time I saw a drone in person. I'll never forget what it was like to see it with my own eyes; to see how it hunts and kills people," Paul said.

Paul hesitated briefly before saying, "There was a farmer who lived near me, in the back country of Chantilly. He recently had his land seized, under the Carbon Tax Law. He wanted to protest the American government giving up their sovereignty to the United Nations. He posted a video to a popular social media website, and told every person in town to assemble at a well-known bridge that was near a popular public park. A large crowd of spectators all gathered there at the time he requested. The video had millions of views, by the day his protest happened. He started throwing his home grown produce off the bridge. He told the crowd to eat all that they wanted; and that farmers were the backbone of America. The crowd cheered louder than anything that I've ever heard before, or since that time."

Paul became somber and said, "Two drones which had been spying on the crowd, eventually lowered their position and began hovering above us. The farmer pulled out his pistol, fired a shot, and hit one of them right in its wing. The drone swayed, and sparks flew from its bullet wound. The crowd roared even louder. Some even burst into tears at his heroic act. He got ready to fire another shot. Before he could pull the trigger, the drone blasted him. The lasers they were equipped with back then, were cruder than modern ones. He didn't explode. He more like...ignited. His body swiftly burned and charred. By the time he was done smoldering, his body looked like it was covered with gasoline before striking a match. Everyone ran away, screaming in terror. I knew then that we were at war; and these drones were sent straight out of Hell to aid our enemies."

Everyone was deeply moved by Paul's tragic story.

"Are you *sure* you're ready to join this war, Sky?" Paul asked.

"I've been fighting in my own way, for a long time. Girls like me...usually choose to prostitute themselves if they want real food. I have so many former friends who entered the sex industry just to buy bags of apples. I swore no matter what, I would never be a whore. Meeting Cameron and his friends was a sign that I made the right choice. That's why I have to protect them. My apartment will be raided. The authorities will search every room in the building, and use the LSA Grid to data mine all of the tenant's electronics. Eventually, they'll find something linking me back to Cameron, Walter and everyone else. I won't let that happen. That's why I'm choosing to fight with all my might," Sky replied.

Sky choked back tears, while finishing her sentence. Samantha patted her on the back in a comforting manner.

"Walter is a good friend. We go back a long time, and he has always done right by me. We need every soldier we can get to help us win this battle. You can stay here until we find you a permanent residence. You can help out around the house and on the farm, to earn your keep," Paul said.

"Thank you, Paul," Sky gratefully said.

Paul tapped his gun holster and asked, "You any good with one of these?"

"No. I've never even fired one," Sky replied.

"I'm not surprised. Yours is one of the first generations to grow up in a predominately gun free America," Paul said. Paul sighed with remorse before adding, "Bullets are too scarce to waste, so you won't get much live ammo practice. I'll give you some pointers and show you proper gun maintenance. You can practice with a few spare rounds, once you understand the philosophy of firearms."

Paul extended his hand, which Sky promptly shook.

"Welcome to the war," Paul said.

Sky was too overcome with emotion to utter a response.

Eiji tepidly said, "Paul, do you think it would be okay if we stayed for a while? Walter said you'd need help if..."

Eiji let his thoughts trail off. Paul understood that Eiji knew the Branson family could be viciously raided by thuggish groups of government enforcers at any time.

Paul nodded his head and said, "If you want to find a free spot, be my guest. We're not really equipped to handle a large group, but we have sleeping bags."

"I'm sure we'll be fine. We just need some time until the heat dies down. Thank you so much, Paul," Vincent said.

Paul motioned for the group to follow him, and they all went inside the house. They walked through the main hallway. They passed the living room, and stairs which led to the upper level. At the end of the hall was a kitchen, where the rest of Paul's family was congregating.

"Everyone, I'd like to introduce you to Sky Solomon. She's going to be staying with us for a while. She has been a great asset to our friends in the Food War. You all saw Cameron's video, the other night. That was Sky's building. She had to evacuate her home so that she wouldn't attract any unwanted attention from the authorities. She has given up a lot to protect us. She is a refugee. Please make her feel welcome," Paul said.

Sky waved her hand and said, "Hi everyone. I'm glad to meet you, even though it's under terrible circumstances."

"I'm Doreen. This is my son, Paul junior. You've already met his oldest sister, Samantha. These are my youngest daughters Abigail, and Lily," Doreen said.

"Pleased to meet you Sky! I can't wait to get to know you!" Abigail said.

Lily ran up to Sky, and gave her a big hug.

"Hi Sky, I'm Lily! You are so pretty! I love your hair!" Lily said.

Sky hugged the small child and said softly, "Aww. Thank you so much, sweetie! You're adorable!"

"Doreen, Paulie, why don't you fix our guests some dinner? I know they must have had a hard day. I shot a mighty fine wild buck yesterday. It was one heck of a task, skinnin' and dissectin' him. We had some for dinner, earlier. Meat's downstairs, in the freezer," Paul said.

"It was *so* awesome, dad! I love venison!" Abigail said.

"Of course, hon. Excuse me, Sky," Doreen said.

Doreen and her son gracefully exited the room.

"I hope you guys are hungry, too!" Lily said.

Eiji began saying, "No, it's okay. We're–"

"Don't be ridiculous. You two are more than welcome to eat," interrupted Samantha.

"Darn right. There's only one good thing about living in Jersey. No matter how many people hunt the buggers, there are always too many dang deer!" Paul said.

Everyone laughed at Paul's keen observation. The group spent the next two hours talking, and eating organic food. They shared laughter, and companionship. They lived like normal humans once did, many decades ago. They eventually went their separate ways, and found spaces in the house to rest. Before Sky fell asleep, she thought about Cameron. She wanted to hold him, and let him stroke her long, flowing, curly, dark auburn hair. Sky did not know what the future held, but she was inexorably prepared to face her destiny.

23 Old Flame

Friday, February 1st, 2217 was bitterly cold. It had been over three weeks since Times and Cameron, had committed their crimes. Fear and uncertainty, had spread across the entire country. People throughout the nation, were deeply affected by the events that had occurred during the past several weeks. All around the country people feverishly talked about the young rebel, who was seen feeding the apartment complex. Folk tales about his heroic armed uprising against a predator drone spurred great admiration and pride throughout a deeply divided nation. Many saw his open disobedience, as a sign that a great battle against the oppressive American government was beginning. Others called him a traitor. Many people thought he needed to be imprisoned, or killed, for his rebelliousness.

There was an equal amount of furor, over the masked murderer called Troubled Times. His violent attack on the hospital was condemned by almost the entire population. Many folks wondered if his origins were from another country. Americans did not want to believe an abhorrent act of terror, was committed by one of their fellow citizens. Surprisingly there were others, who praised Times' rampage. Across the country fringe anarchists and criminal gangs, endorsed Times' brutal massacre. While people were understandably upset by an ever increasing government tyranny, it was disturbing to see that Times had awakened a deep angst, seething in the hearts of American citizens. People had become so filled with hatred towards their way of life that they were happy to see that society might be on the verge of a violent end.

The government wasted no time, implementing draconian policies. President Cho signed several Executive Orders, which placed serious restrictions on law abiding Americans. Curfews between the hours of 10 PM and 6 AM were mandatory for all citizens. Clothing covering one's face in public was forbidden at all hours. The monolithic Liberty Surveillance Agency, used its powerful spy technology called the Grid, to data mine all Americans. They justified their unconstitutional desecration of rights; by saying it was necessary to apprehend Troubled Times and Cameron.

The Grid is a vast network of all communication records from officially approved devices. It is used to monitor a person's every move. Vast amounts of information is taken from devices like television cable boxes, bank accounts, video game systems, cell phones, cars, computers, medical devices, refrigerators, microwaves, washing machines, and dishwashers. Any device that has a computer chip which can access wireless internet will automatically send data logs and activity records back to the Grid. This mass aggregation practice is so controversial, that even LSA employees secretly help disrupt the system. They routinely release hacking software that will scramble data sent from these machines. Rebels and ordinary citizens alike, use these programs to hide their true identities.

Webster Morgan lay strapped to his bed. The Chem-Mech used its mounted head camera laser, to project holographic video feeds from various news networks. The images displayed above Webster's bed. Webster was aware of Times' hospital rampage, but had not seen him in days. The robots who were once his allies, now kept Webster prisoner under Times' orders. The room's door opened, and Times entered. He was wearing his headband, and holding the mask in his right hand. Times pulled up a chair, and sat next to Webster's bed.

"It has been an interesting few weeks. Wouldn't you say, old friend?" Times asked.

Webster waited a moment before softly saying to Times, "You know this will not bring you closure, Gregory."

Times looked at the bandaged stump, where Webster's leg had been severed.

"Looks like you're healing rather well," Times viciously said.

"Gregory, listen to me. It's only a matter of time before they catch you. It will take some time to isolate the appropriate data from the Grid. But make no mistake, they will eventually trace you to the murders," Webster said.

"Let them. I welcome a challenge," Times coldly said.

Webster said, "You're not listening to reason. There's no way–"

"Sir. There is a situation in the lobby, which you need to address," the Chem-Mech interrupted.

"Show me," Times said.

The Chem-Mech holographically projected the video feed, from Rigor's main office camera. Times saw and heard Mallory, talking to the receptionist.

"You don't understand. I need to speak with Webster, *now*. Very serious crimes are being committed in this organization. I have to stop that man, before anyone else gets hurt!" said Mallory.

Times and Webster were both astonished to see Mallory.

"Why would she come back?" Webster asked with shock.

"Have Alice bring her to Webster's office," Times said.

"Yes sir. Immediately," said the Chem-Mech.

"Looks like our chat will have to wait," Times said to Webster.

Times began leaving the room.

"Gregory, please stop! You can't keep using the device! You have no idea how badly it may be damaging your brain's neurological connections!" Webster pleaded.

Times ignored Webster's feeble cries for sanity. Times used Webster's secret passageways, to sneak into his office. Once he arrived, Times placed the mask inside of Webster's desk drawer. A few minutes later, the robot Alice rolled itself into the lobby. Mallory was still arguing with the receptionist.

"It's not that I *don't* want to help you. It's that I *can't*. Mister Morgan hasn't been seen around the office in weeks. They say he is stricken with cancer, and is undergoing treatment," said the receptionist.

"It's all right Kendall. Follow me Missus Times. We were expecting you," Alice said before Mallory responded.

Both women looked stunned by Alice's statement. Mallory immediately followed Alice to Webster's office. Mallory saw a shirtless man wearing faded gray jeans. He was facing away from her. The man slowly turned around, and revealed his identity. Mallory was absolutely shocked when she saw that the man was her husband. He slowly approached his wife. He brushed a strand of hair behind her ear, when she was close enough for him to touch. Times stared affectionately into Mallory's eyes.

"Hello Mallory," Times warmly said.

Mallory was overcome with emotion. She fell into his arms, and began sobbing hysterically. Times held her tightly.

"Shh, it's okay. Please don't cry," Times said.

"Greg, I thought you were..." Mallory said through tearful eyes.

"I know...I know..." Times said.

After a long and emotional sob Mallory said, "Greg, this place...it's evil! Webster is a monster! He–"

"I know, Mallory. But he won't be hurting anyone else. Of this, I will assure you," Times interrupted.

Mallory noticed how much more physically fit Times had become, since the last time she saw him.

"You look...amazing," Mallory said while drying her eyes.

"Thank you, my love," said Times.

The couple embraced each other for several more minutes.

"Greg, what happened to you? What's that contraption you're wearing on your head?" Mallory asked with anxiety.

Times did not know how to respond. He did not want to reveal the extent of his depravity, but he felt guilty about lying. Nevertheless, he decided to withhold the seriousness of his experiences.

"The robots made it for me. This medical instrument is helping repair my damaged brain cells. Webster performed experiments on me. Horrible experiments. He made me his puppet and robbed me of my free will, but that is no longer the case. The enslaved, is now the oppressor," Times said.

Times avoided his wife's gaze, and decided to stay silent. Mallory pulled away from her husband's arms.

Mallory said, "Did you have anything to do with these awful events? The statue, the hospital, the apartment complex in Newark...oh my God, did Webster–"

Mallory could not finish her sentence. She once again broke into tears. Times hugged his wife, and they were both overcome with grief.

"I assure you; I had no control over the situation. He was the one perpetrating those disasters," Times said.

The two embraced each other, while Mallory tried to cope with Times' disturbing disclosure.

"Why would he do something, so awful?" Mallory asked.

"Webster is a very sick man, with extremely deranged beliefs. You cannot begin to imagine the suffering, through which he put me. You have no idea how terrifying it is, to be a deviant's plaything," Times solemnly said.

"I normally wouldn't believe you. What you're saying is outrageous, but I don't think you're lying. He performed ghastly experiments on me, too. He told me to meet him at Rigor for some tests, and said you'd be there. I went into an examination room. He gave me a vaccine, which he said was safe. A few seconds later, I passed out. After what felt like hours, I awoke...and...Oh Greg, it was awful! I've never felt so much pain in my life," Mallory said.

Mallory again burst into tears. Times did not like seeing Mallory so upset. He briefly thought about using his headband to manipulate her emotions, but ultimately refrained from artificially affecting her mood.

"Shh. We will have plenty of time to speak about it later," said Times.

He was only mildly worried that Mallory was hiding further abuse from him. He knew that he had saved her life.

Mallory finally worked up the courage to ask, "What did you do with him? Is he..."

She could not bring herself to finish the question. Even though she hated Webster, she did not want to believe her husband was a killer.

"He is still alive, and in a safe place. He won't be going anywhere, or ruining anyone else's life. Don't worry, I have not been too harsh on him," Times said.

Times knew the last part of his sentence was a lie. Mallory was overwhelmed by a complex mix of emotions. She was happy to see her husband, but was terrified by how much he had changed. She knew that their relationship would never be the same. However, Mallory repressed her negative thoughts, and instead focused on the warmth of Times' body.

"We have to tell the police. Serious crimes have been committed against us," Mallory said.

Times thought about her request, and realized he must quell her train of thought.

"I'm not sure if that's a wise decision," Times hastily said.

Mallory pulled away from Times and said, "Are you insane? This is a high tech torture chamber. Webster has hurt a lot of people. My God, he has made you an accessory to mur..."

Mallory abruptly stopped speaking. She could not bring herself to admit that her husband was a killer.

"You don't understand, Mallory. This place is part of something more dark and sinister, than you could ever imagine. I don't think it's a good idea to contact the authorities, because I don't know if they *would* help us. Webster has a lot of powerful connections. He probably works with the government on these experiments. How else can you explain why he hasn't been caught, in all the years he has been running this sick operation?" said Times.

Mallory fell silent because she knew that her husband's conclusions were accurate.

"We have to take that chance. Honey, the country is being terrorized by the results of Webster's sadistic actions. We have a chance to help people, if we go public about his horrific torture methods," Mallory eventually said.

Times walked around the room, and looked out of Webster's large office window. In the distance, he saw several drones circling the skies above New York. Times looked below at the people walking along the street. They looked like ants from his position high in the skyscraper. Times gazed out of the window, and contemplated his response.

"What makes you think they would care about what we have to say, or even believe us?" Times finally asked.

"I don't know if they will believe us, or if we will make a difference. But it's our job to expose Webster and his abominations," said Mallory.

Mallory walked up to Times, put her arms around his waist, and stared out of the window.

"We've been through Hell and back, Greg. We have to pick ourselves up, and keep fighting. We can't quit. Not until people know the truth," Mallory said.

Times knew he could never allow Mallory to speak with the authorities. He would use his headband, if necessary, to keep her subservient. For now Times understood that he must appear sincerely accepting of her idea. Times turned so that he could embrace Mallory in his arms, and look into her eyes.

"Anything you want, my love," Times said.

Mallory and Times hugged each other.

"Can I see Webster?" Mallory asked after a few moments.

"I'd prefer that you did not. I'm treating him better than he treated us, but he is still a prisoner," Times replied.

Mallory was noticeably uncomfortable with what Times said.

"Oh, I see," Mallory said.

She turned away from Times. Times rubbed her shoulders, and tried calming her nerves.

"It's the only way to keep ourselves safe, until the truth is exposed. He's a very dangerous and powerful man. He'll surely kill us, if he ever regains control of his technology," Times said.

Mallory was ill at ease with the prospect of keeping Webster prisoner, but she knew that Times spoke the truth.

"I suppose if he's alive, then it's okay," Mallory said.

"Come with me. I want to show you the private living quarters," said Times, pretending like she had not already seen them.

Times began caressing Mallory, and kissing her face. At first, Mallory was receptive. But after a moment, she gently put her arm upon his chest and moved away.

"No, Greg. Not here. Not in this awful place," said Mallory.

"I understand," Times respectfully said.

Times stroked Mallory's hair and said, "You know what? I think we should go out. I feel like celebrating."

Mallory was puzzled by Times' peculiar choice of words.

"That's an odd thing to say, at a time like this," Mallory said.

Times grinned slightly and said, "You haven't seen odd, yet."

"Sir, I don't mean to interrupt. There's a situation outside, which requires your attention," the robot Alice said.

Alice holographically projected a live feed, from the lobby's security camera. Times and Mallory saw four police officers, talking to the receptionist.

"God damn it to Hell," whispered Times.

"Go outside, and see what they want," he quickly told Mallory.

Mallory began asking, "What do I tell–"

"Just go!" Times abruptly interrupted.

Mallory was hurt by Times' outburst, but she nevertheless followed his request. After Mallory had left the room, Times opened Webster's desk drawer. He pulled out the mask and placed it upon his face.

"Don't make this hard on yourselves," Times said.

Times watched Mallory approach the officers, and listened closely. The robot Alice produced an audio signal to accompany the holographic video.

"What seems to be the problem?" Mallory asked the group of police.

"Ma'am, are you all right? We got a call about a woman who seemed very distressed," one of the men responded.

"Is that so?" Mallory said.

She gave Kendall a menacing scowl.

"This woman came in here, about forty-five minutes ago. She started yelling and demanded to speak with the corporation's president," Kendall said.

"Is this true?" the officer asked Mallory.

Mallory replied, "Yes, but–"

"Ma'am, I think you'd better come with us," interrupted the officer.

Times opened a small box in the drawer. It contained a mosquito drone. Times activated the drone, knelt behind the desk, opened the office's door, and discreetly threw it out of the room. The drone flew towards the officer, and pricked his neck. The drone's hypnotizing agent rapidly took its effect. The door closed and Times arose.

"You shouldn't be here," Times whispered.

A shiver shot through the officer's body, when he faintly heard Times' voice in his ear.

"Are you okay?" his comrade asked.

The officer once again shivered.

"I...I feel dizzy," he weakly replied.

"I think you need to sit down," another officer said.

This distraction allowed Times to inject Kendall with the mosquito drone's powerful mind altering fluid.

"Make them leave," Times telepathically commanded her.

Kendall twitched, and at first, did not take any action.

"I said make them leave, *now!*" Times said.

He caused her momentary discomfort by very briefly creating the painful ringing sound in her ears. Kendall let out a small squeal, but quickly composed herself.

"I'm sorry for wasting your time. I thought this young lady was in need of assistance. It appears I was wrong," a disoriented Kendall said.

"I suppose...there's nothing to worry about in that case. Come on boys, let's leave," the infected officer said.

Everyone was baffled by the bizarre transaction which had just occurred. Nevertheless, the officers left the lobby without incident. Mallory promptly started walking back to the office. Times ripped off his mask, and threw it in the drawer. Mallory entered the room, and saw that Times was breathing heavily. He was experiencing great discomfort.

"The weirdest thing just happened...oh my God Greg, are you okay?" Mallory said.

She rushed over to her husband. He fell onto his knees, and was in obvious pain. She tried to embrace him, but Times lightly pushed her away.

"I'm fine, I'm fine. Let me rest for a minute," Times said.

"Sir, I'm detecting extreme fluctuations in your brainwave activity. This change is adversely affecting your respiratory, and nervous systems. I think your condition should be evaluated," the robot Alice said.

Times winced several times, and tried his best to hide his agony from Mallory.

"Listen, it's no big deal. This is part of the detox process. Webster gave me very powerful drugs," Times said.

"Shouldn't you go to a hospital?" Mallory asked.

Times shook his head in the negative and said, "No. They can't help me. Only the robots have the antidote."

"You're frightening me," said Mallory.

"Please, relax. Alice, tell the Chem-Mech to meet me in the lab. Mallory, stay here. Use Webster's computer to try and find any information about the experiments," Times said in discomfort.

Times abruptly jumped to his feet. He grabbed a white lab coat, which was dangling from a hanger on the nearby wall. Using his thumbprint, Times locked the drawer containing the mask. Times quickly walked to the elevator, and went to the top level lab research center. Times returned to the room where Webster and he had performed their tests, before all the calamity occurred. The Chem-Mech walked into the room a few minutes later.

"Alice tells me that you're experiencing a rift, in your brainwave functionality," it said.

Times laid upon a large examination chair in the middle of the room.

"My head feels like it's on fire, but my body is ice cold. What's wrong with me?" Times asked.

The Chem-Mech used the camera mounted on its head, to scan a digital image of Times' brain. The Chem-Mech holographically projected the image in front of Times.

"It appears you're putting an enormous amount of stress on your brain's neurological receptors. The electrical connections that occur naturally, are being burnt out by your continued use of the headband," the Chem-Mech said.

"What can I do to fix the damage?" asked Times while gritting his teeth in massive agony.

"I can give you a mild sedative, to help you cope with the pain. It will allow blood to flow more freely through your brain. However I suggest limiting your use of the device, until I can further evaluate your condition," it said.

The Chem-Mech pricked Times' right temple, with a syringe on one of its robotic fingers. Times winced when the needle stung his skin. Seconds later, the pain in his cranium subsided. Times gathered his strength and left the laboratory. He traversed through the corridors, and located a palm print activated elevator switch. He entered the machine, and rode down to Rigor's restricted underground facility. He returned to Webster's room and stood over his bed. Webster saw that Times was weak, and very pale.

"What's wrong?" Webster asked.

"The weapon. Chem-Mech says it's destroying my neurological connections. What's happening?" Times replied.

Webster looked away from him, and tried ignoring the question. Times grabbed Webster's neck, and choked him.

"Explain what's happening to me!" Times yelled.

Webster coughed, and tried to wiggle free from Times' grasp. Times eased his grip, and scowled at Webster.

"I...I...can't tell you," Webster said.

"Why?" Times angrily asked.

"It is too complicated for me to explain. You wouldn't understand," Webster blubbered.

"What do you mean?" Times snapped.

Webster said, "Please, just leav–"

Times abruptly lurched forward and yelled, "Stop *fucking* playing games and answer me!"

Webster panicked, turned his head to his left side, and hyperventilated. Times' face was inches away from his.

"All right, all right! I'll tell you!" said Webster in defeat.

Times retreated, and gave Webster some breathing room.

"It's not simply the device which is harming you. There is something you need to know about the vaccines and injections I've been giving you, these past few months. Those drugs are filled with very special nano-machines. They are meant to eat away specific parts of your brain, over a prolonged period of time," Webster said.

Times was stunned by this revelation. Times ran his hands through his hair, in an exasperated manner.

"Explain," Times said.

"The nano-machines in the vaccines are designed to destroy brain functionality. They were added to drugs containing Selective Serotonin Reuptake Inhibitors, decades ago. Over time they will irreparably damage the neurological connections in your brain. There are many uses for them. The vaccines target particular areas of the cerebral cortex, and force a person to change his behavior. They can make it so that he cannot experience pain, or love. They can make him unable to feel any emotion at all. It's a way to sedate patients, so that they will never question why they constantly need the drugs. It is designed to make them subservient. It is designed...to render them incapacitated," Webster gravely said.

Times was sickened by Webster's explanation. Times took several moments to absorb the revolting information.

"Do you have any idea, how much of a psychopath you are, Webster?" Times asked.

"I don't think you're the best man, to make that assessment," Webster sarcastically said.

Times stared at Webster for a second, before he burst out laughing.

"You think I wanted to be this way? I am *your* creation! *You* did this to me!" Times said.

Webster had no reply.

"How can I reverse the process?" Times asked.

"I don't know if it can be reversed. You can only hope to contain the damage," Webster said.

Times used his cell phone to call the Chem-Mech.

"Find out everything he knows about the drug's nano-machines. Figure out a way to stop this, or slow down the effects," he told the robot.

Chem-Mech replied, "Yes, I shall. You really must refrain from using the devi–"

"I don't need your fucking opinion, you walking holo-top!" Times loudly interrupted.

"Yes sir," the Chem-Mech responded.

"If he doesn't cooperate, kill him," Times ruthlessly said.

"Yes sir," said the Chem-Mech, in a cold robotic voice.

Times left the room, and returned to the upper level laboratory. He fetched a bottle of vodka, he had recently stashed in a cabinet. Times twisted the cap, and began chugging the clear fluid. He momentarily stopped, and opened a bottle of painkillers. He took several of them, and resumed his heavy drinking. After a few sips, he breathed heavily and wiped his mouth. He screwed the cap back on, and placed the bottle back in the cabinet. After taking several moments to reorient himself, he returned to Webster's office. Mallory was sitting in Webster's grand chair.

Times said, "I'm sorry I took so long. Did you–"

"Greg, can we leave? I don't want to be in this place any longer," interrupted Mallory.

Times was unnerved and emotionally conflicted by her request. He did not want Mallory to stay in a facility that upset her; but he also did not like the idea of being away from all his newly acquired technology.

"Yes, of course. Let me pack a few items. Alice, take her to the limo," Times eventually said.

The robot Alice escorted Mallory from the room. Times gathered a duffel bag, a shirt, and a large square box, from the corner. He opened the desk drawer, and removed the mask. He carefully placed the mask inside of the box, closed it, and placed his palm on the box's scanning panel. The box locked tightly. Times gently placed it inside of the duffel bag, and took one last look at his surroundings. Times left the office, and walked to the elevator. He took the elevator down to the parking deck. Mallory was standing next to Alice, who was holding Mallory's purse. Times walked over to his wife.

"This car...it's amazing!" Mallory said.

Mallory marveled at the vehicle's beautiful craftsmanship.

"Wait until you see the inside," Times replied.

Times grabbed the back door's handle, which immediately recognized his hand print. Times opened the door.

"After you," Times said.

The couple entered the car, and Alice closed the door behind them. Times pressed his hand against the glass window nearest to where he was sitting. The interface appeared, and Times typed the address for their apartment. Times double tapped an icon on the graphical user interface, and a map of the city appeared. The map rendered the course which the car was planning to drive, as a jagged blue line. Times pressed his finger on a section of the line, and moved it upwards to recalculate the path.

"I feel like taking the scenic route, if you don't mind," Times said.

Mallory had no objections. A few seconds later, the car began driving along the modified route. Mallory placed her head against Times' chest, and he put his arm around her. She gently stroked his chest with her right index finger. They both stared out the window, and watched the changing scenery. The limousine passed a group of wealthy looking corporate businessmen, and women. The large group briskly strolled along the sidewalk. They were surrounded by a circle of thirteen, rotating, hovering orbs. The round, dense, metallic orbs, were the size of a baseball. They were equipped with cameras, and miniature lasers that could shoot non-lethal pulse beams, at anyone who physically threatened them.

"It's true. They really are not like you, and I," Times said.

"What are you talking about, Greg?" asked Mallory.

"Before everything happened, while I still considered Webster a friend, he shared lots of wisdom with me. He told me how the world's elite view the rest of us. We are the human resources to be preyed upon until we are allowed to retire, shrivel up, and die. He spoke of four classes; and how the upper classes feel the lesser ones are filthy, abject animals. Look around this limousine, Mallory. This belonged to one man. He used it however he saw fit. He made the robots supply his every desire. He made a fortune off thousands, if not millions, of other people's suffering," Times replied coldly.

"We didn't have a bad life. We should be thankful for all of our blessings," Mallory responded.

"Thankful...for what? We're slaves, being manipulated in a psychopathic science experiment," Times bitterly said.

Mallory gently caressed Times' right thigh. He gave his wife a mournful look.

"I have faith that people can change. That's why we're going to tell the world about what happened to us. You *have* to believe in the goodness of human nature. If we expose Rigor, something will change. Something *has* to change. I can't imagine that good people will let abuses like this continue, if the truth is exposed," Mallory said.

Times again looked out the window.

"You feel compassion, because you are a good woman. But you have not been exposed to the full truth. In time you will come to understand the world's true cruelty," he eventually said.

Mallory removed her hand, and softly whispered, "Don't let them change you, Greg. Don't let them take away the person you are, and the man with whom I fell in love."

Times' heart was broken by Mallory's deeply optimistic words. He knew she was totally oblivious, to his truly sinister transformation. Times understood that he was forever vitiated, by his immoral choices. He wondered if Mallory would ever again love him, once she found out that his soul had become vile, and odious. Times needed to put these torturous thoughts, out of his mind.

"I need rest. Wake me, when we're back at the apartment," said Times.

Mallory did not reply. Times leaned his head against the limousine's window, and drifted into an unfulfilling sleep. He was tormented by traumatic memories, of the last few months. He had flashbacks to the night on the New Jersey overpass, the Statue of Freedom, and the United World Hospital. Vivid memories of burning bodies, screaming mutilated corpses, and gunshots, polluted his head. He violently awoke thirty-five minutes later. The limousine had reached his apartment building's street. Mallory saw Times was trembling, and sweating when he awoke.

"It's okay, baby. It was only a bad dream," Mallory said.

Times nervously looked around the limousine, while coming to his senses. Times did not say a word. He simply grabbed his duffel bag, and exited the vehicle. Mallory followed Times, and walked to the back of the car. Times opened its trunk and removed a rectangular computer device, which looked like two sticks pressed together. Times pulled the sticks away from each other. A holographic interface was displayed inside of the open space between the sticks. Times pressed a few buttons on the interface.

"I'm sending the car back to Rigor until we're ready to leave. A vehicle this nice, in a neighborhood like ours, is sure to arouse suspicion," said Times.

Times slid the sticks back together, and the limousine drove away.

"Home at last," Times said with relief.

The couple entered the building, and went to their apartment. Times felt anxious, while standing outside the door.

Times stuttered and said, "I...I don't know if..."

"You're safe now, my love," Mallory said.

Mallory placed her hand on its palm scanning panel, and the door opened. Times slowly entered the apartment, and walked into the living room. He let the duffel bag drop to the floor. Times placed the sticks upon the kitchen counter. Times' hands were shaking. He slowly reached up to his head. He removed the band that he had been wearing for weeks. He gently placed the powerful weapon on the counter. Times was on the verge of tears. He turned to face Mallory.

"You have no idea, how much I've missed you," Times said.

Without saying another word, the mates furiously began kissing each other. They attacked each other's bodies, with a passion neither one of them had ever felt in their entire lives. They rushed to the bedroom, and with wild euphoria, tore off their clothes. They made passionate love for what felt like hours, before falling asleep in each other's arms. Times rested peacefully, and experienced his first relaxing sleep in months. For a while, the whispers inside of his head subsided. For a moment, he felt like his life was complete.

Mallory awoke the next morning in an empty bed. Her heart skipped a beat. She briefly wondered if the previous night, had only been a dream. She saw clothes, strewn about the floor. Mallory grabbed a robe from her closet, and walked to the living room. A pleasing aroma filled the air. It was a scent which she had only experienced, a few times in her life. She entered the living room, and saw Times cooking breakfast in the small adjacent kitchen. Mallory beheld a wondrous sight. In another era, it would have been part of an average person's mundane morning. Times was cooking scrambled eggs, toast, and bacon. Mallory saw from the empty packaging that all the products were purchased from a high class organic food store.

"My goodness, Greg. Where did you get all this food? It must have cost a fortune!" Mallory said.

Times smiled and replied, "Would you believe Alice purchased all this, for only a little more than two thousand Carbon Credits? She dropped it off a half hour ago. That's not a bad deal. We paid more than twice that, for my birthday ham."

"Where did you get the money?" Mallory said.

"We're rich now, remember?" Times replied.

Mallory knew that Times was talking about the money, which they were stealing from Webster.

"Baby, you know that's not our money," Mallory said.

"I beg to differ. I think we've earned the right to live well on someone else's dole," Times said in a callous tone.

Times looked over at the two plates, which he had set upon their living room dining table.

"Please, go relax," Times said.

Mallory slowly walked over to the table. Their personal computer's holographic projector, which was resting in the middle of the table, displayed a video feed of the daily news. A female Chinese reporter was narrating a video report about demonstrations, which were breaking out around the country. Mallory sat at the table, and listened to her speak.

"Riot police, quelled an unauthorized illegal protest in the city of Wichita, Kansas, earlier this morning. Local residents, angered over the curfew issued by President Cho, began setting fires to privately owned crops. The isolated act of terrorism destroyed over thirty-five percent of a wheat field, owned by the world's largest Genetically Modified Food producer, Mancentor," said the reporter.

Times walked over to Mallory, and put a heaping pile of eggs and bacon upon her plate. Times placed the rest on his plate, and went back to the kitchen. He returned a moment later, with freshly baked toast for the both of them.

Before Times sat down he said, "Almost forgot the drinks!"

Times returned to the kitchen, and brought back a pitcher of organic orange juice. He poured the frothy cool liquid into the two cups beside their plates. When he was finished, Times giddily sat upon his chair.

"What are you waiting for, honey? Eat!" Times said.

Times scooped up a big portion of eggs with his toast, and placed three slices of bacon on top. He took a gigantic bite, chewed loudly, and let out a moan of ecstasy. The warm chemical free food tantalized his taste buds. Mallory used the fork which Times had set for her, to pick up and eat a nice sized chunk of eggs. She chewed slowly at first, savoring every bite. Suddenly she was overcome by the taste, and began attacking the food herself. The two of them, shoveled the delicious morsels into their mouths. They were so delighted by the marvelous flavor medley, that they did not bother speaking. Their meal was interrupted, when the Chinese reporter went to her next story.

The reporter said, "...no word if the protesters are connected with the terrorist group, that attacked an apartment complex with illegal food in New Jersey, last month. In other news, the terrorist known as Troubled Ti–"

Times quickly waved his hand in front of the computer's sensor, ending the video feed. Both Mallory and Times went completely silent. They did not exchange glances, even though they sat less than two feet from one another. They awkwardly chewed, and swallowed the bits of food remaining in their mouths. Even though they both had food upon their plates, neither one took another bite. Their eyes finally met. There was a tension so high, it rivaled gravity's force.

Times spoke slowly, and softly said, "Mallory, I–"

"Oh my God," Mallory interrupted in disbelief.

Times said, "Mallory wait, listen–"

"Oh. My. GOD!" Mallory shouted.

She placed her hands over her eyes, and began screaming. Times rushed to her side, and put his arms around her.

Times said, "Shh, it wasn't me–"

"*Liar!*" Mallory yelled.

She tried to wiggle away from Times' grasp.

Times pleaded, "Baby, it wasn't–"

"DON'T YOU FUCKING TOUCH ME!" Mallory frantically shouted.

She tried pushing Times away, but he did not let go. The two of them fell to the floor. Mallory screamed hysterically, and Times struggled to control her. She started kicking him, and flailed her arms wildly. Times momentarily let her go. Mallory got up, to run out of the apartment. Times stood up and felt his body burn with rage, and sadness. He did not again want to lose his cherished Mallory. He heard the all too familiar whispers. He briefly drove his knuckles into his forehead. With his fingers curled, he held out his arms, and arced his hands upwards. Without even using the headband, he miraculously summoned his telekinetic powers!

"STOP!" Times screamed long, and loud.

Mallory fell forward before reaching the door. She landed hard upon the hallway floor. She moaned, and fell into a state of semi-consciousness. Times rushed to her, knelt down, and held her twitching body in his arms.

"Mallory...no. I'm sorry, baby. I didn't mean to hurt you. I love you. Please wake up!" Times frantically said.

Mallory opened her eyes in a dazed state. She gently caressed his cheek, before falling unconscious.

"No!" Times lengthily screamed.

He began sobbing, while holding Mallory in his arms.

"It's okay. It's all right. I'll help you my love," Times whispered.

Times held Mallory for a few moments, before retrieving the computer sticks from the kitchen counter. He slid the sticks apart, and pressed a few buttons on the holographic interface. Times slid the sticks back together, and began gathering his belongings. He grabbed a scarf, hat, and coat from Mallory's bedroom closet. Times dressed Mallory with the coat. She stirred slightly, and moaned. Times placed the hat upon her head, and wrapped her neck with the scarf. Times dressed himself in a jean jacket, and pants. Twenty minutes later, Times heard a knock at his apartment door. Times looked out of the door's viewfinder, and saw the Chem-Mech standing outside. Times opened the door.

The Chem-Mech said, "You've reported a possible overdo–"

"Shut the fuck up you overgrown tin can, and *help* me!" Times immediately snapped.

Times draped Mallory's left arm over his right shoulder. The Chem-Mech supported Mallory's right arm with its left robotic one. The robot picked up Times' duffel bag, with its right robotic claw. The man and the machine dragged Mallory to the elevator, and went outside to the limousine.

They laid Mallory down upon the back seat. Times put his duffel bag in the limousine's trunk. The vehicle's driver's side door opened vertically. The Chem-Mech contorted its body, so that it was able to climb sideways into the vehicle. Times sat in the back seat with Mallory. He held her in his arms, and cried intemperately.

"Patient is in emergent need of treatment. Return to command base," the Chem-Mech said to the limousine.

The vehicle entered Rigor's lower level parking deck thirty minutes later. The Chem-Mech and Times swiftly went to the private elevator. They brought Mallory up to one of Rigor's numerous secret research laboratories. Times took Mallory to the same laboratory, in which he had conducted countless experiments over the course of the past few weeks. Times and the Chem-Mech, laid Mallory upon a medical examination table.

"I don't know what happened. I got upset, yelled at her, and then she collapsed," Times told the Chem-Mech.

The Chem-Mech used the lasers inside of its head camera, to scan Mallory's body. A green beam of light covered her. It expanded and shrank in a triangular pattern. It carefully evaluated Mallory's condition.

"The electrical connections in her cerebral cortex have been over-loaded. There is severe hemorrhaging in her brain. She is in a state of shock," the Chem-Mech said.

"Fix her," Times said.

"I will perform an emergency procedure that will reduce the bleeding. I can give her a tranquillizer to numb the pain. Please be advised Mister Times; she will require intensive surgery to fully repair the damage," the Chem-Mech said.

"Will she be okay?" Times asked.

"Unable to confirm patient's recovery prognosis, at this time," the Chem-Mech said after a brief pause.

Times walked over to a corner of the room, rested his hand against the wall, and bowed his head. Without warning, Times began having an incredible migraine. He screamed, and slid down the wall. He rested on his knees, and the Chem-Mech walked over to him.

It said, "I have not yet perfected the formula, to reverse the effects of the nano-machines. I can administer a–"

"Stop talking and *do* it, goddammit!" Times shouted.

The Chem-Mech injected Times with a powerful painkiller, and gave him two pills to ease his migraine. After a few moments, Times calmed down. He stood up, and walked over to his wife. Times stared at her, and rued his ebullition.

"I don't care how much money it costs, or what surgeries you have to perform. Fix her, and do it well," Times said.

"I will do my best, Mister Times," the Chem-Mech replied.

Times looked at Mallory, and stroked her hair. Times placed a soft kiss upon her lips, before walking over to the duffel bag. Times removed the box, opened it, and placed the heavy mask upon his face.

"I was a fool, to believe I could achieve solace. Men like I, deserve punishment for being obedient servants. My entire existence has been micro-managed by foreigners, and tyrants. I mindlessly accepted a depraved belief system, enormously long work hours, outrageously high income taxes, and authoritarian food restrictions. I fooled myself into believing that I lived a good life. This...was a sadistic lie. Every one of my days, has been spent living in a false reality. I was nothing but a diseased carcass, preyed upon by parasitic elite. I know that my soul is cursed. But I am not the *only* one, damned. Many others deserve reprieve, for their transgressions. I used to believe that there were only a few who deserved retribution, but that is not the case. We are all guilty of wanton degeneracy. I will open the world's eyes, to their putrefaction. I vow to correct this mistake, called the human experience. I vow to cleanse our collective sins through perfidious, anarchistic, artifice!" Times said.

Times clenched his hand into a fist. The mask's cold silver was but a fraction of the icy hatred, he felt in his heart.

24 Visions

Cameron Moss could not sleep. It was 2:41 in the morning on Saturday, February 1st, 2217. He tossed and turned in his bed. His mind was tortured by the thought of immersing Sky, in a world which she did not understand. Cameron never meant to make her an outlaw like himself. Sky was a good girl who deserved a better life than that of a food rebel. Sometimes he wished that they had never met.

Cameron was tormented by the thought, that he was the reason why her life was ruined. Cameron was afraid that one day, she would hate him. That fear was worse than anything he had ever felt, while fighting the food battle. There was no drone that could damage his body, more than Sky would damage his heart, if she ever left him.

He got out of his bed. He put on his dark jean pants, black leather jacket, and black boots. Cameron pressed his finger upon the biometric recognition panel, on the side of his bedroom door. The door slid open, and Cameron made his way out of the compound. The air outside, was chilly. Cameron hated this time of season. New Jersey weather was unimaginably awful.

Cameron chuckled, when he remembered once telling Lily, "We only get four months of good weather during the year. Two good months in the fall, and two good months in the spring. Any other time it's too damn *hot* or too damn *cold*."

He walked a half mile away from the compound and to a small gravel pit surrounded by light foliage. The pit used to be part of a larger parking lot. Over the years, the lack of maintenance had rendered it befouled, and ramshackle. He walked over to a large cement stone that used to be a street lamp's container. The lamp and its post had long since been torn apart. Its rusty deteriorating remnants lay not far from the stone. Cameron imagined the violent riots, which had destroyed the street lamp.

He remembered hearing stories when he was a kid; about roaming hordes of hungry looters and cannibals, killing each other over canned food. Cameron knew that to people of Walter's age, these nightmarish tales were more than gruesome fables. Cameron reflected on his own childhood, and remembered having barren cupboards. His parents constantly argued over money, and food. He wanted to hug them, and see their faces one last time. He wanted to hear them say that they were proud of their son. Cameron picked up a rock, and threw it across the empty lot.

"I'm so sick of this bullshit," Cameron muttered to himself.

Cameron angrily picked up another rock, threw it, and watched it skip across the gravel.

"I am so sick...of this bull, shit," Cameron said a bit louder.

Cameron picked up a palm sized rock, and clutched it tightly.

"I am fucking sick, to my goddamned stomach...of this mother, fucking, bull, SHIT!" he shouted.

Cameron began throwing the rock hard, like a baseball. As the rock left his hand, he saw bright ripples that looked like small lightning bolts, appear in the air. His body slowed down while he was in mid-pitch. The rock slowly left his hand. He felt a powerful gravitational force begin crushing him. Time continued moving slowly. Suddenly the familiar and frightening ashy ripple appeared before him! The Time Shifter stepped out of the ripple, and caught the slowly moving rock in mid-air, with his left hand!

"Stop whining, grow a set, and man *up!*" said the Time Shifter.

Gravity instantly returned to normal. Cameron's motion propelled him forward. He stumbled and fell down. Cameron rolled over, onto his right shoulder. He landed in a kneeling position. The awesome Time Shifter squeezed the rock, and broke it into pieces! He flung the rock's dust from his hand. It blew away like insignificant specks of rubbish. Cameron smiled, and laughed in delirium.

"Nigger, you picked the *wrong* night!" Cameron shouted.

Cameron lurched forward, and grabbed the Time Shifter by the back of his left knee. Cameron used all of his strength, and tackled him to the ground. The two men began trading blows on the floor. Cameron furiously pounded the Time Shifter's side, while the Time Shifter pummeled Cameron's back. The Time Shifter began squirming sporadically, and was able to kick Cameron in his chest. Cameron grunted and rolled away. Cameron quickly sprang to his feet, and saw that the Time Shifter had vanished.

Cameron said, "Come on, you little twat! I thought you wanted to fig–"

Before Cameron could finish his sentence, the Time Shifter reappeared at Cameron's side, and pushed him to the ground. The Time Shifter shook his head at Cameron, while watching him rise from the floor.

"You should know better than to taunt me," the Time Shifter scolded.

Cameron readied himself in a fighting stance. Cameron flinched forward, and tried tricking the Time Shifter into attacking him. The Time Shifter also flinched, before lunging at Cameron. Cameron quickly spun three hundred sixty degrees in place, and delivered a powerful roundhouse kick with his right leg. Cameron's powerful blow sent the Time Shifter reeling backwards. The Time Shifter landed hard upon his back. He slowly recovered, and stood upright. Cameron could tell that the strike had seriously stunned the mysterious fighter. The two men began circling each other, in a very tight formation.

"Why are you hesitating? Fight me!" Cameron said.

"Good. You realize that a man on the defense has the upper hand. This is because he is fighting, not for selfish reasons, but for his own survival. Remember this lesson. It will serve you well in the future," the Time Shifter replied.

The Time Shifter lurched forward, and appeared that he would once again rush at Cameron. Cameron moved to perform another roundhouse kick, but was countered. The Time Shifter teleported behind him, and grabbed him around his neck while he was in mid-kick. The Time Shifter held Cameron in a mighty choke hold.

"You must not assume that you can keep using the same tactic. It makes you predictable to your opponent," said the Time Shifter.

Cameron struggled, and used his elbow to hit the Time Shifter in his midsection. The Time Shifter groaned, and after a few repeated blows, let Cameron free. Cameron turned around and used his right foot to kick the Time Shifter in his shin. Cameron followed up with a flurry of alternating left and right handed punches. The Time Shifter used his teleportation ability to dodge the attacks and confuse Cameron.

"Stand still, so I can beat your ass!" Cameron shouted.

Cameron lashed out in the air, with a series of controlled punches. Cameron desperately tried to hit the Time Shifter, but his mysterious teleportation skill made him a hard target. After a carefully timed teleport, the Time Shifter landed a devastating sweeping forearm to Cameron's back. The blow sent Cameron stumbling forward, and he lost his balance. Cameron landed face down in the dirt.

This only hardened his resolve to defeat his opponent. Cameron punched the ground twice before rising to his feet.

"Stop holding back!" Cameron said.

"After you," his foe replied.

The Time Shifter teleported to Cameron's left side. He struck Cameron hard, with a roundhouse kick from his right leg. Cameron let out an agonized grunt when he felt the impact. The Time Shifter used his lighting speed to teleport by Cameron's right side. The Time Shifter quickly dropped to the ground, and knocked Cameron off of his feet by using a leg sweep. While Cameron was still on the floor, the Time Shifter teleported into the air, and began falling downwards. Cameron rolled away, and heard a loud thud. The Time Shifter had missed the attack, and struck the ground with his fist.

Cameron quickly pounced onto his opponent. He rolled the Time Shifter onto his back. Cameron began punching the Time Shifter in his helmet's visor. Without warning, the glowing orb embedded in the Time Shifter's marvelous gold chest plate, pulsated. Cameron was instantly shot with a low intensity particle beam cannon! Cameron was catapulted upwards, and came crashing down upon his back. He groaned in pain but slowly regained his footing.

"Ionic Shock!" the Time Shifter yelled.

Cameron was hit with another beam of light, and gravitational force wave. The blast sent him flying backwards, and knocked him to the ground. An uncomfortable tingling sensation flowed through Cameron's body. He was disoriented from the repeated blasts. Small bursts of visible electric current briefly fluctuated over his body.

"Is that all you've got?" Cameron defiantly asked after rising to his feet.

The Time Shifter seemed pleased with Cameron's response.

"Hah! Very good! That's the spirit!" the Time Shifter replied.

He teleported in front of Cameron, and began hurling a series of powerful punches and kicks at him. Cameron swerved and avoided the punches. He used his arms to absorb the rest of the attacks. Cameron saw a brief opportunity to counter attack. He lunged forward, and powerfully jabbed the Time Shifter's face. Cameron followed up with a devastating series of hay maker punches, to the Time Shifter's left and right side. Cameron ended his assault by strongly kicking the Time Shifter in his chest. He stumbled backwards, clutched his midriff, and was obviously wounded by Cameron's attack.

"Not bad. I am almost impressed," the Time Shifter said.

"What do you mean 'almost'?" Cameron asked.

He laughed and replied, "You still have a lot to learn!"

The Time Shifter suddenly used his gravitational control, to rise from the ground. He hovered in the air. The Time Shifter positioned himself so that his arms were stretched out, and lowered by his side. The Time Shifter quickly teleported down, and struck Cameron in his chest with a powerful dropping kick. Cameron did not have time to marvel at this awesome maneuver. Cameron was knocked back down, by the incredibly powerful attack. Cameron crawled around on the floor. His vision was blurred, and his body ached. Cameron did not want to lose another battle. He painstakingly pulled himself to his feet. Cameron saw the Time Shifter run forward a few steps.

The Time Shifter jumped up, and teleported high into the air. He began falling at a downward angle. His legs were bent in a kicking stance. At the very last second Cameron rolled away, and avoided the maneuver. The Time Shifter was forced to land at an awkward angle. Cameron seized the opportunity to deliver a strong roundhouse kick to the Time Shifter's ribcage. The shot greatly flustered the Time Shifter. He fell to the ground, and landed on his left side.

Cameron ran forward, leaped into the air, and tried connecting with a falling punch. Before Cameron could finish his attack, the Time Shifter used his glowing orb to fire one more devastating shock-wave at Cameron. He was pushed away in mid-air, by the orb's forceful pulsation. Cameron landed on the ground with a hard thump. Cameron rolled around in pain. He fully expected the Time Shifter was going to pummel him, in his weakened state. Instead Cameron saw the Time Shifter standing over him, clutching his own side. He extended his arm, to help Cameron rise. Cameron accepted the gesture without hesitation. Both men were dazed and quite sore from the damage which they had inflicted upon each other. Cameron struggled to catch his breath.

"You've grown strong, Cameron Moss," the Time Shifter said.

Cameron wiped his lip to remove some of the blood, which was drawn during the fight.

"I'm getting sick of you pulling this shit. It's not funny," Cameron said.

"When have I ever claimed that I was not serious?" the Time Shifter asked.

"Stop fucking around! Tell me why you're always fighting me!" a frustrated Cameron yelled.

"Because I must prepare you for the challenges that you will face," the Time Shifter replied.

"Fuck you. You always speak in riddles. Stop rambling, and give me some answers," Cameron angrily said.

"My time in this world is limited. I cannot give you all the answers you seek, at this present stage of events. However, you have proven yourself to be strong. Therefore I will provide you with knowledge to whatever I can, without revealing information that will affect the natural unfolding of occurrences on this time line," the Time Shifter said.

"First thing you can do, is tell me what you want from me," Cameron said.

"Very well, I will try my best to explain. I come from a wonderful planet that was once rich in beauty, life, and natural resources. In a time that you consider your future, my planet is a barren wasteland. Decisions being made during your lifetime, lead to the destruction of this marvelous planet," the Time Shifter said.

Cameron was stunned by these words. Cameron's mind struggled to cope with the Time Shifter's disturbing revelation. Cameron could not believe this person was a time traveler from a different planet. Yet the pain he felt in his body from their physical confrontation was undeniable.

"How am I involved?" Cameron asked.

"Choices you make in the present have a direct impact on this future. Your actions, and inaction, have a profound effect on my planet," the Time Shifter replied.

Cameron looked away from the Time Shifter, and stared at his own bloodied hands. Cameron gazed around the dilapidated pit, in which they were both standing. He directed his attention back to the Time Shifter. Cameron chuckled softly. After a moment, he began laughing hysterically. Behind his mysterious dark helmet, the Time Shifter stared at Cameron.

Cameron erupted in a fury and said, "Fuck you! I don't give a fuck, where the fuck you say you're from! I'm *nobody!* I'm a fucking *criminal!* You are a fucking lying sack of *shit!* Do you hear me? You are–"

The Time Shifter teleported, and punched Cameron very hard across his jaw. Cameron clutched his face with both hands. This was a mistake. The Time Shifter punched him extremely hard in his midsection. Cameron felt his stomach muscles cramp, and he dropped to his knees. Cameron clutched his midriff with both hands. The Time Shifter violently placed his right palm, on the top of

Cameron's head. The glowing orb in the Time Shifter's golden chest plate began flashing a multitude of different colors. Cameron tried to move, but he was encumbered by a heavy gravitational force. Bright blue fluid flowed from the orb, and began attaching itself to Cameron.

Cameron grabbed the Time Shifter's right forearm, with both of his hands. This action was in vain. Cameron was paralyzed by the intense weight. He struggled to break free from the Time Shifter's powerful grasp. The Time Shifter slowly moved his hand, and clutched Cameron's jaw. The blue fluid poured over Cameron's entire body.

The Time Shifter furiously shouted, "You think this shit is some kind of video game?! You think the future is a joke?! You have no idea the Hell that will be unleashed! You don't believe me? Fine, let me show you! LET ME SHOW YOU EARTH'S FUTURE!"

Cameron suddenly felt himself traveling in a way, which he could not decipher. He felt all parts of his body moving in different directions at once. He saw flashes of bright light. The gravitational force crushing Cameron's body intensified. He eventually felt himself moving in a definite backwards motion. Cameron witnessed an astonishing sight. He saw a still image of himself, held in place on his knees by the Time Shifter. He began moving away from what he perceived was his position. He reached out, and tried to grasp at the image. It appeared like he was looking at a picture inside a tunnel full of light. The image became smaller and eventually disappeared.

Soon Cameron only saw an array of colors, surrounded by black ash. The colors turned into a vast collection of stars. Cameron saw the stars getting further away, and dimmer. Cameron felt like he was falling. Cameron reached to grab a hold of something, but he could find no solid matter to touch. He accelerated with such velocity that he began feeling pain, from the centrifugal force crushing his body. When Cameron thought he could take no more, he suddenly felt himself slowing down. He decelerated, and saw his surroundings come into focus. Cameron found himself staring at blacktop pavement. He looked up, and saw the Time Shifter. Cameron felt extremely cold, and his vision was blurry.

Cameron shook his head, and after a few moments his vision returned to normal. Cameron looked around, and saw a horrible world. Cameron was in the middle of a large city. All the buildings were burnt out, ramshackle, or crumbled. The street was cracked, and broken. Cameron looked up and saw hundreds of black, triangular shaped drones, flying around the sky. The stench of this world was horrific. The smell of sulfur, rotted meat, and burnt wood filled the air. Overturned, vaporized cars littered the area. Crushed military tanks were scattered throughout the city. Destroyed military aircraft were strewn about the road. Cameron felt sick, and even though he tried fighting the urge, Cameron eventually vomited.

"Where are we?" Cameron asked after he recovered.

"New York City, 2331," the Time Shifter said.

Cameron looked around and said, "Impossible. That's over one hundred years in the future. This can't be real."

"It is very real, Cameron. But what you're looking at is only a projection. Follow me," the Time Shifter said.

The Time Shifter and Cameron began walking through the decimated streets. They turned a corner to their right, and encountered more ghastly visions. Burnt skeletons lined the streets. Some of the corpses held laser rifles. This immensely disturbed Cameron; because he knew that they had obviously died fighting for their lives.

"What happened?" Cameron asked.

"A great war took place on Earth, during the first few decades of the twenty-third century. This war plunged the world into one hundred years of darkness. This is what the rest of Earth looks like too, Cameron. I have jumped to many corners of the world, and the devastation across the planet is unimaginable," the Time Shifter said.

"Who was fighting the war?" Cameron asked.

"Humans. They were fighting an enemy for which they were unprepared, and did not understand," he replied.

Cameron saw the burnt skeletons of a mother who had died, clutching her small child in her arms. Cameron once again felt sick, but he forced himself to maintain his composure.

"Who was the enemy?" Cameron asked.

The Time Shifter stopped walking, and placed his hands upon Cameron's shoulders.

"A very ancient and inter-dimensional entity," the Time Shifter said.

The blue fluid oozed from the Time Shifter's chest orb. The two men were transferred into the remnants of an old sky scraper. The structure had been chopped in half. All around the devastated office building were desks, chairs, and computer terminals. Cameron was horrified to see more burnt skeletons, laying on the floor. What most disturbed him was that some of skeletons were sitting upright in their chairs. The Time Shifter walked to the building's edge, and looked off into the distance.

"That is the entity, which has inherited this world," the Time Shifter said.

Cameron saw a man, sitting in a chair made out of human bones. The man was surrounded by giant robots, which Cameron estimated to be over thirty feet tall. The robots were humanoid in shape, and held laser rifles. The man in the chair, held a trident in his right hand. He wore a black and gold colored metal suit of armor. He had a mask in the shape of a Minotaur's head.

"Who is he?" Cameron asked.

"He is the one, who destroyed Earth," the Time Shifter grimly said.

"Well, obviously. But what is his identity?" Cameron asked.

The Time Shifter bowed his head.

"I cannot tell you," he said with remorse.

"Cut the bullshit! You've brought us all the way to 2331! Why can you not tell me his name?" Cameron said.

"I cannot tell you, because I do not know," the Time Shifter said.

"I don't understand," Cameron said.

"Jumping is a complex process. When I jump, the world around me changes. Life is a series of possibilities. This is why there are many different future time lines. Sometimes I jump, and see great changes in the world. Other times there is little noticeable difference. There is a definite universal time line, which people call their present. However their past lingers, because all actions leave a ripple of light in space. The future is different. It is a collection of the most likely events, given the decisions that are being made in the present. That is why I called this, a projection," the Time Shifter said.

"My device allows me to interact with the fading ripple of old light remnants. This is how I can experience the past. My teleportation, allows me to move very quickly around the present. The combination of the two, along with my light orb, allows my creation of realistic portals to probable futures," the Time Shifter continued.

Cameron was awestricken by the Time Shifter's words.

"What do you mean by a portal?" Cameron asked.

"Have you ever held two mirrors, in front of each other?" the Time Shifter asked.

"Not that I can remember," Cameron replied.

"When you hold two mirrors together, they create an infinite reflection. That is essentially how a time line works. Those light reflections are different realities, and different time lines," the Time Shifter said.

"This is insane. I must be going mental. There is no way that this is real," Cameron said.

"It is very real, Cameron. The universe is a complex place, and it changes when it is observed. Time travel is nothing more than observing events at different distances, and velocities," the Time Shifter said.

Cameron stared at the man with the Minotaur head. A shiver of fear, raced up Cameron's spine.

"If you can see different time lines, why can't you stop him? Can't you find out who he is, and kill him?" he asked.

"It's not that simple. Directly interfering with a time line is dangerous. Like I said, the universe changes when it is observed. It also changes, when it comes in direct contact with a person. If I interfere with events, I could possibly make the future worse. I may even wind up being the catalyst, of the very event which I seek to prevent. Even my interaction with you, could have grave consequences. But I feel it is necessary, because this is where my time line stops," he replied.

"What do you mean? How can a time line stop?" Cameron asked.

"My device cannot render any further events beyond this destination. After this point in time, I cannot see the future," the Time Shifter replied.

"Maybe more time needs to pass in the present," Cameron said.

"I thought about that, too. Because time constantly moves forward, I should always have a new reference point in the present, from which I can jump into the future. That is not the case. This is where the time line *ends*. I believe at this junction, there is a cataclysmic event that destroys Earth, and possibly even the Milky Way Galaxy," the Time Shifter said.

"What type of event?" Cameron asked.

"Massive nuclear weapon detonation; the use of an anti-matter weapon that creates an artificial black hole; an early supernova of Earth's sun; anything is possible. I do not know what happens; but I *am* sure, that this is the end," the Time Shifter said.

Cameron continued staring at the Minotaur man. He abruptly dropped to his knees, and put his hands to his face.

"Why me? What have I got to do with any of this, Rasheed?" Cameron woefully asked.

"You have a very strong aura, Cameron. While observing different time lines, I saw you emerge as a great leader in your future. What you did at the Newark apartment complex, is only a preview of the great potential which you possess. After observing you in my past, I looked at the possible time lines which await you. I eventually decided to interact with you, in your present," the Time Shifter said.

Cameron stood up and asked, "So what should I do? How can I stop any of this from happening?"

"You must make your decisions by yourself. What I am here to do, is warn you. The level of tyranny you face in your lifetime is unprecedented. The American empire has become the greatest manifestation of evil, the world has ever seen. At one time it was the shining example of how a free nation, and people, should live. Do not ever take your existence for granted. You are in a special place in the Earth, and universe. I warn you, if the spirit of liberty falls...if *you* fall, then everything falls. All the Hell you see here today will become reality," the Time Shifter said.

"I...I...I don't know how I'm supposed to stop this atrocity," Cameron said.

The Time Shifter looked at the Minotaur man, then at Cameron.

"You will find a way. You *must* believe, that you will succeed," the Time Shifter said.

The Time Shifter looked up at the sky, and Cameron followed his gaze. They saw a dark cloud amid a vast electrical storm, spreading across the atmosphere.

"We have to leave. The projection is becoming unstable. You must return to your time line, or you risk dying in this plane of existence," the Time Shifter said.

Cameron was chilled to his core by the Time Shifter's ominous words. Before he could speak, the Time Shifter placed his hands upon each of Cameron's shoulders. The blue fluid oozed from the orb, and Cameron felt a heavy gravitational force upon his body. Cameron saw the image of himself and the Time Shifter, standing in a ruined world, begin fading away. Soon all he could see was swirling light in the ashy tunnel. Cameron tried steadying his breathing. This time he was better prepared for the effects that deep space travel would have on his body.

Even though his mind was strong, his body failed him. Cameron gasped for air, and panicked when he realized that he could not breathe. He tried screaming for help, but he could not muster a sound. Cameron's vision blurred and he felt himself losing consciousness. He was terrified that he would die. The pain in his body began transforming into a peaceful sensation. He saw blinding flashing lights. Right when Cameron was getting ready to pass out, the ashy void and lights around him disappeared. He dropped a short distance to the ground, and landed on his back. Cameron coughed, rolled over to his right side, and desperately gasped for air.

"Do not be alarmed. The human body has difficulty adjusting to the physical stress, of extremely fast travel," the Time Shifter said.

Cameron rolled around on the floor, and continued coughing. After a few moments, he pulled himself to his knuckles and knees. The Time Shifter stood above him, and extended his right hand. Cameron tried calming himself, and suppressed a few coughs in his chest. In a moment, his normal breathing pattern resumed. Cameron grabbed the Times Shifter's hand, and painfully pulled himself to a standing position.

"Please, leave me alone. I can't help, or save, anybody. You have the wrong guy," Cameron said.

"One person can create, or destroy universes. Your power comes from a fantastic source. It is an infinite consciousness that has been with you, all your life. It resides in the spirit, of every human. It is their most unique gift, and separates them from animals," the Time Shifter said.

"I'm *nobody*. I can't make a difference," Cameron said.

"That is where you are wrong. It is this way of thinking that you must change. All humans, no matter how much they believe themselves to be insignificant, can individually change Earth, time, and space," the Time Shifter said.

Cameron was almost brought to tears by the Time Shifter's deeply moving words.

"How do I know what you're saying, is true?" Cameron finally asked.

The Time Shifter used his right index finger, to press the biological computer interface embedded in his suit's left forearm. A liquid holographic keypad imprinted with strange symbols, appeared on top of his appendage. He furiously pressed the symbols with his fingers.

"When you have seen so many different realities, the truth is not hard to decipher," the Time Shifter said.

The face shield in the Time Shifter's helmet began flashing a flurry of geometric symbols, numbers, and words.

"Nothing in this universe happens by accident. All outcomes are determined by choice," the Time Shifter said.

The Time Shifter stopped pressing the holographic keypad, and rested his hands at his side. The orb's bright blue fluid started flashing an array of marvelous colours. The Time Shifter began rising from the ground, in a vertical direction.

"*Choose* to be strong. *Choose* to leave a powerful imprint of knowledge, upon this realm. *Choose* to endure, and let love be your guiding light through the darkness," he said to Cameron.

Dark black ash began surrounding the Time Shifter. Cameron put his right hand in front of his face to stop the blinding hot multicolored light from burning his retinas.

"I am *positive*, that this knowledge is true. Without it I could never have survived the powerful phase shift, which almost disassembled my body during my first trip through space-time. To be dismantled in an infinite vortex, is a Hell which I would only wish upon the most depraved individuals. However the ability to reconstruct one's self in the face of certain defeat comes from the power of a divine order, which blesses the human species," the Time Shifter said.

Cameron fought the powerful gravitational force that pulled him closer to the ashy ripple.

"I must return to the Time Realm, and study more events. I need to discover what caused the future such destruction. Go, Cameron Moss. Go and claim your rightful place in this world!" the Time Shifter said.

The Time Shifter disappeared into the ashy black ripple. The light created by the orb collapsed upon itself, after being absorbed into the void for a few moments. Cameron was amazed that the void held its solid spherical shape. The light flowed toward its center, before disappearing completely. Cameron looked around the dilapidated pit.

The night was calm, and the air was cool. The only audible sound was that of the wind. It whipped through the thin layer of ice, high upon the tree branches. Cameron was left with nothing but bruises on his body, to prove that he had survived a paranormal encounter. Again he questioned if his experience, was actually real. Cameron's whole body was shaking. He took a few deep breaths to calm himself down. After he had regained his composure, Cameron walked back to the compound. Cameron entered the building, and went to his room to get some rest.

Cameron awoke with his entire body aching. Cameron thought that maybe his surreal experience had only been a terrible dream. His stiff joints, sore muscles, and swollen face, contradicted that thought. Cameron exited his room, took a shower, and changed his clothes. After he had dressed himself, he went to the compound's living room. He saw Eiji and Vincent, playing a holographic video game. Two opened beer bottles were on a nearby table.

"Hey Cam...dude, are you okay? You look like shit!" Vincent said.

"I'm fine. When did you two get back?" Cameron asked.

"A couple hours ago, around two-thirty," Vincent replied.

Cameron opened his cell phone, and checked the time. It was 4:43 PM, still February 2nd, 2217. Cameron closed his palm, and the holographic display disappeared.

"I must have lost track of time," Cameron said.

"Yeah, no shit!" Vincent said.

Vincent did not know that Cameron was making a personal reference to his experience with the mysterious Time Shifter. Cameron went to the community refrigerator, and removed a jug of water. He poured a cup, and took a long sip.

"Did you have any issues at the Branson's?" Cameron asked.

"No. Everything worked out great. They are lucky to have such a strong family and fresh organic food," Eiji said.

Cameron finished his glass and said, "I have to go see Sky."

Vincent and Eiji stopped playing their fighting simulation.

"Cameron, are you sure that's a good idea? She is safe, I promise," Eiji said.

Cameron walked past the duo, and down the stairs. He grabbed his leather jacket from the coat hanger near the garage door, and checked its pocket. A small revolver, which he kept near the inner left breast pocket, was secure in its holster. He swiftly put on his coat.

"I wasn't asking. I'm going alone," Cameron said.

Vincent and Eiji were surprised by Cameron's bold statement.

Eiji began saying, "Cameron, don't be–"

"Let him leave. It's not our problem," Vincent interrupted.

Vincent and Cameron gave each other a stern, yet respectful stare, before Cameron left the room. Cameron entered the garage, walked down the stairs, and over to the locker, where the team kept their armor. Cameron looked at his marvelous body armor. Cameron took off his coat, and put each of his armor components on, one piece at a time. He first put on the protective rubber body suit. He then placed his armored shin coverings, and steel plated boots, around his legs and feet. He followed them with his knee-pads, abdomen covering, chest plate, shoulder pads, arm coverings, and gloves. Cameron breathed heavily. He had not worn his heavy suit in weeks. When he was finished, he again donned his jacket.

Cameron removed his special mask from the post on which it was hanging, and placed it in a duffel bag. He also put two boxes of bullets, a hover camera, and computer sticks with a holographic interface, in the bag. Cameron swung the bag around his shoulder, and exited the compound. Lucia was on top of the compound's roof, using a hand held device to scan for nearby drones. She noticed that Cameron was leaving.

"Hey! Where are you going?" she shouted.

Cameron did not respond.

"Cam! Cameron! Can you hear me?" Lucia yelled.

Cameron still did not answer.

"Shit. What the hell is wrong with him?" Lucia asked herself.

She climbed off of the roof, entered Walter's car, and began driving towards Cameron. He was moving quickly, and had already reached the deserted street. Lucia assumed that he was walking to the nearby bus station. Lucia caught up with him, and drove along Cameron's right side.

"Why are you ignoring me?" she asked.

"Go home, Lucy," Cameron said.

"What's your problem? Stop being an asshole, Cam," Lucia angrily said.

Cameron continued walking and said, "I'm serious, Lucy. I don't have time to talk with you."

Lucia tried being friendly and said, "If you won't talk, at least let me give you a ride to wherever you're going."

"You're pissing me off. Leave me alone," Cameron said.

Lucia stopped driving, and angrily stared at Cameron. He continued walking up the road. Lucia opened the car's driver side door, and held it out with her left arm. She accelerated to ten miles per hour, and smashed the car's door into Cameron's back! Cameron lurched forward, and fell to the ground. He instinctively used his hands to brace his fall.

Cameron stood up and angrily yelled, "What the *hell* was that for, Lucy?!"

"You're being a jerk!" Lucia playfully yelled.

The two stared at each other for a brief moment.

"Sorry," Cameron finally said.

Cameron turned around and kept walking. Lucia was agitated that he was being so stubborn.

"Get in, Cameron," Lucia said.

He attempted to ignore her.

"Don't make me hit you again, mister," Lucia said.

He obliged, and entered the vehicle through its passenger's side door. Lucia turned off the car.

"You going to tell me what's wrong?" she asked.

"There's no point. You won't believe me. I'm not even sure, if I believe myself," Cameron replied.

"You don't sound so hot, hermano," Lucia said in a very concerned tone.

Cameron looked away from Lucia, and did not respond.

"Tell me where you're going," Lucia said.

Cameron sighed and said, "The world is dying, Lucy. I can't explain how I know…but I'm positive that something terrible will happen in our future. We won't survive."

Lucia tried injecting positivity by saying, "We all have to die, someday. That's a given situation."

Cameron shook his head and said, "No, Lucy. You don't understand. I saw something. It was more real than you can imagine, and it was horrible. It was death, destruction, and pure Hell on Earth."

Cameron slumped back in his seat and said, "I don't expect you to understand, or believe me."

"Whatever happened seems like a very unnerving experience for you. If you need to talk about anything, you know I am always available. But please tell me why you're about to walk into town, wearing your war gear," Lucia said.

"Did you see the video that came out of Wichita?" Cameron asked.

"Yeah, that was crazy. I'm so proud of them, for burning all those genetically modified crops," Lucia replied.

"People have had enough of the bullshit, Lucy. They are sick and tired of having their lives ruined by a group of power mad control freaks. People are calling me a hero, but I don't feel like one. There are talks about revolution, everywhere. And who is this sick freak calling himself Troubled Times? The world is getting *crazy*," Cameron said.

"Whoever he is, he sure picked an appropriate name for himself. He certainly is very troubled, to commit such violence," Lucia said.

"That's why I have to leave, and make another video. For whatever reason, it sparked emotion in people. I don't know if this nitwit Troubled Times saw it, nor do I care. All I know is that my video, inspired people to burn a GMO wheat field. *Mancentor's* wheat field, no less. That's *got* to count for something," Cameron said.

"So what are you planning?" Lucia asked.

"There's a small laboratory in northeast Elizabeth which specializes in producing cloned meat. I'm going to steal a truck when one leaves to make a delivery. If I can destroy a few pounds of meat, and upload a video of it, maybe it will inspire people to fight back," Cameron replied.

Before Lucia could respond, the car's dashboard illuminated. Walter's holographic image displayed in-between Lucia and Cameron.

"Isn't that a little dangerous to do by yourself?" said Walter.

Lucia had forgotten that Walter's car automatically sent a textual message to his cell phone, whenever the car started and began driving. The alert was a safety feature, that car manufacturers claimed helped prevent car theft. The device allegedly worked so well, that it was mandated by the government in 2187, as an amendment to the expanding Carbon Tax Law. All modern cars came equipped with software that allowed a user to place and receive phone calls. The car's two-way speakers could be activated remotely. They allowed a cell phone caller to interact with the car's occupants.

Lucia said, "Aw shit, I'm sorry Walter. Cameron just ran out–"

"Save the excuses. Both of you need to get your asses back to the compound," Walter interrupted.

Cameron said, "Walter listen–"

"I wasn't asking for your opinion. Get back," Walter again interrupted.

Lucia and Cameron begrudgingly followed Walter's request. They soon arrived back at the compound, and exited the vehicle. While they were walking up the driveway, one of the garage's large metal sliding doors swung open. Standing inside were Walter, Eiji, and Vincent.

"I can't believe you two little whippersnappers, thought you could have all the fun without us!" Walter said.

Cameron and Lucia were stunned. The men were wearing their combat gear, and specially designed masks! Walter wore his custom gas mask. Vincent held a shotgun underneath his arm. The loose ends of the large cloth bandana tied around the bottom of Vincent's face, flapped in the wind. Covering Vincent's eyes was a reflective visor. Eiji wore a full face ski mask, equipped with night vision goggles. Around Eiji's mouth, was a Japanese anthropomorphic battle mask.

"Get inside. We have to make a plan, quickly," Walter said.

Lucia and Cameron entered the building, and Walter closed the garage's door. Lucia went to the storage locker, and retrieved her personal custom mask. It was a white Kevlar facial covering, with enhanced backscatter optics in its eyes. It was decorated with three pink streaks that extended from the bottom left side, to the top right side. They gave the mask style, and made it look like an animal had clawed the face. She secured the mask snugly upon her face.

"Let's go Iconic-ly kick some ass!" Lucia giddily said.

"Guys, you seriously don't have to help me. This is going to put you all, in unnecessary danger," Cameron said.

"What else are we going to do, Cameron? Hide in our homes like children, because that rat bastard Cho tells us we can't leave? *Fuck* him," Vincent said.

"I've lived through some of the worst times this country has ever seen. I'll tell you all, there has never been a time period crazier than the present. I have no idea how any of this will play out. But I know that now is the time, for a real grassroots revolution. There is social unrest breaking out, all across the nation. We have to be a shining example of the good people left in society. We *must* steer this revolution in a positive direction," Walter said.

"I don't know what else to say except, thank you," a humbled Cameron said.

"Ain't nothing to it, my dude! What's our game plan?" Eiji proudly asked.

"We're going to a meat cloning facility, in Elizabeth. We'll steal a truck, and blow it sky high," Cameron explained.

"Several drones will be patrolling the facility. This will be difficult," Walter said after listening to Cameron's plan.

"We've done this before, Walt. What's the big deal?" Eiji asked.

"Those jobs were different. We studied the truck's route for weeks, before we hijacked one. I'm not sure that we can steal only one truck. We'll have to take out a group, when they leave," Walter said.

"That factory is run entirely by robots. Those farms, and I use that word loosely, don't employ armed human guards. I think that gives us an advantage. We can use high powered weapons, because we won't need to worry about hurting humans," Walter continued.

Walter walked over to the locker. He removed a crossbow, and several explosive arrows.

"These are serious weapons. The arrows are equipped with a high grade plastic explosive on their tips. The bombs can be remotely detonated. If we spread them across a distance, we'll disable multiple trucks," Walter said.

"This is pretty heavy. If we get caught for this..." Vincent said.

Vincent trailed off, before completing his thought. The team knew this was a highly dangerous mission.

"Awesome. We can use the bombs to incinerate that nasty meat," Cameron said.

"We are also going to take out a drone," Walter ominously said.

The whole team was shocked. They started protesting Walter's statement.

"Let's not get crazy!" said Eiji.

"I'm not trying to press my luck!" said Cameron.

"That's way too dangerous, Walt!" said Vincent.

"How will we take it out?" asked Lucia.

Walter put his hand up, and indicated that he wanted the group to calm down. Walter pulled a small cylinder device from the locker. It had blinking LED lights on its top.

"This is a grenade that produces a short EMP burst when it's detonated. These were used for crowd control, during the riots. The police used them to disable electronic devices, like cell phones and cameras, in large crowds. If a drone flies low enough, we can use the crossbow to shoot in its direction. The EMP will detonate, and the resulting explosion will scramble its electronics," Walter said.

The group became stone silent.

"This is fucking insanity," Eiji eventually said.

"Yeah, and it's fucking *awesome!* Whew!" Vincent excitedly said.

"Enough chit-chat. It's time to leave," Cameron said.

Cameron extended his right arm, and made a fist. The others stacked their hands atop Cameron's.

"One, two, three..." he counted.

In unison the team shouted, "Break!" before raising their hands in the air.

The team left the compound, and began driving one of their spare vans. All the supplies they needed were in three separate duffel bags. They drove to Elizabeth, New Jersey. They parked the van on the outskirts of a deserted town, which was about a mile away from the cloned meat factory. They walked through a ruined neighborhood that had been almost completely burned down, during the economic collapse. Lucia looked at all the abandoned houses, and was heartbroken that many of them had been reduced to piles of wood.

"I can't imagine how horrific it was, to live in the old days. Those poor people lost everything," Lucia said.

"You have no idea, young lady. Don't worry; we are going to get it back. That's why we're going on this mission. We are taking back the society that was stolen from us," Walter said.

They saw an abandoned apartment building, which was only fifty yards away from the highway's overpass.

"Follow me," Walter said.

The team entered the building, and had to watch their step. There were holes in the floor, and the structure was unstable. The stench of rotted meat and feces filled the air. The team made their way to the roof.

"I don't think we will get a better spot. We should be able to shoot the trucks from here," Walter said.

"So what should we do now, Walt?" Vincent asked.

Walter sat down, and rested his back against the roof's brick covering.

"We wait. Vincent, you and Cameron should go downstairs, and keep watch," Walter replied.

The men followed Walter's request. The team waited for two hours, but no trucks left the cloned meat factory.

"Hey! It looks like some are finally leaving!" Eiji suddenly said.

Walter and Lucia ran over to Eiji's position. They used their mask's optical zoom lenses, to look in the direction he was pointing. Walter confirmed that five trucks were exiting the building, and driving towards the overpass. An escort drone hovered above the trucks, and followed their movement.

"This is the moment of truth! Eiji, ready the camera. Lucy, prepare to shoot the trucks," Walter excitedly said.

Walter ran to the other side of the building.

"Hey! Go get the van!" he shouted down at Cameron and Vincent.

Vincent and Cameron ran off to retrieve the van. Walter sprinted back to Lucia and Eiji.

"Start rolling Eiji," Walter said.

Eiji twisted a section on the spherical hover camera, and gently lobbed it in Walter's direction. The camera hovered in front of Walter's face. Eiji used the holographic interface on his cell phone, to control the camera with his fingertips. The projection holographically displayed in his right hand.

"I'm saving the video offline, for right now. I don't want to send any location identifying data through the cell towers. It's recording. You have the floor," said Eiji.

Walter took a deep breath and said, "I am an old man. I remember the collapse, quite well. I was only seven years old, the first time I saw someone I loved, die of cancer. My grandmother loved fast food, and she ate it all the time. One day, she was diagnosed with terminal liver cancer. I tried explaining to my family that she got it from eating genetically modified fast food. Nobody believed me. Now, decades later, the world sees the horrors that GMO food has unleashed upon our society.

All across the nation, and the world, people are dying from the lethal cocktail of chemicals, and modified organisms, in their food. We've been conditioned by our government and media overlords, that this is acceptable. It is not. GMOs are biochemical weapons. Mega-corporations that are above the law, have released these weapons all across the Earth. We vow to rid our planet of this plague."

Lucia aimed her crossbow. She hit the leading truck in its windshield with an explosive tipped arrow when it came close to the overpass. Lucia shot another explosive arrow at a truck in the middle of the convoy.

"We do not condone violence against humans, unless it is in self-defense. We are not affiliated with the masked murderer, Troubled Times. We are a group of angry citizens, who demand that our voices be heard. We will make our oppressors listen, through our acts of civil disobedience," Walter said.

Lucia hit the last truck in line, directly in its side. Lucia nodded at Walter to signal that she was finished. Lucia armed her bow with the arrow that was equipped with the EMP grenade. Lucia knelt down and pointed the bow high in the air, to compensate for the extra weight affecting the arrow's trajectory. The trucks came around the overpass' corner.

"Pull the charges," Walter said.

Lucia typed a sequence of numbers into a small keypad, embedded in the crossbow's right side. Two seconds later, the explosives detonated. The trucks crumpled, and came to a screeching halt. Three of the five trucks, were engulfed in a fiery blaze. The drone lowered its altitude, and scanned the highway. Walter knew it would eventually pick up the team's thermal signals.

"You've already met one of our brave freedom fighters. He was responsible for the organic food giveaway, at the Newark apartment complex. He said it best. We are the motherfucking Icons, and we are here to take back our country!" shouted Walter.

Lucia seized her last opportunity to fire at the drone. She shot high into the air, and prayed she would be accurate. The arrow quickly released, but swiftly began falling. As it arced downward, Lucia typed a series of numbers into the crossbow's keypad. The arrow detonated, and a bright spark of electricity scattered near the drone. The strong electromagnetic pulse scrambled its systems, and it immediately lost power. The drone crashed between the last two trucks, and exploded in a gigantic fireball!

"Yes! That's what I'm fucking talking about!" Walter yelled.

Eiji quickly panned the camera, and zoomed in to get a better view of the damage. Cloned meat and twisted metal, burned brightly in the road.

"I think it's time to leave," Eiji said.

Walter ended his message by saying, "We *will* remove these satanic weapons from our society. Remember, you are *all* part of the resistance! Demand these genetic atrocities; be removed from our food supply! Demand these flying death machines; be removed from our skies! If no one will listen then remove them yourselves, by any means necessary! God bless you all!"

Eiji cut the video's signal. The three of them gathered their belongings, and ran into the building. They raced down the stairs, and reached the ground floor. Before exiting they removed their masks and jackets, so they would not be identified by their clothing. Lucia, Walter, and Eiji, placed the gear into an empty duffel bag, and ran outside. Cameron and Vincent were waiting inside of the van. Lucia, Walter, and Eiji, entered the van through its side door. Vincent wasted no time driving away.

"We heard explosions. Did it work?" Cameron said.

"Hell yeah! It was awesome! This woman is an amazing shot," Eiji said.

Lucia blushed and said, "I could be better..."

"Nonsense! You're spectacular!" said Eiji.

He wrapped his arm around her, and gave her a kiss on the side of her forehead.

"I can't believe we did something so bold. We're going to jail forever!" Cameron said.

The team laughed for a moment, but quickly stopped.

"Cameron, that's not funny!" Lucia said.

"Sometimes a man must risk his freedom, to properly fight his oppressors," Walter said.

"I really hope you're right, Walter," Vincent said.

The team let out a cheer, while they drove back to their compound. A few hours later, they uploaded the footage to a video sharing site. They used a cheap holographic laptop, which they destroyed after the video was published. A few hours later, the video started going viral across the internet. Soon, people all across America would see the team's rebellious actions. Before long citizens everywhere would praise the heroic team of dissidents, who called themselves The Icons.

25 Madison Avenue Mayhem

The cool waves splashed Mallory Times' feet. She walked alongside of her husband, across the Coney Island beach. The sounds of birds calling out, while flying high above the sea, was a beautiful compliment to the crashing sounds of the ocean's waves.

"It's so beautiful this time of year," Mallory said.

"Not nearly as beautiful, as you," Times said.

Times stopped walking, and put his hands around his wife's waist. He pulled her close, and kissed her soft lips.

"You are the best thing that ever happened in my life," Times said.

"I'm so happy, baby!" Mallory said.

Mallory placed her hands upon Times' cheeks, and gave his lips a series of soft kisses. The couple heard a distinct clicking sound. They looked out to the ocean, and saw a group of dolphins. They were jumping up out of the water, only a few miles from the coast line.

"They are so cute! Can we keep one as a pet?" Mallory playfully asked.

Times laughed at her joke and said, "Anything for you, my love."

Times stroked a strand of Mallory's hair away from her forehead, and gave her another passionate kiss.

"You need to rest," Times said.

Mallory yawned and said, "I do feel tired, now that you mention it, hon. I don't know what's wrong with me."

"It's all right. You need to sleep," Times said.

Mallory fell forward, and collapsed in Times' arms. Times gently let her slide down to the sandy beach, and rolled her over onto her back. Times cradled her legs and back in his arms. He gently lifted her body from the sand. Times walked several feet into the water. Times laid Mallory down upon her back, and watched the waves begin covering her body. Times fought back tears when he saw a grid of squares, flash brightly on top of the water. Times looked up at the sky. The square grid flashed across the horizon. Times began screaming while the square grid flashed faster, and faster. The beautiful background melted away. The simulation disintegrated, and the laboratory room came back into focus.

Times released one final agonized scream. Shivers ran through his body. He stared down at his wife, who was laying on the laboratory operating bed. She had a clear, plastic breathing mask, covering her nose and mouth. It was attached to an oxygen tank by the side of her bed. Times looked at the beautiful white dress, which he had recently purchased for her. The one piece dress had a skirt at the bottom, and sleeveless straps at the top. An electroencephalogram attached to her head, monitored her brain activity.

"Sir, I have to advise against using the device in this manner. The patient is not sufficiently prepared for extended cryo-stasis," the Chem-Mech stated.

"She's not in fucking cryo-stasis. She's in a goddamned coma," Times snapped angrily.

"You do not want to exacerbate her injury. I have not yet finished repairing her neurological connections. I strongly discourage repeatedly hacking into her subconscious mind," the Chem-Mech said.

"Shut up. Shut the *fuck* up, goddammit! I will not be lectured by a fucking *machine!*" Times yelled.

"As you wish. But it is my duty to advocate on behalf of the patient, that the best decisions be made in the interest of her health," the Chem-Mech said.

Times looked at his unconscious wife, and felt crippling sorrow.

"What are her chances for survival?" Times asked.

"It is hard to say. There are still many cerebral systems that must be repaired. She must be allowed to awaken by herself. Forcing her from a coma, could cause serious damage," the Chem-Mech said.

"How long will she be asleep, once the connections are repaired?" Times asked.

"It could be days. Or it could take months, maybe even years. There is no standard time frame, for a patient to revive from a coma," the Chem-Mech responded.

Times suddenly winced in pain. He grabbed his cranium, and rubbed his fingers around his right temple. He reached into his pants pocket and removed a bottle of white pills, which the Chem-Mech had created for him. Times poured several pills into his trembling hands. He put them in his mouth, chewed, and quickly swallowed their bitter contents.

The Chem-Mech said, "Sir, we should perform an MRI on your brain. The nano-viruses–"

"Don't," Times quickly interrupted.

After regaining his composure Times said, "Listen you walking holo-phone, I don't want to hear any bullshit excuses. Fix her. Understand?"

"I shall do my best," the Chem-Mech said.

Times stroked Mallory's arm, before kissing her breathing mask.

"Don't worry, my love. Your suffering shall not go un-avenged," Times whispered.

It was 6:17 AM on Thursday, February 21st, 2217. It had been almost three weeks since The Icons had dispersed their video throughout the internet. Their heroic actions sparked mass civil unrest, in defiant citizens across the nation. Fast food chains, which were notorious for distributing GMO products, were being repeatedly vandalized by demonstrators. Numerous restaurants were defaced by protesters, who were angry that they were being forcibly fed lethal chemicals. They plastered the restaurants with anti-GMO literature, and rebellious slogans.

Underground organic farmers, who had previously kept their illegal growing operations secret, started doing business in public. They proudly sold their products for reasonable prices, to anybody that desired them. They also donated free organic food to people living in the country's poorest cities. Many upscale commercial organic meat stores, were robbed of their goods by flash mobs. These robberies were committed to protest the price of real organic food, which many people could not afford.

Oppressive police forces violently clashed with dissenting citizens. Protestors, who opposed President Cho's unprecedented crack down on the First Amendment, openly expressed their anger in the city streets. They wore homemade masks and screamed, "We are all Icons!" These protests violated Cho's policy, which banned the use of facial coverings in public. Many protesters were beaten and arrested. There were also groups that resisted, and forcibly restrained the unprecedented police brutality, by using illegally owned guns. Unfortunately these confrontations resulted in several police and civilian deaths. Other government factions responded by supporting food protests.

All Wyoming sheriffs, refused to arrest anyone participating in organic food exchanges. The governor of Georgia signed an executive order, which removed the ban on the sustainable hunting of wildlife. The policy had been in place for over seventy years. The Missouri Legislature voted to restore the state's Second Amendment, and authorized the reopening of gun stores.

The faux news media remained government propagandists. They slandered anyone who supported the Food Movement. They labeled this new breed of political dissidents, terrorists. Some media outlets said the Federal government should use the Army, to invade cities and states that were not doing enough to stop the protests.

Times left Mallory's bedside, and traveled to Webster's holding room. Times entered, and stared at his prisoner.

"Interesting news we have these days," Times said to him.

Webster was watching a newscast on a holographic television that Times had placed by his bed.

"How is she?" Webster asked.

"Mallory is none of your concern," Times replied.

Times walked over to a wheelchair in the corner of the room, and rolled it to Webster's bedside. Times began unfastening Webster's restraints.

"Let's go for a little walk," Times said after unbuckling the last restraint.

Webster painfully rolled out of bed, and sat in the chair. Webster panted and wheezed.

"My muscles are beginning to atrophy," said Webster.

"That's interesting," said Times in a cold and indifferent manner.

Times began wheeling Webster out of the room. They walked down the hall, towards the elevator.

"I know it probably won't mean anything, and I'm sure you won't believe me…but I am sorry, Gregory. I am truly sorry, for making you into the man you are today," Webster remorsefully said.

Times rolled Webster into the elevator.

"Spare me your pity, old man. You've never been sorry for anything, a day in your life," Times said.

A few moments later, the elevator reached the ground level. They exited to the underground parking garage, where the limousine was kept. The robot Alice was waiting next to the vehicle. Times rolled Webster to the limousine.

"Were you able to get all of the supplies?" Times asked.

"Yes. All preparations are complete," the robot Alice replied.

With its robotic claws, it offered him his purple trench coat, fedora hat, and mask. Times handed it his cell phone.

"You are wrong. I *am* sorry. I hope that one day you can forgive me, and yourself," Webster said.

Times put on his coat, and bone chilling mask. Times placed the hat upon his head. He removed his gloves from his jacket pocket, and put them on his hands.

"You're a terrible liar, Webster. You're not sorry for hurting us," Times said.

Times turned around and glared menacingly at Webster, from behind the cold, intimidating mask.

"You're just sorry; you couldn't control your creation!" Times said.

Times opened the back door and said, "After you."

Webster sat up in the wheelchair, and dragged himself into the vehicle. He was careful not to bump the tender stump on his right knee, where his leg had once been attached. Webster pulled himself across the seat, and breathed heavily while pulling himself to an upright sitting position. Times entered the limousine, and closed the door. Times sat back, and stretched his arms out across the large seat.

"I feel like going shopping!" Times said in a very ominous tone.

Times tapped on the window and used its touch screen interface, to enter an address. A few seconds later the limousine started its engine, and began driving away from the garage.

"Where are we going?" Webster asked.

"Don't spoil the surprise!" Times said with excitement.

The limousine rolled down the street. It took Times and Webster fifty-eight minutes, to arrive at their destination. The vehicle drove down the East side of Manhattan, and passed Grand Central Station.

"Can you imagine what people would have said, if you told them eighty years ago, that we'd be living in little Hong Kong one day?" Times asked.

Webster knew that Times was referring to the large Chinese population. The buildings were adorned with numerous Chinese symbols. Dozens of shops, catered to the needs of Chinese citizens. There were even holographic advertisements that were being projected above the streets, which featured Chinese actors speaking in their native tongue.

"I suppose they would have called you, a conspiracy theorist," Webster replied.

"You know they own all of the big cities? New York, Detroit, Seattle, Chicago, and many others, are all controlled by those Communist chinks," Times said.

The limousine turned onto Fifth Avenue, and Times lamented, "They own more, than just land. Whole markets like the film, television, music, and fashion industries, are heavily controlled by the Chinese. Their only competition is those damn, filthy, rat eating Indians. Did you know that ninety-eight percent, of the computer and tech industries' labor force and profits, are split between those two groups? How fucking ridiculous! It's because they have better education systems, than ours. They actually teach their kids reading, writing, and arithmetic. They don't shove all this absurd multicultural, multisexual, bullshit down their throats. They actually give a shit about things that matter. To think, these groups survived a holocaust during the 2090's, when the CIA helped put China's Chairman Dao into power. Over one hundred years later, again using the CIA's help, they've exported his ruthless brand of tyranny across the globe. It's quite amazing when you think about it, honestly."

The limousine stopped in front of a trendy Chinese mega-mall that had been built nineteen years previously. Times reached into a black duffel bag, which the robot Alice had loaded into the back seat, before Times and Webster had entered. Times removed a large rectangular box that was filled with twenty-five mosquito drones.

"I'm sure you are aware that these little fuckers aren't cheap. They cost over five thousand Carbon Credits per model. Oh well. It's a small price to pay, for something so useful," Times said.

Times removed a remote control from the box. The remote control was a glove that was used in conjunction with his brainwave device. It allowed him to control the drone's movement, using hand gestures and thoughts. Times put the glove on his right hand, and quickly made a fist. The drones activated. Times opened the limousine's moon roof, and used his devices to discretely fly the drones out of the car. Times flew the drones to a nearby building, and perched them on its ledge. Times typed a new destination into the limousine's interactive window, and the vehicle began driving away.

The limousine drove two blocks, and came to a stop at the corner of Madison Avenue, and East Forty-Fifth Street. Times flew his legion of drones off the ledge. Times infected twenty-five different targets with the mind control serum. A group of five businessmen, three street food vendors, six college students, two homeless men, four police officers, and three random pedestrians, were infected by the behavior affecting serum. Times used his final two drones, to prick two armed guards that were standing outside of a fancy Chinese sword shop. All of Times' victims were of varying races and ages, but they were all male. Times needed to use their physical strength to his advantage.

The youngest victims were the college students, whom Times assumed were in their late teenage years. When he was finished, he flew the drones to various locations around the street, and perched them on different ledges. Times displayed video feeds from the drones, across the back window, in a square-shaped grid. Times imagined this is how a fly viewed the world. Webster became horrified, when he realized that Times had taken control of so many people.

Webster said, "Gregory, stop. This is madness. Whatever you're thinking about doing–"

Times created the painful ringing sensation in Webster's ears, and Webster immediately stopped speaking.

"Enough with the lectures, old man," Times indignantly said.

Times removed a hover camera from the duffel bag, turned it on, and made it hover in front of his face. Times adjusted the camera, so that a small holographic display projected from its side. He could see everything that the camera was recording. Times adjusted it, so that the only visible image recorded, was his masked face.

"Director, I am ready for my close up shot!" Times maniacally said.

Times cackled, and Webster tried to reason with him.

"Gregory, listen to me. These people have done you no harm," he said.

"It's time for you, to shut your fat fucking mouth," Times said.

He pulled a roll of duct tape from the duffel bag, and strapped a piece over Webster's lips.

"Get ready to see something, spectacular," Times said.

Times started recording and said to the camera, "People of America, it is so good to again speak with you! Over the past few weeks, we have seen much turmoil spread across our nation. The terrorist faction called The Icons, has stricken fear throughout our communities."

Times used his mind control ability, to make the large group walk towards the sword store.

"This band of violent misfits, seeks to lead a countrywide revolution. They speak about wanting to resurrect our lost republic, from a tyrannical government," Times continued.

The group entered the store. The panicked attendant tried to remain calm.

"Ca...Can I help you?" she nervously asked.

The armed guards and policemen drew their weapons and pointed them at the attendant. She screamed and tried to run away, but an armed guard shot her dead. Several store patrons also attempted to flee, and they were also brutally gunned down by the gun toting men.

"This...is a fool's dream. This country has been captured for decades. The only way to fix society, is by purging its dregs," Times said in a menacing tone.

The group inside the sword store began taking different blades off of the shelves. They armed themselves with long katanas, machetes, daggers, and axes.

"Many people have claimed that I am of the same breed as these food terrorists. I assure you, I am not. I am the *antithesis* of freedom. I am *chaos*. I am *anarchy*. I am the unholy *nightmare*, who will teach you the meaning of total despair," Times said.

The group rushed out of the store, and began running around the street like rabid animals. People screamed in terror, and ran for their lives when they saw the heavily armed group.

Times continued his insane rant, "Until now, I have been soft on this society. That changes, today. I must cleanse you, of your sins. I must burn away, your wretchedness. What you saw at the hospital, was only the beginning. I will unleash a brutal wave of attacks that will mortify you in ways that you cannot begin to imagine. I will not stop, until everything has been taken from you; the same way it was taken from me. Now let me show you the evil, of which I am capable. Let me show you, the trouble with Times!"

Troubled Times followed through on his promise, and pure tragedy ensued. Times made the group run into shops all around Fifth Avenue. He forced his victims to maim innocent bystanders with the blades! The five businessmen ran into the subway station, and viciously chopped at passengers exiting the terminal. A young woman screamed; when she witnessed a man get a katana sword shoved through his stomach. The woman put her hands up to defend herself, but this act was in vain. One of the businessmen hacked off her forearms with a machete. The woman, and her appendages, fell to the ground. The businessman proceeded to stomp her head into the pavement, putting an end to her suffering. Blood splattered across the walls, but the carnage was far from over.

The businessmen ran like savage beasts, through a screaming crowd. One of the businessmen shoved an elderly woman to the floor, and pummeled her in the head with his axe. Her cranium split in half, and a stream of blood spurted from her mangled appendage. Another businessman used a short katana to slash at a man trying to protect his girlfriend. The businessman hacked at the man's belly. The man's entrails spilled onto the hard subway pavement.

His girlfriend started vomiting. The businessman wickedly hacked at her neck with his katana. The woman was completely beheaded. The businessman took the severed head, and threw it into the horrified crowd. All around there were sounds of crying, mixed with the unmistakable screams of agony. People were being chopped up, like helpless pieces of meat. Two police women patrolling the subway platform heard the commotion. They raced towards the sounds of madness. One of the female officers used her cell phone to call for assistance.

She said, "We have a code four one five. Serious civilian disturbance, near the Grand Central Station subway–"

The female officer did not finish speaking. She was overcome with horror, when she saw a man crawling on the floor. The man had his right arm severed, and his left cheek was hanging off the side of his face.

"Code two forty-five! Requesting immediate backup! I have serious injuries!" she screamed.

One of the women stayed behind to try and help the severely wounded man. The female officer drew her service laser pistol, and began quickly jogging amongst the scattered crowd. People with various cuts and abrasions, ran for their lives. Others lay mortally wounded, and had deep slash wounds to their bodies. Blood and body parts were strewn about the floor. The officer resisted the urge to vomit. She saw the top portion of a man's head, which was severed at the nose, laying on the ground.

The female officer saw a group of people fleeing from a bloodied businessman. The businessman turned around, and the officer beheld a ghastly sight. The businessman was holding a young woman's severed head in his right hand, and a large machete in the other. The businessman was screaming hysterically. She aimed her gun at the blood soaked man.

"Drop your weapon!" the female officer said.

"Help me! Help me! Help me! He's inside my mind!" the businessman screamed.

"Drop your fucking weapon!" the female officer once again yelled.

The businessman threw the severed head at the female officer. He lunged at her, with his machete held high above his head. The female officer fired one shot from her laser. A hole was burned into the businessman's chest, and he fell dead.

The scene on the street was equally chaotic. The three food vendors had entered a trendy clothing store. One of the vendors, jumped behind the sales counter. He proceeded to stab the female cashier through her chest, with a very large scimitar. Blood sprayed wildly. The woman instinctively grabbed the blade in self-defense. The vendor twisted his scimitar, and the woman's fingers fell off. One of the other vendors frantically ran throughout the store, and hacked up merchandise with a double-sided axe.

The third vendor used a long spear to attack his victims. The vendor lurched forward, and gored an elderly man through his stomach. The vendor twirled the spear in a circular motion, until the old man's intestines fell from his body. The elderly man fell dead while clutching his intestines, in a desperate attempt to keep them inside himself. A chorus of bloodcurdling screams filled the air. The vendor with the scimitar ran towards the changing area. He opened one of the doors, and saw a frightened teenage girl, cowering in the corner of the dressing room.

The girl screamed, "Please don–!"

Her plea fell upon deaf ears. The man sliced her undeveloped body with his scimitar. She put her hands up to defend herself. After a few brutal chops, the girl's hands fell off. She slumped over, on her left side. Tears flowed from her eyes. He knelt down beside her and slit her neck, from ear to ear. Her screams were silenced. The vendor ran out of the room.

"Make him stop! He won't let me stop!" he screamed.

Covered in blood, the vendor continued running through the store. He saw a fleeing young man, running adjacent to his own position. He took the opportunity to slash him across his chest. The wounded man still attempted to run, while blood gushed from the gaping wound. The young man fell down, and succumbed to his injuries.

Two young men saw the unfolding carnage, and decided to take action. They ran up to one vendor, who was wildly swinging his axe. They grabbed some boots and shoes from a nearby display rack, and began throwing them at him. The vendor stopped chopping a helpless woman, whom he had hacked in half with his large axe.

"Why?! WHY?!" the vendor screamed.

He ran towards the two brave young men. The vendor swung his axe, horizontally in front of his body. The two young men prepared for confrontation.

"Let's go, you tweaking motherfucker! Real niggers ain't scared of your crazy ass!" one of the young men yelled.

Before the vendor could reach the screaming man, his friend ran around to the vendor's side, and smashed him with a hard rushing tackle. The vendor fell into a display case, and lost control of his axe. Another man ran over, and helped the two others contain the crazed vendor. They wrestled him, and tried to constrict his flailing appendages with their bodies. Troubled Times let out a howling maniacal laugh, from inside the limousine.

"Hah, hah, hah! Is this dementia, not beautiful? Where now, is your system of belief? Does your God, spare you from this suffering? Do your laws, save you from destruction? How does it feel to know that your philosophy of ignorance, and worship of death, has brought these horrors to your streets?" Troubled Times asked disrespectfully.

Troubled Times felt himself losing the neural connection, with the one vendor scuffling with the brave group of men inside the department store.

"I don't need you any longer. Your service is complete!" Troubled Times said.

He telepathically sent a powerful brainwave signal to the vendor, which caused him to immediately scream out in terrible pain. The vendor's eyes began bulging from his skull. The men rolled away from him, and were afraid that it was them who had caused the injury.

"Take me!" the vendor yelled.

He leapt to his feet, grabbed his chin, and the back of his head. He twisted his arms, snapped his own neck, and fell dead. The small group of men gasped, and immediately ran away from the vendor's warm, twitching body.

"You're welcome!" said a deranged Troubled Times.

Anarchy was spreading elsewhere, around the Manhattan streets. The group of six students had separated and were wildly running along the sidewalk. They brutally massacred innocent citizens by stabbing, hacking, and slashing them. Three students ran up to a fleeing elderly man, and knocked him to the ground. The man slowly pulled himself to his knees.

"Please don't kill me!" he screamed.

The students punched and kicked the man, in his face and body. The man tried crawling away. Two of the controlled students, held out the man's left and right arms.

"No! Have mercy!" the man yelled.

The third student ignored the man's cry for sanity, and began hacking at his left shoulder with a hatchet. The man's arm eventually broke away from his body. The fresh stump spurted a fountain of blood. The student chopped at the man's right arm, until it was also severed. The two students holding the severed limbs used them to beat the man, while he lay twitching upon the ground. Blood covered the students, while they savagely pummeled the man with his own appendages.

Three other students, and the two homeless men, were terrorizing patrons inside a popular fast food restaurant. The group ran into the restaurant, and immediately attacked a line of people waiting to order. The students indiscriminately murdered the patrons with spiked steel maces. Screams filled the air, and people fled for their lives. Those who were unfortunate enough to be hit by the mace attack were viciously impaled by its large spikes.

The mace's heavy mass broke their bones. Its sharp spikes pulverized their fragile flesh. One innocent young female was bludgeoned in her face by one of the students, while she was praying on her knees. The mace got stuck in her facial bones. The student kicked her body over on its side, put his foot on her chest for leverage, and ripped the mace out of her face. A bloody mash filled with holes, was all that remained of her once beautiful face.

The two homeless men jumped over the restaurant's counter. Using steel batons, they assaulted a teenage male worker whom had been taking orders. The bones broke in his arms, legs, and shoulders. The boy screamed in agony, and dropped to the floor. One of the homeless men began bashing his skull with a baton. His head split apart like a coconut. Blood and brain matter splattered the walls.

"I'm sorry! I'm so sorry!" the man screamed.

The homeless men stopped their rampant assault upon the poor boy. They turned their attention to three other workers, cowering in fear near the deep frying station. Two young women, and a middle aged male manager, were begging and pleading for the homeless men not to hurt them. The homeless men slowly walked towards the frightened group.

"Lord, no. I...I can't let you hurt these women!" the manager said.

The manager performed a valiant act. He picked up a pan of hot frying oil, threw it in their direction, and scalded the homeless men. The homeless men howled in pain, when the hot oil seared their flesh. The grease stuck to their skin, and horrifically burned their bodies.

"Follow me!" the manager said.

The heroic manager led the girls away from kitchen. He pushed the girls toward the back of the restaurant. They reached a door which led to a restricted employee area. The manager placed his palm on the door's lock panel, and was granted access to the room.

"Quick! Get inside!" he yelled to the frightened and whimpering women.

The manager followed them, and pressed his palm against a panel on the other side. The door slid shut. The group huddled together and listened to muffled screams of agony, echo throughout the restaurant.

Troubled Times winced in discomfort. Controlling the large group was exhausting. Their collective brainwaves overloaded his mental pathways. It was extraordinarily difficult, managing so many simultaneous thoughts and emotions. He removed a bottle of pills from his coat pocket, and poured a few into his hand. He slipped them underneath the mask's chin, and quickly consumed them. Troubled Times forced himself to concentrate.

"Embrace the Hell being unleashed upon our streets! Embrace it, just like you have embraced corruption! This is the Hell that *you*, the degenerate parasites, have brought upon yourselves! It is not *I*, who is doing this to you! You are being prosecuted for your willingness to embrace immorality, in every aspect of your lives! You submit to tyrannical authority! You promote faggotry, and pedophilia! You bow to degenerate foreigners! You are lazy *scum*, whom worship a glowing god called the television! How long did you think that your decadent, selfish behavior, would go unpunished?!" he yelled.

Troubled Times made the two armed guards, and three pedestrians, enter a large office building. The guards pulled out their guns and started randomly shooting people in the building's lobby. People frantically scattered in all directions. A young woman wearing a tight skirt, tried to take cover behind a large fake plant. She was shot in the back of her head by an armed guard. Her dead body fell into the faux foliage. Another guard saw a receptionist, who was hiding behind the lobby's desk.

The receptionist yelled, "Please don–!"

Before she finished, the guard callously shot her in the chest. She clutched her wound, and fell over. She coughed up blood, while taking her last breaths. The three pedestrians ran to an elevator, and waited for it to arrive. The elevator reached the lobby a moment later. The elevator doors opened. The five people inside were startled by the ghastly butchery. The sounds of gunshots rang loudly throughout the lobby. One pedestrian was holding daggers in each of his hands. He screamed, and ran into the elevator.

He started stabbing the woman closest to the door. She screamed, and fell to the ground. The crazed man continued stabbing her, and gouged out her eyeballs. The other people in the elevator ran out, and tried to escape. Most of them did not get far. Two were immediately assaulted by the crazed men. One pedestrian used a large fireman's axe, to behead a middle aged woman. The other pedestrian, who was holding a large trident, impaled a young male.

Two other women, who had fled the elevator, were lucky enough to escape. They ran around the corner, and found safety in a restroom. The sounds of chaos echoed throughout the lobby. The two pedestrians stepped over their victim's dead bodies, and entered the elevator. One of the pedestrians pressed the button, for the building's top floor. Another pedestrian sat down on the ground. He rocked back and forth, and tried to cope with the nightmare in which he was living.

"My brain, it's burning!" the pedestrian screamed.

Several moments later, the elevator arrived at the 30th floor. The floor housed a competing pharmaceutical company, named Illuminated Pharmaceuticals. Troubled Times chuckled when he saw the drug company.

"This really brings a new meaning to the phrase, 'killing the competition'!" Troubled Times said with sick glee.

The three pedestrians ran from the elevator, and raced down the hallway. They stormed into the front office, and began unleashing death on the hapless workers. One pedestrian leaped over the lobby's front desk, and stabbed the receptionist in her throat with his daggers. He continued stabbing her entire body, until her bloody corpse fell out of its chair. Office workers screamed in fright. The pedestrian with the fireman's axe, ran into a cubicle where a very husky man was working.

The frightened large man started asking, "My God, what are you doi–"

The overweight man did not finish speaking. The pedestrian drove the axe into the top of his skull. The pedestrian wiggled the axe free. The large man slumped over in his chair and died. The pedestrian with the trident, ran into another worker's office. A scared middle aged woman was cowering underneath her desk.

"I'll give you anything you want! Just don't hurt me!" she yelled.

The pedestrian ignored her request, and began stabbing her with the trident. She screamed, and tried to block the attack. Unfortunately this did not stop the man from assaulting her. After poking her several times in the stomach, the woman went limp and began twitching. The man ended her suffering by taking the trident, and impaling her through the chest. Blood soaked the doomed woman's body.

"Somebody stop this madness!" the man screamed.

He left the woman's office, and ran down the hallway. The pedestrian with the axe, ran into an employee break room. An attractive woman was sitting in a chair. She put her hands in front of her face.

"Don't kill me!" she shouted.

"He won't let you live!" the pedestrian screamed.

He proceeded to hack off her forearms, while she screamed loudly. Her bloody appendages fell into her lap.

"No! No!" yelled the woman.

He swung the axe at her face, and chopped her head in half. The top part of her skull flew into the wall. The crazed man proceeded to chop off her breasts. Unbelievable amounts of blood sprayed everywhere, during this vicious abuse.

"Forgive me!" the pedestrian screamed.

He ran out of the room, leaving her mangled body behind.

It had been seventeen minutes since Troubled Times began his horrific rampage. Police units were arriving at the scene. Three heavily armed drones with mounted laser guns, slowly lowered their altitude. The autonomous miniaturized fighter jets, circled the street. The drones took pictures and video of the carnage. They uploaded the data to various government databases around the country. The databases kept records of known terrorist attacks. The databases were filled with countless hours of footage. They also contained the names of convicted and suspected terrorists. This interconnected grid of databases served a legitimate purpose. But many people felt that political dissidents like Food Liberationists, were unfairly listed alongside of real terror organizations, like the Islamic Sisterhood.

"Unknown terror threat, identified. Heavy casualties sustained," said one of the drones.

Two large armored black trucks autonomously drove to the Grand Central Station terminal. The trucks parked on opposite ends of the street. Inside one truck, was a team of eight armed men and women. These agents from the Division of Homeland Safety assessed the situation. All the agents wore the same attire. They had black combat boots on their feet. They dressed in blue, white, and gray, camouflage fatigue pants. Bullet proof vests, which they wore over matching camouflage jackets, covered their upper bodies. Black masks shielded their faces, and black helmets rested atop their heads. They carried semi-automatic laser rifles, and hand-held laser pistols for their sidearm.

The only uncovered portions of their bodies were their fingertips, which were partially obscured by fingerless gloves, and their eyes. A holographic visor projected a user interface in front of their line of sight. The visor wrapped around the front of their helmets. Tiny cameras embedded in the helmet, allowed them to see their surroundings in a three hundred sixty degree panoramic view. The camera's optical zoom lenses magnified objects. Citizens were swiftly identified by using facial recognition programs. Advanced millimeter wave scanning technology, gave them the ability to see through walls. The lead DHS Agent pulled down his mouth covering. He used the dozens of tiny microphones embedded in his helmet, to call the NYPD headquarters.

"This is Commander John Cooper. Authorization code, A-P-X-Seven-Five-One-Zero. Chief Vazquez, do you copy?" he asked.

Chief Vazquez replied, "Yes, this is Lisa Vazquez; Chief of the New York City Police Department. What the fuck is happening over on the east side? Calls are flooding in–"

"Drone intel indicates that group terrorism is occurring. Location seems contained to Fifth Avenue, and its surrounding buildings. Holographic maps are showing victims with catastrophic injuries, and multiple fatalities. We have been authorized by the Division of Homeland Safety headquarters, to use lethal force during apprehension," he interrupted.

"I'm sending support units to your position," Chief Vazquez said.

"Negative. There are still active terrorists at this location. The DHS will assume command and jurisdiction over all New York City police units, until the terrorist threat is resolved. Is that understood?" Commander Cooper asked.

"Yes sir," Chief Vazquez begrudgingly replied.

"Copy. Under the power vested in me by the United States Federal Government; I hereby place the entire resources of the NYPD, under the Division of Homeland Safety's control. This order will be effective for forty-eight hours. At the termination of that time period, the DHS will assess the situation and determine if operational authority can be transferred back to the city," Commander Cooper said.

"Roger. What are our orders?" Chief Vazquez bitterly asked.

"Issue a city-wide 'Cover Inside' directive, to all persons currently located in New York City. Make sure everyone understands that they are required to stay indoors, until the crisis is over. The drones will scan the island for all civilian electronic devices, currently emitting cellular phone frequencies, and send the numbers to you in an encrypted text file. Use the city's message alert system, and disperse the cover order to the provided numbers," Commander Cooper said.

"I understand. Is it all right if I speak with Mayor Wu, and determine the best time to hold a press conference?" Chief Vazquez asked.

"Permission to engage in social media statement, approved. Stand by for an upload of permissible topics, and Federal Press Release Guidelines. End transmission," he said.

Commander Cooper cut the microphone's audio feed, and ended the conversation. Commander Cooper interacted with one of the nearby drones, by using the holographic interface on his DHS cell phone. Commander Cooper flew the drone through the streets at a low altitude. The drone automatically took video, and picture images of the destruction. All around Fifth Avenue, dead and injured victims lay upon the ground, and moaned in agony. Blood and body parts littered the sidewalk and streets. Severed arms, legs, and heads, were strewn around the block. Hordes of screaming people were fleeing with the utmost expedience. Some people attempted to help injured individuals, by bandaging their wounds with their clothes. The drone saw three students chopping a man to pieces.

"Terrorists identified," the drone said.

Without hesitation, the drone fired three hot plasma beams at the students. The students exploded into gory mash. A frightened woman who had managed to escape the slaughter, vomited when the bloody particles of their bodies, splashed onto her face. The drone used high powered wireless fidelity, to see through the walls of the surrounding buildings. The drone located the other three students, who were still inside the fast food restaurant. They had finished their onslaught on the store patrons, but were now directing their attention to the burned homeless men. The men on the ground were twitching in pain.

"Please. Help me," one of the burned men muttered.

"I can't!" a student screamed.

He smashed the man's face with his spiked mace. One of the other students walked over to the other homeless man, and proceeded to stab him in the eye with a machete. The machete went through the homeless man's left eye, and came out the back of his skull. The man's dead body twitched for a few seconds. The student yanked the machete out of the man's head.

"Please, no more!" he screamed.

"Terrorists identified. Unable to eliminate. Thermal weapons will potentially cause structural damage," it said.

"Take them out," Commander Cooper said to two female DHS agents.

"Yes sir!" the women yelled.

They opened the truck's back door and jumped out. The women ran down the street and a few moments later, reached the fast food restaurant. They entered the establishment with their assault laser rifles drawn.

"Division of Homeland Safety! You are under arrest! Drop your weapon!" one of the women yelled.

The students each gave bone chilling replies.

"We can't..."

"He won't let us stop..."

"Tell my mother, I love her..."

The woman used her communication headset and said, "Commander, these are just college kids. They look frightened. Please advise."

"Try to take them alive, but do not hesitate to use deadly force. That is an order," Commander Cooper responded.

The women looked at each other briefly, and acknowledged the unspeakable decision they might be forced to make.

The other woman softened her voice, and said to the students, "Hey, listen. No one is going to hurt you. Come with us. We'll get all this sorted out."

The students did not respond. They all started whimpering, and crying.

"I'm so sorry," one of them said.

In an instant, the three students screamed and rushed toward the women. The agent who was just talking to them, sprung to action.

"Shit! Open fire!" she shouted.

The two agents fired several shots from their laser rifles. The plasma beams ripped holes in the students' chests. They dropped dead before they reached the women.

"Holy fuck!" her companion yelled.

"What happened?" Commander Cooper asked over their com-devices.

"We had to kill them, sir. My God, they ran right at us. They didn't even care about the lasers," the lead female agent said.

"You had no choice. Return to the truck," Commander Cooper said.

The women looked at the dead young men. Without saying a word, they jogged back to the truck.

Troubled Times knew that he could not control the situation. He decided to create a distraction, to facilitate his escape.

"Damn. It seems that some people are not enjoying the show!" Troubled Times said.

Troubled Times used his glove and headband, to fly the small hovering drones into a nearby sewer. He telepathically gave his remaining surrogates their final dastardly orders. Troubled Times instructed the four police officers, to locate two of their squad cars. Two officers entered each vehicle. Troubled Times made the officers override the squad cars' automatic drive feature, by having them place their hands on the dashboard scanning panel.

"Excellent. Now for the magnificent curtain call, to my symphony of misery!" Troubled Times said.

He tapped the window, set the limousine's destination, and began driving away. The squad cars activated their flashing overhead lights. The police drove to the end of the block, and turned the vehicles around. The occupants revved the engines. The cars peeled out and began racing down the street. Bystanders screamed and jumped out of the way, to avoid being hit. The vehicles accelerated faster. A few seconds later, the cars crashed into the DHS trucks, which were sitting on opposite ends of the street. The squad cars crumpled, and the impact killed their occupants. Commander Cooper and his team were rattled inside of their truck.

"This is Commander Cooper, Authorization code Alpha Ion Omega! We are under attack! Initiating anti-terror protocol, forty-one-X-dash-zero-six!" Commander Cooper shouted.

The doors of the other DHS truck opened. Some onlookers screamed in horror, when they saw the object that exited the mangled vehicle. A seven foot tall, humanoid, robotic exoskeleton emerged from the truck.

"Classified DHS protocol, acknowledged. Xavier, model number 41X-06, activated. Orders are to rescue surviving DHS agents, and eliminate remaining terrorists," said the large robot.

Xavier ran over to the mangled DHS human transport truck. Xavier ripped off its doors, using its superior strength. It helped the DHS agents climb out of the truck.

"Do you require medical assistance?" Xavier asked.

"We'll be fine. Go stop the asshole responsible for this shit!" Commander Cooper said.

"Understood. Air reconnaissance has identified three active locations, containing hostile terrorists. Commencing elimination," Xavier said.

Xavier wirelessly interfaced with one of the drones, and made it lower its position to the street. Xavier climbed atop the drone, and began flying around the neighborhood. The armed guards in the ground floor office lobby ran out, and started shooting the robots. The drone immediately used its high powered laser to explode the guards. Pieces of their bodies flew in every direction. Troubled Times felt his mental connection with them, sever when they died.

Troubled Times laughed and said, "Yes! It doesn't get any better than this, America!"

Webster sobbed when he saw bloodied people run past the limousine. The robots flew past the office building, and landed in front of the department store. Two vendors were still on a rampage. Xavier leapt off of the drone and ran into the store. Xavier scanned the store, using its advanced optics. Blood, body parts, dead bodies, and injured victims, were strewn around the store. Some were crying, and begging for help. Others gasped at the sight of the large, human-like robot. The robot used the same Wi-Fi technology as the drones, to see through solid walls. The robot located one of the vendors. He was using his scimitar to viciously kill an elderly woman; that had attempted to hide underneath a pile of clothes.

"Terrorist identified," Xavier said.

Xavier held out its right exoskeleton hand, and shot a powerful laser beam at the vendor. The vendor howled in agony, while the laser's heat melted him into a smoldering pile of flesh.

"Threat eliminated," said Xavier.

The robot continued its scan. The remaining vendor ran up to Xavier, and used his spear to attack it from behind. Xavier quickly turned around, grabbed the vendor's spear, and broke it in half.

"Terrorist identified," Xavier said.

Xavier grabbed the vendor by his neck, and lifted him off of the ground. The vendor struggled for a moment, until Xavier squeezed its hand tightly, and crushed the vendor's neck. Xavier let the dead vendor fall from its grasp.

"Threat eliminated. No more targets identified in this location," it said.

The robot ran out of the department store. Xavier saw the four remaining businessmen, running out of the subway.

"Group of terrorists, identified. Requesting air support," Xavier said.

A drone quickly swooped down, and dropped a pulse bomb on the group. The bomb detonated with a limited-range plasma explosion. The men were vaporized into piles of bloody mash. The spot where the explosion had occurred was heavily damaged.

"Threats eliminated. No collateral damage detected," Xavier said.

The robot was referring to other humans that might have been killed during the air strike. Current U.S. law allows collateral damage during drone strikes. Fortunately, the targeted area was deserted.

"Six targets still at large," Xavier said.

Xavier summoned a drone to its position. Xavier hopped onto the drone, and took flight. It swiftly located the three remaining students. They were brutally dissecting a man, who was laying on the sidewalk.

"Terrorists identified," Xavier said.

It commanded the drone to use particle beams on the students. The students were brutally executed by its high powered lasers. The young men were completely engulfed in bright blue flames, and violently burned to death. People hiding inside of a fancy eatery, screamed at the horrific sight.

"Threats eliminated. Proceeding to final targets," Xavier said.

The automatons flew to the office building. The last three pedestrians alive were still on their vicious rampage. The drone hovered outside of the office's window. Xavier leapt from the drone, crashed through the window, and landed in a blood soaked hallway. Xavier used its Wi-Fi scanner, to locate the remaining pedestrians. One of the pedestrians was in an office supply room. He was standing behind a frightened young female hostage, and held one of his daggers to her neck.

"I'll cut her fucking head off, I swear! Don't fuck with me!" the pedestrian screamed.

"Terrorist identified. Terrorist is holding civilian hostage. Citizen, close your eyes," Xavier said.

The frightened woman followed the robot's order. Xavier held out its left exoskeleton hand, and made it flash bright light in their direction.

"Fuck!" the pedestrian yelled.

He was blinded by the light, and released the woman from his grasp. Xavier wasted no time shooting the pedestrian, with a directed laser beam from its right exoskeleton hand. The small beam hit the pedestrian in his forehead. The beam seared a hole through his skull, and the pedestrian dropped dead.

"Fucking shit!" the young woman screamed.

"Threat eliminated. Stay here, until all terrorists are disposed," Xavier said.

The woman did not wish to be near the dead pedestrian, but she also did not want to disobey orders given by a DHS robot. She sat on the floor, closed her eyes, and followed the robot's instruction. Xavier began walking around the rest of the office. It noticed a group of three women, fleeing from around a corner. The robot ran around the corner, and witnessed the trident wielding pedestrian impaling a male worker, who was still sitting in his cubicle's chair.

"Terrorist identified," Xavier said.

Xavier moved closer, grabbed the pedestrian's head, and turned it backwards. The pedestrian's neck snapped and he immediately died.

"Threat eliminated," Xavier said.

The robot left the cube, and started walking around the rest of the office. Xavier located the last remaining pedestrian. He was using his axe to dismember a woman. He finished severing her hand,

and threw it against a window.

"Final terrorist, identified," Xavier said.

The robot casually walked towards the pedestrian. He turned around and stared at Xavier.

"Fuck you, motherfucker!" the pedestrian shouted.

He swung his axe at the robot. Xavier blocked the attack with its left exoskeleton arm. The axe was knocked away from the pedestrian. He tried to punch and kick the robot. Xavier grabbed the pedestrian, and lifted him into the air. Xavier threw the man against the window. The glass shattered, with a loud bang. The pedestrian screamed, while flying through the air. Seconds later, the pedestrian crashed into the cement. His body was completely pulverized by the long fall.

"Threat eliminated. No further enemy combatants detected. Returning to base," Xavier said.

Xavier summoned a drone to the window, and leaped onto its back. The robots flew to the DHS agents, who were bandaging themselves. Xavier jumped off of the drone, and landed near Commander Cooper.

"Report your status," Commander Cooper said.

"All terrorists eliminated. Aerial units do not detect any further threats," Xavier replied.

"Great. Let's get some medics out here, to clean up this fucking mess," Commander Cooper said.

Commander Cooper called Chief Vazquez and said, "Chief, send medical teams to our location. Also, send several of your detectives. We have to investigate the origins of this attack."

"Understood," Chief Vazquez responded.

The limousine continued driving through the panic filled streets.

Troubled Times said, "People of New York; one thousand nightmares still await the city that never sleeps. I am going to redefine the meaning of repugnance. To the gang of misfits that call themselves the Icons; I advise you to give up your rebellion. Your sacrifices will be in vain. The American people do not deserve salvation. They deserve punishment, and I will gladly oblige. I will watch this city burn to the ground. After its demise, I shall stand atop a pile of corpses; and laugh at the Hell which I have created. I can control *anyone*; and make them fulfill my every desire. Your kingdom of sand, has crumbled. No doubt, you *all* fear me. No doubt, you understand that these are indeed, very troubled times."

Troubled Times cut the signal to the video, and the hovering orb dropped safely into his lap. From behind the limousine's tinted windows, Troubled Times saw crying survivors comforting each other.

Troubled Times looked at Webster and said, "I wish I could drink their salty tears, and devour their agony."

26 The Battle of Manville

Lucia furiously pounded on Cameron's bedroom door.

"Cameron! Wake up man!" she yelled.

Cameron rustled in his bed. He stirred from his slumber and looked at the time. It was 1:43 PM on February 21st, 2217. Cameron had been sleeping a lot ever since his encounter with the Time Shifter. Even though it had been three weeks since their skirmish; the experience had exhausted him mentally, physically, and spiritually.

"Go away, Lucy," Cameron replied.

"Cameron, stop being a dick! Get the fuck up, and answer the door! Serious shit is happening!" Lucia shouted.

Cameron arose from his bed and walked to his door. He opened it using the finger scanning panel.

"Why are you flipping out, Lucy? What the hell is wrong?" Cameron asked.

Lucia grabbed Cameron's hand and quickly walked him to the living room. Eiji and Vincent were watching the holographic television with horrified looks upon their faces. Walter was in the far corner of the room speaking on his cell phone. Cameron watched the newscaster deliver horrific information.

"This is Mei Jia, reporting live from Fifth Avenue. Manhattan is currently gripped in a state of fear, after an absolutely ghastly attack by the man who calls himself, Troubled Times. At approximately 10:13 AM this morning, a large group of citizens and law enforcement personnel went on a violent rampage. The east side erupted in carnage that resembled something out of a horror movie. Perpetrators, using a wide variety of serrated weapons, went on an absolute killing spree. There are hundreds injured, and the number of dead currently stands at eighty-one. That number is expected to rise significantly," Jia said.

"This can't be real. Is this a fucking joke?" Cameron asked.

"Sit down, man. You haven't even heard the worst," Vincent grimly replied.

Cameron sat next to his friends and continued listening to the reporter.

"At approximately 12:41 PM, an encrypted video was sent to Chinese News America through something called a proxy server. It is an anonymous internet server that hides the originating computer's identity. In the video, Troubled Times took responsibility for the attack. He claims this is only the beginning of a larger terror campaign that will be proliferated against the people of New York. Even more disturbing, is the fact that Troubled Times implied his crime is a form of retaliation. He claims to want revenge on the hostile terror unit called The Icons. The radical group released a video three weeks ago, in which they vandalized a convoy of food trucks," said Jia.

"Oh, fuck me. Holy shit," Cameron said.

Cameron put his head in his hands, and Mei Jia continued her report.

"We are now going to show you a segment of the video. We must warn you, it is highly disturbing," Jia said.

The feed cut to a ten second video clip of Troubled Times condemning The Icons for their work.

"This is bad. This is really fucking bad," Eiji said.

Walter was overheard saying, “Yes, yes of course. Be safe.”

Walter ended his phone conversation, and walked over to the group. He opened his palm in front of the projector.

“Mute,” Walter said.

The television's audio went silent.

“I just got off the phone with Paul. I told him what happened, but tried to keep it brief. The Liberty Surveillance Agency probably has a team of robots, analyzing the content of all cell phone conversations in real time,” Walter said.

“Have you watched Troubled Times' video? He is trying to blame *us* for his psychotic outburst!” Lucia said.

“Yes, I'm aware. I've watched the raw video on some deep web servers. It is highly upsetting,” Walter said.

“This doesn't make any sense. Why would he say that we are responsible?” Vincent asked.

“Because this country is on the verge of revolution, and many people think we are its catalyst,” Cameron said.

“Possibly. This could also be a psychological operation, or psyop, for short,” Walter said.

“What do you mean?” Eiji asked.

“We are still trying to determine if Troubled Times is truly an independent terrorist. He could be a government manufactured operative, whose mission is to demonize the new Patriot movement. Or he could be some sort of patsy, that is being allowed to carry out these attacks,” Walter said.

“It seems he was involved in the Statue of Freedom massacre, the United World Hospital attack, and now this atrocity,” Lucia said.

“Yes. These are not isolated incidents. I am worried that he may be using advanced military technology, to commit these crimes,” Walter said.

Walter pressed a few buttons on his cellular phone's holographic interface. When he was finished, he flicked his right index finger. The image transferred from the cell phone to the television.

“Play video,” Walter said.

Walter waved his hand upwards and the volume was reinstated. The video played and they all watched a teenage girl who survived the attack, speak about the incredible evil that she witnessed.

“There were people screaming, and dying all around me! I was running from the subway, and all I remember was this man in a business suit saying that he was sorry, and that he couldn't stop killing! I was running and I saw a lady dying on the ground; getting stabbed in her face with a sword...” said the teenage girl before bursting into tears.

Walter waved his hand in front of the television.

“Off,” he said.

The machine shut itself down.

“I have been scouring social media sites all morning, watching videos posted by survivors. They all confirm what that young girl said. The people committing the murders seemed like they were not in control of themselves,” Walter said.

“That's exactly what happened during the other attacks. Those doctors were powerless to stop him,” Eiji said.

“I remember the statue incident. That weird fucker who almost got us arrested, also seemed like he couldn't use his free will,” Cameron said.

“Holy shit! Do you think that guy at the pier, was Troubled Times?” Vincent asked.

The room fell silent when they realized that their group may have had contact with this masked killer, before he committed his murders.

"We've got to find out the identity of the man you guys interacted with at the pier," Walter said.

"You said that he might be using military technology. What did you mean?" Cameron asked.

"This may just be my wild conspiracy theorist brain, over-analyzing the situation. I think these attacks, may be part of project MK-Zero," Walter replied.

"What the hell is MK-Zero?" Lucia asked.

Walter took a deep breath before giving his explanation.

"MK-Zero is a program started by the Central Intelligence Association, back in the late 2090's. The project's goal was to refine new methods of mind control," Walter said.

The group was stunned into silence by Walter's explanation.

"That's impossible. How could they get away with something so sinister?" Vincent asked.

"Tell us more," Eiji said.

"MK-Zero was officially stopped in 2128, due to public outrage over the agency's numerous illegal activities. They used Lysergic Acid Diethylamide, nano-pharmaceuticals, DNA splicing, and many other twisted scientific techniques; in conjunction with sensory deprivation, hypnosis, and torture, to control human specimens. Truth seeking individuals claim that the government manipulated MK-Zero patsies into performing high profile assassinations. An array of individuals blamed for crimes, including the slayings of known public figures, mass shootings, and car bombings during the 2110's; were rumored to be part of the MK-Zero experiments. The project was declassified in 2126 during a Congressional hearing, after investigations by the Chapel Commission," Walter said.

"Shit, Walt! You're saying they've been fucking with people's minds, for over one hundred years?" Cameron asked.

Walter nodded his head in agreement and said, "Correct. Like I said, the project was officially disbanded over ninety years ago. But this is the United States government we're talking about, Cameron. They have been involved in illegal, and immoral, projects throughout history. There's no reason to think the project was ever fully discontinued."

"This is fucking intense. I want to say that Walt is crazy, but it all makes sense. If they've been experimenting with mind control technologies for all these decades, who knows how advanced they've gotten?" Eiji said.

"So, how can we help? There's no way that we can fight Troubled Times. It's too risky," Vincent said.

"For once, I agree with Vincent. We have no idea where to find him. Even if we did know where he lives, fighting him directly could be a disaster. We can't mess with someone that can control people's minds," Cameron said.

The room once again fell silent. The team hated feeling helpless, but Cameron and Vincent's words were verity.

"We can't just sit here and do nothing," Lucia said.

"I agree. We may not be able to take out Troubled Times just yet, but we can still fight back," Walter said.

"What do you suggest?" Eiji asked with a puzzled look upon his face.

"We'll counter this vile propaganda, by making a viral internet video," Walter sternly said.

Cameron thought Walter was joking.

He said, "Walter, be serious. We can't–"

"Stop it, Cameron. I know they may seem silly, or trivial, but our videos have reached millions of people. We're awakening people to the truth. Like you said earlier, people are angry. Informational warfare is more important than physical combat. In fact, propaganda is ninety percent of warfare. We need to make a movie, and explain that we think MK-Zero technology is being used to proliferate this violence. We will provide solid evidence of the program's existence. We shall put forth the idea that Troubled Times is either using the technology by himself, or with the aid of government collaborators," Walter interrupted.

"I don't know, Walter...that doesn't sound like a very good plan. Do you really think that one silly conspiracy video, will make a difference?" Eiji asked.

"I *know* it will, Eiji. Truth is a powerful weapon, when it is presented in a digestible fashion," Walter replied.

"I like the idea. Walter has a great plan," Lucia said.

"Count me in, guys," Eiji said.

"Same goes for me," said Vincent.

"You all have my full support," Cameron said.

"Great! Here's the plan. First, we have to make a short video condemning the attack. We must make it clear, that we abhor Troubled Times' violent rampages. We cannot let the Food Movement be called terrorists. After we post that video, we need to spend some time researching MK-Zero. We'll comprise a short movie, maybe about thirty minutes or so, detailing the project. At the end, we will propose the theory that this technology is being used by Troubled Times. We will ask our fellow citizens for their help. Together we will determine if Troubled Times is truly working alone, or if he is being helped by the shadow government," Walter said.

The team wasted no time putting Walter's plan into action. Their team video thoroughly decried Troubled Times' latest repugnant rampage. They asked the country to mourn the injured and dead victims. They prayed for the survivors' health. They urged citizens, to resist any illegal attempts by the government, to implement martial law. Their video was relatively short; and only lasted only eight minutes and thirty-one seconds.

They uploaded the video to a file sharing site by using proxy servers, and data encryption methods. Two hours later, the video had been watched by over fifty thousand people. Over the next few days the video went viral, and was eventually seen by millions of viewers. Responses to the video were mostly positive. All their fans praised The Icons for their bravery. Even some of their detractors, admired them for having the courage to remain true to their morals and message, after such a horrific event.

The team spent the next twenty-one days researching the MK-Zero project. Afterward, they created an exhaustive documentary which was thirty-eight minutes and fourteen seconds in length. The video was filled with numerous articles of evidence supporting their research. They explained that MK-Zero was intended to be the ultimate psychological warfare program. The team explained that the project was brought to America in the 2090's by the Nayalites. The Nayalite Communist Party was the official Communist Party of India. They were Chairman Dao's main opposition group when he came to power during what was called the Secret Space War.

In 2091, Communist leaders in China and India formed an alliance. Chinese and Indian radicals stated their ultimate intention was to attack American Moon bases. They claimed America had hidden the existence of these bases for eighty-two years. The American government vehemently denied the existence of the Moon bases. Newly installed Chinese Chairman Dao Sung Te betrayed Indian Prime Minister Ajay Nayal. He accused Nayal and his followers of being unfaithful to the Communist Party. Chairman Dao publicly executed Nayal, and twenty-seven of his cabinet members, by beheading them in 2093. This led to a four year war between India and China.

American anti-war protestors claimed that the war was exacerbated by the CIA. War critics said that America funded different factions, on both sides of the conflict. This was done to prevent both nations from cooperatively exploring the Moon's far side. Conspiracy researchers claim craters on the portion of the Moon that is not facing Earth, contained vast deposits of the super-heavy Element 119. Researchers say that the American government wanted to keep Element 119 a secret. This allowed the American government to covertly create reinforced armor for military vehicles, and soldiers.

Under the code name Operation Thumbtack, top Nayalite science experts were allowed to enter America; with the provision that they would work exclusively for the United States government. Numerous Nayalite psychologists, physicists, engineers, and chemists, shared their research with American scientists. These Nayalite criminal defectors, were given asylum and clemency, to escape the Mumbai trials in 2098. The trials were held to prosecute numerous Indian military and guerrilla fighters, who were accused of committing war crimes. These individuals were eventually convicted on various charges of terrorism and genocide. China narrowly won the Secret Space War, and solidified its world super-power status.

The team discussed the various mind control techniques and explained how human guinea pigs were studied during the ghastly experiments. Subjects would be forced to spend long hours in dark rooms and drugged until they could be manipulated into doing almost anything. MK-Zero's main objective was to brainwash victims into losing their free will. One highly effective method of altering a victim's mental state was the use of television wavelengths. Long hours of watching images at certain flicker rates and frequencies, changed the viewer's perception of reality. Many subjects died during the course of the program. The group pleaded with Troubled Times to think about what he was doing and to stop killing people. They implored him to seek help, if he was not working with the government.

The team eventually found themselves huddled around Lucia. They watched Walter make the video's final statement on Lucia's holographic computer workstation.

"This is why we are asking Troubled Times, to reveal his identity. If you are not a government funded provocateur, then believe me when I say that your brain is *not* functioning properly. I do not know what they have done to you, or who made you into a murderer. I implore you; stop your heinous actions at once. Let us help you expose the real criminals behind these acts. Our government has been wicked and corrupt for many generations. Good people have shirked their responsibilities. They have allowed the most abject, dark-hearted criminals to conquer them. Let us, not fight with each other. Let us defeat the *real* enemy, together. This is an official transmission by The Icons. Stay strong, America," his recorded image said.

"So, what do y'all think?" Lucia asked the team, after the movie ended.

Vincent patted Lucia on her shoulders, with both his hands.

"Nice work, kiddo," Vincent said.

"It looks amazing, girl," Eiji said.

"You've got a lot of talent, Lucy," Cameron said.

"The information is really powerful. I think we will reach a lot of people with this message," Walter said.

"Do you think it will make a difference to Troubled Times?" Eiji asked.

"I can't say yes, or no. We still don't have a solid grasp on his identity. I know I'm probably being an old fool, but I'm hoping the power of reason will change his heart," Walter replied.

"I guess we can hope for the best," Vincent said.

"What's our next move?" Lucia asked Walter.

"You and Eiji are headed to Newark. Find hackable Wi-Fi hotspots, and upload the video to all the big social media sites. You should upload it from several different spots. It will make your location tougher to trace. I'll give you an encrypted portable holo-drive, and disposable cell phone, that you can use to upload the file anonymously. After that, destroy the devices. Cameron, Vincent; you two are going to help me distribute food in Manville. Paul harvested a fresh batch of organic peaches yesterday. They yielded eighty-eight pounds. That's really good for a solar powered winter greenhouse. Paul told me that he traded a twenty pound stash of BPA-free paper towels with another local farmer. In return, he got sixty-two pounds of organic chicken. He is going to keep thirty pounds of chicken, and thirty pounds of peaches. He has found a buyer for the rest. In total, ninety pounds of food will go to Manville's hungry citizens," Walter said.

"Hot damn, that's a lot of food!" Eiji said.

"Damn right. This is going to be epic," Vincent said.

"Let's not waste any time. Move out," Walter said.

The team spent the next hour preparing for their separate missions. They packed duffel bags full of computers, weapons, and ammunition. Walter, Vincent, and Cameron, put on their suits of body armor. They placed their masks in separate bags. They wore regular clothes over their armor to keep it concealed. When they were sure that they had all their necessary supplies, they reconvened in the compound's garage.

"Time to leave. Lucia, Eiji; contact us when you get back to the compound. Good luck, and be safe," Walter said.

The group exited the garage. Eiji and Lucia walked to a nearby bus stop, and rode one to downtown Newark. Vincent, Walter, and Cameron, loaded their supplies into Walter's car. Walter drove, Vincent sat in the passenger's seat, and Cameron sat in the back. Walter placed his hand upon the dashboard's touch screen panel.

"Welcome, Walter. There are two passengers in your vehicle. You have approximately seventy-four miles, left on this carbon card," the car's robotic voice said.

Walter typed their destination into the dashboard's retractable holographic keyboard.

"Destination entered. Please sit back, and enjoy the ride," said the voice before it began driving.

"Why are you so quiet?" Walter asked Cameron.

Cameron stared out the window. He did not want to explain that their new found fame embarrassed him.

"It's nothing. I'm...tired. That's all," Cameron blandly said.

"All right, suit yourself young-in'," Walter said without pressing the issue.

A few moments later, Cameron's wrist band began buzzing. He opened his palm, and expanded the holographic user interface. Cameron saw that Sky had sent him an encrypted textual message from Samantha's computer.

"You still going to stare at the stars, tonight?" Sky's message read.

Cameron knew that Sky was using a clever code, to ask if he was coming to see her.

He typed the words, "Wouldn't miss them for the world."

"Be safe," Sky wrote back.

"Always am," Cameron responded.

"I miss you," Sky wrote.

"I miss you too," Cameron replied.

"Okay. Let me know when you want to fly," Sky said.

Cameron smiled, and was amused by Sky's second play on words.

"I will. I have to go..." Cameron replied.

"Okay. Talk to you later," Sky replied.

Cameron closed his palm, and continued staring out the window. The car drove for another fifty-one minutes before reaching the outside of the Branson's farm. The car stopped and Walter exited the vehicle. Walter looked around the deserted street. He gazed at the rugged dirt road that led from the highway to the Branson's house.

"Anybody home?" Walter asked aloud.

A blurry orb moved from behind a bush. The orb disintegrated, and revealed Lily. She was holding her shotgun.

"Hey guys!" Lily said.

"Hi, pumpkin. Where is your dad?" Walter asked.

As Walter finished asking his question, Paul's image flashed across Lily's bulletproof vest.

"I'm on my way. Hold tight," Paul said.

"No problem," Walter said.

Paul's face disappeared from the vest. Cameron opened his door. Lily walked up to the car and spoke with him.

"Hi, Cam!" she happily said.

"Hey there, kid. How have you been?" Cameron asked.

"Cold! Our heater has been malfunctioning lately," Lily said.

"Sorry to hear that, Lily. How's Sky? She hasn't been giving you too much trouble, has she?" Cameron asked.

"Sky's so awesome! We've taught her how to plant seeds, clean guns, wash clothes, and make bandages!" Lily said.

"Good. It sounds like she's really learning how to survive," Cameron said.

Moments later Paul and Samantha drove their jeep along the dirt road. They arrived and exited the vehicle.

"I'm getting tired of living in an ice box!" Paul said.

"Don't worry, old boy. Summer is only a few months away," Walter said.

The men happily shook hands.

"Hah, hah! I know I'll be wishing otherwise when it's one hundred degrees outside; but I could really go for a nice heat wave!" Paul responded.

The group laughed wholeheartedly.

"So, what's our plan?" Walter then asked Paul.

"We'll go a couple miles up the road, to the next exit. There's an abandoned strip mall not too far from the parkway. The other group will meet us there. If everything is legit, we'll call Sam and have her drive through with the goods," Paul said.

"Sounds cool. Let's get moving," Vincent said.

"I'll wait here with the girls. Cameron and Vincent can keep you company," Walter said.

"That's fine," Paul said.

Cameron and Vincent grabbed their weapons and duffel bag, then entered the jeep. They started putting on their masks, while Paul drove away from the farm's entrance. Vincent checked the amount of ammo he had in his handgun.

"You good?" Vincent asked Cameron.

Cameron pulled his pistol from its holster, removed the clip, and checked the number of rounds in the magazine.

"Yeah. I have a couple more clips in the bag, if we need them," Cameron said.

"These guys are cool. I've known them for years. They never gave me any issues," Paul said.

"There's always a first time for everything," Vincent said while popping the magazine back into his gun.

"I suppose you're right. They almost blew a gasket when I told them I am bringing some members of The Icons! Hah, hah, they thought I was lying. Wait until they see you guys!" Paul said.

Vincent adjusted his mask and said, "This mask thing is starting to seem silly. We never did it for bravado. It was to avoid the facial recognition technology on the drones!"

"I know. I can't believe we're famous for wearing some cheap, anti-spy devices," Cameron said.

"It's more than just a gimmick. People identify with you, because you could be anybody. You prove that the Food Movement is not about one man, or one group of men. It is about *human* struggle," Paul said.

"I've never thought about it that way," Vincent thoughtfully said.

After a brief silence, Paul asked his friends an intriguing question.

"What are you individually calling yourselves?"

Cameron and Vincent gave each other bewildered looks. They had never thought about using individual identities.

Vincent spoke first and replied, "I'm Vestige. A patriot, from the old American glory days."

Cameron was not thrilled about giving himself a name. He felt the idea of being masked heroes was ridiculous. However, he also realized that their captivating costumes, was quickly helping them become folk legends.

"Call me, Doctor Serenity. All I want, is peace," Cameron finally responded.

"Very appropriate names, gentlemen," Paul said.

"Hell yeah! We sound like real Icons! Good shit Cam...I mean, Doctor Serenity!" Vincent said.

Vincent playfully punched Cameron in his arm, while Paul continued driving. Paul followed the exit ramp, and arrived at the strip mall located on the left side of the road. Paul drove into its abandoned parking lot. The group was disheartened by the mall's dismal state. There were several small shops that had been abandoned for decades.

Decrepit stores littered the strip. Some buildings had been reduced to rubble. Other ones had been severely damaged by fire. Their broken windows and rotting structure, was a painful reminder of the horrific American economic collapse. The parking lot's asphalt was in a similarly bad shape. There were numerous cracks in the pavement. Pot holes, and sections where only gravel remained, were prominently scattered across the blacktop.

In the middle of the lot, a group of two women and four men were standing outside of a van. One of the men, who appeared to be around Paul's age, was holding an assault rifle. He steadied it underneath his arm in a non-threatening manner, with the barrel pointing towards the ground. Paul pulled close to the van.

"These are our people," Paul said.

Vincent, Cameron, and Paul, exited the jeep. Paul waved at the man holding the assault rifle.

"Nice to see you again, Jerry!" Paul jovially said.

Jerry transferred control of the gun to his left hand, tucked the stock under his arm, and extended his right hand.

"Glad to work with you again, Paul," Jerry said.

The two men shook hands, and smiled at each other.

"Whoa! Looks like you weren't kiddin' about bringing your friends! Let me introduce them to the group. The guy to my left, is Travis. These two fine fellows to my right, are Lamar and Cody. Those two lovely ladies, are Melissa and Alexis," Jerry said.

"I'd like y'all to meet two members of The Icons. The guy with the visor, is The Vestige! You've already seen the video of the guy with the blue eyes. He calls himself, Doctor Serenity!" Paul excitedly said.

The group briefly laughed, and applauded.

"Doc Serenity and The Vestige. Those are some bad-ass names, man!" Alexis said.

"You guys have no idea how important you are to the Liberty Movement. You've become, well...icons of freedom, and civil disobedience," Jerry said.

"We're nothing but ordinary citizens; who are fed up with the heaping piles of dog shit, the government has been dropping on us for all of these years," Cameron said.

"Yes, we're no more special than any one of you. We can only fight our own individual battles. It's up to good folks like you, to win the war," Vincent said.

"Do you guys have any special abilities?" Melissa asked.

"Nope. Other than some cool technological equipment, we're normal humans," Cameron replied.

"What about that maniac, Troubled Times? He's a real damned *super* villain. He can control anybody. He fucks with their minds, and takes control of their bodies. How are you planning on stopping him?" Travis asked.

The question caught both Cameron and Vincent off guard. They had not yet resolved how they would fight Troubled Times in person. His mind control powers terrified them.

"We're not yet sure. We have to do some research, and figure out how he controls people's free will. We can't defeat him until we know the source of his power," Vincent said.

"Good luck. That guy is bad news," Lamar said.

"So, how are we going to distribute the food?" Paul asked after a short silence.

"We can transfer the goods to this van. We should be safe. Nobody comes around these parts anymore. After we're done, we're going to a nearby apartment complex. I've told a select few people there that we're bringing back the food. That part of the plan has to be done quietly. We don't want to draw any attention to ourselves," Jerry said.

"Sounds good to me," said Paul.

"Yeah. We're glad to help," said Vincent.

Paul used his encrypted holographic cell phone, to contact his daughter.

"Hey beautiful, it's dad. You can come meet us where I told you," said Paul.

"Copy. Pop, is it okay if little one joins us?" Samantha asked.

Paul hesitated for several moments before answering Samantha. Paul looked at the group of people standing in the lot. A feeling of incredible strength overwhelmed Paul and prevented him from speaking. The two young rebels half his age, Cameron and Vincent, stood proudly among Food Liberationists both their elder and their junior. Paul could tell the men that Jerry had chosen to accompany him were obviously in their teenage years. Their strong female companions kept a watchful eye over the young males. Paul was aware that Melissa and Alexis were in their mid-forties. Despite the age, gender, and racial divides that separated this diverse group; they were all united by their love for food, and freedom.

"Let me call you right back," Paul said to Samantha.

"By your estimation, how many people are going to receive this food?" Paul asked Jerry.

"A decent amount. Probably a couple dozen. Why do you ask?" Jerry replied.

Paul took a deep breath and said, "When I was a kid, we used to have a town square that looked a lot like this one. There was this wonderful restaurant, owned and operated by local organic farmers. They had the juiciest, crispiest, deep fried steaks in Virginia. One day we found out, the company who owned the land on which all the shops were built, sold the entire space to Chinese realtors. Three months later, those Communist bastards tore down the entire strip, and built a movie theatre. Have you ever eaten movie theatre food? It's the most fake, nasty, GMO filled trash in existence. It's even more disgusting than fast food."

Paul looked down at his feet. The cool night air whipped around his body.

"I'd give anything, to have one more bite of those steaks," Paul lamented.

Cameron sensed that Paul was becoming emotional.

"You feeling okay, Paul?" Cameron calmly asked.

Paul deeply exhaled and said, "Tell your people to meet us at this lot. We're going to cook the food right here, right now, tonight."

Jerry nervously said, "That wasn't the plan–"

"Take the deal, or do not. It's your choice. Don't worry about the money. I'll transfer the food's Carbon Credit street value to your phone," Paul interrupted.

Paul extended his arm, exposing his cell phone wrist band. He gave Jerry the opportunity to accept the money, by tapping their wrist bands together. Shockingly, Jerry declined Paul's gesture.

"Why would you want to have an open cook out, in the middle of this deserted parking lot?" Jerry asked.

Paul looked at his friends and said, "So these guys can make a recording, and distribute it over the internet."

"That's a bold plan, Paul," Cameron said.

"Yeah it is, and it sounds fuckin' sweet!" Vincent said.

"No complaints from me," Travis said.

"Hell yeah. That sounds like a great idea!" Alexis said.

After a long pause Jerry said, "I guess I can't turn down an invitation, to have a real barbeque with The Icons!"

The group concurred by cheering and applauding.

"Great! Call your friends. I'll tell Sam to bring our portable grill, and any other supplies we'll need," Paul said.

"I'll tell my buddies to bring the utensils!" Jerry said.

"Thank you so much. This is going to be great!" Paul said.

Paul called Samantha and said, "Hey, it's dad. Tonight, we're about to be a part of something amazing. Bring everyone down to the spot about which I told you. We're throwing an old fashioned shin dig!"

"Did I just hear you correctly, dad?" Samantha asked with shock.

"Yes, you did. Now stop wasting time, and get over here! Bring the grill and goods with you!" Paul replied.

"Okay. I really hope you know what you're doing, dad," Samantha said after a brief pause.

"Me too, darlin'," Paul said under his breath.

Jerry called his friend, and informed him of the plan. Jerry instructed him to bring approximately twenty-three people which they were planning on feeding, to the abandoned shopping center. He also told his friend to bring utensils and napkins. Over the course of the next hour, a large group congregated at the parking lot. Paul's family, Sky, and Walter, arrived with the food. They drove to the lot in Walter's car, and an old pickup truck. Walter, who was wearing his Icon armor and gas mask, exited his car. He briskly walked up to the large group.

"Good evening Liberty Lovers! It is I, Mister Daylight!" Walter said.

"Oh shit, that's their leader! I can't believe your team has taken out two drones!" Lamar said.

"You guys are fucking awesome!" Cody said.

"Glad you could make it, Mister Daylight," Cameron said.

Cameron shook Walter's hand, discretely leaned forward, and quietly whispered in his ear.

"Vince is calling himself, The Vestige. I'm Doctor Serenity," said Cameron.

Walter chuckled and loudly said, "Good evening Doctor Serenity, and Vestige!"

Walter walked over to Vincent and shook his hand. The three men took a moment to admire their handiwork.

"Too bad the rest of the team couldn't be here tonight. This is going to be spectacular!" Walter said.

Vincent pulled a small hover camera from one of the duffel bags. Vincent twirled it into the air, and the camera began recording its surroundings. The Icons walked to the back of the pickup truck.

"Organic food! Free for all!" Vincent yelled.

The team began distributing bags of food to the crowd. The camera flew around and recorded the action.

"Yes, it's time to celebrate! Eat up, everyone!" said Walter.

"Doctor Serenity has the cure for tyranny!" Cameron said.

Even though his face was hidden, Cameron smiled widely when a beautiful woman approached him. Her long hair glistened in the moonlight. Sky walked up to him, accompanied by Lily.

"Hey there, pretty lady. You come to help us make history?" Cameron asked Sky.

"Yes! I am so proud of you guys!" Sky happily exclaimed.

Lily grabbed a large bag of food and said, "Ca...I mean, Doctor Serenity! See all the food we've brought?!"

Cameron rustled Lily's hair and exclaimed, "You did a great job. For our people. For our planet, little one."

While the crowd cheered, Doreen tried scolding her husband.

"This is bad. Why are you exposing us?" Doreen asked with concern.

Paul grabbed his wife, and passionately kissed her.

"It's time to stop hiding. We're not bad people. If we don't assert our rights, our children have no future," Paul said.

Doreen softened her tone, and happily kissed her husband.

"You're right. It's time to stop being cowards," Doreen said.

The next one hour, was blissful. The townspeople shared food and friendship. Cameron lectured the group about the necessity of firearms rights. Vincent explained the importance of maintaining privacy and being able to have freedom of expression. Walter explained that America had been captured by powerful corporate interests; and that the only way to reverse their dire predicament was by not complying with an illegitimate control system. They tried to forget that their cellular phones could be hacked by government agencies, and utilized to reveal their location. Everyone wanted to believe that for a few moments, they could enjoy some normalcy in their lives.

They distributed Organic food, like it was not illegal. They were totally oblivious to the fact that a large drone had been dispatched to intercept the crowd. It was shaped like a fighter jet, but was only two-thirds the size. The drone lowered itself, and hovered above the group. At this time, thirty-eight people in total, had gathered in the ravaged shopping mall. The drone projected a holographic video image in the middle of the parking lot. The secretly recorded footage showed the Icons distributing food to hungry Manville citizens.

"Powerful global interests have used our tax dollars, to build a giant surveillance grid! It predicts the future, and unfairly manipulates the economy! The Income, Health, and Carbon Taxes are a form of indentured servitude! They are extortion fees that are directly paid to offshore banks! It does not matter how many taxes they raise! You will *always* be impoverished, because that money does *not* go to repaying our debt!" Walter said in the drone's replayed video projection.

The drone repositioned itself, and menacingly hovered above the crowd.

"Known terrorists, identified. Hostile American jihadists, delivering illegal goods to radical collaborators. Threat level, highly elevated. Commencing with capture, or kill, protocol," the drone's robotic voice said.

"Shit, that thing isn't fucking around! Everybody! Clear the area!" Vincent exclaimed.

"Party's over folks! It's time to get the hell *out* of here!" Walter yelled.

"Dammit, I thought we'd have more time," Paul said to Doreen.

In a horrible display of power, the drone targeted the grill which Paul's family had placed in the middle of the burnt out strip mall. It unleashed a hot laser beam, which violently incinerated the grill!

"Go! Go!" Paul screamed.

Paul grabbed Doreen's hand, and began running towards their vehicles. Panicked people fled in all directions. Several people immediately started crying. Screams echoed throughout the air.

"Kids! Get to the cars!" Paul screamed.

"Good God! It's going to kill us!" Melissa exclaimed.

"Dammit! I'm *tired* of these damn things *fucking* with us! They have no right to treat us like cattle!" Jerry said.

Jerry checked his ammunition. He had ninety rounds, split between three clips. Alexis swiftly ran up to him.

"What in God's name do you think you're doing, Jerry?" Alexis nervously asked.

Jerry disengaged the rifle's safety lock. He had a stone cold look of defiance upon his face.

"It's time to show these bastards who's in charge! These are *our* streets!" Jerry said.

Jerry began running towards one of the mall's abandoned stores. Alexis immediately followed him, and they both took cover inside the building. Jerry aimed his rifle out of a broken window. He bravely fired three shots at the drone! One of Jerry's shots hit the drone and damaged its metal plating.

"Armed rebels, identified. Situation has become unstable. Proceeding with elimination protocol," the drone said.

The drone pumped hot laser particles into the ground, and split the terrain into pieces. People, whom were enjoying healthy food only moments earlier, now wondered if they had just eaten their last meal.

Cameron said to Sky, "We have got to leave! This thing is going to–"

Before Cameron could finish his sentence, a pulsating beam shot the ground beside them. Sky fell sideways into a newly created ditch and cried heavily. Cameron was completely disoriented. The drone continued flying around the lot.

"Terrorists are violating curfew. All citizens are subject to immediate termination," it said.

Lily frantically ran towards the jeep yelling, "Daddy, daddy! Don't let it kill me!"

"Baby, be careful! That drone is weaponized!" Paul worriedly shouted at his little daughter.

Paul Jr. had already reached the pickup truck where Paul and Doreen were waiting. Samantha and Abigail were running not far behind Lily. In the distance, Paul saw Cody distributing handguns and rifles to Lamar, Melissa, Travis, and several other people who were standing behind Jerry's van.

"Don't wait for me. Get the hell out of here!" Paul said to Doreen.

Paul began running towards the van. Several people were desperately looting the remaining food.

"Wait! Paul, come back!" Doreen yelled.

Paul ran by his older daughters, who were pale with fright. They were terrified that he was not evacuating.

"Dad, stop! Where are you going?!" screamed Abigail.

"Keep moving!" Samantha shouted, while pushing her sister towards the truck.

Paul was out of breath by the time he reached the van.

"What the hell are y'all doing?!" Paul asked Cody.

Cody placed a clip inside his handgun and said, "Run away, if you want. We're fighting this metal piece of shit!"

"Are you out of your damn mind? It's going to *kill* you!" Paul angrily replied.

"Any man who is told that he can't eat the food of his choice, is already dead," Lamar said.

"Exactly. We're tired of being treated *worse* than animals," said Travis.

"You can't support them! These boys have their whole lives ahead of them!" Paul yelled at Melissa.

"No one is forcing them to do anything. This is the only way we'll ever take back our society," Melissa said.

Cameron had barely recovered from the assault. He finished helping Sky climb out of the ditch. Cameron saw that Paul was passionately arguing with the group. Cameron knew he had to intervene in the situation.

"Go back to the farm," Cameron sternly said.

"You are *not*, about to take on a drone! I *know* you're not thinking about doing something so *stupid!*" Sky snapped.

"I have to help Paul," Cameron said.

Cameron began running away from Sky.

"Cameron, stop!" Sky frantically yelled.

"Don't worry; I'll be right behind you!" Cameron shouted over his shoulder.

Sky instantly became very angry at Cameron. She momentarily put her feelings aside and ran over to the Branson's vehicles. By the time Cameron arrived at the van, Vincent and Walter had joined Paul, and the rebels.

"This is not a goddamned joke! Do you know how many people I've seen killed by these things?!" Walter yelled.

"Why the fuck is everybody standing around? We all need to leave, right now!" Cameron said.

"Not this time. We're going to show them why they call us the motherfucking Icons!" said Vincent.

Vincent loaded incendiary rounds into his large shotgun. The shells were designed to violently explode on impact.

Cameron held up his hands and said, "No way! You're all *insane!* I am *not* dying today!"

The drone hovered only several yards away from the gathered group. Everyone knew the time for talk was over.

"Take cover!" Cody yelled.

Cody and his friends quickly ran towards the strip mall's decrepit buildings. They hid amongst the ruins of an abandoned shop. Walter, Cameron, Paul, and Vincent, looked at each other.

"This is not our battle," Walter said.

"Do what you want. I've got to help these people," Vincent said.

Vincent left his team, and went to join the rest of the group. Walter tried using his holographic wrist band to contact Eiji and Lucia, but it was a futile effort. The signal was being scrambled by the drone's frequency disruptor. All Walter saw was a distorted image in his hands. Walter let out a heavy sigh and made his decision.

"Paul, go be with your family. Cameron, take care of Sky," Walter said.

Walter began running towards the buildings.

"Aww, shit!" Paul angrily yelled.

Cameron put his hands atop his head. He was in complete disbelief that his friends were about to fight a drone.

"*Fuck* them! We're bailing!" said Cameron.

Cameron and Paul started running away from the van. They had only ran several feet before the drone targeted them.

"Wanted terrorists, cannot be allowed to leave the area," the drone said.

The drone shot a powerful laser at the van, causing it to explode and melt into the concrete. The force from the blast pushed Cameron and Paul away, and violently threw them to the ground. Paul screamed in pain, and grabbed his leg. A piece of jagged metal was sticking out of his left calf. Paul's family watched in horror, from inside their jeep.

"Daddy!" screamed Lily.

Cameron forced himself to stand up, and then helped Paul arise from the ground.

"Come on old boy, I've got you!" Cameron said.

Paul fought through the pain and willed himself to stand. Paul draped his left arm around Cameron, and used him for support. They began moving as quickly as they could towards the jeep. Paul limped heavily, and his injury reduced the speed at which they could escape. From inside the buildings, the group of rebels saw Cameron and Paul were in trouble.

"Let's give them some help! Everybody fire!" Cody said.

The rebels opened fire on the drone! Bullets ricocheted off of its metal, and chipped its powerful armor.

"Terrorists have become extremely violent. Illegal guns detected," the drone said.

The drone charged its powerful laser. It used its wireless fidelity technology to see through the building's walls.

"Fourteen terrorists, located. Elimination protocol, activated," the drone stated.

"Everybody scatter!" Walter yelled.

The drone shot a powerful pulsating laser into the ground and swept it across the terrain. Any area that was hit by the laser was evaporated by the devastating energy weapon. A middle aged man, who was attempting to take cover in a building, was tragically vaporized by the powerful beam.

"Holy *shit!* I've never seen one use that type of weapon!" Jerry said.

"Jerry, we have to leave! This is *suicide!*" Alexis said.

"There's no going back! Either we stop this thing, or it's going to kill everyone!" Jerry said.

Jerry fired five more shots at the drone. Three rounds chipped its shell. The drone was battered and momentarily swayed while it was hovering.

"Aerial Unit, sustaining damage. Navigation systems, becoming unstable," the drone said.

The drone used its laser to slice through the building, in which Jerry and Alexis were hiding. Jerry dove out of the way, and narrowly avoided the sweeping beam. A large piece of falling rock landed near Alexis, while she jumped to safety. She screamed in pain when pieces of debris pelted her body.

Cameron and Paul were approaching the vehicles. Doreen ran over to them and helped Paul walk to the back of the jeep. Doreen and Cameron helped Paul pull himself into the jeep. Abigail was sitting in the passenger's seat, and sobbed heavily when she saw her wounded father.

"Daddy, are you going to be okay?" Abigail asked.

Even though he knew his wound was very serious, Paul put on a brave demeanor for his daughter.

"I'll be fine, darlin'. We have to get home, so I can fix myself," Paul said.

Cameron heard the sound of gunfire in the distance.

"We won't all fit in the jeep. Sky, Sam, Lily, and myself, can ride in the pickup truck," Cameron said to Doreen.

"What about your friends?" asked Doreen.

"They've made their decision," Cameron said with sadness.

The pickup truck was only a few yards away from the jeep. Cameron, Lily, Samantha, and Sky, raced towards the truck. The drone was taking heavy fire from the rebels hiding in the building. The drone had to keep changing its position to avoid taking too much damage. Lily and Sky, hopped in the back of the pickup truck. Samantha climbed into the driver's seat. Cameron opened the passenger's door. He placed his right foot inside the truck, and took another glance at the drone. Cameron saw that the group was waging a fierce battle with the aerial abomination. Cameron knew he could not flee when so many brave men and women, were risking their lives to stop the winged nightmare. Cameron took a very deep breath.

"Take care of them," Cameron told Samantha.

He closed the door and ran away. Sky yelled at Cameron when she saw he was rushing to the battlefield.

"Cam! Stop!" Sky screamed.

Cameron looked over his shoulder and yelled, "I'm sorry!"

"Cameron!" Sky shouted.

One more time Cameron yelled, "I'm sorry!"

He continued running into the war zone.

"You're going to get yourself killed!" Sky yelled.

"You have to trust him," Samantha solemnly said.

She threw the vehicle into reverse, made a U-turn, and began driving out of the parking lot. The Branson family and Sky, left the battleground. Cameron quickly ran to one of the buildings, and found shelter. The drone was still attempting to unleash its full power against Manville's citizens. The armed rebels continued shooting its metallic frame.

"Vestige! Daylight! Can you hear me?!" Cameron shouted.

There was no response.

"Shit, I've got to get closer to them," Cameron said to himself.

Cameron heard several more shots ring out from nearby. The drone responded, by shooting its powerful ground penetrating pulse laser into the terrain. The drone moved its laser forward, and sliced into another section of the building. Cameron saw his chance to move. He ran with lightning speed, to the sounds of gunfire. Cameron jumped over a steaming pile of rubble, and found a small group of fighters. They were tired and injured, but were still standing their ground. Cameron saw a man laying in the arms of a young woman. The laser had severed the man's arm, at the base of his forearm. The man screamed in pain, while the woman used her jacket to stop his bleeding.

"Where are the rest?" Cameron shouted at the woman.

"That way!" the woman frantically yelled.

She pointed to her left. Cameron glanced at the drone and saw that its laser was recharging. Cameron used the opportunity to run into the next building. Cameron dove into the structure and began crawling around on the floor. Cameron saw Vincent was reloading his shotgun. The group was in bad shape. Cody was holding his hand to his bloody right eye, which had been hit by a piece of hot shrapnel. Walter was covered with concrete dust, and repositioning himself behind broken pieces of detritus. He was trying to get a good firing position, while still retaining cover.

"We've got to take this thing out!" Cameron yelled at Walter.

"We don't have many bullets. We need to create some kind of explosion. If we can get it to stop moving, we can concentrate our fire and put it down for good," Walter said.

"Incoming!" Lamar yelled.

The rebels dashed in different directions. The hot laser beam blasted its way through the building. Most of the rebels were able to avoid the particle beam. Unfortunately, one young woman was crushed by falling debris from the collapsing roof. After the beam had dissipated, several rebels ran over to the woman, and began pulling the rocks off of her. The bloody and dusty woman lay motionless. Regrettably, she was dead. The rebels moved her mangled body to the far left corner of the broken building.

"The fuel cells! We can use them to create a small explosion, and electromagnetic burst!" Cameron said.

Walter did not like the idea of ruining their transportation.

"We can't. How the hell will we get home?" Walter said.

"Goddammit we'll be going home in body bags, if we don't destroy that drone!" Cameron shouted over the gunfire.

"Shit. You're right," Walter quickly said.

"Everybody, listen! We need to retrieve explosives from Mister Daylight's car! Our only hope is to blast that thing out of the sky! Vestige, when Daylight gives the signal, be prepared to shoot the fuel cells!" Cameron said.

"Piece of fucking cake. Just like trap shooting," Vincent replied.

He reloaded his pump action shotgun, with more incendiary rounds. Seconds later, Alexis and Jerry came stumbling into the ruined building. Jerry was breathing heavily, and pressing his left hand into his stomach. Alexis had Jerry's rifle tucked under her right arm, and was helping Jerry walk with her left one. Alexis helped Jerry hide behind a pile of debris. Jerry painfully sat down, and assessed the damage to himself. His flesh was blackened, and peeling. His pinky and ring finger were partially blown off.

"Son of a *bitch*. That thing tore me up pretty righteous," Jerry said.

Vincent rushed over to Jerry and said, "Don't worry, friend. We will *not* lose this battle."

"Let's go!" Walter yelled at Cameron.

Without hesitation, Walter and Cameron ran from the building and started sprinting across the parking lot.

"Give them cover!" Vincent yelled.

The group unleashed a fierce barrage of bullets, which heavily damaged the drone. The drone's altitude lowered, and it struggled to stabilize itself.

"Navigation systems, critically impaired. Terrorists refuse to comply with lawful lethal force. Additional engagement necessary," the drone said.

LED lights around the drone's body began blinking. The drone emanated a powerful sound wave, from the tiny sound cannons mounted around its frame. The wave dissipated in all directions. A horrendous pain shot through all the rebels. People screamed, and their entire bodies shook from the sonic vibrations. Cameron and Walter fell to the ground. Both men felt like they were about to completely explode.

Cameron crawled forward on his stomach. Walter groaned in agony beside him; while trying to move forward. Cameron was violently shivering, and his muscles were going numb. Cameron rolled over to his right side, and looked at the menacing drone. It was hovering only several yards above ground. Out of the corner of his eye, Cameron saw the buildings were being reduced to rubble. Cameron thought of all the brave people that were willing to die for their freedom.

"They're using sound cannons!" Cameron yelled at Walter.

"Ouch! I don't...I don't think I can stand," Walter said.

"We have to keep moving! If you can't *stand*, then *crawl!*" Cameron said.

Cameron used his right arm to pull Walter forward. Walter found his strength, and the two warriors continued their journey towards Walter's car. In the building, Vincent was struggling to regain his footing. He and several other people had been knocked down by the sound cannon's force. Vincent used the wall to help pull himself to a sitting position.

"Serenity! Daylight! You have to hurry!" Vincent yelled.

Vincent lurched forward, and began crawling around on his hands and knees. Vincent reached his shotgun, which he had dropped during the sonic assault. He secured it with his left hand. Vincent held the gun by the padding grip, attached to the bottom of the fore-end. He slowly moved back into position. Vincent pressed his back against the wall, and finished reloading the shotgun. Vincent tried to raise it, but the intense pain from the sonic weapon, was wreaking havoc upon his body. Vincent heard the sounds of people yelling in agony. Women were crying, and men were groaning loudly.

"Everybody stay strong! We *are* going to beat this fucking piece of *shit!*" Vincent yelled.

Cameron and Walter continued their harrowing crawl. They were only twenty-five yards away from the car.

"We've got to move faster! That thing is preparing to fire another shot!" Cameron said in pain.

"I know. Cameron, I can't take much more of this assault," Walter said.

Cameron knew that Walter needed his help. Cameron took a long deep breath, and focused his mind. Cameron knelt beside Walter, and slung Walter's left shoulder over his own body.

"Come on old boy; let's finish what we've started!" Cameron said.

Combining their physical strength and collective willpower, the two men screamed loudly, and arose from the ground! In a superhuman feat, the men used all of their strength and energy, to fight the physical pain being inflicted upon their bodies. They scrambled to reach Walter's car. Their muscles twitched, which made their jogging unsteady. They panted and gasped for air, but forced themselves to keep moving. The drone scanned the two men, with its high powered infrared camera.

"Unexpected scenario. Enemy combatants are unaffected by sound wave generated pain compliance. Scanning algorithms, for alternative situational protocol," the drone said.

The drone's powerful laser beam was almost finished recharging. Lamar saw that the drone was going to shoot Cameron and Walter. Lamar made a valiant decision. He grabbed a handgun that had been dropped near him, and crawled out into the parking lot. Vincent and several other people screamed at him, and told him to get back inside the badly damaged building.

"Lamar, stop! Stay inside!" Vincent screamed.

When he was far enough away from the building, Lamar rolled over onto his right side, and aimed his gun at the drone. Lamar took several deep breaths, and knew the sacrifice he was about to make, would be enormous. Lamar began praying. He watched the drone mark Walter and Cameron with its laser optics.

"Lord Jesus, protect my family. Watch over them, and keep them safe. Bless these people, dying here today. Please let our efforts, be made not in vain," Lamar said to himself.

Cameron and Walter barely reached the car without collapsing. Walter used the vehicle to steady his balance.

"Help me open the hood," Walter said.

Cameron opened the driver's side door, and helped Walter pull himself into the driver's seat. Walter reached forward, and pressed his hand against a small circular pad on the dashboard's left side. The car's hood popped open. Walter climbed out of the seat, and started crawling towards the car's front.

"Tape, in...Glove box," Walter said through strained breaths.

Cameron climbed into the car, and opened its glove box. He saw a roll of duct tape inside, which he promptly removed. Cameron moved to the front of the vehicle, and helped Walter lift up the car's hood. Walter reached inside, and ejected two of the car's four fuel cells from the engine.

Cameron handed Walter the duct tape, which he used to bind the two cells together. Walter handed Cameron the cells, and instantly dropped to his knees. His whole body shook profusely.

"I'm too...tired, kid. You've got...to finish by yourself," Walter said.

Cameron spoke no words. He briefly patted Walter on his shoulder. Cameron willed his feet to move, and stumbled towards the drone. His internal organs felt like they were burning with hot lava.

"Vestige! Vestige!" Cameron yelled after a few painful steps.

The drone fixed its laser sights upon Cameron. A three dimensional holographic box was drawn around his body.

"Oh shit! Vestige, get ready to fire!" Cameron said.

Cameron moved with every ounce of rapidity that he could muster. Every step he made, sent coursing agony through his muscles. Cameron momentarily dropped to his knees from the crippling pain. He forced himself to stand, and kept jogging. The drone readied its pulse beam, and was preparing to fire upon Cameron at any second. Lamar saw that Cameron was running out of time. Lamar closed his eyes.

"No fear," he said.

In a heroic act of bravery Lamar shouted, "Fuck you, you robotic Hell demon! You will never keep niggers from having our freedom!"

Lamar began shooting at the drone! He let out a long battle cry, from deep within his belly. His shots were sporadic, but several bullets hit the autonomous flying killer. The drone quickly turned one hundred eighty degrees in midair, and repositioned itself.

"Terrorist threat level, immediate," the drone said.

The drone shot its powerful pulse beam into the ground, and began moving it in Lamar's direction. People screamed, but Lamar truly showed no fear. He kept firing at the drone, until the beam vaporized the entire upper half of his body. Cameron witnessed the brave young man's heroic death, and started burning with a ferocious rage.

"No! You mother *fucker!* I'm going to send you straight back to *Hell!*" Cameron yelled.

Cameron summoned all of his strength, and began running towards the drone. Cameron sprinted fifteen yards, in what seemed like seconds. Even though the powerful sonic weapon was still dispersing its waves, Cameron was unaffected.

"Vestige, it's time!" Cameron yelled when he got closer to the drone.

Vincent fought through his own pain, and forced himself to stand upright. His whole body was trembling, but he did his best to steady his aim. When Cameron was only a few yards away from the drone, he used his remaining strength to hurl the fuel cells high into the air. The cells flew towards the drone's left wing. Vincent traced the cells' flight path with his shotgun. Vincent waited until the very last moment to fire, so that he could get the best possible shot.

"Fuck you," Vincent said, and pulled his trigger.

The cells exploded, and created an enormous fireball! The drone started falling sideways, and rotated in a continuous three hundred sixty degree motion. The drone hit the ground so hard, that the pavement broke apart! It skidded for another eighteen yards, until its left wing broke off. Sparks flew everywhere. It came to a stop, and smoldered atop broken concrete. The fearless warriors stood upright. The intense pain generated by the sound cannon's waves, left the rebels' bodies.

The surviving group was bloody and battered. People had severe burns to their bodies, broken bones, and missing limbs. Sounds of people crying, and moaning in pain, echoed throughout the parking lot. An eerie silence swept across the group. The sounds of agony were soon quelled by the spirit of victory. People started clapping solemnly, and gave each other hugs. The patriots congratulated each other, and tended to the wounded.

"Absolutely amazing. You did it, guys. You beat the drone," Jerry said to Vincent.

"No. *We* did it, together," Vincent said.

Vincent knelt beside Jerry, who was sitting against a wall. Vincent extended his right hand, which Jerry humbly shook. Walter slowly walked back to the remaining rebels. He stopped beside Cameron, who was on his knees, catching his breath. The men surveyed the battle's aftermath. The drone continued burning in the lot. Several buildings had almost been reduced to rubble. Sections of broken asphalt were smoldering. The lot was in even worse condition, than when they had first arrived.

However, it was even more beautiful. The dilapidated old parking lot was now officially a reclaimed American territory. It was home turf that was defended with the blood of defiant citizens. Walter patted Cameron on his left shoulder. He reached under Cameron's left arm and helped Cameron rise to his feet.

"Great job, Doctor Serenity," Walter said.

"You too, Mister Daylight," Cameron replied.

The two men walked over to the gathering crowd. A group of twelve survivors, five of which were badly wounded, were huddled around Lamar's remains. They mourned the loss of their brave friend. Travis comforted Melissa, who sobbed uncontrollably at the sight of the slain man. Cody stared in disbelief, at the lower half of Lamar's body. It was laying in a pool of blood, and gore. Cody's face was partially burned, and his eye was missing.

"Aw shit, dude. I'm sorry," was all Cody could say.

"Don't look," Cameron said.

Cameron removed his tattered jacket, and placed it over the lost hero's body.

"He was a good man, and will be missed," Walter said.

Walter felt great remorse, and patted Cody on the back. He decided to address the survivors.

Walter said, "You are *all* great men, and women. What you did here today took an amazing amount of courage, and resilience. Your courage was–"

Before Walter was finished speaking, the spherical hover camera moved itself close to Walter.

It holographically projected the words, "Fifteen minutes of battery life remaining."

"No way. That thing has been filming the entire time?" Jerry said.

"We started recording the barbeque, before the fighting broke out," Vincent said.

Walter grabbed the hovering camera, and held it in his palm.

"Good. Now, when the world sees this video, they will know that we are *not* terrorists. They will see that our tyrannical government, are the real enemies. It's not even *our* government. Our alleged government is just a bunch of criminals and corporate interests, masquerading as authority figures. You all clean yourselves up, and leave this place. Wherever you go, tell your fellow humans about what happened here today. Never let the sacrifices of these brave people be forgotten. Let everyone know that *you*, the occupied people of a formerly sovereign nation, are *all* ICONS!" Walter said.

"We are all Icons! We are all Icons!" the crowd chanted.

Walter turned off the camera, and the crowd dispersed into the cold night.

27 Found

Samantha sat in the rocking chair on the Branson's front porch. She nervously chewed her fingernails. The cold night air made her shiver, but she did not go inside to warm herself. Samantha breathed a sigh of relief when she saw Walter's car driving itself along the dirt road.

"They're back! They're back!" Samantha shouted.

Samantha arose from the chair and ran inside the home. She bolted into an adjacent living room to her left, where Doreen was treating Paul's wounds. Sky, Paul Jr., Lily, and Abigail, were helping Doreen.

"They're here, you guys! They made it back alive!" Samantha said in an elated voice.

The group stared at Samantha, with shocked looks upon their faces. Paul was still in tremendous pain. He groaned loudly, when Doreen pulled the final piece of metal from his shin. His children waited for his reaction to Samantha's incredible news.

"I'll be okay. Go see what happened," Paul told his children.

Paul Jr., Lily, and Samantha ran out of the room. Sky, who had a solemn look upon her face, did not leave Paul's side. Abigail did not immediately leave.

"Aren't you coming?" asked Abigail.

Sky bit her lip. She shook her head in a manner which indicated she was not going outside. Abigail knew to not press the issue.

"Okay. It's cool," she said before leaving the room.

The Branson children ran outside. They saw Walter's car finish parking itself near the jeep, and pickup truck. Walter, Cameron, and Vincent, exited the vehicle. They held their masks in their hands. They slowly walked towards the Branson's home, with sullen looks upon their faces. The Branson children ran to meet them on the lawn.

"What happened?" Samantha nervously asked the group.

Walter, Vincent, and Cameron briefly looked at each other.

"We won," Walter softly said.

The Branson children all spoke at once.

"Oh my God! You guys are hardcore!" exclaimed Paul Jr.

"You're kidding me! That's wonderful!" said Abigail.

"I can't believe you beat a drone!" Samantha said.

"Yay! No more flying hurty machine!" said Lily.

Walter held up his left hand and opened his palm, which indicated that he wanted the children to calm down.

"We won, but we lost some very good people. Let's not forget the sacrifice of those who have fallen," Walter said.

The Branson children and their friends fell silent for a moment.

"You guys are heroes!" Lily eventually said.

Vincent rustled Lily's hair with his right hand.

"Thanks, kiddo," Vincent said.

Walter, Vincent, Cameron, and the Branson children, walked up the front porch's stairs and entered the house. Walter saw that Paul was still being treated. Doreen finished bandaging his leg, and Paul sat upright.

"Sweet potato pie! I didn't think I'd ever see you again, old boy!" Paul said to Walter.

Walter walked over to Paul, and knelt by his right side.

"They're going to need a whole army of those damn things, if they expect to take me out," Walter said.

Paul stared at his longtime friend, and felt immense sadness.

"I shouldn't have run. I feel like a coward," Paul remorsefully said.

"Stop it, Paul. That's nonsense. You were injured, and you had to protect your family," Walter said.

He rested his hand atop Paul's left shoulder. Paul tapped Walter's hand, twice with his right hand.

"Yeah, you're right," Paul said.

Paul looked around, and saw that his children had once again gathered around him.

"I don't know what I'd do without y'all," Paul said.

Lily hugged her father and said, "I love you, daddy."

Cameron noticed that Sky was sitting on the couch, with her legs crossed. Sky had her index finger and thumb, over her lips. Cameron knew that she was incredibly angry with him. Cameron approached the couch and sat down.

Cameron looked at Sky and began saying, "Listen, I'm–"

"Please, don't," Sky furiously interrupted in a stern tone.

She quickly arose from the couch, and walked out of the room. Cameron heard the front door slam shut. He sank into the couch and sighed deeply. The room fell into an uncomfortable silence.

"Do you want me to talk to her?" Samantha asked softly.

Cameron put his head in his hands and ran them over his face.

"No, no. Just...just give me a minute," Cameron said.

After a few seconds, Cameron got off of the couch and went outside. Sky was standing on the front porch, and staring at the stars. Cameron walked beside her. He tried to get her attention, but she avoided his gaze.

"I'm sorry," Cameron said with sincerity.

"I can't believe you would do something like that to me," Sky coldly said.

Cameron said, "Sky, you don't understand..."

He put his hands on her shoulders, and began massaging her upper body.

"Cameron…no," said Sky.

She moved away from Cameron's grip.

"I can't believe you're so willing to throw your life away. That was the most dangerous thing you've ever done. You think dying is a joke," said Sky.

"You know I don't feel that way," Cameron replied.

Cameron looked up at the moon, which shone brightly above the New Jersey landscape.

"When I was a kid, I got depressed when I saw the stars. They are so far away; and it's so rare that we can actually see them through the pollution. Seeing them made me mad, because I know that I will never reach them," Cameron said.

Sky only pulled slightly away from Cameron, when he put his arms around her waist. He gently caressed her hips.

"I remember the first time I saw someone die," said Cameron.

Sky let her body sink into Cameron's.

"When I was fifteen, I went out partying with my friends. We were laughing and having a great time. It was the middle of summer. My buddies and I were walking along the Atlantic City shore. My friend picked up a rock and threw it into the ocean. We all laughed and thought nothing of his flippant action. Only seconds later, a drone surfaced from beneath the water," he lamented.

Cameron gripped Sky tighter and said, "The drone began threatening us. It said, 'Carbon Violation. Littering on a public beach is a serious offense. Fine is to be paid immediately.' I playfully told him, 'Better do what it says, James! That thing looks like it means business!' Our girlfriends laughed. James said, 'I don't give a fuck about some bossy robot!' and threw a rock at the drone."

Cameron's grip tightened even more, while he continued his story.

"'Fuck the robots, and fuck the future!' said James. He picked up another rock, and threw it at the drone. The drone used its laser to vaporize the rock in mid-air. The drone said to us, 'Terrorism is illegal. Attacking a drone is a capital offense,' before it shot a hot pulse beam from its mounted gun," Cameron said.

Cameron turned Sky around, so that he could look into her eyes.

"James didn't have time to react. The laser exploded his torso. His lower half fell to the ground. The girls screamed and ran. I was so terrified, that I pissed my pants. Soaking wet, I sprinted the fuck out of there; the quickest that my little nigger legs could take me," he said with fear.

"Why have you never told me that story?" Sky asked after a long silence.

Cameron replied, "I don't know. I..."

At that moment, Cameron saw the tree's leaves rustling. Sky and Cameron looked at the stars above them.

"Do you feel that breeze?" Cameron asked.

Sky pulled away from Cameron's embrace.

"Yes. Why?" Sky asked.

Suddenly they both saw a blurry object, moving erratically through the air.

"Holy fuck!" Cameron loudly whispered.

Cameron took his handgun out of his waistband, and looked through its holographic sights.

"Cameron, what the hell did we just see?" Sky frantically asked.

"You should go inside," Cameron replied.

Cameron continued using the gun's holographic viewfinder to scan the terrain, but he saw no movement on the farm's land. Cameron gazed upwards, and did not see any further aerial activity. He changed the viewfinder's light spectrum settings, by tapping the holographic screen. The viewfinder illuminated the entire landscape, in a green and black resolution.

"What do you see?" asked Sky.

"Nothing. Yet," replied Cameron.

Once more, Cameron tapped the screen. He scoured the aerial landscape in infrared vision.

Sky said, "Cameron you're scaring me. What's wron–?"

"Sky, stop talking! I think someone is spying on us!" Cameron interrupted.

Cameron looked through his sights, for another few seconds. One final time, Cameron switched the viewfinder's contrast. The aerial landscape was shown in a yellow, orange, and black resolution. Cameron was horrified when he saw two large stealth helicopters, flying above the farm. Flashing bursts of light from cameras mounted on their back rotors, snapped pictures of the family's dwelling.

"Holy fuck! It's a raid!" Cameron said with total fear.

Sky said, "What do you–"

"You and Sam need to gather the children, and get the fuck out of this house!" he interrupted.

Sky began saying, "We can't just–"

Before Sky could finish her thought, one of the stealth helicopters uncloaked itself. The chopper hovered above the Branson's house. It shone a bright white light upon Sky and Cameron.

"Terrorists located. You are all under arrest," a loud robotic voice said.

"Raid! Raid!" Cameron yelled.

Cameron grabbed Sky by her right arm, ran inside the house, and raced into the living room.

"You and your family need to leave! There are stealth choppers outside!" Cameron said to Paul.

Abigail ran to the living room's large window. She used her right index finger to move one of the blind coverings upward. She saw that there was a large helicopter outside. Abigail immediately moved away from the window, dropped to the floor, and crawled towards Doreen.

"Mom! Mom, they're outside!" Abigail said.

Doreen hugged her daughter. Doreen looked at her husband, with great sadness in her eyes and heart.

Doreen said, "Shh, darling. Baby, they've found–"

"I know, I know," Paul woefully said.

"Help me up, dude," Paul said to Walter.

Walter put his arm underneath Paul's left shoulder, and lifted him to his feet. Paul groaned, and briefly wobbled.

"Get your Mum, and sisters, to the safe zone," Paul said to his son.

Paul Jr. said, "Dad, I'm not leaving–"

"I'm not asking you! I'm giving you a damn *instruction!*" Paul snapped.

"Yes, father," Paul Jr. dutifully said.

Paul Jr. went to the couch and lifted up its cushions. He took the AX-91 semi-automatic laser rifle, and holstered .45 caliber revolver, from beneath the couch. Paul Jr. removed several boxes of ammunition, thermal magazines, and a backpack.

Paul Jr. said to Abigail, "Sis, help–"

Before Paul Jr. could finish speaking, Abigail grabbed the ammunition and started stuffing it into the backpack.

"It's okay, brother," Abigail said.

Paul Jr. loaded the AX-91 with a thirty round, fully charged, thermal magazine. He slung the rifle over his shoulder. Abigail fastened the holster and gun around her waist. Abigail put several more magazines, and boxes of ammo, inside of the backpack. She zipped it up, and threw it over her shoulders.

"Don't worry about reloading. I'll make sure we're stocked and ready to rock," Abigail said.

Doreen said with panic, "How did they–"

"It doesn't matter. They're going to kill the kids. That's a mobile vaccination unit, with a full United Nations escort. Remember that place about which we talked? Go there now, honey," Paul said.

Doreen had tears in her eyes.

She said to her husband, "You're hurt–"

"I'm fine. Take the kids and get out. Please," Paul interrupted.

The Branson family did not have time for long farewells.

Lily began crying and said, "Daddy–"

"It's okay pumpkin. I'm right behind you. You have to go now, okay?" Paul interrupted.

Paul knelt down, hugged his small daughter, and kissed Lily upon her forehead. Vincent, Walter, and Cameron, were already putting on their masks.

"Shit! We left the guns in the car!" Vincent said.

"You're fine. Go to the kitchen, and look behind the refrigerator. Use anything you want," Paul said.

"You heard him, people! Everybody get the hell out!" Walter shouted.

"That means you too, Sky!" Cameron shouted.

Cameron ran from the living room, bolted down the hallway and entered the kitchen. Vincent followed him without hesitation. The stealth choppers continued hovering above the house.

"Terrorist faction. We can see that there are ten of you inside the domicile. You have three minutes to surrender. Use of lethal force is authorized. Firing warning ammunition," the robotic voice said.

The stealth chopper shot a hot particle beam at the house. A significant portion of the front porch was vaporized. Several of the women screamed loudly. Walter shoved Paul behind the couch and dove atop of him for cover.

"Stop standing around!" Walter screamed.

The Branson children, their mother, and Sky, ran from the room. A hailstorm of bullets began penetrating their sovereign home. Abigail, Paul Jr., Samantha, Lily, Doreen, and Sky, screamed in terror. They raced out of the living room, sprinted through the hallway and went to the kitchen. They saw Vincent and Cameron loading a shotgun, and sniper rifle. Vincent opened the back door, ran outside and aimed his shotgun around the yard. When Vincent was sure the path was safe, he motioned for the evacuees to start running.

"Go, go!" Vincent yelled.

Doreen, her children, and Sky, ran from the house and raced towards the nearby woods. The secondary drone helicopter had uncloaked itself, and flown to the back of the house.

"Terrorist farming operation identified. Hostiles are violating United Nations protocol, Agenda 21," it said.

The drone began shooting at the invisible cage placed in the Branson's backyard. The cage flickered for a moment, before its shielding collapsed and exposed fresh produce. The drone shot a blue flame at the produce. The crops violently ignited in a burst of fire.

"Keep moving! Don't come back!" Vincent yelled at the fleeing group.

Vincent turned around and ran back towards the house. He fired two shots at the helicopter. He watched the crops burn for only a moment, before reentering the house.

Once they had reached the woods, Doreen briefly stopped the group.

Doreen said, "There are some underground tunnels, about one mile from us. We have to–"

"I'm not leaving daddy, or our friends!" Lily angrily said.

Doreen snapped at her child, "Don't argue with me! They will be fine. We–"

"We can't keep running!" Lily screamed.

Lily pressed a button on her cloaking vest, and she instantly turned invisible. She began running back to the house.

"Lily! Lily, stop! You come back here right this instant!" Doreen yelled before breaking out in tears.

"Mom if they find all of us, they will enforce the One Child Mandate," Paul Jr. grimly said to his mother.

Doreen knew her son was wise beyond his years.

"Oh, my baby..." Doreen whispered.

She forced herself to regain her composure, before leading the group towards the tunnels.

Cameron ran upstairs, through a hallway, and entered the master bedroom. Cameron went to a large window, opened it, and aimed the sniper rifle at the hovering chopper.

"This is an illegal farming operation. The U.S. Sector of Agriculture, operating under the authority of the United Nations, demands you immediately cease and desist all unauthorized carbon activity," the drone said.

Cameron began laughing and said, "Hah, hah, hah! Keep dreaming, motherfucker!"

He slid the rifle's bolt action into place, and fired a round directly at the vehicle. The bullet created a large spark, when it hit the chopper's windshield. The drone's hovering was disrupted, and it swayed in midair.

"Damage sustained. Terrorist farmers are confirmed to be illegally armed, and hostile," the chopper said.

Cameron reloaded the rifle, and fired another shot at the helicopter. The bullet struck hard and penetrated its nose.

"Violent extremists will not submit to arrest. Capture alive protocol, may not be possible," the chopper said.

Cameron saw that the laser gun attached to the chopper's hull, was preparing to fire. Cameron ran from the room, only seconds before a hot plasma beam tore through the wall. The blast's force made Cameron lose his balance. Cameron hit the floor hard, but quickly pulled himself to his feet.

"We have to evacuate!" Cameron yelled.

He began running back down the stairs. Vincent was running around the bottom floor, and using an extinguisher to prevent pockets of fire from spreading throughout the house. Paul and Walter were in a room adjacent to the family one. They were hiding behind an overturned table, and only emerged to fire shots out of the window.

"We can't take these things out," Walter said while tightly gripping his handgun.

"I know. It's time to leave," Paul said.

"Head out the back! I'll cover you!" Vincent shouted.

"No way! We're not leaving you!" Cameron said.

"Paul's hurt! He needs both of you to help him escape!" Vincent said.

The entire team was startled when they heard a young voice.

"I'll help!" the voice shouted.

A small blurry blob de-cloaked itself while moving down the hallway. Paul saw Lily and became furious.

"What the *hell* is *wrong* with you?! I told you to get out of here, dammit!" Paul screamed.

Lily said, "I'm sorry! I couldn't leav–"

"I can't believe that you would deliberately disobey me!" Paul quickly interrupted.

Lily tried to say, "But I can hel–!"

"I don't want you here! You're going to get *killed!*" Paul shouted.

Lily's lower lip began quivering and her eyes filled with tears.

"I'm not a wimp! I'll prove it to you!" Lily yelled.

Lily reactivated her cloaking device. Before leaving the room, Lily grabbed a pistol off of the floor. Paul frantically tried to stand, but his injury quickly caused him to fall back down.

"Lily! Lily, no! Come back!" Paul screamed.

"Shit, I can't see her!" Vincent said.

Cameron and Vincent fired several more shots at the helicopter. Cameron prepared to run outside.

"Terrorists are attempting to escape," the stealth chopper said.

Vincent pulled Cameron back, and pushed him to the ground. The chopper fired several bullets into the house's wood foundation. Cameron and Vincent rolled out of the way, and narrowly avoided the hailstorm of bullets. They moved to the back of the room, and hid behind furniture. Cameron handed Vincent the sniper rifle.

"Cover me!" Cameron shouted.

Cameron ran to the front door, and hid behind its frame. Vincent repositioned himself next to Walter, who was still firing upon the drone. Vincent raised the rifle and fired a shot which struck the chopper in its side.

"Sustaining heavy damage. Rerouting power from laser weapon systems, to altitude thrusters," it said.

"Lily! Where are you?!" Cameron shouted.

"I hate being called a terrorist! Stop attacking my family! We did nothing wrong!" Cameron faintly heard Lily yell.

Lily tightly gripped the gun with both hands, and began shooting at the chopper. Cameron saw the muzzle flashes.

"Oh my God! Lily, stop! You don't know what you're doing!" Cameron screamed.

The drone helicopter struggled to lock onto Lily. Her cloaking technology disrupted its powerful thermal camera.

"Unknown terrorist is using light manipulation technology. Preparing to activate infrared vision," the drone said.

Lily ran over to the vehicles. She hid between the pickup truck, and Walter's car. Walter and Vincent unleashed another round of bullets. Cameron used this opportunity to sprint through the doorway. Cameron ran wildly around the front yard, and was no longer concerned about his own safety.

"Lily! Lily! Get back inside!" Cameron said.

Cameron felt his heart becoming heavy, and wanted to cry. The chopper shone a bright light on Cameron.

"Terrorist, stop. You are required to follow lawful orders," the drone said.

Cameron put his hands in front of his face. He turned his head to the left, to avoid the blinding glare. Cameron heard the sounds of gunfire coming from the cars' direction. Cameron continued sprinting towards the cars.

"Get off my property! We never did anything to deserve this!" Cameron heard Lily shout.

Cameron ducked low while he was running. The sounds of gunfire coming from all directions disoriented him. The loud banging sounds hurt his ear drums. Cameron stopped beside the pickup truck, when he saw sparks emanating from Lily's pistol. Cameron could barely see the blurry blob that was crouched between the cars. Nevertheless he ducked his shoulders down, and tackled Lily to the ground.

Cameron rolled over and said, "Take off the cloak right now, Lily!"

Lily tuned off the invisibility shield, and sat upright. She had a scared look upon her face.

"Cam, Cam...I'm sorry! I just wanted to help!" Lily apologetically said.

Cameron hugged Lily and even though he was still masked, kissed her forehead. He put his hands on her triceps.

"It's okay, it's okay. You don't have to be sorry. Listen, we have to get out of here right away. Do you understand?" Cameron asked.

Lily shook her head in agreement.

"Good. Take my hand, and stay close," Cameron said.

Cameron grabbed Lily's left hand, with his right one. They both took several deep breaths.

"Okay, you can reactivate the cloak," Cameron said.

Lily quickly followed Cameron's instruction. The sounds of gunfire continued emanating from the house.

"Run!" Cameron shouted.

Cameron and Lily bolted towards the house. Cameron's long strides were difficult for Lily's tiny frame to match. Lily lagged behind Cameron, but never lost her grip upon his hand.

Lily stumbled and said, "Cam, slow down!"

"Terrorists attempting to flee," the drone chopper said.

The drone readied its lasers. Vincent and Walter were hastily reloading their weapons.

"Holy fuck, it's going to shoot them!" Vincent said with great concern.

"Not on my fucking watch!" Walter screamed.

Walter and Vincent immediately stopped reloading. They used their remaining bullets to fire a barrage of ammunition. Their effort was valiant, but they were powerless to stop the drone. It finished charging its lasers, and fired a thin plasma beam right at Cameron and Lily! The blast erupted behind him, and knocked Cameron off of his feet. Cameron fell forward, and landed flat upon his stomach. Cameron was in pain, and out of breath.

He groaned and said, "We've got to...keep moving..."

Cameron felt himself still gripping Lily's hand. Cameron started rolling over, onto his left side. He began moving his right arm upward, and brought it closer to his body. He was sickened to see that the appendage he was holding, was no longer attached to Lily's body. Cameron gasped, dropped the severed limb, and immediately removed his mask. He crouched upon his hands and knees; and started vomiting. Lily's left arm had been separated above her elbow.

Cameron was so paralyzed by horror that he could not move. He saw Lily laying on her back. Her bloody bicep muscle was hanging out of her left arm. Lily screamed in absolute agony. Her mortifying and shrill shrieks sent a terrible chill through Cameron's entire body. Cameron crawled forward, and his whole body was shaking. He reached Lily a few seconds later. Her young body contorted in agony. He wanted to hug her, but restrained himself. He was too afraid that he would exacerbate her suffering. Her clothes smoldered. Small patches of burnt flesh, adorned the left side of her body.

Blood had splashed onto her face. The muscles in her severed left arm, twitched while she convulsed. Cameron looked at the small, innocent child, and felt unparalleled remorse. Lily started heaving, and foaming at the mouth. Her fragile body went into shock. The ruthless aerial abomination kept its laser sights aimed at both of them. Walter and Vincent watched in horror from inside the house.

"Dear, God. No..." Walter said.

"What happened? What did they do to my baby?!" Paul frantically shouted.

Vincent let the sniper rifle fall to the ground. He put both his hands atop his head.

"Holy shit. Holy, SHIT!" Vincent yelled.

"Help me!" Paul screamed.

He extended his right arm, and signaled that he wanted Walter to help him stand.

Walter said, "Paul, I–"

"I fucking said, *help me!*" Paul quickly shouted.

Walter and Vincent obliged, and helped Paul off the floor. The three men walked out of the house.

"Terrorists appear to be voluntarily surrendering," the drone said in a callous tone.

They walked down what remained of the front porch. They reached the front lawn, and walked along the grass. Paul was horrified when he saw his bloody, mangled daughter.

"My baby!" Paul screamed.

Paul lurched forward, out of his friend's grasp. Paul quickly crawled along the cold grass, and rushed to his daughter's side. Lily was still convulsing. Paul cradled her in his arms, and sobbed immensely. He tried to console Lily, while she struggled for her life.

"I've failed you. I'm so sorry, baby. I've failed you..." Paul regretfully said.

The second drone chopper had flown from the back of the house. It was now hovering next to the chopper, which had mercilessly shot Lily. Two teams of four men, dressed in heavy combat gear, used thick black rope to descend from the choppers. The men drew their rifles, and surrounded the group of defeated rebels.

"U.S. Sector of Agriculture! You are under arrest!" one of them yelled.

Cameron stood up, and angrily walked over to the man.

"What the fuck is wrong with you?! What kind of small dick piece of shit, lets a drone shoot a laser beam at a little girl?!" he screamed with rage.

The man aimed his gun at Cameron's head.

"Get on the ground!" the officer shouted.

Cameron used his left hand, to violently slap the gun away from his head.

"Don't you fucking point that shit at me, nigger! I'll fucking take out *all* of you faggot ass niggers! Let's see how fucking tough you are, without your fucking robot! I'm the baddest nigger in these *streets!*" Cameron indignantly screamed.

Cameron continued to stand ready for a fight. Vincent and Walter quickly walked over and tried to calm Cameron down. The raid team's leader approached Paul and Lily. The leader removed a small canister from his combat tactical belt.

"Move. This will stop the bleeding," the leader said to Paul.

Paul let Lily gently fall from his arms. The man sprayed the can's thick foam, upon Lily's arm. He removed a small oxygen mask from his belt. He placed it over Lily's mouth, and nose. Lily started falling unconscious.

"We will transport her to the nearest hospital. She will need surgery. Do you have health insurance?" he asked.

Paul flew into an absolute rage, and started punching the leader in his shin.

"You *motherfucking* piece of *trash!*" You fucking try to *murder* my daughter, and then ask me to pay a fucking Carbon Tax? *Fuck* you!" Paul screamed.

Vincent and Walter immediately grabbed Paul by his arms, and dragged him away from the leader.

"Let me go! Let me fucking *go!*" I'm going to fucking *kill* this piece of *shit!*" Paul shouted.

Cameron showed his support, by resuming his tirade of obscenities.

"All of you niggers are going to Hell! You fucking idiot niggers have destroyed your *own* fucking future, by serving this bullshit system! You niggers are fucking dying from eating the GMO *too!*" Cameron passionately shouted.

"Book them, and take the child to a hospital," the leader told one of his fellow soldiers.

"Roger," the soldier said.

The soldier pressed several buttons on the computer interface, embedded in his suit's left forearm. The helicopter shot Cameron, Paul, Vincent, and Walter with thick glowing green netting. The sounds of screaming were quickly silenced. The netting was equipped with miniature tasers that sent an electric pulse through their bodies. They fell to the floor, and eventually passed out from the painful shock torture.

Thirteen long weeks passed between Cameron, Vincent, Paul, and Walter's arrest. Videos of the drone battle in Manville had spread like wildfire throughout the internet. The repugnant marionette media was forced to cover the events. Survivors from the battle spoke out on various media platforms. They condemned the U.S. government for allowing drones to murder American citizens in their homeland. They called for legislators at the State and Federal level, to nullify the Domestic Defense Authorization Act of 2164. For several decades, the Federal government used the fifty-three year old unconstitutional law to authorize extrajudicial assassinations against American citizens that were declared terrorists.

There was an even more intense public condemnation, for the attack on the Branson's farm. Around the country, protests had been taking place for weeks. Activists demanded that Paul be released from prison, and reunited with his daughter. Lily spent weeks in an intensive care unit, at the New Brunswick Pediatric Hospital. Doreen desperately tried to convince the courts, to release Lily into her custody. The courts did not want to comply, because Lily was considered an undocumented youth. Her birth was never registered with the Child Enforcement Agency. In the eyes of the law, Lily was considered an illegally conceived child. Doreen gave many interviews to news outlets that were not controlled by corporate interests. She vowed to win the custody battle with the State. Every alternative media outlet supported Doreen's crusade.

The corporate media criticized Doreen and her husband for running an unauthorized and illegal home farm. They called the couple tax evaders and wanted the Internal Revenue Society to perform a full audit of their finances, medical records, and internet activities. Samantha, Abigail, and Paul Jr., were hiding at another illegal farm, which was owned by Jerry's friends. Doreen had instructed her children to conceal their location and identities. The whole family feared the kids would be euthanized under the One Child Mandate. Doreen used encrypted communication devices to speak with her offspring once per week. The modified cellular phones were given to her by Eiji and Lucia. They were altered to transmit data over archaic internet connections, which were not governed by the United Nations. Doreen sparingly used the devices. She did not want to risk having her communications intercepted by various government agencies.

Sky moved back into the compound, with the remaining Icons. Eiji and Lucia released numerous videos, and demanded that their friends be freed. They wore their masks and used aliases while they were on camera. Eiji called himself Magnificent Sight; because he felt that the animating spirit of liberty was a marvelous sight to behold. Lucia called herself Lady Fore-shock; because she was part of the Liberty Movement that was a precursor to the great second American Revolution. The two of them vowed to rally other factions in the Food Movement. They swore to commit acts of civil disobedience; like spray painting the outside of fast food stores with pro-liberty messages, and destroying street light surveillance cameras; until their friends were given a full pardon. They were praised by their followers, who proclaimed that the videos were a powerful tool of resistance.

Free speech in America had been increasingly eroded, when the Chinese took greater control of the country following the economic collapse of the 2180's. Political dissenting was a dangerous act. A person could have his wages garnished, bank account seized, travel restricted, and United Nations' authorized internet access revoked; if he was publicly declared a conspiracy theorist. The Icons completely revolted against this brazen First Amendment violation. Their videos inspired others to speak their mind, protest, and resist the unjust laws that had been placed upon them.

Troubled Times released videos of his own. He mercilessly ridiculed the captured Icons members. He claimed that they had failed their mission. He urged citizens to create rampant chaos across their city streets. Troubled Times promoted anarchy, and vowed to commit a new string of attacks. His threats of real terrorism, spread fear throughout the public. It was well known, that Times possessed superhuman abilities. Witnesses who had survived his brutal Fifth Avenue massacre, told stories of how the people doing the killing were not in control of their own bodies. After the release of the video that Eiji and Lucia had uploaded the night of the farm raid; people conceded that Troubled Times might actually be using advanced MK-Zero mind control technology, to enhance himself.

It was 10:07 AM on Friday, May 23rd, 2217. Walter, Vincent, Cameron, and Paul, were being transported to the Mercer County Superior Court House in Trenton, New Jersey. They sat in a windowless armored van, while it drove through the Trenton streets. They heard crowds of people loudly protesting their imprisonment. Some were saying that they should be released. Others were shouting obscenities, and agreed with the notion that The Icons were violent terrorists. The group was handcuffed and their feet were shackled to restraints underneath their seats. They wore dark black jumpsuits on their bodies, and black burlap sacks over their heads. None of the men dared speak to each other. The van eventually stopped, its back door opened, and a sheriff's officer entered. She began unlocking the foot restraints. Four other officers pointed sub-machine laser guns at the group, while they were being unchained. The woman promptly finished, and exited the van.

"Everybody out," the female officer said.

The men slowly stepped out of the van. Their hands remained shacked, and they were chained together at the hip. The female officer proceeded to lead them through the back of the courthouse. They walked through a series of corridors, and up to the main floor. They traveled down a long hallway, and arrived at the court room. A mass of observers was anxiously awaiting the trial. The prisoners were led to the defendant's area, and seated next to each other. Vincent sat in the far left chair, Paul and Walter sat in the middle, and Cameron sat in the far right chair. The female officer finally removed their burlap head sacks. Observers spoke in hushed whispers. They pointed their fingers, and snickered at the defendants. The prisoners nervously looked around the room.

"This place is packed," Vincent said to Paul.

"It's a damn circus," Paul replied.

Moments later, a five foot tall robot rolled itself to their council table. Its semi-humanoid torso had a large cylinder for its body. Attached to the body, were thick tubes. It had robotic claws for arms. Its head was a rectangular camera. Its lower half was attached to a square box, with six wheels.

"Good morning," the robot said.

The group was unnerved by the sight of the awkward-looking automaton.

"What are you?" Walter said.

"I am PD-3100," the robot replied.

"PD? What the hell does that mean?" Vincent asked.

"Public Defender, thirty-one hundred. I will be your acting attorney, for the duration of this trial," PD-3100 said.

The group became enraged, and started protesting this gross miscarriage of justice.

"Are you kidding me? You're a fucking tin can!" Cameron said.

"This is a human rights violation!" Walter shouted.

"You have no right to speak for us!" Paul said.

"Whatever happened to the Sixth Amendment?!" Vincent angrily asked.

PD-3100 said, "I've tried approximately six-hundred thirteen thousand, seven-hundred and fifty-one cases. This with be my–"

"I don't care if you've tried one *million* cases! I want a *human* attorney, dammit!" Cameron loudly interrupted.

The Prosecutor entered the room. She was a middle-aged Chinese woman, who wore a fancy business suit. She was accompanied by another robot, which looked similar to the PD-3100. Vincent immediately addressed her.

"Miss! Excuse me, Miss! I think there has been some mistake! This thing is saying it's our lawyer!" Vincent said.

The Prosecutor giggled, and said something in Chinese to the other robot. The defendants did not understand her. They were highly disturbed when both the Prosecutor, and her robot, shared a laugh. Even though the robot did not talk, it made a bleeping sound which the group assumed was its way of laughing.

"Well, this is pretty fucking rotten," Walter said to his friends.

Vincent was visibly upset.

"Falun Gong forever, bitches!" he defiantly said.

"We have the *right*, to be represented by *real* people!" shouted Paul.

A male sheriff's officer entered the room.

"All please rise," he said.

The observers sitting on the court benches, and The Icons, arose from their chairs. A rhythmic musical song began playing over the courtroom's loud speakers. The song was an instrumental tune, with chunky distorted guitars churning a heavy riff. The drum beat was thick. The bellowing bass guitar gave the song's rhythmic groove, a powerful tone.

"Ladies and gentleman! Boys and girls! Welcome, to the Mercer County Court House!" the officer shouted.

"Are they serious? They can't be serious," Paul said to Walter.

Observers began swaying, and moving in sync with the rhythmic music. The Icons watched in bewilderment, at the absurd scene unfolding in the courthouse.

"You've seen her on T.V! You've read about her online! Now, I want you all to put your hands together; and give a warm welcome to the most Judging-est Judge, in *all* of New Jersey! Please give it up for the one, the only; the Honorable Judge Sheila Bailey!" the officer yelled.

The mawkish scene became even more bizarre. The room erupted with cheering and applause. The Judge began walking down the aisle, and was accompanied by two female officers. One officer walked in front of the Judge, and the other walked behind her. The three women moved in rhythmic fashion to the music. They took two steps forward, while simultaneously raising their arms. They extended their appendages, and bent them at the elbow.

They formed a closed fist with their palms facing outward. They simultaneously locked their other arm in a similar fashion with their palms facing inward, in front of their stomach. They continued moving in this asinine manner, until the Judge walked up to her bench. The Judge performed more grandstanding, and danced for a brief moment. She was a rotund, youthful looking, black woman in her mid-forties. Her wig was styled immaculately, with long flowing, curly brown locks of hair. The song ended, and the Judge sat down.

"All y'all muthafuckas, *sit* yo' asses *down!*" Judge Bailey said to the courtroom.

The crowd laughed and clapped once more, before taking their seats. The court room became eerily silent. An absolutely dumbfounded Paul, stared at his friends in disbelief.

"Oh, Lord. We're toast," Paul said.

"Prosecutor! Who these fools?" Judge Bailey loudly asked.

The Prosecutor did a curtsey and said, "Cao Mingzhu, representing the State. As always, it is a pleasure to serve you, your Honor."

"Oh, please. You don't have to sweet talk me girl," Judge Bailey said.

The courtroom's observers softly laughed.

"The State intends to prove that this consortium of criminal terrorists, was responsible for leading an attack on a Neighborhood Aerial Protection Unit," Mingzhu said.

"That's what you call a mobile killing machine? A 'protection unit'?!" Walter angrily snapped.

Judge Bailey slammed her gavel down with passion.

"Shut yo' old ass up, and let her finish!" Judge Bailey said.

"That thing murdered *teenagers!*" Walter said.

Mingzhu ignored Walter and said, "Furthermore, the State will prove that this group of criminals, is also responsible for distributing illegal food."

"This is insanity," Cameron quietly said to Walter.

"Little nigger, is there something you want to say?" Judge Bailey angrily asked Cameron.

Walter whispered to Cameron, "Cam...stop. Let it g–"

He abruptly stopped speaking, when Cameron arose from his chair.

"Your Honor, with all due respect, this is a fucking joke!" Cameron said.

The court room observers let out a shocked gasp at Cameron's accurate and controversial statement.

The PD-3100 said, "Your Honor, what my client meant to say was–"

"Shut up, dammit! You are *not* speaking for us! Justice Bailey, I'd like to fire my attorney!" Cameron interrupted.

"Why? What's wrong with him?" Judge Bailey asked.

"Because *it's* a damn *robot! It's* not a *'him'?!*" Cameron shouted.

"Who you think you getting uppity with, young nigger? Don't you yell at me!" Judge Bailey said.

"We have a right to a fair trial, by a jury of our peers!" Cameron said.

The courtroom erupted with laughter. The ignorant observers blissfully enjoyed watching the ridiculous spectacle. Judge Bailey slammed down her gavel, with authority.

"Order in the court!" Judge Bailey said.

"I move to declare a mistrial," Vincent said.

"Shut up! I'll mistrial you!" Judge Bailey said.

"What the hell does that even mean?" Vincent asked.

"This is so fucked up," Cameron said.

"Order dammit, *order!* I've heard *enough!* You muthafuckas are giu'ty! G, I, U, T, Y, GIU'TY!" Judge Bailey yelled.

The Icons were absolutely awestricken that the Judge could not even spell the word, under which she was convicting them. Paul tried pleading for sanity.

He said, "Your Honor, I think we should at least hear the evidence–"

"Keep yo' pasty behind, *quiet!* We already *saw* the evidence. Everybody saw the evidence! You assholes are the ones dressed up like clowns, leading terrorist attacks around the State! You *all* giu'ty as *shit*, and I sentence all of you to fifteen seasons, on *The Yard!*" Judge Bailey emphatically said.

The wild sounds of cheers and applause erupted from the court room observers. Judge Bailey stood up, and did a victory dance. She placed one hand behind her ear and the other hand on her hip. She bent her knees, and thrust her pelvis forward twice. She switched hands, and repeated this process several times.

"Fuck you, lady! Fuck this whole kangaroo court! I want my due process! I want a Prosecutor, who isn't a foreigner! I want a Judge who's not illiterate! I want a defense attorney, that isn't a walking blender!" Cameron yelled.

The two female officers walked up to Cameron. They began spraying him with red liquid from their steel plated batons. Cameron dropped to the ground, and starting writhing in pain. The robot Prosecutor's assistant rolled itself up to the rest of the defendants. It used its right robotic claw to shoot taser beams at them. The PD-3100 used its left claw to shoot sticky glowing netting at the newly created convicts.

Gregory Times sat in what was formerly Webster Morgan's personal penthouse bedroom. On a large holographic projector he watched the live internet feed, streaming from the court room's cameras. Times twisted the cap off the bottle of his specially designed medication. After swallowing four pills, he chuckled with amusement. Webster sat half-naked, like a dog, beside Times' feet.

Webster wore a specially designed shock collar that Times controlled with his brainwaves. The robot Alice had created the device for Times. It was designed to give Webster a specific dosage of medication, every several hours. It was embedded with a tracking chip that would alert Times of Webster's every move. Times sat upon a large chair, loudly crunching on organic pretzels. He heard the penthouse's door open. The Chem-Mech, and the robot Alice, entered the room.

"Sir, I have wonderful news. The patient seems to have made a full recovery. Her neural connections are repaired. Her physical therapy is complete. She has requested to see you," the Chem-Mech said to Times.

Times turned slightly in the chair, looked over his left shoulder, and cracked a wide smile.

"Honey, is that you?" Times giddily asked.

Times could barely contain his excitement. He heard soft footsteps slowly approaching him. Times turned further to his left, and saw his beloved Mallory. She was wearing a gorgeous, one piece, red dress. She looked like a movie starlet. The expensive dress had sleeveless straps, and a flowing skirt. Her lightly colored, peach lip gloss was a beautiful contrast to her ginger colored hair. Mallory knelt beside Times, and they passionately gazed into each other's eyes. Mallory gently reached her left hand behind Times' ear and caressed him. Mallory leaned forward, and softly kissed her husband's lips.

Times said, "You look, stunning. I–"

Before Times could continue, Mallory placed her right index finger over his lips.

"Shh. I can hear you inside my head, my love," she softly whispered.

Mallory gently caressed Times' face, and kissed him repeatedly.

"I understand why it's so dark. I understand…everything," Mallory said.

"I'm glad that you finally know the truth," Times said.

Times tossed the bag of pretzels at Webster's face. Webster grabbed its spilled contents, and rabidly began eating.

"Thank you. I know it wasn't an easy task, to merge our memories without killing her. All the recollections of our pain, suffering, and torture, are unified," Times said to the robots.

Times looked at Mallory and said, "Now my love, we are one. Our emotional connection has been enhanced, through our amalgamation in The Reality. I understand the unbearable heartbreak you endured; the night our children were ripped from your womb."

Mallory softly stroked Times' cheek and said, "And I understand why you must make the degenerates suffer, for ruining this diseased world."

Times arose from the chair. He extended his hand, which Mallory used to help herself stand. Times grabbed her waist, and pulled her close for a loving embrace.

"Forever in chaos, my love?" Times asked Mallory.

"In chaos, forever," Mallory coldly replied.

28 Capital Punishment

Cameron Moss lay upon his bed. His heart was heavy with sorrow. It was 8:49 PM on Saturday, June 21st, 2217. The burgeoning heat wave, made the black jumpsuit which he was wearing, chafe his skin. He could hear the screams of madness, emanating from outside of his dirty prison cell walls.

"You going to get it tonight, nigger!"

"It's time for the fucking Yard!"

"Show these pussies how we roll in Jersey, Cameron!"

"Fucking hope you ate good for your last meal, you organic faggot!"

"Nigger, bet to hope you win, or we're going to beat your ass!"

"That's my nigger! Go fuck them up, Moss!"

"That nigger's about to get *crippled!*"

"You the best! Show these niggers why you an Icon!"

The horrendous chorus of vulgar threats and twisted encouragements, chilled Cameron to his core; but he did not dare show fear. Had he been an average food criminal, his sentence would not have been so harsh. The Yard was originally reserved to punish only the most violent offenders. The show's popularity allowed its creators to fill its roster with high profile convicts. Famous political dissidents were routinely forced to compete in the brutal competition. The Yard was one of the most common ways to punish people who violated the Carbon Tax Law. However, it was rare that inmates convicted of food related crimes, were forced to complete in death matches. Cameron knew that he and his friends were being persecuted for their civil disobedience.

Even though their actions had resulted in the injury and deaths of noble citizens; they had never purposely harmed other humans during their years of rebellion. Any lives lost, were scarified during the struggle to liberate the greater population from the enslavement under which they lived. Cameron and his friends had risked their own lives countless times, during the battle for freedom. The State wanted to make an example of them, so that others would be discouraged from replicating their actions. Numerous authoritarian bureaucrats and their ignorant followers, wanted to see The Icons dead. Cameron, Vincent, Walter, and Paul were slated to be executed like common thugs. It seemed like their wild, bloodthirsty naysayers, would soon get their wish.

The small window on his cell door began projecting a holographic image of a female face. The computer generated face resembled that of a Chinese female. The face abruptly spoke in a computerized voice.

"Inmate number nine hundred million, seven hundred thousand, eight hundred and sixty two; you are required to report for mandatory rehabilitation, in thirty-one minutes. How are you feeling this evening?" the animation asked.

Cameron briefly tilted his head to his left, and viewed the image. Cameron spoke no words, and returned his gaze to the ceiling.

"Iris scans and bio-environmental analysis, indicate that your testosterone levels are excessively high. Pharmaceutical reduction of these levels is mandatory. Would you like to choose a pill?" the holographic face asked.

The rectangular slot embedded in the front door of Cameron's cell, slowly moved a few inches forward. A tray containing several different types of pharmaceutical drugs was offered to Cameron.

He cleared his throat, and continued staring at the steel walls above him. The tray rescinded after Cameron did not accept a pharmaceutical.

"Inmate refuses to abide by Carbon Control Protocols. Visitation time limit will be reduced," the animation said.

Cameron looked at the cartoon and said, "You want to repeat that a bit more slowly, robo-chink?"

The computerized voice said, "Racial hostility detected. Multicultural training does not yet appear to be effective. Enrollment in Diversity Appreciation course is–"

"Cut the psychological warfare bullshit, and let me see my visitor," said Cameron.

He quickly rolled off of the bed, and into a standing position. The holographic display began projecting soft laser beams. The beams scanned Cameron from his head to his feet.

The computerized voice said, "Inmate guest seems to be experiencing–"

Cameron walked forward and started calmly punching the window in a controlled fit of rage. The window fizzled and a few random sparks fell to the ground.

"Stop acting like you give a shit about my welfare," Cameron calmly said.

"Destruction of state property is prohibited. Further outbursts, will be met with severe physical reprimands," it said.

Cameron let out a deep sigh, before he pressed his hand against the interactive window. The panel scanned his hand print. Afterwards, it projected another holographic image.

"Bio-signature, accepted. Communication authorized. Incoming call time limit is restricted to seven minutes. Thank you for your cooperation, Cameron Moss," said the machine.

Cameron's heart sank when he saw the image of a beautiful woman; rendered inside of the small, dirty panel. Even though the woman wore tinted glasses, a fleece hood, and silk scarf, Cameron knew her identity.

"What the hell are you thinking? You know this isn't a secure line," Cameron angrily said.

"Do you *always* have to be such an asshole?" Sky sternly replied.

Cameron timidly said, "I'm sorry. I'm not mad at you; but you can't stay on this connect–"

"Fifteen seasons, Cameron. They gave you fifteen *seasons!*" Sky furiously interrupted.

Cameron replied, "Yeah, I know. Yard sentences are usually only ordered on a yearly basis. It's rare that convicts get more than five or six seasons in a row. I spoke to a human lawyer today. She said I can probably get the conviction overturned on appeal–"

"Cameron, you have no idea how much trouble you've gotten yourself into, this time. You've signed your death warrant one thousand times over! Most people only have to do twelve weeks over the course of one summer. You, have to serve fifteen summers in a row," Sky interrupted.

"It's not that bad. I can be out by the time I'm fifty-one. Maybe if I win enough matches, I'll get time off for good behavior," Cameron said.

Sky ignored Cameron's wishful thinking and said, "This may be the last time, we ever talk to each other. I don't want to spend our last conversation fighting with you."

"I don't, either. I guess...it's just easier to fight. If we fight, then we can ignore our true feelings," Cameron said.

"That's no way to act. What if this is our last chance to express our emotions?" Sky asked.

Cameron could tell Sky was experiencing an intense amount of heartache, by the exasperated tone in her voice.

"They are going to trace this call, and run your voice and face prints through a recognition database. I don't want to ruin anyone else's life. You're better off, without me. Now, you can finally be happy. Goodbye," Cameron said.

Cameron terminated the call, by pressing his hand against the window panel.

"God, *damn!*" Cameron screamed at the top of his lungs.

He punched the panel several times. The door to Cameron's cell horizontally slid open. Six masked policemen dressed in riot gear, entered the cell. They shoved Cameron into the corner, and began tasering him.

"Cameron Moss, you are hereby required to pay your debt to society; by participating in entertainment on a social media platform," a seventh officer said.

Cameron yelled, "Aw, fuck! Wait, WAI–!"

The cops tasered him more, until he slumped over two of the officer's outstretched arms. Cameron was carried out of his cell, and would soon be transported to The Yard's holding pen.

From their position one half mile away; Eiji and Sky watched Lucia feverishly type commands into a holographic keyboard. The interface emanated from a headband projector which she was wearing. Moving images, and computer code text, flashed brightly. Lucia winced from the high resolution projection that was burning her retinas.

"What the hell? I can't believe he just hung up on me," Sky said.

"Silencio, nina!" Lucia said.

Eiji patted Sky on the back and said, "Relax. She's not mad at you. She always speaks Spanish when she's upset."

Lucia typed for several more seconds, before removing the black gloves she was wearing. Lucia ripped the band from her head, and painfully extracted the corresponding eye lenses.

"Joder!" Lucia exclaimed.

Lucia whimpered in pain, and her hands shook uncontrollably. Eiji put his hand upon her back, and comforted her.

Eiji said, "Easy–"

"Hoja de puta! Why do people use this goddamned biotechnology? The shit burns so bad!" Lucia interrupted.

Eiji immediately embraced her and said, "Shh, shh! You did great."

After a moment, Lucia stopped breathing heavily. Eiji gently released his grasp.

"Look at me. I know you're upset; but did you finish the configuration?" Eiji asked.

Lucia blinked a few times, and gave Sky a remorseful look.

"Si, si. Lo siento, hermana," Lucia said.

"It's okay. We're all upset. This is unbelievably wrong. They didn't even let him have a human lawyer," Sky said.

"None of them were prosecuted fairly, but it's out of our hands," Eiji said.

"We have to trust in a higher power. God will take care of Cameron's spirit, no matter what happens to his Earthly body. I'm sorry that you didn't get a chance to say a real goodbye; but neither did we," Lucia said.

"Amen, sister," Eiji said.

"I hope you two know what you're doing. This is absolutely crazy," Sky said.

"I do too, Sky. We've never done something this bold. Broadcasting a live video so close to a prison, is hellishly nuts...even for us," Eiji said.

Lucia reached into a backpack, which the team had brought with them. She pulled out a miniature drone, which was shaped like a small airplane. Lucia pressed several buttons on the drone, and then typed a series of commands into her holographic cell phone. The sensor attached to its nose cone, blinked several times before starting the drone's engine.

"Okay, here goes nada," Lucia said.

Lucia grabbed the plane by its hull, and launched it into the air. The drone flew towards the prison, at a low altitude. She controlled the drone by using her phone's interface.

"Hack the T.V. signal. We have to monitor the show," Lucia told Eiji.

Eiji removed a small hover camera from the backpack. He quickly pressed the camera against his cell phone.

The phone holographically displayed the words, "Synchronizing devices."

After a moment it said, "Synchronization completed."

Eiji navigated to The Yard's official website. He streamed a live video feed of the show to the hover camera. Eiji twisted the bottom half of the camera, three times. Eiji twirled the sphere into the air, and it began hovering.

"Video is ready. We have about two hours of battery life," Eiji said.

"That will be more than enough," Lucia replied.

Eiji removed Lucia's mask, and his own, from a different backpack.

"Stand out of the way. We don't want to record you by accident," Eiji said to Sky.

Sky moved away from the camera's line of sight. Eiji and Lucia put on their masks.

"Creeper's signal is spoofing a government IP address. Any devices that ping it, will think it's a friendly machine. It's only accepting trusted connections. Our friends can sign into the server at any time," Lucia said.

"Great. I'm going to start recording in a few moments. Send everyone in our network the server address, and have them connect right away," Eiji said.

Lucia quickly sent a mass group text message from her phone. Eiji stood in front of the camera. He slid his right index finger vertically downward over the camera's projection. A blue line divided the image in its center. Eiji pressed his fingertips into both sides of the cropped rectangle. Eiji slowly moved his arms outward, and away from each other. The image split into two squares. One square projected The Yard's live steam. The other projected Eiji's reflection. Eiji watched a middle aged, gray-haired, Caucasian announcer, commence with pre-fight commentary.

"We are broadcasting live, from the New Jersey Trenton State Penitentiary! We're over an hour into tonight's events, and you can really feel the excitement in the air! We've already seen three terrific contests, from a variety of people helping repay their debt to society. Lisa, why don't you give us a recap of tonight's action?" the Caucasian announcer said.

The broadcast cut to footage of a young colored woman, who was standing outside of the cage.

"Sure, Tom. First, we had a team brawl. Two members of Nuevo Raza, a powerful drug gang that has its roots in Northern Mexico; battled two doctors convicted of operating an illegal child birth clinic. The doctors were found guilty of helping patients violate the One Child Mandate. It is reported that their heinous actions, subverted over one million legal corrective terminations during the course of seven years. Even more startling, is that their practice helped prevent mostly low income and minority women from having access to affordable health care, and birth control choices," Lisa said.

The TV station played full screen clips of men fighting in a steel cage. One member of Nuevo Raza was seen smashing a doctor's head, into the side of the cage. A second clip showed the other doctor, punching the second member of Nuevo Raza in his groin. The doctor proceeded to smash the gang member's head into his knee. More videos of the men brutally beating each other, played in a small holographic window, displayed by the left side of Lisa's head.

"Nuevo Raza scored a big win tonight, after four minutes and eighteen seconds of fierce competition. As we see in this highlight; Doctor Patrick Fisher accidentally bumps into his partner, Doctor Roger Williams. Fisher was trying to recover from a nasty uppercut, dealt by Luiz Vega," Lisa said.

The video showed Patrick getting punched in his face. He stumbled backwards into Roger, upsetting his teammate's balance. Roger's head bounced off the cage's floor. He twitched for a few moments before passing out. Luiz and his fellow gang member started violently assaulting Patrick. A humanoid robot that was walking around inside of the cage, prevented them from further beating Patrick. The six foot tall robot ran into the middle of the brawl, separated the men and held up the gang members' hands.

"Representatives from cell block D, victorious," it said in a callous robotic voice.

The broadcast cut back to Lisa.

"Next, a group of four female inmates with crimes ranging from prostitution, to illegal rain water possession; engaged in a spectacular free-for-all battle royale!" Lisa said.

Clips of women pulling each other's hair, punching, and biting one another, was played in the small square projection beside of Lisa.

"Health Insurance Tax evader Sarah Kopiec, was eliminated early in the match," Lisa said.

The video showed three women viciously assaulting Sarah. The robot stopped the women, and removed Sarah's battered body from the cage. The match resumed, and the three women continued fighting. One of them was thrown into the cage, and fell to the ground. The other two women dragged her around the floor by her hair. She kicked wildly into the air and tried to stop the other women from attacking. Her assailants started stomping on her face and body. The robot immediately interrupted the carnage.

"In the end Marisol Parker, a 35 year old mother of two who was convicted of deep web Internet domain name laundering; emerged as the winner," Lisa said.

The video showed Marisol sneak attacking her opponent. Marisol smashed her foe into the cage, while the robot evacuated the second badly beaten female. Marisol punched and kicked the remaining combatant until she toppled over. The woman hit the ground at an awkward angle, and broke her wrist. The robot ran over to Marisol and raised her hand.

"Representative from cell block E, victorious," it said.

Sky was repulsed by the ghastly violence. She winced while viewing the graphic clips.

"This is sick. Dear God, this is so unbelievably sick," Sky said.

Sky put her hand to her mouth, to prevent herself from crying. Lisa finished summarizing the night's events.

"A one-on-one battle between thrice convicted drug dealer Willis Jennings, and first time inmate Naseem Stroud, who was convicted of illegally possessing unregistered handgun ammunition; ended with an intense display of power," Lisa said.

The edited video highlights showed Naseem and Willis fighting each other. The men harnessed real boxing techniques and athletic skill, while attempting to compete in a fair test of strength. They utilized powerful knee strikes, quick jabs, and devastating roundhouse kicks. They mercilessly beat and bloodied each other.

"After two rounds of action, lasting five minutes and thirteen seconds; twenty-two year old Naseem Stroud ended the match by unleashing a powerful barrage of punches," Lisa said.

The video showed Naseem push Willis into one of the cage's corners. Naseem unleashed a flurry of well-controlled punches upon Willis' head and body. One of Naseem's punches hit Willis' jaw so hard, that he was knocked unconscious. Willis fell sideways to the floor while his back was still pressed against the cage. Naseem happily jumped around, before dropping to his knees and triumphantly pounding his chest. The robot walked over, and pulled Naseem to his feet. It raised Naseem's right arm high above his body.

"Representative from cell block B, victorious," it said.

"That wraps up our replay. Back to you, Tom!" Lisa said.

"Thanks, Leese! Now we're going to give our viewers some more information, about tonight's highly anticipated main event," Tom said.

"It's almost time," Lucia said.

"I'm ready," Eiji said.

He waved his hand in a downward motion at the camera's sensor, and it began recording.

"Friends, if you are out there watching my transmission, then you know tonight is an incredibly sad day for the Liberty Movement. Our lawless government intends to execute local hero, fellow Icon, and our dear friend, Cameron Moss. This is a despicable, and barbaric, ritual human sacrifice. We will document this disgusting event, in an effort to refute the marionette media's continuing disinformation, and propaganda campaign against us," Eiji said.

The Yard's broadcast continued.

"Tonight, convicted thief Juan Lopez is battling a dangerous criminal; who calls himself an Icon. Juan will battle the convicted food smuggler and terrorist, Cameron Moss; who goes by the moniker Doctor Serenity," Tom said.

"They lie, and call us terrorists. Yet they have been running a campaign of dehumanization, and pure eugenics, for decades. Many people ask, who are 'they'? 'They' are a group of Fascists, Socialists, and Communists who conspire to control Earth's resources; thereby controlling its human inhabitants. One can call it oligarchy, tyranny, Sociofasciunism, or any other fancy word he wishes," Eiji said.

"This dangerous individual is part of a domestic extremist cell; which calls itself The Icons. This group has committed countless acts of terrorism," Tom said from his ringside seat.

"The truth is that, the most accurate word to describe this global cabal of lunatics is *evil*. They are connected by their wanton desire, to commit heinous acts of evil against their fellow man," Eiji said.

"Governor Sarah Hawthorne has authorized the use of Maximum Deterrent rules, which will be in effect during tonight's big event," Tom said.

"The Governor requested authority from the Federal Justice Department, for the permission to use MD rules. In addition to the various crimes we've previously mentioned; it is believed that the group led an armed assault on a FEMA food transport last year. This brazen revolt left sixty-eight people dead. Governor Hawthorne stated that the imminent danger this group poses to society, justifies the harsh punishment," Lisa said.

"It is a shame that one of these young men will lose his life tonight. However, justice must be served. All those who violate the law and create social chaos, must be punished accordingly," Tom replied.

"For voluntarily participating in this dangerous fight, Juan's family has been assured that if he loses; they will receive a one hundred thousand Carbon Credit deposit into their bank account. The prize will go up to five hundred thousand Carbon Credits, if Juan is victorious," Lisa said.

"We must fight this evil, in any way we can. Whether that evil comes in the form of corrupt politicians, police brutality, corporate greed, manipulative media, banker occupation, genetically modified food, high taxes, invasive spying technology, brain chips, political correctness, elitism, fluoride, illegal immigration, climate change alarmists, fake feminism, anti-male propaganda, carbon controls, fascist mandatory health insurance, Second Amendment loathing gun grabbers, Communist educational systems, a militant anti-family agenda, sexism, racism, eugenics, trans-humanism, global government, or any other detestable institution; we must resist it with all of our collective will power!" Eiji said.

"Looks like the match is about to begin!" Tom said.

He saw that Cameron was being forcibly pushed towards the cage, by a group of armed prison guards. They menaced him, and poked him in his back with their large laser rifles.

"Most importantly, we have to condemn this type of vile exploitation of our citizens. This is *not* justice. This is a public execution! The despicable media, aren't even showing the protests taking place outside of the prison at this very moment!" Eiji said.

Eiji nodded his head at Lucia. She used the Creeper's camera, to show a group of people that always gathered outside of prisons during Yard broadcasts. They were called the Coalition for the Humane Treatment of Inmates.

"Oh God, they're bringing him to the cage," Lucia said.

Eiji looked over at Sky. Her body was shaking unsteadily, and she had her hand pressed against her forehead. The crowd's screaming was deafening. Cameron approached the cage, and saw that Vincent, Walter, and Paul, were chained to a bench near the ring's outskirts. Before he reached them, he was approached by a clunky robot. It resembled a garbage can, and rolled around on four wheels. It was attached to a crude, semi-human torso.

The robot said to Cameron, "Request for conversation with fellow inmate acquaintances, has been granted. Communication time limit is six minutes. I am required to offer you a reading of your last rights. Please state your religion. Say one, for Muslim. Two, for Buddhist. Three, for Jewish. Four, for Satani–"

"Shut the fuck up, and let me see my friends," Cameron interrupted.

The robot moved out of his way. The human guards continued marching Cameron down the aisle. Cameron reached the bench, and decided to entertain his friends with a dose of gallows humor.

"Well gentlemen, our journey's level of sucktitude has reached epic proportions. But this is still less painful than being forced to buy overpriced health insurance!" said Cameron.

"Please take this more seriously, son," Paul said, with a deeply serious expression on his face.

"If it makes you feel any better, we won't be far behind you," Vincent said with sorrow.

Cameron saw that Walter was not even looking at him. Walter was staring directly at the floor.

"What's wrong with you? I know the food in here sucks, but it could be worse. They could have sent us to the Mexican salt mines!" Cameron said to Walter, who did not respond.

"Walter hasn't said a word all day," Vincent said.

"He hasn't been the same since the trial," Paul said.

Cameron said to Walter, "Look, either way, it'll be over soon. There's nothing to worry abou–"

"I wish I could apologize to your parents, for corrupting you," Walter interrupted.

Cameron was shocked by Walter's statement. Cameron, and the rest of the group, did not speak. Walter gradually looked up, and stared Cameron directly in his eyes.

"I'm sorry that I let you down, kid," Walter said remorsefully.

The guard behind Cameron poked him with the barrel of his rifle.

"Wrap it up, Moss. It's time to leave," the guard indifferently said.

Cameron took one final look at his friends. He knew that the time had come, to say goodbye.

"My Mom always said, 'You only get to use it once, so make sure that it counts.' Don't feel sorry for me. We did *not* fail. Even if we only helped *one* person, we did not fail," Cameron said.

The guard once again poked Cameron in his back.

"I love you guys, like you were my own brothers. I'll see you all, in the next one," Cameron calmly said.

Cameron walked up the stairs, which led to a circular caged dome. Once Cameron was inside, the robot referee removed the shackles from Cameron's wrists, and ankles. Cameron was given a set of sparring gloves, with the fingers cut off the tips. The robot handed Cameron a rubber mouth piece, upon which Cameron slowly bit down. The sonic vibrations created by the crowd's noise, rattled the cage's walls. In two large sections on opposite sides of the room, inmates stood behind fences, and howled in excitement. The rest of the room was garnished with stadium-style seating. Cameron felt nauseous when he looked at the hordes of people, cheering in support of this dehumanizing spectacle.

Cameron and Juan met in the middle of the ring. Juan had a stocky build, and was physically larger than Cameron. Cameron estimated that Juan was around six feet, three inches tall. Juan was not overly muscular, but he was in decent shape. Cameron had a fairly athletic build, but at only six feet tall, Cameron felt he was at a physical disadvantage in this fight. The robot referee stood between the two men.

"Inmates, it is time to repay your debt to society. Weapons will be distributed at two minute intervals. Touch fists, and then separate. You will begin when the timer reaches zero," the robot said.

Cameron removed his mouthpiece, and looked Juan in his eyes.

"We don't have to do this, man," Cameron said.

Juan held out both of his fists, which Cameron begrudgingly tapped with his own. Juan removed his mouthpiece.

"Sorry, ace. I have kids to feed," Juan replied.

The robot pointed its humanoid fingers towards opposite ends of the cage; signaling that it wanted the two men to wait in those spots.

"We are only moments away from this magnificent main event!" Tom said.

"Please pray, for both of these men. Especially pray for the safety, of the valiant Doctor Serenity," Eiji said.

A holographic numeric counter began projecting in the middle of the ring. It counted backwards, starting at five. The counter reached zero, and the word 'ENGAGE', projected for three seconds. The crowd cheered fanatically. Juan formed a boxing stance, and quickly started walking towards Cameron. Cameron went into a defensive posture, and began rapidly moving around the cage's edges. He kept a close watch on Juan's every movement.

The men moved closer to each other and tried to trick one another into attacking. They both threw a few quick left handed jabs, to gauge their punching reach. Juan quickly lunged forward. He threw two heavy, right handed, roundhouse punches. Cameron put up his left arm to defend himself.

He winced in pain, when the blows struck him in the side of his head; but it was part of his strategy. Cameron was able to entangle his left arm, with Juan's right, when he attempted to make a third strike. Cameron used this leverage, to uppercut Juan twice in his rib cage. Cameron stepped forward, and head butted Juan in his chin. He pushed Juan away, and continued circling the cage in a fighting stance. The crowd roared loudly.

"Here we go, ladies and gentlemen! What an exciting start to this fight!" Tom said from ringside.

"Moss looks like he's in trouble. He can't take many more of Lopez's powerful hits!" Lisa said.

Cameron backed himself against the cage, and waited for Juan to get close. Juan fell for the trap. He lurched forward, and tried to tackle Cameron. Cameron quickly jumped to his right, which sent Juan crashing face first into the cage. Cameron quickly moved behind Juan, and started punching him in the small of his back. Juan turned around and used his right elbow, to hit Cameron in his cheek.

Cameron placed his left hand over Juan's face and attempted to gouge his eye. Cameron pressed Juan's head backward, causing the back of Juan's head to scrape the cage. Juan used his right arm to prevent Cameron from gaining an advantage. After a few seconds of locking up, Cameron quickly twisted himself, reached his right arm across his body, and placed it upon Juan's hand. Cameron tried to twist Juan's arm, but Juan backhanded Cameron's chin. Cameron pushed away and quickly plotted his next move.

"Beautiful technique by both of these fighters!" Tom said.

"Absolutely! You can tell that these men are experienced at hand-to-hand combat," Lisa said.

Juan lightly punched himself in the side of his head with his right hand, to get his adrenaline flowing. The two men moved closer to the ring's center. Juan rushed forward, and threw a left handed punch, immediately followed by a right handed one. After making the strikes, Juan would speedily jump back. Juan repeated this action several times. Cameron was able to chip Juan's face, with swift jabs of his own. Several of Juan's punches, grazed Cameron's chin and cheeks. Juan rushed forward once again, but instead of throwing a punch, he dove for Cameron's legs. Cameron lurched forward, and skillfully fell on top of Juan to avoid being tackled.

Cameron was able to roll at an angle, and put Juan in a headlock; but Juan struggled fiercely. He snapped his head back and forth, painfully striking Cameron in his nose. The blows made Cameron loosen his grip. Miraculously, Cameron held on to Juan's neck, and attempted to strangle him. Juan fought back, and grabbed Cameron's forearms. Juan used his strength to flip Cameron over his shoulders. Cameron lost his grip and became dazed. Juan was able to rise to his feet. Juan dropped to the ground, and crushed Cameron with a falling elbow strike. The crowd cheered madly.

"Lopez pulls an *amazing* maneuver, to escape a ground lock!" Tom said.

Cameron rolled around wheezing, while blood began flowing from his nose.

"This is horrific!" Eiji shouted.

Juan wasted no time trying to regain the upper hand. Juan mounted Cameron, and began using alternating punches to smash the sides of Cameron's head. Cameron put his arms up and curled up in a fetal position to absorb the blows. Cameron locked his legs around Juan's back. Juan tried to stand up so that he could gain a better strike point. Cameron hooked his hands around Juan's ankles and began sitting up, which made Juan fall backwards. Cameron promptly dove to Juan's right side. With his right forearm, he began bashing Juan's face. Juan rolled to his left and tried to avoid the assault. Seeing a chance for a powerful strike, Cameron let Juan stumble halfway into a standing position. A second later, Cameron used his right foot to kick Juan hard in his stomach. Juan fell over onto his right side, and grimaced in pain.

"Moss uses a great counter on Lopez!" Lisa said.

"I thought Moss was in trouble there, when Lopez had him on the ground. Amazingly, Moss was able to fight his way out of the situation!" Tom said.

"Indeed, Tom. That's why terrorists like Moss are so dangerous. They usually study martial arts, during their radicalism training," Lisa said.

Both bloody men stumbled around, trying to regain their breath. Suddenly, a holographic image began displaying at the cage's top. The crowd roared, in a wild frenzy. The image rapidly scrolled through an array of weapons. Knives, bats, swords, hammers, rope, pipes, sharp sticks, brass knuckles, hatchets, chainsaws, braided chains, sickles, ice picks, axes, blowtorches, and spiked maces; were shown in a random fashion. Cameron and Juan walked back to the middle of the cage. They started boxing with each other, while the images flashed above them. The picture array slowly stopped scrolling, and eventually selected the image of a hatchet. The image blinked several times and the words, "Deterrent Selected!" holographically displayed. The crowd howled with excitement.

"Oh God, they just selected the execution method," Lucia said.

"How can people applaud such barbarism?!" Sky shouted, with tears streaming down her face.

"These are real people, for God sakes! It is absolutely *crazy*, that they are being forced to *kill* each other!" Eiji said.

Cameron and Juan continued sparring near one of the cage's walls. Cameron's back was against the cage. He was defending himself by grappling the back of Juan's head, and continually driving either one of his knees into Juan's stomach. Cameron attacked using whichever knee gave him the most ability to keep his balance. Juan tried blocking the attack, while simultaneously striking Cameron's body, with his fists.

The holographic counter began counting backwards from five. When the counter reached zero, the cage's top opened. A hatchet began dropping into the middle of the ring, from a chute that was attached to its top. The circular chute extended into the room's ceiling, and was used to quickly drop weapons into the ring. The hatchet hit the floor. The crowd erupted in an absolutely insane chorus, of cheers and applause.

Cameron could tell that Juan was fatigued. Cameron released his grip on Juan's head. He slapped Juan in his neck, and unleashed a flurry of quick alternating punches to Juan's face and body. Juan stumbled backwards and Cameron delivered a powerful standing side kick to Juan's stomach. Juan fell down and clutched his abdomen. Cameron stumbled around and gasped for air.

Cameron and Juan quickly realized that the hatchet had fallen into the ring. Juan was closest to the hatchet. Cameron tried to run forward and retrieve it, but Juan reached the hatchet one second before Cameron. When Cameron realized he would not recover the hatchet, Cameron dropped to the ground, and rolled over onto his shoulders. Juan grabbed the hatchet and swung it wildly. Cameron dogged and weaved, to narrowly avoid being sliced.

"Oh my God! I can't watch!" Sky said.

Sky turned away from the projecting image, and sobbed heavily. Cameron quickly ran to the cage's other side. Juan menacingly held the hatchet in his right hand.

"This is it, folks! Lopez appears to have the upper hand! It's only a matter of time before the terrorist Cameron Moss, pays for his crimes against humanity!" Tom said.

Juan slowly moved forward. He held the hatchet above his head, and prepared to strike. Cameron firmly planted his feet, and held his open hands up, in a defensive position. He had his left forearm pointing upward, and his right forearm pointing inward. Cameron watched Juan's every movement. He knew that he could make no mistakes when Juan attacked. Juan finally made his move, and swung the hatchet in a downward motion, right at Cameron's head! When Cameron saw that this was the way Juan chose to swing the hatchet, he instantly countered. Cameron used his right forearm to block the attack. Cameron pushed his right forearm down allowing the hatchet's motion to continue its strike path. Cameron used his left hand to further push away Juan's attacking arm.

Cameron grabbed Juan's forearm with his right hand. The hatchet fell downward and narrowly missed Cameron's body. Cameron used his right hand, to help guide the hatchet toward Juan's shin. He simultaneously used his left hand, to help him maintain total control of Juan's arm. Cameron pushed Juan's arm inward, and the axe struck Juan's right shin! Juan howled in pain, and dropped the hatchet. Cameron continued his fluid motion, and proceeded to twist Juan's arm backwards.

Cameron pivoted his feet so that he could complete the shoulder lock. He passed control to his left arm and completed the motion. With Juan's arm locked in a firmly controlled position, Cameron brought his right hand to Juan's elbow. He used his leverage, and opposing force, to break Juan's arm! Juan howled in immense pain, and fell over on his left side. Juan tried to cover the bone protruding out of his right arm with his left hand, while letting out agonized shrieks.

"What?! How can this be happening?! Cameron Moss just disarmed the axe wielding Lopez...and then broke his goddamned arm!" Tom said.

"He missed! He missed!" Eiji shouted.

"Holy shit! I've never seen anyone move that fast! Where the hell did he learn that move?!" Lucia said.

Sky turned back around and said, "What?! He's still alive?! Let me see!"

Vincent, Walter, and Paul, cheered loudly from their ringside seats.

"Fuck yeah! That's my boy!" shouted Vincent.

Cameron was bloody, and bruised. He had knots on his face. His eye was swelling shut. His nose was puffy and oozing blood. Cameron looked around at the masses of people, who were worked up into a frenzy. They had never witnessed such a marvelous maneuver, in all of their lives. Cameron knew that the crowd still wanted blood.

He heard people screaming, "Kill him! Finish him off!"

Cameron picked up the hatchet. He stood over Juan, who now had tears streaming down his face. Cameron looked over his shoulder, and saw the robot standing several feet away from them. Cameron slowly raised the hatchet. He knew what he must do next.

"It looks like Moss is about to win his first match. We'll see a deterrent handed down, at any second!" Tom said.

Cameron took several deep breaths. He quickly turned around, and threw the hatchet directly at the robot's head! The hatchet crashed into the robot's skull, and became lodged in its cranium. The robot awkwardly stumbled around. Sparks flew from the area where it was damaged. The robot removed the axe, and dropped it on the floor.

"Neural pathways, compromised. Navigation systems, disrupted," the robot said.

Cameron let out a full bellied yell and ran towards the robot. He jumped into the air, and delivered a crushing falling roundhouse punch directly to the robot's skull! The robot stumbled backwards. Cameron pushed it against the cage. Cameron used his fists to violently pummel the robot. Cameron kicked the robot off of its feet, and then stood atop its robotic arms. Cameron grabbed the robot by its head. He screamed loudly and twisted the robot's head from its body! Sparks flew everywhere. Cameron took the head, and threw it to the cage's other side. The crowd screamed in absolute hysteria.

"Cameron just tore that thing's goddamned head off!" Eiji said.

Sky laughed, and smiled when she saw Cameron destroy the machine.

"This is unprecedented! In all of my thirteen years covering these fights, I've never seen a robot attacked so viciously! This man is truly an abominable radical!" Tom said.

Cameron picked up the axe and walked over to Juan.

"Quiet! Quiet, all of you! Be quiet!" Cameron screamed.

Cameron put his finger over his mouth, indicating that he wanted the crowd to stop screaming and applauding.

"It looks like this criminal, is about to give some kind of speech. Let's turn up our microphones, and listen to what this wretched extremist has to say," Tom said.

Cameron held the hatchet high above his head.

"You want me to kill this man?!" Cameron yelled.

In a unanimous chorus the crowd responded, "Yes!" while hooting and hollering.

"You want to see him *die?!*" Cameron asked.

The crowd once again erupted in unanimous applause.

"Then what the *fuck* is wrong with all of you?!" Cameron shouted.

A stunned silence whipped through the arena.

"You should all be *ashamed* of yourselves!" Cameron shouted.

Hushed whispers began fluctuating throughout the crowd. Cameron looked down at Juan.

"What is your crime? Why are you here?" Cameron asked him.

"I robbed a convenience store; then carjacked some old guy and made him drive me out of town," Juan said through deep amounts of pain.

"Do you hear that, people? You want me to kill this man, for being a petty thug!" Cameron said to the crowd.

Cameron knew he had the attention of everyone in the crowd, and everyone watching the live broadcast. He used the opportunity to make a heartfelt speech.

"I've done a lot of really bad stuff in my past. I've hurt people. I've gotten them killed. Do you know what makes me different, from the people you see killing each other, on this demented form of entertainment? I never *chose* to be a criminal. The cause for which the Food and Liberty Movement fights, is the cause to restore freedom in our society. I was made into a criminal because people like you, many years ago, allowed your society to become decadent and rotten to its core. You have allowed your civil liberties to be fully eroded. By doing this, you have allowed your own government to become your biggest enemy, and oppressor," Cameron said.

What were once cheers had now turned into deafening silence. Cameron continued speaking.

"Look where your lack of empathy has led us. This is what your laziness, and refusal to be involved in your own governance, has brought to our nation! We've reverted back to a gladiatorial society! This is the complete opposite of human progress! National spy agencies, that track your every move; a group of armed goons who molest you at the airports, train stations, and shopping malls; socialist health care which robs you of your right to seek the treatment which you desire; outrageously high taxes paid to a global world bank; a paramilitary police force that points guns at you any time they want; drones that murder citizens without any hesitation; a Communist regime controlled by the red Chinese; a horrible education system that places more emphasis on being politically correct, than it does on teaching kids reading, writing, and arithmetic! These are only some of the plagues, which you've allowed to infect this country! But your worst crime, and the reason that I am here; is you don't even respect yourselves enough to eat real food," Cameron said.

The stunned crowd listened to Cameron's every word.

"There are people that are willing to steal, prostitute their bodies, and even die, for their *right* to eat healthy food. Now, in your wanton desire for blood, you want me to kill a man who should be in here serving his time, and working towards rehabilitation. You should all be *disgusted* with yourselves. Your fore-bearers would be *mortified* that they ever spilled *one* drop of blood; to found this country on the idea that all men are created equal, and deserve to be free; if they could see how you've *all* collectively squandered your birthright. No. I will not kill this man for your pleasure. I would rather take his place, than live in a world where this type of brutality, is considered legal justice," he said.

Cameron flippantly tossed the hatchet away from himself. He knelt upon the ground, and put his hands to his face. The crowd did not cheer, nor did they jeer him. Instead an eerie silence, echoed throughout the packed stadium. After a few awkward moments, Tom addressed the audience.

"Ladies and gentlemen, I don't know what to say. It seems Cameron Moss, has refused to deter his opponent. This has never happened, in The Yard's twenty-eight year history," Tom said in a solemn voice.

The silence was soon disturbed by the sound of heavy footsteps. Prison riot police, were rushing to extract Cameron and Juan from the cage. Cameron heard the cage door open. Cameron stood up and was ready to face his captors.

"You will be all right. Your body, and spirit, will heal one day," Cameron said to Juan.

Riot police wearing black body armor, helmets, and face shields, surrounded Cameron.

"Get on your knees!" one of the officers yelled.

"No," Cameron sternly said.

He repeated the command, while aiming a laser gun at Cameron.

"I said get on your knees, right *now!*" he shouted.

"I said *no*, motherfucker!" Cameron yelled.

The officer shot Cameron with the laser. A low voltage current flowed through Cameron's body. Cameron snarled at the officer and still refused to get down. Two other officers rushed at him and started beating him with their nightsticks. Cameron let out a fierce battle cry, while he attempted to block their attack. Three more officers wrestled him to the ground. Cameron was mercilessly beaten, and shot with lasers. It took a total of eight prison guards to subdue Cameron, before he passed out from exhaustion. They dragged him out of the cage by his arms, and let his knees scrape across the floor. Sounds of people crying could be heard amongst the terrified and awestricken crowd. Cameron was hauled back to his cell.

Lucia and Sky were crying and hugging each other, while they watched the broadcast end. Lucia had walked away from the hover camera's line of sight. She had removed her mask because she did not want her tears to stain its inside.

Eiji said to the camera, "You've just witnessed something amazing tonight, my friends. Our dear friend Cameron Moss has escaped death; and brought an unprecedented message of freedom, to everyone watching this transmission. This battle may be over, but the war continues. Doctor Serenity needs your prayers. All of us need your prayers. Together, we *will* defeat this tyranny! This is Magnificent Sight, signing off."

29 Behold; My Masterpiece

It has been several days since Cameron Moss' extraordinary speech on The Yard. The video Eiji released that night, is the most popular piece of media in the country. All across the nation, people are demanding that Vincent, Walter, Paul, and Cameron's convictions be overturned. There are highly emotional, but largely peaceful, protests in every state. Large groups of concerned citizens are calling for an end to The Yard.

Even the mainstream media, which usually is nothing more than a propaganda machine, that regurgitates information which only government and corporate interests approve; have had to reverse their rhetoric against The Icons. The media suggests that maybe The Icons can be deported to another country, or possibly serve time in a less restrictive facility. The media is also putting out talking points, which concede that The Yard is barbaric. Journalists around the country, say that Congress should open an investigation into the mistreatment of inmates.

Gregory Times stood on the balcony of Webster Morgan's Manhattan penthouse apartment.

"Do I really have to leave? I don't want to go, without you," Mallory asked him.

Times put his hands on Mallory's biceps.

"You know we can't stay here any longer. It's too risky. Too many people are getting suspicious at Rigor. Webster has been a great help to us, but he has outlived his usefulness," Times softly said.

Mallory leaned into her husband, and hugged him.

"I can't believe those gangsters, are now being called heroes. What kind of stupid name is The Icons?" she asked.

Times stroked a piece of hair behind Mallory's ear, and kissed her forehead.

"They won't be relevant in a few hours," Times said.

"Are you sure you know what you're doing?" Mallory asked.

Times kissed his wife and then said, "Absolutely, I am. The robots have perfected my device. I can control anyone that I desire. After I'm done with the next phase of my plan, the city will be mine. Soon I will take control of the state, then the country, and ultimately the world."

Mallory giggled, and tapped Times on his nose with her right index finger.

"You're so sexy, when you get all ambitious!" she said.

Times smiled and said, "Stop! If you keep talking like that, I won't be able to let you out of my sight!"

He gave his wife another hug. The two of them playfully caressed each other.

"It's time for you to leave, my love. The car is downstairs," Times said.

The couple walked into the penthouse. Mallory picked up a small suitcase and walked to the front door.

"Your route is already programmed. All you need to do is instruct it to drive. Once you get to the tunnel, you should have no problem leaving the city. You're only going to Saint Lawrence, so you won't need a passport to leave the state. The house is in an isolated area, where you will be safe. I'll join you at the earliest moment that I can," Times said.

"Don't keep me waiting too long, sweetie," Mallory said.

Mallory gave her husband another passionate kiss. The couple took one final look at each other, before Mallory opened the door and left the penthouse. Times closed the door behind her, and rested his back against it for a few moments. Times removed his headband from the small holder which he had hooked onto his belt buckle. Times placed the device on his head and walked to the guest bedroom.

Times opened the door by placing his palm on its rectangular biometric scanning panel. Times calmly entered the room. The Chem-Mech was standing in the room's far left corner. Webster was sitting upright, on the right side of the bed. Webster stared out of the bedroom's window and was obviously deep in thought. His black suit, and white tie, looked immaculate. Times dragged a small chair that was sitting by the doorway, over to the bed. Times placed the chair across from Webster, and sat down.

"I'm sure you've known this day was coming…for a long time, old man," Times calmly said.

Webster directed his gaze to Times.

"Oh, yes," Webster sedately said.

"Did you have enough to eat? It looks like you hardly touched your breakfast," Times asked.

An undisturbed plate of eggs, bacon, and toast, sat upon the nightstand near the left side of Webster's bed.

"I'm all right," Webster said.

After a lengthy pause Times said, "Let me ask you something. Why did you so desperately crave this device's power? You lived about the most charmed a life that anyone could imagine. Money, fancy cars, cool machines. These, are every man's dream. Most people would have been content to wallow in luxury. Why would you need anything else?"

"Does it really matter?" Webster replied.

"I suppose not," Times said.

Webster continued gazing out the portion of the large window that was not blocked by Times.

"You know, none of it really mattered. All these years, I really did think that my work was serving a higher purpose," Webster said.

"Yeah? What made you feel that way?" Times asked.

"I thought if I could control people, manage them, then maybe they wouldn't be so pitiful," Webster said.

Webster paused briefly before saying, "People have been hurting each other, for thousands of years. It seems like we are destined to be nothing more than cavemen; fighting for freshly killed meat."

"Everyone wants to be top dog. I suppose your greed is understandable," Times said.

"Yes, but it doesn't *matter*. None of it, *matters*. I realize now, that destroying what others have built, doesn't give a man *real* power. Real power, comes from helping to build society; not leading it into destruction. All the money I've made by taking advantage of my fellow man, and betraying my colleagues, is all worthless. True wealth comes from having friends, and a family, that care about you. True power comes from being independent, and teaching others how to be successful," said Webster.

"I beg to differ. True power, comes from the raw exercise of force," Times said.

Webster smiled and said, "I now know, that it does not. That is why I am in this situation. You'll discover that too, one day. That is why I want to thank you, Gregory. Thank you for opening my eyes, to what truly matters in life."

Times cracked a sadistic smile and said, "I don't think you should be thanking me."

Webster finally looked at Times and said, "You know, there is still time for you to be saved,

Gregory. There is a reason that men like you and I, don't win."

"And what is that reason?" Times asked.

"We are disconnected from reality," Webster said.

"Speak for yourself, old man," Times said.

Times stood up, and walked closer to Webster.

"You know I never thought I'd say this, but I'm actually going to miss you. You had a certain...charm," Times said.

"Those boys will never let you get away with your plans. They are special. That's why I hated them for so long. I knew from the beginning that they were unique; but I never imagined they'd actually change the world," Webster said.

Times smiled and said, "I wouldn't worry about them. They are powerless to stop me. No one can stop me. This device is the most almighty weapon the world has seen; since the creation of the Antimatter Bomb."

"I hope that one day, you find peace in this world, Gregory," Webster said.

Times, did not respond. He placed his right hand, atop Webster's head.

"Let me show you, why I am troubled," Times finally said.

He began overloading Webster's neural pathways with horrible images of destruction. Dead animals, burned bodies, crumbling buildings, and crawling bugs, were all seared into Webster's mind. Webster began convulsing, and moaned in agony. Times continued blasting Webster with more ghastly images. Webster could actually feel all the pain, from the suffering victims that he was seeing. Webster saw nightmarish visions of people being slaughtered, during the Fifth Avenue rampage. Times showed him a hospital full of people with missing limbs. It was a representation of a video which had been leaked online during the height of the United States' war with Syria.

Webster cried out in agony. Times tightened his grip upon Webster's head, and continued bombarding his brain with more images of violence. Mass shootings at banks; riot police on every American street corner; a child with her legs blown off, sitting in a Seattle hospital; maggots crawling out of a dead soldier's eye socket; were all displayed in vivid detail. Webster coughed three times before falling backwards onto the soft bed. Times watched Webster's body twitch. Webster began vomiting. He choked on his own upheaval. While Webster was dying, Times stared at him with a cold look upon his face. Eventually Webster's body stopped moving. Times looked at the Chem-Mech.

"Examine him," Times said.

The Chem-Mech walked forward, and Times moved out of its way. The Chem-Mech used a laser embedded in its head camera to scan Webster's body.

"Patient's vital signs are critical. No ventricle circulation occurring. No neurological activity detected. Death occurred at approximately zero seven hundred, and thirty eight hours; plus nineteen seconds. Day four, July. Calendar year, 2217," the Chem-Mech said.

Times grinned slightly, before releasing two low bellied laughs. His laughter quickly grew louder. He ripped the headband from his skull.

"I beat you, you twisted old fuck!" Times shouted.

Times looked at Webster's dead body. His suit still looked perfectly pressed even though it, along with Webster's face, was covered with bodily fluids. Webster's face was contorted, which signaled that he had obviously died in tremendous pain.

"I fucking *beat* you," Times softly said.

He triumphantly stared at the lifeless body of the man who had made him into a cold, remorseless, vindictive, shell of a human being.

"Pump him full of drugs. Make it look like he overdosed," Times told the Chem-Mech.

The Chem-Mech promptly followed Times' command. Times walked out of the room and placed the band back on his head. He picked up a large duffel bag that was laying on the kitchen table. Times left the apartment, went downstairs, and exited through the building's front door. Times placed the duffel bag on the ground, removed his fedora hat, and placed it upon his head. Times used his holographic cell phone to summon the limousine. It drove from a nearby parking lot and rolled up to Times' location.

Times grabbed his bag, entered the vehicle, closed the door, and tapped on the window. A map of New York City began displaying in the frame. Without warning, Times' body violently shivered. He felt an intense migraine shoot through his cerebral cortex. He quickly reached into the bag, and pulled out a bottle of his anti-nanomachine pills. Times quickly tore off the cap, removed several pills, and swallowed them.

"God, *damn*. I need a stronger dosage. These aren't working long enough," Times said.

His body shook for several moments, before the pills finally took effect. After he regained his composure, he threw the pills back into the bag.

"Take me to Chinese News America's main headquarters; located at Forty-Second Street, Times Square," he said.

The limousine began driving Times to the requested location. Times pressed a small circle embedded in the window's image. A menu bar rendered itself on the screen. Times pressed the bar and selected the television mode. Times tuned the channel to CNA's station. Two Chinese reporters sat behind a large desk. It was oval in stature. Its shiny glass centerpiece was surrounded by finely carved wood. He watched the broadcasters speak from behind the lavish studio desk.

"Good morning and thank you for joining us. It is almost eight AM, here on this beautiful July Fourth afternoon. I'm Chao Bo. Sitting next to me is the lovely Mei Jia," said Bo.

"A lot of festivities are taking place today. A holiday with highly grotesque origins, formerly observed by only the most deeply racist Americans, is quickly becoming a celebration of world progression," Jia said.

Times continued watching the corporate shills, degrade the fallen Constitutional Republic.

"The holiday was created as a sadistic homage, to the alleged Founding Fathers of the United States. For many generations, American history distorted the true facts about those supposed men of honor. For centuries, a large group of peasant ruffians were revered American folklore heroes. Centuries later, the world knows that they were nothing but arrogant, untrustworthy, slave masters; who committed high treason by disobeying their King. On July Fourth, 2105; newly elected President Pedro Diaz marked the passage of the Safe Immigration Act. The controversial bill granted full amnesty to all illegal immigrants that were currently living in America. It vastly reformed other immigration laws across the country. It also declared July Fourth, a national day of remembrance. Instead of celebrating the anniversary of a violent rebellion against a benevolent nobleman; President Diaz stated that the holiday would be observed in honor of all the indigenous people, who had their land stolen during the American empire's numerous conquests. Today is also used to stand in solidarity with global citizens around the world; who wish to create a more peaceful, and integrated planet. The United Nations gave President Diaz a World Peace Prize, for his courageous actions," said Bo.

Times reached into his bag. He extracted a set of silver colored, leather gloves. Times adjusted his purple tie. He used his hands to iron out the few wrinkles in his white, two-piece, dress shirt. Times began slipping the gloves upon his hands, while the broadcast continued.

"We have a great show today. We will be covering all the celebrations here in New York City. Joining us a little later, the man who is called the most highly reclusive person in the world, breaks his decade's long silence," Jia said.

The station played a video clip of a man wearing a brown cowl, dark sunglasses, and surgical mask. He walked through a large gathering of screaming fans and feisty reporters. The man politely waved his hands at the group, but kept his head down. His two large, humanoid, robot bodyguards, helped him gently push his way through the crowd.

"Alistor DeMarcco, heir to the DeMarcco Technologies fortune; has not given a public interview in twenty-seven years," Bo said.

"Mister DeMarcco was rumored to have been badly disfigured in a horrible accident, which occurred when he was only eight years old. Since that time, he has rarely made public appearances. Adding to the mystery, on the rare occasions that he *has* been spotted publicly, it was never without a facial covering. Mister DeMarcco shocked the world last week; when he posted a public statement on his personal website about a controversial episode of 'The Yard'," Jia said.

Bo said, "Mister DeMarcco publicly condemned the brutally violent show. But in a bizarre move, he praised the dangerous terrorist Cameron Moss, for refusing to deter his opponent. Mister DeMarcco also stated that he was deeply saddened to hear about the story of young Lily Branson. Lily sustained catastrophic injuries during an early morning USSA raid of her family's illegal farm. The trial proved that Lily, who was home-schooled, unregistered, and not vaccinated; was being held captive by her parents. This radical and dangerous family, was part of a larger terrorist cell–"

Times waved his fingers in a downward motion and the television's volume was muted. Times reached into his bag and pulled out his mask. He looked at the shiny, silver apparel. He slowly ran his fingers across the eyes and cheeks.

"So many people in this world wear masks to hide their true identity. When I wear you, I expose my true self. I no longer have to feel afraid. My sinful mistress; whom comforts me in madness. You see the unbridled ugliness, of this disgusting planet. The childish silhouettes of men; emasculated by their bossy wives. I travailed for many years; while my life was plundered of significance. Preyed upon by kleptocratic banks, Communist politicians, Fascist corporations, and even my cretinous fellow man; it is obvious why my heart is annealed with contempt! But you, have never tried to deceive me. Your benignity, has allowed me to find solace in iniquity. This is it, my friend. We now stand at the precipice of acquiring eternal glory. Together, our violent crusade will purge society of its collective human trash. You understand the importance of vigilante adjudication. You, and only you; understand why I am troubled," Times lovingly said to the mask.

For a few more moments, Times gleefully gazed at the mask, before delicately placing it back in the bag.

Times rode for another seventeen minutes. He had almost reached the CNA's main corporate building. The limousine rolled up to a police barricade that was blocking the path to Forty-Second Street. A uniformed female officer tapped on the vehicle's tinted window.

"Excuse me. You can't drive down this road," she said.

Times used the door's thumb scanning panel to crack the window ajar. Times leaned against the door and looked downward to obscure his face.

"What's the problem? You know I'm supposed to be here," Times said with a grin.

His headband sent out a strong signal, which disrupted the officer's brainwaves. He began overriding her free will.

"I need to leave. I have an important appointment at the CNA building," Times said.

Times made the woman experience a sharp pain in her stomach. The woman grabbed her abdomen.

"You feeling okay? Maybe you should take the rest of the day off," Times said.

"Damn. I must be getting cramps," the officer said to herself.

"Listen lady, I'm with the press. I'm already late for my meeting. Hurry up and wave me through," Times said.

Times rolled up the window. The woman signaled to her fellow officer that Times was allowed past the blockade.

"It's okay, he's with the media. He showed me his credentials," the woman said.

The other officer pressed a few buttons on his cell phone. The four foot high, portable metal barricade retracted. Times' limousine drove itself to the next block. It pulled beside the street curb, and parked itself underneath the enormous building. Times zipped up the duffel bag, grabbed it by the handles, and exited the vehicle. Times kept his head down while walking towards the building's entrance.

Times entered the studio's lobby. He saw a middle aged female security guard sitting behind a desk. Holographic projections of various security feeds, projected from the desk. Beside her sat a crude, older model robot. It had a cartoonish looking generic male torso, attached to a rolling cylinder. The torso swiveled from side-to-side, and its arms were able to rotate. Its face was bland, and expressionless. The lobby itself was barren. Times was not surprised that it was empty because it was a national holiday. Times was sure that there would not be many visitors, and the building's staff would be minimal. Times casually sauntered up to the reception desk.

"Turn that thing off," Times said to the guard in a soft, but firm tone.

She was quite surprised by his arrogance. She had no idea that beneath his fedora hat, was Times' powerful brainwave amplifier, that could manipulate her subconscious mind.

"I don't think I'm allowed to turn him off," the guard replied.

"Why do people personalize these abominations?" Times asked.

The guard said, "Sir, I–"

"Can't you just do me a favor?" Times slyly asked before she finished speaking.

He distorted the woman's emotions, and made her feel sexual attraction towards him.

"I suppose I can make an exception, for a nice young man like you," the guard playfully said.

She pressed her palm against a panel embedded into the robot's back. A large keypad holographically illuminated above the panel. She typed a short series of commands, which Times did not care to see, into the robot's back. He nervously looked around, and ensured that he was not arousing suspicion. The robot made a low humming sound when it shut down.

Times smiled and said, "Good. Let's go speak to the chief of security operations. Lock the doors, turn off the cameras, and deactivate any other security systems that you can access."

The woman was obviously puzzled by this request, but she could not resist Times' artificially manufactured charm. She was ignorant to the fact that Times was using his brainwaves to control her. Times understood that most people functioned in a lucid dream state. He knew that the general population was hypnotized by an endless parade of media, which was streamed to them via numerous electronic devices.

He had read dozens of Webster's private business documents. The classified memos admitted that pharmaceutical drugs had drastically reduced most people's intellectual functioning ability. It did not matter if the drugs were taken willfully, like Times did; or whether people digested them unknowingly through the food, water, and vaccines. The drugs were his gateway to hacking the human mind.

Times finally understood why Webster wanted this amazing ability. Times was able to control any person on Earth using a powerful form of telepathy. Control, was immensely important to Times. He had experienced the helplessness that comes from having a lack of control; before taking his freedom back from Webster. He had experienced what it felt like to control others; during the ghastly United World Hospital, and Fifth Avenue attacks. Now, Times was embarking on his boldest journey. Times wanted this attack to bring New York City, and eventually the rest of the defunct United States, to its connective knees. Times intended to use the television station's powerful wireless fidelity broadcasting signal, to amplify the range of his psycho-kinesis.

The woman typed a few more commands into the digital keyboard. The front doors locked, and several cameras in the lobby went dead. The woman arose from her chair. Drool had begun dripping from her mouth.

"Follow me, sir," she said to Times.

Times walked through a large body scanner next to the reception desk. It did not make a single sound. Times smiled and proceeded to follow the woman. They traversed through a short series of hallways, until they reached a large office. Inside, a security manager was typing commands into a holographic keyboard. There was a large wall of holographic monitors placed in front of him. The monitors showed various security camera feeds from around the building.

He heard the door open and said, "Fucking shit...Brenda, is that you? The system is acting retarded agai–"

The man stopped talking when he looked at his room monitor and saw Brenda shaking in fear. He swiveled in his chair and looked at Times, who had a devious look upon his face.

"Umm...Hank? This man wants to speak with you," Brenda said.

Hank arose, and began walking forward.

He said, "Who the hell are y–?"

Before Hank could finish his sentence, Times wildly swung his bag and smacked Hank across the left side of his face. Hank fell over, and used his right arm to break his fall. Hank wheezed in agony. His portly body was not built for such a hard landing.

"You will delete all of today's security footage. I want every file, on every database, erased," Times said.

Brenda rushed to Hank's aid and began helping him to his feet. Times turned around and dropped the bag on the ground. Times knelt down and ripped the hat from his head.

"Are you out of your damn mind?! What the hell do you think you're doing?" Hank frantically asked.

Times rapidly removed his mask and strapped it to his face. Its cold metal sent a chill down his body, when it touched his skin. In one smooth motion; Times grabbed his hat, placed it atop his head, stood up, and faced the guards. They were immediately overcome with a paralyzing fear. The masked killer named Troubled Times was standing only a few feet away from them!

"Oh, sweet mother Mary...it's YOU!" Hank shouted.

Troubled Times rushed over to Hank, and head butted him in the nose. Hank grabbed his face with both hands and felt blood begin flowing.

"Kneel," Troubled Times calmly said.

Hank could not resist Troubled Times' psychic assault. With the sole of his right foot, Troubled Times kicked Hank in his stomach. Hank clumsily fell over, and rolled onto his back. Brenda screamed in terror.

"I see that you know who I am," Troubled Times menacingly said.

He put his heel against Hank's throat. Hank began choking and grabbed Troubled Times' shoe.

"That's good. That means you know *I*, am in control. This will end very badly for both of you, if you do not follow my instructions," Troubled Times said.

Brenda's eyes swelled with tears. Hank started coughing, when he accidentally swallowed some of his own blood.

"Please! We are not bad people! We never hurt anybody!" Brenda said.

"Silence," Troubled Times replied.

Brenda said, "But, my fam–"

"I didn't fucking tell you to speak!" Troubled Times shouted, before he made Brenda's ears ring.

He immediately said to Hank, "You had better think real well, before you make any idiotic moves. Disobey me? I'll kill you. Try to call for help? I'll make you eat your own testicles, *before* I kill you. Follow my instructions, and *maybe* I'll let you live. Do you understand?"

Troubled Times eased the pressure upon Hank's throat.

"Yes, yes," Hank garbled.

Troubled Times looked at Brenda and asked, "What about you, baby-cakes? You comprende?"

Brenda shook her head in staunch agreement.

"Good. Get up, you pile of dog piss," Troubled Times said.

Troubled Times removed his foot from Hank's neck. Hank immediately wiped his face, and sat upright.

Hank rubbed his neck and said, "Please don't ki–"

Troubled Times viciously kicked Hank in his leg. Hank screamed loudly.

"Stop blubbering like a goddamned faggot!" Troubled Times snapped.

Troubled Times went to his bag, removed his purple trench coat, and gracefully slung it around himself. The trench coat was snug and warmed Troubled Times' icy cold soul. Troubled Times buttoned his apparel, and then removed a set of handcuffs from the bag. He threw them at Hank.

"Chain yourselves together," Troubled Times said.

Hank gave Brenda a woeful look.

Hank said, "I'm so sorry–"

"It's okay," Brenda softly said.

Hank strapped one part of the handcuffs to his left hand. He immediately snapped the other end, to Brenda's right one. They sat in chairs placed in front of the large, holographic computer terminal.

"Get working," said Troubled Times.

They began disabling the remaining security cameras, and erasing all the data on the computer's hard drives. Troubled Times removed a dual gun holster, which held two black, nine millimeter pistols. Troubled Times strapped the holster to his waist.

"How long will you need, to complete your task?" he asked Hank.

Hank nervously said, "It will take some time. There are a lot of connections, firewalls, and–"

"Spare me the technical bullshit," Troubled Times quickly interrupted.

Hank chose his words more carefully.

"At least a couple hours," Hank said.

"That's better. Short, and simple," Troubled Times said.

He walked up to Hank and Brenda, and placed his hands upon the tops of their heads. Troubled Times created a graphic hallucination in their minds. He made them think that their entire bodies were engulfed in flames. The guards wildly howled, in extreme distress.

"That is only a sample of the pain, which I can make you endure. Betray me, and you will suffer an agony one thousand times worse, than what you feel at this moment," Troubled Times said.

Troubled Times removed his hands and ceased their torment. The guards whimpered heavily.

"I'm going to the main control room. I need to use the broadcasting station. Tell me, on which floor it is located?" Troubled Times asked.

"Eighteen! It's on the eighteenth floor!" Brenda shrieked.

"Very well. Be sure to lock this door once I leave. It has been a pleasure to make your acquaintance. Thank you, for your kindness," Troubled Times sarcastically said.

Troubled Times picked up the duffel bag and walked out of the room. Hank and Brenda cried, and remorsefully began following Troubled Times' orders. They were mortified, and powerless to resist Troubled Times' psychic attack. They awkwardly typed commands into their holographic workstation. They found it extremely difficult to work together, while handcuffed.

Troubled Times went to the main lobby and entered the elevator. While he was riding, Troubled Times reached into the bag and removed his pill bottle. The Chem-Mech had specially designed the pills, to enhance the strength of Troubled Times' telekinesis; while simultaneously preventing the nano-machines from eating away parts of his brain.

"I've got to stay focused. It's going to be a long day," Troubled Times said to himself.

He removed six pills, lifted up his mask, and consumed them. Troubled Times moved his mask back into place, and put the bottle inside his coat's inner left breast pocket. Troubled Times removed a small data stick from the duffel bag. The data stick was a four inch long cylinder, with a fine groove carved along its entire height. The elevator arrived at the eighteenth floor. Its doors slid open.

The noisy floor was filled with busy workers that were dutifully performing their tasks. Some talked on communication devices and barked out orders to other employees. Technicians were sitting at a complex computer terminal. They used head bands, with iris scanners on their tips, to monitor and control video feeds. Technical and managerial assistants helped their colleagues run the show.

The astonishing room was enormous, and circular in nature. A large pane of specially cut glass covered a huge section of the wall. Numerous images appeared inside of the glass. Others holographically projected outward. The consoles were linked together, and several teams worked at different stations. There was a section for audio mixing, a section for video operation, and several sections where graphics and text could be added over live broadcast streams.

Troubled Times marveled at this impressive command center. He felt like he was inside the cockpit of a large space ship. The command center overlooked the main studio theater. From this position, the people inside of the control room could see everything that was happening on the floor below them. Troubled Times could only briefly enjoy the high tech room's complexity.

Several seconds after he stepped off the elevator, a young woman in a business suit recognized him. The woman screamed, and dropped her computer sticks on the floor. The computer sticks shattered when they hit the ground. The crew looked in her direction. They were all petrified by the sight of this most vicious and infamous madman. Panicked cries filled the room.

"Have mercy, he *is* real!"

"That can't be *him!*"

"What's he doing here?!"

"God help us!"

Before the situation got out of control, Troubled Times dropped his bag and raised both of his hands into the air.

"Be, fucking, QUIET!" Troubled Times screamed.

Troubled Times used his powerful brainwave signals, to generate the painful ringing sensation in everyone's ears. People covered their ears and howled in pain. The deafening sound rattled their eardrums. His sonic torture method made them feel like their entire brain would explode. Even though Troubled Times did not generate an actual audible tone, the pain produced by the imagined noise, brought many people to their knees. Troubled Times slowly silenced the ringing.

The group followed his orders. Faint whimpers echoed throughout the control room. People did not dare say a word. They had no idea what punishment would befall them, if they disobeyed his instructions. Troubled Times began slowly walking around, and menaced the hapless workers.

"Even though it would be an insult to your intelligence, and a belittlement of my achievements, to pretend that you all do not know who I am; I still feel the need to properly introduce myself. I am chaos; a bonafide living nightmare. I will bring savagery to your lives. I cannot be bribed with money, or worldly possessions. I wield the power of *God.* My only desire is to bring a little anarchy, to your otherwise boring existence. You have already seen examples of my extraordinary gifts. Today, you will witness even *more* wonders. Today, you will all experience the trouble, that is Times," he said.

Troubled Times walked over to the audio station. He stood above a frightened young lady, who nervously trembled in her chair.

"I assume you can broadcast an audio signal, from that machine," said Troubled Times.

She sheepishly replied, "I...suppose..."

Troubled Times immediately created the painful ringing inside her head.

"Careful, my young friend. It is not polite to act stupid," Troubled Times said.

"Yes, yes!" she screamed.

Troubled Times stopped tormenting her and handed her the device.

"Good. Take the audio file on this device, and mix it with the signal that is currently broadcasting," he said.

She took the stick, and inserted it into the console's appropriate slot. She uploaded the file to the machine's hard drive. Suddenly a well-dressed man in a fancy shirt and tie, screamed from across the room.

The man said, "You can't help him! Are you mad? He–"

Before the man could finish speaking, Troubled Times created the ringing sound in his head. Troubled Times pointed his finger at him.

"Stop acting like you're dictating this situation's outcome!" Troubled Times shouted.

The man covered his ears, and trembled in pain.

"You *will*, respect me. That goes for *all* of you. Do you understand?!" Troubled Times shouted.

He sent out a painful telepathic shock wave. Screaming briefly erupted, before Troubled Times allowed the ringing to stop. The woman finished uploading the file, and mixed it with the broadcast's audio feed. A distinct pattern emanated. It would alternate between a deep vibration, to a high pitched squeal, then back to a low frequency. Several people removed audio monitoring devices from their ears. The disturbing vibration pattern made them feel nauseous. Others were entranced by the hypnotic sound. Their bodies swayed in synch with the rhythmic noises.

"Wonderful!" Troubled Times exclaimed.

He removed the data stick from the socket in which it was inserted. Troubled Times walked over to the graphics station, and confronted a frightened middle-aged woman.

"Do the same thing with the video file," Troubled Times said.

The woman did not hesitate to grab the stick with her trembling hands. She inserted it, and transferred the file to the control console's hard drive. In a moment, the upload was finished.

"Superimpose the graphic over the current image. Blend them together, and make sure the signal is broadcast with a high flicker rate," Troubled Times said.

The woman immediately followed Troubled Times' commands. A pattern of colors and waves began mixing together with the video feed. The pattern created a ghoulish looking effect on the screen. The complex pattern mesmerized the spectators. A series of blurry gray waves, flickering images, and bright colors, played in sequence. Troubled Times manically laughed, like a hyena on LSD.

"Give me one hundred percent output! I want the *highest* possible wattage! This signal will permeate through the airwaves, at *maximum* strength! My malevolent, marvelous, mayhem shall now commence!" he yelled at the operators.

Troubled Times reached into his right side holster, and pulled out one of his pistols. Shrieks of fright erupted in the command center. Troubled Times pointed the gun at a group of people, who were huddled together.

"You fucking dirty creatures are coming with me!" Troubled Times said.

Troubled Times waved the gun at the elevator, signaling that he wanted his hostages to enter. One woman, and two men, held up their hands. They quickly walked to the open elevator doors.

"Smash your cell phones!" Troubled Times yelled.

Again he created the ringing sensation in his victims' ears. They all feverishly ripped off their cell phone wrist bands. They threw them to the floor, and the devices shattered.

"Well done, you execrable beasts. I think for now, I'll let you live," Troubled Times said.

Troubled Times stepped into the elevator and pressed the button for the seventeenth floor. The elevator traveled to the main television studio, in the lower room. The elevator doors opened; and for a moment there was nothing except blissful silence. Program coordinators, camera operators, and the television studio's audience; had noticed that the broadcast's signal was going haywire for the past one hundred forty-eight seconds.

Even Chao Bo, and Mei Jia, realized that the small projectors which they were using to monitor their own broadcast images were not functioning properly. Everyone who was paying attention to the projection emanating across the airwaves, was rightfully confused by the odd audio-visual distortions that were occurring. Troubled Times shoved one of the men, and motioned for the rest of the hostages to exit the elevator. All three people walked out in a single file line. Their hands were placed atop their heads. Troubled Times followed them out. He was startled when he heard a loud roar erupt from the audience!

Applause filled the room. Troubled Times quickly looked around, and saw that the audience which was viewing the live broadcast euphorically cheered his arrival. Troubled Times was beyond shocked when a middle aged man, who was an obvious homosexual, scampered up to him. The man wore a white feather boa. His skin tight leather body suit was painted pink. His obviously dyed hair was cropped short and dyed a fake orange color. The audience momentarily silenced. The man spoke in an annoyingly light and high pitched tone.

"Cool how! You couldn't made entrance better! It was for *so* trending!" the gay man said.

The man waved his hands about, in a flippant manner. The audience cackled and moronically applauded this baffling nonsense. The man pressed his index finger against his right temple.

"Okay, so we're, right. Totally switch back, going to cell-cam. Even though it's, umm, very back dated. Chip brain future!" the homosexual man said.

The gay man's holographic cell phone illuminated in his right hand. Troubled Times saw the man's own image render inside his palm. He continued speaking in a wispy voice.

"This is Inter-Web's favorite tranny; Fawn! I'm broadcasting! Yes...so the, in studio. Here on CNA...my girl Emm Jay. Hi 'lo!" Fawn said.

Mei Jia smiled widely, and happily waved to the crowd. Troubled Times' hostages kept their hands on their heads. They looked around and nervously laughed. Troubled Times realized what was actually happening. The sissy man, who called himself Fawn, placed his open palm near Troubled Times' chin.

"Still trouble having get service with new brain web. Only implant got last week. But much love, to all fans. On cam! Give it up for new costume! Say?" Fawn said.

The crowd erupted with euphoric laughter and applause.

"You can't even talk," said Troubled Times with disgust.

"I know it's so...on, right?!" Fawn ecstatically replied.

Bo placed his index finger up to his ear, and nervously smiled.

"What Mister-Missus Fawn means; is that she-he did not realize...this is our show's Halloween segment!" Bo said.

Troubled Times started walking down the small walkway which led to the studio's stage.

"That's right, Bo! Glagoole searches show; the most trending costumes this year are outfits that resemble American Terrorists!" Jia said.

"Maspro Toys has been coy about the specifics; but it is rumored that they are set to release a line of Halloween costumes, based upon this year's most controversial real life public figures. Pre-orders for The Icons' and Troubled Times' replica masks, are reaching astounding numbers!" Bo said.

Troubled Times motioned for the hostages to wait aside a nearby camera operator, who was recording their ascent to the stage. The operator pointed his opened palm at the group. His cell phone recorded every millisecond of the action. Troubled Times, followed by Fawn, stepped onto Chinese News America's large stage. Troubled Times slowly turned around, and viewed the entire room. He saw bright lights flashing. The studio's audience was blissfully unaware that they were in real danger. A group of highly paid public figures acting like morons; real hostages scared for their lives; and a group of terrified gargoyles watching silently from their voyeuristic perch; were all fixated on Troubled Times.

"I...understand. I finally...understand," Troubled Times said.

He looked at Fawn's open hand. It was still placed underneath Troubled Times' chin, and recording him.

"You are so…lost. So brain dead...so out of touch with reality; that you can no longer comprehend the truth. You think the events you've seen taking place these past few months, are a form of Reality T.V. You think that *I* am part of your show. I thought that my frequency manipulator would be the catalyst that put you into a trance, but I was wrong. You are already hypnotized," Troubled Times said.

Troubled Times looked at the monitors. He saw that the distorted images and sounds, were still broadcasting from the command booth. Troubled Times put his own gun to his head.

"No wonder you let me walk in here, holding this in my hand," he said.

The entire room nervously laughed.

"I mean this obviously can't be real, right? New York outlawed guns over ninety years ago!" Troubled Times said.

Troubled Times lowered his weapon, and activated the gun's safety lock. Troubled Times recklessly pointed it into the air, and pressed the gun's trigger.

"See? It doesn't even work! It's a toy!" Troubled Times exclaimed.

Fawn, Chao Bo, Mei Jia, and the studio audience laughed hysterically. They were completely fooled by the safety mechanism. For a moment, Troubled Times was saddened. He realized that Americans had become so disenfranchised with gun culture, that they did not have the slightest concept of how they worked. Even more startling, was the fact that they could no longer tell the difference between a real gun, and a toy. The only guns they had ever seen were replicas, or "professionally" wielded by bureaucratic enforcers. He put the gun to his right temple, and pulled its trigger several times.

"See? It doesn't hurt me!" Troubled Times said.

Troubled Times lowered the gun. He casually disengaged its safety, while the room busted out with laughter.

"Hah, hah! Of course I'm actually a real person, and live in reality. Let's see what it does to a loser; like *you!*" Troubled Times said.

Troubled Times pointed the gun at Fawn's forehead, and pulled the trigger. The gun exploded with a loud bang. Fawn's brain matter ejected backwards. His eyes closed, and he immediately dropped dead to the ground. Screams instantly erupted. The hapless onlookers realized that this was not an imposter, or a promotional gimmick. They knew they were in the presence of a real sadist. Panicked statements were shouted by mortified spectators.

"Stop! This is not funny!"

"He just killed him-her!"

"Quick! Change the channel!"

"Somebody call the D.H.S!"

Troubled Times took a deep breath.

"Silence!" he mightily roared.

The mask amplified the sound of his voice. The headband amplified the power of his brainwaves. A panoptical undulation emanated throughout the room; and visibly distorted electronic equipment. The subliminal messages in the audio, and visual signals, were magnified by Troubled Times' powerful technology. People felt intense heat and pressure upon their bodies. The painful ringing sensation filled their entire head. The shrieks of agony were uncontrollable. Troubled Times basked in the pandemonium.

"There are no words to describe the magnificent events we have seen, over the last several months. It seems like almost every few weeks, our entire perception of the world changes in an instant. We continually lose our morals, freedoms, and loved ones; to an increasingly insane society. This nation has undergone radical changes over the last several decades. We have seen war, famine; degradation of law, order, and morality. It is no surprise that people can no longer differentiate between fantasy, and fiction," Troubled Times powerfully said.

Troubled Times walked around the stage and said, "I was once like all of you. I had a decent job. I followed the restrictions placed upon me by 'the system'. I truly believed that if I submitted to the tyranny controlling my life; that I would eventually be rewarded by my slave masters."

Troubled Times walked around Fawn's dead, twitching body. He looked down upon it, and genuinely felt remorse.

"Part of me feels sorry for you, my fallen comrade. You believed every piece of propaganda, which the Super Elite 'gods' spoke. Perhaps we might have been friends, had our lives crossed at different paths. But unlike you, I have seen behind the veil of lies that obscures the hideous, mutilated face of truth. I understand why elite hate you with such a passion. They have told me themselves; you are *nothing* but animals. *They* are ruthless wolves, and *you* are their prey. But the lesson my misguided mentor did not learn, was that there can *never* be order out of chaos. He, and his acquaintances, believe the best way to gain power...is through the creation and management of crises," Troubled Times said.

Troubled Times looked up, and started walking towards Chao Bo and Mei Jia. They trembled in fear when they saw him approaching their large, lavish desk. Troubled Times stared at them from behind the mask's glowing red eyes.

"I loathe you. You are ventriloquist dummies, who cowardly enjoy their servitude. You know that every word which spews from your wretched mouths has been carefully selected by your puppet masters. You serve this beast because it gives you shiny trinkets, and vacuous fame. In exchange, you have discarded your credibility and integrity," he said.

Troubled Times turned and looked at the audience.

"There is no way for you to truly understand the evil that runs this world; unless you have seen the entire creature in its bare naked form. This is why I have chosen to release you, from your collective prisons. I understand that there is no negotiating with the unwashed masses, or the pampered elite swine," Troubled Times said.

It was 9:51 AM. For the past thirteen minutes, viewers watching the Chinese News America broadcast had been subjected to Troubled Times' brutal onslaught of trauma. The hypnotic signal created by combining a very specific pattern of wavelengths, amplified the real feelings of shock induced by seeing the commission of a graphic murder. The audio and visual patterns were designed to combine with the flicker rate, and disrupt the normal functioning of a viewer's neurological signals.

This made anyone watching the broadcast, more susceptible to the effects of Troubled Times' amplified brainwaves. Scientific studies proved decades ago, that watching television puts the viewer into a highly suggestive, dream-like state. This is one of the reasons that governments and corporations pay over ten million Carbon Credits a piece, to place thirty second advertisements or propaganda commercials during prime-time television events; like the yearly football Mega Bowl.

Troubled Times had perfected his methods of telekinesis after escaping Webster's control. Troubled Times knew very well, that he could easily manipulate the average members of society, by using these advanced mind control techniques. The average person operated in an arrested stage of development. The poor American education system, combined with the chemical drugging of the food and water supplies, had rendered most people unable to use any form of critical thinking. The psychological damage already inflicted upon the American people was devastating. Troubled Times' sophisticated technology only increased their ability to be hypnotized.

"I intend to give you *all* a gift; that you will remember for the rest of your lives. I am going to give you something, which the controllers do not want you to have. I am going to give you, *freedom*," Troubled Times said.

Troubled Times focused his thoughts, and stared straight into one of the cameras.

He said, "Pay attention to my voice, and obediently heed my words. At this very moment, you will release every last one of your inhibitions. I want you to unleash the animal, which your overlords have sought to suppress. You are vicious, rambunctious, violent, unhinged, hostile, insane, bloodthirsty, unsuppressed, uncaring, psychotic, demonic, *ruthless* criminals. You shall no longer follow the restrictions placed upon you by reality's masters. I want you to cast aside the shackles of a civilized society! I want you to pillage, maim, torture, loot, riot, rape, and *kill!* Embrace *darkness!* Embrace *dementia!* Go forth; and create all the destruction that your heart desires! Now is the time for you to indulge in every vile, corrupt, and twisted impulse, that you have repressed for too long! For you see, anarchy *is* the goal! There can be no order, out of chaos. For chaos and catastrophe, *is the ultimate order!* Lawlessness and blood are the only solutions to fixing a decadent, putrid, rotted culture! Go forth; and show the world that we *all* live, IN FUCKING TROUBLED TIMES!"

Troubled Times shot his pistol five times at random audience members. Screams filled the air. One of the bullets struck an overweight woman in her stomach. Another bullet tore through an elderly man's throat. Troubled Times looked up at the control booth.

"I want you to put that speech on continuous replay! Every fifteen minutes, splice in your most violent stock footage! Pollute the airwaves with my corrupted message! These docile sheep will have their thoughts poisoned, until social unrest tears this city apart! If any attempts are made to stop me, or to infiltrate this studio, I will have every person in this room rip each other limb-from-limb, with their bare hands!" Troubled Times yelled.

The time had reached 10:12 AM. News was spreading of Troubled Times' siege upon Chinese News America's studio. Reporters from around the city frantically rushed to CNA, and documented the carnage. Troubled Times' mind control weapon was quickly disrupting people's sanity. Panic was breaking out in isolated pockets, all around the city. Certain groups of people were overwhelmed by feelings of rage. The weaponized auditory hallucinations, made people functioning at low forms of consciousness go absolutely insane. On a crowded city street, one man who had been watching the broadcast on his holographic cell phone became blind with anger.

"This son of a bitch speaks the *truth!* Fuck *all* of you!" the man yelled.

He ran into a deli, and began attacking random patrons. He punched an elderly woman in the face, knocked over a table, and kicked a teenage girl in her stomach. Three other men who had been eating breakfast, jumped up from their chairs. They ran over and attempted to restrain the crazed individual. They repeatedly punched the man, until he fell down. They tried to roll him onto his back, but he continued fighting. The group struggled to restrain the assailant.

"Call the goddamned cops!" one of the men screamed.

Inside a private dwelling, Troubled Times' words were having a different effect. A young, frail, lonely, and mentally unstable woman was watching the program from inside of her apartment. The woman began rocking back and forth on her couch. She got up, and frantically paced around her living room. She bit her nails, until they bled.

"There's nothing left for me. He's right. This world is shit," she finally said.

The woman walked over to her refrigerator, and pressed her hand against its large door. A user interface began displaying. The interface had several items including: a number pad for making calls; a small clock; a weather monitor which displayed the current temperature; and a meter which showed how many Carbon Credits remained in her bank account. It also displayed the amount of food her health insurance company said that she was allowed to eat during the month. She pressed one of the buttons, and a large electronic notepad was rendered.

The woman used the holographic keypad to type the words, "I'm so sorry. Please forgive me. Love, Jess – 7/4/2217." She walked over to her kitchen counter and removed a large butcher knife from the drawer. Jess pressed the knife against her chest. She allowed herself to fall forward. The entire way down, she kept the knife in front of her heart. Jess hit the floor with a loud thud. She let out a scream, when the knife impaled her flesh. Jess flopped around for several seconds, before tragically bleeding to death.

Violence was permeating throughout the city. Numerous people had been seduced by Troubled Times' venomous words. Years of watching television, taking prescription drugs, drinking fluoridated water, breathing geo-engineered air particles, and eating genetically modified food, had left their minds weak. They were unable to resist his devastating mind control weapon. In addition to altering a person's brainwaves, the weapon was designed to activate nano-particles that had attached themselves to their inhabitant's DNA.

The nano-particles were embedded into the numerous poisons, which people consumed in every aspect of their lives. The particles were activated by specific audio and visual frequencies. Troubled Times was beaming these frequencies from the television station. Upon hearing or seeing the signals, the nano-particles became receptors. Once a message was delivered, people fell under a hypnotic trance. Troubled Times used this method of hypnosis, to deliver his twisted message of anarchy.

The nano-particles altered the flow of chemicals, which naturally occurred in the human brain. The nano-particles forced the brain's pituitary glands, to release high levels of adrenaline and norepinephrine. The secretion of these endorphins released deposits of excess glucose, which was stored in human livers. This effect created uncontrollable hostility in Troubled Times' victims. People watching the broadcast, became extremely violent.

All across Penn Station, fights were breaking out between pedestrians who were drunk on fury. Two business women were viciously assaulting one of their colleagues. She was on the floor, crying hysterically. The crazed coworkers were dragging her around by her hair. The women punched their helpless victim in her body, and face. Their brutal violence was a stark contrast to their professional business attire. Several people tried to stop the fight, but the women were not deterred from committing their savage beating. One of the aggressors removed the shoe from her left foot. She began hitting the victim, with the shoe's three inch long heel. Large chunks of flesh fell from the helpless woman's face.

In another part of the station, vandals were ransacking a small kiosk. They knocked snacks from the shelves, broke trinkets that were designed for tourists, and threw bottled drinks at the angry store owner. From behind the counter, he menaced the crowd with a baseball bat.

"Get the fuck out of here, you crazy assholes!" said the store owner, in a pronounced Eastern European accent.

The crowd became even more hostile. They used small novelty lighters, to set t-shirts ablaze. They threw the flaming shirts around, in an effort to burn down the kiosk.

"Oh, no! I'm not going to die over this shit!" the owner yelled.

He jumped over the counter, and ran away. He swung his bat at anyone who tried assaulting him. He wasted no time exiting the station. Police were helpless to stop the hostilities. All around the city, violent outbreaks were being reported. The station was being flooded with calls, asking for help and assistance. Police at Penn Station had no choice but to react with extreme impunity, to contain the wild mob. They bashed out people's brains with their nightsticks, and shot tempestuous rioters with high powered laser guns.

To make matters worse, many of their own brethren were driven berserk by Troubled Times' behavioral manipulation. A male officer removed the large shotgun on his back, and indiscriminately fired at anyone in his path. People screamed and fled from the officer. The shotgun's blasts mercilessly tore through its victims. A teenage boy had his forearm blown off when a cluster of pellets hit him at close range. A woman's head was blown completely open, when she was shot in the back of her skull.

Back inside of the studio, Troubled Times took a deep breath. He thoroughly savored the disorder, for which he was responsible.

Troubled Times said, "I can feel the complete madness disseminating across this city. My device has made me hypersensitive to people's emotions. I can feel the fear in this room. I can sense the hopelessness in my victims. They are being driven insane by my thought manipulation weapon. This, is only the beginning. As the collective dementia spreads, I will ensure that no one is unaffected. I will not stop, until I have plunged this Hellish Babylon into total despair. Fires will burn in every building. Thousands will lay dead across every borough. Bodies will be stacked one hundred feet in the air. Before the day's end, the streets will run red with blood!"

Victims cried, and hugged each other. Many individuals knew they would never make it out of this nightmare alive. Troubled Times laughed like the truly mad individual, into which he had transformed. Gone was the shy, weak, and innocent man, named Gregory Times. He had been fully replaced by an unhinged lunatic, who had no mercy for humanity.

He raised his arms and said, "Now, you truly understand what it means; to be troubled LIKE TIMES!

30 Unexpected Allies

Sirens blared in a high pitched tone.

A female voice repeated the message, "This building is under total lock-down. All inmates are required to remain in their cells. If you have an emergency, please contact personnel using the touch pad in your quarters. Use of Lethal Force, is authorized. Unauthorized movement around the premises is forbidden. Violators will be shot on sight. Thank you for your cooperation."

The wild howls emanating from angry prisoners, echoed throughout the prison's hallways. Cameron Moss was fashioning a shank. He rubbed a piece of his broken, plastic meal tray, against his cell wall. Cameron wrapped one end of the shank in a sock. He lightly stabbed the wall, to see if it slipped in his hand.

It was 12:07 PM; July 4th, 2217. For the past two hours, the New Jersey Trenton State Penitentiary has been in complete disarray. Several riots are still happening. All television, cell phone, and internet communications, are disconnected throughout the prison. As a security precaution, all incoming and outgoing data, is being delayed for fifteen minutes. It is scanned on a special server that searches for specific keywords, and content. This prevents the distribution of messages that might be used for criminal activity. This practice controls the flow of information from outside media sources, which might contain material deemed unacceptable by the Warden. This serves a legitimate purpose by preventing some forms of crime; but it also limits a prisoner's access to uncensored political and social information.

Inmates earned Carbon Credits by working menial jobs as barbers, cooks, carpenters, and janitors. The Carbon Credits were used to purchase luxury usage minutes for internet, television, and cell phone services. All luxury activities were heavily monitored and regulated. Web sites and shows containing violent, pornographic, or conspiracy theorist related material, was banned. Inmates who were caught viewing restricted media could have their sentences increased, or be forced to work in the Robot Repair and Maintenance hard labor camp. The camp was a grueling and dangerous fourteen hour per day job. Inmates learned how to build and repair numerous robots and their parts.

Critics of the labor camps made numerous attempts to stop their usage in prisons across the nation. The anti-labor camp movement claimed that the prison industrial complex, exploited the inmates for the robotics industry's benefit. Because many prisons were privately run institutions owned by robotics manufacturers, they required states to keep a high inmate population at all times. Due to the fact that alarming numbers of people were arrested for unjust and trivial crimes, the prisons had an endless pool of cheap labor. They used these human resources to build expensive machines, which they sold for astronomical profits.

The aftermath of Troubled Times' attack was deeply affecting the prison. Because streaming television shows were automatically time delayed, the prison guards were able to prevent the mind control weapon from infecting too many inmates and staff. Cameron had been in his cell at the time of the incident; and had not personally viewed the broadcast. He did not know if the people he had overheard screaming about seeing Troubled Times on TV, were spouting anything more than rumors. To Cameron, it did not make a difference.

His performance on The Yard had made some of Cameron's fellow inmates wildly jealous of his success. Historically, prisons were always violent places. Just because the number of prisoners incarcerated for non-violent and petty crimes had increased, it did not mean that jails became safer. Cameron knew that if necessary, he would have to protect himself with lethal force. Cameron stopped what he was doing, when he heard voices outside of his cell.

“I don't give a shit what the fucking document says! He's a dangerous man!” a woman loudly said.

“Miss, we've been over this with you. You've already seen my orders. This inmate is a convicted terrorist, and must be transferred to a more secure facility,” a male's voice replied.

A confused look spread across Cameron's face.

“I'm not covering your ass if this is some kind of mistake. I do not approve of any transfer, dammit!” she said.

“Understood. But it's not your decision, or mine. Open the door. He's the last one we need. The others have already been extracted,” the man replied.

Cameron hid the shank underneath his mattress, and quickly laid down upon the bed. His cell door opened.

“Cameron Moss, this is Warden Tina Schawles. Stand up, and face the wall,” the female said.

Cameron was extremely nervous. He did not trust the Warden, or the man whom accompanied her. Cameron slowly arose from the bed, and faced Warden Schawles. She was a husky, physically fit, athletic woman. When he first saw her, he thought she was a lesbian. He was surprised to hear from other inmates, that she had been married to a man for thirteen years, and had a seven year old daughter. Next to Warden Schawles, stood an athletic man. He wore black and blue camouflage fatigues, a matching t-shirt, and bulletproof vest. His entire head and face, was covered by a dark black helmet. He held a large gun, which was obviously a military grade laser rifle. Cameron knew that he was not an average policeman.

“Warden...you know I've never caused you no trouble,” Cameron nervously said.

“Mister Moss, don't sass me,” Warden Schawles replied in a remorseful voice.

Cameron saw two additional men dressed in the same camouflaged attire, standing outside of the cell. Cameron knew that he was not going to negotiate his way out of this situation.

“Dammit, you can't let them take me, Warden! They could be black ops! They're going to *kill* me!” Cameron said.

“Mister Moss...Mister Moss, calm down. Nobody is going to kill you,” Warden Schawles firmly stated.

“Horse shit! You know what you're doing is wrong!” Cameron frantically said.

“Cameron, stop!” Warden Schawles forcefully said.

Cameron sensed that Warden Schawles was complying against her will. Cameron begrudgingly held out his arms, and allowed himself to be handcuffed. The Special Forces soldier placed a thin black veil over Cameron's head.

“Okay boys. Take him away,” the soldier said.

Cameron was led out of his cell by the lead enforcer's subordinates. The thin silk veil only allowed Cameron to see a portion of what was happening in the prison. Inmates screamed, while confined to their cells. Some were tearing up their mattresses, and eating them. On the tier's lower section, Cameron saw a small fire burning in one of the room's corners. Several inmates were fighting riot guards, dressed in heavy combat gear. Cameron was unnerved to see that the inmates were not only confronting the peacekeepers in such a violent manner; but that the heavy armor which the guards were wearing did not seem to provide much protection against the crazed convicts.

Cameron was overwhelmed by the chaotic situation. He also sensed that there were heavy footsteps following him. Cameron was escorted down a large corridor. At its end, was a giant elevator that led to the bottom level of the five-storey facility. Cameron heard the extraction team's leader, yelling at several other inmates.

"Get back! Stay *back*, or else I'll let it eat you!" the leader said.

Cameron tilted his head to the left. He saw the object, from which the noisy footsteps originated. The robotic growls emanating from the beast, served as a vicious warning. A heavy clunking sound occurred, when its large metal paws hit the ground. It menaced anyone who dared oppose its awesome power. The animal was five and three quarter's feet tall, and six feet long. Its four foot tail had a sharp spike on its end. Everyone knew, that this was no ordinary dog.

The mighty beast called the Uncanihound, intimidated all who dared threaten the extraction team. Its name was a mash up of the phrase, Uncanny Companion Hound. The term was coined in 2177 by its inventor, Sebastian DeMarcco. At one point in time Sebastian, the founder of DeMarcco Technologies, was one of the most brilliant and prolific inventors in the world. He was responsible for numerous technological innovations. Advances in the development of robotic animals, anti-gravity devices, and commercialized human organ cloning, were all created by his ingenuity.

In 2190, Sebastian left the public spotlight to care for his son, Alistor. It was rumored that Alistor had been permanently disfigured, and brain damaged after a car accident. The accident was caused by human error. Even though he never again spoke publicly, Sebastian donated billions of dollars to lobby for the passage of laws that mandated the use of automated vehicle driving systems, all across the United Kingdom.

The Uncanihound was a fully robotic replication of a very large dog. It used advanced electro-optical cables to connect all parts of its frame. Its tail was made from flexible metal blocks, connected by thin strands of wires. Its paws and body were synthesized metallic rubber, crafted from a highly refined mixture of silver, clay, isoprene, amber, and copper. A detachable laser cannon was mounted on its shoulders. The quantum computer chip in its head was programmed with highly sophisticated artificial intelligence. The beast's eyes produced a powerful scanning wave.

The specially calibrated optical lasers projected a green circle, upon any object that it focused. Any offenders that dared threaten it were immediately declared hostile. They were given warnings when the Uncanihound growled viciously. When attacked it would bite offenders with its razor sharp, serrated metal teeth. In extreme situations, it would shoot them with its cannon. Cameron continued his journey towards the elevator. Cameron felt the large muzzle of the leader's laser rifle poke him in the back.

"Keep moving," the extraction team's leader said.

Three inmates, who were beating a prison guard in a corner near the elevator, abruptly stopped their vicious attack.

"Hey, where do you think you're going? Get that nigger!" one of them said.

The three inmates rushed towards Cameron and his extraction crew.

Cameron heard the leader yell, "Stop! We have no issues with you!"

The leader's plea was in vain. Before anyone could react, one of the inmates tried to stab Cameron in his stomach, with a crudely made prison shank. Cameron twisted his body, and wrapped his handcuff's chains around the shank. Cameron struggled with his attacker. He felt the blade randomly pricking his skin. He lurched forward out of his captors' grasp, and head butted his assailant in the face.

Cameron was able to push the goon against a nearby wall. Cameron violently smashed his head into the nose and mouth of the man who was trying to kill him. One of the extraction team's members separated the two men. The Uncanihound pounced forward, and bit the attacker upon his left leg. The man fell to the ground, and the Uncanihound proceeded to rip out a large portion of his thigh. The Uncanihound stood atop the inmate, who was screaming in agony, and howled. The piercing directional based noise prevented the other two assailants from further approaching the group.

"Hurry up and get him to the elevator!" the leader yelled.

The leader pointed his large laser rifle at the hostile group. His two companions quickly escorted Cameron to the elevator. The Uncanihound continued menacing the attackers. Warden Schawles used her cell phone to call for help. The lift arrived, and Cameron was shoved inside. The extraction team's leader and the Uncanihound immediately followed. The leader pressed the button for the main floor. Before the doors closed, Warden Schawles gave the team an ominous warning.

"You're on your own, boys. Good luck," Warden Schawles said.

The leader did not reply. The elevator's doors slammed shut. Cameron grabbed his side, and checked the damage.

"Ow, ow! Oh man, did that nigger get me?" Cameron asked.

One of the extraction team members looked at the spot where Cameron had been assaulted.

After a moment the guard said, "No. It wasn't that sharp. Just looks like a few scratches."

"Why do I have to wear the hood?" Cameron asked.

"For your safety. People are rioting. There are violent criminals running rampant. Someone with your notoriety is a high valued target. You've already been attacked, and they didn't even know who you are," the leader said.

Cameron knew that the leader's words were true.

"You know, if you're going to kill me…just do it already," Cameron said.

"Relax. We're not going to kill you," the leader said.

"Yeah, right," Cameron replied.

The elevator reached the ground level. The team walked Cameron through another corridor. The group exited out the back of the prison, and Cameron was led to a large van. The team helped Cameron into the van, and sat him next to another prisoner. Once he was settled, they locked his shackles to a bench. Cameron saw the shape of two other inmates sitting on a bench across from him. The other inmates were wearing hoods, which prevented Cameron from seeing their faces. The van's doors closed tightly. The extraction team's leader used a computer embedded in his suit's left forearm to program a driving route.

"Destination set," said the robotic voice in the van's dashboard.

"We're out," the leader said.

The extraction team and the Uncanihound entered another van. Within seconds, both vans drove themselves away from the prison. Cameron's heart raced. He leaned back against the van's wall, and closed his eyes. Cameron tried to calm his nerves. He accepted the fact that he was not in control of the situation. The van only drove for twenty-seven minutes, before it stopped. The journey felt like hours to Cameron. After a moment, its back doors opened.

"This is the last stop, boys. We're unchaining you. Don't try anything stupid, or I'll have the Uncanihound rip off your nut sacks," Cameron heard the team's leader say.

Another team member entered the van, and unlocked the inmates' shackles. He removed them from the van, one at a time. Cameron saw that his captors had brought the inmates to a secluded wooded area.

"You don't have to execute us," Cameron said.

"Cam? Cam, is that you?" he heard Vincent ask.

"Vincent? Aw damn, they got you too?" Cameron replied.

"Stop talking," the leader said.

He then told one of his companions, "Take off the hoods."

The group's hoods were promptly removed. Cameron saw that Walter, Vincent, and Paul, were the other inmates!

"Praise Jesus! You're all still alive!" Paul said.

Walter looked at the leader and said, "This is wrong. You can't just bring us out here, and gun us down like dogs!"

"Yeah! Take off these fucking cuffs, and fight us like men!" Vincent exclaimed.

The leader raised his left hand, and opened his palm.

"Relax. I already told you, we're not going to kill you," the leader said.

He slung his rifle over his shoulder by using the strap that was attached to the gun. The leader and his teammates, unlocked the prisoners' handcuffs. The leader pressed a button on the side of his helmet while he walked over to Cameron. His helmet opened and the man's face was revealed. His other teammates did the same. Cameron looked at the man and was shocked when he recognized him.

"Do you remember me?" the leader asked.

Cameron looked at the other two men. One was a short, youthful Caucasian male. The other one was a tall black man, who appeared to be in his late thirties or early forties. All the men were very physically fit.

"You're Dominic, right? You were there that night, on the turnpike," Cameron replied.

"Glad to see you haven't forgotten," Dominic said.

"What the hell is happening? Why are you helping us?" Vincent asked.

"Let me introduce you to my friends. This young chap, is Nathan Miller. The big guy, is Rex Hammond," Dominic said.

Nathan and Rex gave the group a nod with their heads. Cameron's team returned the favor.

"If you're not a hit squad, why on Earth would you bring us out here? We're felons," Cameron said.

"Are you aware of what occurred today?" Dominic asked.

"No," Cameron replied.

"I've heard a few rumors, back at the prison. Something really serious happened this morning," Paul said.

"Let me show you something. I'm warning you, it's pretty intense," Dominic said.

Dominic pressed the touch screen interface embedded in his suit's left forearm. Footage from a television news report began holographically projecting out of the device.

The frantic female reporter said, "...for the past two hours. Riot police have moved us behind this portable metal barrier. Chaos and mayhem are spreading–"

She abruptly screamed. Only a few feet away from her, crazed rioters began violently clashing with the police.

"Oh my God! We have to get out of here!" the reporter shouted.

The feed cut back to a male reporter, who was sitting behind a desk at the television's studio.

"Uhh...I think we are experiencing technical difficulties. We will be right back," the man said.

Dominic pressed the interface, and the holographic projection stopped.

"What the hell was that about? Christ, the city looked like a war zone," Walter asked.

"It *is* one," said Rex.

Dominic took a deep breath and said, "A few hours ago, that crazy asshole Troubled Times took over a TV studio in midtown Manhattan. He released some kind of weapon, that's driving the whole city insane. The mayor has suspended all electronic communications. Only the big media outlets are being allowed access to the airwaves."

"That's not surprising. The people in power want to control the official narrative," Cameron said.

"I agree with you. But I think the mayor is doing the right thing, in this case. Times' weapon is affecting people through the broadcast signals. It's making everyone who sees it, go delirious," Dominic said.

"That's terrible. But seriously man, why are you telling us?" Cameron asked.

"You want to explain, Nate?" Dominic asked Nathan.

Nathan somberly said, "When I got back from Syria, I needed help. I saw a lot of bad things out there–"

"We all did," Rex briefly interrupted.

"Veterans Affairs enrolled me into a therapy program. They said it would help me get my shit straight. I met this guy there. He seemed decent. I didn't think anything about it, until a few weeks later. When I first heard about Troubled Times, I almost hit the ceiling. You know what he said his name was?" Nathan asked.

"The guy in therapy?" Vincent asked.

"Yeah. He said his name was Greg. Gregory *fucking* Times! Dude had missed several sessions, before the first Troubled Times incident," Nathan said.

"That's heavy. Do you think it's the same person?" Cameron asked.

"Maybe, but the story gets weirder. I told my adviser at the VA, about Greg. They allegedly started an investigation. Three weeks later, my adviser told me that there was no connection, and to shut up about Gregory Times," Nathan said.

"What happened next?" Walter asked.

"There was another couple at therapy, who spoke about the turnpike incident. I knew it was a long shot, but I called in a favor from a buddy of mine who's an Army Corporal. He got me the travel itinerary for the military convoy that was there that night. I contacted everyone who was on the list. None of the other guys wanted to talk, except for Dominic. I told him what happened, and that the VA wasn't going to investigate Times," Nathan said.

"Dear God, are they insane? Why would they ignore the possible connection?" Paul asked.

"We did our own research, and found out some startling information. The company where Nate was receiving treatment is called Rigor Pharmaceuticals. Rigor has a huge contract with the military. They are the sole supplier of our vaccines, and medications. It is highly possible that they are also involved in black ops. If this guy Troubled Times was part of a covert weapons program, Rigor and the military would want to keep it a secret," Dominic said.

Cameron kicked the ground and said, "Dammit! Why does the government always have to be so fucking evil?!"

After a long silence Walter asked, "What does all this have to do with us?"

"After we saw Cameron on The Yard, we knew we had to help. Your friends Lady Fore-shock and Magnificent Sight, have been rallying thousands of people around the country. There is a huge movement that is protesting on your behalf. A lot of people want to see you released. We were planning on busting you out today, and hopefully giving you a chance to clear your names. Now, with everything going on with Troubled Times, that plan has changed," Dominic said.

"Whoa, whoa, whoa...calm down for a minute. We are *not* superheroes. We've all seen what Troubled Times can do to people. He controls their minds, and hijacks their free will. There's no way we can handle something of that magnitude," Vincent said.

"Yes. No offense to present company, but we're just farmers and petty crooks," Paul said.

"You underestimate yourselves. I've seen what you can do, not only on the turnpike, but in your videos. You are very resilient. You guys have some amazing technology. You've taken out at least three drones, by my count. That's no easy task," Dominic said.

"Son, I appreciate the kind words. But how can we fight something, which we don't understand?" Walter asked.

Everyone fell silent for a few moments. No one denied that The Icons were severely disadvantaged in this fight.

"If we decided to help, how would we get into the city?" Cameron asked.

Dominic began saying, "I don't kno–"

"Cam, have you gone mad? What makes you think that we can go up against Troubled Times?" Vincent interrupted.

"These guys took a huge risk, extracting us from jail. We owe it to them, and everyone else who believes in us, to try and stop that psycho," Cameron replied.

"How do you know that we can trust these guys? This could be a trap!" Vincent said.

"Hey! Watch who you accuse, tough guy! Who's to say that we can trust *you?*" Rex said.

Vincent and Rex started arguing. Their friends tried to calm the situation.

"Enough, enough! Stop fighting, dammit!" Cameron loudly shouted.

The commotion quieted down, and there was a brief silence.

"Look. We've already been sentenced to death. The government has no reason to entrap us. If these guys wanted us dead, they could have already shot us," Cameron said.

"Listen, we don't have time to fuck around, or argue with each other. I figured you'd be skeptical, so I brought something to ease your concerns. Rex, show them the stuff," Dominic said.

Rex walked over to the back of the van, in which his team had ridden. He removed two large duffel bags and threw them on the ground.

"See for yourselves," Rex said.

Cameron and Walter walked over to the bags and opened them. They were shocked to see that Dominic's crew had retrieved the gear; which was confiscated by the arrest team the night Cameron and his friends were captured!

"This is amazing. How did you get these out?" Walter asked.

"It wasn't easy. We had to forge several electronic documents, which allegedly 'authorized' your transfer. One of the documents said that these could potentially be weapons of mass destruction, and they had to be confiscated for the staff's safety," Nathan said.

Cameron held his mask in his hand. The diamond shaped mouth and nose coverings, were scratched with numerous battle scars. Its straps were frayed; but they could still keep the mask steady upon Cameron's face. The blue eye pieces embedded into the mask were murky, but they would not prevent Cameron from seeing his opponent.

"We've got to do whatever we can, to stop this madness," Cameron said.

"Cameron, hold up, I didn't agree to *any* of this nonsense! I have a family! You guys can play vigilante by yourselves!" Paul said.

"We're not *all* going after Troubled Times. We need to infiltrate Rigor Pharmaceuticals. If you and Walter can get inside, we might be able to steal information about these secret experiments that Nathan mentioned," Cameron said to Paul.

"How would we get into the city? It's probably under lock-down at this point," Vincent asked.

"Any suggestions?" Cameron asked Dominic.

"Well, I'm not sure that we can give you too much assistance. Keep in mind, we'll get in deep shit if any of our commanding officers find out that we've helped you," he replied.

"I understand. Would you be able to let us borrow that thing?" Cameron said while pointing at the Uncanihound.

"It depends. What did you have in mind?" Dominic asked.

"Uncanihounds can run wicked fast, and they're strong as hell. There are some abandoned train stations in Newark. It's a long shot, but Vincent and I might be able to reach midtown Manhattan if we follow one of the defunct rail lines," Cameron replied.

"Yeah, I suppose that would work," Dominic said.

"How would we get inside Rigor?" Walter asked.

"You said you can forge electronic documents, right? We should be able to trick border patrol, using one of these vans. You can drive this van up to the check point and show the guards a fake extraction document. We'll make it look like there is an emergent order to evacuate foreign diplomats from the United Nations building. Once you're past security, you can take Walter and Paul to Rigor. They will handle the rest. It's a holiday and there's a crisis happening. It shouldn't be too hard to break inside," Cameron said to Dominic.

Nobody spoke. They were impressed by the enormous complexity of Cameron's plan.

"All of this sounds hellishly bold, but I don't have a better suggestion," Dominic said.

"You guys have all lost your damn minds! There's no way that I can be a part of this tomfoolery," Paul said.

"Paul what if doing this, meant getting your family back? I know our mission requires a huge amount of faith; but we have to expose the truth about Rigor, and defeat Troubled Times," Walter said to Paul.

"What's our other option? Do you really want to be thrown back into that Hell hole? Our only choices are to be killed on The Yard, or to rot away in our cells for the rest of our lives," Vincent said.

Paul reflected upon his friends' wisdom.

"You've all gone kangaroo shit crazy, but Vincent's right. What choice do we have left? We're damned either way," Paul said.

There was a brief and uncomfortable silence. Cameron rummaged through the bags and inspected all the items.

"We have ammo, weapons, armor, and masks. Everything that we need to pull this off is in our hands. Is everyone ready?" Cameron asked.

"No, but it appears that I'm outvoted," Paul said.

"We can get you inside the city; but I can't promise that we'll be able to extract you. Shit is going to get pretty crazy. This is most likely a one way ticket," Dominic warned the team.

"It doesn't matter. In a couple of hours we'll probably be back in the slammer, or dead," Cameron said.

Cameron strapped his mask to his face, and holstered his pistol. The teams separated. Rex, Nathan, Walter, and Paul, rode in one van. Cameron, Vincent, Dominic, and the Uncanihound, rode in another. The vans drove up the New Jersey turnpike at speeds reaching upwards of ninety miles per hour. The flashing lights atop the vans helped clear the road of what few cars were still traveling. Paul prayed for his safety, and the safety of his companions. Both teams were monitoring news reports of the hellish events unfolding in the city. Holographic video feeds were projecting from the vans' dashboards.

"We are in our news copter, flying above Times Square. It has been over three hours since the terrorist known as Troubled Times, seized control of Chinese News America's studio. It is believed that he is holding a large group of hostages. Violent outbursts are still erupting all around the city. Early this morning, Troubled Times released an extremely powerful weapon. Its effects are creating fits of mania in his victims. There has been talk of bringing in the National Guard to deal with the situation. Furthermore...wait, wait! I see someone in that window!" a frantic male journalist said.

On the seventeenth floor, a bloody woman pressed a sign against the glass.

"Zoom in and get a shot of that person!" the reporter said.

The operator inside the helicopter used the camera's high powered lens, to get a close up shot of her.

"No one escapes," the sign read.

The sign had obviously been written in blood. The message was scrawled on a large sheet of white cardboard. The woman abruptly dropped the sign, and disappeared from the window.

The reporter said, "It appears as if one of the hostages was momentarily trying to signal for help. She seems to have disappeared–"

Without warning, a chair crashed through the window. It tumbled through the air, and shattered upon the ground.

"There appears to be some kind of struggle. I think...oh, oh no!" the reporter said.

The camera operator zoomed out, but not before he captured footage of the bloody woman leaping through the broken frame. She tumbled to her death.

"Cut the feed, cut the feed!" the reporter screamed.

"Holy fuck! This is *bad.* I haven't seen such horrors since the riots in '85," Walter said.

"I agree. At least there was a reason behind those riots. People were broke, and starving. This is just mindless mayhem," Paul said.

The convoy was quickly approaching Newark. Dominic used the communication device embedded into his suit's forearm, to speak with his team members.

"Rex, we're getting off at the next exit. We've been looking at old train station maps. There's an old PASS route that was deactivated in the late '90's. It looks like the rail ends somewhere near the Empire State Building," Dominic said.

"Copy. We're going to the Abraham Tunnel. We'll be in contact soon. Over and out," Rex said.

Dominic quickly drove another mile, through what remained of the decimated city. Broken streets, dilapidated buildings, and homeless drifters, were scattered throughout Newark. The van reached an old train station, which was near a partially collapsed bridge.

"This is the place," Dominic said.

The van drove up to a gated area by the bridge. It was marked with a tattered old sign that read, "No Trespassing."

"Wait here for a minute," Dominic said.

He exited the van and walked around the tracks. After a couple minutes, Dominic opened the back of the van.

"Time to ride," Dominic said.

Cameron and Vincent stepped out of the van. They had changed out of their prison garments, and were wearing their body armor and masks. Vincent had a large shotgun strapped to his back. Cameron had two pistols holstered at his side. The men were low on ammunition. They only had a few rounds, which had not been spent during the farm raid. They hoped that they would not need to engage in a prolonged firefight. Their suits, combined with the hot summer day, made them uncomfortably warm.

"I'm roasting. I hope we don't get dehydrated," Vincent said.

"We'll be underground soon. Hopefully, it will be cooler. We won't be on the street for too long," Cameron said.

Dominic handed Cameron a device, similar to the one he was wearing on his forearm.

"You'll need this to control the Uncanihound," Dominic said.

Cameron clamped the flexible computer to his left forearm. Dominic grabbed Cameron's left hand, and tapped the device against his own. The Uncanihound opened its jaw.

"Device synchronized. Authorization accepted," a robotic voice said.

"Familiarize yourself with the user interface. It has GPS navigation, millimeter wave scanner, encrypted cell phone connections and more. Uncanihound has unbelievably sophisticated AI. It will know how to handle any threats that you may encounter. Right now it's configured to be non-lethal. You won't be able to override the setting, without special pass codes," Dominic said.

"That's fine. The last thing we want to do is contribute to this bloodbath," Cameron said.

"Give me a hand," Dominic said to Vincent.

Vincent helped Dominic unhook the large laser cannon mounted to the Uncanihound's back. Vincent was surprised by the cannon's light weight. He swung it over his right shoulder.

"How does it work?" Vincent asked.

"You'll need this to free fire, when it's not attached," Dominic said.

Dominic reached into a small pouch attached to his belt buckle, and removed a thin headband. Attached to it was a transparent, plastic square eye piece. Vincent placed the laser cannon on the ground. He removed his visor, and sheathed it in his tool-belt holder. He put the band atop his head, and mounted the square over his right eye.

"Press your finger against the target finder," said Dominic.

Vincent placed his right index finger on the square. One second later, the target finder was activated.

"Ow! That's different," Vincent said.

It used a series of flashing laser light patterns, and calibrated itself to the dimensions of Vincent's eye.

"Give it time," Dominic said.

After several seconds Vincent saw the words, "Authorization required," projecting.

Vincent said, "It says I need–"

Before Vincent could finish speaking, Dominic placed his right finger on the target finder's back.

The words, "Authorization accepted. Calibrating Optics for New User," flashed in front of Vincent's right eye.

Vincent asked, "Should I–"

"Don't talk just yet. Wait for the next screen," Dominic interrupted.

Soon the words, "Repeat this phrase: Test. Weapon aim. Test," were displayed.

Vincent repeated the words aloud.

"Thank you. Repeat this phrase: Test. Weapon fire. Test," the screen displayed.

Vincent followed the instructions, and repeated the second phrase.

"It will follow your eye's motion. Point the cannon in the direction you want to fire. You can't see it, but there are small microphones inside of the headband. At this moment, they're only calibrated to your voice. Just say 'weapon aim, weapon fire' to launch the laser. Give it a try," Dominic said.

Dominic pointed at the fence's 'No Trespassing' sign. Vincent swung the cannon over his right shoulder. Vincent stared directly at the sign.

"Weapon aim. Weapon fire!" Vincent shouted.

A powerful laser beam incinerated a portion of the fence and the sign.

"Holy shit!" Vincent exclaimed.

"Right now, it won't fire if it detects body heat signatures emanating from the target. You won't be able to directly shoot at large groups; but you will be able to use it to take out solid objects, including drones," Dominic said.

Vincent and Cameron looked at each other, and knew they shared the same concern. The men understood that they had the potential of facing deadly robots, which would not hesitate to immediately kill them.

"Well, let's hope that doesn't happen," Cameron said.

"You had better get moving," Dominic said.

Cameron climbed on the upper portion of the Uncanihound's back. Vincent mounted its lower hind.

"Just like riding a horse!" Vincent said.

"Yes. A very weird and metallic horse!" Cameron said.

They shifted their weight, and secured a good grip on the large artificial beast.

"Listen, if I don't see you again...thank you for your help, Dominic," Cameron respectfully said.

"Don't thank me. Just stop that sick son of a bitch, before he hurts more people," Dominic said.

Without another word, Cameron pressed his forearm's computer interface. The Uncanihound gave a loud howl, ran past the gate, and stormed into the tunnel!

The Uncanihound started gaining tremendous speed. Cameron and Vincent held onto small grips, welded to the Uncanihound's back. It leaped over concrete debris that was strewn about the rotted metal tracks. Vincent saw that there was a collapsed portion of the tunnel ahead.

"Duck!" Vincent yelled.

Vincent aimed the laser cannon and yelled, "Weapon aim. Weapon fire!"

The laser shot a powerful beam which melted the debris. The Uncanihound continued running.

"I'll blast anything that gets in our way! I don't want this thing to stop!" Vincent said.

"Be careful! We'll get caught in a damn collapse, if you shoot the wrong spot!" Cameron yelled.

"Don't worry man, I got this shit covered! Weapon aim. Weapon fire!" Vincent shouted.

The laser blasted another piece of debris. The Uncanihound continued barreling along the tracks.

Paul and Walter were still thirty-eight miles from the tunnel. They continued watching the carnage unfold on the live television news broadcast. They heard the reporter continue speaking from the chopper.

"We have confirmed that Troubled Times is murdering his hostages! He is demanding that the CNA broadcast signal be restored! He said...wait...I think there is someone else in the window!" the reporter said.

The camera operator zoomed closer. Two men were seen walking a woman up to the seventeenth floor's broken window. She struggled, and desperately tried to pull away from their grasp. All three of them were crying. They slowly moved closer to the opening.

The two men struggled to resist. From a position on the seventeenth floor where he could not be seen, Troubled Times overpowered their free will. He forced them to push the young woman out of the window! In an even more sadistic act of violence, Troubled Times immediately made the men jump to their own deaths!

"My God! This is the most repulsive thing I've ever seen!" the reporter yelled.

"Cameron and Vincent need to get to that studio! This is a total massacre!" Walter said.

"Times has gone completely insane. He is publicly executing people for his own sick pleasure. It's not about making a point anymore. It's about causing the most havoc and suffering possible," Paul said.

"Do you have any phone lines that are secure?" Walter asked Nathan.

Nathan handed Walter a clunky old cell phone.

"This is an encrypted communication line. It won't give away the receiving or sending number, but don't stay on it for too long. The LSA still records the conversation in backup servers," Nathan said.

"I'll only be a minute," Walter said.

Walter quickly dialed Lucia's cell phone number. She answered after a few rings.

"Hello?" Lucia asked.

"Lady Fore-shock, this is Mister Daylight. I need you to listen to me very carefully," Walter said.

"Are you for real? How the hell are you calling me?" a stunned Lucia asked.

"Under much duress. Listen, you and Magnificent Sight need to start streaming a live broadcast. Use public satellites and focus them on the CNA's studio. I'm sure you've already heard that Troubled Times has flipped the fuck out! He is wantonly murdering people. Help is on the way; but we need real journalists to document the events. We can't let the defunct mainstream media, control the flow of information!" Walter said.

"Of course, Mister Daylight. We'll record everything," Lucia replied.

"I'll contact you later. You *have* to make sure the truth gets out. There are going to be a lot of people asking questions, after this is all over. We have to be sure that they get *truthful* answers. Mister Daylight, out," Walter said.

He ended the call before Lucia could reply. Walter handed the phone back to Nathan.

"What else can you tell me about the man you met at therapy?" Walter asked.

"He sure didn't act crazy, like this Troubled Times guy. He was quiet, and had a wife. I'm not even sure that he and Troubled Times are the same person. I'm just going off of a hunch, you know?" Nathan replied.

"A wife. Do you remember her name?" Walter asked.

"I think it started with an M. Marcy? Mary? Mallory! Her name was *Mallory Times!*" Nathan said.

"Hand me a computer. We have to find out every bit of public information that's available about Gregory and Mallory Times," Walter said.

Nathan reached into the glove box and handed Walter a pair of computer sticks. Walter pulled the sticks apart. A computer interface rendered a holographic projection in the space between the sticks. Walter used various public search engines to find information related to Gregory and Mallory Times. Several searches returned no results, because those were rather common names.

"Nate, do you remember why they were in therapy?" Walter asked.

"Yes. They said they were victims of the CEA," Nathan said.

"Walter, the hospital! Check the records for the United World Hospital!" Paul said.

Under the revised health care laws of 2163, a person's health information was controlled by the Internal Revenue Society. Therefore, it was public information. These public databases were accessible to anyone with a computer. Walter performed another search.

"Everyone, look at what I've found!" Walter exclaimed.

The group focused their attention on Walter's screen.

"UWH records show that late last year, Gregory and Mallory Times were fined for violating the One Child Mandate!" Walter said.

"Now it makes sense why Troubled Times attacked that place! Walter, how could anybody miss that connection?" Paul asked.

"Nate already explained it to us. Something very serious is going on here. There appear to be a lot of forces involved with concealing the truth," Walter said.

"Why would anyone let a maniac like Troubled Times loose, if they had even the slightest chance of stopping him?" Rex asked.

"There are a lot of reasons, son. Governments, and the corporations that own them, don't ever waste a good calamity. There may be powerful interests, which *want* Troubled Times to proliferate destruction. They can exploit the crisis to gain more power," Walter replied.

A concerned look fell upon Nathan and Rex's faces.

"Look, I can't tell you too much. There has been, let's call it, heavy chatter...about implementing Martial Law nationwide," Nathan said.

"That's why we knew we had to help. Everybody on the inside has been hearing rumors that President Cho, will use some kind of catastrophe to implement Martial Law," Rex said.

"We're not trying to shoot our fellow American citizens. There are awake individuals within our own ranks, who say those orders are inevitable. Most military members hate to admit it, but there are rouge special-ops factions who have been training to fight the American people, for a very long time," Nathan said.

"We have to hurry up, and get to Rigor," Walter responded.

The van continued racing down the highway. Walter resumed his search of the public databases.

"Nathan, is there a way to send Cameron a message?" Walter asked.

"Yeah. Give me a minute," Nathan said.

Nathan called Dominic by using his forearm computer.

"Dom, did you give them any coms?" Nathan asked.

"Yep. He has a Muscle. I'll text you the number," Dominic replied.

Muscle was the slang term used to describe the forearm computer. A few seconds later, Nathan handed Walter the old cell phone.

"Send them a text. The satellites may not be able to forward calls, if they're underground," Nathan said.

Walter sent Cameron a text message that said, "Wife is named Mallory. Kids killed under OCM."

"We'll be at the tunnel soon. I'll let you know if I find any other useful information," Walter said.

The group remained silent. The van sped along the highway, and valiantly drove towards the Abraham Tunnel.

31 Infiltration

"Hold up, this is the spot," said Cameron to the Uncanihound.

Cameron, Vincent, and the Uncanihound had been traveling through the abandoned subway tunnel for the past thirty-one minutes. Their bodies were sore from riding the mechanical beast. Their suits were dirty, from the dust inside of the tunnel. They had reached a large wall, which was blocking their forward mobility. They both got off of the Uncanihound, and walked up to the blockage. Cameron pressed several buttons on his forearm computer. He held out his arm and gray light began shining on the wall. Its millimeter scanner allowed Cameron to see through the bricks. Cameron saw that there were more tunnels, and a platform, on the other side.

"This is where they sealed it off. According to the GPS, we are right underneath Thirty-Third Street. All right, man. Bust this fucker open," said Cameron to Vincent.

Vincent used the laser cannon to blast a large hole through the concrete. Vincent and Cameron walked through the opening, and continued traveling along the tracks. The site was incredibly eerie. They both adjusted their masks, so that their faces were exposed. The old Thirty-Third Street PASS Station was completely untouched. It had not changed since it was closed due to budget cuts, over two decades ago. Vincent and Cameron climbed onto the subway platform. The Uncanihound followed their every movement. The platform was dusty and worn. The yellow line near the platform's edge was barely visible.

The group began walking down the corridor. They followed tattered signs that marked the route to the exit. Along the tunnel were old advertisements for devices long forgotten. Ads for hand-held cell phones, human operated motor vehicles, tablet computers, flat screen LCD TV's and paper magazine publications, were still plastered to the walls.

"Wow! It's like stepping into a time machine! How long has it been since they shut it down?" Vincent asked.

"Twenty-two years, if I remember correctly. Hey, check it out!" Cameron replied.

Cameron pointed to an advertisement for a television set.

"This is the H.G. 1000. It was one of the first mass produced holographic devices that working class people could afford. I was a kid when they first came out. I remember wanting one so bad, but my parents didn't have the money to buy one," Cameron said.

The duo stared at the advertisement. It showed a clunky square box, projecting an image above itself in midair.

"It's hard to believe they became so cheap. We use them all the time, without a second thought," Vincent said.

They stared at the advertisement for a few brief moments, before they continued walking down the long corridor. They made a right turn at the end of the path, and began traveling through another huge passageway. They saw the remnants of old pizza shops, gift stores, and ticket dispensers, scattered throughout the room. Cameron looked over at a small, empty coffee shop. A few tables and chairs were still set, like they were about to be used.

"What do you remember, about being a kid?" Cameron asked.

Vincent took his time, and pondered the question.

"The terrible living conditions. Our neighborhood rarely had power. The lights were always off, the water was rationed, and it was always too cold, or too hot, in our tiny apartment," Vincent said.

Cameron stopped walking when he saw a state financed anti-terror advertisement. The advertisement had the symbol of a single opened eye, next to an upright palm. Beside the hand was a banana, inside of a universal prohibition sign. The three symbols were imposed over a menacing, dark black background.

The sign's text read, "See Terror, Stop Terror. Report illegal food dealing to the NYPD."

"Older folks like Walter, always say they want to get things back to normal. While we were locked up I realized that for me, this *is* normal. For folks our age, the world has always been shit. I can't imagine a world without constant police check points, spy drones, biometric scanners, outrageously high Carbon Taxes, or where I didn't have to fight niggers for food," Cameron remorsefully said.

Cameron looked down at the ground. He let the seriousness of the situation sink into his mind.

"Maybe we've been wrong about everything, Vincent. Maybe Troubled Times is right. What else is left for society, except anarchy?" Cameron finally asked.

Vincent was speechless. He was extremely disheartened that he shared Cameron's impuissance.

"Hey. Look at me, dude," he told Cameron.

Cameron looked up at Vincent. Both men were fighting back tears of rage.

"There's always hope that the future can change. If we give up, then all the sacrifices we and others have made over the years, will be in vain," Vincent said.

Cameron took a moment to reflect upon Vincent's wise words.

"We need to keep moving," Cameron sternly said.

The duo and their robotic companion continued traversing the corridor. Eventually they reached a large set of stairs. They started walking up the stairs, but soon discovered that the exit above them had been sealed shut.

"This used to be the exit to the ground level; but it has obviously been blocked," Cameron said.

Cameron activated the millimeter scanner, and attempted to see through the concrete.

"Damn, it's too thick. I can't see anything," Cameron said.

"We have no choice except to blast through. There doesn't appear to be another way out that's any less dangerous," Vincent said.

"We have no idea what's on the other side of that concrete. It could be nothing except pavement, or it could be a damn building for all we know," Cameron said.

Vincent adjusted his mask, so that it again covered the bottom half of his face.

"Only one way to find out," Vincent said.

Cameron nodded his head, and readjusted his mask. Cameron stood back, and Vincent aimed the laser cannon.

"Weapon aim. Weapon *fire!*" Vincent yelled.

A powerful laser blast shot from the cannon. The wall started breaking apart.

"Fire!" Vincent once again yelled.

The powerful directed energy beam started melting the concrete.

Vincent yelled, "Fire!" one more time.

The laser beam ripped a hole through the rock. Vincent and Cameron jumped back, and let the dust settle. They saw that the opening led out of the tunnel.

"We're right on the corner of Thirty-Fourth Street. The station is only ten blocks away. Uncanihound, cover us!" Cameron said.

The Uncanihound raced up the broken concrete, to clear the path for Cameron and Vincent. Cameron climbed through the rubble, and exited through the freshly created opening. Cameron rolled forward after pulling himself out of the hole. He crouched upon his right knee, and looked around the city.

They were in the middle of a small park that was located near the Empire State Building. Cameron helped Vincent out of the subway tunnel. They were horrified to see pandemonium was ensuing all around them. People were causing havoc throughout the streets. There was rioting, and fighting everywhere. Arsonists were setting the surrounding buildings ablaze. Looters wildly pilfered stores. Drones flew above city streets, and shot people with laser beams of varying lethality.

"Sweet Jesus! This is fucking nuts!" Cameron said.

A crazed man wildly ran through the park. He quickly approached Cameron and Vincent.

"We're all fucking dead!" the man screamed.

"Wait!" Vincent shouted.

The man did not stop. Vincent was forced to use his laser cannon, to smash the man in his face.

"Get down!" Cameron yelled at Vincent.

Cameron and Vincent swiftly took cover behind some shrubs. They saw an eight wheeled Humvee, rolling down the street to their right.

The Humvee blasted the words, "Mandatory curfew is in effect. Return to your homes. All citizens are required to remain indoors," from a loudspeaker mounted atop its hood.

Cameron and Vincent continued surveying the area, and tried to cope with the frightening situation. They saw a large group of people clashing with police. Some of the police looked like they were genuinely trying to quell the violence; but other police were actually contributing to the madness by rioting themselves.

"There's no order. These cops aren't trying to get control. They're fighting for their lives!" Vincent said.

"You're right. We need to get in touch with Walter," Cameron said.

Cameron noticed a small gift shop across the street. Its lights were off, and its windows were busted out. After surveying the streets for a few more seconds, Cameron was positive that they had a clear path to the store.

"Follow me," Cameron said.

The group ran towards the shop, and immediately took cover inside. The Uncanihound continuously scanned its surroundings for threats. Cameron tried calling Walter by using the Muscle's communication system.

"Daylight? Daylight, can you hear me?" Cameron said.

"...erenity? ...s that ...u?" a crackly voice replied.

"Yes, it's me. Can you speak louder? I can barely hear you," Cameron said.

Cameron fiddled with the settings for the signal strength, and was able to get the device to work a bit better.

"Doctor Serenity, do you copy?" Nathan clearly asked.

"Yeah, it's the good Doctor. Where's Daylight?" Cameron replied.

"Let me get him," Nathan said.

Nathan motioned for Walter to speak into the microphone, embedded in the Muscle.

"It's Mister Daylight. Did you and Vestige make it to the city?" Walter said.

"Yeah we did, and it's real bad. The news stations aren't even coming close to accurately portraying what's happening. This place has turned into pure Hell on Earth," said Cameron.

"Shit. I'll call you back. We're almost at the checkpoint," Walter replied.

"Damn. Okay, I understand," Cameron said.

"Get to the back of the van, you guys. We're about to enter the tunnel," Nathan said to Walter and Paul.

There was very little traffic near the toll booths. All civilians attempting to enter or exit the tunnel, were being thoroughly searched. Police with hand held body scanners were only allowing one lane of traffic, to flow through the tunnel in any given direction. Usually, both outbound and inbound sides of the tunnel had several lanes of moving traffic.

Currently, only emergency personnel were being allowed to travel in the far right side lanes. Members of the Army, who wore green camouflage fatigues, patrolled the road. They pointed guns at families inside of vehicles, while their identities were confirmed. Rex saw a ten foot tall humanoid DHS robot that was holding a large laser rifle. It walked around the streets, and kept a watchful eye over the entire operation.

"Damn, these guys ain't playing," Rex said to Nathan.

"No shit. This may be harder than we anticipated," Nathan said.

"Relax. We're incognito," Rex said.

The van rolled past one of the initial toll booth checkpoints, and had no problem entering the Abraham Tunnel.

"Okay, that was easy. The interstate checkpoint is the big one," Nathan said.

"I've got to close the doors. The scanners will obviously be able to tell that there are four people in the van; but it will be tough to explain why you are wearing street clothes," Rex said to Walter and Paul.

"Yeah, or why there are prison garments back here with us," Paul said.

Rex smiled, and pressed a button near the left driver's side dashboard. The large metal door, which was used to separate the cabin, slid shut. The van continued driving towards the interstate checkpoint. It swiftly reached the large scanning tube, and barbed wire gate. Even though the van was clearly marked as a law enforcement vehicle, the military guards made it stop for inspection. A female Army guard walked up to Rex's open driver side window. She noticed that Rex was a fellow military member.

"Forgive me sir, but why the hell are you trying to get into the city? It's a fucking loony bin! There are reports of people tearing each other apart with their bare hands, in the goddamned street!" she said.

"We have orders to evacuate some high valued allies," Rex sternly said.

"Thermal scans detect two in the back," the woman said.

"Yeah, they're special ops," Nathan said.

"You know what? Fuck it; I don't even want to know your orders. The scanners haven't detected any bombs, or radioactive signatures. Go through the next section. If nothing requires further inspection, then good luck completing your mission," the woman said.

"Not a problem," Rex said.

The van drove through the tube. The gates opened and the van was allowed to pass into New York City.

"Can you believe that bullshit? She waves us through like it's fucking nothing. Those people back there will be lucky if they don't have to go through cavity searches," Nathan said.

"I know, man. It hurts me every time I see something like that happen. This is all ass backwards. Drones, FTA thugs, body scanners, passports, checkpoints, and everything else. It's nothing but security theatre; and a way to remind the American people that they're slaves," Rex said.

The van continued driving, and soon exited the tunnel. Rex rolled up his window and opened the cabin's door.

"Okay, we're clear," Rex said.

Walter began to say, "We have to get to Rig–"

Before Walter could finish speaking, a soda bottle smashed against Nathan's passenger window. Nathan looked to his right. He saw a group of people, pelting cars with various bottles and food objects.

"Good Lord, look at their eyes. They have no spark. It's like someone sucked out their life force!" Nathan said.

One angry man stopped his car. He got out to argue with another man, who had hit his car with a water bottle. The man began assaulting the driver, who ran back to his car. He sped away, and narrowly avoided being beaten to death. Rex activated the truck's manual drive mode.

"This weapon has taken away their humanity," Rex said.

The crew sped through the city streets and frantically rushed to the Rigor building. All around them they saw fires burning, people fighting, and frightened individuals fleeing from the destruction.

"I really hope the boys are safe," Paul said.

Cameron and Vincent were still inside of the temporarily abandoned store. Cameron had tried several times to call Eiji and Lucia. The cell phone communication lines were still being jammed by signal frequency interference. Cameron used the device's wireless internet, to send Lucia a message by electronic mail.

"Yes! It worked! Lucy just wrote back!" Cameron said to Vincent.

Cameron clicked the blue hyperlink, which Lucia had sent him in her reply. The link opened a connection to a messaging service. It allowed people to communicate using video chat, without using cell phone frequencies. Lucia's and Eiji's masked faces rendered on Cameron's Muscle screen.

"Gracias a Dios! I never thought I'd get another chance to see you guys!" Lucia exclaimed.

"We can't believe that you're still alive!" Eiji said.

"I know the feeling, but there's no time for pleasantries. Did Daylight tell you what's happening?" Cameron asked.

"He has been sending us information. We're aware of everything," Lucia said.

"Good. Vestige and I are about to confront Troubled Times. Is there anything you can tell us about how he manipulates his victims?" Cameron asked.

"At this point, we haven't a clue," Eiji replied.

"It has something to do with microwave, light, and audio frequencies. He released some kind of virus over the airwaves," Lucia said.

"Yeah, and it's making people go fucking insane. Any idea how we can protect ourselves?" Cameron asked.

"I wish I could help, but I can't. We don't know exactly how he's infecting people," Lucia said.

"Our advice is to say a prayer, and take him out quickly," Eiji said.

"Okay. We have to get moving," Cameron said.

"Roger. We're using an encrypted connection to stream live video of your journey. Everything that happens will be documented," Lucia replied.

"That's right. You probably have thousands, if not millions, of people watching you at this very moment. Everyone can see what The Icons are doing to help the people of New York," Eiji said.

"Wow. No pressure, huh?" Cameron said.

The group chuckled.

"Okay, we're out; and tell her that I...I'll see her soon," Cameron said.

"Absolutely. Be safe, hermano," Lucia said.

Sky nervously stood in the corner of the living room. Eiji gave her a raised thumb, to indicate that Cameron was okay. Cameron switched the interface back to its GPS mode.

"This is it, man. We're about to ride. We only have ten blocks to go," Cameron said.

Cameron and Vincent mounted the Uncanihound. Cameron pressed several buttons on the Muscle's interface.

"This thing is about to run at top speed. Hold on for dear life!" Cameron said.

Cameron pressed one more button. The Uncanihound let out a loud howl. It jumped out of the store and ran through the park. The Uncanihound turned, and began running along the chaotic street. Vincent saw an armored SUV in the middle of the road. It pointed the laser cannon mounted on its rooftop at them.

"I don't think so, motherfucker! Weapon aim. Weapon *fire!*" Vincent yelled.

Vincent's laser blasted the armored SUV, causing it to partially melt.

"Damn! Tore that shit a new one!" Vincent exclaimed.

"Over there!" Cameron shouted.

A triangular shaped drone flew from around the corner of a building on the next street. Vincent shouted his command. His laser shot the drone with precision accuracy. The Uncanihound jumped over the drone, when it crashed and slid in front of their way.

"Fucking *toast!*" Vincent said.

The Uncanihound turned around the following corner, and continued running to the CNA station. A large crowd was rioting along the sidewalks and streets. People who had not lost their minds, fled from the violent crowd. Cameron saw a group of three teenagers, throwing Molotov cocktails into a popular fast food restaurant.

"Damn, I can't blast through this crowd!" Vincent said.

"Don't worry. Uncanihound has got this covered!" Cameron said.

Cameron pressed a button on the Muscle's interface. The Uncanihound emanated a powerful, directional sonic wave. Hordes of people threatening the team immediately scurried away. The sound wave released a strong and high pitched ringing tone, combined with the barks of a real dog. Its high decibel level caused people immediate discomfort. The Uncanihound tilted its head from side-to-side. It effectively herded the crowd, and dispersed them in different directions.

"We're almost at the station! Only six blocks left!" Cameron yelled.

The Uncanihound continued its sprint. Cameron and Vincent vigilantly watched for other potential threats.

Rex, Nathan, Paul, and Walter, had reached Rigor's Fifty-Eighth Street corporate headquarters. Rex drove the van around the block. Nathan pointed to an adjacent alleyway.

"Over there," Nathan said.

Rex pulled the van into the alley.

"This looks like a good place to let you guys out," Nathan said.

"Did you see that poor woman, getting beaten by those EMTs? They were hitting her pretty hard. I hope they didn't kill her," Rex said.

"Yes, it was awful. We must pray for her," said Paul.

"Don't worry. Vestige and Serenity will stop this bastard," Walter said.

"You should get going. We can't wait here for too long," Rex said.

Nathan grabbed a small backpack that was resting on the floor, and handed it to Walter.

"Here are some tools that will help you hack security. You can take the computer sticks with you. I personally knew the guy that ran the main program. His name is Webster Morgan, and his office is on the seventh floor," Nathan said.

Walter grabbed the bag and said, "Thank you. You fellas are real heroes. Don't let anyone ever tell you otherwise."

"No need to thank us. Just infiltrate that building, and find solid proof of corruption," Rex said.

Without another word Paul and Walter exited the van, and hurried to the Rigor building. They kept their heads down, to avoid the street camera's prying eyes. Paul pulled the main door's handle, and was not surprised that it was locked.

"Check around for the security interface," Paul said.

Paul and Walter searched the outer walls, until they found a large panel on the side of the building. The panel was a standard touch screen biometric interface. It allowed authorized personnel to lock, and unlock, the building.

"There we go. Let's see what we have in the bag," Walter said.

Walter opened the backpack, and rummaged through its contents.

"Find anything useful?" Paul asked.

Walter removed a customized rubber glove, a can of aerosol spray paint, and a roll of a clear adhesive tape.

"This will work," Walter said.

Walter sprayed the panel with the paint.

"The paint is infused with nano-machines that decrypt the machine's fingerprint pattern. The tape is a flexible bio-signature detector, that mimics a touch-screen interface," he explained to Paul.

Walter slapped the adhesive over the panel. He put the glove on his right hand, and tapped the panel.

"The glove has special fibers that can send fingerprint sequences. The nano-machines encrypt the prints, and submit them to the system in a bio-sequence that the computer recognizes," Walter said.

"Welcome to Rigor Pharmaceuticals. Please press your thumb against the area of the screen you see below, to begin confirmation," the screen's text read.

Walter completed the machine's request. After a few seconds the text, "Authorization accepted," was displayed.

After gaining access to the security module, Walter deactivated the alarm system and unlocked the main doors.

The screen flashed the words, “Thank you. This building is now open for business.”

“Simple enough. This is a standard flimsy security panel. I don't know how well it will work on the high tech systems,” Walter said.

“No time to worry about that, old boy,” Paul said.

The duo walked to the front door, which now opened for them. They rode the elevator up to the seventh floor. The duo started walking around the deserted building.

“What do you think we should be looking for, in terms of evidence? It's not like they're going to have a sign that says, 'Illegal Lab Experiments, and Evil Weapons Development Behind This Door',” Paul said.

Walter chuckled and said, “Let's find the office that Nathan mentioned.”

Paul and Walter searched the floor, until they found Webster's room.

“Bingo! This is what we want,” Walter said.

Walter hacked the security panel using his equipment, and gained access to the dimly lit room. Paul walked over to the window, and placed his hand upon its glass. It turned transparent, and the room was illuminated with natural light.

“Much better,” Paul said.

Walter and Paul noticed that there was a computer terminal in the middle of Webster's desk. Walter waved his hand in front of the computer's sensor. A moment later, the computer began holographically projecting an interface above the terminal. Walter pressed a few buttons on the user interface.

“That's weird. The security boot screen is disabled,” Walter said.

“Why would he leave his stuff unsecured?” Paul asked.

“That's usually a sign that the device has been hacked. Maybe the person who hijacked the machine, turned off its security so that anyone could use the device. They probably forgot to restore it, when they were finished,” Walter said.

“Let's hope they didn't clean everything out,” Paul said.

“Hand me the sticks,” Walter said.

Paul reached into the backpack, removed the computer sticks and handed them to Walter. He synchronized the devices by tapping them together.

“I'm going to copy the contents of his hard drive to our machine. Hopefully, we will find something useful. These guys usually store the real stuff on isolated servers. But you can always find out valuable information about a person, by looking at the contents of his personal computer,” Walter said.

Walter began the transfer. While the machine was making the copy, Walter searched through Webster's virtual folders. Walter found a video file named, 'Interview with Subject Thirty-One,' in a directory labeled, 'Previous Subjects'. Walter played the file. It showed a very young boy, around the age of six. He was wearing a straightjacket, and was being interviewed by a woman with a British accent. The woman was not visible.

“Describe the nightmares you've been having,” the woman said.

“I'm not asleep, when they talk,” the boy said.

“Who are 'they'?” she asked.

“The people who whisper in my ear,” he said.

“What do they say to you?” she asked.

“Bad things, Doctor Mandy. Very bad things,” he replied.

"Like what?" she asked.

"It's good I hurt myself. It's good I hurt those girls. My daddies deserved to die," the boy answered.

The men were highly disturbed by the boy's shocking admission of guilt.

"These bastards know their drugs cause hallucinations and dementia. The SSRI's make people highly suggestible. I'm sending these files to Lucia and Eiji. They need to post them online," Walter said.

From one of his many encrypted accounts, Walter sent Lucia an e-mail and asked her to contact him. A few moments later, Lucia responded with the link to a video conference site. Walter opened the connection.

"Lady, I need you to remotely log in to this computer, and make copies of its files. Give me a minute. I'll send you the specs," Walter said.

Walter sent Lucia the required information. She synchronized the machines.

"Okay, it looks like we're connected," Lucia said.

"Good. Copy everything in that folder. It's a backup of Webster Morgan's personal computer hard drive. He's the company's owner. Extract every bit of important data that you can find," Walter said.

Walter and Paul continued searching the contents of the hard drive, while Lucia made a copy to her machine.

Cameron and Vincent were only one block away from the CNA studio.

"Over there! That's the building!" Cameron said.

"It looks like the entrance is blocked off...damn, look at the size of that mob!" Vincent said.

Cameron saw that citizens and police were fighting with each other.

"That group is massive! We can't let them stop us from reaching that building!" Cameron said.

Cameron saw a crazed woman, stomping another female's head into the pavement. The victim's head bounced off the concrete. Blood, pieces of her skull, and brain, spewed everywhere.

"Get that laser ready. You need to blast the door, when I give you the signal!" Cameron said.

The Uncanihound raced forward, and used its sound cannons to disperse the crowd.

"Oh, dear God. Look over there, Cam!" Vincent said.

Cameron looked around, and saw that the street was littered with numerous dead bodies. They were pulverized into piles of red gore, and human mash. One of the bodies had crashed through the top of a nearby police cruiser.

"What a nightmare! These must be the people that jumped from the building!" Cameron said.

"Don't worry man; we're going to stop this sick asshole!" Vincent said.

While they were traveling, Cameron heard a policewoman yell, "Hey! It's those terrorists! Stop them!"

Cameron and Vincent were only thirty yards from the building. Cameron saw that the path ahead was clear.

"Now, now! Blast that motherfucker!" Cameron yelled.

Vincent aimed the laser at the lobby's front door.

"Weapon aim. Weapon fucking FIRE!" Vincent said.

A powerful beam blasted the structure. The doors melted, its glass windows shattered, and a smoking hole was created at the energy weapon's impact origin.

"Yes! We're almost there!" Cameron yelled.

The Uncanihound sprinted closer, and stopped in front of the smoldering rubble. Cameron and Vincent immediately got off the contraption. Cops and rioters alike tried moving closer to them. They wanted to assault, or arrest, the duo. Vincent pointed the laser cannon at the uncontrolled crowd. The Uncanihound used its powerful sound cannons, to keep the horde at bay. It continuously waved its head back and forth, which created a small protective perimeter. Cameron heard nothing but unintelligible screaming emanating from the mob.

"This is a full-fledged terrorist attack! I need a D.H.S. tactical unit, and drone support!" a policewoman shouted into her cell phone.

"We're not terrorists! We're here to help!" Cameron shouted.

"Doc, we don't have time to explain ourselves. This place is about to get raided," Vincent said.

Cameron started typing commands into his Muscle.

"I'm giving the Uncanihound instructions to wait here, and buy us some time. Give it the cannon, so it can shoot any robots that try to breach the perimeter," Cameron said.

Vincent strapped the laser cannon to the Uncanihound's back.

"Run!" Vincent shouted.

Cameron and Vincent ran inside, and immediately raced into a stairwell. Vincent removed his eyepiece, and replaced it with his visor. Cameron activated Lucia and Eiji's video communication link.

"We're inside CNA. Do you know where we can find Troubled Times?" Cameron asked.

"The news is reporting, that people are being thrown from the seventeenth floor's windows," Lucia said.

"We saw the aftermath. Trust me, it's not pretty," Vincent said.

"According to CNA's web site, that's the main broadcasting studio. There's a guest greenroom on sixteen and a control room on eighteen," Eiji said.

"We're going to floor seventeen. We have to stop Times, before he kills anyone else," Cameron said.

"Be careful, hermanos!" Lucia said.

"Get ready, dude. There are a lot of stairs ahead, and we have to move fast," Cameron said to Vincent.

The two men began running up the stairs, with the maximum rapidity that their legs would allow.

Meanwhile at Rigor Pharmaceuticals, Walter and Paul had finished making electronic copies of Webster's computer hard drive. Walter was simultaneously uploading the drive's contents, to Lucia's server.

"That's the last of these files. Do you see anything else in this room that may shed some light on this conspiracy?" Walter asked Paul.

"Check this out," Paul said.

Paul tapped a section of the wall, near the fireplace's mantle.

“Hear that sound? It has an echo. A portion of this wall is hollow,” Paul said.

“Hit that spot one more time,” Walter said.

Paul punched the wall thrice, while Walter closely listened to the reverberations.

“I think you're right. It sounds like there's space behind this fireplace!” Walter said.

Walter inspected the fireplace. He discovered a tiny fingerprint scanner, hidden behind a porcelain doll that was sitting on the mantle. Walter picked up the female doll, and briefly admired its beauty. It was adorned with a full bodied, red dress skirt. Walter did not know that the doll was made in Mallory Times' image.

Walter gently placed it on Webster's office desk. He used the spray paint, glove, and adhesive tape, to hack the panel. The fireplace's center, rotated. A rusty ladder replaced the holographic images that were projecting inside of the faux fireplace. Walter knelt, and looked down the opening.

“You see anything?” Paul asked.

“Yes. This ladder looks like it leads to some kind of underground facility,” Walter replied.

“We're going down,” Paul said.

Walter thought for a moment before replying, “No. You need to take what we hav–”

“That wasn't a question, old boy,” Paul interrupted.

Walter smiled and said, “Grab the bag.”

Paul and Walter began their descent. Walter was the first to reach the ground.

“Easy! I've got you!” Walter said.

He helped Paul cushion his two foot drop from the ladder. Walter and Paul saw a large corridor extending far into the building. They began cautiously exploring the vast corridor. Walter aimed the computer sticks outward, so that its camera could record the surroundings.

“Incredible! Are y'all seeing this?” Walter asked Eiji and Lucia.

“We are, and it's totally spooky! Are you still inside Rigor?” Lucia asked.

“Yes, we're in a secret passageway! There's an entire laboratory hidden inside of this place!” Walter said.

Walter continued recording, while Paul walked slightly ahead of him.

“Over here!” Paul said.

Paul pointed at a crudely written sign on a laboratory door. Walter jogged forward, and took footage of the sign.

Its text read, “Neural Programming in Progress. Do Not Disturb.”

“There might be something really nasty, on the other side of this door,” Paul ominously said.

Walter said, “Listen, Paul. You can turn back now and–”

“Is she recording this, dude?” Paul interrupted.

Walter asked Lucia, “Lady Fore-shock, are you–”

“Still recording. Everything is being saved on our private storage drive,” Lucia interrupted.

“Let's get that door open,” Walter said.

Paul used the biometric hacking kit to operate the fingerprint scanning panel. The door slid open, and Paul slowly entered the room. After several steps, he abruptly bumped into a large workstation. Paul let out a loud gasp when he saw what lay upon the table.

A chimpanzee, whose arms and legs had been surgically removed, was strapped to the table. A holographic projector was beaming images directly into the chimpanzee's eyes. Violent pornography was being mixed with real videos of human suffering. Images would quickly cut between scenes of naked women being abused, and graphic videos of humans being mutilated. A horrible compilation of terrible suffrage and depravity was steadily pumped into the chimpanzee's mind.

Unclothed women being choked by abnormally muscular men; crying children being sodomized with florescent light bulb tubes; females who were bound and gagged, being punched in their stomachs; horribly deformed burn victims receiving physical therapy; a crying woman who had her head repeatedly shoved into a toilet; tribal cannibals in a jungle, enjoying the flesh of a crudely cooked human; and other ghastly images seared their way into the chimpanzee's brain.

"Lord, let it go mercifully!" Paul exclaimed.

He grabbed the tiny chimpanzee's fragile mangled body with his left hand. He cradled its skull, and twisted it with his right hand. Its neck snapped, and the animal immediately died. Paul dropped to his knees, and was overcome with grief.

"My Lord, please forgive me!" Paul screamed aloud.

Walter raced to Paul's side. Both men were trembling with anger.

"I've seen enough! We're leaving this evil place!" Walter said.

Paul took several deep breaths, and forced himself to regain his composure.

"No. There's more to see in this satanic den of iniquity. Demonic spirits are strong in this abode," Paul said.

Walter nodded his head and said, "Okay, then we keep moving."

He arose from the ground, and extended his hand. Paul immediately grabbed it, and pulled himself to his feet. Walter nervously looked at the computer.

Walter said, "My Lady, I hope you didn't–"

He did not get a chance to finish his sentence. Lucia held her hand over her mask's mouth, arose from her chair, and walked out of the camera's line of sight.

Eiji remained seated and said, "Yes, Mister Daylight. That was truly hideous."

"I've only read about stuff like this in declassified CIA documents. We're in a high-tech brainwashing facility. They hook animals up to these machines for hours on end; and show them that type of sick garbage. Different flicker rates are used to reprogram their brains. I'm now positive that Rigor has performed these experiments on humans," Walter said.

"If Times gained access to these laboratories, he could have easily perfected a mind control weapon," Paul said.

The men exited the room, and continued walking through the corridor.

Cameron and Vincent panted heavily. They were exhausted, but had finally reached the seventeenth floor.

"We're here. Hold up for one second," Cameron said.

Cameron checked his Muscle's interface. He noticed that Walter had sent him a message, over an hour ago. Cameron opened the file and read the text.

"Walter said that Gregory was married to a woman named Mallory. Their kids were euthanized under the One Child Mandate," Cameron said.

"That's intense. I guess that explains why he went crazy. Having his children murdered, would make the best of men lose his humanity," Vincent said.

"I agree. I'm not surprised that Times is angry, but nothing justifies this type of wanton killing," Cameron said.

Cameron drew his pistol, and placed his left ear against the door.

"I can't hear anything," Cameron said.

"These walls are probably sound proofed," Vincent said.

"Shit, you're right," Cameron said.

He used the Muscle's millimeter scanner, to see through the walls.

"There are definitely people inside. I can't tell if Times is with them," Cameron said.

"Only one way to find out," Vincent said.

Vincent and Cameron breathed deeply. They looked at each other, and knew that they had to complete their task.

Cameron solemnly said, "Listen man, we don't know if we can handle what awaits us on the other side of this door. If I lose my...you know...if I can't..."

Cameron let his thoughts trail off, while staring at Vincent. The two men completely understood that they may have to kill each other, if either one of them lost their minds.

"I know. Same goes for you, Cam. If I can't...well, you know what to do," Vincent said.

Cameron and Vincent did not speak for several seconds.

"Okay, clear everything on the right. I have the left side covered. We move, on three," Cameron finally said.

Vincent removed the shotgun strapped to his back, and clutched it in both of his hands.

"No problem," Vincent said.

Cameron slowly and quietly counted, "One, two..."

On the count of three, Cameron smashed the door's operating panel with his left forearm. It swung open, and the duo ran into the room. Cameron aimed his pistol to his left. Vincent aimed the shotgun to his right. A few loud gasps emanated from startled hostages. Cameron and Vincent did not see any signs of hostility. Cameron slightly lowered his pistol, and further walked into the room. What he saw, emotionally disturbed him beyond belief.

32 Confronting The Darkness

Blood was splattered upon the floors and walls. A broken window in the corner of the room, whistled while wind swept through its shattered frame. Several people were sitting in a circle, on the far right side of the room. They cried over the body of a young man, who had been shot in his face. A woman who had been bludgeoned to death, lay dead near the news anchor's desk. Several dead people were hanging out of the control room's broken window. Their necks were wrapped with thick electrical cord.

"This is the worst shit I've ever seen, in my entire life," Vincent said.

He and Cameron walked to the studio's broadcasting set. As they were stepping onto the stage, a man emerged from the shadows. There was no mistaking his identity. Troubled Times stood before them, dressed in his full regalia! His long purple trench coat covered Troubled Times down to his knees. His black pants fit snugly to his body. The gray ring around his black fedora hat, matched the color of his gloves.

His glistening silver mask, which had become a symbol of pure evil, was firmly strapped to his face. The small bump of its nose was barely visible. The circular plate covered with mesh netting, attached to its mouth and jaw, was sternly pronounced. Its shiny red eyes, burned hot with the fires of Hell. Troubled Times slowly clapped his hands together.

"Well, well, well. The Icons. In the flesh, and soon to be *much* blood. We meet at last!" Troubled Times said in a deep, raspy, and bellowing voice.

Troubled Times slowly walked around Cameron and Vincent. His demeanor was highly threatening. Troubled Times abruptly stopped walking, and held his arms out by his side.

"What do you think of my infernal masterpiece?" Troubled Times unfeelingly asked.

"Times, you have to stop. This is lunacy. These people have done you no harm," Cameron said.

"Innocent people don't deserve to be tortured in such a cruel manner," said Vincent.

Troubled Times began slowly pacing around the stage.

"You know...when I was a kid, I wanted to be a journalist. I dreamt of working in a nice studio, like this one. I wanted the world to know my name," Troubled Times said.

Troubled Times sickly laughed before saying, "Look at me now, boys and girls! Dreams really do come true when you use hard work and perseverance!"

Vincent angrily pointed his shotgun at Troubled Times.

Vincent said, "*Fuck* this guy! I'm about to blast him–!"

Troubled Times waved his right finger and interrupted Vincent.

"Now, now, now. That wouldn't be proper. Famous people like ourselves can't just kill each other, before we've been properly introduced. My name is Times, and I am Troubled," he said.

Troubled Times did a disrespectful and overly dramatic bow, to show Vincent and Cameron mock chivalry.

"So let's see if I remember correctly. You're Doctor Shitty, right?" Troubled Times asked in a completely mordacious tone.

"That's Serenity, you jackass," Cameron snapped.

"Oh, that's right...that's right. Forgive me! My mistake! This muscular gentleman is, the Vulva?" Troubled Times asked.

"It's VESTIGE! Serenity, stop fucking talking to this crazy asshole! He's trying to get inside our head!" Vincent said.

"Oh, I haven't gotten inside of your head…yet," Troubled Times said.

He paused for a moment before saying, "So is this the part where you become superheroes? You're pathetic. You're two grown men playing dress up, like some bad video game protagonists."

"I don't think you can lecture *us* about fashion sense," Cameron said.

Troubled Times laughed and said, "Hah, hah! So true, so true!"

There was an extremely tense moment of silence.

"You're not going to save anybody. You know that, right? All you are is a couple of hungry fools; who have come a long way to die," Troubled Times finally said.

"What is your problem? Why are you Hell bent on causing bedlam and misery?" Cameron asked.

"Because these swine must be forced to pay for their insolence. This repugnant, decadent, domesticated society must be obliterated," Troubled Times replied.

"What do you mean?" Vincent asked.

"You and I both agree that this is a nation fraught with problems. Our entire future has been stolen by a criminally insane group of ruling elite. People have tried to reverse the evil for decades. Something *must* be done to upset the balance of power. I am offering, a permanent solution," Troubled Times said.

"So this is your answer? Add fuel to the flames by inciting violence?" Vincent asked.

"There is no other option. Ask yourselves; what great reward has your little crusade brought you? For your entire outlaw heroics, what great change have you achieved? You've done nothing but bring suffering, pain, and death, to those who so blindly follow you. What makes you think that you are any better than me?" Troubled Times asked.

Cameron and Vincent felt tremendous guilt. They were always remorseful when people got injured during their countless battles. Nevertheless it was tough to hear Troubled Times' somewhat accurate criticism.

"I don't pretend that I'm a hero. I know we've made some terrible decisions that have wrecked the lives of those who we call our friends. That happened because we chose to fight our evil, criminal, oppressive, corrupt, murderous government; that implemented U.N. Agenda 21 to reduce our standard of living. Can't you see the *real* villains? It's these trendy hipsters, and corrupt politicians. It's the laziness of our fellow man. It's everyone who *collectively* let America turn into a toilet. We're *all* guilty of letting tyrannical bureaucrats run every aspect of our lives," Cameron said.

Cameron continued, "Countless wars we allow to be fought in our name; relentless atheists who vehemently deny Creation; genetically engineered food; a Communist education system that teaches collectivism over individualism; a counterculture of pedophile sexual deviants that want to destroy traditional families; the flippant 'I-don't-give-a-shit-about-anyone-except-myself' narcissistic attitude, that we've been sold by Hollywood; a mainstream media that mindlessly vomits talking points; *these* are some of the real enemies. It is because we've gotten so arrogant, indolent, and decadent, that we've allowed ourselves to be captured by legion of anti-American *foreigners!* I agree that our society and culture has decayed, but this is not the way to get it fixed!"

Troubled Times took a moment to absorb the heavy wisdom of Cameron's words.

"Touching, but foolish. What you fail to understand, is that you have no power. I once was like you; empathetic and hopeful. What I did not realize is that to truly create change, one must be in *control.* Let me show you a demonstration," Troubled Times said.

Chao Bo and Mei Jia, had been forced to sit in their chairs for the last several hours. A steady stream of tears had caused Jia's mascara to completely run down her face. Bo was equally flustered. His tie was disheveled, his hair was disorderly, and he looked exhausted beyond belief. With his left index finger, Troubled Times pointed at Bo.

"You see this dirty slope? He's not in *control* of *himself.* He's an abject voyeur with wild sexual urges. Tell me, sir. What is your favorite type of pornography?" Troubled Times ruthlessly asked.

Bo feebly replied, "I...I don't watch–"

"Don't lie to me, you fucking Chinaman! I asked you, what is your favorite type of porn?!" he abruptly interrupted.

Troubled Times created the painful ringing sensation in Bo's ears. Bo screamed in agony.

"Cougars! I like older women!" Bo shouted.

Troubled Times cackled and said, "You hear that, everyone? This perverted, slant-eyed, motherfucker likes touching himself to photos of your grandma!"

Bo was in extreme pain. Cameron knew that it was time for action.

"Enough! Goddammit, enough!" Cameron yelled.

Cameron and Vincent raised their guns and were about to fire upon Troubled Times. He abruptly looked at them and extended his right hand.

"I don't think so!" Troubled Times said.

Cameron and Vincent immediately began feeling intense heat inside their brains. Troubled Times created the horrible ringing sound inside of their minds.

"Oh, shit! What the fuck is he doing to us?!" Vincent screamed.

Cameron and Vincent's bodies began shaking.

"You know, I'm not a big fan of the Second Amendment! I think guns kill too many innocent people! Why don't you help keep our streets safe, by getting rid of them?!" Troubled Times said.

Cameron and Vincent lost their free will. They struggled to resist Troubled Times' powerful brainwave disruptor, but were overpowered by his psychic barrage. Against their wishes, they threw their guns halfway across the room!

"*Much* better! Now accede to my illustriousness!" Troubled Times said.

Troubled Times forced Cameron and Vincent to kneel down. They struggled to regain control of their bodies.

"Let me tell you about *control.* People like this sack of filth, like to watch porn because it makes them feel like they are in *control!* This son of a bitch doesn't realize that porn is legalized rape! He's an *abuser!* See how he likes to hurt women?!" Troubled Times said.

Bo let out an agonized yell. Troubled Times forced him to punch Jia in her nose! Jia screamed in pain, grabbed her face, and began crying. Troubled Times continued taunting his victims.

"Is that all you've got? You chicken-armed, yellow faggot! Don't be such a pussy! She can take *more!*" he shouted.

Bo was forced to violently grab Jia by her hair; and repeatedly punch her in the face. Jia screamed, and tried to block the horrific assault.

"No! Stop!" Cameron screamed.

Cameron forced himself to fight the intense physical pain, which was flowing throughout his entire body. He fell on his hands and crawled forward. When he was only a few feet away from Troubled Times, Cameron forced himself to lurch upwards. He hit Troubled Times with a diving shoulder tackle! Troubled Times landed on his left side, quickly rolled away, and sprang to his feet. Troubled Times was surprised that he had lost control of his foe. Cameron coughed heavily and tried crawling back to help Vincent.

"Fine. Let's see if you're *really* the tough motherfuckers that everyone says!" Troubled Times yelled.

Troubled Times delivered a strong right kick to Cameron's stomach. The blow knocked Cameron off of his knees and made him gasp for air. Cameron rolled onto his right side, and was momentarily disabled. Vincent rushed forward and tried punching Troubled Times. He swiftly ducked Vincent's sweeping, left handed punch. Troubled Times jabbed Vincent in his stomach, which made Vincent stumble backwards.

Vincent quickly recovered and continued fighting. He kicked Troubled Times in his shins. Troubled Times absorbed the attacks and countered with a powerful standing kick. Troubled Times used his left forearm, to block Vincent's right handed hay maker. Vincent tried throwing a left handed uppercut to Troubled Times' stomach. Troubled Times swung his right forearm downward, which blocked the attack. Vincent quickly used a series of alternating jabs, with his left and right hands. Troubled Times dodged and weaved.

Troubled Times avoided being stricken by using his incredible speed. His heightened sense of awareness, enhanced by his brainwave amplifier, hastened his reaction to his opponent's assault. Vincent unleashed another series of powerful punches. One of Vincent's fists eventually connected with Troubled Times' nose. Troubled Times' head quickly snapped back. Troubled Times responded by delivering a hard frontward kick with his right foot. Troubled Times moved so fast that Vincent could not block or dodge the attack. Vincent was pushed backwards by the devastating blow. His body made a loud thud, when it hit the ground. Vincent coughed and clutched his stomach.

Cameron tried lunging at Troubled Times while his back was turned. Without even turning to face him, Troubled Times whipped his torso around, and performed a defensive palm strike. Cameron was forced to block, which interrupted his movement. Troubled Times twisted his torso in the opposite direction, and used his palm to deliver the same type of strike. Cameron blocked using both of his hands. Troubled Times pivoted his body, and delivered a chipping sideways kick with his right leg while he was turning. Cameron had difficultly blocking the attack. He was forced to absorb the blow by using his right leg. Troubled Times followed through with his left leg, and executed a powerful roundhouse kick.

Cameron was barely able to block the kick. Troubled Times immediately followed up with a powerful right handed punch. Cameron blocked with his left hand, and tried countering with a strong right punch of his own. Troubled Times swatted Cameron's hand away by swinging up his left forearm. Cameron yelled, and angrily lunged forward. In a desperate attempt to inflict damage, Cameron threw a strong flurry of forceful alternating punches. Troubled Times gracefully stepped backwards, while flippantly swatting away Cameron's fists. Cameron was exasperated; and tried kicking Troubled Times in his left shin with his right foot.

Troubled Times countered by bashing his right knee into Cameron's foot. Cameron tried the same tactic using his left leg. Again, Troubled Times countered the attack. Cameron threw a hay maker with his left arm. Troubled Times stepped sideways into the attack. He entangled Cameron's left arm with his right one. He pounded Cameron's chest three times with his left fist. After the third strike Troubled Times pushed down on Cameron's arm, which caused him to bend forward. Troubled Times took his right knee and smashed it into Cameron's face. Cameron's torso was immediately driven upwards. He lost his balance and fell to the ground. Troubled Times proudly walked around and laughed. He raised his hands upward and taunted his battered adversaries.

"Am I supposed to be impressed?" Troubled Times arrogantly asked.

Inside of the Rigor building, Walter and Paul were inspecting laboratories, one at a time. They came upon the old room, which both Webster and Times had used to confine each other. Walter was still recording video.

"Look at this bed. It has shackles. They strapped people to this, and held them here against their will!" Paul said.

"This is like something out of a movie. I've only read about this kind of stuff in science fiction novels," Eiji said.

"Actually, this is exactly what I would expect to find. Remember I told you guys about MK-Zero? These are the exact tactics that they utilized. The experiments performed in this lab, are frighteningly sadistic. But they correlate with the information I've read, about MK-Zero," Walter stated.

"I agree. This is MK-Zero on steroids," Paul said.

Lucia had finally calmed her nerves. She was watching newscasts on the living room's holographic television.

"Hey guys, look what they're reporting!" Lucia exclaimed.

Lucia waved her hand upward, which raised the television's volume. Lucia, Eiji, and Sky, watched the helicopter's live footage. The Uncanihound was still patrolling the studio's perimeter. It diligently prevented any entry into the edifice.

"We have confirmed that two members of the terrorist cell known as The Icons, were seen entering the building! We have received footage taken moments ago, from inside the CNA studio. We've had to cut the audio and apply a gray video filter, so we will not further disseminate Troubled Times' weapon. We will now show you our exclusive footage, of this highly disturbing development!" the reporter said.

The newscast cut to a short black-and-white video clip, of Troubled Times pummeling Cameron and Vincent. The video paused on a still frame of Troubled Times gloating over his foes. The video zoomed out and was placed in a small window, near the screen's upper right hand corner. The broadcast continued streaming live footage from the chopper.

The reporter said, "It appears that these extremists are now working together! Our analysts can confirm, that the terror organization called The Icons, has combined forces with Troubled Times–"

"Do they think people are fucking stupid?! They just played the damn video! It's obvious that they are trying to *stop* Troubled Times, not *join* him!" Sky yelled with rage.

"That's why nobody with a brain, believes these lying propagandists. They should all be ashamed to call themselves professional journalists. The truth doesn't matter to them. They will only promote the version of a story that fits their agenda. They don't care if the video evidence contradicts that story," Lucia said with disgust.

"This is more ridiculous than their explanation, for why World Commerce Center building seven imploded into its own footprint, at free fall speed," Eiji said.

"We should leave. We already have a ton of evidence. We don't have our guns to protect ourselves, and we can't predict what else we'll encounter," Paul said.

"I agree. Let's grab whatever we can carry, and get back to the van. We have to escape from the city," Walter said.

Walter and Paul took several final video recordings of the underground laboratory. They ran back through the corridors, ascended the ladder, and escaped Rigor's nightmarish torture dungeon.

Inside of the studio, Cameron and Vincent were still locked in a vicious battle, with a herculean adversary.

"Are you ready to become believers in anarchy? Have you suffered enough, to finally realize the error of your ways?" Troubled Times smugly asked.

"Fuck you!" Cameron shouted.

Cameron swiftly ran towards Troubled Times. Vincent did the same, and they simultaneously attacked their opponent. A heap of body parts collided with one another. Cameron used his forearm to smash Troubled Times in the back of his head. Troubled Times easily absorbed the blow. He countered by swinging his right arm around, and backhanding Cameron in the side of his face. Troubled Times avoided Vincent's left handed punch, by ducking. He mercilessly punched Vincent in his stomach. Cameron stood behind Troubled Times. He connected a hard right handed punch to Troubled Times' right side. The powerful impact caught Troubled Times off guard. Troubled Times spun around, and assaulted Cameron with a devastating series of hay maker punches.

Cameron winced in pain while blocking the vicious strikes. Cameron saw an opportunity to counterattack. He jumped backward, when Troubled Times lunged at him. Cameron used his right leg to roundhouse kick Troubled Times in his stomach. Troubled Times stumbled, and instinctively grabbed his abdomen. Vincent seized the opportunity, to place Troubled Times in a choke hold. Troubled Times struggled to break free from Vincent's grasp.

Cameron ran forward with the intention of walloping his enemy. Troubled Times grabbed Vincent's forearms, pushed backwards, and extended both of his legs. The acrobatic move collided Troubled Times' feet, with Cameron's chin. Cameron grabbed his jaw, and was momentarily dazed. Troubled Times used both of his elbows, to jab Vincent's side. In one smooth motion, Troubled Times tucked his body, and flipped Vincent over his shoulders. Vincent lost his grip, and grunted heavily when he landed on his back. Troubled Times jabbed Vincent in his throat, which made Vincent gasp for air. Cameron screamed, and dove at Troubled Times' legs. He knocked Troubled Times down. Troubled Times quickly rolled away, and began rising from the floor. Cameron seized the opportunity to attack him from behind.

Cameron grabbed Troubled Times and tried putting him in a headlock. Troubled Times flicked his head backwards, and knocked Cameron in his nose. Troubled Times followed this action, by elbowing Cameron in his right side. Troubled Times pivoted to his right, and escaped Cameron's grasp. He used his right hand to punch Cameron several times in his kidneys. The brutal attack, made Cameron keel over on his right knee. Vincent tried to tackle Troubled Times by ducking his head and rushing forward.

Troubled Times rolled over Vincent's back, and flipped over him to avoid the maneuver. Troubled Times quickly regained his balance. He was momentarily stunned when Cameron hit him in his face three times with alternating left and right handed jabs. Troubled Times blocked Cameron's fourth shot, with his left arm. He used his right fist, to smash Cameron's face. Cameron instinctively grabbed his mouth. Troubled Times used this opportunity to punch Cameron several times in his abdomen.

Cameron bent forward and clutched his midsection. Troubled Times grabbed Cameron by his neck. He squeezed hard and walked Cameron back a few paces. He placed his right leg in back of Cameron's. Troubled Times tripped Cameron's leg and shoved him by his neck. Cameron was instantly knocked to the ground. Vincent leaped over Cameron, and threw a series of fast punches at Troubled Times. Troubled Times continuously blocked the majority of blows, using his forearms and hands. Several punches grazed Troubled Times' face, chest, and midriff. The barrage did not seem to cause any significant damage. Vincent moved closer; and attempted to drive his right knee into Troubled Times' groin. This was a poor decision. Troubled Times countered by hooking Vincent's knee with his left arm. He knocked Vincent off balance, by pushing against his chest with his right hand. Vincent fell to the floor and groaned in agony.

"Your fighting abilities are atrocious. Your inutility is deplorable," Troubled Times derisively said.

Troubled Times casually walked around the two warriors. He exultantly displayed his dominance over them. Cameron rushed to Vincent's aid and helped him sit upright.

"You okay?" Cameron asked.

"I'm hurt, man. This guy is intense," Vincent replied.

Cameron helped Vincent rise to his feet.

"I know. I never imagined he'd be so strong," Cameron said.

"Why are you making this so difficult? Why are you willing to throw away your lives for a group of strangers, who don't even care about you?" Troubled Times asked the men.

"It's not about saving one person, or one billion people! It's about upholding morals, and being honorable! You have no right to decide who lives, and who dies!" Cameron said.

Troubled Times gazed upon the frightened people, who were watching this magnificent event unfold.

"People make those types of decisions, every day. How am I any more Mephistophelean than them?" Troubled Times asked.

Cameron made a bold decision, and tried to reason with Troubled Times.

"Are you speaking about the health care death panels, that euthanized you and Mallory's children, Gregory?" Cameron asked.

Troubled Times felt a blinding rage, boil in his blood. He slowly turned to face Cameron.

"What did you just say to me?" Troubled Times asked with disbelief.

"You heard me, Gregory. I'm right. Aren't I? That is why you are so angry, and want to hurt people. You never had a chance to properly grieve for the loss of your family. You want everyone to feel helpless and insignificant; the same way you felt, the day the government murdered your children," Cameron calmly said.

Troubled Times' whole body began shaking with fury.

"How dare you. You don't know anything about me," Troubled Times coldly said.

Cameron knew that Nathan was right. Gregory and Troubled Times are the same person.

Cameron softly said, "This won't bring them back, Gregory. You're hatred will only destroy you, if you give in to darkness, and pain. Please, let us help yo–"

"YOU DON'T FUCKING KNOW ME!" Troubled Times loudly shouted.

Troubled Times pointed his right index finger at Cameron and Vincent. He caused their ears to ring in an excruciatingly uncomfortable manner. Troubled Times ran forward and strongly backhanded Vincent, which made Vincent fall to the ground. Troubled Times punched Cameron in his abdomen so hard that Cameron dropped to his knees. Cameron trembled uncontrollably, while pain coursed through his entire body.

"Stop! You *must* listen to reason!" Cameron yelled.

Troubled Times said, "Shut up, you motherfucker! You think *you* have any idea, what it means to experience *pain?* You think *you've* seen darkness? You haven't seen *shit!* Let me show you. Let me show you, why I am so fucking troubled!"

Troubled Times placed his right hand on top of Cameron's head. He began performing the same neural overload, which he had used to kill Webster. Cameron felt his entire skull rattle. The electrodes in his brain were burdened by an influx of electrical impulses. Cameron screamed when terrible images from his own past vividly formed themselves in his mind's eye. He remembered seeing his parent's fighting, over not having enough to eat when he was a child. He recalled the day that he was sickened, after receiving a mandatory flu vaccine when he was in high school.

Cameron envisioned the first time he participated in a foot riot, when hungry looters set fire to a GMO food truck. He recalled memories of the numerous battles that had taken place over the last several months. Images of screaming burn victims on the NJ Turnpike, raced through his mind. Gunshots from the drone battle in Manville rang loudly in his ears. He smelled the sweat and blood in the dirty cage during his torture on The Yard. Cameron felt himself losing consciousness. Cameron's chest tightened and he cried out in agony.

"You are close now, Doctor Serenity. You can feel it, can't you? All the suffering and hardship you've experienced, and caused others to experience, is coming back to you. Soon you will succumb to negativity, despair, and pain. You will merge with the darkness, and be cleansed by anarchy," Troubled Times said.

Cameron felt his overworked heart pumping blood, too fast through his veins. Cameron gasped for air, and knew that he was about to die. With all the strength in his body, he forced himself to stop recalling such abominable images. Cameron willed himself to resist Troubled Times' powerful brainwave manipulator. Instead of remembering the bad experiences he had endured, he filled his mind with memories of happier occasions. He recalled the time that his father taught him to ride a bicycle, when he was six. He remembered the first time he kissed a girl, when he was thirteen.

Cameron remembered when he tasted his first bite of organic ham, on his twenty-first birthday. He recalled meeting Walter at a food protest, on a cold night, eight years ago. He remembered Lily, and how strong she was to have survived a drone attack. He remembered Sky's beauty. He remembered how he loved her laughter, kindness and soft, gentle spirit. These memories gave Cameron a superhuman strength. He let out a powerful scream that emanated deep from within his soul. Cameron raised his right arm, clenched his fist, and smashed it down upon Troubled Times' forearm!

Troubled Times howled in pain, and released Cameron from his grip. Troubled Times grabbed his forearm with his left hand and stumbled backwards. Cameron fell forward and took several deep breaths, but he did not rest for long. Cameron seized this open window of opportunity, and immediately took decisive action.

"Vestige, get all these people out of here! Evacuate the building!" Doctor Serenity yelled.

Cameron pulled himself to his feet. He sprinted forward, tucked his shoulders, and tackled

Troubled Times. They hit the ground with tremendous force. Both men were dazed, and wobbled while they began standing.

Troubled Times muttered, "How, how–?"

He did not have time to finish speaking. Cameron used his right hand to repeatedly uppercut Troubled Times' ribs. He ended the flurry by smacking Troubled Times' face, with a powerful left hook. Troubled Times grabbed his cheek, and staggered to his right. Vincent promptly retrieved the discarded weapons. He looked at Bo and Jia, while securing the guns.

"Let's go! We're leaving!" Vincent loudly shouted at them.

Bo and Jia immediately fled from behind the desk. Audience members, who had been terrorized for hours, arose from their seats. Several people had to be helped out of the bleachers by fellow patrons. All those who were still fortunate enough to be alive, began orderly evacuating the theatre.

"The door is over there! Use the stairwell!" Vincent yelled at the crowd.

Vincent assisted people out of the room, and assured them that they were safe. He looked up at the control booth, and addressed the remaining people.

"Leave! You're free! Get out of here, while he's distracted!" Vincent said.

The Vestige gracefully assumed leadership, and courageously helped the large crowd escape to safety.

Cameron and Troubled Times continued waging a spectacular battle. Troubled Times threw a wild swinging punch with his left hand. Cameron blocked the punch with his right arm. He countered by using his left hand to twice jab Troubled Times in his face. Troubled Times stumbled for a moment, but quickly regained his footing. Cameron swung around with his right arm and hoped to land a powerful blow. Troubled Times blocked with his left arm, and entangled their limbs. Cameron knew that Troubled Times would break his arm if he did not quickly react.

Cameron jerked his arm to his right side, and pulled it closer to his body. Troubled Times refused to release Cameron's appendage, but this worked in Cameron's favor. Cameron continued his motion, which made Troubled Times stagger to his left. With his left hand, Cameron dealt a punishing strike to Troubled Times' chin. Troubled Times released his grip but was not deterred. He countered by performing a spinning backhanded punch.

Cameron blocked the attack with both of his hands. Troubled Times continued rotating, and subsequently followed with a strong, left handed hay maker. The punch struck Cameron across his face, which momentarily stunned him. With lighting fast speed and agility, Troubled Times leaped into the air. He arced his body into a crescent shape. He grabbed Cameron by the padding around his shoulders. Troubled Times stiffened his body and flipped over Cameron. Cameron felt his feet rise from the ground.

While somersaulting over Cameron, Troubled Times extended his feet to brace his fall. Troubled Times used his momentum, to toss Cameron over his head. Cameron's whole body vertically rotated one hundred eighty degrees. Cameron slammed face first into the floor. Cameron was seriously hurt, but he did not quit fighting. Cameron stood up and ran towards his mighty opponent. Troubled Times extended his arm and strongly pointed his right index finger at Cameron.

"Suffer! Submit!" Troubled Times shouted.

Cameron's blood boiled like hot lava in his veins. He briefly stopped moving, while the unbearable ringing sensation furiously pounded his ears. Cameron fought through the pain, and continued running. Troubled Times stepped forward and kicked Cameron in his chest. Cameron was catapulted backwards. He landed hard, but quickly pounced back to his feet. He used both of his hands to make a motion, which disrespectfully indicated that Cameron wanted Troubled Times to move in his direction. Troubled Times became furious at this mockery; and rushed to attack him.

Troubled Times flung his right arm and tried upper cutting Cameron. The attack was skillfully prevented when Cameron rapidly swooped his left hand down, and pushed away his aggressor's arm. Troubled Times threw a fast left hook, which Cameron blocked using his right forearm. Cameron countered by punching Troubled Times' body several times. Cameron ended his alternating quick punches, with a hard strike to Troubled Times' jaw. Troubled Times was weakened, and was forced to fall upon his right knee. Troubled Times recovered and slowly stood upright.

"You're defeated, Times. You've got to stop this charade," Cameron said.

"Not before I take you to *Hell!*" Troubled Times screamed.

Troubled Times lunged at Cameron, and tried to strike him with a series of fast punches. Cameron gracefully blocked the assault, using his forearms and hands. Cameron interrupted Troubled Times' barrage with a quick left handed jab. Cameron continued his offense by dealing Troubled Times two hard, right handed punches. Troubled Times instinctively grabbed his face. Cameron jumped forward, and shoved his right knee into Troubled Times' midsection. Troubled Times bent forward, and Cameron smashed his right elbow into Troubled Times' back.

Troubled Times dropped to his knees. Cameron kicked Troubled Times in his ribs incredibly hard. Troubled Times rolled onto his right side. Troubled Times burned with rage. He arose from the ground, released a monstrous scream, and swiftly ran at Cameron. Troubled Times threw a series of powerful overhead strikes at him. Troubled Times grunted while violently swooping his forearms down at Cameron. The hurricane of punches was difficult for Cameron to defend. Cameron had to continuously step back to avoid being overwhelmed.

Cameron fluidly raised his arms to prevent the blows from hitting him. Troubled Times did not relent. He continued alternating his attacking limb, until his left forearm finally smashed into the top of Cameron's head. Cameron was stunned and thrown off balance. Troubled Times stayed on the offense. He quickly decked Cameron across his right cheek, which further disoriented Cameron. Troubled Times pointed his left finger at him.

"Equilibrium disruptor!" Troubled Times shouted.

Cameron felt a painful vibration flow through his entire body. He heard a low humming noise inside of his head. Cameron began feeling dizzy, and nauseous. He was briefly compelled to shut his eyes. He shook his head erratically and desperately attempted to recover his equanimity. Cameron quickly regained his vision, but was immediately stricken with panic. The entire room looked like it was swirling and shaking. Even more alarming, was the fact that he saw seven different instances of Troubled Times!

The six hallucinations stood in a hemicycle around their origin. The apparitions and their leader began walking around Cameron. Troubled Times laughed manically, while Cameron felt wild anxiety. Cameron gasped and blinked several times. Cameron tapped his fist against the right side of his head. His worries increased, when Cameron realized that the counterfeit clones were not dissipating. Troubled Times chuckled with mirth, at Cameron's obvious exasperation.

"What's the matter, Doctor? You look a little...*confused!*" he arrogantly asked.

Troubled Times smashed his fist into Cameron's right knee. Cameron screamed in agony.

Troubled Times used Cameron's disorientation, to strike him with three more punches. Troubled Times began by punching Cameron in his left side. He instantly repeated his attack upon the right side of Cameron's rib cage. He finished this battery by strongly upper cutting Cameron's jaw with his left hand. Cameron toppled sideways and hit the floor. Troubled Times, and his imaginary body doubles, paced around a wildly confounded Cameron. Troubled Times reached down with both hands.

He mockingly said, "For someone who claims to be serene..."

In an amazing feat of strength, he lifted Cameron by his collar and belt. Troubled Times hoisted Cameron high above his head.

"...you don't look very *calm!*"

Troubled Times finished his sentence, while throwing Cameron thirty feet across the room! Cameron crashed into the extravagant news anchor's desk, and it shattered underneath his weight. Cameron was absolutely devastated by the punishing maneuver. He rolled around in broken glass and wood. The fragments scratched his protective armor. Cameron knew that he had to immediately stop Troubled Times from maintaining his advantage. Cameron fought through all the painful sensations flowing through his entire body, and forced himself to stand. He limped around, and exaggerated his injury. Troubled Times ran forward in a crooked motion. His specters appeared to dash in multiple directions.

Cameron strafed to his right, and activated his Muscle's millimeter scanner. Cameron swept his forearm in front of his body. The wavelength reflecting technology allowed Cameron to dissipate the phony images of Troubled Times! Cameron hurried his pace to a light jog, and continued sweeping his forearm. As he was moving the Muscle to his right, the light fixated on a solid object. Cameron saw the real Troubled Times clearly x-rayed by the device!

Troubled Times had almost reached Cameron. He flung his right arm and tried striking Cameron in his neck. Cameron immediately dropped to his knees. He slid forward and smashed his right forearm, into Troubled Times' right shin. Troubled Times was tripped off of his feet. He did not have time to brace his fall, and landed on his face. Troubled Times pulled himself to his knees. He pounded his left fist into the floor three times. Troubled Times sprang to his feet.

"You're fucking *dead!*" Troubled Times shouted.

Cameron assumed a defensive stance, while Troubled Times moved closer. He wildly swung his left fist at Cameron's face. He ducked and punched Troubled Times in the side of his pelvis. Troubled Times grunted in agony. He clasped both of his hands together, and tried smashing Cameron's head. Cameron put up both of his hands, and stopped the attack. He continued pushing his arms' weight down upon Cameron. The two men briefly contested each other's strength.

The vigorous combat had driven both men beyond the point of exhaustion. Their flesh was bruised, and swollen. Their muscles quivered with exhaustion. Immense pain, shot through every bone in their body. Troubled Times' overuse of his telekinetic headband was starting to short circuit his neurological pathways. His once unrelenting attacks had lost their fury. Cameron knew that this was the moment of verity. Cameron released a warrior's roar, and used all of his strength to push Troubled Times' arms away. Troubled Times was thrown backwards.

Cameron wasted no time unleashing a relentless onslaught. Cameron began throwing a series of punishing hay makers. Troubled Times' head bounced around like a basketball, when the alternating punches struck his face. Troubled Times was forced to stumble backwards. This poor decision placed his back against a wall. Cameron did not yield his assault. He continued punching Troubled

Times in his face, chest, and stomach.

Troubled Times was so exhausted that he could not defend himself against the brutal punishment. Cameron smashed his right forearm, into Troubled Times' face. He immediately performed the same move with his left forearm. Cameron followed with a hard right handed hook to Troubled Times' abdomen. He repeated the attack with his left hand. Cameron shoved his right knee, into Troubled Times' ribcage. He quickly did the same with his left knee. Cameron pivoted three hundred sixty degrees, on his left foot. He raised his right leg, and ended the combination with a spinning roundhouse kick to Troubled Times' chest!

Troubled Times fell to his left side, and hit the floor with a loud thud. Troubled Times slowly sat up and rested his weary back against the wall. Troubled Times breathed heavily and knew that he could no longer fight. Troubled Times brushed away his hat. He pulled the mask from his bloody, swollen face. Times reached into his coat pocket, and removed his medicine bottle. He lifted the cap, and chugged several pills.

"Now I know...I know why...why they all believe in you," Times begrudgingly said.

Doctor Serenity slowly removed his mask. He saw the headband that Times wore atop his head. He reached down and delicately removed the device.

"Is this your secret weapon? Is this what you use, to control people?" Cameron asked.

Times grinned sadistically.

"You should...wear it, Doctor. It will...give you great power," Times said.

Times tilted the bottle to his mouth, and consumed more pills. Cameron held the band in his hands, and was humbled by its potential power. It was one of the most powerful, and dangerous technologies, the world had ever seen. Deep down inside, Cameron knew that Times was right. He thought about the positive influence that he could affect, using this awesome ability. Cameron genuinely considered using it, for the Freedom and Liberty Movement's benefit. Cameron stared at the device for a few more seconds.

"This, can never give me true power," Cameron decisively said.

Cameron held the device by its tips, and snapped it in half. Cameron placed the pieces, inside of his belt buckle.

"Real power comes from being honorable, trustworthy, and righteous. Any person will discover this truth when he chooses to fight injustice, corruption, and tyranny in all its forms," Cameron said.

"A fool's dream. You will *never* defeat the system, you so strongly seek to abolish. It's bigger than you. I've seen Hell. It is all around us," Times said.

"That remains to be seen," Cameron said.

Cameron extended his hand and offered to help Times rise from the ground. Times angrily slapped away Cameron's hand. Cameron repeated the gesture. Times defiantly spat at him. He did not again offer Times assistance.

"I remember you. I saw you on the pier that day, during the shooting. You weren't in control of yourself, at that time. You sounded frightened, and lost. Even with your incredible power, you still don't seem to be making your own decisions. What made you become such a vile, wicked person?" Cameron said.

Times smiled and coldly said, "You should have worn the device."

Times swallowed another pill. Cameron knew that he was not going to have a rational conversation with Times.

Cameron took a deep breath and said, "I hope that one day, you find your true human spirit. I hope that you can atone for what you did, and make peace with your anger. I don't know what happened to make you so troubled, or if we will ever know what turned you into a hollow, empty, shell of a man. What I *do* know is that history will remember you, as nothing more than a vicious psychopath. Your name will be eternally cursed. Like every other murderous tyrant who preceded you, your petty quest for dominance has failed. I feel sorry for you, Gregory. You are a victim."

Cameron took one last look at the man who called himself Troubled Times. Cameron turned around when he heard the sound of heavy footsteps. Two humanoid DHS robots had entered the room. Their transport drone hovered outside of the floor's broken window. The robots approached Cameron, and pointed their laser rifles at his chest. Cameron dropped to his knees, held his hands upward and out to his side.

One of the robots said, "Hostile terrorist appears to be surrendering. Extermination protocol, possibly unnecessary. Proceed with detention."

33 Embracing Tomorrow

"May I see him?" asked the well-dressed man.

The guard outside of the interrogation room said, "I'm really surprised that your request was approved. Yeah, you can enter."

The guard placed his palm against the door's biometric scanner. A second later, it slid open.

The guard said, "Listen, he's a dangerous man. You might want to–"

"It's all right. There will not be any issues," the well-dressed man said.

The well-dressed man walked into the room, and saw Cameron sitting in a chair. In front of him, was a rectangular table. Another chair was placed across from him. The well-dressed man walked over to the unoccupied chair.

"How are you feeling, Mister Moss?" he asked.

Cameron marveled at the impeccably dressed man. The man spoke with a thick English accent. His voice had a crisp bass tone. He wore a dark blue suit, and white collared shirt. His ocean blue tie matched the color of his eyes. The man was tall, and athletic. He looked like he could run for miles without tiring. His extraordinarily handsome face was smooth shaven. His ravishing, neatly cropped hair was a light shade of brown.

Cameron said, "I already told your boys, I'm not talking. The video speaks for itself and–"

"I'm not with the bobbies," the English man quickly interrupted.

"Oh...well, what do you want?" Cameron asked.

"I wanted to personally thank you, for saving my life," he said.

Cameron was completely confused.

"Saving your...what are you talking about, dude?" he asked.

The well-dressed English man slowly pulled the empty chair away from the table. He comfortably sat upright, while maintaining impeccable posture.

"My name is Alistor Beaumont DeMarcco. Eighty-eight people were rescued from the telestation, with you and your friend's help," the man said.

Cameron proudly said to himself, "He got them out," before asking Alistor, "What's today's date?"

"July ninth, Wednesday," Alistor replied.

"Damn. I can't believe it has been four days, since the robots locked me in solitary," Cameron said.

"How did you like Chompie? I'm impressed you were able to operate him so effectively, using a computer interface. That particular model is not designed to bind with human DNA. It makes the entire command process, a bit less precise. They respond much better using bio-interfaces. Forgive me, I'm rambling," Alistor said.

"Do you want to explain anything that you just said to me?" Cameron asked.

Alistor laughed and said, "I call our Uncanihounds, Chompies. One of the early prototypes was a replication of a poodle. It used to run around our chateau, constantly biting all the furniture. Father had not yet perfected its Emergency Response Logic. Every time we let our cell phones run out of battery power, Chompie would eat his way through any non-carbon object that stood in his path; trying to find the source of the terminated signal. My mother would get so huffy. She always complained that they wouldn't stop chomping. That's why I gave them that name. I'm sorry, I digress."

Cameron paused for a moment, when it dawned on him the importance of the man, to whom he was speaking.

"DeMarcco? Like, from *the* DeMarcco family?" he asked.

Alistor smiled and replied, "Yes. It's not that big a deal, really."

Cameron slapped the table.

"Not a big deal? Dude, your dad was a damn *rock* star! Every nerdy kid who loved science wanted to be like him! Wait, I thought you were supposed to be..." he excitedly said.

Cameron abruptly stopped speaking. He did not know if he would upset Alistor, by questioning his tragic past.

"Yes. I've heard all the stories and rumors. Am I alive? Am I dead? Some have claimed that I am nothing but a deformed trust fund baby; who lives atop a floating castle replete with gold. They say I remain hidden from the world because I am a hideous, grotesque, monstrosity," Alistor said.

"I'm sorry. I didn't mean any offense. I'm still in shock. It has been a wild past few months; and it's hard to have a real conversation while we're in this wiretapped room," Cameron said.

"I understand. I've lived in my own personal prison for twenty-seven years. My first public interview in almost three decades was scheduled to occur last Friday, at CNA," Alistor said.

"Wow, that's incredible! Yeah, I think that would have been more interesting, than what they aired. Television wasn't very good that day," Cameron said.

Alistor could tell Cameron was making a sarcastic joke.

He joined Cameron by saying, "Really? Well some people would disagree. It's not every day that one gets to watch ordinary men, save the world."

Cameron talked over Alistor and said, "Naw, it was ridiculous experimental programming. Not very good. Stupid, really. Bunch of guys running around in masks."

Alistor laughed briefly and said, "You have a good sense of humor, Cameron Moss. Being able to laugh is very important, these days."

"I agree," Cameron solemnly said.

"The little girl...have you seen her since the incident?" Alistor calmly asked.

Cameron was shocked that Alistor would ask about Lily.

"I...can't talk about her," Cameron said.

"I understand. That's all right. From what I hear, she is doing very well. On Monday, the state granted custody to her mother. Tragically, they were not able to save her arm," Alistor said.

Cameron did not know what to say. He stared down at the table for a moment.

"I'm glad that she survived," Cameron finally said.

Cameron was overwhelmed by an influx of different emotions. He felt joy, pride, exhaustion, pain, anger, sorrow, and happiness all at once. He put his hands to his face. He released two, short, emotional screams of frustration. He quickly composed himself and slowly lowered his hands.

Cameron said, "I'm sorry. I–"

"It's all right. I only ask, because I was hoping to help her," Alistor said.

"How?" Cameron asked.

Alistor reached into his suit's right breast pocket. He removed an index card, and gracefully slid it across the table.

"That's my personal contact information. Call me any time," Alistor said.

"Thank you, Alistor. That's a really kind gesture," Cameron appreciatively said.

Cameron was confused why Alistor had not delivered this information to Paul. But Cameron remained silent, because he did not want to say anything that would endanger the Branson family's safety. He had been in isolation for four days, without contact from the outside world. He had not even known that Vincent had successfully rescued the hostages.

"Well, I won't keep you from your business. I'm sure you have a lot that you want to accomplish," Alistor said.

"I wouldn't worry about bothering me. I don't think I'm going anywhere," Cameron said.

Alistor smiled and said, "They haven't told you? That's peculiar. It has been all over the news. All right then, I won't spoil the surprise."

Alistor stood up and extended his right hand. Cameron noticed it was covered by a thin blue glove. Cameron arose, and shook Alistor's hand. Alistor had an extremely firm grip, but his hand felt surprisingly cold.

Before he could respond Alistor said, "It has been a pleasure speaking with you, Mister Moss."

Alistor released Cameron's hand and exited the room.

Several moments later, Warden Tina Schawles entered the room. Warden Schawles sat down across from Cameron and cleared her throat.

"Governor Hawthorne feels, in light of recent events, that it would best serve public interest if you were temporarily released on parole; pending the outcome of your appeal," Warden Schawles said.

"You're saying...you're saying that I can leave?" Cameron asked with shock.

"For now, yes. You may leave. The officer outside will explain the release process. He will also take you to retrieve the belongings, which we are allowing you to keep," Warden Schawles replied.

Cameron knew that his gun, and Muscle, would be confiscated. However that was not important at this moment. He was simply happy to be a free man. Cameron picked up Alistor's card, and started walking out of the room. Warden Schawles spoke to him before he left.

"Cameron?" she asked.

He glanced over his left shoulder.

"Yeah?" Cameron replied.

"I like your mask," Warden Schawles said.

The Warden tried to repress her smile. Cameron grinned before he exited. Forty-five minutes later he was escorted to the prison's front gate. He held two duffel bags that contained his clothes, body armor, and even his custom built mask; that was now a truly iconic symbol of heroism. Cameron smiled as the gates opened. He walked towards the two men who were standing in front of a small, worn out, pickup truck.

"Good Lord, Paul. Look! It is Doctor Serenity, in the flesh! How are you doing today, good Doctor?" Walter happily asked.

Walter playfully bowed, like he was saluting a man of high stature. Cameron rolled his eyes and felt embarrassed.

"Oh, please. Enough with the superhero shit! I'm retired! I'm never again putting on that mask!" Cameron said.

"Never, say never," Paul said with a wide grin.

Cameron dropped his bags. The men gave each other a strong group hug.

"Glad to see they released you guys," Cameron said.

"Yes, it's wonderful! They even gave Paul, an exemption to the One Child Mandate! They said his situation met the 'extraordinary circumstances' requirement...whatever that means," Walter said.

"CEA wouldn't have even found out about my other children, if Lily hadn't accidentally told a nurse about her sister, Abby. Doreen didn't officially admit to having more kids, but she still accepted the exemption," Paul said.

"I'm so happy to hear that they're safe. Have you spoken to our...assistants?" Cameron cautiously asked.

Paul and Walter knew that Cameron was referring to their military companions.

"Paul and I left the city without them. We didn't want to put them at further risk. They had already given us an incredible amount of aid. After we escaped from Rigor, we told them to bail. We got snagged at the Brooklyn Bridge, when we tried to sneak past border patrol," Walter said.

"Damn. I wanted to thank them," Cameron said.

"I'm sure that one day, we will get that chance," Walter said.

"Okay, enough with the small talk. We have to go eat!" Paul said.

Paul, Walter, and Cameron, entered the pickup truck and drove back to the Newark compound.

"Oh, good Lord! I never thought I'd be so happy to see this dingy old pile of bricks!" Cameron said as they rolled into the compound's parking lot.

Paul parked the truck. Cameron saw Eiji, Lucia, Vincent, Sky, and the entire Branson family, was standing outside and anxiously awaiting their arrival. Lucia ran to Cameron and hugged him.

"Bienvenido a casa, hermano!" Lucia said.

"Moochie gracie me, uhh...girla?" Cameron said.

Lucia playfully punched Cameron in his shoulder.

"Oh Cameron, you really need to learn Spanish!" Lucia replied.

"I'm absolutely ecstatic. I never thought I'd see any of you again, in my entire life. Is it true what Walter was telling me, during the ride? Did you really find out that Rigor was conducting MK-Zero experiments?" Cameron said.

"Hell yeah, we did! Walt and Paul infiltrated Rigor like stealth ninjas! They found all types of twisted science projects," Eiji said.

"It gets even better. There are some high level public officials that are righteously pissed! They are actually talking about indicting people," Vincent added.

"We are still leaking documents, and videos. A lot more information will be revealed to the public. This is going to be a national news story, for quite some time," Lucia said.

"Incredible. I'm so proud of all you Icons," Cameron said.

A beautiful young woman pushed her way to the front of the crowd. Her hair reflected the mid-day sunlight. Her bright red lipstick matched her dress' color. Her tight pink shirt, accentuated her womanly figure. Cameron held out his arms, and passionately embraced her. They shared a deeply intimate kiss.

"I love you, Sky. I love you so much," Cameron said.

"I love you, Cameron," Sky immediately said while staring into his hazel eyes.

"Eww, gross!" Lily playfully said.

The group erupted with laughter.

"Come on, let's get some food. I haven't had a decent meal in months!" Paul said.

The reunited family and friends walked into the crumbling old building. No longer was it a den of criminal activity. It was a place which made them feel safe. It was their home; and was now a command base in the fight for human freedom and liberty.

The group spent the next several hours bonding, while they prepared an organic meal. A grand feast consisting of turkey, potatoes, corn, oranges and squash, was devoured by the hungry group. They sat at a long rectangular table.

"Lord, have mercy! I've never been so full in my entire life!" Paul exclaimed.

"God has truly blessed us with this food, and by bringing us all back together," Doreen said.

Walter raised his glass and said, "A toast. May the future, be brighter than the past."

The group toasted to Walter's inspirational words. Cameron stayed seated for another brief moment.

"I need to stretch my legs. I'll be back," Cameron eventually said.

Cameron arose from the table, and walked out of the compound. The sun had set, and the heat wave had broken. The warm summer air felt wonderful, as it blew against the hair follicles on Cameron's skin.

Cameron leaned against the compound and closed his eyes. It had been a long time since he had heard the calm sound, of peaceful silence. A strong breeze swept across his body. The faint aroma of burning charcoal, wafted through the air. Suddenly a deep voice broke the silence.

"Hello, Cameron," he said.

Cameron opened his eyes. He was shocked to see the Time Shifter standing before him! Cameron raised his fist, and prepared for a confrontation.

"No! Not you! Get away from me!" Cameron shouted.

"Calm down, calm down. I just want to talk," the Time Shifter softly said.

The Time Shifter placed his hand on Cameron's left shoulder. Cameron abruptly shook it off.

"Don't touch me! Do you have any idea what has happened, since the last time you decided to appear? Oh wait...that's a dumb question to ask a damn *time traveler!*" Cameron angrily said.

Cameron took a few steps forward and angrily turned his back on the Time Shifter. Cameron placed his hands on his hips, and looked over his left shoulder.

"Let me ask you a question. Why do you refuse to take action? Why do you stand idly by and let people suffer?" Cameron coldly asked.

"I've told you before, I am not omnipotent," the Time Shifter replied.

Cameron turned around and angrily said, "Why didn't you warn me about everything that was going to happen? You could have told me about the Manville raid! For Christ's sakes, Lily lost her fucking arm! You could have at *least* stopped Troubled fucking *Times!* Do you have any idea how many people he killed?"

Cameron briefly paused.

"What do you want, Rasheed?" he asked.

"I know you think that I am being callous and selfish, but you still do not understand. It is not that simple, Cameron. I must not abuse my abilities. A fast traveler *must* remain an observer of events. It is the only way to prevent a disaster," Rasheed said.

"So you don't think that hundreds of people dead, and a little girl with her fucking arm blown off, is a disaster?" Cameron heatedly asked.

"All suffering is unfortunate," Rasheed said.

Cameron angrily said, "You're unbelievable! That's what you call it, Rasheed? Unfortunate?"

The Time Shifter placed his index and middle finger, against the side of his helmet. His visor slowly opened. For the first time, Cameron saw the face of the mysterious man who called himself Rasheed Wallace, the Time Shifter. He had a well-pronounced, short goatee. The sides of his face were scruffy. The coarse hair upon his head was unkempt and knotted. His dark skin was wrinkled, and tattered with age spots. The most fascinating aspect of his face, were his eyes. Both of his lenses were discolored a dark shade of black. His left pupil was tinted a light hazel color.

The center of his right eye contained a small white dot, where his pupil should have been located. Cameron could not believe how elderly Rasheed appeared. Cameron had personally witnessed Rasheed's marvelous strength. Cameron knew that Rasheed was in wonderful shape, and moved like he was not much older than a teenager. But his face was obviously that of an old Negro gentleman's.

"Yes, it is unfortunate. It is unfortunate that even though you and your allies have sacrificed so much, the world is still not ready to hear your message," Rasheed said.

"Rasheed, what do you mean? People are calling us heroes. They're saying we're responsible for defeating the world's first genetically enhanced super villain. How can you say that we have failed?" Cameron asked.

"You misunderstand me. I am immensely proud of you, Cameron Moss. You are not the angry young man, whom I first battled almost one year ago. You've grown strong. You have achieved a higher consciousness that most people will fail to obtain, even if they lived several life times," Rasheed said.

"So why do you sound hopeless? Why do you incessantly belittle me?" Cameron asked.

"Again, you misunderstand. I am far from hopeless. Hope is one of the emotional constructs, that allows my body to remain intact during the phase shift," Rasheed answered.

Rasheed Wallace pressed the computer embedded in his suit's left forearm. The thin layer of sand, covering the concrete upon which Cameron Moss stood, began vibrating. Particles of dust swept through the air.

"She really is quite beautiful. You are a lucky man, Cameron," said Rasheed.

The Time Shifter's visor closed, while he arose from the ground. The black ashy void swirled in all directions. All visible light, focused upon Rasheed.

"All humans, are beautiful. The universe is manifested by a collection of thoughts. Reality is literally a projection of ideas. Your choices can save this time line. Your inaction will bring it to ruin. It is your duty to help humanity achieve their ultimate destiny; amongst the stars. If you fail, many planets will crumble. If you succeed, entire galaxies will be explored. I anxiously await the outcome of your decisions. I know that incredible blessings are written into your future. Farewell, for now, Cameron Moss," Rasheed said.

The Time Shifter disappeared into the dark, ashy ripple. Cameron closed his eyes, and raised his right forearm; to shield himself from the blinding light. He felt intense heat emanating from the void, into which Rasheed had vanished. Cameron felt his body being pulled towards the ripple. He began screaming in fright. Cameron opened his eyes, and was dumbfounded to see that he was still standing against the compound's wall. He heard a soft female voice speak to him.

"Cam? Cam are you okay?" she asked.

Cameron realized that Sky Solomon was staring at him. She had a concerned look upon her face. Cameron took several deep and panicked breaths. Sky caressed Cameron's face.

"Baby...hey, look at me. What's wrong?" Sky asked.

Cameron calmed himself. He grabbed Sky's waist and pulled her close.

"I'm still...trying to cope with everything," Cameron said.

Cameron passionately kissed Sky upon her soft lips.

"I can't imagine what you're feeling. Nobody should have to endure the hardships that you've faced. You can tell me anything. You know that I am always here for you," Sky lovingly said.

"You are an incredibly strong woman. I do not deserve your love," Cameron said.

Cameron kissed Sky, and held her soft body in his arms. He gazed into her magnificently beautiful green eyes.

"Hey, y'all! Why you hiding? Come inside! Uncle Walt is about to slice the yam cake!" a young girl shouted.

Lily ran over to Sky and Cameron. Her short-sleeved shirt had a patch sewn over its left arm. Even though they wanted to cry, Sky and Cameron smiled at the small, mutilated child. Lily gave Sky a hug.

"You smell like Christmas," Lily said.

Sky laughed and said, "Little miss, what is that supposed to mean?"

Lily giggled and said, "I don't know!"

Lily released Sky, and ran back inside the compound. Sky and Cameron held each other's hands, and followed the little girl. The stars above them flickered brightly. A cool and calming mist, began spreading across the New Jersey terrain.

Epilogue

Mallory caressed her husband's face, while he lay upon the examination table. A large humanoid robot stood in the corner. A frail and elderly doctor was the only other human in the room.

The doctor said, “He has been stagnant for quite some time. His body and brain appear to be functioning normally. It is possible that he will recover from his coma. I believe that I have identified a potential brain tumor. It could be a hemorrhage, or permanent damage from a stroke. There's no way to tell unless I perform a full autopsy. Obviously we can't proceed with the operation, unless you authorize–”

“He is only sleeping. Give him time to rest. He will recover,” Mallory interrupted.

Mallory grasped her husband's cold right hand, with her left one.

“Don't worry. You've fooled everyone, my love. I know that we are still united in chaos. I will not let your sacrifice be in vain. Forever, I am your soul mate. Forever I...am your Malcontentress,” Mallory telepathically communicated to her husband.

Mallory stepped back and began emanating crocodile tears.

“I know people think he is a monster, but he is still my husband. I love him. Please do not take his life,” she said.

The doctor wheezed and said, “Yes, miss. Whatever you wish.”

Mallory walked over to the large door by which the eight foot tall humanoid robot was standing. The robot shot a small non-lethal laser beam at Mallory, which scanned her entire body.

“Biometric scan completed. Target is not determined to be a threat. Lethal force needed to quell potential terrorist, deemed unnecessary at this time. Subject may exit. Have a nice day, ma'am,” the robot said in its artificial voice.

The robot moved out of Mallory's way when the door opened. Mallory pulled down over her eyes, the dark black sunglasses which were previously perched atop her head. She walked down the hallway at a fast pace. Her breasts jiggled obnoxiously because the tight dress which she was wearing, was not appropriately fitted to her body size. She clutched her diamond studded white purse in her left hand. Her white fur scarf flapped while she moved. She swiftly reached the end of the long, winding corridor.

“Let me out, woman,” she said to the female guard.

The guard pressed her hand against a panel, which opened the large doors in front of her. Mallory impatiently tapped the tip of her shoe against the ground. In a moment, the doors opened. She exited the building and quickly walked to the limousine. The robot Alice awaited her arrival.

“Missus Times, are you still traveling to your previously requested destination?” the robot Alice asked.

Mallory sat upon the limousine's back seat. Her feet were firmly rooted on the concrete floor beneath her. She pushed her shades to the top of her head.

“Yes. I can't remember...did I give you the address?” Mallory asked.

“It is in my data banks,” the robot Alice replied.

Mallory smiled and said, “Splendid. Alert me when we arrive at the hotel.”

Mallory adjusted her legs in a proper womanly way, and sat forward in her seat. The robot Alice closed the door, and rolled itself to the car's driver's side. The robot Alice extended its robotic arms, and lifted itself into the vehicle.

"User has confirmed destination. Proceeding with transportation to the Center for Disease Containment. Location is Alpharetta, Georgia," the limousine's robotic voice said.

The limousine began driving itself away from the psychiatric institution. Mallory stared out of her passenger's side window. Mallory used her eyes to control the images being displayed in the window. She looked at news articles, school records, and videos uploaded to public file sharing sites.

Mallory focused upon the photograph of a strikingly handsome Negro faculty member.

"Maybe you can help me, Professor Brown. Maybe you can help me understand, why this world is so troubled," she said.

She brushed back the long hair that was overlapping her ear. A small LED light connected to her headband, blinked softly. Mallory terminated the computer's signal by closing her eyes for half of one second. She stared sorrowfully out of the window. The limousine continued driving along the poorly paved gravel road. Mallory gazed at the clouds.

"What a beautiful sky," Mallory said.

ABOUT THE AUTHOR

James H. Wiggins III was born in New Brunswick, NJ. He graduated Summa Cum Laude with a 4.0 GPA from DeVry University, and has a Bachelor's degree in Video Game and Simulation Programming. He is also a member of the Phi Theta Kappa Honor Society. He has worked as an actor, musician, sound engineer, computer programmer, and writer.
His website is www.drisium.com.

www.ingramcontent.com/pod-product-compliance
Lightning Source LLC
Chambersburg PA
CBHW080742250626
47162CB00010B/2991
9780692328668